THE BORROWED DAYS

A Novel

by

Susan M. Walls

WAKING
EDGE
PRESS

THE BORROWED DAYS

PRINTED IN THE UNITED STATES OF AMERICA

Acknowledgements

My mother awakened in me a love of books and history; both have been important parts of my life nearly all my life. My father took my sister and me to movies almost weekly from the time I was in elementary school into my high school years. Like books, movies fired my imagination by the stories they told.

My own storytelling began with my dearest friend, Maggie Garfield, an author herself. Over the years, for hours on end, we would take turns spinning long, involved tales that went on for months, a clear indication of what was to come. She encouraged and inspired me, gave me feedback, asked me questions, was my technical advisor at times, and told me when more work was needed. Her friendship, love and support have been an enormous part of my life and I thank her from the bottom of my heart.

I owe a huge thanks to my friend Philip Bigler, author, educator and 1998 National Teacher of the Year. He formatted the text and guided me through the steps to publish this book. I will forever be grateful for his willingness to spend his valuable time working with me to let this story finally see the light of day.

The exquisite cover is the work of Victoria Racine, a graphic artist and long-time friend who said to me over a decade ago that, if I ever decided to publish, she'd be interested in working on the cover. I'm beyond grateful we had that conversation as she has translated beautifully my vision and I'm overjoyed with the result.

And I want to thank my husband, Bill, for his support and understanding the time and energy it takes to create a story I hope readers will enjoy and characters I hope they will come to care about.

Chapter One

"*Fia, help me,*" Mary cried and raced past her.

Fia leapt from her bench, mending tumbling to the floor, and ran outside knowing only that her friend needed her. Her step faltered. The byre before her was a roaring inferno; flames erupted from the roof and licked over the stone walls from the gaping door and windows. At first, she saw only the frenzied horses running toward the lane and noted, with relief, all three. Then, "Dear God, no!" she cried. There, lurching across the schoolyard, body nearly engulfed in flames, was Mary's husband, Robert MacInnes. Fia stepped back inside long enough to grasp a lap blanket and rushed toward him.

While Mary had managed to push him down, Fia threw the blanket over him and, together, they smothered the flames. In the confusion, Fia became aware of terrified cries from the students and frantically searched around her.

"Joan," she hollered at one of the older girls. "Go get the doctor."

Joan stood stock still in shock until Fia yelled, "Now!" then sped toward Fort William.

Fia turned to another student and gripped her arm. "Help me get them inside!"

The wide-eyed girl nodded dumbly and, shaking with dread, began to shepherd the other students toward the school. As soon as they entered, Fia said urgently, "I know it's hard but you all need to try to calm yourselves. Isla, please take them upstairs. When I know something, I'll tell you." She grabbed a blanket and, hastening back to Mary, crouched beside Robert's tormented body. "Let's try to get him inside."

The women clumsily placed Robert on the blanket. He was not a big man, but carrying him was difficult; he was in agony. To lessen his cries and moans, they had to move slowly and stop often, but finally got him into the drawing room.

Fia paced the hallway and wondered for the hundredth time what was keeping the doctor. From the next room, Mary's soothing voice broke Fia's agitated thoughts. "There, my love, the doctor will be here soon. He'll tell me how to ease your suffering, and we'll make you well–I promise you."

Fia paused at the drawing room door, her eyes fastened on her two friends. She knew in her heart Robert wouldn't live, and her own helplessness sickened her. She owed them so much. In anger and frustration, she ground her fist against her palm. "How could this horror have happened?" she thought.

The door opened with such force it hit the wall with a bang and the doctor entered behind the anxious Joan. "Where...?"

Fia clutched his arm, steering him toward Robert and Mary. "I'll be right here if you need me." She shut the door behind him and turned to put her quaking arms around Joan, squeezing her tightly.

"Thank you for fetching the doctor, Joan; you were very brave."

"Will...will Master MacInnes get well?"

"We can only pray that he will, Joan. He's badly burned though. Why don't you go upstairs and rest? You must be exhausted; the other girls are there." She smoothed the girl's hair and smiled weakly at her. "I'll let you all know what the doctor says."

Joan nodded and left her teacher at the bottom of the stairs. Fia sat on a step, stared at the drawing room door, and waited.

Two torturous days followed before Robert let go. In anguish, Fia and Mary watched his suffering knowing none of the doctor's remedies would heal him. But the two women dutifully followed instructions. They boiled cream until it became oily, cooled and applied it as best they could to Robert's pitiful body. They crushed elder leaves into an ointment of chalk, wax and oil of roses, but that didn't help either. Over and over Fia begged God to ease Robert's agony and, mercifully, he was unconscious until he released his last breath. He never spoke.

Now Fia gazed sadly into the cloud-mottled sky. "Finally, he's at peace," she murmured. Mary clung to her for support but, as the first shovel of dirt landed with a thud on Robert's coffin, she slipped to the ground. The aging vicar struggled to carry Mary's limp form into the school but Fia steered him away from the drawing room chaise where Robert had suffered and died.

The vicar deposited Mary in a wingback chair in the office. The effort winded him, and he settled his creaking body heavily in a matching chair as Fia tucked a blanket around the woman. Sitting beside her, Fia waited for Mary to revive. There was no sense in bringing her back to reality any sooner than necessary.

Reverend Grant stretched his feet toward the comforting fire and spoke quietly, "You're exhausted, child; you need rest. Mary told me earlier you've run the school since Robert's accident and managed to attend to her every need as well." He nodded toward the motionless woman. "Do you know when her sister is expected?"

Fia slid tapered fingers under her dark tresses and rubbed her neck wearily. "No, I don't. I sent word to her the day before yesterday. Don't worry; I intend to remain here until she arrives. Mary won't be alone."

The vicar nodded his approval, rising stiffly to leave. "It was fate that brought you here, my dear. Will you go home now?"

With a sigh, Fia confirmed, "I've no choice. Aye, I'll leave when Mary's affairs here are settled."

The vicar's smile was sympathetic. "Take heart, Fia. Perhaps Struan will be a kind husband. You've been a good friend to Mary and Robert. God will reward you."

"As good a friend as they've been to me, I hope," she murmured, lightly touching Mary's shoulder and ignoring his remark about the man she'd met only once; the man her uncle insisted she marry. "It was a beautiful eulogy Reverend Grant. I know Mary would want me to thank you."

He nodded his appreciation. "I'll show myself out. Remember, Fia, try to get some rest. It won't do for you to get sick."

The lowering sun lit the western sky so brilliantly that it seemed an insult to the solemnness of the day. Mary now slept in her bed, her face pinched and wan, but the sleep was blessedly dreamless. Fia wished for such relief herself and, with panic beginning to flutter her belly, memories of her four months at the MacInnes' school crowded her, robbing her of that luxury.

"How fortunate that Uncle George sent me to you," Fia spoke to the sleeping woman. "Since the day I arrived you and Robert have been my friends," she declared, remembering the morning Robert MacInnes had smiled tentatively at the new arrival.

"Frankly, I'm confused, Miss Graham. From our brief conversation, you seem well educated, and, if I may be blunt," he added hesitantly with a glance at his wife, "you're too old to be enrolled as a student at all. We were led to believe you were younger."

Fia apologized that they had been misled. "If I may tell you honestly, I wasn't sent here to learn anything, just to pass time under supervision." To Robert and Mary's mystified expressions, Fia murmured with embarrassment, "My uncle and I are at odds over his intention that I marry someone of his choosing. He wants me cloistered here until the wedding; it's no more than that…except to me." Fia gulped in sudden apprehension, eyes shifting between the Headmaster and his wife. "You…you won't send me back will you?"

Robert shrugged his shoulders. "You really are too old to—"

"Oh, please," Fia interrupted anxiously, leaning forward in her chair. "I don't need to be schooled. Uncle George has many books; I've read them all. I was allowed, at times, to observe when my cousin was being tutored. Isn't there something–anything–I might do to assist you and Mistress MacInnes? I'll gladly work for the room and board."

"Your uncle has already paid us," Robert returned.

"But isn't there some way I can be of service? I don't want to burden you, but I can't go home, not yet, please. I… need this time to think," she begged.

The MacInnes' exchanged questioning looks and the spark of an idea lit Robert's eye. He took his wife's hand and asked, "What do you think, my dear? Can we make use of this windfall?"

Mary, who had remained silent until now, nodded enthusiastically. "Of course, we can. She can take Miss Porter's position while we search for a permanent replacement." She turned to Fia. "A teacher who left not long ago to care for her ailing mother," she explained.

"So," Robert said, "this is a very unusual situation. I feel that we should let your Uncle know." He stopped as the young woman paled noticeably. He glanced at his wife who shook her head ever so slightly, then continued. "Perhaps we'll rethink that. In the meantime, we might come to some agreement that will benefit us and keep you away from home for the time being."

Her relief was palpable. "Thank you, thank you both so much," Fia exclaimed, eyes bright with unshed tears of gratitude. "You won't regret your decision."

Robert forced a smile; he was beginning to simmer with disgust that someone had made the thought of returning to her home so repugnant to her. Why, she was little more than a pawn in someone's game. So he made his offer. "If you assist in the teaching duties and the care of the students, we are prepared to offer you room and board, the freedom of the library and," he winked at his wife, "a small salary. Is that acceptable to you?"

"Oh...oh I couldn't accept a salary," Fia's eager smile died with her protest. "Your kind offer is such a blessing to me...I'm so grateful, I couldn't—"

"Miss Porter was paid," Mary insisted, "you shall be, also."

"You're...you're very generous." Fia reluctantly added, "My uncle won't like it."

Mary's expression softened with compassion. "He won't know, dear, unless you choose to tell him."

Fia had easily adjusted to life at the school. The younger girls in her charge liked her, and she enjoyed helping them with their letters and reading, instructing them in needlework and, occasionally, chaperoning outings when they practiced their drawing. During the busy days, she had no time for thoughts of what the future held for her. Night was a different story. Memories fueled her anxieties about the proposed marriage, and made her restless now. Fia glanced at Mary MacInnes who stirred briefly, her brow furrowed. In the weeks since Hogmanay, when her uncle had introduced her to the man he'd chosen for her, Fia Graham had pushed all thoughts of marriage and her intended groom into one simple vow to refuse—at the alter if it came to that. She knew she had hardly a hope of converting her uncle's intentions to her way of thinking.

Fia rested a comforting hand on Mary's arm and confided, "My problems are so few compared to yours."

As midnight approached, Fia rose and crossed to the window. Beyond the yard, she saw the charred remains of the byre, stark in the dusky light, and she shuddered at the changes the fire had wrought. "Robert rests, and Mary's sister will arrive soon. After the school closes...." Unable to finish the thought, Fia pressed her forehead against the glass and, despondent, tears spilled down her cheeks.

By the time Mary's sister, Alice, arrived nearly a week after the funeral, Fia had packed the library and assured that most of her young charges were delivered safely into the hands of their relatives or servants. With the help of Reverend Grant, she had also seen to it that the horses Robert saved from the fire were sold.

Mary was eager to leave the school, and her sister immediately spoke to Fia about it. "You're capable of closing the school by yourself; you've shown that by doing nearly everything for Mary humanly possible. I'm grateful to you."

Fia conceded, "I would do anything in my power for your sister. When Robert lay dying, I could do very little."

"On the contrary," Alice disagreed, "you relieved Mary of the burdens of running the school and looking after the students. Because you did that, my sister could concentrate on caring for her husband. She couldn't have managed without you."

"You're very kind to say so," Fia said.

Alice shrugged. "I only speak the truth as my sister has told it to me. Now, if you agree, I'll leave the day after tomorrow and take Mary home with me. When you've finished the work here, you can lock up and leave the key with the vicar. I'll talk to him; Mary's certain he'll see to selling the school on her behalf."

And when the time to say goodbye came, Fia stood in the cold morning mist choking back tears as Mary MacInnes took her leave. "I'll remember your friendship and kindness always. You and Robert hold special places in my heart."

"Fia...thank you for everything. I...I'm so glad I didn't have to face this alone. That's selfish of me, I know, but true just the same. I wish you well, dear. Please, don't let your uncle rob you of the happiness you deserve, or of a life of your own choosing."

The two embraced and before long, Fia and the five remaining students were waving after the coach, and continued to wave until it was out of sight.

Fia bade farewell to the last of the students a few days after Mary's departure, and the contents of the library were shipped the following day. There was nothing left but to take her leave.

A heavy moon hung over the knoll where Robert lay buried. By its light, Fia could see the whole yard almost as though it were day. "Robert MacInnes, born 1727, died 1760," Fia read, then sat to speak to her friend. "I've made sure Mary's in good hands, Robert. I'll give Reverend Grant the key before I board the boat tomorrow. He's been kind enough to arrange my passage to Oban and from there I can pick up the post chaise." After a pause, she whispered, "I wonder how Uncle George will react when I arrive in Glasgow, and then there's Elizabeth." She shook her head knowing her cousin would be difficult.

Her gaze shifted back to the stone marking Robert's resting place. "I'm not foolish, Robert. If my parents hadn't drowned, I doubt I'd ever have seen George Graham. Letting me live under his roof is a duty to his dead brother, nothing more." Suddenly, Fia was perversely glad that her early return would likely annoy the Grahams. After the events of this past Hogmanny, Fia found the thought appealing and it lifted her spirits a little. After saying a last goodbye to Robert, she wandered back to the empty school.

Her mantle pulled close against the penetrating damp and chill, from her spot in the bow, Fia scanned the shore looking back toward the town. But the mist shrouded almost all from her sight. If the weather didn't improve, it would be a miserable trip home just as the trip to Fort William back in January had been. And, if the borrowed days came, bringing back the full cold of the Highland winter, Fia prayed that it would be after she completed her journey.

There was only a slight breeze to ruffle the small sail, but the rhythmic splash of the oars sent the little boat skimming down Loch Linnhe. Reverend Grant's friend was a reticent little fellow called Murray. Fia marveled at his ability to propel the boat for seemingly endless hours without complaint. The fog lifted after a time, and Fia watched the passing countryside, but with little interest. Though the circumstances under which she began her journey to the school were unhappy ones, she remembered the trip as promising. Then, the scenery had been engrossing and she was excited to be out from under the watchful eyes of her cousin, Elizabeth. Fia had planned to make the most of her time away from those eyes, time now so cruelly cut short by Robert's tragic death.

As the distance stretched between her and the MacInnes' school, Fia became increasingly apprehensive about the confrontation to come. A heaviness seemed to be taking hold, and she found herself grateful for Murray's silence which allowed her to sit undisturbed in her end of the boat.

Fia's reflections turned to the eve of the Hogmanny ball–the only such event she'd ever attended though her uncle's wealth and standing would normally have dictated her inclusion at such social events. Every detail of that night was etched in her memory beginning with the new violet silk dress with pearl-gray lacings over a matching brocade petticoat and stomacher that suited her coloring. It was, by far, the finest dress she'd ever worn. Her hair had been dressed in a becoming fashion; a ribbon matching her lacings woven into her piled curls.

Hundreds of tapers created a warm golden glow in the ballroom. Decorations of seasonal greenery twined with rowan twigs and parsley, to ward off demons in the coming year, were artistically draped in every conceivable corner, strung on the bannister, and hung over each door. It was breathtakingly beautiful and in complete contrast to the events that followed.

Fia spoke with several people she knew before hearing the strains of the sarabande as it began. Her portly uncle claimed the first dance of the evening. Fia was immediately wary; the honor should have gone to her cousin. As that dance ended and her uncle released her hand, Struan Forbes stood before her, supercilious grin slicing his pale face. "I claim this dance, Miss Graham." His arrogant presumption made her wish she could refuse. But, she knew her uncle and cousin well. If she did anything that displeased either of them, her first ball would be her last.

Despite his slender, almost gaunt frame, Forbes was not graceful. More than once, he tread heavily on Fia's slippered feet as he lead her stiffly around the room. Thin strands of straight black hair fell from under his powdered wig and clung to his damp brow. His too-close eyes were a pale, watery blue that Fia found particularly objectionable.

One dance, she told herself, fighting the urge to abandon him there on the floor, for he studied her boldly. She chided gently. "Sir, you really mustn't stare, it is quite rude."

He merely grunted in response and, when the music finally stopped, he didn't ask for another dance. Neither, to her dismay, did he leave her side. Instead, to her bewilderment, he began an awkward discourse on hunting.

"There is nothing quite as exhilarating as shooting," he declared. "I'm particularly fond of birds, grouse, you know."

"Grouse?" she questioned, never having heard that hunting the bird was of special interest to anyone except if it put food on the table. While he was thin, she felt sure he could afford to buy his birds.

"It has a delicious flavor when properly prepared," he was saying. Forbes' pale eyes rested on her neckline and Fia deliberately spread her fan in between his leer and her bodice.

Finally, she exclaimed, "You should find another dancing partner, Mr. Forbes."

"I like it where I am, Miss Graham," he assured her. "Besides, there's more you should know about me. I'm also an excellent swordsman."

Puzzled, Fia asked, "Why would you think I should know that? Am I in danger?"

Forbes tossed back his head and laughed loudly. "Oh...oh hardly, Miss, hardly in danger."

His presence made her very ill at ease and she longed to move away from him. However, with his ungainly presence beside her, seemingly in conversation, no one else approached. Finally, desperate to be away from him, Fia reached out for the arm of a passing soldier, his hair the color of ginger.

"There you are...Lieutenant," she smiled broadly. "You promised me earlier that we might dance before midnight." She hoped the young man would be a gentleman and not expose her deception.

The Lieutenant's gazed flicked over Forbes and came to rest on Fia. He bowed. "Indeed, Miss, and we just have time." He then looked squarely into Forbes' flushed face. "Excuse us." With a smile, he led Fia onto the dance floor.

While they danced, Fia thanked the young man profusely, and he responded by declaring, "I'm delighted to assist. I know something of that man; he has a less than sterling reputation."

"I've never seen him before tonight and he will not leave me alone. It's very strange; he's very strange," Fia concluded.

"Perhaps we might sit together at supper, in case he returns. I'm Charles Drummond."

"And I'm Fia Graham. I would be very pleased to sit with you at supper, thank you."

The music halted abruptly to a small commotion at the front door. "Ah," said Drummond spying the time, "it's midnight, so that must be the 'first-foot'."

Fia craned her neck to glimpse the first visitor of the new year, a dark man bearing the traditional gifts to ensure a trouble free year ahead for his hosts: whisky, bread, salt and cake. A toast to the visitor and one to the host were drunk then the guests were called to supper.

Accompanying Lieutenant Drummond into the dining room, he sat on her right. Still, Forbes hovered at her left elbow. Her raven-haired cousin, Elizabeth, sat directly across the table. In short order, Fia discovered that Elizabeth knew Struan fairly well.

Lieutenant Drummond was recounting an episode with smugglers he had recently encountered, when Elizabeth rudely interrupted. "Lieutenant, everyone knows how ineffective the army is at trying to suppress the free traders. I'm surprised you boast of it."

"That was not my intention, Miss. I do my duty to protect the excise men and capture these criminals as I am ordered. I believe legitimate merchants are grateful for our efforts."

"Perhaps but, even when you *do* manage to capture them, it's not the army that ensures they pay for their crimes. It's our noble solicitors, like Mr. Forbes, who see to that." She smiled haughtily nodding toward Struan.

"Then we are all in his debt," Drummond responded dryly.

Elizabeth regarded Drummond disdainfully. "Indeed. Mr. Forbes is an excellent solicitor, Sir."

"I must take your word for it, Miss," Drummond allowed, "I don't know Mr. Forbes personally, only by reputation."

A sharp retort was on Elizabeth's lips and, puzzled though she was by her cousin's disagreeable manner, Fia offered hopefully, "Elizabeth, we should be celebrating the new year. Let's speak of something more festive."

Bestowing an icy glare on Fia, Elizabeth nevertheless agreed. "You're quite right, Cousin. But I must say, I'm surprised that you and Struan have never met before tonight. Why he and his brother, Andrew, are practically our neighbors. It's unfortunate that Andrew is away on business or you could have met him as well."

Through each course, Fia heard nothing festive, just praise for Struan Forbes who sat smirking and silent on her left. She was at a loss to explain it. She only knew that it was unusual behavior even for Elizabeth–and that worried her.

As the women prepared to leave the table, Lieutenant Drummond asked Fia for the first dance when the time came for the men to rejoin them. Elizabeth frowned at the exchange and Fia's smiling acceptance and pulled her cousin aside when the ladies entered the drawing room. "The attention you are paying that soldier is disgraceful, Fia. I insist that you stop."

Astonished, Fia's eyes widened. "I hardly spoke to him. I barely got a word in while you prattled on about that oaf Forbes."

Black eyes narrowing, Elizabeth hissed, "Well, you'd better get used to that 'oaf', dear Cousin, and leave Lieutenant Drummond alone." With a swish of emerald silk, Elizabeth briskly strode away, leaving Fia disconcerted and even more troubled.

Not long after the music resumed and under the scrutiny of Struan Forbes, the Lieutenant guided Fia around the room and, using the other guests as a screen, deftly led her out a door and into a small library. "This is the farthest away from Forbes that I can manage, Miss. A few minutes away from his constant glower will do you good, I dare say."

"That's very thoughtful, and I'm grateful. But I think I must tell my uncle that I want to go home."

"You'll let Forbes force you to leave?" he questioned.

"It's not only Forbes. My cousin is scheming–I'm not sure what, but I think it involves Forbes." Fia shook her head and said, "She's warned me to stay away from you."

His brow lifted in surprise. "Did she? Now that's intriguing. Is she always so...blunt?"

Fia smiled apologetically. "I'm sorry about Elizabeth. She's very temperamental, but even I've never seen her as rude as she's been tonight. That's part of my concern."

Drummond frowned. "It's not for you to apologize for your cousin. Miss Graham, I'm glad I could assist you tonight and you've made my evening enjoyable in return. I won't have more opportunities like this for some time since my unit goes south to Luce Bay next week. No matter what your cousin thinks, the excise men need our help. Illicit trade in that area is out of control. And the locals are no help at all," he said in frustration.

"I'm not surprised since many people depend on smuggling just to feed their families."

Drummond stared at her. "You sympathize with them?"

"I sympathize with their hunger, Lieutenant. I've heard it said that there is a certain amount of honor among free traders and that could be another reason many find support throughout the countryside."

"I know first-hand that some of these men are ruthless cutthroats who would stop at nothing to fill their purses; they are not 'honorable'. But you're right. If people benefit from smugglers, they will support them," Drummond's eyes narrowed as he studied her. "Forgive me, but I'm intrigued that you are interested in smuggling."

"My uncle owns a small fleet of ships; it's important to him since it directly affects his business." She grinned, "And you might be surprised at the information you can pick up at Market if you aren't wearing a uniform."

Drummond's round face relaxed into a pleasant smile. "I suppose I might be," he chuckled then asked, "May I call on you before my unit leaves?"

"No, you may not!" a voice blurted from the doorway. Fia and Drummond started and were stunned to see Forbes, George Graham and Elizabeth glaring at them. Forbes pointed a bony finger at Fia and accused, "So this is where you've been hiding!"

Lieutenant Drummond rose. "No one is 'hiding'; the door is wide open. And I don't see that the whereabouts of this woman is of particular concern to you."

"Oh, you don't? Well it does concern me as I am betrothed to this woman," he finished smugly.

Fia's face turned stark white in shock, then scarlet with rage and humiliation. "That, Sir, is a lie! I demand an apology for myself and for the Lieutenant." Why would her uncle and cousin allow Forbes to say such a thing without coming to her defense?

"It's no lie, Miss Graham." Forbes inclined his head toward her uncle. "Tell her, Graham."

There was a long moment of silence. Finally, looking greatly discomfited, George Graham mumbled, "Aye, he...he speaks the truth, Fia. I planned to tell you at the end of the evening after you had a chance to get acquainted with Struan."

Fia was indignant. "Not once have you ever spoken to me about marriage, Uncle George, *not once*. No one arranges marriages anymore unless there's something valuable at stake. It's not as if I have property or money. Why would you do this?"

"You will have an inheritance from your father–money and property," George declared then blustered, "You must think of what is practical and sensible."

"I just met this man but I know I won't marry him!" Fia declared.

"I've already made the arrangements. There will be no further discussion or hysterics." Her uncle spoke firmly, but would not look at her.

"You'll get used to the idea, Cousin. Did I not say as much earlier?"

Elizabeth's smugness was almost too much to bear. Fia took a deep, steadying breath and turned to the Lieutenant. "I must apologize. Had I known of this..." She extended a trembling hand which he took immediately and bowed over. "Thank you for your company. It made my evening... bearable," she finished lamely.

"Miss Graham." Drummond bowed curtly and left without another word.

She faced her uncle squarely. "I wish to go home now."

"Fia, there is still time this evening for you to better acquaint–"

"Uncle," she cut him off and spat through clenched teeth, "you owe me this much if you plan to sell me for an inheritance!" Without waiting, she pushed past him, her head high. Fia had a sinking feeling that all the pleading in the world would not save her from this dilemma. Instinctively, she also knew that Elizabeth was behind this betrothal.

"Oh cheer up, Fia," Elizabeth said as the carriage traversed the snow-covered streets. "He's young at least, and from a fine family."

Fia would have laughed if she could have found anything humorous about her situation. "If you think him a fine young man, then you take him with my blessing."

Elizabeth's laughter filled the coach. "Why would I do that when any man I want would be mine for the asking?"

Fia was livid and, because she was trapped, it was that much harder to stand Elizabeth's gloating. "Uncle George, I won't marry Struan Forbes." Perhaps, if she said it enough, it would come to pass.

"Well, there will be no changing Father's mind on this match, will there Father?" Elizabeth smiled sweetly, tucking her hand into George's.

A silent George sat ill at ease between the two hostile young women. He was not entirely sure that his daughter's plan would work, but Elizabeth did not wait for his answer. "You've been enough of a burden to us these eight years, Fia. You'll marry Struan the day before your eighteenth birthday when you will inherit. So, be good and do as you're told. We'll all be happier for it in the end."

Fia doubted that. She had not thought much about marriage and she was far from sure what kind of man she could love. However, of one thing Fia was certain; Struan Forbes was not a man she wanted to share another minute with much less a lifetime. It seemed, however, that this was to be her destiny–Elizabeth and George had planned it so.

An unexpected thump scattered Fia's memories and abruptly returned her to the present. Murray had beached the boat so they could spend a few minutes stretching their legs. Fia gratefully left her gloomy thoughts behind in the cramped bow of the little boat.

It was two bone-chilling days of travel to reach Oban, and Fia was exhausted when she stumbled to shore. The long hours of uninterrupted confinement were taking their toll even on her young body. She could not get warm, she felt groggy and her voice, little used in the past few days, was raspy. She bade farewell to her morose companion, thanking him again for his care and help. They had spent last night at a croft where she was able to stretch out on a pallet offered by the generous owner and his wife, friends of Murray's. Except for that welcome relief, from the time they left Fort William, the travelers had taken their meals while on the water and there had been few stops for resting, stretching, and none for freshening up. In Oban there was time for all for it was still a few hours until the post chaise was due to leave.

The hot food served at the inn was plentiful and tasty; it did wonders for the aches and the dull cold that had plagued her since the end of the first day of travel. While she ate, Fia listened to snatches of a drunken disagreement about whether the King's army would ever succeed in liberating Montreal as they had Quebec the previous September. The war with the French in the American colonies had never been a topic of conversation in the Graham house except as it affected shipping and any special commercial privileges to be had. It was Robert MacInnes who had explained that the constant juggling to maintain a balance of power in Europe corresponded directly with the English and French ability to expand trade in the colonies. Their converging interests resulted in overlapping territorial claims and contested commercial rights. Thinking of Robert brought a wave of sadness and she signaled the tavern keeper. "Have you a room where I can freshen up?"

"Aye, Miss. Follow me."

Once in the room, Fia sagged against the closed door. There was a nervous gnawing in her belly that simply would not go away. She washed, and changed into something warmer. Her fingers shook as she fastened her quilted, fitted bodice and adjusted the sleeves of her frock-cut coat.

Sighing, she surveyed her handiwork in the small looking glass above the wash stand. She closely resembled her mother whom she remembered well: the same abundant walnut-brown hair, oval face and slender figure. But it was her father's eyes that stared back at her, dark gray, flecked with blue. They were pleasantly large and framed with thick lashes. The hot water had brought a little color back to her cheeks, and she brushed a stray curl from her forehead before smoothing her midnight-blue camlet petticoat a final time; soft leather gloves extended beyond her wrist-length cuffs. Fastening her mantle at her neck and picking up her valise, Fia felt as ready as she thought possible to resume her journey and face her family's displeasure when she arrived in Glasgow, for she was sure they would not be pleased.

The post chaise looked top heavy with her valise, a small trunk and the box of mail lashed to the roof. However, Fia was delighted to see she would share it with only two other passengers both of whom sat on the seat opposite her. One of the men was rather large and friendly looking. She cleared her throat as best she could and asked, "Where are you bound, Sir?"

He smiled amiably, "For Inveraray, Miss. I'm going home to see my wife and our children–all seven of them."

"Seven? I imagine you must get lonely when you're away from them."

"Oh, aye. Once you're used to a crowd it's hard to do without." The man chuckled. "Of course, it doesn't take long with the lot of them to make me want to be back on the road either."

Fia smiled at him and turned to the other man as the driver urged the team of horses away from Oban. "And, you, Sir? Are you going to Inveraray as well?"

The man scowled, "It's nobody's business but mine where I'm going."

Fia was surprised at his surliness."I beg your pardon, Sir," she apologized and, feeling rebuked, retreated into her own thoughts. In the low light, she just barely saw the look of distaste on the pleasant man's face and his apologetic shrug to her.

As they traveled on, the air turned measurably colder. Fia occasionally wriggled her toes inside her boots to make sure they were still there.

Bounced and jostled for what seemed an eternity, the road smoothed out and turned south around the end of a loch, which was far behind when Fia awoke with a jolt after finally having succeeded in dozing off. The chaise had come to a sudden stop and, in the darkness; she could not distinguish the faces of the two men opposite her. "What's happening? Why have we stopped?"she asked, trying to shake her confusion.

"Dunno, Miss," the man traveling to Inveraray answered.

At that moment, the door swung wide and a cold, sibilant voice commanded them to get out.

"Sweet Jesus," one of the men muttered as he followed her out, "we're being robbed."

Behind a brace of pistols, was a man, face obscured from the dim light of the chaise lamp by the shadow of a large slouch hat. It was further concealed by a thick woolen handkerchief. She saw no trace of the driver. Fia shivered and pulled the hood of her mantle forward against the night air. The movement brought a swift reprimand from the armed man.

"I wouldn't do that again, Miss, if you hold your life in high regard," he hissed.

"The chill, Sir," she responded, voice hoarse, lowering her head slightly, "I sought only to keep it out."

"Do that again, you'll not need to worry about the cold any more, I promise you." Quickly, he turned his attention back to the men. "Now, lads, turn out your pockets."

The surly passenger panicked and pointed at Fia. "She's got plenty of money. I saw her put it in her bag back at the inn!"

Fia stared aghast at the man. "What a lying coward you are," she accused, momentarily forgetting the man with the pistols. But the robber was not deterred.

"I'll get to her in time, don't worry. The lass isn't wrong though. You are a coward." With that, the man discharged one of his pistols with a crack and Fia jumped back against the coach as the passenger fell, already dead, at her feet.

The other man, terrified, was rooted where he stood. The murderer turned to him. "You. What's your name?"

"E…Edward," the man answered nervously.

The venomous voice almost whispered to him, "Right you are, Edward. Get what he has on him and add your own to it. Be quick."

Edward obeyed with all the speed he could muster. With numb fingers, he felt through the dead man's pockets, then emptied his own. Edward set everything on the ground next to the outlaw.

"Ah, that's fine, Edward. You've done well. Now," the man ordered, pointing the still charged pistol past the horses, "start running. Inveraray's not so far away."

Tentatively, Edward stretched his hand toward Fia. "Come along then."

As Fia reached for his hand, the robber lowered his pistol at Edward. "This one is still loaded. I told you to start running. You."

Still, Edward hesitated until Fia nodded. Then he turned and ran down the road. When he was out of sight, the killer turned his full attention to Fia. "Now, my bonnie lass," he purred, "where's all this money I've heard about?"

Plucking up her courage, Fia faced him. "We're not wealthy people, you can see that. Why are you attacking us in the dead of night?"

Amused, he answered, "Would you prefer that I rob and kill in the light of day?"

Instead of becoming flustered by the way he twisted her words, she simply stood her ground. He slithered nearer and whispered, "In truth, my business is smuggling. This just keeps me from getting bored between shipments." The deadly voice washed over her like icy water. "Now, lass, where's the money?"

"In my handbag," she answered with a calm she did not feel.

"Why I'm surprised you'd give up so soon, lass. I'm disappointed."

Behind his scarf, Fia knew he was laughing at her. "You'll have it sooner or later so why not sooner so that I may be on my way?" she rasped.

The bandit threw back his head and guffawed as he opened her bag. He was enjoying sparring with her. "This is hardly what I'd call a fortune, Miss. Nine pounds?"

"I can't be responsible for the lies of another." She pointed to the dead man. "He was just trying to save himself."

"Aye, and look where it got him. But," he added, tucking the money in the pocket of his frock coat and tossing the purse aside, "I'll wager there's more where this came from." His fingers clamped like a vise on her upper arm and he laughed again as the unexpected pain made her cry out. "Where is it?"

"There is no more, Sir," she gasped, "and I would appreciate it if you'd let go of my arm. You're hurting me."

Bending nearer, he pointed to the roof of the chaise and, menacing, whispered, "I'll wager, it's either in your bag, or somewhere on your person. Now, where shall we start looking, hmm?" She felt suffocated by his nearness and thanked God that her hood helped conceal the panic that his words brought to her. Nervously, she glanced toward the chaise to see if she could spot the driver, but the thief read into it another meaning. "So, it's in your bag. Let's get it down, shall we?"

Before she realized what was happening, Fia was thrust toward the empty chaise and, with his arms around her knees, the man hoisted her to its roof. Off balance, she grabbed the rope binding the baggage, and pulled herself up the last bit, sprawling across the boxes and her bag.

"Now don't waste time. Just toss it down." That voice made her shiver uncontrollably and she was glad that the space and night between them didn't allow him to see it.

"I have to find it first," she said, her thoughts racing ahead. There was no more money in her valise; no more money anywhere. "It's back here," she volunteered. What would he do when he found out?

Fia pulled at the heavy mail box in front of her valise, freed it from its binding ropes, and pushed it toward the edge of the roof. Then she reached for the valise. She could think of nothing that would save her from whatever fate awaited her at the thief's hands.

"Well?" he growled impatiently.

"I have it here. But to open it, I need my purse. The key is in it." She got to her knees behind the box she had just moved. "There," she said pointing behind him to where he had dropped her purse.

He snarled at her. "I'll open the valise. Just throw it down." Fia could only comply. With the valise in hand, the man turned to pick up her purse.

Before Fia consciously thought of it, she thrust the heavy box with all her might and sent it hurtling through the air. It landed squarely on his neck and shoulders, knocking him to the ground under its weight. The horses, startled by the sudden commotion next to them, leaped forward; Fia lost her balance and was thrown from the roof. She lay, momentarily stunned, hearing only the sound of hooves as the horses set a frightening pace down the road.

Slowly, she sat up and looked about. The body of her fellow passenger lay within arm's reach. The outlaw was sprawled face down on the road at her side. Rising cautiously, Fia found herself loath to touch his body, but she pushed him over and pulled the handkerchief from his face. A thick silver scar, running from the corner of his mouth to his square chin, gleamed unnaturally in the darkness. Under his jaw, she found his pulse. It beat wildly beneath her fingertips and she was terrified, realizing suddenly that she was stranded with him. Frantically, she wondered how long it was until daybreak; there was no way to tell. "I can't wait here." she thought anxiously. Standing, Fia gratefully discovered no real damage from her fall. Eyes darting around, she saw no sign of the man's horse, or of the coachman. She couldn't carry her valise but was reassured knowing there was nothing in it he could trace to her. Bending, she hastily retrieved the nine pounds, picked up her purse and, without looking back, ran from the road onto the nearly frozen moor.

The ground was uneven, the footing treacherous. Run...it seemed that she had done nothing else for hours on end, yet the sun had not risen since she'd left the bodies of the dead man and his murderer. The frosted heath crunched beneath her boots endlessly until she left the moors and entered a sparse forest. In short order, Fia was surrounded by trees as the forest became more dense, forcing her to a slower pace. Only twice had Fia stopped to rest, her throat and eyes burning. The cold air in her overworked lungs finally forced her to stop again. Wearily leaning her forehead on the rough bark of an oak, struggling for breath, Fia wondered what to do next. No thought came but to continue running, and she pushed herself onward.

Numbness and exhaustion crept through her and Fia began to stumble frequently, always pulling herself upright to stagger on. When she tripped and finally did fall, she cried out. Panting, she lay with tears running down her flushed cheeks trying to clear her head and think; but it was impossible. Her chest and throat ached and she was scratched, bruised, and bloody. Through clenched teeth, Fia fought an onslaught of chills. "Concentrate," she muttered in frustration and closed her eyes.

Pounding. That pounding in her head–it wouldn't stop. "*Hooves,*" her mind screamed as she struggled to wake, "*He's found me!*" She crouched against the tree, fingers clawing the bark in panic, and listened as the rhythmic thundering grew louder. Glancing about, Fia noticed thin shafts of pale light beginning to brighten the forest around her. She bit back a frantic scream of fury at the betraying light.

Suddenly, the monstrous shape of horse and rider appeared bearing down on her. All her dread rushed back; she had to get away. But in her confusion, she stepped directly into the path of the animal and dropped to her knees.

Chapter Two

Martin Ross had risen early from Jean MacNab's bed, ashamed and annoyed with himself at having stayed the night. It certainly hadn't been his intention, and now he'd made things far more difficult.

Jean was painfully aware that he hadn't visited often since the harvest; and now he wanted to end things. So he said. She studied him as he dressed in the dying firelight, trying to decide how to change his mind. "Martin, have I done something to anger you? Is that why you teased me so cruelly yesterday?"

Martin tucked his shirt into his breeches and tied his neck handkerchief. "You've done nothing. I wasn't teasing though."

"Shall I come to you then?" she hopefully asked, rising to wrap her arms around him and rest her cheek against his back. The feel of his shirt on her bare breasts excited her. "It's been a long winter."

He stepped away from her, turned, and shook his head. "No, Jean. I don't want you to come to me." He shrugged into his wool broadcloth frockcoat.

Twisting from him, Jean wrapped herself in a blanket and sat down hard on the bed. Beneath her anxiety that he was serious about not seeing her anymore, she was angry that he was pushing her aside. She had refused to think of her life without Martin in it since they'd met the previous spring, a few months after her husband's death. Jean had decided then that she would have him, whatever it took. His preference for solitude was a challenge to her; he was young and pleasing to the eye. On the summer solstice, Jean invited him into her bed.

Stunned by her proposal, his eyes had flicked over her shapely form before he glanced away, embarrassed, and responded, "Any man would be tempted and flattered. But, you're hurting from your husband's death. You need someone to lean on. That person isn't me."

"No, that's not it. You may think ill of me, but I'll be blunt, Martin. You can provide exactly what I need. I'm young; I miss the...physical side of married life. Surely you understand." Jean hastily added, "I see no woman with you. Have you no wish for what I'm offering...willing company?"

"I truly believe you need more than you're telling me...more, perhaps, than you even realize."

She pouted, "I've thrown my pride aside to confess that a man in my bed is exactly what I want. But I'm particular as to which man it is." She saw the doubt flicker across his face and hurried on. "Let me prove it; I'll make a bargain with you. At any time either of us wishes to end the arrangement, we'll do so without argument, without casting blame." With a bit more coaxing and that promise, he had finally relented because she was right. He had needs as well. But her offer had been a ploy because Jean believed that, in time, Martin would come to care for her. In fact, she counted on it. Now she shook her head to clear her thoughts and scowled at Martin's back. Well, he might care–but he didn't love her. "And now", she thought fiercely, "I want him to love me."

When her thoughts returned to the moment, Martin was repeating, "I'll not visit again."

"And you think I should believe you? Just like you weren't going to stay last night after you delivered your edict?" she threw at him.

Martin kept his gaze on hers though he flushed slightly. "I deserve that. It was selfish of me to stay, I shouldn't have done it. Still, we agreed at the beginning that if either of us wanted out..."

Jean suddenly wanted to hurt him. "You are selfish...and cowardly."

"I obviously agree that I was selfish. But if I was cowardly, I'd have never told you that I'm done with this. I'd have left and just not returned. I was weak to have stayed and I regret that."

"You think you can come in here and use me for your pleasure and toss me aside," she accused.

His eyes narrowed. "Now you're being selfish. We both got what we agreed to…what you suggested…out of this affair." Undaunted, Martin continued, "There's no future for us together and there never was. You're young; I don't think you'll look for anyone to rebuild your life with unless I'm out of it. It's best that we go our separate ways, Jean."

"Oh, so you're doing this for me? Martin, you sound so sanctimonious, telling me you won't love me again when you stand there with my scent still on you," she scolded.

"I told you last night was a mistake," he said, trying to keep his exasperation in check. "And you said that if either of us ever wanted out…Yet here you are trying to stop me. I won't make that mistake again," he declared, "I promise you."

In panic, Jean dropped the blanket and pressed her body against him, grasping him around the waist. "You'll come back, Martin. There's hunger in you, and nowhere else for you to feast."

Firmly, he pushed her back and held her at arm's length. "I won't return, Jean; I wish you well."

In the clear, pre-dawn air, Martin saddled and mounted his towering gelding, Odhar. He whistled once for the black dog sleeping at the corner of Jean's croft, and wheeled the horse northwest toward home.

The ground fell away beneath the horse's stride and, while Martin tried not to think about Jean, one thing she'd said nagged him. Upon reaching the ambling burn that crossed his path just two miles from her croft, Martin reined in and dismounted.

The hound sat panting while his master stripped to bare skin, waded into the frigid water, crouched and began to wash. Jean was right–her scent clung to him. Never before had he paid it any mind, now Martin just wanted to be rid of it, rid of the last vestiges of his liaison with her. For him, their affair had been just what she'd asked for–release. Martin had never been wholly comfortable with the arrangement and, though she professed to be happy with it, Martin was ashamed at using her thus. His conscience plagued him.

Martin scowled. It was no wonder Jean doubted he would stay away. Again, he cursed his weakness for having stayed the night. "Never again," he vowed a final time, tired of feeling guilty, tired of being part of a liaison he didn't really want.

He thrust his head under water, the shock of the cold good therapy for his self-flagellation. He waded to shore and palmed the water from his limbs and torso, pulled his clothes on, and with burnished curls and beard still dripping water, remounted Odhar. "Come, Arthur," he called, touching heels to Odhar's flanks.

The horse burst forward and, gradually, thoughts of Jean MacNab and their few months of dalliance slipped from Martin's mind as the cold air whipped his face, feeding his relief at being free again.

He entered the sparse woods where thin ribbons of light dotted the forest floor like shooting stars in the night sky. Martin breathed deeply. When he thought about it, this was always his favorite part of his visits to Jean. His chest filled with contentment at the peace and beauty of the forest around him. His homeland was the one thing that he loved of which he had not been stripped. Much of the ancient way of life his grandfather had lived, and Martin remembered vividly, no longer existed. The horror of 'the '45', the battle of Culloden, that last futile and bloody attempt to place Charles Stuart on the throne, had changed the life of every Scot–the English were not merciful conquerors. But the land was still here; still tangible, still hauntingly beautiful, always stirring his blood. It had been his lifeline and no one could rob him of it. Knowing that Arthur would find his way, Martin forced Odhar into a gallop across the frosted ground.

Without warning, almost beneath Odhar's pounding hooves, a dark form stumbled and fell. Martin reined the horse in hard causing him to rear up dangerously close to the crumpled figure. Once his mount was under control, Martin leapt from its back. Furious, he grabbed a handful of cloak and wrenched the rogue around to face him. The angry curses momentarily froze in his throat as waves of dark curls tumbled from beneath the cloak's falling hood. A woman's arms flew to protect her down-turned face. Recovering his surprise, Martin's ire returned and he swore, "God's blood, you fool. What did you think you were doing?"

"I…it was an accident. Please," her plea was ragged. "There was no more money. Please don't kill me."

Taken aback, Martin replied, "K…Kill you? I…I don't intend to hurt you at all." Then he remembered his ire and added, "We're all lucky you caused no harm. You could've easily been killed when you jumped in front of Odhar, and he and I might be lying with our necks broken!" Martin released her and sat back on his heels. He watched her body became rigid. Lowering her arms, she lifted her scratched, dirt-smeared face to his. In her eyes, Martin saw recognition, but didn't understand it.

Fia focused her gaze on his lips, barely discernable in the man's bearded face. Gingerly, she extended her hand–that voice, the beard. She pulled her hand back. "You aren't him," she whispered then, as if to convince herself, again exclaimed, "you aren't him!" With that, she cradled her face in both hands and sobbed with relief.

Thoroughly mystified and anger vanished, Martin stared. But before he could speak, the girl began to recover. "I...I'm so very sorry," she gulped. "Are you and your horse really unharmed?" She wiped her eyes and looked at him again.

Fia caught her breath in a hiccup; his nearness was intimidating and his appearance wild compared to what she was accustomed to in men of her acquaintance. Lazy reddish-brown curls lay unruly and unqued on his shoulders and his eyes, the color of dried heather, were intense–spellbinding. After a long moment, Fia realized that he was studying her as well. She turned her head and closed her eyes briefly against his searching gaze, trying to gather her thoughts which scattered again abruptly when he took her hand. She snatched it from his grip.

Martin assured, "It's all right, Miss." Her hand was hot. He rose and walked to the sleek black horse.

Fia panicked, thinking he was going to leave her where he'd found her, not that she'd blame him if he did. But she was lost and lightheaded. If he did leave her, her chances of finding her own way to safety were slim indeed. She started to call to him, but he was already beside her again with a flask.

"You'd better have some of this. You're not just cold, you're ill."

"How–"

"Your eyes are glassy, your color, high. Your hand is hot." He pushed the flask toward her lips. "This will warm you a little."

With a shaking hand, she accepted and swallowed a little of the whiskey it held. A shudder went through her and Martin smiled sympathetically. "Better?" he asked, taking the flask from her.

"I'm not sure," she admitted.

Martin knelt before her again. "Where are you going, Miss?"

"Glasgow, though I wasn't expected–" Fia bit her lip, silently cursing her recklessness. She was about to tell a complete stranger that no one would miss her if she failed to arrive at her destination. Fortunately, the man did not seem to notice.

"And how did you get here? Why did you think I would try to kill you?"

She ached all over and needed desperately to get warm, so Fia's answer was brief. "An outlaw stopped the post chaise I was traveling in and killed one of the passengers. I was afraid you were him." She shivered violently and the man urged her to take another sip of whiskey.

"And how did you escape this man?"

"I knocked him out."

Martin sat back slightly and his eyes narrowed.

"By accident," she added, emphatically, seeing his doubt. "And I ran."

"Aye, you did that," he exclaimed. "The post road and your outlaw are far away."

She let out the breath she was holding. "I'm more than relieved to hear it."

Fia made motions to rise and Martin offered his hands to help her. She swayed a little once on her feet, and kept her gaze on the ground, concentrating on pulling herself together.

Martin's gaze quickly took in details he hadn't seen before: dirt stained her torn clothes; bits of leaves clung to her; scratches and blood dotted her hands as well as...he started as his glance returned to her face to find her watching him. "You have had quite a journey," was all he could say.

She nodded then asked, "Which way is Inveraray? Do I have a long way to go?"

"Surely you don't think you're going to walk there?" he asked, incredulous.

"Is there another place where I can pick up the chaise? Which way?" she repeated and pulled her cloak close as she shivered.

Martin studied her again. If she was still afraid, he couldn't see it. And there was no confusion in her expression now, only a dignity and resolve he found intriguing. A frown tugged at his mouth; he made his decision quickly. "No you won't walk and you won't go to Inveraray today. I'd take you there or wherever you chose to go if you were in condition to travel that far. But you aren't."

She started to protest, but he asked, "Can you ride astride?"

"I've never tried," Fia admitted.

Without warning, he scooped her up and carried her toward the grazing horse.

"Where will you take me if not to Inveraray?" she demanded, concern suddenly piercing her thoughts.

"We are taking you to my croft. It's a league north–twice as close as the road to Inveraray."

"We?"

"Aye, we. This is Odhar. I think you should ride to the side; I'll see that you keep your seat." He set her easily at the front of his saddle and tucked her mantle around her booted feet. His expression was as warm as the touch of his hand on her leg. "There, how's that?"

Fia's voice froze in her throat. She nodded briefly and the man swung into the saddle behind her, his arms on either side of her as he picked up the reins.

"Are you ready?" he asked.

Again, she nodded.

Satisfied, Martin whistled sharply, making Fia jump. Instantly, a large hairy beast of a dog appeared. "That's Arthur." Barely touching the horse's flanks with his cuffed boots, Martin urged Odhar forward.

The hands on the reins before her were lean and strong without obvious signs of heavy toil. It made her wonder how the man earned his living if not off the land. Fia was too tired to ask though. Silence accompanied them for some minutes and as Fia drew a bit of warmth from the man's body, she began to relax. Soon she was leaning against the stranger.

The lass was soft and slight in his arms, unlike the sturdy Jean MacNab. Annoyance flashed through Martin that he'd made that comparison so easily, and he asked, more harshly than he intended, "You live in Glasgow?"

Her head beginning to throb and her thoughts to muddle, Fia nodded, the ire in his voice confusing her.

"And you say that no one is expecting you?"

So, he'd caught her blunder after all. "I...that's right."

"Have you been off visiting?" he inquired.

"No. I...I left school before the term was over."

Martin puzzled, "A bit old for school aren't you?"

Fia didn't respond.

"So are you running away?" he persisted. "Why? Was the Headmaster pestering you?"

Fia felt so wretched she didn't noticed the sarcasm in his voice. "His death was so horrible; Mary had no choice but to close the school. She couldn't bear to go on," she replied, nearly choking on her sadness.

The silence that followed her admission was so complete that, when it seeped through Fia's grief and her befuddled mind, she felt a chill crawl up her spine. Pulling away to look at him, she saw undisguised embarrassment and had to think to remember just what he'd said to her. Then, angry at her own naivety, bewildered and offended by his question, Fia spat, "Robert was a fine man and loving husband to Mary." Abruptly, she faced forward and sat away from him as best she could. Almost immediately, a shudder ran the length of her body, but she kept that small distance between them.

Martin cursed himself, furious for upsetting her and embarrassing them both for no reason that involved this young woman. After a few moments, he said, "Forgive me, lass. I...it was a poor, vulgar jest to make. I'm truly sorry."

Fia didn't reply–she didn't know what to say. They rode in silence for what seemed hours. Once or twice she caught herself nodding and hoped the man behind her hadn't noticed. However, she realized quickly that he didn't miss much for, when it happened yet again, he wrapped his arms more tightly around her.

"Stop that," she snarled and plucked at his fingers.

"No, please," he protested. "I'm so sorry to have upset you, Miss. But you need to rest. Here," he urged her resisting body closer until she leaned stiffly against him. He placed his lips near her ear, whispering, "Go to sleep if you'd like, lass." His voice was deep and soothing and his arms cradled her. "We'll not let you fall."

Fia's wounded pride kept her from immediately surrendering to sleep. At length though, she turned a flushed cheek against his coat surprised at how comfortable she could feel in the embrace of this irascible stranger.

"God's blood, what have I stumbled upon?" Martin pondered silently as Odhar carried them homeward. Glancing down, he could see little of her face as she slept against him. But the skin was smooth and heavily flushed beneath the crescent of her lashes. A stray lock of glossy hair lay across her cheek and over Martin's arm. He felt a moment of unexpected tenderness which quickly deteriorated, so certain was he that the peaceful life he'd just that morning hoped to regain once again was out of reach. Martin had looked forward to ending his affair with Jean so that he could answer only to himself again. And now this. "Be reasonable," he scolded silently, with a shake of his head. "This is temporary. Just nurse her back to health and get her to Inveraray." Once more he looked at the sleeping girl. He was curious about her, a slip-of-a-lass who could knock out and escape a killer. But one thing he already knew, she was young and vulnerable, and Martin would have to be careful with her. He vowed he would be, more so than he'd been already, at least.

What seemed to Fia only a moment later, Martin pointed slightly to her left. "There, can you see it?"

Fia roused herself with difficulty. Ahead, she could see a mortared stone croft set near the bottom of a hill from which a shallow burn tumbled. "This is yours?" she asked noting two multi-pane windows, the door and an open entrance to the right. The croft was covered with a heather-thatched roof.

"Aye." Martin dismounted when they reached the croft. He lifted her from Odhar's back and carried her inside before letting her set a foot down. Inside, he hung her cloak on a peg beside the door before leading her to a fiddle-backed chair that faced the hearth. He lit the fire and nursed it to a blaze. Without warning, he grasped first one of her boots then the other, pulling them off. He chaffed her feet and calves in their woolen stockings before tucking a blanket around her. "Stretch your feet toward the blaze," he instructed. "I'll be back when I've tended Odhar."

While relishing the warmth of the fire, Fia tried to focus her attention on her surroundings. There were two candlesticks and one lanthorn on the hewn mantle and, not far from where she sat, stood a bed against the wall. It was not the usual box bed with curtains. There was a trunk at its foot. At the far end of the croft was a large object which her fevered mind refused to identify, but it made her think of an enormous spider's web. To the left of the door was a cupboard against which leaned a musket, and to the right, directly under the window, was a small table and second fiddle-back chair. Few pieces, but all looked well made. The croft appeared neatly kept and the floor, except for the stone hearth, was not beaten earth, but wood which she found a puzzling luxury in this unusual croft in the middle of–God knew where. And the man? What kind of man was he? There were few personal articles visible to give her any clues. Just some pieces of clothing hung on pegs near her cloak. She closed her eyes and it was the opening and closing of the door that woke her once again.

The man approached the hearth and hung a small pot on a hook over the flames. He turned to look at her. "You need something hot to eat before you go to sleep."

Fia shook her head. "I'm not hungry."

"Nevertheless," he insisted, "you will eat. You have to trust me on this."

He was right; she had to trust him. She hoped she could. "You're very kind taking me in like this. I don't know where I am or who you are. I only know this is your croft, that your horse is Odhar and your dog, Arthur."

Martin's brows drew down; he was worried that her words were beginning to slur and, while he was near perspiring from being so close to the fire, she was shivering. He inclined his head slightly. "Martin Ross. Welcome to my home. It's a good two hours from any road and more than one from the closest croft."

"And your family?" she asked as he spooned an aromatic stew into a bowl.

Handing her the bowl he grinned. "You've met them all."

Puzzled, she said, "You...you live by yourself?"

"Aye, except for the animals." He realized that, ill as she was, she was struggling with the revelation that she was alone with him. "It's all right, lass," he tried to reassure.

After a few moments when doubt plagued her expression, she extended a scratched hand. "I'm Fia Graham. Thank you again for helping me." He took her hand and impulsively touched it to his lips. Her fingers were burning.

"Eat up now, Miss Graham, so we can put you to bed."

He sat on the floor opposite her while she ate half-heartedly. When she started to doze over the bowl, he rose and took it from her. At his urging, she took another drink of whiskey which made her shudder violently. "Hold to me, lass." Martin scooped her up, blanket and all, and carried her to the edge of his bed. "Can you undress yourself, preferably down to your shift? If you're wearing stays or even a boned bodice, they come off."

Fia was too wretched to worry about modesty. Feebly, she nodded and removed her coat, waistcoat, and petticoat. She rested a moment then removed her under-petticoat and bodice. Martin steadied her while she stepped out of her pocket hoop and, when she sat, clad in her knee-length linen shift and stockings, he again chaffed each foot and calf.

"All right, climb into the bed now," he instructed.

After she lay down, he pulled the woven covers up to her chin. But Fia slipped a fevered hand onto Martin's arm as he began to move away. "I am sorry to be such a bother."

Tucking her hand back under the covers, Martin patted her shoulder. "Don't trouble yourself. Just rest now, Miss."

"Please, call me Fia. I would very much like to call you Martin."

"Very well, Fia. Sleep now."

She turned her face to the wall and slept instantly. Martin sat in his chair to wait. It wasn't noon yet and he wished he could work at his loom; it would have helped pass the time. But he didn't wish to disturb Fia Graham's badly needed rest.

Chapter Three

As the day passed, Fia's fever remained, much to Martin's consternation. Periodically he would rouse her from sleep long enough to give her a few sips of mistletoe tea. Martin hoped that keeping her warm and getting plenty of tea and maybe some broth into her would break the fever. He had no meadowsweet or blackthorn berries and there was no time to ferment spruce beer–even if he had molasses to make it with. She needed help now. Martin shared all this with Fia, not really thinking she understood, but saying it aloud helped him think. It also forced him to admit how unprepared he'd let himself become for treating even a simple illness. When again Fia slept, he wrapped warmed stones and placed them in the bed before doubling another blanket over her.

Late that night, Martin took one of his medical books from the trunk at the foot of the bed. Perhaps there was something he'd forgotten. He'd been sure it was nothing more than exposure to the cold or exhaustion causing her illness. She had no symptoms of anything more serious, but the ever-present fever plagued him.

As the vaporous light of early morning crept across the floor, Martin picked up a rough bag stuffed with clumps of raw wool. He carded and spun wool through the early morning hours, but grew restless and stiff from inactivity. Stepping outside near mid-day, he checked Odhar in his byre and spent a few minutes tossing a stick to Arthur. When he returned, he found Fia standing beside the bed looking uneasy and confused. "He can't mean it," she rasped. "Why would he make me do this?"

Martin quickly crossed to her and gently took her arm; "Fia, get back into bed; you shouldn't be up."

She turned on him; there was no hint of recognition in her eyes. "I know my duty," she swore, agitated, "but Uncle George…he asks too much."

"We'll deal with your uncle later. Now," he coaxed, "back to bed."

Fia grasped and tugged at the front of his shirt in desperation. "What if he comes looking for me? Where will I go now that the school is closed?"

Holding her hands against his chest to still them, Martin soothed, "You will stay here with me. If he comes, he'll not take you anywhere. I promise you that. Now back to bed, lass. Your rest is important."

It was a bit of a struggle to calm her but, when she had fallen into a fitful sleep, Martin pondered the exchange between them; he could make little sense of it. Staring down at her, Martin decided to stay close in case she woke again in such an anxious state.

As the hours of idleness drew on, Martin's thoughts strayed to memories prompted by Fia's arrival, the Headmaster in particular. He would rather have kept most of them locked away, but they jabbed and plucked at him, offering no peace. Absently scratching between Arthur's ears, Martin rested his head against the back of the chair. He knew those memories well. Once awakened, they would hold all else at bay like a snarling hound until he gave them the time they demanded of him. With a resigned sigh, he surrendered.

The years he'd spent in Edinburgh studying medicine with Alexander Monro were full of challenge and promise. The renowned doctor had taken Martin in training as a courtesy to an old acquaintance, Meriel Campbell, Martin's grandmother. Monro told him later that he never regretted the favor; not only did Martin become one of Dr. Monro's most dedicated students, but the two became fast friends–as close in some ways as Alex and his own son, Martin's classmate. For seven years, Martin studied and stayed to practice with Alex: physic, surgery, midwifery. But, with all that to prepare him, and two years of his own successful practice behind him, Martin could not prevent the death of his own wife and her child. When he let himself dwell on it, Martin could almost believe he was responsible for their deaths–Bridgid's and her bairn's;

aye, hers...and that of his brother, Hugh. His brother's tirade in the immediate aftermath of their deaths had revealed the truth.

"You're not a doctor, you're a *butcher!*" Hugh screeched at his younger brother. "You *killed* them." He wailed piteously, "You took them from me."

"I didn't kill them–there was nothing else I could do for them," Martin insisted, his features pinched white in anguish. "And what have I taken from you? Bridgid was my wife, he was my son. You should be thanking God that you still have your wife and children."

"How long were you a husband? Less than eight months? And how eager was Bridgid to marry you?"

A chill crept up Martin's spine. He turned a questioning look on his brother, but the malevolent stare Hugh returned made Martin's belly lurch. "Bridgid was...the bairn was ...yours," he stated quietly.

Hugh glared his triumph for a split second before remembering that she was dead; his son was dead. His face twisted and grew dark with anger. "And you killed them," he snarled.

In his shock, Martin managed to ask, "If you loved Bridgid, why did you urge me to love her? To marry her?" But he already knew the answer. "You sacrificed me to keep your lover under your wife's nose."

Hugh flung his arms wide and railed, "Don't try to blame me. You killed her because she loved me. Me," he sneered, pounding his chest, "the lowly schoolmaster–not you, the lofty physician. And you despise me for it."

"How could that be when I didn't know?"

Hugh thrust his massive fist in his brother's face; and while Martin reeled from the blow, his head struck the stone wall and fingers clawed at it for support.

Hugh's twisted ranting continued. "You saw your chance to get even with me and grabbed it. But you won't get away with it. Oh, no. I'll make sure you regret what you've done this day you *murderer.*" Hugh's rage exploded in another swing at his dazed brother who tried to side-step the blow. It caught only his shoulder and Hugh fell heavily to the floor with the force of his misplaced swing.

Martin shook his head to clear it and begged in desperation, "Hugh, listen to me." Blood from his nose and brow dripped onto Hugh as he bent to help his brother up. But Hugh thrust Martin and his offered hand away.

"I will have my revenge, you son of Satan," Hugh seethed. "I swear it." Those words, Hugh's last to his brother, had echoed in Martin's memory a thousand times over the last three years. Martin had relived that night again and again, always coming to the same conclusion. The child was stillborn–beyond the reach of his or anyone's skills. And Bridgid had overdosed on laudanum. If he was at fault, it was for leaving that damned bottle too close to her. He used the drug as a last resort. The babe was so large that Bridgid was ripped badly and he had a terrible time trying to stop the bleeding. The more she writhed in pain, the more she bled. Eyes bulging in her sweat-covered face, she clutched at him then struck his chest with all the power she had. "Give me that laudanum now! Stop this pain or I swear you'll be sorry."

He knew if he didn't quiet her, she'd surely bleed to death, so Martin relented. And who knew? By easing her suffering, perhaps he could ease his own. Martin was wretched. The child he had longed for had died and his wife was in agony. He'd left the bottle next to the bed and it was drained when he returned with more toweling.

As Martin's horrific memories began to fade, he covered his face with his hands and wondered, as he always did, "Why didn't I see it?" His courtship of Bridgid had been a whirlwind. They married quickly and Bridgid had been attentive enough as a wife. It had puzzled Martin that soon after he married Bridgid, Hugh had turned cold and distant. He thought they were fortunate that she got pregnant right away. He didn't know that she married him already pregnant. "I should have known; I'm a doctor," he scolded himself. Hugh's selfish and ugly plan had cost them both dearly. Hugh had lost his lover, his son, and his wife, Olwyn, and her children though it was clear, to Martin at least, that the last was insignificant to Hugh. And Martin too had lost a wife and a son–along with his home, his standing as a physician and, periodically, his peace of mind.

Hugh kept his oath, telling a tale of jealous rage over and over until everyone believed Martin had committed murder and Hugh had somehow been wronged even as he cheated on Olwyn.

And with emotions running high, Martin could not undo the damage. Hugh had his revenge, and Martin was cast out.

Emotionally exhausted, Martin was startled by the crack of a log falling into the fire. Rubbing his eyes, he turned from the flames to look at Fia. She moved restlessly and Martin could see from where he sat that her skin was still heavily flushed. "Fia Graham," he murmured and wondered about her yet again. Several times since she had stumbled into his path, her presence had annoyed him. It was not her fault that she was in this predicament, and Martin was ashamed of his flashes of discontent. Running long fingers through his unruly hair, Martin sighed. His experience and the years alone had made him cautious; that was part of his present frustration. He was used to his aloneness, but his reaction to the young woman's presence concerned him. Perhaps his privacy had become too important to him if he so resented her temporary intrusion into his life.

Again, Martin focused his gaze on her and his expression softened. She intrigued him. The bits of information she had given him on the way to the croft, and some of her fevered utterances, had piqued his curiosity. "And she needs me", he thought; and the thought shook him. "Needs me?" he puzzled aloud, and Arthur raised his face to his master's. Medically speaking, it was true. With some surprise, he realized it had been a long time since he'd felt really needed–too long since feeling his skills were vital to anyone but himself. The appearance of Fia Graham already was beginning to affect him; he had to think again instead of going through the motions of living. Martin walked to the bed, cautiously excited by this reawakening. Sitting next to her, he studied Fia's face in detail. Dark circles were beginning to show under the shadow of her lashes. Her lips were parched from the fever. "I can ease that." From his depleted supplies, Martin drew and gently applied a salve to her lips and to the scratches on her face. He then placed his fingers under her jaw. Her pulse was a bit fast. Hesitantly, he stroked her soft cheek and whispered, "Break that fever, lass."

Throughout the remainder of the day, Martin alternately sat beside her and moved aimlessly about the cottage. He had a few blankets but, no matter how many blankets he doubled over her, Fia still had bouts of chills. Sometime after midnight, she again began to move restlessly, muttering largely unintelligible words and phrases. Each time she reached this stage, Martin sat with her, spoke in quiet, soothing tones and stroked her forehead and face repeatedly. Once or twice, she looked at him with pain-filled eyes, and it hurt Martin that she was in such distress. When once again she was calm, he left her side.

In the early morning hours, he moved through the croft with a purpose. Taking two blankets with him, he spread them before the fire which he stoked to a high, hot blaze. Martin then stripped to his breeches and went back to the bed.

"Come, lass," he murmured, "this had better turn the tide." He gathered Fia up, along with her remaining blankets, and carried her toward the hearth. He laid her, facing the blaze, on the pallet he'd fashioned. Blankets now underneath and on top of her, Martin slid in behind her and pressed his body against the length of hers, his arm across her waist. He fervently hoped that the combination of blankets, the fire and his own body heat would finally drive the stubborn fever from her. Unresponsive till now, she shifted once and, to Martin's surprise and consternation, she only moved to fit her body more snugly against his. He was chagrinned to feel a mounting pressure in his loins. For the first time, he consciously admitted she was more than comely. He shook his head and chided himself for his thoughts and his reaction to her nearness.

Several hours later, Martin awoke to find himself drenched in sweat–partly his own, but mostly Fia's. Her forehead was noticeably cooler. Rising, he stoked the fire again to ensure the success of his treatment and turning back, caught his breath at the sight of her. Fia's shift was soaked through, the shadows and curves of her body too thinly veiled now. Shaken, Martin quickly covered her, dried himself off and wavered only for a moment before climbing back in behind her. He wanted her to sweat until she rid herself of the last traces of the clinging fever, and he felt a small rush of pleasure at this positive turn of events. Propping himself on one elbow, Martin leaned over her. In the firelight, her cheekbones cast angular shadows across her perspiring skin, flawless except for the scratches suffered from her escape into the woods. Her lips were slightly parted. Hesitantly now, he touched her face and listened to her breathing which was steady, stronger. Martin nodded his approval. He lay back and closed his eyes. When he next opened them, he was looking directly into Fia's gray, wide-eyed gawk. "Ah, lass, good–you're awake." He smiled sleepily and stretched.

She watched him intently as he sat up and rested his hand lightly on her forehead. Fia was afraid to move. She didn't understand why she was sleeping with Martin Ross, but his nearness and obvious familiarity with her in their mutually half-clothed state, transfixed her.

Martin beamed with relief. "No more fever. Very good." Her eyes continued to bore into his and he believed he had some idea of what she was thinking. "It's all right, lass, we sweat the fever from you. The important thing is that you should recover fairly quickly now." He brushed a damp curl from her forehead. "How do you feel?"

"Confused," she admitted weakly.

"As well you might. But, physically, how do you feel?"

"Leaden. Would you help me sit up?"

Martin put one arm around her shoulders and took her left hand in his to help her into a sitting position.

"Oh, Lord," she whispered clinging to his arm with her other hand as well. "I...didn't realize...I'm really weak. And I ache."

Supporting her back against his chest and shoulder he remarked, "The aches are partly because you slept on the floor. The rest, and your overall weakness, is because you've been fighting a high fever for several days and eaten only what I could force into you during that time."

She looked up at his bearded face and earnest brown eyes just above her and her voice faltered. "S...several days?" she asked in a breathless voice, suddenly acutely aware of the warmth of his bare skin against her.

"Aye. We'll talk more later. Right now, you need to get into dry clothes and back into a real bed. Do you think you can stand?"

Fia nodded and Martin pushed all but one blanket from her. Leaning heavily on him, Fia got to her feet and walked to the bed where she sat, slightly dizzy, holding her head in her hands. He arranged the blanket around her shoulders then Fia heard him rummaging around and looked to the end of the bed. The movement of muscle in his chest and shoulders as he searched the contents of his trunk jolted her. She was unprepared for his raw vitality, lean and muscular, so close to her; she could still feel the hardness and the heat of his body.

He looked up, some unidentified treasure in hand, and she glanced away quickly least he see something she would keep hidden. "Are you all right?" he asked, having noticed her shifting gaze. He came to her side.

"Aye." Her whispered answer was barely audible. She was breathing rapidly, which Martin attributed to exertion.

"You're still far from well, Miss." Placing a soft woolen shirt into her hands, he asked her to put it on. "Get out of that damp shift. I have to feed the animals so you should have plenty of time to change." With that, he pulled his own shirt and coat on, stockings and boots, then left her alone.

The only thing Fia wanted to do was think about what she'd just experienced. But she had to change quickly so, for a time, she put off thoughts of Martin Ross.

Fia sat holding her shift feeling a little lost in Martin's shirt, but it was wonderfully soft and warm and comforted her aching body. She'd rolled the sleeves up above her fingertips and looked up as Martin reentered followed by a blast of cold air.

"Looks like we won't escape the borrowed days this year after all," he said closing the door. When he turned toward her, he stopped abruptly.

"I had wondered if we would." In the silence that followed she asked, "Is something amiss?"

Martin shook his head slightly. "No," he answered somewhat gruffly and moved toward the cupboard. "You should get under the covers now and try to sleep. I'll have food for you when you wake." Without a word, he took her shift and draped it near the fire to dry.

"I need to thank you." Her voice was low but steady. "I can only guess how much trouble I've caused you since I fell in front of your horse–I'm sure it's considerable. I'll be out of your way as quickly as I can." She climbed into the bed, drawing her knees toward her chest as he placed a warm, wrapped stone between the covers. He straightened and looked down at her.

"There's no hurry, Miss." His voice was solemn and matched by his expression.

Fia sighed inwardly. On some level then, her presence was acceptable to him. "You promised to call me Fia, remember?" She thought his expression gentled somewhat.

"Aye...Fia," he responded obediently. "I'll be outside for a bit. I'll try not to wake you when I return."

"Do what you need to," she stifled a yawn. "I'll be fine."

Martin closed the door behind him and walked to the burn, oblivious to the frigid air and Arthur's playful antics. The man was at a loss. He knew so little about Fia Graham–bare sketches only of why she had left school and how she'd come to be in the woods. And for some reason, she feared her uncle finding her. But he did know that the sight of her in his shirt, dark hair spilling around her face and shoulders took his very breath. "You'd think I'd never seen a woman before," he spoke absently to Arthur. Thoughtfully rubbing his hand across his mouth and down his bearded chin, Martin murmured, "I'll do well to keep my distance–and my head about this. The sooner I can get her to Inveraray, the better for us both." He looked over his shoulder at the croft where the lass slept. With Fia inside, the croft looked different, less empty somehow. Suddenly, Martin rolled his eyes and shook his head in exasperation. "Damn. This won't be easy."

Fia could see by the light of the dying fire that her host slept on the makeshift pallet they had shared on the floor. "He must be exhausted," she mused. She remembered waking off and on during...what did he say...several days? Always he was nearby, waiting to feed her, talk to her, or force her to stay in bed. How could she ever repay him?

Slowly sitting up, Fia placed her bare feet on the bare wood. While she didn't want to disturb Martin's sleep, neither would it do to let the fire go out.

With considerable effort Fia stood, then slowly approached the hearth. She stopped to look at him; his face not quite relaxed even in sleep. The defined sculpture of his chest was softened by a dusting of lightly curled hair and shone, darkly golden, in the fading firelight. Fia was embarrassed at her bold perusal of him and forced her attention back to the problem of the fire. When she bent over to pick up a peat brick, her head throbbed with such ferocity that she cried out.

Martin was on his feet instantly, fully alert. "What do you think you're doing?" he demanded crossly.

"I...the fire needed tending. I didn't mean to wake you."

"God's blood, I'm not upset that you woke me. What the devil are you doing out of bed? If you needed help you should have called me."

"Please don't scold me," she murmured, hand on her forehead. "I meant no harm."

"Well, I hope you did none." He picked up a heavy coverlet from his pallet and leaning over, wrapped it none too gently around her. He shoved peat onto the fire, stood with his back to her a moment and finally forced himself to take a deep breath. "Are you hungry?" he asked abruptly.

"Famished," she admitted in soft tones.

"Sit then." He tugged his shirt on then swung a pot over the fire to heat a stew of barley, vegetables and rabbit to go with cold oat cakes. In a short time he handed her one bowl and he took the other then sat on the floor facing her.

"Are you still angry with me, Martin?" Absently, she stirred the contents of the bowl awaiting his response.

His sigh was almost audible. "I don't want you to have a relapse, that's all. We've worked hard to get you this far." Then, belatedly, he added, "No, I'm not angry. But tell me, do you understand my concern?"

Nodding, she assured him that she did. "And you're right–it was a thoughtless action." She was silent for a few moments while she ate. "You know, you make a very tasty stew."

"It's nice to have a second opinion. With only me to judge, I'm never quite sure how the food really tastes."

Glancing at the darkened window, Fia looked frustrated. "I've lost track of time, sleeping and waking as I have. How long have I been here?" She scraped her bowl with the last bit of oat cake.

"Almost five days."

Resting her head on the back of the chair, Fia said, "When I left the school, I thought I'd arrive in Glasgow before the borrowed days set in."

"You're anxious to be home then?" he asked in a casual voice as he watched her reaction with more than casual attention.

Her gaze dropped to her empty bowl. She took a deep, resigned breath. "No, no hurry." She started and glanced at him nervously. "Not except to be out of your way, of course."

He watched her discomfort with a hooded gaze. "Well," he stated, "as your doctor, I'll decide when you're well enough to leave. And there'll be no arguments on that count."

She smiled a little. "As you say."

Martin rose and took her bowl from her. In response to a sudden noise at the door, he opened it to the woolly black dog. "Come, Arthur...inside now." He gave the dog a healthy whack on the rump as it entered. For a brief moment, Arthur laid his large head on Fia's arm in acceptance of his new friend then settled by the hearth with a non-committal snort, head between outstretched paws. Martin vowed that Fia was in good hands with Arthur and, donning his coat and boots, excused himself to tend the horse.

As she sat resting, Fia noticed a book lying on the hewn timber above the hearth. She stood briefly and reached for it. Thumbing through it, she was surprised to find what looked to be a medical text, *Primitive Physic*. Unexplainable guilt caused her to glance quickly toward the door, but Martin wasn't there. The door was still closed and her interest was aroused by the discovery of the book. Hadn't he been speaking in jest when referring to himself as her doctor? Not by the looks of the volume in her hands. "Arthur, this is strange, don't you think?"

The dog raised his eyes to her without lifting his head from its resting place.

Was he truly a doctor? Fia couldn't imagine why any doctor would live miles from anyone who might need his help; it made no sense. The opening door interrupted her thoughts.

"I'll need to exercise Odhar a bit in the morning. He's restless." Martin approached with more firewood and peat bricks. "This should keep us for–" He stopped in mid-sentence, gaze resting on the book in her hand.

"Are you really a physician?" she asked pointedly.

Kneeling beside the hearth, Martin stacked the logs and bricks and answered without looking at her, "I'm trained as one."

"But you're by yourself here. You could be helping people. Aren't you wasting your training?" she blurted.

Hardened eyes bored into hers; controlled anger swelled his voice. "My training wasn't wasted on you, Miss." In one fluid motion, he rose, took the book from her and deposited it back on the mantle.

His reproachful use of the title "Miss" and his unsuccessfully concealed wrath made her cringe. Taking a deep breath, Fia scolded herself. After all, she barely knew him. Furthermore, how he led his life was not her business. She stood up and, with bowed head offered, "It was wrong of me to pass judgement and I apologize. I've been rude and offended you. I hope you'll forgive my blunder." Suddenly weary, she moved past him intending to retreat to the bed, but stopped and stared ahead at the large object at the far end of the croft.

His own gaze following hers, Martin offered bluntly, "That, Miss, is how I make my living."

"I don't know how I failed to recognize it before." She moved toward the loom, careful not to touch it or the beautiful unfinished cloth on it. "You're an accomplished weaver," she murmured.

"Most of what you see here is mine." His voice right behind her startled her. So close was he that her shoulder brushed his chest when she turned causing her to step back as if burned.

"Then I'm right, you are accomplished," her voice was barely audible. With the firelight behind him she could scarcely distinguish his features. She only hoped her own face did not reveal how disturbed she was by his nearness. "I...I'm tired," she whispered. Then, lifting her chin a notch, Fia's eyes seemed to challenge him.

The moment stretched between them until in a low, thick voice, Martin said, "Good night, then," and stepped aside.

Tired she was, but Fia lay awake for some time puzzling over Martin Ross. He must not have found being a physician to his liking. She believed him young enough to have a thriving practice and build an excellent reputation if he were a good one. Here her thoughts took a turn. It was hard for her to imagine him not being a good physician–or weaver–or anything he chose to be. While his moodiness confused her, she liked much of what she saw in Martin Ross: compassion, humor, intelligence. She turned over abruptly as if to quell the thoughts now crowding her mind; but they would not be stilled. His body was taut and sinewy on a smallish frame, and his undeniably commanding presence made him seem larger than his physical size. "What am I thinking?" she murmured. The promised wedding to Forbes loomed before her. Surely when she returned to Glasgow, Uncle George would push to move the date up. She had sworn never to marry Forbes, and now...Fia stifled a moan. Now, there was Martin Ross. And while they were little more than strangers, Fia knew that she could never be content to be Struan's wife now–not in her wildest dreams.

"Lass, don't cry, please." Her eyes flew open as Martin sat gingerly on the edge of the bed, regret etched on his face. "I didn't mean to be so harsh with you."

Fia struggled to sit up, wiping her eyes; she had not realized that she was in tears. "Your life is just that, yours, and none of my affair," she gulped, not knowing what else to say.

"It was a reasonable question and I am sorry for my reaction." Reaching out, Martin wiped the tears from her cheeks, fingers lingering a moment against her jaw line.

She caught his fingers in her own and pushed them gently away. "Please," she could barely speak, "I'm fine; don't trouble yourself. I'd really like to go to sleep now." The attraction to him she felt was almost tangible–it was suffocating.

Nodding, Martin rose and left her side, chiding himself. Was this what he considered keeping his distance? He shook his head in disgust. She drew him like a moth to flame. Curiosity to know more about her began to nag at him and that made him worry. He was so close to her during her illness that they already shared an intimacy many people never experienced. Maybe that was clouding his thinking. He sighed ruefully. Perhaps it was he and not the croft that was less empty since her arrival.

Chapter Four

When Fia awoke the next morning, the only evidence of the bed on the floor was a pile of folded blankets atop the trunk. The air in the croft was chilly and she snuggled down into the warmth of the bed. She heard movement near the fireplace and turned to focus on Martin, sitting in his chair, absently rubbing Arthur's head. When Fia sat up and pulled her knees under her chin, making a pyramid of the covers, Martin and the dog turned to look at her. Her soft, sleep-tousled expression warmed him.

"Good morning, Fia. How are you feeling?"

"Better, I can finally feel my strength returning."

"And you slept well?"

"Aye," she replied, "better than you did I'll warrant."

"The floor isn't that bad, though I don't think Arthur was too keen on sharing it with me." He ran his fingers down the dog's back.

"If I continue to improve at this rate, you shouldn't have to share much longer. I'll be able to leave soon and you can have your bed back."

Martin studied her briefly before averting his gaze. "There's no rush. Besides, there may be more to contend with than your recovery. It's snowing."

"Truly?" she gasped and, stumbling from the bed, yanked the door open. A cloud of small white flakes swirled in as cold air rushed over her. Eyes closed, Fia turned her face upward, exhilarated by the delicate sputters of snow settling on her skin. She had little time to savor it though for Martin abruptly shut the door, leaned hard against it, and glowered at her.

"I don't take it lightly that you've been ill," he said tersely. "What happened to your promise to be more careful? I don't want to see you relapse nor do I wish to play nursemaid indefinitely. There are other things I'd rather do."

His rebuke stung. Fia fought to control her voice and, when she finally replied, her tone was taut, her words curt.

"I did not intentionally break my word. You're right. It was impulsive of me. But you're wrong about me not taking my illness seriously. I'm feeling much better thanks to you." Her eyes narrowed. "You've told me that I'm not a bother but I see that I am. From this point, I'll not trouble you more than I must. I'll take care of myself and stay out of your way." Purposefully, she marched to the bed and began straightening the covers.

The tension between them hung in the air and, though Fia felt his eyes bore into her, she refused to look at him. She simply didn't understand his shifting moods and thought it a good thing that she really was feeling better. Though she wasn't eager to go on to Glasgow, clearly, the sooner he was rid of her, the happier he'd be.

Martin, still leaning against the door, scrutinized her from the top of her head to her bare feet. Closing his eyes a moment, he silently cursed himself for lecturing Fia so sternly and causing additional strain between them. He wanted to mend the rift but realized it was a wide one. After a few minutes, Martin moved several steps closer to her. "While I wish you hadn't let the cold air wash over you, it doesn't excuse my outburst. I owe you an apology, Fia." He paused staring at her back. "You may not believe me when I say that your presence isn't a hindrance, nor would I blame you considering I've snapped at you more than once." Again, Martin hesitated. "I want to do whatever I can to help you recover your health. I ask you not to doubt that at least–please."

Fia hesitated before responding, trying to decide what hid behind those words. "I believe you want to help me otherwise you'd have left me in the woods where you found me. But I barely know you, Martin. You keep apologizing for getting angry at me, and I apologize for making you mad." Fia turned to face him and the silence stretched between them again while he waited uncertainly for her to continue. Reticent, she crossed the room to stand in front of him, and offered peace. "You've brought me through my illness, Martin, the fever is gone and I'm on the mend. Perhaps we could put our differences aside and start anew, not as doctor and patient, but maybe as friends."

Martin smiled gently and took her hand in his. "You're generous, lass." For the second time, he kissed her fingers. "I'd like that very much."

While they ate porridge and treated themselves to the luxury of tea for breakfast, Martin suggested that he heat some water. "I thought you might like me to wash out your clothes. You'll want to put them back on soon. I'm afraid they're not in very good condition though."

Fia shook her head. "I'll wash them. You should do something for yourself–maybe work at your loom."

After a moment's hesitation, Martin confessed, "I've been itching to do just that. As long as you don't tire yourself," he ordered.

"It's settled then."

Martin went about setting up a large kettle and filled it to overflowing with snow. "I'm not sure how well this will work; there's not much room in here."

"Leave that to me. I believe," Fia pointed to his loom, "you have something else to do." Martin smiled, bowed slightly and moved to the loom. When the snow melt was hot enough, Fia set about cleaning her clothes. It was a laborious task in the confined space around the hearth and, though she wouldn't admit it to Martin, she was spent. The rhythmic sounds of his loom set a pace by which she was able to finish her chore. As she spread the last of the wet clothing by the fire, Fia spoke over her shoulder. "When my things are dry, I'd like to repair them. Do you have a needle and thread I might use?"

"Aye, I have everything you'll need for your mending."

"Can I wash anything for you? I've finished my own."

Martin shook his head. "Even though you feel better, I really don't think you should do too much."

"Perhaps later then," she remarked, silently relieved. "Martin?" He looked up at her again. "Do you think I could have a bath?"

After a long moment, his gaze dropped back to his work. "It's too soon yet, Fia. The pitcher and bowl will have to do."

"Maybe so."

Though he didn't see the disappointment on her face, he heard it in her voice. After a brief silence, Martin asked if she knew anything about weaving.

"A little; I'm more familiar with finished cloth."

"Then, if you're interested, come and sit."

Fia sat down on the bench at Martin's side, pulling a blanket around her shoulders. "What lovely colors," she said.

"This russet brown," he began and pointed to a yarn in his cloth, "is made from lichen and this grayish-blue from the root of yellow flag." He pointed into the rafters above the loom where bunches of plants and roots hung upside-down in various stages of dried fragility.

"And all these you use to make dyes?"

Martin shook his head. "Some are medicinal." His profile was expressionless and Fia decided not to pursue the remark.

"Do you spin your own wool?"

"I do." He continued to pass the shuttle back and forth, slowly lengthening the fine woolen cloth. "I card the wool to remove all the debris and, at the end of the carding, when the wool fibers are all aligned in the same direction, I roll it off, hold it in my palm, and guide it with my thumb and forefinger onto the spindle. With practice, it's like anything else–once you get the feel of it, it doesn't leave you."

His tone suggested to Fia that weaving was more than a way for Martin to make a living; it was something that he enjoyed. He appeared relaxed for once, and Fia enjoyed this easy rapport. She sought to prolong it.

Watching him for several minutes she asked, "Where did you learn to weave?"

"My grandfather taught me when I was tall enough to work the loom. It was his trade; he was a true wizard at it." Martin turned a brilliant smile on Fia whose heart thudded unexpectedly in return. She was afraid he could hear it; it was so loud in her own ears.

"Your grandfather was very special to you."

Her statement brought a raised eyebrow from Martin. "Aye, you're perceptive."

Fia blushed slightly. "Your feelings for your grandfather are written clearly on your face."

Martin turned his attention back to his work, and Fia thought the pleasant interlude at an end. So it surprised her when he said, "More than any one person, my grandfather has influenced my life."

"How did he do that?" Fia waited, hoping for a glimpse into this complex man. She wasn't disappointed.

"Hugh was an Appin Stewart who married a Campbell–Meriel Campbell. The families forbid it, but Hugh and Meriel adored each other so married anyway. Their decision caused them a great deal of personal pain. My brother...older brother...is named for Grandfather. But I inherited Hugh's looks and temperament. People always said that I was the elder Hugh's favorite–the son he never had. And Grandfather used to say that my brother inherited too many of the less desirable Campbell traits to suit him." Martin chuckled, but Fia noticed a hardness cloud his expression. Thinking it curious, she tucked the thought away for later.

"Hugh not only taught me his trade, but also the properties of plants; how to use them for my dyes, to tend wounds and treat certain illnesses." His voice distant, Martin paused staring out the window at the falling snow. Then he turned to look at Fia. He stared at her for so long she became uncomfortable.

"Perhaps you'd rather continue this later." Fia suggested and rose. But Martin's hand closed gently over hers, and drew her back down. When she was seated again, Martin released her and continued.

"Hugh was a man of strong convictions. He was a confirmed and outspoken Jacobite who believed that Charles Edward Stuart was Scotland's path to salvation. And he hated Clan Campbell with the exception, of course, of my grandmother. For years, the Dukes of Argyll ran Scotland for the monarchy and helped destroy many of the smaller, weaker clans." He paused then huffed, "Some folk claimed he married a Campbell just to make her life miserable. It wasn't true though, he was devoted to her. Meriel's family disowned her." His expression clouded momentarily before he continued. "It wasn't until my mother married a Ross that Grandmother's existence was even acknowledged again."

"I don't understand what difference marrying a Ross would make."

"As a clan, the Rosses supported the crown, not Bonnie Prince Charlie." In silence, Martin surveyed the inside of the cottage as if searching for something, someone. "This place, this land I live on, Grandmother gave me when I was merely a child. The Campbells either don't know or don't care that I live here–probably have forgotten I'm alive. To them, I was never significant except for my connection to Meriel. And, in the end, Meriel did renounce Hugh and return to her family."

"Renounce him?" Fia gasped, unable to hide her shock. "She gave up her family for him... loved him that much. How...why then did she renounce him?"

Pausing in his tale, Martin watched her with appreciation in his brown eyes. Her indignant question on his grandfather's behalf touched him. "In truth, Grandmother gave the land to me so that Hugh would always have a home no matter what happened–even if it was under the very noses of the Campbells he loathed. She loved her family; but Hugh was her life. Meriel knew his politics were dangerous. By shifting her family's focus away from him, separating from him, she was trying to help ensure his survival."

Martin began to move the shuttle again, back and forth across the loom, as if it helped him remember. Fia had many questions but dared not speak; she wanted to hear the rest of the tale.

"When the Prince landed at Glenfinnan, Hugh was there with his kinsmen. All of them were disappointed; they had expected more clans to rally to the cause. It didn't stop them though. I guess they believed men would join them along the way, especially if they could win battles as they went. Hugh fought at Prestonpans and at Derby and celebrated both victories with the Prince. Hugh was away a long time, but returned to Meriel and me on his way to Culloden."

An uneasy shiver ran down Fia's spine at the mention of Culloden. She pulled the blanket closer around her as though it would block out her own memory of scarce food and rampant fear that plagued Inverness after the battle. Only three years old when the English poured into her hometown, the impression on her was a lasting one. She swallowed hard and whispered, "What happened?"

"One more sound victory was all they thought they needed to advance to London and claim the throne. Hugh predicted the decisive battle would be soon and he was right. He just never considered that the enemy might win."

"So...he was at Culloden during the battle?"

"Aye. He was killed there with many of his kinsmen." Martin's hands faltered on the loom.

"I'm truly sorry, Martin. It must have been devastating when you and your grandmother received the news."

"It was the hardest thing I ever did, telling her that he was dead. Her one consolation was that Hugh wasn't alone when he died."

Fia struggled to understand. "I suppose that dying with others who believed strongly in the same cause would be of some comfort."

"Aye, but I meant that Grandmother's consolation was that I was with him when he died."

Staring at him, Fia shook her head as if she hadn't heard correctly. "You?" she whispered. "You were there?" Martin nodded and she continued to stare, not wanting to believe it. "But surely, your grandfather wouldn't...but you were just a lad!"

"Not after that day. After seeing the agony, gore, and cruelty, I was suddenly the oldest lad of twelve you could imagine."

Fia's eyes were bright with tears. "But they butchered everyone: soldiers, spectators, women and children; everyone for miles around," she croaked. "How did..."

"By some miracle, they didn't find me."

The air was thick around them and Fia put her hand to her throat. She couldn't breathe; she needed to distance herself from Martin, yet she could not move. How could he have escaped? With difficulty, she focused her attention on what Martin was saying.

"I wanted to be with Hugh and decided to accompany him when he left to rejoin his clansmen. He respected my decision. But I was to work behind the battle line, tending wounded soldiers as best I could. When the battle started, our men were hungry and exhausted from the march. The weather was bad. When they began to fall, the wounded seemed grateful for whatever comfort I could give them. Of course, there was little time to do anything that the enemy didn't undo within minutes. The grapeshot alone shredded our lines. We had muskets and broadswords; the English knew what a bayonet was for." Martin drew his hand across his mouth and down his beard as if shaking the memory. "It all happened so fast though it seemed a lifetime to me as it unfolded." His eyes hardened and his voice was edged like one of those swords–sharp and cold. It made Fia shudder. She closed her eyes and tears slid down her cheeks thinking of the misery and carnage he'd seen.

"The soldiers moved in before the battle was over, killing those too weak to move or too slow to get out of the way. They took everything of value. It was barbaric; just how the English liked to think of us." The pain and anger Martin harbored were obvious, and Fia felt helpless to respond to such passion.

"As I worked, I found myself being overrun by the battle. It was hard to walk through the freezing rain and, half of the time I could hardly see fifteen feet in front of me. Hugh came from nowhere, hurled me to the ground bellowing at me to stay down. He'd never raised his voice to me so I knew I was in danger. But, when he looked at me, there was no emotion in his eyes– nothing. Then I saw that his sword arm was nearly severed. As I lay sprawled on the soaking ground, his life was spilling from that wound." Martin seemed suddenly exhausted. "His last words were, 'Use me or you'll die with me,' and I lay, pretending to be dead too, his body shield-ing mine, his warm blood covering us both. Occasionally, I heard a scream from some wounded man being murdered or mutilated. But I was completely numb and that probably saved me. I lay still for a long time after the battle subsided. I didn't even realize that, when an English bastard ran his bayonet through Hugh to make sure he was dead, he wounded me in the process." Un-moving for a long moment, Martin shut his eyes concealing further thoughts of Culloden. When he opened them again, he saw Fia's slender fingers gripping his arm and frowned.

Fia's own gaze followed his. She hadn't realized that, while listening to him, she had reached out. Casually, Fia removed her hand hoping not to call undue attention to the gesture. Deeply touched by the tale, she wanted to reflect further on it and its effect on Martin. But he would not let her do that just yet.

"You're very quiet," he observed sharply.

Raising her stunned face to his stormy one she challenged, "And that surprises you?"

He clamped his lips together so she tried again. "Are you upset with me?"

"I'm not," he replied bluntly.

"Martin," she responded hotly, "you're obviously displeased–I just don't understand what's caused it. You've told me a frightening, tragic story that's also an amazing tale of devotion and love. I'm honored you chose to share it with me."

Abruptly, he shifted his eyes from her face and Fia sat staring. Suddenly she pushed herself from the bench and stood away from him gaping in disbelief. "Martin Ross! You're incensed because I heard your tale, aren't you? You dropped your guard and now you're unhappy with me for what you did."

He didn't deny it. "I said before that you were perceptive."

"I am also worthy of your trust."

It was Martin's turn to rise from the loom. He crossed to the hearth busying himself with preparations for a meal. The silence between them stretched unbearably. As she watched the muscles in his back and shoulders work, a feeling of tenderness toward him broke through her outrage and tears shimmered in her eyes. Desperate for a moment alone to collect her thoughts, Fia dropped the blanket, drew on her mantle and boots and shut the door behind her.

This was the first time Fia had left the croft since her arrival. Now she wasn't sure where to go. Light flakes of snow still fell around her. "No doubt he'll scold me for this, too. But I don't care." She was bewildered by and tired of his moodiness. Arthur startled her as he brushed against her legs.

"Is that a proper greeting for your guest?" She stroked his broad, black head then picked her way through the snow to the edge of the burn. Thin ice lined each bank and crystallized delicately where the water met the rocks. The dog came and sat beside her. Taking deep breaths of the sharp, cold air, Fia looked carefully around her, taking in the details of the snow-covered yard and the shrouded woods across the burn. After some time, she turned to Arthur. "Would you tell me how I'm supposed to deal with your master?" Fia touched his nose leather and Arthur's tongue flashed out and licked her finger. "You see? You trust me." She shook her head. "Just a little earlier, we agreed to try to get along. And now he's irritated again. Is it my presence he resents or is this just his way?" Fia sighed. "What do you think Arthur?" She crossed her arms, hugging herself against the cold outside and the ache inside her. "I feel sad when I should still be cross." The dog rubbed the side of its face on her thigh, and she scratched his ear.

From the doorway, Martin watched the exchange between Fia and his dog. He wasn't sure how to react to the fact that the two had struck up such a friendship. Arthur normally had little use for other people; he wasn't used to them. Though he knew he should call her back into the croft out of the cold and snow, Martin was reluctant. Once again, he had let his past come between them. Now his unhappiness was aimed at himself. Why couldn't he keep himself under better control? There was no reason to punish Fia; she'd done nothing wrong and would be gone soon enough. His actions had driven her from the croft and he was at a loss as to how to approach her now. Then an idea struck him. "Perhaps you'd like to visit with Odhar as well." Martin's voice carried across the hush of the snow-covered yard. Fia turned to see him–unsmiling, arms crossed–propped against the door frame. Pointing to the far end of the croft, Martin moved toward the gaping doorway she'd noticed on her arrival.

While his expression was not particularly inviting, Fia felt she had little choice but to accept his gesture at peace-making, if that's what it was, and trudged toward the byre. She reached it just behind Martin who stood aside for her to enter. In the confines of the stable, Odhar looked even bigger than Fia remembered him; and she remembered him as the largest horse she'd ever seen barring draft horses. "He really is huge."

"He's not small, but perhaps he looked larger because of the angle from which you first saw him." He rested his hand on the horse's withers.

Fia fanned her face with her hand. "It's warm in here."

"Aye." At least he'd gotten her out of the cold. "Odhar gives off a lot of heat. It's a pleasant heat if the smell of horse doesn't bother you."

Fia reached out and ran a hand lightly over Odhar's glossy coat. "It doesn't bother me in the least." They were silent, Martin watching Fia, Fia eyeing Odhar. Finally, she looked across the horse at her host. "How did you come to name him 'Odhar'."

Martin grinned, "Have you ever heard of Coinneach Odhar, the Seer?"

"Do you mean the prophet of Culloden?" she asked warily.

"The same. He was a brave and honest man who didn't misuse his gift of prophesy, someone to look up to. This lad," he slapped Odhar's hindquarters, "used to be a bit of a runt." Fia's mouth opened to protest, but Martin raised his palm to stop her, "I swear it's true! The Seer seemed just the kind of example Odhar needed to overcome his poor beginning."

"That's all very well but, didn't the Seer come to a bad end?"

Martin leaned forward to see her better over the horse's back. "It depends on your point of view. Coinneach Odhar was a great friend to the Earl and Countess of Seaforth. The Earl had traveled to France and, when he didn't return as scheduled, the Countess asked Odhar to tell her how her husband fared. Odhar refused at first; he didn't want to upset the Countess. But she insisted and, relenting, the Seer told her that her husband was in a luxurious room with a beautiful, amply endowed woman on his lap. The Countess was so angry, she ordered the Seer put to death, which he was, burned in a barrel of tar at Fortrose."

Fia shuddered. "That's monstrous."

"It is," Martin agreed. "You may be pleased to know that he didn't die before placing a good curse on the House of Seaforth."

"I hope it worked," she vowed. There was an awkward moment, when only Odhar's breathing could be heard, before Fia said, "We always seem to be at odds, you and I. I'm not sure why." When he didn't respond she pressed on. "If you didn't want me to know about your grandfather, why did you tell me? You could have stopped."

"It wasn't a question of wanting or not wanting to tell you, it just came out. And you're wrong. I couldn't stop once I'd started. Only one other person living knows that I was with Hugh at the end. And here, to you, a virtual stranger, I've poured this out. I...I can't explain it," his voice faltered.

"Perhaps I'm not quite the stranger you believe me to be. Martin, I wouldn't betray your confidence."

"No, I don't believe you would. It was not your fault. I'm not as good at apologizing as I am at creating the need to, but I am sorry."

Fia smirked. "You'll get better if you keep practicing."

Martin threw back his head and laughed heartily. "Well said and deserved. But this time, I even drove you out into the cold. At least you have discovered the truth–at times, Arthur and Odhar are better companions than I am." His gaze softened as he asked, "Will you come in soon?"

"I will when you're ready."

He offered his hand. "Come then."

Even now, Hugh's death was painful to Martin perhaps because he had held it close all these years. Until today, only Alex Monro, his old friend and teacher, knew the truth about Hugh's death. Lacing his fingers in front of him, Martin gazed over them at Fia, mending her woolen petticoat. Why did she have this effect on him? Martin rejected the obvious reason for telling Fia about his grandfather–increasingly, he was drawn to her. Silently, Martin reminded himself of his promise when Bridgid died and his life began to fall apart. Never again was he going to let himself be vulnerable to a woman. But he never counted on Fia Graham.

"Have I sprouted horns?"

Pausing to clear his thoughts, Martin asked, "Horns?"

"Well, the way you were staring at me, I thought perhaps I had suddenly grown horns." Fia suppressed a laugh at his momentary confusion.

"No...no horns." Martin rose abruptly. "I'm going out to check on Odhar." Without another word he was out the door, leaving Fia bewildered, as he often did.

The snow had stopped, but the clouds looked more leaden than ever. Martin walked the bank of the burn with Arthur. The dog's breath visible in the frigid air, Martin laughed at him. "You look like a dragon whose flame has been snuffed." Arthur turned sullen eyes on Martin and was rewarded when Martin reached down and scratched the animal's black muzzle. "I doubt things will ever be quite the same for us thanks to Miss Graham." The dog looked appropriately sympathetic with its large, dark eyes. Again, Martin laughed, truly grateful for Arthur's presence. The burn curved around the base of a large hill and, just out of sight of the croft, was the crumbling stone of an old cairn. Martin leaned against it hoping the cold air and solitude, heightened by the earlier snowfall, would help clear his thoughts. Over these last three years, he had purposely separated himself from most outside contact. And, in a matter of days, Fia Graham had stumbled into his life and, without trying, found a chink that he hadn't known existed in his carefully constructed armor. Martin hung his head in denial. "When she's gone, I'll realize that I've made too much of this." He spoke aloud as if hearing it would make it true.

Chapter Five

Fia hung her clothing back on the pegs beside the door. It was going to take longer than she'd thought to finish her mending. The hems of her petticoats were in tatters from her flight, and there were several small tears in the body of the skirt. But right now, she needed to be of some use to her host. Since Martin was still outside, she decided to reheat their earlier meal. "It must be time for supper," she thought, "I'm so hungry." When the soup was nearly bubbling, the door opened and Arthur bounced in followed by a more sedate Martin.

"The sky still looks like slate, but I don't think it'll snow any more today."

Fia gently pushed the dog's nose away from the kettle. "I've always loved snow–the soft rattling sound of snowfall–the exquisite silence when it's finished. That silence seeps into every corner of the soul and banishes emptiness." With that, Fia fell silent and resumed stirring their meal.

As he watched her, Martin's expression softened, and he pondered briefly her statement. What emptiness did she have to banish? But he was soon distracted by the lush dark hair framing her serene face which was lit softly by the firelight. The smallest of smiles teased the corners of her mouth. He caught his breath. Fia wasn't just comely, she was beautiful. Entranced, he approached and knelt beside her at the hearth. "You didn't need to do this," he stated quietly.

Fia's smile broadened easily, "You did all the work; I only warmed it. Besides, I wasn't sure when you'd be back and, to be honest, I was getting hungry."

"Ah, so that's how it is." He peered into the kettle. "It looks hot enough." Martin held two bowls while she ladled them full, then he nodded toward the table. She pulled over the second chair and they ate in comfortable silence.

Near the end of the meal, Fia leaned back in her chair and glanced around. "Martin, I hope you know that I appreciate everything you've done for me. I'd like to do something for you in return."

"What are you talking about?"

"Well, your croft is immaculate and you're a better cook than I am. It doesn't look like you need any help with anything. But I'd really like to make myself useful in some way–to repay your kindness."

Martin scoffed. "Fia, as many times as we've done battle, we both know that I haven't always been kind. There's no need–"

"Please, Martin...I'm serious." Impulsively, she reached across the table and touched his hand.

"So am I."

"I'd be dead now if not for you," Fia persisted. "Please, isn't there something?"

Martin traced her fingers briefly with his own. "All right, there is something I need. Can you sew, not just mend?"

"Do you mean...clothing? Can I sew clothing?" When Martin nodded, Fia grinned. "What have you got in mind?"

"A shirt. I really could use a new one." He held up his wrists to show her the frayed cuffs. "My skill with cloth ends when I take it off the loom."

"You're talking about something for daily use?"

Martin nodded, walked over and opened the lid of the trunk. He quickly produced a pale blue piece of wool broadcloth which he handed to her. He pointed to the small leather box she'd used during her mending. "Everything you need is in there, isn't it?"

Fia nodded, turned the soft fabric over, and ran her fingers across it appreciatively. "Martin, this is much too fine for daily wear. Are you sure you wouldn't like me to make something else for you–something special?"

"I haven't much use for something special."

She nodded and, for a moment longer, she fingered the cloth. "Would you be willing to leave it to me?"

Intrigued, he simply said, "Why not?"

"Good." Fia began sifting through the little box. "Take your shirt off, Martin. I need to do a little measuring." Martin hesitated and Fia glanced up at him. "Today, Martin."

Martin snickered, "I see you enjoy being in charge."

"I don't know how much time I'll have," she explained, "and I do want to make you a nice shirt."

"Of course," he thought with a pang. "She wants to leave as soon as the weather allows." Martin felt obliged to agree with her and, as he removed his shirt, commented, "This project should help you pass the time until I can take you to Inveraray."

Foolishly, his remark caught her off guard and Fia almost dropped the box. So, he was humoring her. No matter what he said, the sooner she was gone, the happier he'd be. Well, he was right. She could throw herself into making this shirt. After all, as long as he kept it, he had part of her. She drew a resigned breath and faced him. "That's right, it'll help pass the time. Now let's get started." With the knotted string she pulled from the leather box, it didn't take long for Fia to complete the measuring. Martin was surprised at how poised she appeared to be as she worked; his own pulse quickened considerably at her nearness and the warmth of her fingers on his skin. She faltered only once. In hushed tones she asked, "That soldier–the English soldier–he did this?" Her fingers almost caressed a scar just under his right rib cage.

Martin stepped away from her touch. "Aye."

Fia blushed scarlet. "Forgive me that was rude." Quickly, she turned away. "I think that's it. I can get to work now." Walking to the table, Fia cleared it and began to spread the fabric, the shirt already taking shape in her mind. It would be different from the standard stitched rectangles and squares. Martin was handsomely narrow in the hip, and she had an idea to taper the shirt slightly, not enough to be uncomfortable, but enough to allow her extra material for a slightly fuller sleeve. After all, a man who worked at a loom might find the additional width helpful.

Martin put his shirt back on. "You don't have to start tonight."

"Ah, but I do. I don't know how much time I have to work."

She was totally preoccupied with her chore within minutes and Martin fidgeted while she worked. He let Arthur out and tended the fire. Now he sat in front of the fire, drumming his fingers on the arm of his chair unable to concentrate on the book lying in his lap. When he could no longer stand her absorption in her work, he asked, "Would you like some tea?"

"Martin, we had it for breakfast. It's a nice offer but, I couldn't–it's too extravagant."

Shaking his head, Martin said, "It's a ruse. I want to talk, but I don't want to disturb you."

"I can work and talk at the same time," she assured lightly. "What do you want to talk about?"

He draped one leg over the arm of his chair. "I want to know more about you and about your life in Glasgow."

Fia hesitated. "Why?"

"Because we're friends, remember? I don't really know anything about you. I'm curious."

Straightening, Fia's brow creased in a frown. "What do you want to know?"

"Anything...everything. Tell me about your uncle."

Fia took her time pinning the first two pieces of fabric together, planning what she was going to say before beginning. "My parents drowned eight years ago; it was a sudden squall in the Moray Firth. Uncle George came to Inverness to fetch me to his home in Glasgow."

"Was there no one left in Inverness to care for you?" Martin questioned.

"My mother's sister. But Uncle George had more influence and more money than she did. He wanted to keep me away from my mother's family so they couldn't lay claim to my inheritance–some money and a little land."

"Is that true? He took you in because of your inheritance?"

"That's what Uncle George told me...but not until recently. He's a businessman–that's how he thinks."

Martin felt numb. "Do you mean your uncle thought that taking you in was a good business decision? Had he no sympathy for you, an orphan, or love for you as his niece?"

Fia avoided his eyes. "That was the first time we'd ever met and, well, he's always been...

direct about his feelings regarding me. He likes me, he doesn't love me–I look too much like my mother to suit him."

Martin frowned, "I don't understand."

"Uncle George is convinced that my mother cast some sort of spell on my father, otherwise Father never would have married her and left his brother alone to run the shipping business."

"Isn't your uncle successful?"

Fia nodded. "The trouble is that George is the older brother. He always counted on Father to help him carry on the family business. When Father decided to go his own way–with my mother–Uncle George took it very hard. He had to blame someone and that was my mother. He never forgave her for coming between them."

Martin swallowed hard, voice grating, "That's difficult to live with."

Eyes darting to his, Fia said, "You speak as if you know from experience."

A shrug of his shoulders dismissed her comment. "Please go on, lass."

Fia sighed. "I live in Glasgow with Uncle George and his daughter, Elizabeth. Her mother died shortly after she was born and Elizabeth is the center of Uncle George's world. She's well educated, clever and beautiful." Fia left the table, settling on the floor, closer to the firelight, where she threaded her needle. "Elizabeth had her coming out in London. It was a huge success; several marriage proposals."

Martin was impatient. He didn't want to hear about a woman who couldn't possibly be as interesting as the one before him. "But you? How have you spent your time since moving to Glasgow?"

"Mostly I keep to myself, though sometimes I go riding. I've spent a great deal of time with my head in books, and I practiced and experimented with the sewing instruction my mother gave me–now I can make clothes."

"You haven't mentioned your schooling."

Fia slowly pulled a stitch through the cloth. "I used to be allowed to join in when Elizabeth's tutor was at the house. But the only time I attended a real school was when I was sent to Fort William in January." Her gaze softened. "I so enjoyed being with Robert and Mary. They owned the school and we became good friends. They let me teach the younger girls."

"You were a teacher?"

She nodded. "They always treated me as an equal. If I didn't love them for any other reason, I'd have loved them for that. It was a short but wonderful time." Tears blurred her eyes and, over her basting stitches, her voice faltered, "That is until Robert died."

"You said it was tragic, didn't you?" Martin gently urged her to continue. Acutely, he felt the loss and pain he heard in Fia's voice.

"Aye. The byre...it caught fire with Robert inside. He...well, he died later. Mary and I...we didn't get to him fast enough." A tear slid down her cheek and she wiped it away and smiled shakily. "It won't do to cry on this lovely cloth."

Martin moved to the floor and sat facing her. "Your tears won't hurt the cloth, Fia...but they hurt me. It must have been an unspeakably dreadful ordeal for you watching your friend die so horrendously. I'm very sorry."

Fia nodded her appreciation, but wouldn't look at him. "Being a physician, you'd understand his suffering."

He protested, "I'm sorry for the pain it causes you. Still, Fia, I'm puzzled. Why did your uncle send you to school to teach?"

Fia's belly churned at the thought of Struan Forbes. She could not bring herself to talk to Martin about him. Her life story sounded pathetic even to her–she couldn't tell Martin what awaited her in Glasgow. "He...Uncle George, never planned for me to teach. We had a disagreement last Hogmanny and he...he simply sent me away."

Martin persisted. "What disagreement could have been so bad that he'd send you off like that?"

Tears so obscured her vision now that Fia could barely see. She concentrated on not letting them fall as she suggested urgently, "My life really isn't very interesting, Martin. Can't we talk about something–ow!" Fia cried out as she jabbed the needle deep into her finger. The cloth fell from her lap as she leapt from the floor and stumbled blindly toward the door, consumed with the need to escape her strangling emotions.

But Martin was fast and caught her before she got half way there. He held her from behind while she struggled in vain to pull away. "Fia, please, you're safe here," he murmured soothingly. "Safe," he repeated, holding her until her struggle ceased and she panted leaning stiffly against him. Reaching for her hand, Martin raised it to examine the injured forefinger. "It's all right, lass," he assured and sucked the droplet of blood from it. Turning her palm in his hand, Martin pressed his lips against its soft flesh.

Completely undone by his tenderness, Fia wrenched from his embrace. Her breath came rapidly; she fought to calm her pounding heart. If her emotions were choking her before, the conflict raging in Fia now threatened to tear her apart. Her future loomed coldly before her, another hollow episode in the life she'd led since her parents' death. When she cared for someone–each time she cared–something horrible happened and they were ripped from her: her parents, Robert. She was unnerved to realize how much she cared for Martin Ross–God, if only she didn't care for him.

Fia shook with the effort to regain her composure and, seeing this, Martin's need to comfort her grew. He extended his hand. "Fia..."

"No, p...please," her voice cracked as she stepped back from the smoky warmth in his eyes. "I'm tired, Martin, that's all. I'll work on the shirt some other time, perhaps when my mending is done." Cautiously, Fia stepped around him, picked up the pieces she'd been basting and folded them.

A persistent scratching at the door finally drew Martin's attention away from her and he opened it for Arthur to enter. When he turned to her again, Fia was already in bed. She faced the wall, cutting off any chance for further conversation. Reseating himself by the fire, Martin sighed raggedly and leaned his head on the chair back. Silently, he wondered what had happened; what was it all about? She wasn't tired, he knew that much. He didn't know if he'd offended or scared her. God's life, he hoped not. Martin shivered remembering how Fia felt in his arms. He pressed the heels of his hands against his eyelids as he began to realize why he was shaken. Without trying, Fia had reached in and touched something deep inside him. He wanted to protect her, to make her forget the indifference of her uncle and the pain it caused her. Quickly, he rose and left the croft to stand in the chill night air. Here, he could breathe, and here, when his mind cleared, he remembered how she'd fought to pull away from him while he only wanted to hold her closer. "This will never do; she doesn't need you complicating her life," he scolded himself. "Accept it and stay away from her." But how many times had he already said that to himself?

Fia pretended to be asleep when Martin returned. He stood beside the bed a moment looking at her tear-stained face then, stripping to his breeches, retired to his pallet. For hours afterward, Fia stared into the shadows at the ceiling rafters, the palm Martin had kissed resting on her breast. She heard Martin's breathing change as he stopped tossing, relaxed and finally slept. When she could no longer stand it, she got up and silently approached him. Kneeling, she studied his face in detail–the straight nose, expressive mouth. His hair and beard were like burnished copper in the firelight. The gentle rise and fall of his chest was hypnotizing. He was so beautiful it pained Fia to look at him.

Martin woke in the semi-darkness, not sure what had disturbed him. Rolling to his side, he was startled by Fia, ghostly in the faded firelight, staring out the window. Martin rose on one elbow. "Fia?"

"It's snowing again," she answered simply.

He stood and rubbed his hands across his face. "How long have you been standing there? You're probably chilled to the bone." He stopped behind her so that they reflected as one in the glass.

Fia wiped her cheeks. "I'm not sure how long I've been here."

"Are you cold?" Fia nodded and Martin reached for a blanket and draped it softly across her shoulders, careful not to touch her. "I've made you cry again, haven't I?" His voice was laced tight with regret. "Tell me what's wrong or, at least, how I can help."

"I was just thinking, the new snowfall will keep me here longer."

"Is that so terrible a prospect?" he asked gently.

Over her shoulder, Fia studied him with furrowed brow. "Just hours ago, you talked of getting me to Inveraray. Who knows how long I'll be here now?"

An ache squeezed his heart. "Fia...is that the cause of your tears, because you have to stay here with me?"

She ignored his question. "You need me to go. You seem torn between a sense of duty and your need for privacy and that confuses me. I never know which of your needs will assert itself. Martin, being alone is your choice. I can't say I understand it because I've been alone for a long time and I'm tired of it. But I respect your inclination and I won't inflict myself or my needs on your generosity any longer than necessary. You've been–"

"Enough." Martin stepped quickly in front of her and gripped her icy hands tightly. "In the last few years, solitude has suited me well. I won't deny it. But that has nothing to do with you. I'm not unhappy you're here. On the contrary, I'm surprised at how much I've enjoyed your company. I'm just not used to it. I'm sorry I've confused you, truly. But as long as you're with me, you needn't feel alone. No matter how badly I sometimes behave, we're friends; I'm here for you, Fia, if you want me."

Fia was shocked to realize how much she did want him. But to Martin, she croaked, "I... appreciate that."

"Yet you don't believe me," he surmised. A step toward her and Martin whispered his vow, "I swear to you, lass, you aren't alone." He gathered her into his arms hoping she wouldn't fight him. To Martin's surprise and relief, Fia's unyielding body slowly relented and she clung to him so tightly, he couldn't tell whose heart he felt pounding against his chest. As they stood in their silent embrace, Martin could feel his old wounds healing and a sense of long forgotten peace returning. Calling on every ounce of willpower he possessed, Martin finally pulled back far enough from Fia to look into her eyes; her beautiful, gently curved lips, inches from his, stunned him into silence.

There were fresh tears in Fia's eyes and her voice was husky with emotion, "I don't feel quite so alone now, Martin." She eased herself from his embrace and added, "I think I'll try to sleep now." But, once again, she lay awake, her stomach and heart tied in such knots that she could barely breathe. Despairing, she admitted to herself that she'd fallen in love with Martin. He was all she wanted. In his arms she felt whole and safe as he'd told her she was. Fia swallowed her tears. Her memories from these few days with Martin would have to last her a very long time– perhaps a lifetime as Struan Forbes' wife.

The snow blew wildly throughout the day. Fia watched from the window, each time Martin left the croft. He didn't want her to budge unless he ran into trouble. Neither spoke of what had passed between them in the early morning hours, but each privately savored the moment and the serenity and upheaval it brought them. That evening, Fia bent over the mending she hadn't finished. Back in her shift, under-petticoat and stays, she at least felt presentable. When Martin began rummaging through the trunk, she stopped to watch him. "That trunk of yours must be a treasure chest in disguise, judging by the interesting items you always pull from it."

Flashing a smile that washed over her like a balm, Martin conceded, "I never thought of it that way, but you're not far wrong. Things I value are kept in here." He held up a short sheathed blade with an agate set in the handle. "Grandfather's dirk. I never found his sword on the battle-field...couldn't really stop to look with the soldiers about. Someone probably took it anyway." Before Fia could respond, Martin had replaced it and added, "I have his plaid as well. That's warm enough to have driven out your fever; I didn't think of it at the time."

"The method you settled on was good," Fia offered, quietly happy to have shared the intimacy of sleeping with Martin though she remembered none of it but the waking.

Martin raised warm eyes to hers. "I agree. Ah, this is what I've been searching for." His hand waved the slender tube of a tin whistle at her. Closing the trunk lid, Martin squatted near the hearth.

"Can you play that?" Fia asked, surprised.

"Aye, since I was a lad. I've also played the fiddle," he reflected, "though not for years now. I don't know if I still could." He turned a tender gaze on Fia. "I thought some music would be appropriate."

"Appropriate for what?"

"Why for our Beltane celebration, of course," he answered with an impish grin that received Fia's stare in return.

"It's the first of May? I...I've been here nearly three weeks?" she said in disbelief.

"Aye, and who would ever let Beltane pass without music?" Martin's expression was a dare.

"Do you think with all this snow, it's fitting to celebrate the renewal of spring?"

"I think the grasses and trees need all the help they can get," he responded, "though there'll be no bonfires tonight, I'm afraid."

"This fire," Fia nodded to the blaze behind him, "will do very nicely. Please, I'd love to hear you play."

Martin placed the whistle between his finely sculpted lips and began with a lilting jig, then a reel, even a hornpipe. As he continued to play, Fia found it difficult, then impossible to sit still. Finally, she rose and stepped off the different dances to the melodic, high-pitched tunes until she found herself lost in a full-blown jig, collapsing in a heap as it drew to an end. Damp curls clung to her face and neck. Laughing and breathless, her face shone joy as she said, "Thank you so much, Martin. Your music is enchanting."

"And you dance enchantingly. I've never enjoyed playing so much as I have for you." He reached out and gently pushed hair from her forehead, his fingers lingering. "This Beltane, I will always remember. With warm lips, he brushed her glistening cheek and immediately rose, trembling, to return the whistle to the trunk. It was reckless of him to touch her at all; he wanted to fold her into his arms, to kiss her until they were both bruised with passion. He should not want these things–had no right to them. Distance was the answer. If only he'd listened to his own counsel in the beginning, he wouldn't ache for her now.

Fia was grateful to be able to bury herself in her mending. She thought she could hide her longing if she didn't have to look at him. But if he had kissed her lips instead of her cheek....Fia quavered with delight at the prospect, and with a stabbing disappointment.

By the time the sun reappeared the following day, Fia had finished her mending and had begun work, in earnest, on Martin's shirt. Because of the snow, she was taking her time and, over the next few days, asked Martin several times to try on the shirt so that she could judge her work. Fia ceased to be surprised at the tantalizing ache that radiated through her each time she looked at or touched him. She recognized it, and silently basked in her love for him. It was fine to dream, she convinced herself; no one could take that from her.

The steady drip of the melting snow was driving Fia crazy. "It means the end of the borrowed days," she told herself, "and the end of days borrowed from Martin Ross as well." Fia was tired and cross; she hadn't slept well knowing that she had little time left with him. She bit the thread as she finished a seam.

From his seat at the loom, Martin wondered what Fia was thinking; she was withdrawn this morning. Since the morning of the new snow, when they'd embraced so fiercely, he'd been trying to deal with his desire to be with her, not just to protect her. Rising, Martin approached the hearth tentatively–the fire did need tending. However, when he knelt before it, he did nothing, feeling suddenly spent. "Fia, we've not said ten words to each other all day."

Fia set her sewing aside. "I slept poorly and feel a bit out of sorts." She studied him for a moment then rose. "I think I'll go outside for a while–I need to stretch."

Also standing, Martin asked, "Do you mind if I come along?"

"I'd really like that." Almost before her words were out, he took his coat from its peg by the door then held her cloak for her.

When Fia stepped outside, she was surprised at how much of the snow had disappeared. The snow-melt pressed the banks of the burn till it threatened to overflow. It made her sad that this beautiful, peaceful place soon would be part of her past. Fia drew a shaky breath and Martin, who had been playing with Arthur, came and stood next to her. He lifted his face to the warmth of the sun as it sliced the frigid air. "I think spring has really arrived this time."

She ached when he smiled at her. "Aye. No more borrowed days."

Martin was puzzled by the finality in her voice. He searched for something he might cheer her with. The answer came quickly and he grinned down at her. "I think that, early tomorrow, I'll bring water in so that you can have that bath I promised you. You're probably tired of using the basin."

His words were a tonic to Fia. Her face lit up. "Oh, Martin, I would love that!" She grasped his arm excitedly. "Thank you so much."

"While you bathe, I'll ride over to Loch Awe and see if I can catch a fish for our dinner. That should give you plenty of time to enjoy a leisurely soak."

Fia beamed, "I know I'll feel so much better." She could hardly contain her delight. Once bathed, she could dress and feel like a human being again. And, for the first time, she'd be on a truly equal footing with Martin.

In the morning, Martin set water to heat in several kettles which, together, covered the entire fire. Next, he brought in a wooden tub which he positioned in front of the hearth. "Enjoy yourself, lass, and don't worry about the tub. I'll empty it when I return." The joy etched on Fia's face made Martin whistle happily as he headed to Odhar's byre.

She watched Martin ride off, Arthur in pursuit, then waited impatiently for the water to get hot. When she finally had filled the tub, she let her shift fall from her body and stepped in. The tub was small. The tops of Fia's knees and everything above the middle of her back was exposed to the air. But Fia had never appreciated a bath more in her life. She did exactly as Martin suggested–she soaked as best she could.

In the light of day, after a good night's sleep, Fia's thinking was clearer. So often, Martin had shown her compassion and concern, and she realized, rather belatedly, that she wasn't accustomed to such treatment; it touched her deeply. For a moment, she puzzled Martin's tenderness which captivated her, and the swift mood swings that made him so unpredictable yet compelling. He was infinitely complicated and fascinating to her. Resting her hands on the side of the tub, Fia wondered about the irony of her situation. When she'd been at school, she'd spoken at length to Reverend Grant, seeking his counsel. As a result, Fia had come close to thinking she could endure marriage to Struan if no other choice was left her. If a loving relationship wasn't in her future, so be it. Now she knew better, knew what her uncle and cousin were asking her to live without. Her eyes surveyed the neat, cozy room and strayed to Martin's bed. Nervously, Fia tried to guess what Martin's reaction might be if she were to tell him that she longed to lie with him again by the fire–this time to love him–so that no one could ever take the memory from her. The idea was exciting and intimidating. She didn't think her inexperience would matter; where Martin was concerned, her instincts seemed to have taken over. Hadn't it been the most wondrous and natural feeling to be held in his arms? Remembering the scent of his skin and touch of his body sparked a liquid warmth below her belly that made her breathing difficult. She made her decision. "If I can live on the memory of loving him once...."

When Fia realized that the water was almost cold, she got down to scrubbing herself and washing her hair. After rinsing, Fia reached for a cloth and briskly dried off. She'd just pulled her shift over her head when the door swung open.

"Martin, my lad, are you here?" The door closed behind a woman, her head covered by a woolen shawl, her body buried in a man's greatcoat.

Fia froze and the two women stared at each other. "Martin?" The woman called more loudly, her eyes not leaving Fia.

Fia drew a deep breath. "He's not here."

The woman moved cautiously into the room and removed the coat revealing a broad shouldered, shapely figure. "And who might you be?"

"My name is Fia Graham. I'm a guest of Martin's."

"Is that right?" the woman responded curtly. "And what exactly does that mean? She removed the shawl and shook loose her thick fiery hair.

Fia was starting to get irritated. She picked up her cloth and began drying her own hair. "It means just what it sounds like. Now, I'd like to know who you are."

Jean ignored her. "Where is he?"

"He's out catching our dinner." Fia began to pull a comb through her tangled curls. She sat nervously in Martin's chair. Who was this woman?

Jean studied Fia suspiciously and decided, after a few moments that, while Fia was pretty, her slender body could not compete for Martin's favor with her own well-endowed one. But what was she doing here? Jean made herself comfortable, purposely lounging on the bed as though she'd done it many times. "So, dear, how did you come to be Martin's 'guest'?"

As Fia continued to work with her hair, she decided that she did not like this woman's demanding and possessive questions. A gnawing fear began to take root as she wondered about the woman's relationship to Martin. Jean repeated her question and, this time, Fia responded.

"By accident."

Jean bristled. "That's not good enough."

"It's going to have to be because I don't make it a habit to speak about myself to people I don't know."

"I'm Jean MacNab. Now you know me, and I expect an answer."

"I already answered you, it was by accident."

"Maybe you'll cooperate a little better if I tell you a few facts, Miss Graham. Let's see, how shall I put this?" Jean purred running her hands suggestively over her breasts and belly to her thighs. "Martin and I are not strangers. In fact, we're very close and have been for some time. So, you see, I think I deserve an explanation for your presence in his croft."

Jean's gesture was not lost on Fia. As the nature of Jean and Martin's relationship screamed at her, Fia felt weak and broken. "I've been ill. Martin's been treating me."

"You look healthy enough to me." Jean quipped.

"He is a talented healer."

Jean stretched as sensuously as a cat in heat to drive home her point. "You'll be leaving soon then." It was a statement of fact, not a question.

Fia was dismayed at her own lack of sophistication. Why hadn't this idea ever crossed her mind? Of course Martin would have a woman somewhere. He was, after all, a fascinating and comely man. She shook her head. Did she hurt so much because she loved him and was too naive to see this coming, or because she was face to face with a woman who'd been loved by Martin? Fia had to work hard to appear unaffected by Jean's presence. She refused to give the woman that pleasure. "When Martin tells me I'm well enough to go, I'll be leaving. Tell me, Miss MacNab, where do you live?"

"South of the woods. You do know where the woods are don't you?"

"Aye. And I know you've come a long way this morning. Can I get you something to drink?"

"You aren't mistress of this house." Jean growled at her.

"If you and Martin are so close, wouldn't he want me to offer you something in his absence? As I said, it's a long way that you've come." Jean glared at her in silence so Fia continued, "What brings you here today? Was Martin expecting you?"

Jean snapped at her. "If he'd been expecting me do you think he'd be somewhere else?"

"I can't answer that—he's never mentioned you."

Jean bounded from the bed, stung by Fia's remark. She quickly decided that she had nothing to lose and perhaps everything to gain by her next words. Angrily, she hissed, "Well, Fia Graham, let me tell you what brought me here today. Martin and I need to finalize the details of our wedding next month. The weather is the only thing that's kept us apart. And if he hasn't mentioned me, I'm sure it's because he felt no need to discuss something so personal with an absolute stranger. You see now why I'm surprised to find you here."

Only the momentary hesitation of Fia's hand as she combed her hair betrayed her anguish. Martin was to be married. So much became clear to her in that instant. And Jean was right. Why would he discuss his upcoming marriage with her? It was not her business. Her shoulders drooped in defeat. When she began listening again, Jean was in front of her, hands on her hips. "...that's why I have the right to know what you are doing here and why I want you gone. Martin will take in any rover that's hurt, but you look fine to me. I won't let Martin's weakness for strays get in the way of our plans."

Jean's face was an angry red when Fia focused on it. She didn't understand why Martin's taking care of her should cause Jean McNab to sound so bitter. But she said nothing. If Martin was going to marry this woman, it was between them. "You'll stay until he returns then?" she asked flatly.

Slowly, Jean straightened well aware that she may have gone too far. If she stayed and Martin saw her, he would refute everything she'd told this tart. "No...I won't let your presence become an issue between Martin and me. If he doesn't know I was here, it won't be necessary to discuss you unless, of course, he wants to." Jean casually drew on her coat and picked up the shawl. With her hand on the latch of the door, she turned to Fia. "And I don't believe he'll consider you important enough to mention to me. Goodbye, Miss Graham. Forgive me when I say I don't want to see you again. And please, don't create problems by telling Martin that I was here. You wouldn't be doing him any favors and he's probably been very good to you. I'm sure that you wouldn't want to be that selfish and ungrateful." With that, Jean McNab was gone. Fia heard the muffled clop of her horse's hooves, and then there was silence.

Chapter Six

The ride to Loch Awe was exhilarating and Martin's spirits soared. He spurred Odhar into an easy canter marveling at how deeply Fia Graham had rooted herself in his mind and heart.

As he approached the Loch, Martin slowed Odhar to a walk. His favorite spot for fishing was in the shallows just off the spit of land that was home to Kilchurn Castle. It was rare for him to run into anyone else here, but he was careful just the same. Though the castle hadn't been occupied since the '45, it still belonged to the Campbells. And while he was kin to these Campbells, he respected their power enough not to cross them if he could avoid it. Thus far, he'd been successful. He understood perfectly their desire to keep intruders away. Martin reined in his horse and sat looking at the massive fortress ruin. Its reflection, with the rolling mountains behind it, was unblemished in the still waters of the Loch.

Martin waited patiently until he decided he was alone, then dismounted and led Odhar out onto the peninsula. He called Arthur, ordering him to stay close. Hobbling the huge horse close to the castle wall, Martin settled himself and dropped his line into the water. Staring into the depths of the Loch, Martin envisioned looking into Fia's eyes. Sitting here now, he found he could think of nothing but Fia. With quickening pulse, he recalled how her body fit neatly against his when they lay together before the hearth, and how their hearts beat as one that snowy morning when he reveled at the feel of her in his arms. And the more he got to know her, the more he thought that he couldn't have wished for more in one woman: compassion, intelligence, wit and spirit. Thinking again of lying with her–that stunning glimpse of her body shrouded in the damp shift– aroused him mercilessly. As he shifted uncomfortably, Martin admitted that he no longer wished to keep his distance. In fact, he very much wanted to be close to her in every way imaginable. But, how did she feel about him? She trusted him, he was sure of that. And, the attraction between them was strong–he'd felt it often. Doubt surged forward and he shook his head mumbling, "Maybe that's just what I want to believe. After all, she may not hold anything more than a friendly affection for me because I 'rescued' her."

The dog nudged Martin's elbow in response to his master's muttering. Martin rubbed Arthur's neck in return. "Right. The fish won't bite if I ramble on." For a moment, Martin closed his eyes and wondered, "How much longer can I keep her with me? She's strong now and, if not for the snow, would already have been in Inveraray." A dull ache gripped Martin at the thought of her leaving; he recognized it–loneliness.

Sitting in Martin's chair by the fire, Fia lost track of time. Her comb hung limply from her hand and the fire was almost down to embers. Emptiness shrouded her. Over and over she repeated, "I have to decide what to do," but no thoughts came to mind. When the last peat brick crumbled and fell to the hearth, Fia roused herself, Jean MacNab's words coming back to her, "You will be leaving soon."

Fia nodded to herself. "Aye. I'll be leaving soon. There's no reason to stay any longer. I can finish the shirt today; I can leave tomorrow."

She rose, transferring her pain into action. "No more feeling sorry for yourself, Fia. You should thank God that Jean MacNab showed up when she did–kept you from making a complete fool of yourself." Furiously, she rebuilt the fire, then began the laborious chore of emptying the tub. Once the tub was outside, propped against the side of the croft to dry, Fia finished getting dressed. She tied her hair back with a strip of cloth she'd found in the leather sewing box and picked up the shirt, determined to complete it quickly. "No more dawdling. It'll be a beautiful shirt for Martin to remember me by–just as I'd planned." Without putting it into words, Fia knew that she had to make her break from Martin as complete as possible. The only way she could live in peace and keep her dignity was to plan her own return to Glasgow–to take the decision out of Martin's hands.

Fia looked up from her sewing when Martin entered. She fixed her gaze, not on him, but on the fish he held up for her inspection. "They're nice," she said.

"Nice?"

"And...large." Fia resumed her sewing. "Can I help you clean them?"

"No, I'll do it." Martin looked at her quizzically. "I saw the tub outside; I told you I'd empty it."

"I had time to take care of it myself."

"Do you feel better? Did you enjoy your bath?" he asked hopefully.

Fia smiled stiffly. "Very much, thank you again."

Martin stared at her, his hopes for her restored good spirits dashed–she was as distant as he'd ever seen her. "Fia..."

"Really, Martin. You should take care of the fish soon. My appetite is back and I'm starving."

Without another word, Martin picked up a shallow pot and left the croft, baffled. What had happened?

Feeling sick, Fia covered her mouth with her hand. "How can I look him in the eye knowing what Jean MacNab means to him?" she thought and began to pace the room, fighting off tears she swore she wouldn't shed. Looking out the window, she watched Martin kneeling by the burn cleaning his catch. The lowering sun caught the copper in his hair which shimmered like liquid fire as he moved. Fia's heart thudded painfully.

Martin made quick work of the fish then cleaned up in the icy water of the burn. When he turned back to the croft, he saw Fia at the window and smiled at her. Fia turned away.

Now he was sure that something had happened. She may laugh at him, chide him, or any number of things, but Fia was never indifferent to him. He left the fish and sprinted to the croft. Fia stood near the fire and he moved to her quickly. Grasping her shoulders with still dripping hands, he looked into her pale face and, without thinking, pulled her into his arms.

"Lass, lass, whatever is it? What has happened to upset you so?"

Fia remained stiff and unyielding. Though part of her desperately wanted to cling to him, she knew now that it wasn't her place to be in his arms. That knowledge cut her to the bone. Gently, but firmly, Fia disengaged herself from his embrace, looked him straight in the eye, and lied, "Nothing."

Shaking his head in disbelief, Martin insisted, "But *something* has happened. I'd hoped you'd be happy when I returned. Instead, you hardly speak to, or look at me. We've not known each other long, Fia, but we've been on better terms than this from the beginning."

"Shouldn't you go get the fish?"

Frustrated, he turned away, then back to her. "God's blood, Fia, forget the fish. What's wrong?"

Taking a deep breath, Fia began to break her ties to Martin Ross. "Nothing at all. Being here by myself today I've been doing a lot of thinking about my upcoming marriage and...I realize it's high time I got on with my life and let you get back to yours."

If Fia had struck him, Martin could not have been more taken aback. It was a long moment before he could croak, "Marriage? To whom?"

"His name is Struan Forbes. He's a Glasgow solicitor. We're to marry before my next birthday." Knees beginning to weaken, Fia picked up the shirt and sat down.

Through great effort, Martin kept his voice calm. "Why didn't you tell me this before?"

Fia wondered why he hadn't told her about Jean, but instead answered, "Marriage is a somewhat daunting prospect. But I'm...eager to marry Struan."

Martin's voice shook. "Do you l...love this Struan Forbes?"

In her own anxiety, Fia didn't hear Martin's distress. "We'll have a good life together."

Martin pressed her. "If you don't love him, why marry him?"

She looked up sharply, her voice harsh. "We'll have a comfortable life based on mutual respect."

Martin's face darkened like a thunderhead. "If comfort is all you want Miss, then you're welcome to it." With that, he stormed from the croft to retrieve the fish. "God's life," he spat scornfully. "I wouldn't have believed it if she hadn't said it herself. Well, she has set her path and embraced it–so be it."

They sat at the table in strained silence until Martin could no longer stand it. He pushed his fish aside, scarcely touched. Fia usually wore her emotions on her sleeve; he just couldn't fathom this coldness in her. He was angry and disappointed that Fia had decided to marry for any reason other than love; she had such passion. He thought he knew her at least that well. Apparently, he was mistaken, and he'd have to resign himself to it no matter how it pained him. "Fia, we need to talk."

Pushing her own plate away, Fia waited.

"Your announcement...surprised me, truly surprised me." His head felt like it would split open. "But, I should not have questioned you as I did. It's not that I didn't want the answers...."

"Maybe I shouldn't have announced it so bluntly," Fia cut him off. "I should have shown you more consideration than that."

He looked at her hopefully. "Why?"

"Because you've been good to me. I owe you a great deal."

Martin's eyes narrowed and, exasperated, he sighed.

Fia looked away from him and her teeth tugged at her lower lip. "I think we should talk about Inveraray. The shirt will be finished tonight; I should go tomorrow." She continued to look away from him and missed the undisguised anguish that crossed his face.

Martin whispered, "There's no hurry, lass."

"I don't think that's true, Martin. We've been friends, but I see that, by not telling you sooner about Struan, I've made a mistake. I'd like to part as friends, so it's probably best that I go quickly."

After a heavy silence, Martin reluctantly agreed. "We'll leave for Inveraray in the morning." Standing, he picked up his plate. "I'll clean up while you finish your work. Then, you'd better get some sleep. It'll be a long ride."

"I'm sorry about the fish, Martin."

"Don't be–Arthur will love it." In his heart, Martin felt that there was much more that needed saying. He wondered if it would make any difference to her if she knew that he loved her, but he dismissed the thought. "She's made it clear what is important to her," he thought bitterly. "What I have to offer, Fia doesn't want."

Fia had very little work left on the shirt but was having trouble finishing. It was as if completing it would sever her last tie to Martin. But, finally, it was done. Folding it, she rose and gently laid it in Martin's lap.

For some time, Martin had been staring into the flames of the fire. It was several seconds before he focused on Fia. She gestured to his lap. Martin looked down and slowly unfolded the shirt. He was quiet for so long, Fia got nervous. "I'm sorry I didn't finish it before...before today."

Without a word, Martin stood and stripped off his shirt. He was so close to her that Fia could feel his body's heat; it made her weak with longing and sadness for what she would never share with him. Carefully, Martin drew on the new shirt and walked to the window to see himself reflected against the night.

"I folded the collar so you don't have to wear the stock unless you want to," she offered.

Martin blinked, but his voice was steady, "It's the most beautiful shirt I've ever worn."

Hastily, Fia said, "I'm glad you like it...you...look splendid in it." She would have turned away, but he caught her hand and held it pressed to his breast.

"Thank you, Fia. I'll take good care of it."

Fia eased her hand from his, nodded, and began to put the last of the brass pins back in their case.

After a long, sleepless night, Martin bent to wake Fia, but it wasn't necessary–sleep had evaded her as well. She rose to dress, feeling leaden and stiff. While Martin saddled Odhar, Fia took a last look around the croft that would soon be Jean MacNab's home. Carefully, she folded the shirt she'd made and laid it on the bed. Picking up the oatcakes that would sustain them until they reached Inveraray, Fia left.

The Borrowed Days

Much of the snow had melted and what was left crunched under the black's hooves. Fia sat away from Martin more successfully than she had on her first journey with him. They were both quiet on the ride and spoke only when they had to.

"Is there someplace in Inveraray where I can wait for the post chaise?"

"Aye. A friend of mine owns the 'Rowan and Thistle'. You can stay there." Martin flicked Odhar's reins and the horse tossed his head in response.

Fia's stomach lurched–Jean. "Tell me something about your friend," she asked tensely.

She heard the smile in Martin's voice. "Oh, you'll like Annie, she's the salt of the earth."

"Annie?" Fia repeated weakly.

"Aye, Annie MacAuly. The 'Rowan and Thistle' is hers. I've known her since I came here to live." Martin felt some of the tension leave Fia. "Are you comfortable?"

"Fine, thanks." She was so relieved that the friend Martin spoke of wasn't Jean MacNab, she felt giddy. Where she had been numb before, suddenly she was acutely aware of Martin's nearness. With everything in her, Fia wished to forget that Martin was marrying Jean. She wanted to rest against him, to stroke his bearded cheek and kiss his beguiling mouth. Squeezing her eyes shut, Fia's mind screamed at her to let go of Martin Ross.

When they finally arrived at the 'Rowan and Thistle', Martin helped Fia dismount and, hearing an excited yelp, turned as a young boy flew at him from the doorway and wrapped his arms around Martin's waist. "Donald," he exclaimed, staggering from the impact, "you're a head taller than when I last saw you." He clasped the lad's shoulders.

"And you've been away too long, Martin. Mam was saying so just last week."

Martin chuckled, "And how is your sweet mother?"

"The lad's 'sweet mother' is much better now," boomed a voice from the door. "Martin, what a welcome sight you are, lad. Come here." He handed Donald Odhar's reins just as a wiry, fiftyish woman engulfed him in a huge embrace that he enthusiastically returned.

Still holding her hands, he stood back. "Let me look at you, Annie." He quickly took in her pink smooth cheeks, honey-colored hair slightly faded by the addition of gray. She was immaculate in a deep blue broadcloth petticoat and striped waistcoat over a bleached linen shift. "It's good to see you."

She swatted playfully at his shoulder. "You, my friend, have been missed. And you're still a comely rogue." She studied him thoughtfully. "There's something different though." A movement caught her eye and she peered around Martin at the young woman behind him.

Annie's mouth dropped open and, before she had a chance to say anything, Martin put his hand under Fia's elbow and brought her forward. "Annie, this is Fia Graham. Fia, Annie MacAuly." Fia and the surprised Annie bent their knees to a curtsey and lowered eyes in proper greeting.

Martin leaned slightly toward Fia. "As I told you, Annie owns the inn; Donald is her son." He turned back to Annie, hand still at Fia's elbow. "We could use rooms for the night, Annie, and something to eat."

Her eyes now fastened on Fia, Annie responded, "A room for the lass I'll find. But, Martin, you'll probably have to share a bed; depends on how many lodgers I get."

Martin knew Annie well and could tell that her curiosity was about to get the better of her. "Let's go inside," he suggested quickly. "Fia's been ill and I'm sure she'd like to rest a little before supper. She'll be catching the chaise to Glasgow in the morning."

"Oh...oh, certainly. Please follow me."

As they entered, dim light surrounded them, the air was warm and smelled of good food and tobacco. Annie called a young girl over and told her to show Fia upstairs. "We'll call you in time for supper, lass. There's water in the room if you'd care to wash up."

"Thank you, Mistress." Fia forced a small smile at Martin and trailed after the girl.

"You must call me Annie," the woman called as she watched Martin's eyes follow Fia until she was out of sight. "So, it's like that is it", she thought. She laid a hand on his arm. "Come, Martin. You look in need of some ale." "Make it whiskey," he muttered.

Leading the way to a well-scrubbed table in the taproom, she fetched a cup and sat down, waiting expectantly. She didn't have to wait long.

"I'll save you the trouble, Annie. I found Fia in the woods. She was ill and I nursed her back to health. Now she's going home." Martin gulped his drink.

"So, you care for Fia Graham?"

"Aye, of course I care about her. I just told you that I've nursed her back to health."

Shaking her head, Annie persisted. "I said care 'for' her, not 'about' her. There's a difference and that difference was written clearly on your face just minutes ago."

Martin narrowed his eyes. "You imagine things."

"I don't think so, and I must say I'm glad. I've long prayed for you to find someone special– someone that you'd let inside the Martin Ross you try to keep buried. Does she feel the same way?"

Martin purposely turned the empty cup in his hand. "I told you, it's your imagination."

She sat back, arms folded and studied him for a moment. "Why are you lying to me and to yourself?"

Martin's eyes rolled toward the ceiling. "Annie, I know exactly how I feel about Fia. I know you mean well, but let's drop it."

She realized that she wasn't going to get anywhere now; this would take time. But she couldn't let him have the last word. "All right, you know your feelings. But I guess, since she's leaving tomorrow, you haven't told her."

He reached for her hand and squeezed it. "Please don't say anything to her; you'll only make it worse."

It was as close to an admission as he would come, but it was enough for Annie. Her smile was reassuring. "I knew I was right. I just wish I understood why you're hesitating. Now, I have work to do. And, in case you're wondering," she rose and leaned toward him, "she's in the second room on the left."

The serving girl closed the door behind her and Fia stood looking around the room. The table beside the bed also served the chair next to the hearth. A washstand was the only other piece of furniture in the tiny room.

Fia sat on the chair and closed her eyes. Mistakenly, she thought herself too tired to think. Moments later, she was pacing the cramped space, trying to rid her mind of uneasy thoughts. Her relationship with Martin was so strained that she had little hope left for kind words from him when they went their separate ways in the morning. Fia shook her head, "It's just as well. If he did try to say goodbye in some tender way, I'd probably crumble, and that wouldn't do."

She poured water into a basin. Splashing her face, she vowed, "I will not make a fool of myself the last time Martin ever sees me." A knock on the door put Fia's heart in her throat.

"It's Annie. Are you ready for me to take you down to supper now?"

Fia dried her face, took a deep breath and opened the door. "Aye, I'm ready."

"You don't look a bit rested, lass." Annie sympathized as Fia accompanied her downstairs.

"Oh, the room is quite comfortable, Annie. I'm afraid it's me. I have a lot on my mind."

"Well, if there's anything I can help you with, just let me know. Don't be stubborn like Martin."

Fia smiled unsteadily at her hostess. "You two are good friends aren't you, Annie?"

"Aye. He's a fine man."

Fia nodded. "Martin's been good to me."

Annie noted the slightly muffled tone of Fia's voice and, as they entered the now crowded taproom, watched with interest as Fia searched for Martin. The apprehension on her face was replaced by relief when she recognized him. So, Annie thought with satisfaction, Fia is every bit as taken with Martin as he is with her. As she left them together, Annie could not help but wonder again about their strange behavior toward each other, but decided to keep her nose out of it. Martin didn't care for folk mixing in his business. "It's a shame though," she murmured sadly, "a real shame."

Holding Fia's chair for her, Martin asked, "Is your room suitable?"

"Aye, though it seems strange after being at your croft." Fia sat down.

"How is it strange?"

Fia wanted to say it was because he wasn't there, but instead answered, "It doesn't feel like a real home. I suppose that's normal for an inn."

"Haven't you ever stayed at an inn before?"

Shaking her head, Fia responded, "I haven't. But then, this trip is full of firsts for me."

They ate quietly, a silent island in the bustling room around them, occasionally commenting on Annie, the inn, or the food, which was very good, but which each had to force down. Bits of discussions floated to them and provided some distraction from their strained conversation. From a nearby table, one man addressed his companion. "If General Wolfe was still alive, I bet that, by now, Montreal would be in British hands, not French."

His companion seemed agitated, "Aye, but at least with Pitt running things, we've got some victories to show. And those damnable French have to fight more of their own battles. I hear there's trouble between them and their Indians."

The first man snorted, "If I had to trust the French–or those natives–I'd have trouble deciding which to turn my back on!" Both laughed boisterously, causing Martin and Fia to exchange fleeting smiles.

When the meal was over, Fia pleaded fatigue, the effort to make conversation with Martin too taxing. At the bottom of the stairs, Fia turned to him. "Where will you be staying?"

"I'm not sure yet. But, judging by the number of men I see here, I'll wager I'll be sharing a bed as Annie predicted. Goodnight, Fia."

"Goodnight." Fia held her chin up, forcing herself not to look back as she went up to her room.

Undressing, Fia wrapped her shivering body in a blanket and, sitting on the floor, rested her head against the chair. She was so tired.

It was only minutes later that there was a knock on her door. Pulling the blanket close around her, she opened the door slightly to Martin's intense stare.

"May I come in?"

She stood back and opened the door, closing it behind him.

Never taking his eyes from her, Martin reached past her and slowly slid the bolt. Fia's heart began to race.

"I don't want you to go." His hands moved up her arms and she could feel their warmth through the blanket.

She could not break the spell his eyes cast on her. Neither could she speak.

"In so many ways, we're connected to one another. You feel it, don't you?" His hands stroked her hair. "I need you with me, lass, and I want you more than you could possibly know."

His kiss was gentle at first as though he feared hurting her. But, Fia responded hungrily and pressed herself, against him. The blanket fell to the floor and suddenly feeling her smooth, warm skin beneath his hands, Martin stepped back to look at her. Sharply, he drew in his breath. "How can you be so lovely?"

Martin lightly ran his fingers from her throat, across her breast and down her belly to rest on her hips.

Fia reached to pull him nearer, fingers eagerly plucking at his shirt.

Quickly, Martin stripped his shirt over his head and Fia wrapped her arms around his neck. But when she saw her arms, she suddenly became confused and flustered; something was dreadfully, frighteningly wrong. The arms weren't hers. "What's happening?" she cried, but he appeared not to hear her.

Martin's lips nipped one pink, freckled arm. "It'll be so good to lie with you again, I've missed your touch."

"What do you mean, 'lie with me again'?" Alarmed, Fia pushed herself from him.

Martin laughed, playfully reaching for her. "Why pretend we haven't loved before?"

"What are you saying?" Fia looked down at her body, larger and more rounded than her own, crowned by a mass of red curls between her thighs. Panic gripped her as she ran to the tiny looking glass over the washstand. Jean MacNab laughed back at her. "No...no!" she howled and, with a mind-numbing jolt, woke up.

Dripping with sweat, Fia shed the blanket and stumbled to the washstand. Trembling, she splashed water on her face and over her body till there was no water left. Then she sat on the floor and sobbed.

Hours later, fully clothed, Fia was again pacing the room wondering if she could find Martin without creating trouble. A young woman roaming the halls of an inn crowded with men was dangerous but, since waking from her nightmare, Fia was desperate to see him. Once, she reached for the latch on the door but stopped herself. Martin loved Jean. "Don't be a fool! And don't think," she muttered, "that because you've spent these last weeks with him, it changes anything." A sudden thought hit her like a slap in the face. She was truly alone now; there was no one else: her parents, the MacInnes' and now, Martin–all beyond her grasp. Shaken and without hope, Fia rested her head and palms against the rough wooden door. A tear slid down her cheek and she tasted its salt on her lips.

Martin stuck his head inside the taproom. It was empty now and the fire reduced to glowing embers. Sleep had eluded him–he wasn't sure if it was the snoring of his roommates or the emptiness he felt from Fia's absence. Martin had lost count of the times he tried to convince himself that, whatever he felt now, it would pass quickly after she'd gone. And, if it took a little longer? Well, no matter. Fia was to be married soon and that would be that.

The room was suddenly too small. "I need to get out of here." He took the stairs two at a time intending to fetch his coat, but stopped in front of Fia's door. Thinking he heard movement inside, he put his hand on the latch and raised his other to knock. But he hesitated and backed away. There was nothing more he could say; she'd made her desires clear. Abandoning the quest for his coat, Martin retreated down the stairs and hurried out the front door.

Arthur sleepily rose from beside the byre where Odhar was stabled. He lumbered toward his distraught owner. After drawing a steadying breath, Martin said, "It's all right, lad. Go back to sleep." The dog tilted his head but, when Martin gestured toward the stable, Arthur yawned and returned to his bed.

Martin walked every lane and path in Inveraray several times waiting for the sun to rise. On the Garron Bridge, he stopped to look back over the water at the slumbering village, barely discernable in the sliver of the quarter moon. Distance was his ally–Fia may have made it clear that she preferred Struan Forbes, but that didn't stop Martin from wanting her. If he couldn't sleep in her bed, he still wanted to sleep beside it. It was maddening knowing that she was on the other side of the door, and he was no longer free to just walk in.

"God's blood," he cursed, "I hate that door." And he could not shake his disappointment in Fia for the choice she had made. He didn't want to believe she'd settle for just a comfortable life. She felt things too deeply–he'd seen it time and again. She must really care for Forbes. His stomach tightened at his next thought–Fia must have guessed his feelings for her. That sad look in her eyes...it was pity.

By the time the sun's first rays graced the town, Martin's mood was foul. "I should have heeded my own counsel, kept the distance between us," he berated yet again. "But I didn't–and I didn't fight it hard enough when I realized what was happening to me." He looked at the last morning star through bleary eyes and whispered the truth, "I didn't want to." Searing loneliness turned to fury and he struck his fist against the stone house on his right, his heart anguished, his mind bruised.

"I swear I don't know where Martin's gone this morning." Annie MacAuly bustled around Fia who sat poking at an oatcake and cheese the woman had given her. All Fia could manage to choke down was tea. Annie kept talking, hoping to keep Fia's thoughts occupied. "You'll have to do better, lass. It's a very long way to Glasgow. I can't vouch for the food along the road."

"Could I wrap it and take it along, Annie? I'm not really hungry."

Patting Fia's hand, Annie agreed sympathetically, "Of course dear." She picked up the plate and took it back to the kitchen. "Where is that man?" Annie grumbled. Fia had been downstairs for an hour and the post chaise was to leave in less than ten minutes. "If he doesn't get himself back here before she leaves, he'll hear plenty about it from me!"

"What did you say, Mam?"

Annie glanced around having forgotten her son's presence. "Nothing, Donald, just talking to myself."

After wrapping a second oatcake, Annie returned to Fia. "There you are, dear. I added another; and I do expect you to eat them. My oatcakes are famous."

Fia smiled and took the woman's hand. "I promise I will. It's just...right now...I can't."

Annie sat beside Fia, her heart breaking for the young woman. "Can I give him a message, lass?"

Fia thought of all the things she might say to Martin, but nothing seemed right. Throughout the night, she'd rehearsed how she would say farewell never imagining that he wouldn't even be there to see her off. Fia blinked as tears filled her eyes. "Only 'goodbye', Annie. I'll leave it at that. I think it's clear that he has nothing more to say to me."

"I'm truly sorry, Fia."

Fia flashed a shaky smile. "Aye, well...." She looked up as the door opened and a disheveled, wild-eyed Martin entered. He had never looked better to Fia.

"Chaise is loading," was all he said.

Annie jumped up. "Where have you been?" she demanded.

"Feeding Odhar and Arthur." Martin's eyes dared her to challenge him.

She pushed past him and hissed, "We'll talk later."

Without Annie's presence, Fia suddenly felt vulnerable. She rose and, picking up her packet of food, clutched it against her. As Fia passed him, Martin's hand closed firmly around her arm. His touch jarred her nerves, already raw.

"Will you not say goodbye?"

She answered with all the courage she could muster. "As you have said, the chaise is loading. I'd given up seeing you, so talk to Annie–I left a message with her."

Fia tried to move on, but Martin held tight. His voice softened, "And will you pay my fee before you leave?"

She wrenched her arm from his grasp and faced him, insides churning as she railed, "Ah, your fee for medical services." She tossed her purse on the table. "What I have left is yours. If you need more, I'll send it by way of Annie."

"Put your money away, Fia. The payment I seek is far sweeter." Taking her face in his hands, Martin covered her mouth with his in a fierce kiss, unwilling to let her go.

Fia's heart leapt at the feel and taste of him. In a split second, her joy turned to fury and she thrust him away crying, "This is the payment you want? Never! I won't let you treat me like a harlot." Pain threatened to crush her and her hand shot out and solidly slapped his bearded cheek. "I'll send money," she choked and stalked from the room.

Martin bit his lip to keep from calling out to her and watched as the dark blue dress disappeared through the door. A dismayed voice came from behind him.

"Martin, how could you do this?" Annie hurriedly picked up the dropped cloth containing the biscuits, Fia's purse, and darted after her.

Fia was seated and the last call had been sounded when Annie handed everything through the chaise window. Her hand closed over Fia's. "I'm so sorry, lass."

Squeezing Annie's hand, Fia thanked her with a trembling voice, "I won't forget your kindness."

Annie smiled sadly and backed away as the driver called out to the horses and cracked his whip in the air above their backs.

Fia saw Martin standing in the doorway, an odd expression on his face. Her lips still burned from his kiss; her hand stung. But looking at him for the last time, her anger drained from her–only the pain remained. Fia held his eye until the forward lurch of the chaise took the 'Rowan and Thistle' out of sight. Her mind was paralyzed. She continued to look out the window, dry-eyed and numb.

On the verge of tears, Annie glared at Martin. "I love you dearly, Martin, but you're a fool."

His voice was tight and controlled. "And I love you, Annie, but you don't understand."

She sniffed at him. "You're right, I don't. I only have one thing to say. If you'd kissed her sooner, she probably wouldn't be on that chaise right now." She muttered, "I have work to do," shook her head ruefully and left him.

Quickly, Martin saddled Odhar and led him from his stall. "Arthur, come." Martin commanded as he mounted the big gelding.

All the way to the croft, Martin rode Odhar hard. But it made no difference–it was the longest ride Martin had ever made. Arthur gave up the pace early and would make his own way home.

Once Martin arrived, he delayed entering the croft as long as he could. He spent a great deal of time rubbing down Odhar and cooling him off. "I shouldn't have run you like that," he apologized to the horse who tossed its head and snorted as though in agreement.

Finally inside, Martin rebuilt the fire in the cold hearth and swung the pot of leftover potatoes and cabbage over the flames. As he rose, the shirt on the bed caught his eye. His stomach surged and he turned away briskly rubbing his hands together, holding them out to the blaze "Why isn't this fire throwing off any heat?" he grumbled impatiently. Crossing the room, Martin began to work at his loom which had always soothed him before. Perhaps it would help now.

He worked until an acrid odor reached him and, glancing at the forgotten kettle, he strode to the hearth, angry at himself for being so careless. He grabbed the smoking pot off its chain, opened the door and heaved it into the darkness before slamming the door so hard it bounced open again.

Fists clenched, Martin stood and let the cold night air wash over him. He closed his eyes trying to regain control of his emotions. Arthur's persistent nose against his fist forced Martin to open his hand and the dog fit his head under Martin's palm.

"So you're finally home." Martin rubbed the dog's head lovingly, gratefully. "Come in then."

Martin latched the door this time and sat in his chair. "I'm tired, Arthur; tired and sick at heart." He stared at the bed. Rising he stripped and, picking up the now familiar stack of blankets, Martin spread them on the floor. He could not face sleeping in the bed–not tonight.

Arthur lay down beside his master and yawned. Martin touched his cheek to the dog's head. "You're tired too, I know." Arthur licked Martin's face.

Tears stung Martin's eyes. "Thank you, laddie. Thank you."

Chapter Seven

Fia walked listlessly toward the house on Virginia Street, the squawk of a hooded crow high in a budding beech mocking her dejected return. She felt as though the last day and a half in the cramped chaise had taken a year off her life. When she was awake, memories swirled mercilessly in her head; when her head hurt too much, Fia slept fitfully. The intimate, special moments shared with Martin were the ones Fia wanted to remember, but those last, painful ones were those that plagued her. "There can only be one reason he tried to drive a wedge so deeply between us by calling a kiss payment. Somehow, I showed him how I felt, and he wanted to be sure that I left with no illusions about having a place in his life." She shook her head knowing she no longer had such illusions. "I love him; he loves Jean." As she trekked on, she thought to plan what she would say when she got home. But, when she reached the door of the hulking, stone house, Fia's mind was blank. Her hand on the doorknob, she was surprised when it was pulled from her grasp by Elizabeth who was on her way out.

Elizabeth gasped, "What are you doing here?"

Annoyance surged through Fia and she snapped, "I live here," and pushed past her cousin. "I see you're leaving, don't let me stop you."

Elizabeth's jaw dropped but she recovered quickly. "I mean what are you doing here *now*? You're supposed to be at school." She followed Fia into the drawing room.

"News travels slowly, I see. The Headmaster died over a month ago and the school was closed."

"A month ago?" Elizabeth's brow furrowed thinking she must have misunderstood.

"Aye."

"Well, where have you been since then?"

Fia studied Elizabeth's heart-shaped face and the widow's peak of shining black hair just visible under her flat-brimmed hat. She would never tell her cousin about Martin. To Elizabeth, she replied, "I helped close the school then came here."

Elizabeth said hesitantly, "You're home earlier than planned...but I suppose that'll work to our advantage."

Fia laughed sharply. "You mean to *your* advantage, don't you?"

Elizabeth conceded. "Aye, that really is what I meant. You'll be happy to hear that your intended husband is still anxious to marry you. Struan will be pleased that you couldn't wait and rushed back to be with him."

Fia shrugged. "Tell him what you like."

Elizabeth straightened and searched her cousin's face–it revealed nothing.

Fia moved toward the stairs. "I'm going to my room and rest. The journey was tiring."

Bewildered, Elizabeth's eyes followed Fia. "All right. I was on my way out, as you noted, so I'll see you at supper."

On the front stoop, Elizabeth leaned back against the door, a frown creasing her delicate features. Something was wrong–or different–she wasn't sure which. But it troubled her. It wasn't like Fia to be abrupt or abrasive. She hurried toward the Forbes townhouse on Jamaica Street; Andrew would want to know about Fia's return.

In a matter of minutes, Elizabeth was ushered into the Forbes' music room. Neither Andrew nor Struan was musically inclined, but their mother had been gifted on the spinet and this was Andrew's favorite room. He sat fingering the keyboard absently and, without looking up, dismissed the servant who announced his guest's arrival. When he heard the door close, he turned a hooded gaze on Elizabeth. "Lock the door and come here."

Elizabeth shivered in anticipation as she turned the key and approached him, her eyes a mirror of her desire.

Andrew turned on the small bench as she stopped in front of him letting her short cloak slip to the floor. His eyes held hers as he unfastened the stomacher which fell to one side and he pushed the neck of her shift below her breasts. Andrew began to rub and pinch her nipples. First one then the other, his mouth tugged at her breasts while she swayed slightly, eyes closed, head back. Elizabeth was soon squirming, begging him for relief. When his fingers slid between her thighs, she moaned and opened her eyes to see that he'd freed himself and was ready for her.

"Now, Andrew," she urged and eased herself onto him with a shudder.

Beneath her petticoat, Andrew's large hands gripped her hips tightly as the couple moved together slowly, then frantically seeking and finding release.

Elizabeth leaned her head on Andrew's shoulder and smiled appreciatively. He pushed a lock of hair aside and kissed her throat. "As always, my love, you knew what I needed." She kissed the heavy scar that ran from the corner of his mouth to his chin.

Andrew caressed her breasts again and, while his right hand stayed teasingly at one nipple, the left traveled to her jawbone. "And you, beauty," he hissed in her ear, "are a whore."

Elizabeth's eyes sparkled. "Only for you, Andrew, only for you."

"I wonder."

She sighed and reluctantly rose. As she adjusted her clothing and pinned her stomacher, Elizabeth said lightly, "You'll never guess who's at the house."

Rearranging his own clothes, Andrew grunted, "How would I know?"

"Fia."

Andrew stopped and looked up quickly. "What? She's in Glasgow?" When Elizabeth nodded, he finished buttoning the fall of his breeches. "Why? She's supposed to be at school."

"What she says is that the Headmaster died and they closed down the school. Do you think it's true?"

"Probably. The story's easy enough to confirm. When can I meet her?"

Elizabeth noted a change in his voice, a subtle excitement that she didn't like. "Do you really think that's necessary?" she asked coolly.

Andrew's brows went up in mild surprise; she was jealous. "That's been the plan all along, my beauty. After all, I'm to be...related to her." Amused, he decided to push Elizabeth. "Tonight will be fine."

"No!" The word spilled from her mouth before she could stop it. "She's...she's tired from the trip. Even now she's resting." Elizabeth lightly stroked his thick, dark hair. "There's no real hurry. We have almost six weeks before she turns eighteen. Why not wait until Struan returns from Edinburgh?"

Andrew caught her hand in a cruel grip. "Tomorrow," he growled, "no later."

She grimaced and relented. "Of course, love, as you wish. You know best how to handle Fia."

Fia heard the door close and Elizabeth calling for the maid. Any moment, Fia expected to hear her cousin mounting the steps, but there was nothing. The coolness of the window pane soothed Fia's pounding head. This window seat had been her refuge in the Graham house for eight years. "I will stop thinking about Martin," she swore silently and shivered at the bleak emptiness that faced her. How bad could it really be to be Struan's wife, she wondered? He was conceited and self-centered; he probably wouldn't notice her after awhile. Lost in thought, Fia jumped when her door swung open with a bang. "Elizabeth, don't you ever knock?"

"I did, little cousin, apparently you didn't hear me. And my, my, aren't we grouchy."

Elizabeth settled herself on the bed. "I thought you'd be asleep."

"I'm just resting. Elizabeth, is there something I can do for you?"

"Well, since you mention it, it's as plain as day that you're unhappy about something. Now...I know we've never been close but, well your absence has given me a better appreciation for the times when you were here. I just thought, if you needed one, I'd make a good confidant."

Fia's eyes opened wide; she began to laugh and continued until she cried.

Elizabeth stood and sputtered, "I don't see what's so funny. I'm only trying to help."

"Oh, Elizabeth," Fia finally gasped. "You have. Thank you...thank you so much. That's the first time I've laughed in days." She wiped her eyes, still chuckling.

"I still don't see what's so funny." Elizabeth repeated indignantly.

"You are, Cousin. Don't grin from ear to ear when you want me to think you're concerned about my welfare. And please...please don't insult me. I know exactly how much you missed me."

"All right, so I didn't miss you," Elizabeth admitted. "But you must agree you aren't yourself. I thought I could help."

Fia shook her head. "It's been a long few weeks since Mr. MacInnes' death." Fia sighed, "If there's any other point to this visit, I'd really like you to get to it."

"As it happens, there is something else. Tomorrow we're having a guest for dinner. Not Struan," she added as Fia opened her mouth to protest. "But since you're home, Father and I will expect you to join us. So...rest up tonight. I'll have Una bring something up."

Fia was puzzled. "Don't you want to tell me who this guest is?"

Rising to leave, Elizabeth grinned wickedly. "It's one of my very favorite people. Dress nicely." She stopped at the door, glancing around. "By the way, where's your valise?"

"Lost along the way," Fia responded.

It was nearly sunrise when Fia fell asleep still in the window seat. When she awoke at mid-morning, she rose stiffly, every muscle aching. Rubbing water over her face, Fia realized that she was still in her traveling clothes. "I need a bath," she mumbled and tried not to think about her last bath. She removed her dress and donned her wrapper. Downstairs, Fia found the maid and asked her to heat water for the tub.

Una immediately complied, chatting easily with Fia. "It's good to see a friendly face in this house again, Miss. I'm glad you're back."

"Thank you, Una. Yours was certainly the only face I missed while I was away." Poking around in the larder, Fia pulled out a platter of scones, took one and spread it with jam.

"Have you seen your uncle yet, Miss?"

Shaking her head, Fia broke a piece off the scone, "No, is he here?" she asked and popped it into her mouth.

"He's gone to the docks at Port Glasgow. He and Miss Elizabeth were talking at breakfast. The master was certainly surprised to hear of your return."

"I guess he would be." Fia licked jam from her fingers. "I'd nearly forgotten how good your scones are, Una. God's blood, I didn't realize I was so hungry." Una gaped at her. "What is it?" Fia asked.

"I've never heard you say that before." Una responded.

"Say what?"

"God's blood," she whispered, glancing toward the dining room door.

Slowly, Fia lay the scone down and stared at it. "I must have picked it up somewhere. I didn't realize I'd said it." She smiled apologetically. "I'll be more careful."

"Oh, Miss, I don't mind. It's your uncle I'm worried about."

Fia patted Una's hand. "It's all right. I might as well carry some water up with me." Fia reached for a cloth and picked up a kettle.

"But, you said you were hungry. I can take the water up."

"I'm not as hungry as I thought."

Elizabeth's laughter floated up the stairs. As Fia descended, two muffled male voices slowly became distinct. Her uncle's she recognized, the other–there was something vaguely familiar about it.

At the bottom of the steps, Fia stopped to take a last look in the mirror. But she didn't see the maroon and cream-striped open robe and embroidered petticoat; she saw Martin's countenance in her reflection. Stretching her hand toward the mirror, she touched it, and Martin disappeared, leaving her own strained face looking back at her. Fia stifled a cry and muttered, "I can't sit through this dinner. I can't, not yet." As she reached for the newel post, the second voice penetrated her grief and she froze. "It can't be," she whispered. There it was; that voice: cold, venomous, threatening–the voice of a murderer. Panic gripped her and Fia clutched the post for support. "Why is he here? How did he find me? *Who is he*?" her mind screamed. Fia cast her mind back to the night the chaise was held up; she was sure there was nothing that he could use to track her. Elizabeth said that she knew him... coincidence? It had to be. While desperately trying to convince herself, Fia heard her uncle.

"Where is Fia?"

Fia fought to regain her composure. When she stepped into the room, her color was high and she stared wide-eyed at the man next to her cousin. The scar she remembered was stark in his tanned face. Fia's interest in him was not lost on Andrew Forbes; he smiled invitingly as she reluctantly approached.

Elizabeth looked from one to the other and silently cursed them both. She recognized Andrew's hooded gaze as the mask of desire it was. She'd seen it herself only yesterday. And it was obvious to Elizabeth that Fia was deeply affected by Andrew's presence. Bristling, she concluded that it could only be for one reason–Fia liked what she saw.

George Graham came to his niece's side and awkwardly pecked her cheek. "Welcome, home, Fia."

"What?" Fia pulled her eyes from the guest to look at her paunchy uncle, his graying hair curling gently to his heavy side-whiskers.

George looked at her with concern. "I said 'welcome home'. Fia, are you well?"

"Aye," she murmured, her gaze returning to the man with the scar.

Elizabeth couldn't stand the tension between her cousin and her lover. "Fia, don't be rude. You're staring at our guest. If you can't be more civilized–"

"Finally, we meet." Andrew left Elizabeth's side and stood before Fia. "I thought it about time since, soon, we'll be related."

Fia gaped at Elizabeth. "Are...are you to be married, Cousin?"

"Not me, goose. You. This is Andrew Forbes, you're future brother-in-law."

Fia's palms turned cold and she fought the urge to run from his smothering presence. His bulk was intimidating and, as his hard eyes examined her, she saw a sinister version of Struan's watery gaze. Fia stiffened with fear realizing that he might recognize her from that night on the road to Inveraray. Desperately, she tried to calm herself. Swallowing hard, Fia forced a slim smile and managed a curtsey, her wobbly legs barely supporting her weight. Though she had not extended her hand, Andrew took it firmly in his and deliberately prolonged bringing it to his lips as he executed his bow.

Without taking his eyes from Fia's, Andrew spoke in a husky voice, "Elizabeth, my dear, why didn't you tell me that beauty runs in your family?"

Momentarily, Elizabeth was speechless, watching the exchange between them. There was an obvious connection there and, for the first time, Elizabeth was forced to look at her cousin in a new light. Finally, with barely controlled anger, she responded, "I didn't think you'd be interested."

Andrew let go of Fia's hand and sauntered back to Elizabeth's side. "Sheath your claws, my dear." His reprimand further incensed her.

Fia was so tense that, when Andrew released her hand, she nearly fell backward. Her uncle steadied her. "Are you sure there is nothing wrong, Fia?"

"I'm still a little tired, that's all," she muttered.

He offered her his arm and addressed the others. "I think we should go into supper. Fia is still somewhat worn from her trip. A late night is probably not a good idea. Shall we?"

Supper was a painfully slow affair, and Fia was beginning to feel distressed. Everyone was interested in the circumstances of her early return, so she was forced to remember, in detail, Robert's gruesome death. Finally, she pushed her plate away, the memories too vivid.

"Forgive us. We've been insensitive and upset you," Andrew simpered. "Why don't you tell us instead about your journey home. Was traveling alone uncomfortable for you?"

The concern in his voice crept into Fia's dulled mind. For a fleeting moment, she feared he had indeed recognized her. But one look at his mocking face and Fia knew she was still safe. The concern she'd heard was false, and scarcely concealed his wicked smile and taunting laugh. No matter what Forbes said, he didn't care about her or anyone else except maybe... Fia glanced at Elizabeth who sat glowering at her and wondered how her cousin would feel if she knew Andrew Forbes was a murderer. But she addressed Andrew. "The trip back was uneventful, and I am grateful for that." After a sip of claret, she asked, "Mr. Forbes, where is your brother?"

"He's gone to Edinburgh on business after a few days of grouse hunting. Unfortunately, I don't expect him back until the week after next. I hope you will call on me in his place should you need anything."

Andrew's smile did not reassure Fia of the sincerity of his intentions. "That's kind of you, but I can't imagine what I could possibly need."

"Nevertheless, I am your's to command." Again, the hooded gaze, the sibilant voice. He held up his wine glass. "And I hope to see a great deal more of you."

The days crawled by punctuated only by Andrew's visits and Elizabeth's corresponding mood swings. To minimize the time spent in their presence, Fia frequented the stalls and carts at the Glasgow Green market and, occasionally, a few of the shops. She had ceased being terrified of recognition by Andrew, but his recurring visits kept her on edge. This morning, the market was exceptionally warm and noisy. Fia was constantly jostled by sellers and buyers alike and, once, was nearly overrun by tumblers entertaining the throng in hopes of receiving a few coins. To catch her breath, Fia stepped into a recessed doorway to stand looking at the myriad of faces before her. A moment later, a hand at her elbow pressed her firmly back against the door–Andrew.

"Fia Graham, how lovely seeing your beautiful face on this beautiful morning." His voice washed over her like icy water and she shivered. Her motion brought him a step closer. "Do you know that, since the moment we first saw each other, I've noticed that you tremble when I'm near you?" He fingered a lock of her hair that curled near her breast.

"I believe you may be mistaking the reason for my trembling. It is Elizabeth who desires you, not I." Firmly, Fia pushed his hand away.

Andrew's laugh was low and calculated. "Now don't tell me you're concerned about Elizabeth. Is it that you have your heart set on Struan and are saving yourself for him?"

She forced herself to look into Andrew's callous, blue eyes. "No, as a matter of fact, I don't want to marry your brother at all."

Andrew looked thoughtful. "I'd heard that rumor–but dismissed it. Your uncle made a bargain and you will uphold the honor of his good name by keeping that bargain. Of course, if you fear that you won't be appreciated or desired, you mustn't despair." He pressed so close to her that Fia thought the door handle would go through her back. "Struan and I are quite close and share almost everything–everything I want, that is. Believe me when I say you will never want for companionship." He began to caress her waist but she angrily knocked his hand away. Andrew stepped back, smiling lewdly. "I'll see you soon, my dear."

For a few seconds after he'd gone, Fia's mind refused to work. But when it did, the implications of Andrew's promise stunned her, making her knees buckle. She grabbed the door's latch to steady herself.

"What a curious exchange this seems to be." Watching with interest, the muscles in Simon MacLaren's compact body tensed. He stood unmoving, oblivious to the bustle of the market around him, as a husky man with a distinctive scar forced a young woman into the corner of an entryway. The sound of their voices carried to him, but not their words. Seeing the man's hand caress the woman's hair, he decided that they must know each other. Then he glimpsed her eyes and began to ease his way toward the couple. "This is none of your business," he muttered under his breath. As he neared the stoop, there was a quick movement. The girl struck out at the man who left so suddenly that he bumped Simon's arm as he passed. The lass looked disoriented. Simon groaned inwardly as he reached her. He realized long ago that something in him responded instinctively to people in need. "Protector of innocents", his father had dubbed him, so he approached the young woman. "Are you all right, Miss?"

Fia's head snapped up, and fists clenched. She stared into a most fascinating face–long and angular, surrounded by a halo of pale golden curls fighting to escape their queue. Looking into his vivid blue eyes was like looking into a clear autumn morning sky. The effect was startling, but pleasantly reassuring. He watched her curiously.

"I'm sorry if I scared you. I asked if you were all right?" he repeated.

"I will be...thank you," she replied, hesitantly.

He pointed to the stoop. "Would you like to sit down?"

Fia shook her head. "I think walking will help more."

"Well, if you don't mind, I'll walk along with you." When her eyes narrowed with sudden suspicion, he flashed a broad smile. "I assure you," he pressed his palm against his chest empha-sizing his next words. "I'm relatively harmless. It's just that I noticed the man bothering you. Actually, I was about to come to your rescue when he left. If you are of a mind, I'll keep you company for a while in case he returns. And, just so you know who your champion is, Simon MacLaren." He swept a small bow.

Fia studied him trying to determine what kind of help he might be if Andrew returned. Though small in stature, he looked powerfully built. Her instincts told her that she could trust him. "My name...."

Before she could tell him, Simon stopped her with a dramatic wave of his hand. "No, please...I've already named you. I shall call you Arabella."

"Arabella?" Fia suddenly wondered about his sanity.

Simon's smile was so innocent and beguiling that Fia wasn't sure she could refuse anything he asked of her. She found herself returning his smile. "Arabella, it is." But she quickly grew serious again. "If you're going to walk with me, Simon, you should know something about Andrew...that man you saw with me. He's dangerous; he's a murderer." Spoken in the morning light, in the middle of the crowded market, the words sounded ludicrous–even to Fia.

"I'd like to hear more about that while we walk."

Fia's jaw dropped. "What I told you...that doesn't bother you?"

"Well, I wouldn't say that. But, I think it's all the more reason why I should walk with you. You may really need me to rescue you. Old Scarface looked as though he wanted to get very friendly."

Fia began to walk and he fell into step. "Aye, he promised me as much when I marry his brother."

Simon stopped abruptly and frowned. "I don't think I like what you're getting into."

Fia gazed appreciatively at him. "That makes two of us." Suddenly, Fia felt awkward; her self-appointed protector must be at market for a reason. And here he was spending all his time with her. "Isn't there something else you should be doing? I don't want to take you away from your business."

He feigned shock. "What? We've just met and already you want to get rid of me?" Simon shook his head. "I must be losing my touch. Normally, I devastate women with my charm in less than five minutes. I see you're going to be difficult!"

Fia looked at him wide-eyed, not sure whether he was joking. "I don't want to get rid of you, and I don't mean to be difficult. I only assumed that you probably have you're own reasons for being here and would want to tend to them."

Simon linked his arm through hers. "That's reassuring. Actually, my business here is con-cluded. It turns out that I'm just passing through. I returned from the colonies a short while back, spent some time in London, and now I'm looking for a cousin of mine who's gone and gotten himself lost." Simon frowned.

Noting it, she prompted, "Is something wrong?"

"Well, you were speaking of murder. As it happens, my poor cousin was unjustly accused of that very crime: his wife and her child. He was turned out by virtually all who knew him."

"You say 'unjustly accused'? How do you know?"

"I've seen what's left of his family–a miserable, drunken, guilt-ridden brother–and discovered the truth. It was the brother's child and it was the brother who killed her by accident, gave her too much laudanum."

"What a terrible thing for your cousin."

"Aye, that's why I'm searching for him. If I ever find him, I'll tell him he's no longer being blamed."

Fia grinned at him. "So you're out to save yet another troubled person?"

Simon blushed unexpectedly. "You've discovered my secret quickly, Arabella. This is a dreadful habit of mine, you see, trying to help people whether they want it or not."

"Not so dreadful. Anyway, I wish you luck finding him; no one should have to live under such an injustice. Tell me," she continued, shifting subjects, "what were you doing in the colonies?"

"Touring. I'm an actor by trade."

Excited, Fia gushed, "I've never met an actor before. Are you famous? What kind of roles do you play?"

"I'm well known in the colonies, not here. And as far as roles go, I play just about anything. Versatility is my specialty." He tilted his head skyward, thinking. "This season, the troupe performed 'The Tempest' and 'Romeo and Juliet'. We also performed my personal favorite, 'The Beggar's Opera'. Sometimes, they let me sing, you see, though not during Shakespeare, of course." His laugh was infectious.

Eyes sparkling, Fia laughed with him. "No, I suppose they wouldn't want you to do that. I'd love to see you on stage sometime. It must be an exciting way to live."

"It can be. Depending on what colony I'm performing in, I get the chance to meet fascinating, sometimes powerful people. And I like the colonies. Everything has a vitality and freshness to it that I find addictive." He allowed himself a moment to relish his memories then declared, "That's enough about me. What about you? And how do you know Old Scarface is a murderer?"

"He shot a man who was riding in a post chaise with me. It was night, and Andrew didn't see my face clearly."

"You haven't turned him in; is that because you know him?"

Shaking her head Fia said, "No, it's because I haven't any proof."

Simon was intrigued. "And you are to be his sister-in-law. How did you get to be so lucky?"

"It was arranged."

The bluntness of her response caused him to prompt her. "And?"

"And what?"

Simon patted her hand. "There's more to it than that, I'll wager. Is it Andrew? Come, you can confide in me. We're friends, aren't we?" The fleeting pain that touched her face took him by surprise. "I'm sorry. I've said something to upset you."

She shook her head. "It's all right. It's just...well...there was someone special, not long ago. We used to say that we were friends."

"Forgive me."

"You haven't done anything wrong," she assured. "That part of my life is over; I'm just having trouble letting it go."

"Is it over because of your marriage?"

"He's marrying also. Do you mind if we change the subject? Tell me more about your travels."

Simon and Fia continued their talk as they strolled through Glasgow and, before she knew it, Fia was almost back to Virginia Street. Stopping, she turned to him. "It's not a good idea for you to come any farther. I don't want my family's questions to spoil this. I've enjoyed speaking with you so much; like catching up with someone I've known for years."

Simon smiled at her. "Strangers, who've known each other all along. I feel it, too. A word of advice; if I were you, lass, I'd think of a means to stay out of Old Scarface's way."

"Don't think I'm not working on it. Thank you again. And I hope you find your cousin. By the way," she grinned at him, "you haven't lost your touch."

He held her hand between his. "Thank the Lord my reputation is intact!" He kissed her fingers and bowed. "Our paths may cross again, Arabella–who knows?"

"I hope so. Godspeed, Simon." Fia watched his golden curls disappear back toward the market.

Chapter Eight

The image of Fia in the arms of another haunted Martin. He tried to counteract it by remembering every tiny detail of the night he'd held her in his arms for a few cherished moments. However, his chosen remedy only lasted until his physical need for her became so acute it pained him. It had been a week, one wasted except for his incessant weaving.

"Enough," Martin groused, disgusted with himself. He took the finished cloth off the loom, rolled it and two other pieces in leather for protection, and tied the bundle. He stuffed some personal items into his saddlebags and added a few oatcakes on top. Arms shoved into the sleeves of his great coat, Martin then filled his whiskey flask, slung it over his shoulder and knelt to scatter the embers of the hearth fire.

Arthur watched all this activity with interest and started prancing excitedly around the room.

"Aye, laddie, we're going on a journey." Martin hesitated, trying to decide what else he might need or was forgetting. From the trunk, he hoisted a small pouch of coins and the dirk and plaid that had been his grandfather's. He picked up what medical supplies he had then took a last look around. His gaze fell on the shirt Fia had made sitting on the bed where it had been since she'd left. Drawn to it, Martin lifted the shirt, folded it gently, and placed it at the top of his bag. Arthur shot through the opened door and leapt and danced around the yard. With Odhar saddled, they were soon on their way–Martin just didn't know where.

"You're back sooner than I expected." Annie wanted to greet Martin coolly but, as soon as she saw him, she melted with concern. "Lad, you're a sight; you've lost weight. You aren't taking care of yourself."

Martin smiled wryly. "So you're talking to me after all."

"I'm worried about you."

"I'm sure I don't look that bad." But he could see in her eyes that he did. "All right, Annie. I promise to do better."

"You can start right now." Gently, she pushed him into a seat and nodded to the servant girl. When a slab of ham and a thick slice of bread were put before him, Martin groaned. But Annie was determined, and sat opposite him. "Now, eat," she ordered.

"Annie, I only came...."

"Hush. I said eat. You can talk to me after that plate is empty." Annie folded her thin arms across her bosom and waited.

Exasperated, Martin gave in but found it difficult to finish. Setting down his tankard, Martin thanked her. "It was excellent, as it always is."

Annie smiled smugly. "I'm glad you appreciate it."

"You know I do. But what I came for, is to tell you that I'm going away for a while."

Annie nearly leapt from her chair. "Oh, Martin, you're going after Fia! Oh, lad, it's the right thing to do. I know you care deeply for each other. Why you're both so stub...born..." Annie's voice trailed off as Martin shifted his gaze away from her–but not before she saw the hurt in his eyes.

He struggled to keep his voice steady. "I'm not."

Annie was confused. "Well...why else would you leave?"

Martin sighed. "Just to get away."

"You mean to run away, don't you?" she shrewdly guessed. "Lad, don't you know that you can't escape your feelings for her? Just look at yourself. Stop this foolishness! She loves you– what are you afraid of?"

For a long moment, Martin studied her, considering her last statement. "If she loves me, why is she marrying someone else?"

Annie started. "Who? Who is she marrying?"

"A solicitor her uncle chose for her. She wants to be 'comfortable'."

"Did she say that?"

Nodding, Martin replied, "Exactly."

"I tell you, Fia's in love with *you!*"

The man stared at her. "Did she tell you that?" he asked quietly, not daring to hope.

"In every way possible without saying the words."

Martin's eyebrows went up. "Oh, now I understand. She showed you that she loved me. Well, why didn't she show me?"

Annie rested her hands on the table and leaned toward him. "Did you show Fia how *you* felt? Did you ever tell her?" Annie waited. "Well?"

Martin shook his head. "No. Fia told me she was eager to marry Forbes. So, no...I said nothing."

Annie patted his hand in sympathy. "Lad, I'm sorry. But you didn't sit with Fia while she waited to say goodbye to you. You didn't see the pain in her eyes each time someone came into the room and it wasn't you." She smiled tenderly at him. "More important to me, though, is I know you love her. It breaks my heart to see you suffering, especially when I don't believe it's necessary. At least talk to her, Martin," Annie urged.

Martin's hand covered hers and his eyes were bright with unshed tears. "I do love her, Annie, God knows," he whispered.

"But Fia needs to know, Martin."

He kissed her work-roughened hand and stood abruptly. "I brought you a present." He unrolled the leather covering his cloth and removed one. "I was working on this when I met Fia; I'd like you to have it."

Annie's eyes shone with delight. "Oh, Martin, are you sure? It's so beautiful!"

"It's yours, Annie. It's a small token to someone very important to me. I'll be on my way now." He rerolled and tied the leather, tucked it under his arm and kissed her on the cheek.

"Any idea when you'll return?"

Martin shook his head and walked to the door. "I'll send you word if it's going to be very long. Thanks, Annie. Try not to worry."

"I won't if you promise to eat," she shouted after him, then added to herself, "well, not much."

As the 'Rowan and Thistle' faded from view, Annie's words, 'Fia's in love with you', continued to ring in his head. It sounded incredible–it sounded impossible. The memory of the words and actions that passed between them that last time belied Annie's statement. He ached with disappointment and suddenly realized that, what he thought he wanted most–to be alone–he didn't desire at all. He guided Odhar eastward. "We can be there tomorrow afternoon, and it'll be a blessing to see Alex after all this time."

The pink-orange glow of the setting sun reflected warmly in the windows of the Edinburgh house. Martin knocked sharply at Dr. Monro's door and a handsome woman with upturned nose and flecks of gray in her pale brown hair answered. "You wish to see Dr. Monro?"

"Aye, I'm an old acquaintance, not a patient." Martin gazed appreciatively at her, trim in a soft blue, quilted petticoat and short, embroidered jacket.

"And your name, Sir?"

"Martin Ross."

A ready smile touched the corners of her eyes in fine lines that hinted she smiled often. "So, you're Martin." She stood back. "Please, come in. Alex...uh...Dr. Monro will be so very pleased to see you."

"Arthur, stay," he commanded and watched the hound settle. Closing the door behind him, Martin asked warily, "You know who I am?"

"Indeed I do. The Doctor speaks of you with great affection; he also wonders, from time to time, what's become of you." She grinned.

"I suddenly feel guilty for not having visited sooner."

"Oh, I'm teasing you because I feel I know you already. But forgive me. You don't know me, so I've put you at a disadvantage. Please follow me; he's in the library."

Susan M. Walls

As they approached the library, the sound of Alex's violin reached Martin's ears and reminded him of the first time he'd met Alexander Monro twelve years earlier. He was playing the violin then as well. "It's good that some things in this world don't change."

"I beg your pardon?"

Martin shook his head. "I'm just thinking aloud. The sound of Alex's music brings back pleasant memories." In the doorway, Martin waited patiently behind the woman until Alex finished his tune and she stepped forward and announced his arrival.

Alex whirled in surprise, a broad smile swallowing his face. "Martin, dear God, man! Where have you been all these years?" Monro walked swiftly to Martin with energy that belied his nearly seventy years. He clasped Martin's hand then embraced him.

"Alex, you look wonderful."

Holding Martin at arm's length, Alex studied his protégée. "Emma, dear, please bring us some sherry. We'll take it in here."

"Of course, Doctor." The woman left, discreetly closing the door behind her.

Monro turned his attention back to Martin and frowned. "I can't say the same for you, Martin you don't look well at all. Have you been ill?"

Martin grinned ruefully. "Only sick at heart, Alex."

"Is that why you've come to see me after all this time? I thought I taught you that physicians can't mend broken hearts."

Martin chuckled, "Aye, you did; and you're right. But you are my oldest and dearest friend as well as my teacher, Alex, and I could use your sensible, prudent counsel."

"That sounds ominous. Still, whatever the reason, I'm delighted to see you; it's been far too long. Come, sit down. We should have our sherry in a few moments and we can talk each other's ears off while we enjoy it."

"How's Alexander?" Martin inquired.

"Ah, my son does well, still lectures at the School. I spend less and less time there though I'm still Professor of Anatomy."

"And founder of the School," Martin reminded with admiration and ran his fingers over the polished wood shelves full of leather bound volumes. "I don't think this room has changed a bit since I was last in it."

Alex beamed. "The only change that's occurred here since you left is Emma...Mrs. Rose...a delightful woman."

"And lovely," Martin added smiling.

Alex laughed. "That she is, Martin."

They were chatting when Emma returned. Martin rose and took the tray from her asking her to join them. The woman's eyes darted to Alex's face and, reassuringly, he took her hand. "It's all right, Emma. Join us if you'd like. I want you to get to know this Martin you've heard me talk about."

Emma Rose's expression relaxed into a gentle smile and she dipped a curtsey to Martin. "It's nice to finally meet you."

Martin bowed. "It's my pleasure. Alex has never looked better, and I think the credit must belong to you. Will you join us?" he repeated.

With a shake of her head, Emma declined. "There'll be time later. I'm sure you two have a great deal of catching up to do. I'll leave you to it." She touched Alex lightly on the arm then left them.

"You're a lucky man, Alex." Martin stated with envy.

"I agree wholeheartedly. Emma is all I could ask for in a companion and more. Now tell me what's troubling you."

Martin didn't expect the quick shift in Alex's train of thought and hesitated. "It...it can wait."

Alex leaned forward. "We haven't seen each other in nearly three years. You came all this way, it can't wait."

Suddenly bone-weary, Martin wove his fingers through his unruly curls. "I hardly know where to begin, Alex."

"This isn't about Bridgid is it? Have you been back to Skye since her death?"

Martin shook his head. "I haven't been back. I...if I didn't tell you before, I was grateful to see you after her death."

The Borrowed Days

"I was grateful you came to me. You were shattered and desperate and I'd have gone any-where to help you, you're that dear to me. I know you feared that someone would look for you here, but I can tell you now that never happened."

"They were just glad to be rid of me," Martin mused glumly. "But I'm glad to hear it, Alex. I was afraid of involving you, but I had to be sure you knew the truth."

"I understand, but I know you, Martin. I'd have known it was a lie. So, if this doesn't involve Bridgid...?"

Martin frowned. "It does in an odd sort of way. I've...found love again."

"But...that's good news, isn't it?" Alex puzzled at his friend's dour expression.

Rubbing his forehead, Martin said, "It's very complicated."

"Forgive me lad, but love usually is," Alex declared. "Why don't you just tell me about her."

"I chose solitude to help me deal with all the pain that came with the deaths of my wife and her child. I've had no emotional entanglements. Fia, Fia Graham, was lost and alone in the woods when I came upon her. She was ill so I took her home and, over time, discovered she'd been through some truly harrowing experiences. We were alone together night and day for almost a month, first while she recovered and then waiting for a break in the borrowed days so I could take her to Inverary."

" So far, I don't see the problem," Alex admitted.

"The problem was me. I was so wary, so used to being alone, that I was not always kind; I kept pushing Fia away, all the while knowing she was innocent. I was holding my past like a protective shield." He took a deep breath. "I was afraid to let myself love her, of making another mistake, of being hurt again, of hurting her. I failed so terribly with Bridgid."

"Martin," Alex began quietly, "Bridgid was...to let that tragic episode rule your life...Remem-ber that it was she who deceived you from the beginning. It was not *your* 'failure'. I tried to tell you that when you came here, but you were too wretched to hear or accept what I was saying."

"I know that now. And what I felt for Bridgid was genuine. But it isn't what I feel with Fia, I feel...whole in a way I never felt with Bridgid, or in my life for that matter. And I would never have believed it possible, but Fia has healed the pain I've carried these three years.

"Then let go of Bridgid."

"It isn't that easy. Fia knows nothing of Bridgid, yet, the whole time we were together, she suffered the effects of that time in my life by how I treated her. I was quick to judge and ashamed to say I was not very fair to her. And I am full of remorse that I can't make it up to her." Shoulders slumped, Martin finished, "Fia's gone to marry someone else."

Alex started at this revelation. "When did that happen? Did you know that all along?"

"She never mentioned it until the day before I took her to catch the post chaise in Inverary." Martin replied, voice tight. "Truly I don't believe she loves him, but she would say nothing except that they would have a comfortable life with mutual respect. Alex, she's sweet, compas-sionate, intelligent, breathtaking..." his voice trailed off as his memories took hold.

Alex's voice gentled. "And does Fia love you?"

Martin raised his gaze to his friend's. "I had hoped so, but those words never passed between us. We have a strong bond and shared some intimate moments that made me love and want her all the more." He paused then confessed self-consciously, "I told her about my grandfather."

Brows lifted in surprise, Alex exclaimed, "That clearly says what this woman means to you." Alex studied his friend. "You say that Fia doesn't love this other man?"

Martin shrugged his shoulders. "She didn't say when I asked, but I'm almost positive she doesn't. She's determined to marry him anyway."

"Are you sure? Would she marry him if she saw you again, if you talked with her before the wedding?"

Sighing, Martin sank back into his chair. "I don't think she'll agree to see me. We didn't part on the best of terms."

Folding his arms across his chest and, stretching his legs toward the fire, Alex studied the tips of his shoes. Finally, he offered, "You don't know if she loves you, if she doesn't love the other man. You assume she'll marry him regardless, and you don't think she ever wants to see you again. Martin, you're a man of science. What facts do you have?"

Eyes narrowing, Martin mulled over Alex's question. At length he replied, "I know that I love Fia. Without her, part of me is lost. And...I'm afraid."

"Afraid of what?"

"Of living my life without her, that I'll never be with her again, and that I mean nothing to her."

Alex leveled his gaze at Martin. "My best advice is what I believe you already know deep down. You must go see her."

Tears sprang to Martin's eyes and he dashed them away with the back of his hand. "You must think me a fool."

"Never. However, you are a man too caught up in his past to embrace his future when she stares him in the face."

There was a soft knock and Emma opened the door. "I'm sorry to interrupt. I just want Martin to know that I've prepared a room for him and I'll expect you both for supper in an hour." She blew Alex a kiss and closed the door behind her.

Martin couldn't remember the last time he felt he belonged anywhere other than in his own croft. But that night with Alex and Emma was different. Their love spilled over and surrounded him with its warmth like a balm soothing his frayed emotions. When finally Alex showed him to his room, Martin exclaimed, "I can't thank you enough for letting me share the evening with you and Emma. Watching you together is enough to make any man envious. I'm so very happy for you, Alex!"

Alex clapped his hand on Martin's shoulder. "It'll be this way for you too, Martin. I promise this, if you and Fia are meant to be together, it will happen. God will see to it. Now, get some rest. Stay with us a few days. Young Alexander would enjoy seeing you again, and we can go over to Hospital for a bit."

"I'd like that very much, my friend. Thank you." Martin closed the door behind his host and drew a ragged breath. As much as he enjoyed it, the evening was also painful. Martin washed at the basin beside the bed and held the towel over his face for a long moment, appreciating its comforting softness. He suddenly felt isolated and lonely. He wondered if sharing his life with Fia could be as full of warmth, passion and tenderness as Alex and Emma's. Was it really possible that she might love him as Annie so strongly believed? Martin tossed the towel down and stripped. "She's not here, you fool," he scolded. "If she wanted you...." Martin let the thought trail off because it led nowhere.

Too jittery to sleep, Martin picked up a copy of the *Edinburgh Evening Courant*, thoughtfully provided by Emma. He was pleasantly surprised to find it was Tuesday's paper, only two days old. He scanned the pages filled with bits of news from London and the North American colonies. But as pleased as he was to see the newspaper and be distracted by it, it didn't take long before Martin's eyes began playing tricks on him, and he set the paper aside. He climbed into bed and sank in the feather tick. "God's blood, I don't remember the last time I slept on a bed like this. How will I ever go back to the ground with Arthur?" Still, Martin slept fitfully. In the night, he woke with a jolt. Stumbling to the window, Martin let the light from the waxing moon envelop him. He panted, his head aching and raised the window to let the cool air dance over his skin. He felt anxious, almost panicked as slivers of the dream that woke him flashed before him. Reluctant to move from the light, Martin pulled a blanket from the bed and sat on the floor staring out at the night sky as details of the dream surged into his consciousness.

Soaked in sweat, Bridgid lay straining against the pain that racked her battered body. When she didn't scream in anguish, she shrieked at Martin for doing nothing to ease it.

"You...you don't know what real pain is—I'll show you. Bring me your brother," she gasped. "He should see what his bairn has done to me."

For a moment, Martin sat gaping at her. Then, in shock, he rose, opened the door and motioned his brother in. But when Hugh ran to the bed he turned back to Martin. "You've killed her," he wailed.

Martin shook his head in disbelief. "No. She isn't dead." He came quickly to his brother's side and what he saw made him cry out in despair. Fia's lifeless eyes, not Bridgid's, stared up at him. That was what had jolted him awake and now Martin shuddered violently. He pulled the blanket closer. Huddled on the floor, he knew he wouldn't sleep again that night.

Alex and Emma kept Martin so busy that, almost before he realized it, four days had passed. He sat in on lectures at the Edinburgh School of Medicine, some given by young Alexander who had become a joint Professor with his father in 1754, the same year Martin had returned home to Skye to open his own practice. And, at the moment, the younger Dr. Monro was trying to persuade Martin to accompany him to an assembly. Martin declined saying, "I haven't danced in the company of young ladies since I left Edinburgh. I'd certainly tromp their delicate toes."

"Not you," scoffed Alexander, "you were always the most agile fellow when it came to the dance. Why the only rest the ladies ever gave you was when refreshments were served, and then they were just making sure you were ready for the country dancing that followed. Besides, you haven't seen the 'Comely Gardens' behind Holyroodhouse. They opened in '55. I tell you it's every bit as refined as Vauxhall."

"To which I've never been so couldn't make an adequate comparison," Martin protested.

"What does it matter?" Alexander declared, arms open wide in invitation. "Good music, good food and lovely, willing dance partners whose toes you can doctor if you tread on them. Come, it'll be like old times."

Martin laughed aloud at his colleague's enthusiasm. "How does a busy man like you find the time for such pleasures?"

Alexander confided with a grin, "I haven't a wife yet."

"I'm sorry, Alexander, I really can't. Tomorrow I'm leaving; I want to spend this evening with your father and Emma."

"Oh, all right," Alexander relented then brightened. "I guess that leaves more ladies for me."

Hand clapping Alexander's shoulder, Martin vowed, "I'm certain you'll do your best to entertain them."

In the darkness of the night, Martin tossed in his bed, loins aching from the spiraling need thoughts of Fia brought–how she smelled, the feel of her skin, the taste of her sweet lips. Once again, sleep was slow to claim him and, early the next morning, Martin said goodbye to Alex and Emma.

"Promise you'll visit again," Emma urged, "and stay longer next time."

Alex covered Martin's hand in both of his. "Send me word, Martin. I'd like to know what becomes of your Fia."

"My Fia," Martin mused as he urged Odhar down the street. In his dream, Fia was lost to him. He thought about what it might really mean and decided he needed the answer. Of one thing he was sure. "If I don't see her soon, she really will be lost to me. I have to know, either way, if I'm to get on with my life." He swung Odhar west onto the Glasgow road.

In the kitchen, Fia made tea and thought about Simon MacLaren and how he'd befriended her. Twice, in just over a month, strangers had come to her aid. The thought brought tears to her eyes. "Come, Fia," she scolded impatiently, "there are other things to consider now." Gulping the hot tea, Fia silently admitted that Simon was right. "Somehow, I have to stay out of Andrew's grasp." She forced herself to examine her options and quickly concluded that she had none–none that were rational, anyway.

Fia picked up her tea, and retreated to her room to think. She realized that, in the absence of protest from her, Elizabeth was forging ahead with the wedding plans. Fia determined to have more say in her future. But how?

Despair began to settle over her and she twisted the curtain sash in her fingers. At that moment, she noticed Andrew approaching the house and, instinctively, she pulled back from the window. Her reaction to his arrival infuriated her. Fia's expression hardened and, returning to the window, she watched Forbes dismount and tie his horse. Fia suddenly realized that, if she didn't find a way out of this, she truly would lose all control of her life. The thought frightened her but awakened her determination. "Martin doesn't love me, but I won't lie down and die. I will, at least, choose my own husband, even if it takes a lifetime to find him."

Sitting down, Fia took a deep breath to clear her mind and, a few minutes later, she stood again, a plan forming. Her best chance was to see the solicitor. Perhaps, he still had some loyalty to her father's memory and would be willing to help. "And, I might as well go now," she said, throwing her capuchin around her shoulders. The cloak came just to her elbows and would keep her comfortable in the spring air. Silently, Fia crept downstairs, listening for Andrew's voice. She heard Elizabeth's first.

Susan M. Walls

"Lord, Andrew," Elizabeth giggled deliciously, "what if someone should catch us?"

"Why are you fretting? You told me the maid's out and you never see your cousin except at meals. Besides," he grunted huskily, "the idea of getting caught with your skirt around your waist and me inside you excites you. Why, if I buried my face between your thighs right now, I dare say, I might drown."

Fia stood at the bottom of the stairs listening in fascination. The thought of Andrew and Elizabeth together both intrigued and repulsed her. But, outweighing either reaction, was envy. Fia had lost count of the times she'd imagined loving Martin and, the thought that it would never happen.... Elizabeth's moans wound their way through Fia's thoughts, and she fought back the emotions that threatened to overwhelm her. She hurried though the hall and out the front door.

"What was that?" Elizabeth jumped. "Was that the door?"

Lost in the urgency of his need, Andrew hurried to reassure her, "It was your imagination," before lunging into her brutally so that she cried out in pain, surprise and ecstasy.

Fia read the engraved plaque beside the massive blue door, "Lindsay and Sutherland, Esq." She was nervous and self-conscious, not even knowing whether to knock or walk in. She decided knocking was the safest approach, and her rap was answered by a woman not much older than herself.

"May I help you, Miss?"

"I've come to see Mr. Sutherland, if he's available."

The woman smiled. "He's engaged at the moment but, if you'd care to wait, he should be free soon." She stepped aside for Fia to enter. "May I have your name?"

Fia gave it then added, "Mr. Sutherland doesn't know me." It was almost half an hour later when the young woman opened a door in the back hall, past the staircase, ushering Fia into Mr. Sutherland's presence.

The man unfolded his long-limbed body and rose from his chair to greet her. "Douglas Sutherland, Miss Graham. His sharp green eyes swept from Fia's head to her toes, quickly sizing her up.

"I'm Fia Graham–you were my father, James', solicitor." She noticed a slight change in his expression at the mention of her father, but continued, "I need your help."

The solicitor held a chair for her. "Please sit down, Miss Graham. Of course, I know who you are. Your father was a good friend and helped me get started in my law practice."

Sitting, Fia looked solemnly at him. "I'm happy to hear that. Is that the only reason my name is familiar to you?"

Sutherland reseated himself, leaning back in his chair, thin fingers laced over his flat stomach. "Why would you ask?"

"Because you've probably been contacted by my uncle, who is my guardian, regarding my inheritance," she replied bluntly.

The solicitor smiled tentatively. "True. But please tell me why you're here and how I might help you."

Fia leaned forward, resting one gloved hand on the edge of his mahogany desk. "You were a friend of my father's, but we've never met. I don't know if your loyalty still lies with my father, or if my uncle now influences you."

One eyebrow arched as he regarded Fia critically. "You don't waste words."

"This is important to me. I'd like an answer."

He cocked his head. "If I tell you that your uncle has no influence over me, will you believe me?"

Fia's face softened. "Whichever it is, I believe you will tell me the truth. I trust my father's instincts–my father trusted you. He believed in your integrity."

Sutherland swallowed hard, moved by her words. "That's quite a compliment coming from your father–he was a fine man. Your uncle has been to see me and I've listened to him. I know he wants you married before you come into your inheritance. I assume because he has plans for it." A crooked smile cracked his face. "But your father was a dear friend and you, Fia Graham, must be my first concern."

Fia released her breath in relief. "You can't know how much it means to me to hear you say that."

There was a knock, and the woman entered with a tray. "I thought you might want some tea."

"Quite right, Agnes. Here would be fine, thank you." Sutherland indicated the corner of his desk. Agnes poured the tea and left.

Sutherland turned his attention back to Fia. "Now, Miss Graham, what kind of help do you need?"

Not knowing where to start, Fia replied, "I'm not sure what to expect in the way of an inheritance but, if I got a position somewhere to supplement it, could I live off it?"

"My dear, you could live in reasonable comfort without ever having to augment your income. And, there's a piece of property east of Inverness along the coast that's to be yours. Why, if worse came to worst, you could sell it. But what does it matter? You will have a husband soon to provide for your needs."

Fia shook her head vehemently. "I've decided that I won't marry."

Douglas Sutherland set his cup into its saucer. "May I ask why?"

"I can't abide him; he's a conceited oaf."

"You're a shrewd judge of character." Sutherland replied, amusement tugging his lips.

Puzzled, Fia asked, "Do you know Struan Forbes?"

"I do know him. I was surprised, to say the least, when George Graham mentioned your intended's name."

"What do you know about him?"

"Professionally, he's a bit unscrupulous when he's not being just plain lazy. His reputation in this town is so bad that he works mostly out of Edinburgh now. They haven't caught on to him yet." Sutherland shook his head, loosening pale hair from its queue.

Fia squared her shoulders. "Well, I won't marry him."

Sutherland looked at her with increasing interest. "And, have you told anyone this?"

"Not recently," she answered cautiously. "I needed to see you first to know if I had any real options."

The solicitor nodded. "Your inheritance will come under the administration of your husband– so, choose wisely. But tell them soon, if you're going to refuse."

"I will. Struan is due back in about three days. I should tell him first, then Uncle George."

Tapping his chin with a forefinger, Sutherland inquired, "When do you turn eighteen? Soon?"

"On the thirteenth."

"Well, your uncle promised I'd be invited to the wedding. So, I'll just wait to see whether you come back to my office, or whether I'm summoned to the kirk for the ceremony." He smiled grimly. "I don't envy you your task."

"I don't look forward to it either; but, my mind is made up." Fia stood and caught his hand between hers. "Thank you so much."

"Miss Graham–"

"Fia please."

"Fia then. I haven't done anything yet. But, one more thing before you leave." His brows drew down in a thoughtful frown. "Have you given any thought to where you'll go if you do refuse to wed? I don't recommend staying in Glasgow if you defy your uncle or Forbes for that matter."

Fia's face went blank. "No. I...I hadn't thought about it at all." Inveraray came to mind but she immediately pushed the thought of being so close to Martin and Jean away. Instead, she said, "Probably Inverness. I have an aunt there, my mother's sister. At least, I believe she's still there. She might let me stay with her temporarily."

"Well, you need to decide quickly."

Fia beamed at him, feeling hopeful at last. "I will and thank you again."

"Where have you been all afternoon?" Elizabeth demanded, hands perched on her slender waist.

"Out," Fia answered curtly, then grinned mischievously. "How's Andrew today?"

Caught off guard, Elizabeth blushed crimson. "What makes you think I've seen Andrew today?"

Wide-eyed, Fia replied, "He was here when I left. It seemed that you were seeing a great deal of him. And I clearly heard him say you were excited by his visit...or was it because you were hoping to get caught?"

Elizabeth stamped her foot and huffed, "You're a jealous little witch to eavesdrop like that."

Fia started upstairs. "Not because you've had Andrew Forbes, I assure you."

Elizabeth called after Fia, "Word's come; Struan will be home tonight. That means he'll be here for supper tomorrow. It won't be long now, Cousin, until your wedding night." Elizabeth sneered, "I hope when you eavesdropped, you picked up some pointers. Struan is not Andrew, and you'll never know the kind of pleasure that a man like Andrew can give a woman."

Fia smiled sweetly. "That's not what Andrew promised me at market yesterday." She watched as her words sunk in, then left Elizabeth sputtering and glaring after her.

Elizabeth blustered, "What happened at market?"

Fia stopped on the stairs and glanced back at her cousin. "Ask Andrew."

Fia dressed soberly in dark brown for her visit to Struan. The fact was she hated the itchy, wool sack-dress and wearing it helped put her in the appropriate mood for telling him of her decision. Struan answered the door and Fia was repulsed at how gaunt and sickly he appeared without the benefit of candlelight. His black hair was tied limply with an overlarge ribbon, his diluted eyes barely showed blue in his pasty face.

"Miss Graham, this is unexpected, what brings you here? Do I dare hope you've missed me?"

"May I come in?" Fia asked hesitantly.

Forbes bowed and stepped aside. "Certainly."

Fia glanced around the entryway. "Your brother isn't here, is he?" she inquired, trying to sound casual. "I don't want to disturb him."

Struan's eyes narrowed. "You shouldn't be concerned about Andrew–did you really come to see him?"

"Why would you think that?" Fia asked, surprised.

"Andrew seems to affect women that way–they chase after him like...well, they do," he finished lamely. Aye, he thought. Women were always drawn to Andrew; Struan had never been sure why. He and Andrew were brothers, but Struan's own effect on women was nothing to brag about. He could only conclude that the fair sex enjoyed Andrew's brooding cruelty–that they enjoyed rough treatment–not refinement. Elizabeth surely did. Several times, Struan had listened outside the door when Andrew had taken Elizabeth. Aye, he knew Elizabeth was common in that regard. Beads of sweat appeared on Struan's upper lip at the memory. He wondered if Fia would like it that way too. He promised himself to try it on their wedding night. He'd teach her that Andrew wasn't the only man who might satisfy her.

"Struan?" Fia asked warily.

Abruptly, he glared at Fia. "Andrew's not here."

Fia assured him, "I came to talk to you."

He grunted in response, "Do you want to come into the music room?"

"Fine." Fia followed him into the airy room and nervously blurted, "That's a beautiful spinet; do you play?"

"It was Mother's. I can't play a note; neither can Andrew, in case you're interested," Struan pouted.

Fia turned her attention to the ungainly man. "I'm not."

A strained smile showed Struan's uneven teeth. "Well, enough of this idle chat. To what do I owe the honor of a visit from my bride-to-be? Perhaps some minor wedding detail you wish me to consent to?"

Straightening, Fia answered, "I have come about the wedding–but not to settle minor details." She couldn't swallow. "I can't think of an easy way to say this so...I don't want to be your wife, Struan. I've made my decision; I won't change my mind. I'll tell Uncle George tonight, but I thought I should tell you first." Fia waited for his reaction; she didn't have to wait long. Struan twisted her arm in a grip of iron. His unexpected strength startled her and she gasped in pain.

His voice reeked sarcasm, "Oh, how kind, how very considerate of you to tell me first. You'll be sorry you didn't speak to me *before* making your decision. You've made a big mistake for, I promise you, we will be married."

Fia's anger overcame her fear. "Let go of me," she demanded, wrenching her arm free. "You don't know me. Why would you want to force me to marry you? What is it you really want?"

"Oh, there's something in this for all or us–Andrew and me, George and Elizabeth–even you, if you play along." Struan's eyes glazed over as he looked into the future. "Just think of it, our own little country manor house on the coast. It will make us very wealthy, indeed."

Fia was baffled. "The land...you want the land? I don't understand. Is it special? How could it make anyone wealthy?"

Dreamily, Struan replied, "Aye, it's special. It has a large, sandy beach, a natural cave. Why, it's paradise!"

Fia shook her head. "I still don't understand; you talk as though you'd seen it."

Struan snapped at her, "Well, of course I've seen it. Do you think we'd make this deal blindly? No!" He raised his hand. "I'm tired of your questions. If you fight this marriage, Andrew...." Struan stopped and stared at Fia; she had actually shuddered when he mentioned Andrew. How interesting, he thought. Then, smirking, Struan goaded her, "What's wrong, Fia? Does the prospect of what Andrew might do make you think twice about how good it might be to be my wife?"

"No second thoughts," she spat. "I loathe you."

He pulled her into a cruel embrace. "Get used to me, Fia. I will marry you, and you'll be my wife in every sense of the word, as often as I desire." Struan's lips crushed hers.

Repulsed, Fia twisted her face aside, pushing him hard and backing away. Panting, she watched him warily. "You swine. I'll die before I marry you!"

Struan laughed in delight. "Be careful, or you'll get your wish." He gestured toward her dress. "By the way, when you're Mistress Forbes, don't ever dress in those monk's robes. I won't allow you to look like a beggar. Your father left you money and you'll dress the way I want you to; to emphasize your figure and to please me.

"Never," she replied coldly.

"Mark my words, Fia."

Not only Struan, but Andrew Forbes promptly arrived at the house for supper. Hearing them, Fia was convinced they would try to wear her down because they outnumbered her. Not a chance, she promised herself determinedly and, taking a deep breath, entered the drawing room. Two pairs of eyes glared at her; the third stared coldly; the fourth, George Graham's, skittered across her face and turned away in discomfort. Fia raised her chin a notch in defiance. "I see that Struan has told you of my decision." She expected Elizabeth to rail at her, or George to lecture her; but she didn't expect what happened next.

In an instant, Andrew was beside her, gripping her already bruised arm. His callous, reptilian voice was at her ear. "You don't seem to understand, my dear; what you want is of no consequence."

Struan chimed in, "That's right. Your uncle made a deal; you'll belong to me very soon."

Fia would not acknowledge either brother; her eyes remained on her uncle. "Uncle George didn't ask me how I felt about his deal–I'm not interested," she declared.

Andrew's grip tightened. "Since when is the bride-to-be consulted in these matters?" He scowled, "I want to speak to Fia alone."

"No!" Elizabeth protested. But a quick jerk of Andrew's head toward the door sent the other three from the room–Elizabeth reluctantly.

Releasing Fia, Andrew stepped back and glowered at her. "Now, what's this all about?"

Incredulous, Fia replied, "You know what this is about–I don't like your brother and won't marry him. She glared back at him, her gray eyes suspicious. "Why are you questioning me? Isn't this Uncle George's concern? I'd like to know why he's not here."

"My, you are demanding, this evening." He closed the space between them again and leered wickedly. "I'll tell you this much, you have no choice in this. If you're smart, you won't fight it. If you insist on fighting, I'll make sure you regret it, starting now."

Fia's heart was pounding–she knew well what Andrew was capable of. But Fia was frustrated and angry; her voice rose as she responded, "This is my life we're talking about. How can you tell me that I have no choice? I won't give in; it's that simple." Her legs were shaking beneath her skirt, and Fia starkly remembered her vow to Struan...she'd rather die.

Andrew turned slowly from her. "I'm sorry you feel so strongly about it." He swung around and hit her so hard she crashed into the wall, knocking over a candle stand in the process. Blood spurted from her nose and lip. Again, he struck her. Yanking her head back, fingers entwined in her dark curls, Andrew rubbed his body hard against hers, feeling her slimness and the frantic racing of her heart–like a trapped hare. "I'd rather not hit you again." He buried his lips against her neck. Easily, Andrew caught both her wrists in one huge hand and, with his other, groped her breasts.

Though her head reeled, panic bubbled in her throat and she strained frantically against him. A scream of rage tore from her and she sank her teeth into the skin above his wrist.

Andrew jerked his arm free and seeing the half moon of blood, slammed his fist into her stomach. Fia crumbled to the floor and Andrew started to free himself from his breeches, so engorged with excitement he hurt. "You bitch," he spat at her.

"That's enough, Andrew!" George Graham ran to him from the drawing room door. "You can't do this."

Andrew pointed a finger at Graham, his voice deadly, "You let me handle this."

"No, not this way." George went to Fia's side. "You need my ships–don't forget that."

Andrew hissed, "Old man, watch out–don't threaten me."

George stood his ground. "It's not a threat, just the truth. This may be your idea, but this is my niece. I'll marry her to your brother, but I won't let you beat or misuse her." Graham's gaze rested for a moment on Andrew's swollen groin.

"My, how righteous you've become," Andrew sneered. "You'll let me have her inheritance to do with as I please because you'll make money. But you won't let me have her maidenhead because she's your brother's daughter."

George tried to muster some dignity. "Even I have my limits."

"Then lock her up until the wedding," Andrew roared. "Don't let her out of your sight. I won't have her trying to run off."

George's mouth dropped open. "Two weeks? You want me to keep her locked up for two weeks?"

"No, I'm moving the date up." Andrew glanced briefly at Fia. "Day after tomorrow. Now, get her out of my sight," he growled.

Silently, Struan and Elizabeth advanced and, one on either side, hauled Fia up. Shaken by what they saw, neither wanted to challenge Andrew. Elizabeth was shocked that her father had. He was normally so meek. They half walked, half dragged Fia to the top of the stairs where Elizabeth pushed Fia into her room and locked the door.

"You were a bit rough with her," Struan accused watching Elizabeth carefully.

"*Be quiet,*" she screeched. Elizabeth was furious at Andrew for wanting Fia. His marketplace promise to her cousin still stung and Elizabeth had clearly seen Andrew's condition a few moments ago. And she hated Fia for arousing such passion in Andrew. "Silly trollop doesn't know that Andrew likes to play rough; the rougher the better."

"What did you say?" Struan asked, leaning against the wall, mopping his brow.

Elizabeth retorted, "I said she was foolish to cross Andrew."

"She didn't really know she was crossing Andrew. Fia thought she was defying your father. Shouldn't we make sure she's all right?"

"You can coddle her when she's your wife," Elizabeth spat. "I don't think you want to give your brother any reason to find fault with you right now."

Struan silently agreed. He had no idea that Andrew was personally interested in Fia. He speculated silently, "I thought he had his hands full with Elizabeth. No matter," he tucked his snuff handkerchief in his lace cuff and followed Elizabeth down the stairs. "As long as I get her most of the time, Andrew can have a piece, now and then."

Chapter Nine

Livid, Andrew paced the room. "Never challenge my authority again or I'll call off the whole venture," he demanded, glaring at George. "Do you really think this plan will succeed without me? Need I remind you whose idea this was?"

"No, Andrew, you don't need to remind me. I'm...grateful that you've included Elizabeth and me in the profit part of the plan," George fawned, glancing furtively at his daughter's brooding face. "But Andrew, how will we explain changing the date? The invitations have been delivered."

Andrew poured and downed a glass of brandy in one motion. "Struan came home to find his betrothed returned to Glasgow. He couldn't wait to make her his wife and moved the wedding up." Andrew spread his hands in exasperation, his glower sweeping his conspirators. "Do I have to think of everything? It's too simple."

George Graham looked doubtful; Struan yawned.

Elizabeth refused to acknowledge Andrew. Instead, she marched to the spot where Fia had lain and announced with disgust, "I don't know if that blood will come out of the carpet."

"Oh, Daughter, hush." George rubbed his forehead hard, trying to think clearly. "Suddenly, it's all gotten so complicated," he lamented piteously.

About to retort, Elizabeth stopped herself. After all, it was only her father's intervention that had succeeded in stopping Andrew's intent upon Fia. It was Andrew she wanted to hurt; her wrathful stare shifted to him.

Andrew cursed silently under her glare. His mounting desire to bed Fia might ruin everything—he had to be more careful. As it was, he'd have to work hard to regain Elizabeth's trust. He wanted her around for the foreseeable future. She enjoyed his appetite for sex, was an innovative partner, and key to his plan. George loved her so much that, if Andrew crossed her badly enough, George just might stop being afraid; he couldn't allow that. Look what had happened just now with Fia; George had stood up to him. Andrew clenched his fists as, even now, his thoughts returned to Fia. It was infuriating to have her interfering with his plans, but he admired her spirit and fight and imagined she might be an exciting lover as well. When the time was right, he would find out.

In the silence, Struan cleared his throat pretentiously. "Your explanation should take care of questions about moving the wedding up, dear Brother." His watery gaze slid across Andrew. "Do you have any suggestions to explain how my intended looks?"

Elizabeth's black eyes bore into Andrew as she snarled, "I've never seen her look better."

Fia opened her eyes slowly. It was dark except for a square of gray light that was the window. For a few minutes, she wasn't sure she was in her room. A searing pain tore through her head. When the pain dulled to an ache, her mind began to clear and frightening details of her encounter with Andrew returned. When she tried to move, Fia found her arms and legs unresponsive. She strained again and gradually pulled herself to a sitting position. Every part of her body throbbed. Trying to rise, Fia collapsed in a heap, whimpering. She crawled the short distance to the door and reached up to open it. The handle rattled under her grip, but the door didn't budge. The effort left Fia breathless and she rested, gathering her strength. "This time," she swore and, using the handle to pull herself up, tried again. Fia fumbled for the key—it was gone. The explanation dawned quickly. Leaning her forehead on the door, she choked, "You fool. There's no key because they've locked you in; you're a prisoner!" She sank back to the floor, tears of despair streaming down her battered face.

"Wake up," Elizabeth shook Fia's shoulder hard, but her cousin was slow to rouse. "Have you been on the floor all night?" she asked curtly. "Really, Fia, don't be so dramatic."

Fia finally opened her eyes, the left one, barely, and lifted her face to Elizabeth. She heard her cousin gasp.

"Well?" Fia's word slurred through her swollen lips.

"You're a mess! Scarlet and purple–like heather. I brought you some breakfast and some news. You're marrying Struan tomorrow. I'll make sure you have something to cover that," she gestured vaguely toward Fia's face.

"Will you answer one question for me, Elizabeth? Why is this so important–that I marry Struan, I mean."

"Because he loves you, naturally."

In disgust, Fia spat, "Get out."

Elizabeth paused at the door. "I'll tell you two things. First, you can't escape; the street is being watched, just in case you're stupid enough to try. Second, stay away from Andrew."

Fia's head was about to split and she grimaced, "I'd love to oblige you on Andrew. Why don't you tell me how?"

"That's easy," Elizabeth responded with a regal toss of her silken locks. "Don't make him mad, don't fight him–it arouses him. Be placid and boring, as I know you can be, and you'll be fine."

"I should have asked you sooner."

The metallic rattle of the key in the lock sent waves of hopelessness through Fia. She hugged herself and was reminded, painfully, of how powerful a force Andrew Forbes had become in her life. "Without him, I would never have been pledged to Struan, I'm certain. And, Elizabeth and Uncle George are too deeply involved with him to listen to me–even if I were to tell them what I know about Andrew." The sound of her own voice, muffled as it was by her swollen mouth, soothed Fia as she rose, unsteadily, and shuffled to the wash basin. "Uncle George actually tried to help me, but he's no match for Andrew." She looked into the mirror and cringed. The left side of her face was horribly bruised. Her eye was swollen almost shut, both her lips split, and dried blood caked her from nose to waist. Gingerly, she touched a damp cloth to her nose. It was tender, but not broken. After she cleaned the blood from her skin, Fia painstakingly removed her clothes and examined herself. Radiating from a hard red core was a bluish-purple bruise just in the center below her rib cage. "The size of Andrew's fist," she said dryly. Drawing on her dressing gown, Fia lay on the bed and had one last thought about Andrew's role in her life. "Without him, I never would have met Martin. Odd that Andrew should be responsible for the worst and the best things in my life."

"I don't understand, Mr. Graham." Douglas Sutherland leaned forward in his chair. "I thought the wedding was set for the twelfth of June?"

"It was but, you know how impatient young people can be," George Graham answered. "When he found that my niece was back, young Forbes suggested an earlier wedding–insisted on it, in fact. It fits his schedule and, well, they're so eager. I hope you'll still be able to attend–that's why I came personally. It's such short notice, we certainly would understand if you were unable to join us."

"It is short notice. But, aside from you, I'm her only link to her father. I'll rearrange my schedule if necessary to be there."

Graham forced a smile saying, dully, "Splendid."

Sutherland replied casually, "Fine, then. By the way, would it be best for me to stop by the house today about the letter or see her tomorrow before the ceremony?"

Confused, George asked, "What...what letter is that?"

"Why the one from James to his daughter; the one I told you she's required to receive upon marriage or coming of age, whichever occurs first."

George shook his head. "I don't recall you mentioning a letter from my brother."

The solicitor studied George Graham. He was nothing like his late brother, James. There was a physical resemblance, though time had thinned George's hair and plumped his belly. But in character and manner, there was no similarity. Sutherland didn't trust George as far as the door–he'd have trusted James with his life. "I was sure I'd mentioned the letter; if not, I am remiss."

Graham wanted to be done with Sutherland–at least, until after tomorrow. "Well, no matter. Give the letter to me and I will see that Fia reads it."

The solicitor spread his arms in a helpless gesture. "It certainly would be easier for me to give the letter to you. However, I can't. Legally, according to James' instructions, I am required to present the letter, and remain with Fia while she reads it–only me, no one else."

Alarmed, George recklessly charged, "That's ridiculous. Leave it to that half-wit brother of mine to think of something like that."

Sutherland's green gaze hardened. "Nevertheless, he was specific. So, today or tomorrow, which is it to be?"

George hesitated in his response so Sutherland continued, "I will bring the Sheriff with me to enforce this, if I must."

"No need for that," Graham hurriedly assured. "Tomorrow; you can have a few minutes before the ceremony."

Before Sutherland could say another word, George bowed stiffly, and departed.

"You promised him what?" Andrew bellowed, making George shudder and hurry to explain.

"I had no choice, Andrew. He said he'd bring the Sheriff."

"What do I care? We can deal with the Sheriff."

George tried again. "But Sutherland could stop the wedding. The fewer people involved, Andrew, the better."

"You don't have to tell me that," Andrew snapped. "By God, I'll make sure your niece pays for the trouble she's causing." He shot a heated glance at Elizabeth, who was barely speaking to him, and swiftly appraised her ripe figure, eyes coming to rest on the swell of her breasts. He wasn't likely to find release between her legs today. Of course, he could force her; once she got started, she'd warm up quickly enough. Andrew imagined her silken thighs parting for him and stifled a moan. It was worth a try. "George, could I have a few minutes alone with Elizabeth?"

Eager to be out of Andrew's sight, George readily consented. "Take your time. I have to go down to the docks anyway. We'll see you and Struan here, 12:30 tomorrow."

Andrew waved him away. "Of course, as we planned." He rose behind George, locked the drawing room door, and turned to Elizabeth. "I want you naked," he leered.

"Do you now?" Elizabeth challenged. "What about what I want?"

"And what is that, my dear, if not the same thing that I desire?" Andrew slowly circled behind her.

"I don't want you to act like a rutting stag!"

His hands caressed the back of her neck. "Except with you, you mean."

Elizabeth fought to stay angry. He'd wounded her deeply and she wanted him to pay for it. "Leave my cousin alone," she demanded. "I'm all the woman you need."

Andrew grinned at her back and let his fingers travel over her shoulders and down to the top of her stomacher where his fingers traced the curve of each supple breast. He was gratified to hear Elizabeth catch her breath. His hands kneading her flesh, his mouth resting against her ear, Andrew repeated, "I want you naked."

"Andrew," she mewled, protest weakening.

Languidly, Elizabeth stretched in the tangle of clothing beneath her. Andrew had rolled from her onto his back, eyes closed, sweat glistening on his face and chest. She studied him, a mixture of emotions jumbling her thoughts. When they'd first met, it was always like this between them; passion with emotion that assured Elizabeth theirs was more than a physical attachment. Lately, he still craved her, but Andrew's thoughts were elsewhere and, during their time together, they had shared little more than release. Not that that wasn't good, Elizabeth hurried to reassure herself, just...different...less satisfying. But today, it was like the beginning. She smiled broadly remembering the night at the play when she'd first met him. There was a charming arrogance about Andrew that captivated her. His dark good looks, piercing blue eyes, even his unusual scar fascinated her. He had asked her to tea at his home the next day. When she arrived, he swept her into his arms and into his bed. Andrew wasn't her first lover, but he was the only one who mattered. Admittedly, when Andrew first approached her father about uniting the families, Elizabeth thought it would be a marriage between her and Andrew. She was stunned when the proposal turned out to be for her cousin, Fia. Andrew, sensing her anger and disappointment, escorted her to St. Andrews where he spent a week pampering her, and pushing her to levels of ecstasy she'd never experienced. It was there that he entrusted his secret to her and the reason Fia was to marry Struan.

"How do you think I earn my living, dear Elizabeth?"

"I...I don't know. You travel at your own leisure. I assumed you were comfortably situated. Why?"

His hand caressed her naked belly. "I think I can trust you. Can I, Elizabeth? Can I count on you?"

She pushed his hand lower, till it cupped between her thighs. Her eyes were hot with passion and burned him as she replied, "Have no doubt, Andrew."

"All right then...I'm a free trader."

Elizabeth's eyes widened in astonishment and she giggled. "You...a smuggler?"

"You find that amusing?" Andrew forced a smile, his grip on her tightening almost imperceptibly.

Shaking her head, Elizabeth assured, "Not funny, I'm surprised...and intrigued. I want to know more."

"Many people work for me–they don't all know it. But there's a problem. The excise men are becoming more and more of a nuisance. They have actually shut down several of my minor operations. It's increasingly difficult–and challenging–to keep ahead of them." Andrew began moving his fingers teasingly amongst her short black curls and pretended not to notice the effect. "Your father has a generous tongue when he's had too much claret," Andrew smiled slyly.

"I don't...understand." Elizabeth moved slightly so his fingers would touch where she wanted them.

"I went to see him at his office. I told him I knew you, and he offered me wine. We talked for a time about his ships, how he sometimes barely breaks even on a shipment, how hard it often is to sustain those losses. Two bottles of claret later, he blurted how grateful he was that he wouldn't have to provide a dowry for his niece. He told me your cousin would inherit not only money, but a piece of land on the shore northeast of Inverness, land with a sand bottom, a cave and no one around for miles. Elizabeth, I need land just like that, with no dangerous shoals, a protected landing site and temporary storage for my goods." He hesitated. "Do you remember my last trip?"

Elizabeth pushed herself against him, stroking his hardness. "Of course I do," she answered breathlessly.

"I went to see that land–it was just as he described it. When I returned, I made your father a business proposition to which he agreed. My brother marries your cousin before she comes into her inheritance; I get the use of the land, Struan gets a comely wife, and you and your father receive a generous share of my profits." Andrew moved to cover her body with his, entering her in almost the same motion, making her gasp. He watched her liquid eyes carefully and vowed, "You are too important to me to risk. If anything should go wrong, I'll see that it's Fia who gets the blame."

Elizabeth was dumbfounded. "Father agreed to this?"

"Aye...once we had talked it through, he saw how lucrative the proposition was. I asked your father's permission to share this with you, and to court you openly. I saw your cousin from a distance once–I know Struan will be pleased, especially when he hears what his share, beyond your cousin, will be." Elizabeth wanted to think about Andrew's proposal, but he began to move inside her, slowly, until she moved with him and forgot everything but her urgent need for release. Elizabeth cried out.

Andrew reached over and shook her abruptly, "What is it?"

Her eyes flew open and she was, once again, in the rumpled pile of clothes on the drawing room floor. She drew his head to her breast. "Love me again," she commanded.

Andrew grinned triumphantly. "My pleasure, my dear."

Daylight had barely pierced the window pane when Elizabeth breezed in, Fia's wedding gown over her arm. Fia glanced at the dress she was to be married in. The gown was hurriedly redone from one of Elizabeth's sack dresses. New lace had been added to the elbow length sleeves, and the stomacher was new. It was ivory–a color Fia never wore.

"It's absolutely the perfect gown for you," Elizabeth bubbled. She took a long look at Fia. "Well, at least the swelling has gone down a bit. Here," she dropped a small jar into Fia's hand. "I promised you something to cover the bruises."

"So you did," Fia responded dryly.

Elizabeth fidgeted for a few moments. Finally, she hesitated at the door and said, "Be ready at quarter past noon...we'll have some wine before we leave," and hastily retreated.

"Aye, we'll need the wine." Fia turned away, her glance falling on the dress. Perfect? Maybe it was the perfect gown–for this wedding anyway. She dressed slowly, her mind refusing to help her fingers. She ran a brush through her hair and pulled it back from her face securing it at the nape of her neck. Sitting on the window seat, Fia waited. She'd done a great deal of thinking last night when sleep eluded her, even trying to look at her situation from another perspective. Was the marriage proposed so terrible? Struan seemed to want to bed her...and wanted her land too. Otherwise, he seemed almost indifferent and might well leave her alone. The proposed match could have been worse. But then there was Andrew. How could she willingly submit to a future promising pain and defilement? Fia drew a ragged breath remembering, again, her vow to Struan, "I would rather die," she whispered fiercely.

Fia shivered violently and turned her thoughts to Martin, with whom she had felt safe and whole. There were times when he resented her being at his croft, times when he was so tender it made her cry. And he trusted her enough to speak of his beloved grandfather. She considered that the supreme compliment he could have paid her–even though it had caused them to argue again. Fia did not pretend to understand Martin's actions, but she knew what kind of man he was: generous, loyal, compassionate, not selfish or cruel. Fia clutched at her aching heart. "What I wouldn't give to see the warmth in his eyes or the firelight play over him while he sleeps." A tear coursed slowly down her cheek. Fia straightened her shoulders and calmly wiped it away. "I have one last chance; I'll take it no matter the consequences. When the vicar asks if I will have Struan, in front of witnesses, I'll refuse him." She turned from the window as Elizabeth swept into the room to escort her downstairs. Her cousin was striking in pale rose watered silk, with a snowy petticoat, her glossy curls pinned becomingly at the back of her head.

Elizabeth halted just inside the door, her face twisted with rage. "*What are you doing?*" she screeched. "Your face is as purple as the King's coronation robes. Why didn't you use the cream I gave you?"

Fia's eyes bore into Elizabeth's and she quietly declared, "I have nothing to hide." Rising, she picked up her mantle and left the room.

At the bottom of the stairs, George Graham waited. Looking up when he heard the women, he stifled a gasp, horrified at what he saw. "My dear," he choked, "I didn't realize–"

"Oh, Father, save your sympathy," Elizabeth interrupted. "She can't go like this, and she's being stubborn." Elizabeth grabbed the ribbon binding Fia's hair and yanked it off, pushing and pulling her cousin's hair close to her face to hide some of the discoloration. "I'm going to get that cream." Elizabeth grumbled and, hoisting her skirts, stormed back to Fia's room.

George and Fia stood in strained silence which was broken by a knock on the door. "That must be Andrew and Struan," George mumbled, and went to open it.

Fia forced her quaking legs to carry her into the drawing room. She was petrified at the thought of facing Andrew again, but refused to give him the satisfaction of showing it. Bravely, she lifted her chin and looked Andrew square in the eye when he entered. His mouth was rigid; the scar, pale in contrast to his swarthy darkness. He stood directly before her and whispered menacingly, "You were lucky. Next time you defy me...you're mine. I swear it!"

Raw hatred overcame her fear; Fia spit in his face.

His jaw muscle twitched ominously as he glowered at her, waiting for her to cringe and back down. But Fia returned his glare unwaveringly. "Soon, my dear, very soon," Andrew sneered.

From the entry, neither George nor Struan could hear the exchange; but they clearly saw it. Each held his breath waiting for Andrew's reaction, and released it unsteadily when he simply mopped the spit away. In the silence that followed, George spotted the maid standing, rooted, by the fire. He signaled impatiently to her. "We won't have time for the wine...take it away."

Una curtsied nervously, picked up the tray, and left quickly, but not quickly enough to avoid

72

Elizabeth who reached the bottom of the stairs just in time to collide with her. The tray flew from Una's hands, crashing to the floor–crystal splintering, wine and the covering cream staining the front of Elizabeth's gown. "I'm so sorry Miss Elizabeth, let me help." Una reached to blot the silk, but Elizabeth shoved her away.

"You clumsy hag, look at my dress," Elizabeth raged. "I swear I don't know why we keep you here." She turned to her father. "What am I suppose to do now? I can't go like this!"

George hastened to his daughter's side. "You go change, my dear. We'll wait for you."

"No, we won't," Andrew cut in bluntly. "We have a schedule to keep." He turned to Elizabeth. "We'll go on in our carriage. Change your clothes and follow in yours. Make it fast–we can't keep the vicar waiting."

Elizabeth seethed at Andrew's curt reaction but, underneath, she knew what he said made sense and pouted, "All right, go on, I'll catch up." Turning, Elizabeth grabbed Una's arm. "You can help me change; then clean up this mess."

Martin reined Odhar in at the end of Virginia Street and brushed what dust he could from his clothing. Except for the nervous fluttering in his stomach, the warm sun might have made Martin sleepy. He'd gotten little rest the night before, wondering what would happen when he found Fia again. Annie was so positive that Fia loved him, but he was plagued by doubts. Even if Fia didn't love Forbes, that didn't mean.... He shook the thoughts from his head. "Well, Arthur, the clerk at the shipping office had better be right: second house from the corner." It was an imposing, two-story stone structure; only the numerous windows kept it from being oppressive. Martin knocked loudly to help bolster his courage. He heard some commotion inside and the door was quickly opened by a flushed woman in a mobcap.

"Sir?"

"Is this the home of George Graham?"

"Aye, sir, it is."

"Is Miss Graham at home?" His voice was hopeful, "Miss Fia Graham."

The woman looked nervously behind her at the sound of footsteps, and then replied, "No sir, she left a short time ago to..."

"Who is that, Una?" Una was pushed aside by a scowling woman with raven-black curls. "What do you..." Elizabeth's voice died in her throat. She stared unabashedly at the man facing her. A momentary glance toward the floor, and Elizabeth had gathered her thoughts sufficiently to greet him. "May I help you, Sir?"

"Are you Elizabeth Graham?" Martin inquired.

"I...I am Elizabeth Graham. How did you know that?"

"Your cousin described you to me; I'd like to see her please."

"My cousin? You know Fia?" Elizabeth asked doubtfully.

"I do." Martin asked, "Is she here?"

His impertinence annoyed Elizabeth, yet she was intrigued, especially wondering about the nature of this man's relationship with her cousin. "Not at the moment Mr...."

"Ross, Martin Ross."

"Well, Mr. Ross, I expect her back in less than an hour. Please come in and wait." Elizabeth stepped aside for him to enter, but Martin hesitated.

"I don't want to disturb you. You're obviously dressed to go out. I'll come back."

"Really, I wasn't going anywhere important, I assure you. We can wait in the drawing room." Elizabeth retreated inside leaving Martin no choice but to follow her. "Watch out for the broken crystal," she advised airily over her shoulder. "Please sit down, Mr. Ross. I'll have Una bring us refreshments."

"I don't want to be any trouble, Miss Graham."

Elizabeth waved a delicate hand rejecting his protest. "No trouble. Ah, Una. Please bring us some...tea."

"Excuse me, Miss Elizabeth, but you'll be late for–"

"That's all, Una," Elizabeth ordered sharply.

With a sidelong glance at Martin, Una retreated.

"Your maid seems upset," Martin observed.

"Aye, and well she might be," Elizabeth's reply was steely. "She may lose her job over that broken crystal, not to mention she spilled an excellent sherry all over one of my favorite gowns. I believe it's ruined."

Martin's eyes narrowed. "She said you were going to be late. Late for what?"

Elizabeth suddenly bestowed a brilliant smile on him. "Now, Mr. Ross, I said you weren't interrupting anything important, and I meant it. I'm curious though," she continued, sitting opposite him, "how do you know Fia? I'm sure I'd have remembered if she'd mentioned you."

Her question seemed innocent but the fact that Fia had never told Elizabeth about him made him cautious. His smile was pleasant, but held no warmth. "I wouldn't be surprised if Fia hadn't spoken of me."

"So, you haven't known each other long?"

Martin responded casually. "We met when she was returning here from school. From our conversation, I gathered the death of the Headmaster caused her much grief. I'm passing through, and simply thought to inquire after her."

Elizabeth cooed sympathetically, "It was hard on her." Abruptly, she brought the subject back where she wanted it. "So, are you and Fia intimately acquainted?" She studied Martin from beneath her lashes. His attire was not fashionable; it was simple and functional. A laborer, she decided haughtily, and a Highlander judging by the bonnet he carried instead of a tricorne. For a Highlander, he wasn't bad to look at; his clothing enhanced his muscular frame in a way that made her breathing a little difficult, but he had a slightly untamed look that made her uncomfortable. She found herself comparing him to Andrew, who won the contest easily. Well, Martin Ross wasn't her type, but she was certain he was too much of a man for that simpering cousin of hers! She wet her lower lip with the tip of her tongue. Suddenly, she was aware that he watched her with an intimate, but detached gaze, as though he knew her thoughts. For the first time in years, Elizabeth blushed. "Forgive me," she murmured, "that was a presumptuous question."

"It was." Martin agreed rigidly.

While Una served the tea, Elizabeth pondered how to get the man to open up. So far, she was unsuccessful–her eagerness getting in the way, her curiosity outweighing her tact. After the maid left, Elizabeth handed a cup to Martin. "So you are a casual acquaintance."

"I'm here only to see how your cousin fares. When I saw her last, she was sad."

"Were you in part responsible for that?" Her black eyes glittered in delicious anticipation of his answer.

Martin set his tea down, untouched, and rose. "I told you it was the death of the Headmaster. I think I'll wait elsewhere for Fia's return. I don't appreciate being the object of your examination, Miss, and it's becoming difficult for me to remember that I'm a gentleman. Thank you for the tea." He reached the door just as the clock struck one.

"A moment more, Mr. Ross." Mustering an expression of concern, Elizabeth swept toward him. "I really don't think you should leave just yet. We've only begun to get acquainted and you may be in need of a friend before the day is done." She placed a hand at his elbow and indicated the chair he'd just vacated. "Perhaps you should sit; I have news which will interest you."

Martin stepped away from her touch, but sudden dread clutched his heart. "I don't understand. What news would you have as I leave that you didn't have when I arrived?" Martin braced himself for her response and Elizabeth drove home her verbal knife.

"You should stay, Mr. Ross, because you'll want to congratulate Fia when she returns home... with her husband. You see, as the clock struck the hour, my cousin was married." Elizabeth was not disappointed by Martin's reaction; the shock on his face clearly told her that the news hurt him. But her satisfaction was short lived as Martin's survival instincts took over.

"Forbes?" he asked harshly.

Surprised, Elizabeth replied, "Why, she...she told you about Struan?"

"Aye. She told me about him." Bitterness made Martin sharp. "I don't think I'll stay, Miss Graham. Give my regards to the bride."

The room where Fia waited for the ceremony to begin was small and sparsely furnished, just like the gray stone kirk that housed it. Her uncle had locked her in, making her a prisoner in the house of God. Fia stared wistfully out the window. When she was young, she had regularly visited the kirk with her parents. Uncle George never attended services; he'd lost his faith when he lost his wife. Since he didn't observe the Sabbath, Fia's only form of worship since moving to Glasgow had been her own humble prayers offered directly to God. School had brought her in touch again with the Presbyterian rituals of her youth. She sometimes talked to the vicar; he seemed a wise and good man. More often, she found solace in the austere chapel, the winter wind sweeping under the door to swirl around her ankles, the damp cold penetrating the sheltering walls. There was no comfort for her here in a strange kirk, her fate just outside the door. She cringed, hopelessly thinking, "Only a few minutes more." A short time ago, the sun had glared mockingly through the window. Now, as she looked out the second floor panes, the wind coming off the river buffeted heavy, grey clouds overhead. "I understand how you feel," she murmured to the dark shapes being pushed toward their unknown destinies.

There was a knock on the door. "Fia, dear," George Graham cleared his throat, "you have a visitor. Mr. Sutherland needs to speak with you briefly before the ceremony." George turned to go but added, "I told Mr. Sutherland about your riding accident."

Fia waited for the door to close before she choked, "I'm glad for a friendly face."

Sutherland approached slowly, the light from the window casting her face in shadow. When he could see her clearly, he gasped, "Fia, good Lord above, what have they done? This was no riding accident!"

"No, no accident," she murmured.

He grasped her hands in his long, bony fingers. "Did they get you medical attention?" He angrily answered his own question, "Of course they didn't. This is monstrous; they beat you!"

Fia offered a lopsided smile. "I appreciate your coming today. You don't know what it means to me. Uncle George said you wanted to talk. What about?"

Sutherland stared at her. "I must say, Fia, your calmness mystifies me."

Fia wanted to laugh but winced at the pain it brought her. "You only think I'm calm, Mr. Sutherland. I'm terrified." She gently touched her face with a gloved hand. Her voice quivered, "Unless I reject Struan at the altar, which I plan to do no matter the consequences, I'm lost." Fia gulped, unwilling to voice her next thought.

Sutherland cupped her chin in his hand and raised her sorrowful guise to his gentle smile. "That's where you're wrong, my dear," he whispered.

Her desperate eyes searched his. "What are you saying?"

"When your Uncle came to me about the changed wedding date, I knew something was wrong. This happened too fast and, knowing your plan, I had to see for myself. I told your uncle that your father's will stipulated that, before you married, I give you a certain letter he left with me–and that I give it to you in private."

"A...a letter from my father?"

Shaking his head, Sutherland continued, "There is no letter, Fia, I'm sorry. But it was the first thing I thought of that would ensure I had the chance to see you." He frowned. "I had no idea the bastards would treat you so contemptibly. Put your mantle on."

"W...why?"

"My horse is tied at the back of the kirk, a bay with white stockings. I'll stall them as long as I can." He opened the window and leaned out glancing quickly around. "We're in luck, there's no one in sight. I'll lower you as far as I can. Ride to my office and wait. Hurry, there's no time to lose."

Fia threw the lace covering her hair to the floor, grabbed her mantle, and took Sutherland's hands. She swung her legs over the window ledge, and Sutherland carefully lowered her almost to the ground story below. She dropped down the last few feet, landing easily, and he waved her on, watching as she ran swiftly behind the building. "It'll look odd if the window is closed," he thought. "They'll know that I helped her." He left it open, waited a few minutes and, returning to the vestibule, Sutherland stepped up to George Graham. "That was the most dreadful spill Fia took. I'm sure her husband-to-be will be gentle with her; she says she's stiff and very sore."

Uncomfortable, George shifted his gaze from the solicitor's. "Aye, I'm sure he'll be gentle. Well, I must get Fia. It's almost time."

Sutherland laid a hand firmly on George's shoulder. "Give her a few minutes. Reading her father's letter...well, she's very emotional right now. She needs time to compose herself, you understand."

George looked past him to where Andrew and Struan waited impatiently. "Oh...very well. A few minutes can't hurt."

"And they'll do Fia a world of good," Sutherland added. "By the way, Graham, is your daughter here? I'd be honored if you'd introduce us."

George brightened at the mention of Elizabeth. "Unfortunately, our maid spilled wine on her. Elizabeth didn't want to come to her cousin's wedding in a stained gown. She should be arriving at any moment."

"I look forward to seeing–"

"Go get Fia," Andrew demanded coming up behind the two men.

"Andrew, I'd like to wait just a while longer," George said soothingly.

"Why? My brother's anxious to see his bride."

"Andrew, have you met Mr. Sutherland, the solicitor for my brother's estate?"

Andrew eyed Sutherland suspiciously. "I *know* who he is, why's he *here*?"

Sutherland responded for George, "I'm here because I'm an invited guest, and because I had a duty to perform, as you are no doubt aware. I delivered a letter to Fia from her father."

"Ah, the letter. Well, you've done that now, haven't you?"

The solicitor's eyes narrowed. "Aye, and I've asked Mr. Graham to give Fia a few moments to collect herself. She was quite surprised and moved by her father's words."

"Aye, that's all Andrew, just a few minutes," George coaxed.

Andrew replied evenly, "I'm not an unreasonable man, just anxious to see my brother happy."

"We'd all like to see Struan Forbes get what he deserves." Sutherland smiled innocently. "By the way," Sutherland looked thoughtfully at Andrew. "Who was with Fia when she had that horrible accident?"

"Accident?" Andrew snapped, eyes darting to George then back to Sutherland. "She was alone."

Sutherland shook his head and walked toward the chapel. "It's such a pity to be so battered and on her wedding day. Almost makes you want to destroy the beast responsible."

Andrew muttered under his breath, "He should mind his own damned business." To George, he growled, "Get her out here. I'm tired of waiting."

Graham knocked gently on the door, then loudly. Still, there was no response. Opening the door, he peeked in. "Fia?"

Impatiently, Andrew pushed the door wide and saw the lace on the floor before the window. "Damn," he shoved George aside, ran to the window and thrust out his head. He slammed his fists on the sill. "She's gone!"

George shook violently. "She can't be gone...she wouldn't leave," he whined.

"*She did*," Andrew roared.

Chapter Ten

Elizabeth hummed contentedly to herself. There was no point in going to the kirk now. They'd all be home shortly and she couldn't wait to see Fia's reaction when she told her about Martin Ross' visit. Hearing voices, she hurried to the window. "Ah, finally." She turned away as her father left the carriage. Before she even reached the entry, Elizabeth was startled by the crash of the door as it opened. "What...?" Andrew pushed her aside, his face thunderous. Elizabeth stuttered, "A...Andrew...what is it?" She tugged at George's sleeve. "Father?"

"Fia's run off," George lamented, casting a wary glance at Andrew.

Elizabeth gaped in disbelief. Finally, she noticed Struan leaning against the drawing room door and, grasping his arm, demanded, "Struan, how did this happen?"

Petulantly, he threw off her grip. "Out a window. It must have been that damned letter."

"Or the damned lawyer," Andrew snarled.

Elizabeth's eyes darted between the three men. "What letter? The one from her father?"

George sat heavily, his head in his hands. "The very one. Sutherland brought it to the kirk and asked that we give her time to compose herself after reading it and...she vanished."

Elizabeth did not respond. Guardedly, she watched Andrew's back as he stared out the window. What if Martin Ross had somehow gotten word to Fia? "Impossible," she muttered, "he didn't know."

Andrew turned to her. "What did you say?"

Elizabeth's head snapped up and she gulped. She'd been ready to taunt Fia about Ross. Now that Fia was gone, Elizabeth suddenly wasn't sure she wanted to tell Andrew. "I said, 'impossible'. I'm shocked that she had the nerve to do something like this. You mentioned Sutherland? Do you think he has something to do with this?"

Andrew cast a malevolent eye on George. "I'd bet your father's life on it."

"It wasn't my fault, Andrew," George cried, leaping from his chair. "Struan, talk to him."

"Seems to me you're all at fault." Struan sat, and propped his feet up. "I've gone along with this scheme from the beginning; just taken orders. I'm tired of being consulted only when things go wrong–I should have had more of a say in this whole business."

"It's been such a hardship on you, little brother," Andrew sneered.

"Oh, I'm not saying that I didn't look forward to spending my spare time bedding Fia. And her land is perfect for our trading activities. But I've done my part. You," he pointed at Andrew, "you scared her off. There was no reason for you to beat her. You just wanted an excuse to lift her skirts."

"You self-righteous ass." Andrew lunged at his brother knocking him over and sending the chair tumbling. George stood by helplessly while the brothers grappled on the floor, trying to prove their points with their fists.

Elizabeth was incensed. When she'd had enough, she emptied a large vase of flowers over the two men who sputtered apart. Pushing stems and blossoms aside, they glared at Elizabeth as she said acidly, "I hope you have it–and her–out of your systems. There's enough blame to go around. We have to decide what, if anything, we can do now to salvage this."

"Elizabeth's right," George ventured timidly. "Why don't you go change your clothes and return for supper. Then we can discuss this calmly."

"I'll see Una about it." Elizabeth started for the hall.

"Elizabeth, wait," Andrew's command froze on his lips as Elizabeth looked at him, no emotion in her eyes. There had always been something there–anger, passion. A shiver ran up Andrew's spine, but he shook the feeling. If his quick anger over Struan's observation pushed this black-eyed beauty too far, he'd just have to work harder to warm her up again. "We'll come tomorrow," he uttered lamely.

Elizabeth nodded curtly and went looking for Una thinking, "She'll need to keep her mouth shut about Martin Ross."

Douglas Sutherland closed the shutters before lighting the candle on the table beside the bed. "I don't think it will take them long to suspect my role in your escape, Fia. The question is, how far will they pursue it?" He faced her across the candle. "At the very least, we can expect the office to be watched." Fia nodded and hugged herself. "Are you cold, my dear?"

"No."

"Well, I'm sorry I can't provide anyplace more respectable for you where you'll be safe. My partner is the family man. I live here, but always keep this alcove room for him in case he needs to stay. I hope my dressing gown will do until I can get Agnes to bring you something else to wear," he said. "Your...ahem...wedding dress, I'm sure you don't want to wear it anyway but... smells a bit horsy."

"It does and you're right," she giggled, then placed a hand on his arm. "You are very good to do this for me. I'll be fine here, Mr. Sutherland."

"Douglas, please." He patted her hand. "I could do nothing less for James Graham's daughter. I hope you sleep well."

When she was alone, Fia undressed, washed and wrapped herself in the dressing gown. Lying on the bed, she basked in the feeling of security the tiny room afforded. There was no fire; the brick chimney provided comfortable warmth from the blaze in the first floor hearth. Fia couldn't fool herself, though–she knew the peace she felt was temporary. When morning came, it was likely that a Forbes or Graham would be pounding on the door. Sighing, Fia climbed under the covers and stared at the candle flame, pondering the strange twists of fate that brought her to be lying snug in this alcove bed. The betrothal, less than six months ago, had started it all. "Betrothals and marriages are supposed to be a normal part of life; they aren't supposed to turn your life upside down," she thought. "Yet here I am–no home, no family, and an emptiness that only seems to worsen." Muffled tears slipped to her pillow. "I hope you're content, Martin. You'll marry the woman you want. At least, I escaped a man I abhor." With a quick breath, Fia snuffed the candle.

Dazed, Martin rode Odhar west, then north toward Loch Lomand and home. He kept the horse at an easy gait; there was no reason to hurry. It was all over now–no more wondering, no more hoping in vain for a life with Fia. He just wished he understood why she'd married Forbes. The reasons she'd given him had sounded lame, rehearsed, like someone else had said them.

Martin shifted his thoughts, concentrating on the countryside he traveled through for the small comfort its beauty afforded him. The sloping hills were coming to life as the heather greened and prepared to bloom. Bluebonnets splashed color along the road. Occasionally he saw a croft, but since he'd left Glasgow, Martin had seen only a handful of people. That suited him; he had no interest in being chatty, or idly passing the time of day. When he stopped for the night, Martin tended the animals, munched, without tasting, an oatcake Emma had provided, and washed it down with water from a nearby burn. His sleep was restless and, in the morning, Martin moved sluggishly, taking his time getting back on the road. When Inveraray came into view late in the day, Martin didn't think twice. He passed on the far side of the castle, skirting the town completely and crossed the river, continuing north. Briefly, Martin considered stopping at his croft, but dismissed the idea as quickly as it had materialized. "If I stop there, Arthur, I may never leave home again; that won't do. I'll not sit and lick my wounds." Arthur barked and ran ahead on the road where it forked to the left. "All right, lad," Martin decided, "we'll go where you lead." He guided Odhar onto the hound's chosen trail.

For the next few days, Martin did just that; wherever, Arthur lead, Martin and Odhar followed. And when Arthur rested, so did his companions. This routine kept Martin from having to think. The day came when, surprised, he found himself riding into Fort William. And, as if he knew exactly what he was doing, Arthur led Martin through town and onto the west road. They stopped within sight of a large stone building, several smaller ones, and the charred remains of a byre... the MacInnes school. Martin looked at Arthur suspiciously. "Traitor!" he exclaimed. Dismounting, Martin led Odhar into the yard and tied him to a post. Arthur sat just inside the dry-stone wall fronting the property.

Martin stood in front of the blackened rubble where Robert MacInnes had suffered his fatal accident. "I don't know what this is going to prove," he accused Arthur impatiently. Glancing around, Martin spotted the hillside where he assumed the Headmaster was buried. And, as he drew closer, Martin noticed the low mound of earth and read the marker, "Robert MacInnes, born 1726, died 1760." Martin hugged himself, as though chilled, and closed his eyes. Suddenly, he felt the crushing weight of the truth–Fia was gone, lost to him forever. It didn't matter how or why anymore. "Never in my life have I felt so alone," he confided to the man in the grave, the man Fia had known and called friend. Sitting next to Robert MacInnes, Martin wrapped his arms loosely around his knees and stared ahead unseeing, remembering how Fia's presence had touched him. "I should have told her I loved her when I had the chance." His voice trailed off to a whisper, "I think it would have been right with us."

"Young man," a voice floated up from the bottom of the hill. "Young man?" it repeated.

Startled, Martin looked down and saw a man with a white clergy's collar, tricorne perched on his head, walking stick in his hand. Rising, Martin took a last look at the inscription and went down to meet him. "Aye, Vicar?"

"What are you doing here?"

"I'm not sure," Martin responded thoughtfully, more to himself than to answer the man's question.

The vicar's furry eyebrows shot up. "This is private property in my keeping until it can be sold. I want to know what your interest is in the school."

Martin shook his head, clearing his thoughts. "My name is Martin Ross. I'm not really interested in the school. Robert MacInnes was very dear to someone I know. I...I came to pay my respects and to...think. I apologize for the trespass, Sir."

The vicar relaxed a little. "That's all right, Mr. Ross. I needed to be sure, you understand."

Martin smiled fleetingly. "Of course."

The vicar rubbed his chin with the knob of his walking stick. "I'm Reverend Grant. Would I perhaps know this friend of yours who knew Robert?"

"Probably, so. Her name is Fia Graham."

Smiling broadly, Grant's eyes began to sparkle. "Fia, oh aye. A fine lass, and so helpful to poor Mary. How is Fia; when did you see her last?"

Martin swallowed hard. "The last time I saw her...it will soon be a month. And she was... well."

"Oh, then you saw her after she left Fort William." Reverend Grant nodded, inviting confirmation of his statement.

"That's right," Martin agreed.

"Fia and I had many pleasant chats while she lived at the school."

Martin's interest was piqued. "You saw her regularly?"

"Aye, on the Sabbath and on frequent visits here–school trustee, you know." The man leaned heavily on his cane. "Do you mind if we sit down?"

"Of course not; I'll follow you."

Reverend Grant sighed heavily as he sat on the front stoop. "That's better. I've had an attack of the gout that's just beginning to improve. I don't want to aggravate it if I can help it." He smiled into Martin's serious face, wondering what the young man's interest in Fia really was. "You know," he said casually, "I don't recall Fia ever mentioning you."

Martin grinned at him. "You're fishing," he accused good-naturedly.

Laughing loudly, Reverend Grant sputtered, "G...guilty, as charged."

Martin liked this man, and he was another link to Fia. "You knew Fia before she met me."

"Oh, then that explains it, because she did talk from time to time about acquaintances."

Hesitantly, Martin asked, "Did she ever mention Struan Forbes?"

Reverend Grant's bushy brows drew down in a frown. "Aye, he was very much on her mind. As a man of the church, Fia confided in me. Why?"

"I'm going to ask you to break her confidence and tell me what she said about him."

"And why would I do that?" Grant asked pointedly.

Martin looked down at his fingers. "I care what happens to her. She married Forbes."

"Did she?" The vicar shook his head. "So she did her uncle's bidding after all; she seemed set against it. She must have taken my advice."

"Your advice?" Martin faced him.

Grant nodded. "Fia was troubled. She didn't want to marry Forbes but, deep down, she knew that she shouldn't disobey her uncle. He raised her after she was orphaned, you know. I advised her to think very carefully before choosing her path. That God commanded us to honor our mother and father. Fia's uncle was the closest thing she had to a father. And, if she didn't love Forbes, she might grow to love him. She might still have a comfortable life based on mutual respect."

Martin's face paled. Those were the same words Fia had used; they tore him like a knife. "Aye," he murmured, "she took your advice."

"We can only pray it works out well for her then," he nodded to himself. "Well, lad, I've enjoyed our visit. But come," he lay a hand on Martin's shoulder. "I must move on. Help an old man onto his horse, will you?"

Martin accompanied Reverend Grant back into Fort William where the man offered a meal and a place to stay the night. But Martin was preoccupied and thought it would be ungracious of him to accept under the circumstances. "It's a kind offer, Sir, but I won't trouble you." Martin extended his hand, which the vicar shook. "And try a poultice of crushed elder for that gout," he offered. Then, calling to Arthur, Martin nudged Odhar forward.

"If you see Fia," Grant called after him, "give her my regards."

Elizabeth stood in the doorway of Fia's room, staring vacantly at the empty window seat. Of all the possible outcomes she envisioned since joining forces with Andrew, this wasn't one of them. Elizabeth never believed that Fia would assert her own will over that of George Graham. "After all," Elizabeth huffed, "didn't we provide her with a home, clothes and food? Who would guess Fia would be so ungrateful?" She banged the door shut, and started down to breakfast, wondering what time Andrew and Struan would appear. During the night, Elizabeth had thought about what Fia's disappearance meant to them. Remembering yesterday's display by the two brothers, rolling on the floor, fighting, Elizabeth decided both men were thinking in a fog—their brains addled by their bulging breeches. It was up to her then to keep a clear head and suggest the next move.

Frowning, Elizabeth trailed her slender fingers down the banister. She was unable to shake the troubling revelations the brothers' row had forced on her. The quarrel was useless, disgusting, childish—and about Fia, of all people. Elizabeth had seen a side of Andrew she didn't care for. He seemed to have lost his perspective about this plan. His pride and his physical needs were overshadowing everything. It made Elizabeth wonder about the true nature of their relationship. The passion between them was so consuming, she'd never stood back and looked at it objectively. Until now, she never felt the need to. Instinctively, Elizabeth knew that Fia had become too important to Andrew. The question was, how did Andrew feel about Elizabeth now? Was she no longer of value? That was a role Elizabeth would not tolerate.

George was late coming down to the dining room, so Elizabeth seated herself and distractedly accepted the tea Una offered her. As the maid tiptoed about doing her chores, Elizabeth remembered a dream she'd had last night—a strange dream, because it meant nothing to her. In a grove of birch and elm, she stood amongst numerous, scattered standing stones. The grove was hushed, the light an unearthly hue as though before a gale. Behind her, in a clearing were large round piles of stone—taller than she and, so broad, Elizabeth could not see around them. A name, she called a name over and over. But what name? "I was looking for someone," Elizabeth muttered, trying to force her memory to clear. Something else, there was a man crouched near an opening in one of the piles of stones. Was it he she called for? She started toward him at a stumbling run, heard the crack of thunder behind her and fell, pain searing through her back. The man's face was almost clear....

"Good morning, my dear," George greeted her with forced gaiety, but small talk was beyond him this morning. "When do you think Andrew will arrive?"

"Early," came her blunt reply. Elizabeth saw the worry etched on George's face and smiled faintly. She squeezed his hand. "Don't fret, Father. I've been thinking a great deal about Fia and her land. This may actually have worked out for the best."

George's eyes grew wide. "How can this possibly be better than having her married to Struan?"

"Have your breakfast. By the time the Forbes brothers knock, I'll be ready to tell all of you." Elizabeth's confident smile reassured George a bit, and he attacked the eggs, toast and fish Una placed before him.

Poor Father, Elizabeth thought. He really is no match for Andrew–so easily intimidated. For his sake, she almost regretted that she had blessed his participation in this scheme. Yet, occasionally, signs of the confident, successful businessman, George Graham, peaked through. Elizabeth was glad to see it despite the fact that Andrew's temper made her wary. What was Andrew capable of if pushed too far?

Agnes swung the blue door wide. "Gentlemen?" She looked from one dark-haired man to the other. As Mr. Sutherland suspected, it had taken no time for them to come around. She smiled graciously.

The gangly one responded, "If Mr. Sutherland is in, my brother and I would like a word with him."

"And have you an appointment?"

Andrew started to reply, but Struan cut him off, afraid of what he would say in his aggravated state. "We don't. However, if he is here, I believe Mr. Sutherland will see us. Please announce Struan and Andrew Forbes. We'll wait."

"Then please wait inside, gentlemen. For June, the morning is brisk." She stepped aside for them to enter then left them to find her employer, seemingly at breakfast, but, in truth, coming down the back stairs. Closing the dining room door behind her, Agnes noted, "They've arrived."

"So predictable," he purred. "I'll see to the callers now, Agnes. You be careful."

"Aye, sir."

Straightening his waistcoat, Sutherland approached the entry. "Gentlemen, you are about early, especially after yesterday–a horribly disappointing day for you, Struan." His brows drew together with concern. "Any word from Miss Graham?"

"None yet, Sutherland. And you're right, it was a great disappointment to me–not to mention the anxiety she's caused by disappearing. I'm terribly worried for her safety." Struan wrung his hands. "In fact, that's why I'm here."

Sutherland looked puzzled. "Do you wish me to alert the Sheriff? Haven't you taken care of that already?"

Struan stuttered, "We...we haven't yet."

The solicitor shot back, "Why in God's name not? I thought you said you were worried?"

Struan paced, his agitation obvious. "Sutherland, please. May we speak in your office? I would appreciate privacy."

"Very well, follow me." He led the way to his office, but stopped and looked back at Andrew. "Mr. Forbes, will you join us?"

"No," he replied coolly. "I'll wait."

"As you wish." Sutherland closed the door behind Struan. "Now why haven't you contacted the Sheriff?"

"You must try to understand, Sutherland. I'm respected in this town. It's bad enough that I'm crushed because my love left me at the moment we were to be joined for life. I don't want all of Glasgow to know that I've been treated as a...a buffoon. Not if I can help it. That's why I've come this morning. Before I bring the law into this...very personal affair, I wanted to ask if you have any idea–any at all–where Fia might have gone."

"It seems your reputation is more important than Fia's safety. I don't think I can help you, Forbes. Besides, it wasn't until your brother came running into the chapel with his face as black as pitch that any of us knew something was amiss."

"But the letter," Struan persisted, "was there anything in the letter from her father? You said she was moved by it. Could there have been anything there that might have caused her to flee?"

Sutherland shook his head. "It's doubtful. Fia only read parts of the letter aloud. What I heard were loving words to a daughter from a doting father." Douglas stared unblinking into Struan's watery eyes. "It must have been something else."

Struan shifted uncomfortably and, more loudly than necessary proclaimed, "I'm sure I don't know what that could be."

Douglas perched on the corner of his desk and folded his arms. "It really doesn't matter now, does it? The point is Miss Graham's gone and, for all anyone knows, may be in danger. You should notify the Sheriff without further delay. He will be discreet."

"I suppose you're right. I'd so hoped you could shed some light on her disappearance. I've taken up enough of your time; I'd better get Andrew."

"Let me show you out." As Sutherland led the way to the front of the house, he heard Agnes' shrill voice.

"Sir, Mr. Sutherland's apartments are up there! He'll be most unhappy to learn you've been–"

Andrew took her arm firmly and, leaning in close, threatened, "He'll not find out if you don't tell him."

"Tell me what?" Sutherland asked sternly, appearing next to the staircase. "Release Miss Sinclair, Mr. Forbes, and explain yourself." When Andrew's grip relaxed, Agnes moved swiftly to stand next to Sutherland who asked, "Are you hurt?"

"No, Sir," but she rubbed her arm gingerly.

Andrew pointed a finger at Agnes. "This woman–"

"I don't really need to hear your story. I heard enough to guess what's happened. You've searched my home while your brother kept me occupied. You are not welcome here," he said and turned to Struan. "We've concluded our business. Douglas opened the door and stood clear. "Get out, both of you. If you return, I'll call the Sheriff myself."

"This is not finished, Sutherland." Andrew vowed, "I promise you, we will find Fia Graham."

"It'll give me great pleasure to shut the door behind you, Forbes. I said get out!" And when the door was bolted, Sutherland turned quickly to Agnes. "Are you sure you're unharmed?"

"Aye, he did everything you said he would."

"We were lucky that Struan and I came out when we did. You're involved in this mess only because you work for me. I apologize for that."

"It's easy to see why Miss Graham ran away from those loathsome creatures."

"Will Murdoch walk home with you tonight as usual?"

"Aye."

"Good. Have him walk you over in the morning as well. I've got a plan to get Miss Graham out of Glasgow and I'll need Murdoch's help. And, could you bring clothes for Fia; you're about the same size. I'll replace them. Now," he finished, "I'd better see how our guest fares."

Sutherland took the stairs two at a time, passed the alcove room that he and Fia had straightened at daybreak, and hurried toward his own quarters where he lifted the lid of the trunk next to his shaving stand. Pulling out the inner tray, he extended his hand. "Come, my dear, they're gone. Let's get you out of this thing."

Slowly, he extracted her from the cramped confines of the trunk and, as she stepped out, Fia clutched his arm for support. "I don't feel well," she gasped.

"Rest here a moment." He led her to a chair where she sat heavily. "Will you be all right?"

Nodding, Fia took several deep breaths while Douglas put the trunk to rights. He sat on the closed lid and faced her. "I'm sorry I had no better place to hide you, Fia."

"You never expected to have to hide a fugitive. Please don't apologize, Douglas. I'm so grateful to you and Agnes. Though my body disagrees at the moment, I don't think I'm really any worse for it." Fia stiffly twisted her upper body from side to side.

"You were in there a long time with little air." He scrutinized her. "Feeling better?"

"Uh huh." She stretched her arms and rolled her shoulders. "Tell me what happened."

"Both brothers came. Struan kept me occupied while Andrew searched the house. Agnes caught him."

Fia flinched. "She's all right, isn't she?"

"Aye, Agnes is fine–she caught him on purpose. We had to give him a quick look around to satisfy his curiosity, but not enough time to search too carefully." Sutherland rubbed his chin in thought. "I shouldn't have let Agnes take a chance like that; when I got to the front hall, he had her by the arm. I did get the pleasure of throwing them both out, but that would've been no consolation if he'd harmed her."

"Thank God he didn't, " she exclaimed.

"Her brother, Murdoch, always walks her home, so she'll not be alone this evening. I've asked her to have him escort her here in the morning as well. The key is to get you out of here quickly. Tomorrow Agnes will bring you clothes, and she and I will leave in my carriage. I will arrange for Murdoch to get you to Inverness after we've gone. I trust the Forbes brothers will follow Agnes and me and, by the time they make their move, you'll be long gone."

Fia's eyes narrowed. "You're going to be decoys?"

"Don't fret, my dear. I'll protect Agnes; Murdoch will protect you."

Fia's mouth was rigid with determination. "I can't let this 'Murdoch' risk it."

Douglas shook his head vehemently. "This is not open to discussion. Murdoch works for me from time to time carrying out more difficult tasks than this. It won't be a problem–he loves a challenge. Besides, you can't take a chaise or a boat–you certainly can't travel alone."

Sudden shivers coursed through her body as she remembered her last attempt at traveling alone–her jarring encounter with Andrew. Her shoulders drooped in sudden defeat. "Of course, you're right, Douglas. I wasn't thinking."

Tilting his head, he studied the change in her demeanor. Obviously something weighed heavily on her mind. "Can I help, Fia?"

Swallowing her memories with her tears, Fia smiled gently. "You have already. I can't begin to thank you properly. Few people have shown me kindness such as this. I won't forget it, Douglas."

Awkwardly, he patted her hand. "Let's just see to it that this strategy succeeds, shall we?"

Throughout the day, Fia stayed on the upper floor so as not to chance being seen by any of Douglas' clients. Douglas' partner was in Edinburgh which helped immensely. The long day was marked by the tantalizing prospect of finally being rid of the Forbes brothers, but also by the fear that Douglas' scheme might fail.

Douglas went about his daily routine, even taking dinner alone in the dining room. He and Fia had agreed that, even though neither Struan nor Andrew knew his daily habits, anything that remotely appeared unusual might draw unwanted attention. Agnes had seen to it that Fia had everything she needed and would bring her a dress in the morning. Now it was a question of waiting. Fia wondered if Murdoch would really want the job of seeing that she got safely to Inverness, and asked Douglas as much when he came upstairs to his sitting room that night.

"Fia, please don't worry. I told you before, Murdoch will enjoy it. Besides, he's between jobs right now; the money will come in handy."

"Douglas, you're going to take whatever is needed to pay for all this from Father's estate, aren't you?" He opened his mouth to protest, but she stopped him. "I insist. You are already a dear friend to me, but I was your client first."

Sutherland nodded. "Fine, lass, the fee won't be large."

She replied sincerely, "Most of what you've done for me can't be measured in coin. Father was right to trust you. You are as true a friend to him now as you were when he lived."

The solicitor covered her hand with his, his voice thick with emotion. "My dear, you could never say anything to me that I would cherish more."

Her expression was hopeful. "Will you visit me at Inverness?"

Walking to the hearth, Douglas sighed, "I don't think that's a good idea–at least not right away."

Fia twisted to see him. "But maybe after awhile, when Andrew and Struan lose interest in me."

"I'm not so sure they're going to lose interest. Both are tenacious and they want something from you."

"Oh, I forgot to tell you!" She rose excitedly. "They want my land; they don't even talk about money."

Douglas was confused. "Why your land?"

Fia shrugged, "I really don't know. But Struan was very clear about it."

"Well, I suppose it doesn't matter now that you're almost free of them. You'd better go to bed, Fia. Tomorrow is likely to be a long day for you."

On tiptoe, Fia kissed his cheek. "Good night, Douglas. I'll see you early."

George fidgeted and, standing, paced the drawing room once again. "Where are those two? Shouldn't they have been here by now?"

"I thought so, Father. Please," Elizabeth begged, "your constant back and forth is making my head ache."

"Forgive me, my dear. It's not knowing–ever–what's going through Andrew's mind that bothers me so. He's very shrewd." George added sternly, "He's also cruel."

"Not cruel, father: dangerous, unpredictable...exciting." Her eyes focused on some distant memory.

Rushing to his daughter's side, George pleaded, "Be careful, Elizabeth. I know you're...fond of Andrew. But, honestly, at times, he frightens me. Obsessions are always perilous for others, and he has become quite obsessed with having Fia's inheritance."

"You mean with having Fia, don't you?" Elizabeth fiercely countered.

Dismayed, George searched for a response to soften her ire. "I believe Andrew's desire may be mistakenly directed toward Fia. After all, she's made this much more difficult than it should have been. If she hadn't resisted, Andrew wouldn't have looked at anything but Fia's land. He's desperate for a new location, and he's willing to pay handsomely for it."

Elizabeth rose, smoothing her petticoat and conceded, "You may be right, Father. He may simply have his desires confused. But Andrew had better determine quickly the difference between sweet cousin Fia and her land or, aye, he will pay handsomely for it."

"Elizabeth, please don't cross–" His words froze at the sharp rap of the brass knocker against the door. "Oh dear," he muttered miserably.

Reassuringly, Elizabeth offered. "Father, we'll be fine...I promise you."

Andrew sauntered in, Struan close on his heels. "No one here is the worse for wear I take it?" He turned solicitous eyes to Elizabeth's proud figure.

"We expected you at breakfast," she replied frostily. "Now, you might as well join us for supper."

Sliding into a chair, Struan grunted, "We've been busy. Do you have any claret?"

George moved quickly. "I'll have Una bring us some."

After speaking to the maid, George returned to the thick silence of the drawing room, took a deep breath, and plunged ahead. "So what have you been busy doing all day?"

Andrew slowly wandered the room as though examining it for the first time. "We paid a visit to Sutherland earlier. He claims to have no knowledge of your niece's whereabouts."

"But you don't believe him?" George prompted.

"Hardly."

"Andrew did get a quick look around," Struan chimed, "while I kept our friend occupied."

"And...?" Elizabeth was already tiring of this game.

"Found nothing." Struan's bony shoulders shrugged.

George held up his hand for silence as Una entered. He motioned for her to set the wine on the table and leave. When she had, he poured a glass for Struan. "Even if Fia's not there, Sutherland may still know where she's gone."

Andrew fingered a Chinese porcelain dove on the mantle. "We thought of that, so arranged to have Sutherland watched. It's only a matter of time before he makes a mistake, and we'll be there to catch it." He turned to Elizabeth. "You're very quiet."

"I just wonder why you're going to such lengths to find Fia. If you stop to think about it, we don't need her at all."

Trying, unsuccessfully, to stifle a belch, Struan stared in disbelief. "Surely, I didn't hear you correctly. Of course we need Fia."

"No, we don't; not for our original purpose." Pointedly, she addressed Andrew. "If your purpose has changed...," she left the thought unfinished, so that its full weight might sink in.

"Go on, Elizabeth," Andrew urged. Until he knew what she was thinking, he wasn't going to give voice to his opinion.

"We thought that marrying Fia to Struan would be quick, easy and accomplish our mutual goal of gaining her land."

"Aye," Andrew carefully checked his impatience.

"However, we miscalculated. Fia balking at the idea has made life hell for all of us and has caused some of us to lose sight of what's really important." Her eyes were locked with Andrew's as if no one else were in the room. "We don't need her, we need access to the land. There is nothing to prevent us from doing what we intended to all along. The difference is that, now, we do it without any legal right to establish Struan on the land. It is still isolated, still protected, still perfect–if you can separate it from Fia."

Struan laughed delightedly. "Congratulations, Elizabeth. It's so obvious; it's brilliant. If anything goes wrong, we steer the authorities to Fia and stay clean ourselves. That would teach the shrew a lesson."

Coming to stand before Elizabeth, Andrew sneered wickedly. "You are a woman after my own heart. Let me also congratulate you, my dear–it really is perfect." He held his hands out to her and, after a moment's hesitation, she took them. Pulling her from the chair into his arms, Andrew chuckled, "I knew I could count on you to keep things in perspective."

"It appears that I'm the only one who can." She eased herself from his grip. "You can begin now to prove me wrong. Take the spies from Sutherland and get on with the business at hand."

Andrew's eyes narrowed slightly as he raised her fingers to his lips. "As you wish, my dear."

The Forbes brothers declined supper and Andrew was thoughtful on the ride home. He knew Elizabeth wanted him to stay away from Fia; her demand that he remove his spies from Sutherland was proof enough. She was right about one thing though–they really didn't need Fia to achieve their goal. And, as Struan had stated, this approach actually offered more protection from the excise men and their soldiers–anonymity. While they had uncovered Andrew's operations near Luce Bay, they knew nothing yet of him. This new plan really was ideal–he should have thought of it himself. Lacing his fingers, Andrew loudly cracked his knuckles at which Struan winced.

"Must you do that?" he complained.

Andrew rolled his eyes in the murky light inside the carriage. "Sometimes, I wonder if we had the same father. The things you find to object to are a marvel."

"There's no need to be insulting–you know I hate it when you do that though, God knows, you do worse."

Andrew watched his brother through half closed eyes. "It went well with the Grahams, don't you think?"

"I think you're lucky Elizabeth didn't skin you alive. Obviously, she's vexed with you." Struan grunted. "When are you going to dismiss the men watching Sutherland's place?"

"I don't intend to."

Throwing back his head, Struan's guffaw filled the cramped space. Finally, he gulped, "You really do love to live dangerously, don't you, Brother? Elizabeth really will kill you if she finds out."

"She's not likely to make that discovery. Besides, you and I will be leaving town within the next few days. You to Edinburgh and I...well, I have several places to go. I'll send you word when and where to join me because I'll need your help getting the new routings and landings established. It will give Elizabeth time to begin to miss me. And, if I'm out of town, she'll have no reason to think I'm still waiting for news of Fia."

"Have it your way, Andrew. But don't look to me to use sweet words to persuade Elizabeth to spare your life if your plan goes amiss."

"The dress is perfect, Agnes. Thank you." Fia turned so the young woman could see for herself.

"All right, ladies. If you're both ready, we should get started." Sutherland helped Agnes with Fia's mantle. "Pull the hood close about your face...that's good." He handed Fia the wrap Agnes had worn to his office. "Murdoch will let himself in, Fia. You'll see the resemblance to Agnes and he's wearing a green waistcoat and gray breeches." He placed his hands on her shoulders. "Don't worry; Murdoch is a good man."

"The best," Agnes declared.

Quick tears stinging her eyes, Fia smiled bravely and embraced the young woman. "Thank you, Agnes, for everything."

Turning, Fia embraced Douglas then stepped back. "I'm not worried. Thank you again, Douglas; I owe you my life. You know how to reach me?"

He nodded. "I do, and I promise you'll hear from me as soon as it's safe." Turning to Agnes, he motioned toward the door. "It's time for us to go. Thomas has the coach out front." Agnes kept her head down, even after she and Sutherland were seated and the horses sprang forward at the crack of Thomas' whip.

On the upstairs landing, Fia waited. It seemed an eternity, but Murdoch Sinclair appeared at the bottom of the staircase only twenty minutes after the carriage had disappeared.

"Miss Graham," he announced and bowed deeply, arm sweeping his tricorne wide. "Murdoch Sinclair, come to rescue you."

Fia wasn't sure how to react to this performance and cautiously made her way toward the burly man. She was beside him before he straightened, an impish grin splitting his tidily bearded face, gray eyes sparkling with mischief.

"Oh dear," she murmured and smiled in spite of herself. "You aren't what I expected Mr. Sinclair," Fia confessed, "but I'm very happy to meet you."

"And pleasantly surprised, I hope, at least once you get to know me." Over his graying black hair, he patted his hat back into place and, taking the mantle from her, swung it round her shoulders. "You will be interested to know that a certain scruffy looking lout followed Sutherland and Agnes. Another fellow took off in the general direction of the river. I saw no one else, but it's a good idea to hide your face just the same."

Fia raised her hood and tied the ribbon at her neck. Already, she liked Murdoch. His ability to get right to the point tempered with a dash of humor was appealing. "I'm ready when you are Mr. Sinclair. No doubt you know I'm traveling with only what's on my back."

"Aye, and it's Murdoch. Get used to it." He stroked his neatly trimmed beard. "We're newly wedded and you're mad for me."

Fia's mouth dropped open and Murdoch gently pushed her chin up to close it.

"Sutherland left the details to me, Fia. Traveling as man and wife is the only way I can assure keeping you in my sight constantly. So please don't gape at anything I might do or say in public."

"I'll...try not to."

"I must ask you just one question before we leave. How long ago were you beaten?"

Fia's hands flew to her face. She'd almost forgotten the bruises. "Five days ago," she murmured.

Murdoch gently touched her shoulder.

"Look at me. Douglas told me you're running from the men who did this to you. On the way, if someone is bold enough to ask, tell them it was your father–he didn't want you to marry me so we ran away together."

"I'll remember."

"Good. Let's go then."

Out in the stable, two horses waited. Murdoch gave her a leg up onto a chestnut gelding named Barley, and closed the stable door behind them. "Let me have a look first." Urging his horse just to the gate, Murdoch surveyed the street before him and motioned for Fia to follow.

Fia reached down to close the gate then pulled along side Murdoch. She didn't know what to expect except an adventure. Her traveling companion had already surprised and endeared himself to her. His confidence was infectious and Fia was sure all would be well–at least until she arrived in Inverness.

Chapter Eleven

From Fort William, Martin drifted once more. As he did almost ceaselessly these days, the man pondered his time spent with Fia. Always he ended berating himself for his displays of moodiness, wondering if she would be with him now if he'd been in better control and trusted his instincts instead of avenging old angers on her. He'd turned on her after talking freely about his grandparents. Obviously Fia inspired his trust even though he'd used it against her, probably fearing he'd shared too much of himself, left himself vulnerable again.

With a shuddering sigh, Martin slowed Odhar to a halt before an expanse of rolling blue, flecked with white foam and recalled that he and Fia had shared moments so sensual, so charged with passion that they crackled and threatened to ignite. The night of the snow when she stood, a pale specter in the darkened croft, their hearts had pounded like the sea that heaved itself onto the shore before him. His arms ached to clench her to him again and his eyes glowed at the memory then dulled as the illusion faded. It was torture.

For a long moment, he closed his eyes against the pink sun perched atop the hills far across the bay. It spread the fingers of its last light along the black ridges and into the high valleys. Martin shivered. Before Fia, he'd been stagnating–she pushed him back into the world, but left him with no direction and no retreat. Alex's counsel had given him the faintest hope that, if he were meant to be with Fia, God would see to it. A God that Martin had not forsaken, only forgotten over the years. Someone or something had brought Fia to Martin, had graced him with time to grow to love her. Maybe, just maybe, Alex was right–or perhaps God had already given Martin all he was destined to have. With that disturbing thought, Martin rebelled and determined to put his future back into perspective. He shook his head till the thoughts scattered, then breathed deeply until he began to feel the blood coursing through his body, renewing his strength and firming his resolve. It was time, at long last, to move forward again. His life on Skye belonged to his past and, for the time being, so did the solace of his croft. Not until he shook the lingering cobwebs of his misery could Martin safely return home.

An abrupt fluttering near Odhar's head startled Martin. A lapwing swooped past him, twisting and plummeting, chattering her warning that her nest was in the heath nearby. At last alert, he rose in the saddle and surveyed his surroundings. With a jolt, Martin realized that what he stared at across the sound was the Cuillin Hills of Skye and, just to the east, lay his past. Martin's heart pinched in a wave of bittersweet memory. He'd roamed these mountains many times both as a lad and as a young man. Long and hard, he studied the distant scene till a peach glow rose from behind the range, smooth and flat in the silhouette of dusk. Many times, Martin had wanted to return to his youthful haunts; it didn't matter now. It was time he accepted his fate and let go of his dreams–all of them. He didn't want to waste any more time. His glance swept wide. "I've shut myself off far too long." Whistling sharply for Arthur, Martin turned Odhar's back to the island and, gripped by the fever to move on with his life, kicked the horse soundly, sending him bounding forward into the gathering darkness.

Donald whooped, throwing his arms skyward. "Martin, you're back."

Martin wrapped his arm around the boy's shoulders. "Aye, laddie. You didn't expect to see me so soon."

"No, but Mam said you wouldn't be gone long."

"God's blood, so she's become a seer," Martin teased. "Is your mother here?"

Donald giggled, "She's inside counting the rum bottles."

The boy led Odhar to the stable and Martin called behind him, "Don't unsaddle him yet, Donald. I'm not thinking of staying long."

"Mam will be disappointed," the boy returned solemnly, watching Martin disappear inside.

Before Martin's eyes grew accustomed to the light, Annie had him in a crushing embrace which he warmly returned. Her first thought was to ask about Fia, instead, she offered, "I know you're parched. Let me fetch you a dram." Martin followed her to the taproom, gratefully accepting the whiskey, draining it before he sat. Annie cocked her head toward the young serving girl who scurried, fetching and placing a plate of bread, boiled potatoes, turnips and a little mutton before Martin.

Martin swallowed a mouthful of bread and mumbled, "I'm surprised you didn't ask right off about my trip."

Annie chuckled, "You know me well, lad. When I saw you I hoped...maybe...you had good news."

Martin shook his head somberly. "What you want to hear, Annie, I can't tell you. I was too late."

Her eyes searched his face. "You mean...." Martin nodded and Annie's gaze quickly retreated to her apron.

"Fia is now Mistress Forbes. I was at her uncle's home and, no," he hurried on, "I didn't see her." Martin's finger traced the rim of his wooden bowl. "I handled my time with Fia badly from the start, and...I bungled it in the end."

"And you regret it," she finished in a broken whisper.

"Aye." The confirmation sprang harshly from his lips. "I can't tell you how much."

Annie gripped Martin's arm. "I'm so sorry, lad. Is there anything I can do?"

"No," he answered ruefully, "but I'm not returning to the croft yet; I've made a decision. Annie, I've been hiding for three years and running for weeks now."

"Hiding? I...I don't understand."

Martin shook his head. "It doesn't matter. What does matter, and what I want you to know, is that I'm done with both. I'm going on a pilgrimage, Annie. I'm not sure what I'll discover—maybe myself. At any rate, this time my eyes will be wide open and I'll be looking up, not down in shame or anguish."

Completely baffled, Annie simply promised, "We'll be here when you come home."

In the warm sun, the woolen mantle irritated Fia's skin. She longed to discard it but kept silent; a little discomfort meant nothing if it helped her avoid being found by Forbes. Fleetingly, Fia's pulse quickened thinking they might take the road running through Inveraray. Her relief was tinged with regret when they traveled east instead. Early in the afternoon, Murdoch reined in and dismounted within sight of a narrow, gurgling burn. He helped her from Barley's back suggesting, "We'll rest by the water while the horses drink their fill."

"Do you think I can go on without this awhile?" She flapped the edges of the mantle hoping to urge cooler air underneath.

"I think it's safe." Murdoch took Barley's reins. "But we should still try to hide your face, so take this." He drew a white kertch, modestly trimmed with lace, from his saddle bag and handed it to her.

Fia inspected the cap and, twisting her curls to the back of her head, she settled it over her hair and ears. "Now I truly look the part of a married woman." Quickly, she removed and folded the mantle, handing it to Murdoch. "You know, I didn't realize Agnes was married. She's so kind to let me use her things."

Murdoch cleared his throat, "Aye, Agnes is a generous lass. She's not married though–the kertch, belongs to my wife."

Fia started, "You...your wife? No one told me you had a wife. Children?" Murdoch held up three fingers and Fia flushed with embarrassment. "Why didn't you tell me? If I'd known you had a family I'd never have consented–"

"That's why no one told you," Murdoch interrupted, stuffing the mantle into his bag. "Fia, you need protection. I need money." He grinned mischievously. "Besides, I do enjoy a challenge."

"So I've heard, but 'challenge' hardly describes this. What if something were to happen to you," she moaned. "What would become of your family?"

"I don't expect anything to happen, I'm good at my job. But if it did, Sutherland would see that they're cared for. He's a good man."

Fia protested, "That's not the point."

"Lass, it's done, and nothing's going to happen except that I deliver you safely into the welcoming arms of your aunt."

Fia folded her arms, pouting, "She doesn't know I'm coming."

"Nevertheless," he reassured, "she'll greet you warmly; you'll be happy and safe with her. Come, let's eat before we move on."

Fia sat beside the burn, trying to choke down some cheese and a biscuit. It was bad enough, this unsettling revelation that he'd left a family behind in order to protect her, now doubts hurried to plague Fia that Murdoch's prophesy was a false one. What if her aunt turned her away? She might not be in a position to keep Fia, even for a short time. And happy? How, Fia reflected morosely, could she ever be truly happy until she accepted Martin's love for Jean MacNab? Unwisely, she allowed herself a few moments to picture what it might be like to be in Jean's place. A pall settled over her so completely that it was visible to her companion. Murdoch roused her from her reverie when he dropped an arm across her shoulders.

"Lass, stop. There's no need to be upset." He produced a plain linen handkerchief. "We'll all survive this."

Twisting the linen around her fingers, Fia turned brimming eyes to him. "You don't understand, Murdoch. My whole world has been turned upside down since Hogmanny. It wasn't anything special before, but at least I knew what to expect. Now..." her quivering voice trailed off.

"I'm a good listener, Fia," said Murdoch, his gray eyes sympathetic.

Fia managed a weak smile. "I believe that. Did Douglas tell you about the people who..." Fia started and turned an incredulous glare on Murdoch. "How could I have forgotten to tell him?" She leapt up and wrung her hands. "Oh, Murdoch, I've made a terrible, *terrible* mistake," she cried. "I saw Andrew Forbes kill a man and I never told Douglas."

Murdoch sat in stunned silence. Finally, he shook his head. "Tell me what happened."

"I was travelling home. Andrew robbed the post chaise I was in. He shot one of the passengers who fell dead at my feet."

Murdoch frowned. "You know absolutely that it was Forbes?"

She nodded vigorously. "I'm sure. He has a very distinctive voice and an equally unusual scar on his face. It was dark and, by some miracle, he's never recognized me."

"Did you notify the Sheriff?"

"No. The only other passenger disappeared. It would be my word against his."

"And Sutherland knows nothing of this?"

Fia shook her head and began to pace. "Why didn't I tell him? Everything happened so fast; I was so anxious not to marry Struan, I never thought I'd be putting others in danger! Douglas has seen the results of Andrew's handiwork on my face, but he doesn't know–"

"I wish you had given this information to Douglas; he should have every possible weapon against Forbes at his disposal."

"You're so right. How could I leave him vulnerable like that? Of course I–" Slowly, Fia straightened, her brows drawn down as she searched for some shred of memory.

Murdoch placed his hands on her shoulders. "Fia, what is it? What else is there?"

"Something Andrew said to me when he made us leave the chaise," she whispered hoarsely, then gasped in disbelief. "God's blood, why didn't I remember this before? It's all clear to me now. I was to marry Struan because they wanted my land. I've never seen the land, but Struan described it: sand beach and a cave."

"Lass, you've lost me."

"Andrew said robbing was something he did to kill time between shipments–that he was really a smuggler!"

"That seems a very unlikely combination. Are you sure?"

She smiled broadly at him, "Positive...Andrew told me so himself." Excitedly, Fia grabbed Barley's reins. "We have to tell Douglas."

"What do you mean 'we'?" Murdoch seized her hand. "I'm taking you to Inverness. I'll tell Douglas everything when I return to Glasgow. It's not safe for you to go back just because you've solved this puzzle."

"But I owe him so much more than this."

"Remember, Forbes isn't alone in this. There will be others watching and waiting." Murdoch's sober warning brought Fia thudding back to earth. She nodded reluctantly. "Still, it's a relief to have the pieces finally fall into place–to know what was behind my sudden betrothal."

"Aye, greed!" Murdoch surmised. "Come, we need to put distance between us and Forbes."

They rode until well past supper, Murdoch outlining his plan. "We should be all right if we keep this simple. In case Forbes has someone watching for you that we aren't aware of I want to stay out of sight as much as possible. If we have to be in public, I want people to remember us as a couple, newly wed, and wanting every moment alone together we can get. We'll ask to take our meals in the privacy of whatever lodgings we can get each night. Fia, we have to be convincing."

She nodded, "I understand, Murdoch."

The lengthening daylight of summer should have encouraged their progress, but the lowering sun hazed blood red before ominous clouds. Murdoch stopped, his eyes searching the horizon. "Much as I hate to, we'd better double back to Stirling and look for lodgings before it storms." He wheeled his mount west and Fia urged her horse into an easy canter. They quickly reached the town they'd passed a short while before and stopped before a small tavern. "Remember," Murdoch whispered as he set her on the ground, "keep your eyes on me as much as possible so no one gets a good look at your face...and you're name is Elspeth."

"Elspeth," she repeated and smiled with confidence.

Murdoch took her hand, leading her through the low doorway as the first rumble of thunder reached their ears. It took several moments in the smoky light before they could distinguish crude wooden tables, benches askew, jammed into every available space. The room stank of stale ale and sour wine. Fia forced herself not to cover her nose with her handkerchief, and swallowed hard against the bile rising in her throat. This wasn't the 'Rowan and Thistle' by any stretch of the imagination. A man with wisps of fiery red hair above his ears approached, wiping soiled hands over the expanse of his apron-covered belly.

"Can I assist you and your lady, Sir?" he greeted them.

"Aye," Murdoch responded, "if you have a room where we could stay the night."

The tavern-keeper glanced from one to the other and grinned. "I have one. It's small, but... that'll be no hardship, will it?"

"None, Sir," Murdoch replied gently caressing the curls escaping Fia's kertch, "as long as there's a bed."

Fia colored, and smiled coyly at Murdoch, trailing her slender fingers down his chest. "Aye, love. I didn't marry you to spend my nights between cold sheets."

It was Murdoch's turn to blush, but he bluffed his way through it by clutching her hands, "I fear we may do something rash, my love, if we don't retire soon." He glanced at the leering tavern-keeper. "We'll take the room and...could supper be brought up in say...an hour?"

"Of course," the man agreed, vigorously bobbing his head. "Follow me." He heaved his bulk up a narrow stairway to an equally narrow door. Fia entered the room while Murdoch counted coins into the tavern-keeper's palm. When the door was closed, Murdoch complimented, "You fell into character very neatly."

"And you turn a lovely shade of scarlet," she giggled.

"You might not think it so funny if you'd seen your own face," he teased in return. "We've got our friend downstairs intrigued...I think I actually saw him lick his lips in anticipation of our evening." He scanned the room. "We'll have to make sure we leave all the right evidence of a night well spent. Here, Fia, help me with this." Murdoch pulled the blankets awry and proceeded to rumple the bed. Fia pounded the pillows and pushed them together. The fire sputtered behind her as a few drops of rain found their way down the chimney.

"I think a few articles of clothing strewn about would be a good effect, don't you?" Fia asked and, without waiting for an answer, turned her back to Murdoch and removed her shoes and gartered linen stockings. Artfully, Fia draped the stockings over the bedpost, only then noticing the look of discomfort on Murdoch's face. "Murdoch...?"

"I think it's a good idea, Fia, but I don't want to embarrass you."

"Nor I you; and there's no need to. I'm just trying to make sure we're believable. That means you have to take off something as well."

"Aye, that's what it means," Murdoch mumbled, removing his own boots and stockings and letting them land wherever he tossed them. He untied his stock, opened the collar of his shirt, and pulled its tail free of his breeches. He turned at the muffled thump of Fia's pocket-hoop settling on the floor. "That will do, I think," she murmured and promptly placed it on the room's only chair. "I can always pull the blankets up to my chin to hide my dress."

"And I thought I enjoyed a challenge; you've taken this task to heart," Murdoch pronounced as they settled on opposite ends of the bed.

"We have a great deal riding on the success of this charade. Besides, your wife could tell you how uncomfortable a hoop can be. Murdoch," Fia asked, "will you tell me about your family, I'd love to hear what they're like."

He grinned broadly, "One of my favorite subjects!" Once settled against the bedpost, Murdoch began, "My wife, Elspeth, and I grew up together. When we were quite young–I think I was six or seven–she told me that, one day, I'd ask her to marry me. I laughed at her, claimed she was daft, but promised that I wouldn't let it get in the way of our friendship. One raw day almost twelve years later, we were coming home from the kirk, walking on some rocks beside the river. Elspeth slipped and, when she disappeared under the frigid water, I felt its chill in my very soul. I've never experienced such numbing fear as I did at that moment." Murdoch paused, the feeling washing over him anew. "I jumped in and, before I even got her to shore, I begged her to be my wife." His face became serene. "The children are wonderful, and I love them dearly. But Elspeth...there's no one like my Elspeth."

Moved by the strength and clarity of Murdoch's love, Fia could only croak, "You're both extremely fortunate."

Nodding his agreement, Murdoch declared, "We're also lucky enough to know it." A sharp rap on the door made them jump. "Aye?" Murdoch responded gruffly.

"I've brought your supper, Sir," boomed the innkeeper. "If you're...busy, I'll leave it."

"One minute," Murdoch responded.

Fia dove under the covers as Murdoch untied and mussed his hair, then opened the door enough to give the man a glimpse of the room beyond. But as the innkeeper took a step forward, Murdoch blocked his way. "I'll take it," Murdoch ordered, and relieved him of the tray. Disappointment flitted across the man's pudgy face, but with a resigned shrug, he turned and waddled away.

With a triumphant grin, Murdoch assured Fia, "We'll be leaving our friend with exactly the impression we'd hoped. Now," he said risking a tentative whiff of the unrecognizable contents of the bowls on the tray, "I hope you're hungry."

The days of travel that followed were much the same as the first. But the storms of that night in Stirling had brought steady, soaking rain and, with each day's ride, a chill that could only be dispensed by an evening before a roaring blaze. The weather slowed their progress along a circuitous route chosen by Murdoch. But, to keep their minds off the rain and muck while traveling, Murdoch entertained Fia with tales of his children's' antics and stories of the Sinclairs. "You know, for many years, my ancestors were buried in full armor at Rosslyn Chapel outside Edinburgh."

"An uncomfortable way to spend eternity," Fia observed dryly. "I imagine you're glad they don't do that anymore."

Murdoch grinned, "I'm just over a century too late and delighted to say so." He turned suddenly pensive and Fia leaned forward, peering at his face through the curtain of drizzle falling between them.

"What is it Murdoch?"

His gentle gray eyes studied her. "Do you trust me?"

"With my life," she replied, bemused by his question.

Murdoch reined-in, water dripping from each point of his tricorne. "Will you tell me about the sadness I sometimes see in your eyes?"

Unsettled, Fia fumbled for a response. "I...well...I'm running away from a murderer and must put all my trust in new-found friends and an aunt I haven't seen since I was a child."

Slowly, Murdoch shook his head. "No, lass. While that's all true, there's something deeper. I first saw it at the burn when we began this journey."

Fia opened her mouth to deny it, but the words wouldn't come out. Silently, she urged her horse forward. As Murdoch's sorrel kept pace, Fia finally answered in a small voice, "I thought I hid it better than that."

"Perhaps from others. Is it anything I can help with?"

Fia shook her head. "It's an old story," she answered with a shaky smile, "I love someone who doesn't love me."

"I'm sorry, lass," Murdoch's soft tones soothed.

"So am I." Staring at her gloved hands, Fia began, "I met him while running away from Andrew Forbes, the first time. I was sick but didn't know it. I was also lost. When Martin found me, he took me in and nursed me back to health. It took several weeks between regaining my strength and the snow to melt so that I could return to Glasgow." She struggled for the right words to continue her tale.

"Martin's moods were unpredictable, and me...well, I was impulsive and naive."

"Not a good combination," Murdoch guessed.

She bestowed a fleeting smile on her companion. "No."

Hesitantly, Murdoch inquired, "Was he...kind to you?"

"Oh, aye," she quickly assured. "And I felt safe," Fia declared. Then, in a wistful tone, she added, "Just looking at him gave me such pleasure...it was hard for me to breathe when he was near. It was frustrating and exhilarating to be with him. When I realized I had come to love him, I made up my mind...well...before I could act or even speak of it, I discovered Martin was promised to someone else." Her voice rose slightly as she admitted, "I should have guessed that such a man would have a woman somewhere, but I didn't. And I should be grateful to have found out in time to keep from making a fool of myself. But I'm not grateful. I regret not having had the chance." She paused, pensively taking in the soggy world around them.

"Maybe it was for the best," he offered.

"Well, I'd like to think so because of how it turned out."

"But you don't believe it," he surmised.

"Murdoch, I was so sure there was something strong between us; some tie or bond. I feel it even now, and wonder when it will go away–or if it will." Fia paused, straightening in her saddle. "When I learned of Martin's plans to marry, it suddenly seemed important to save my dignity and break from him on my terms. So I told him I was marrying Struan. And, for a brief time, I thought that maybe I should marry Struan." Fia laughed at the absurdity of it. "At least I didn't make *that* mistake!"

"Fia, how did Martin react when you told him about the betrothal?"

Fia searched her memory and shook her head, slightly perplexed. "I'm not sure, Murdoch...I was in such a sorry state myself that I have no clear recollection. Certainly he was surprised but, I can't remember more than that. Our parting was bitter though."

"I'm so sorry." Murdoch reached over and squeezed her hand. "You've been hurt too much, lass. Thank God you're strong; and thank you for confiding in me. If I could help you, I would."

Fia assured. "You have helped. No one else knows about Martin...I didn't want to talk about him but I'm grateful you listened. To have you as my protector and friend, Murdoch, makes me realize that I'm very fortunate indeed."

Andrew fingered the keys of his mother's spinet, his brooding quiet barely masking the fury seething inside him. Fia had slipped through his fingers because his paid spies were worthless. At their instruction, Andrew thundered after Sutherland's carriage, catching it halfway to Port Glasgow where he forced it to stop.

Sutherland was incensed, "What do you think you're doing, Forbes? Who gave you the right to block my way?"

Thrusting his finger at Sutherland's companion, Andrew demanded, "I want her."

Agnes raised her face to Forbes, inched closer to Douglas and bravely declared, "I work for Mr. Sutherland and have no wish to change employers."

Andrew's jaw fell. "*You*," he bellowed. "Sutherland, what game do you play?"

Douglas scrutinized his adversary. "I have business in Port Glasgow. This was your move, Forbes. Why don't you share your intentions with us?"

Andrew leaned forward in his saddle and sneered, "I will only ask you this once–"

"Good, because you're a tiresome fellow. The quicker you ask your question, the sooner we can be about our business."

Eyes narrowing, Andrew hissed, "Where is Fia Graham?"

Douglas returned Andrew's glare. "I find it infinitely intriguing that you are more interested in finding Miss Graham than your brother."

"Don't waste my time Sutherland."

"On the contrary, Forbes, it is you, wasting our time," Douglas returned coldly. "I don't know the whereabouts of Miss Graham. However, as I think back on each of these little exchanges we've had, I find myself fervently hoping that she's far away, out of your monstrous grasp."

Andrew leapt to the ground and took two swift steps toward the carriage when he abruptly halted, staring into the unwavering muzzle of Douglas' pistol.

"I prefer not to shoot you in front of this young woman, but will do so if you force my hand."

Andrew growled, "I've never known a solicitor who could shoot straight."

"The choice is yours, Forbes," Douglas challenged. "Do you fancy gambling?"

A murderous scowl on his face, Andrew remounted. "You'll pay for this, Sutherland."

Deadly calm, Douglas assured, "Harm me, or anyone in my employ, and I promise you the Sheriff will see you hang. And, my word is good anywhere, Forbes."

Remembering Sutherland's final words made Andrew thirst to squeeze the solicitor's neck until his eyes popped. "I detest that sanctimonious bastard," he snarled, fist striking the spinet.

"Oh, you're finally speaking," Struan chimed petulantly as he entered the room.

Andrew snapped, "Did I ever tell you that you're a dullard?"

"No, but father used to, and did it better than you, I might add. When are you going to stop moping? You may never get to bed Fia, but you still have Elizabeth. She fairly drips with anticipation every time she sees you." Struan's eyes glazed over, imagining his face buried between Elizabeth's thighs. He licked his lips and shifted uncomfortably in his chair. He was rudely surprised when Andrew hauled him up by the collar.

"So, you fancy Elizabeth, do you?" Andrew whispered menacingly.

"No...I...no, Andrew! She's a...a beautiful woman...I mean...any man would find her desirable. But...no. She's yours, Andrew."

"I know she's mine—I don't want *you* to forget."

"Never, Andrew, I swear it!"

Andrew swatted Struan's sallow cheek with his palm and hissed, "I'm happy to hear it. Now, I think I'll pay a call on that lovely lady."

Not until the door closed behind his brother, did Struan let out his breath.

Watery lavender light filtered through the glass and Martin crawled to the foot of the bed to look out over the dreary town. The gray stones of Inveraray were black, the limewash dingy from the night's drenching rain and, as the dawn struggled to become day, Martin pulled the covers over his head and thought back to last night. He'd decided to stay at the 'Rowan and Thistle' after all and help out by doing some odd jobs for Annie. It was late, and Donald long abed, when Annie collapsed on a bench by the immense hearth. "I vow, Martin, what a night. I think I'm too tired to sleep."

Martin raised his head from the leather binding of a fire bucket he was repairing. Just when he'd thought his chores completed, the handle had given way and the bucket had fallen from its hook, spewing sand all over the back hallway. "You were pulled in all directions this evening, Annie."

"I do feel as though I've had a good stretch," she laughed heartily. "Martin, I do appreciate your help; but you didn't need to work here all night."

"It's good for me, and saves you from having to hire someone you don't trust. Besides," he grinned rakishly, "you offered me a room to myself, and that is well worth whatever I've done tonight." He rested the bucket on the floor. "There, finished. I'll refill it before I turn in."

Annie sighed. "It's comforting to have a man around. Times like this...you know, in the quiet after a frantic evening...I miss talking to the lad's father. I'm sorry you never knew my Donald." Annie's eyes misted.

"So am I," Martin gently replied, studying her face, still remarkably smooth and clear for all its character.

"It's hard when they're gone: no talk, no touching, no closeness." Glancing sidelong at Martin, her voice took on an edge, "That reminds me, Jean MacNab was asking after you last week."

93

He raised his eyebrows. "What did she want?"

"To know if I'd seen you; she said she hadn't in a while." Boldly, Annie blurted, "I didn't know you saw her at all!"

"I like to think I can be discreet about some things."

"Like lovers?"

"Like lovers," Martin responded, voice low and clear.

Perplexed, Annie charged, "You mean you're not going to deny it?"

Martin shrugged, "Why should I? If Jean wants to tell the people of this town, I can't stop her."

"Well...she didn't come right out and say it."

"But she left no doubt in your mind did she?" Annie shook her head and Martin wondered, "Why would she wait until it was finished to make an issue of our tryst?"

Annie perked up, "Finished? You...you're not seeing her anymore?"

Martin watched Annie for a long moment, trying to decide what was really on her mind. Annie squirmed slightly under Martin's scrutiny and it suddenly was clear. "This is about Fia, isn't it? Somewhere in your romantic soul you think I've been disloyal."

Annie's fingers brushed imaginary crumbs from the bench and she mumbled unhappily, "The thought crossed my mind."

Martin sat next to her and rested his hands on his thighs. "Annie, you are a dear and loyal friend, to Fia as well as to me. Please look at me."

She examined his intense brown eyes, his earnest, slightly baffled expression, and fondness tugged at her heart. They'd been good friends to each other–dependable friends. He even made sure Donald learned useful, practical things, and taught him in such a way that Donald thought it fun. Most importantly, Martin showed a true affection for her son; she'd always be grateful for that.

"Annie," Martin touched her shoulder, "are you all right?"

Scalding tears spilled down Annie's cheeks. "Martin, forgive me. You don't owe me explanations; I have no right to ask for them–or to interfere."

"I know I don't owe you explanations. But I want to explain because I care what you think." He produced a handkerchief, "You've had a long night and you're tired. Now, dry your tears and listen. I saw Jean occasionally for about half a year. I'm fond of her, but I wasn't happy; nothing was going to come of us together. For me, that isn't going to change."

"I think Jean loves you," Annie sniffed.

"If true, all the more reason for ending it when I did. Only hours before I found Fia, I told Jean I would not be back, and I haven't been."

"It was f...fate!" she hiccupped.

Martin sighed, "You wouldn't know it the way things have turned out."

"Will you go back to Jean now?"

"No, she needs to move on and I only want Fia."

"I only want Fia," he repeated to himself and rolled onto his back. Martin groaned and threw the covers aside. Bleak day or not, it was the first day of his quest. Dressing quickly, Martin sought out Annie and Donald to say his goodbyes. When Odhar was saddled, Martin rode from the stable yard into the slate gray morning, Arthur trotting behind.

"Murdoch, look...the clouds are finally breaking up." Fia splayed her fingers on the dirty window. "Do you think it's a good omen?"

Rubbing his eyes, Murdoch yawned, "Probably so, lass. It'll be a fitting day for your triumphant entry into Inverness." He sat up on his pallet, noting she was already dressed. "Didn't you sleep at all last night?"

"A little." She flopped back onto the bed. "How long will it take to get to my aunt's?"

"About two hours. We'll get started right after putting some food in our bellies."

Nervously, Fia muttered, "I'm not hungry."

Turning from the washstand, beard dripping, Murdoch declared, "I am. And I'm not going to let you faint from hunger on Mistress Matheson's stoop. Are you suddenly in a hurry to get there?"

"Only to get it over with. I've spent a lot of time imagining what might happen when we arrive."

Murdoch rolled his eyes in exaggerated agreement. "That's an understatement."

Fia sheepishly admitted, "I've made myself crazy with it. And you're probably ready to divorce me."

Murdoch howled in genuine delight, "I confess, one wife is plenty for me," and his merry eyes became tender. "But I have to tell you, lass, I honestly will miss you. And, if I'd been your Martin, I'd have snatched you up in a moment, and never let you go."

"That's the most wonderful thing anyone's ever said to me, Murdoch," she whispered unsteadily.

"And I mean it, lass. I feel sorry for him."

Fia handed him a towel. "Don't feel badly for Martin. He married the one he loves, just as you did."

As they reached Inverness, Murdoch noticed Fia grimace. He reassured, "I'll tell you again... your aunt will be thrilled to see you. But, if it'll help ease your mind, I promise you this—if for any reason she can't keep you with her, I'll stay until I see you settled elsewhere."

Fia bit her lip to stop it from quivering like her voice, "I'll miss you dreadfully, Murdoch." She pulled the address from her saddlebags and handed the paper to her companion.

As they traversed the streets, Fia observed many homes and, she guessed, some shops that were little more than thatched huts. Her spirits, such as they were, wilted.

Murdoch's voice was apprehensive as he eyed the same simple, diminutive dwellings. "I wonder if she'll have room for you."

"I've been thinking the same thing," she admitted gloomily.

Yet as they neared Douglas Row, huts were fewer and fewer, replaced slowly by stone and granite structures. And, when they reached the Row, the queue of narrow houses looked friendly, even inviting. And at the one she believed to be her aunt's, rich brocades adorned the windows, softening and warming the stone facade. Fia was heartened by the effect and noted, when she glanced at Murdoch, that he looked cheered as well.

"Shall I go up with you?" Murdoch's hands circled Fia's slender waist to help her dismount.

"Please," she begged.

Taking a deep breath, Fia lifted and dropped the brass knocker several times. Murdoch was on the verge of urging her to knock again, when the door swung wide. A regal, trim woman with a full, slightly petulant mouth looked first at Murdoch, then at Fia. On seeing Fia, bewilderment and pain flashed across her face before the blood drained from it and she collapsed into Murdoch's hastily outstretched arms.

Chapter Twelve

"*God's life, what* caused this?" Murdoch knelt, frantically fanning the woman's face.

"I don't know," Fia glanced around anxiously. "We'd better get her inside before someone notices."

"Right." Somewhat awkwardly, Murdoch lifted the woman and grunted, "Is this your aunt?"

"She looks like the woman I remember." Fia closed the door after him and, while Murdoch set the woman in the nearest chair, searched for some brandy.

"She doesn't look much like you," Murdoch called over his shoulder.

"Here," Fia said handing him a goblet. "I could only find water."

"Should I make her swallow it or douse her?"

Fia gawked, and then burst a nervous giggle at Murdoch's innocent expression.

A small moan swiftly sobered her and brought their attention back to the woman. "Aunt Kate?" Fia questioned. "Aunt Kate?"

Katherine Matheson's eyelids fluttered open and, as she focused on Fia's face, her eyes grew saucer-like. "Dee..." she muttered brokenly. "Dee, is that...no...no, you can't...can't be Dee."

"Who's Dee?" Murdoch whispered.

"My mother, Deirdre," Fia answered and leaned toward her aunt. "Don't worry, Aunt Kate. I'm Fia, Dee's daughter. Here, have a sip of water; I didn't mean to give you such a fright."

Kate pushed the goblet aside and searched the face before her, but seemed no less confused. She pointed to the kertch Fia wore. "Take that off," she commanded softly, and Fia complied, masses of dark curls spilling past her shoulders. Kate's face suddenly brightened. "You are Fia! Oh, child, I never thought I'd see you again!" She rose and wrapped Fia in a joyously tearful embrace which made Murdoch's gray eyes mist. When Kate held Fia at arms' length, she noticed Murdoch. "Oh, oh my, I'm sorry, Fia. This must be your husband. A fine first impression I've made." Dabbing her eyes, Kate offered shakily, "Welcome...?"

"Murdoch," he supplied. "You've had a shock–and there's more to come."

Kate looked from one to the other. "More?"

"I'll tell you everything, Aunt Kate," Fia glanced at Murdoch. "But, first, Murdoch is not my husband. He's my dear friend and protector."

"Protector?" Kate frowned at him.

Murdoch intervened, "It's a long story; it's the reason we're here. Are you up to hearing it now?"

Slightly insulted, Kate huffed, "I'm not an invalid."

"No, you faint gracefully," he smirked.

Kate's peat-brown eyes studied him until a grin played at her mouth as well. "You have a point," she conceded. "Now, though I have a million questions for my niece, I'll hold them until I hear this 'long story'. I'm quite ready," she insisted.

"Aunt Kate, I'm not here for a visit. Murdoch has brought me to Inverness to live–hopefully, to live with you until I can get settled."

"Fia, I would lo–"

"Please don't say anything until you hear me out. I don't want you to feel obligated by something you may say out of devotion to Mam."

As her gaze shifted between her two guests, Kate's bewilderment was obvious. "If that's what you want, Fia, of course I'll listen first."

"Thank you." Fia took a steadying breath and began, "The reason I refer to Murdoch as my protector, is that I've gotten myself into serious trouble."

Murdoch broke in, "Be fair, Fia, your uncle caused this trouble."

"George? George Graham?" Kate asked, and at Murdoch's nod snarled, "What did that mongrel do to you, Fia?"

"He betrothed me to a loathsome man in order to use my inheritance."

Kate's sharp eyes narrowed. "I don't understand. Use for what? Is the shipping concern bankrupt? Not that he wouldn't deserve it," she added.

Shaking her head, Fia continued, "Struan, the man he promised me to, has a brother–"

"A vicious, despicable, murdering bastard of a brother," Murdoch interjected heatedly.

"What?" Kate asked, head spinning.

Fia affirmed, "Andrew's all that, and a smuggler as well. He wanted the land Father left me for his smuggling operations, so Uncle George was going to wed me to Struan."

Kate was incredulous, "And did he expect you to become part of this scheme?"

Fia shook her head. "No, only to provide the land. They have no idea I know why they want it. That's a different part of the story. But," she said emphatically, "I refused to marry Struan, so Andrew...." Fia faltered, trembling.

Murdoch rose and gently pushed Fia onto the footstool where he'd been perched. Turning to Kate, he picked up where Fia had left off. "When she refused, Andrew beat her severely. The Grahams let him get away with it. Two days later, Douglas Sutherland helped her escape. He's an old friend of Fia's father and was his solicitor as well. Douglas asked me to bring her here. He's convinced that Forbes...Andrew...will not give up easily, that Fia is still in danger. I agree with him."

In a small, quaking voice, Fia added, "I didn't know where else to go Aunt Kate, but I don't want to lead these people to you. I really will understand if you'd want me to go somewhere else. Murdoch will see to it that I'm settled before–"

"Nonsense," Kate snapped. "You'll stay here. George Graham has caused no end of despair in this family. First, it was his hatred of Dee, then the threats he made over custody of you, and now this obscene action." Her voice quivered with rage, "You should have stayed with us. I'd have raised you with Muir–he'd have been a brother to you. But when Graham threatened to ruin us, we believed he had the power to do it." Her hand closed over Fia's. "It's late, dear, and you've suffered because I let George intimidate me. But it's not too late to make some amends." Kate stated confidently, "A long time ago, I stopped worrying about George Graham. As long as you like, you may stay with me."

Fia, overcome with relief, could only hug her aunt mutely. Over her head, Kate and Murdoch exchanged satisfied looks: Kate, because she had a second chance and Murdoch because he could tell Douglas that Fia was safe.

The window was raised to the balmy June breeze and the sound of Glasgow going about its business. Out of that subdued din, Elizabeth picked up the sounds of Andrew's horse. It had been nearly a week since Andrew had visited. She knew he was preparing to leave; he'd neglected his business too long. On this trip, Andrew also planned to set up his receiving site and the distribution network using Fia's property. Briefly, Elizabeth wondered where her cousin had gone off to, but dismissed it with a growled, "To the Devil, I hope." She had more important things on her mind today. Her face was composed, though tightly drawn, as Una announced Andrew. When the maid retreated, Elizabeth offered flatly, "What a delightful surprise, Andrew."

Frowning, he studied her. "That wasn't your most sincere or enthusiastic greeting, my dear." Stepping up to her, he whispered huskily, "It *could* be delightful". But Elizabeth glided away.

"I was beginning to wonder whether I'd see you before you left." Elizabeth kept her eyes from his face.

Tossing his tricorne on the gaming table, Andrew sat. "Didn't I tell you I wouldn't go without saying goodbye?"

Elizabeth nervously twisted a lock of hair around her fingertip. "Aye, it's just that...I've missed you."

One black eyebrow arched, and Andrew snorted, "Is that why you pulled away from my touch?"

"Andrew, it's...it's not just your touch I miss," she insisted awkwardly.

"Then I beg you, tell me. Is it my rapier wit? My tender demeanor?"

"I didn't miss your *sarcasm!*" Elizabeth thundered.

Slowly, Andrew rose and, standing behind her, wrapped one arm across her shoulders and tilted her chin so that his lips could easily nibble her neck. Between nips, he murmured, "What is it Elizabeth? You're behaving strangely–like you're mad at me and for me all at once."

Turning swiftly, Elizabeth caught his face and pulled his head down to press her lips to his until she was lightheaded and Andrew, breathless. "Andrew, I'm going to have a child."

He searched her jet black eyes, inches from his, hoping it was a joke. No hint of jest lingered in their depths. "You're sure?" he asked warily. Elizabeth nodded and Andrew turned away from her. He wasn't interested in a little stranger sharing his life. There was too much he wanted to do. What concerned him most was Fia and Sutherland and getting even.

Quaking with dread, Elizabeth prompted, "Andrew?"

His hard eyes met hers. "Is it mine?"

Elizabeth flushed angrily; that was one response she hadn't anticipated. "You know damn well it's yours."

"Do I? Just the other day, Struan was slavering at the thought of crawling between your legs. Maybe it wasn't a whim, maybe it was a memory."

"You're vile, Andrew. You know well that, since we met, I've only lain with you."

Coolly, Andrew prodded, "And how would I know that?"

Elizabeth thrust her body against his and hissed, "Because your spies tell you so." His eyes narrowed and she barked, "What...you didn't think I knew that you have me watched whenever you go away? Of course, you keep me satisfied when you're in town; that's when your spies get to rest."

Andrew's face darkened and he sniped, "Lose the child, Elizabeth."

"W...what?"she gasped, believing she'd heard him incorrectly.

He grabbed her arm, twisting it cruelly, making her wince. "I have no use for a brat, my pet. Get rid of it."

Tears of pain and humiliation stung her eyes. "Andrew, this is your child. I want your child. I...I love you," she whimpered.

Releasing her suddenly, Andrew replied icily, "All the more reason not to ruin things by presenting me with a whelp for which I have no use."

Elizabeth gaped at him. "Do you care about me at all?"

"I don't want you to throw away what we have together; it's good for both of us." He reached to touch her face, but stopped when she stepped away.

"I'm having this child."

"Then you won't have me," he growled.

She smiled oddly, "You'll want our babe once you see it."

Enraged, Andrew bellowed, "I'll show you *exactly* what I want from you!" One huge hand ripped the stomacher and stays from her body. Pushing her to the floor, his mouth tugged and teeth tore at her breasts till blood flowed. He pushed her petticoat to her waist and, tearing his own breeches in his haste, plunged into her, pounding and battering until he spilled convulsively into her. Only then did Andrew realize Elizabeth had uttered no sound. He glanced at her and was unnerved to see that her face radiated ecstasy, her hands soothingly rubbed her wounded breasts, smearing blood everywhere she touched.

Panic rocked Andrew, and he scrambled away, staring at her. She must be demented. How else could she look so serene after he'd taken her so savagely? He'd always played rough with Elizabeth; he knew it excited her. This time, his fury had driven him to new extremes of brutality, yet such contentment and utter rapture as shone from her face, he'd never seen. Andrew shamefully realized he was trembling with fright. She had to do his bidding; he had to control her! What game was she playing with him? "I'll wipe that look from your face," he promised and slapped her hard. A spasm racked her body, then Elizabeth looked at him kneeling over her, sat up and spat, "I'm keeping this child, you son of Satan."

"*May I offer* you more to eat, Mr. Sinclair?" Kate's maid inquired.

"Thank you, Miss Flora, but I must say no. It is tempting though; your meal was delicious," he replied with a flashing smile.

"Are you sure you have to leave so soon, Murdoch? One night's sleep is hardly enough rest after nearly a week on the road." Kate placed her napkin beside her breakfast plate.

"I must leave; I need to see Sutherland soon." He took her hand and bowed slightly. "I'll happily tell him that Fia is in excellent and loving hands."

Kate sighed, "Fia, I will miss this charmer." Then, to Murdoch she smiled and said, "You are always welcome in my home. Thank you for bringing my niece to me."

Fia stood, "I'll see you on your way, Murdoch." She opened the door and saw only Murdoch's mount. "Where's Barley?"

Murdoch smirked, "Barley is Douglas' wedding present to you. He's in the stable." Fia's delighted squeal rang through the entryway and she threw her arms around his neck in a quick embrace. Murdoch laughingly vowed, "I'll tell Douglas you're pleased with his gift." He became serious and grasped her by the shoulders. "Your aunt is thrilled to have you with her just as I predicted; you'll be safe here. Goodbye, lass."

Shimmering tears suddenly spilled onto Fia's cheeks, "And you take care of yourself, Murdoch. I owe you my life."

"Then I order you to make the most of it. Find your happiness, Fia." He kissed her cheek. Almost before she could blink, the sorrel had carried Murdoch away.

Kate approached putting her arm around Fia's waist. "Murdoch's a nice man," she soothed.

"Aye," Fia agreed sniffling, "he's very special. I'll miss him; I hope I see him again."

"You will, my dear. Come back to the dining room and let's talk. We have to do some planning for your future. We've missed a great deal of time with each other while George Graham has been busy playing his ugly games," she said, a bitter edge to her voice.

Fia shut the door and, linking her arm through Kate's, sighed, "I don't want to think about Uncle George, but I do want to hear about you and Muir. How is he? Where does he live now? I remember how he used to run barefoot down by the Loch and I'd always tell him to watch for the thistles just about the time he'd step on one, start howling and–" Fia stopped abruptly and searched Kate's drawn, ashen face. "Aunt Kate, are you all right? What did I say?" Dread crept over Fia as her aunt avoided her piercing stare. Faintly, Fia whispered, "He's not...Muir's not...."

Kate thrust her chin up and said bravely, "I don't know where my son is. I don't know if he's well or even...if he's alive."

Stunned, Fia stuttered, "What...what happened?"

Flora, who had been about to clear the table, heard the question and quietly withdrew.

At the head of the dining table, Kate sat, mustering all her dignity to hold herself together. "My husband died the same year your parents did–the year Graham took you away. Losing his father was very hard on my son. I too was grief stricken and, after losing so many loved ones, I became terrified of also losing Muir. I kept him with me constantly, determined to protect him from everyone and everything." Her voice quavered.

"That's understandable," Fia offered. "He was just a lad."

"But he grew, and so did his resentment of me. As he got older, Muir started sneaking away, never giving a thought to how I worried." Kate swallowed the lump of bile rising in her throat. "Just over four years ago, Muir married."

"Married?" Fia repeated, surprised at the apparent shift in her aunt's thoughts.

"Aye. His wife, Alayne, was very young and the marriage was against my wishes. Still, since they were determined, I offered them a place to live, with me. They moved in, though not to please me. Muir had no money of his own, and he abandoned his apprenticeship to the miller without telling me. Well, shortly after they joined me here, my son began to gamble openly, heavily and... imbibe more than he should have. He abused Alayne...Alayne's love," she quickly corrected. "About five months after they wed, he went to one of the harbor taverns–he often did. But this time, he never came home," she choked.

"And no one knows what happened?" Fia prompted in disbelief.

Kate shook her head. "Alayne thinks he might have been pressed to serve on one of the Royal Navy ships. His Majesty's recruiters were roaming the quay that night. I don't know; there's no proof. Maybe he owed money that he couldn't pay and whoever he owed got tired of waiting." Kate dabbed her nose with her napkin.

Fia stared aghast at her aunt, trying to imagine the pain she had suffered all these years. "I don't know what to say Aunt Kate. I'm so very sorry."

Kate waved her napkin as if to dismiss Fia's sympathy. "There's nothing you can say child that makes it hurt any less. But, Alayne is still here. She stays with me from time to time; her own family immigrated to America. You'll meet her shortly when we go over to the shop. You'll need clothes and I have work to do.

Fia was a little astonished at how quickly Kate had retreated to such mundane matters as shopping. "I will need clothes that's true enough; what I have on isn't even mine. Douglas advanced me some money from my inheritance–"

"Fia," Kate interrupted, "clothes won't cost you anything."

"But, how can that be?"

Kate cupped her niece's chin between thumb and forefinger. "Because, I own the shop, a millinery, and more. Alayne works there." Kate looked thoughtfully at her niece and asked, "I don't suppose that, after all these years of living with George Graham, you can do anything useful with a needle?"

"As a matter of fact," Fia assured, "I'm quite handy with a needle."

A delighted laugh escaped Kate. "Excellent. I think Alayne could use the help–business has been good. And working will keep you occupied which, I dare say, is a good idea."

The prospect intrigued and worried Fia who asked, "Do you think she'll mind working with me?"

"I see no reason why she would mind, but, to be honest, time will tell. Alayne can be a little hard, defensive too–she's not had an easy time of it. And she sometimes acts rashly. Still, she has a good heart and doesn't hesitate to speak her mind. You'll always know where you stand with my daughter-in-law."

A short while later, as she and Kate reached the corner where the shop stood, Fia felt her confidence lagging. Even the airiness of the pink granite walls, in contrast with the gray of the shops on either side, failed to lift her spirits. Glancing at the window, Fia noted a tasteful and decorative display of ladies' accessories: a cream silk hat with gauze trimming, an oriental fan of painted and silvered paper leaf, a handkerchief, cotton with silk chain stitch needlework, a handbag of pink silk taffeta and two framed miniatures of flowers and birds strung with ribbons to be worn around the neck. There was also a small vase of bluebonnets in the center. Inside, Fia saw wooden shelves at eye level stacked high with colorful splashes of shimmering silks, rich brocades and taffeta. The upper shelves held the linens, cottons and broadcloth. There were stays and panniers discretely displayed on one dress form near a curtained doorway in the back, and display counters to her left and right. The variety, abundance and pleasing arrangement of it assaulted Fia's senses. She liked what she saw–and felt she belonged there.

"Good morning, Mistress Hays," Kate greeted the lone customer.

"And to you Mistress Matheson. Alayne is just fetching the waistcoat I ordered, ah...here she is."

Fia turned eager eyes on the curtained door as her cousin's wife passed through it. Fervently she prayed that she and Alayne would like each other–Fia very much wanted to work here.

Alayne Matheson glanced quickly from Fia to her mother-in-law, nodded a greeting, and addressed her customer, "Here you are, Mistress Hays. I pinked the edges, just as you requested. It was a good choice; I think this will be lovely on you." Alayne spread the garment across the counter for her client's inspection and heard, with satisfaction, Mistress Hays' gasp of pleasure.

"My dear, you've outdone yourself. Why, it's simply elegant."

Alayne beamed at the praise. "You're very kind, Mistress."

"Indeed," Kate agreed. "Alayne's work with a needle is art. I'm very proud of her and the fine reputation she has earned. Of course, if she ever opened a shop of her own, half my customers would go with her."

Mistress Hays nodded sagely, "It was a stroke of genius to marry her to your son; she surely would be a loss if she left you."

It was apparent, even to Fia that her aunt stiffened at the woman's thoughtless remark. Alayne still smiled, but the warmth was gone. Her brilliant hazel eyes fell back on Fia who stared at her and Alayne said, "Kate, you and Mistress Hays may wish to chat for a moment. If you'll excuse me, I'll see if I can assist–"

"Oh, Alayne, forgive me." Kate's hands flew to her face in embarrassment. "Mistress Hays, you might as well also meet my niece, Fia Graham. She's come to stay with me for a time."

It was Alayne's turn to stare and an awkward moment for Fia. She'd rather have met Alayne without an outsider present; she could read nothing in the expression of her cousin's wife.

"Why, Kate, this isn't poor Deirdre's daughter is it?" Mistress Hays boldly took Fia's chin in her puffy hand and studied her intently. "Praise God, it is! She has much of her mother's look about her."

Fia's interest piqued, "You knew my mother?"

"Aye from the time she was about your age. I even met you once when you were toddling about. What brings you here, lass, just a visit with your aunt?"

Fia hesitated and Kate stepped in, "Fia has moved to Inverness and is staying with me for the time being. I thought she might help Alayne here at the shop and free up more of my time to do the accounting and buying."

"Well, it's a pleasure to meet you again," Mistress Hays said.

"The pleasure is mine," Fia responded. Glancing back at Alayne, Fia's belly lurched. Except for the slightest color feathering her cheeks, Alayne's face was still blank. Fia eased herself away from the two older women, whose conversation veered to the illness of a mutual friend, until she stood before the inscrutable eyes of Muir's wife. Alayne might be her age. Her pale red hair was splashed throughout with sunlight gold that highlighted her skin, creamy and clear except for a few fair freckles across her nose and cheeks. Her nose crooked ever so slightly just below its bridge, her mouth was full–even when set as it was now in a grim line. And though Alayne was petite, Fia was sure the word 'frail' would never be applied to this woman. She had the distinct impression that, as Elizabeth had been in her way, Alayne Matheson was also a woman to be reckoned with. Fia didn't want to talk about working at the shop–that was for Kate to do. Nervously, Fia picked the one thing she knew they shared in common–her cousin. "I barely remember Muir...," she began tentatively.

"That makes two of us," Alayne responded dryly.

Slightly taken aback, Fia tried again. "Aunt Kate told me about his disappearance."

"Before you tell me you're sorry, I should explain something to you." Alayne's eyes hardened like her voice, "Kate still loves her son; I don't."

Fia pondered Alayne's declaration remembering that Kate had said Muir mistreated his wife. If Alayne had been hurt by a husband she once loved, believed she knew and could trust, she might well be wary of strangers. Maybe she needed a friend–Fia certainly did.

"What are you staring at?" Alayne demanded under her breath, barely masking her annoyance.

"I was just thinking that, maybe we have something in common. I'm glad you told me how you feel about Muir. Now I won't have to tiptoe around wondering if I might offend you–at least, not about him." Fia grinned and added, "Aunt Kate said you spoke your mind and I'd always know where I stand with you. I'm looking forward to it."

Alayne's face clouded in confusion. She'd heard Kate mention Fia's name once or twice, with a sighed resignation to never seeing her again. But here she was, as though raised from the dead, and Alayne wondered what that meant for her. Sometimes she and Kate were close; other times, they tolerated each other. Maybe Fia would be the daughter Kate always wanted Alayne to be after Muir disappeared. A shudder of uneasiness flitted through her and she abruptly asked, "Are you living with Kate?"

Fia nodded, "At least for now. I arrived yesterday. I had no...I don't know anyone else in Inverness. Where do you live?"

Alayne lowered her eyes as she straightened some lace gloves which were already perfectly displayed. "Most of the time, I live here."

"In the shop?" Fia asked, mildly surprised.

"Upstairs–sometimes I work very late."

Fia hesitated, "And you live with Aunt Kate the rest of the time?"

"I have a room at Kate's."

Fia thought Alayne's choice of words odd. It was fast becoming clear that there was some tension between her aunt and this woman. Maybe it was just what Alayne had told her–Kate loved Muir; Alayne didn't. Maybe it was more. Alayne seemed vexed, restless, and Fia couldn't blame her–she knew she wouldn't appreciate having Alayne sprung on her if the situation were reversed. At least Alayne seemed open, and Fia welcomed the change from Elizabeth's plotting.

Kate called to Alayne who left Fia with a whispered demand, "I want to know why you're really here."

"In time, I'll probably tell you," Fia replied bluntly, receiving a frown in return.

Kate's smile was strained, "Mistress Hays is ready to leave, Alayne."

"Fine, I'll just be a minute." Alayne picked up the waistcoat, disappeared through the curtained door and reappeared almost immediately, the waistcoat neatly bundled. "There you are Mistress; I hope you enjoy it."

"How could I not help but enjoy it?" The older woman patted Alayne's hand. "You're a dear, thank you."

When the door closed behind Mistress Hays, Kate turned to Alayne and praised, "You did do a lovely job."

"Thank you, Kate," Alayne said flatly. "Now, what do you have in mind for your niece?"

"Well, you've never been one to waste time," Kate mumbled, then blurted, "I'd like her to help you here with the sewing and the clerking."

"As equals?" Alayne asked pointedly.

"Aunt Kate and I didn't discuss that, Alayne," Fia quickly stepped in. "Forgive me, Aunt Kate, but it makes sense to me to work as Alayne's assistant. I'm good with a needle, as I told you earlier. But I know nothing about operating a shop. Alayne also knows your patrons, their likes and dislikes. I can learn a great deal from her, if she'll teach me."

Kate blinked at her niece. "This is truly what you want?"

"I do," Fia assured. "I'm sure you see it makes sense; you've never seen my work."

Kate realized that Fia had just deftly eased her out of what might have been a very awkward confrontation, managing also to present them with a sensible plan; she gratefully accepted the help. "That is what I'd prefer also. Alayne, would that be agreeable?"

Alayne's gaze fixed on Fia, also suspecting what she'd done. She didn't mind though. Actually, she was pleased that Fia had grace enough to be uncomfortable, and sense enough to address it in the context of a good business decision. Maybe it would be nice to have someone her own age to talk to for a change. For now, Alayne decided she could live with having Fia's help in the shop. "Her instincts seem sound. Given some time, she might well make a good businesswoman," she allowed. "Welcome, Fia." For the first time, the two young women smiled at each other.

Murdoch dismounted in front of the 'Rowan and Thistle'. This was where he'd find Annie MacAuly who would, in turn, lead him to Martin Ross. He'd also worked up quite a thirst; a pint of ale sounded like heaven on earth. Just inside the door he noticed a lad, about ten years old, sweeping with a broom almost twice his size. "Which way to the taproom, laddie?"

Donald looked up from his task and grinned at the stranger. "Through that door, Sir," he replied, pointing the way.

Murdoch removed his hat, entered the near empty room, and glanced around.

"What can I get you, Sir?" a cheerful voice erupted next to him.

Murdoch turned to its source, a tallish woman with a smile on her heart-shaped face. "Ale and conversation," Murdoch replied brightly, deciding that she had probably turned many a lad's head in her youth.

"I'm sure I can arrange it. Why don't you sit down?" Annie fetched a brimming tankard, placed it before Murdoch, and sat across the table waiting for her customer to quench his thirst and start talking. Quickly, Annie assessed him: late twenties, lively eyes, a little worn at the cuffs and elbows, but clean and well groomed. She liked what she saw; she wished he was a bit older–or herself a tad younger.

"Ah...that's better. Fine ale, Madam." Murdoch's smile dazzled her. Immediately, she added 'charming' to her list of his attributes.

"You must have traveled far, Mr....?"

"Sinclair, Murdoch Sinclair–and I have traveled far."

"And how much farther are you going, Mr. Sinclair?"

"To Glasgow. I've been away on business and I'm anxious to see my family."

"Of course." Annie was surprised at her pang of disappointment when he mentioned family. She chided herself for being silly and decided she'd just enjoy his company while she could. Annie started from her thoughts. "I'm sorry, Mr. Sinclair, what did you say?"

"I said, you must be Annie MacAuly, the proprietress."

"I am but...I'm sure I'd have remembered if we'd met before."

"Oh, we've never met. Your reputation as a gracious hostess precedes you."

"As long as it's a good reputation, that's fine." Annie's curiosity was aroused. "Where did you hear about me?"

"Along the road, as I traveled." Murdoch took a long draft of ale. Technically, what he told Annie was true–Fia had talked about her on the way to Inverness. But he wasn't sure yet that he wanted to mention Fia. He set the tankard down. "I thought, as long as I was coming this way I'd do two things."

"And what are they?"

"I thought to sample your hospitality, and try to locate an old acquaintance of mine. I understand he lives near here. The first, I've already accomplished. The second is a problem. I'm not sure exactly where he lives."

Murdoch hesitated just long enough before widening his eyes and staring at her. "A woman of your position, you probably know everyone for several leagues in every direction."

Annie preened under his flattery, "That I do; I can help you find your friend."

"I'd be in your debt, Madam. His name is Martin Ross." Murdoch watched Annie's open face and friendly demeanor dissolve.

"What do you want of Martin Ross?" she asked, immediately on guard for her friend.

Murdoch chose his next words carefully. "It's obvious that I've caused you some distress. I certainly didn't intend to. Martin isn't ill is he?"

"Not the last time I saw him." Annie's eyes narrowed slightly, "I'll be frank with you, Mr. Sinclair. I know Martin well; he's never mentioned you."

Murdoch spread his hands, palms up. "Why would he? I haven't seen him in a very long time."

Annie studied the man. Her instincts were usually good, and they told her that Murdoch Sinclair meant Martin no harm. But her loyalty to Martin was strong and his privacy far more important to her than to risk placing blind trust in a passing stranger. "I'm sorry, Mr. Sinclair," she declared. "I can't help you." She noted the disappointment which flickered across Murdoch's comely face and she softened a bit. "Anyway, he isn't home now. He's traveling, like you. When he returns, I'll happily tell him you were here."

Murdoch leaned forward, arms resting on the scrubbed table top. It irritated him that his mission was about to fail. But he had no reason to doubt Annie was telling him the truth. Now it was his turn. "To be honest, Madam, my name would mean nothing to Ross. I only know of him through a mutual friend. The same friend who told me about you."

"Then why are you looking for him? Do you have a message from this 'friend'?" Annie asked warily.

Murdoch shook his head. "No message was given to me. I just wanted to meet Ross and ask him one question, to satisfy my own curiosity."

Confused and tense, Annie stammered, "Wh..what question?"

"I want to know if he's happy with the choice he made."

"Choice? I don't understand."

"Ross is a friend of yours." As Annie nodded dumbly, Murdoch continued, "I've no right to pass judgment on your friend. But I can tell you that he was a fool to let her leave. I wanted to tell him that to his face, because that's exactly what I told Fia."

"Fia!" Annie cried, gripping the edge of the table, knuckles white. "You're talking about Fia Graham?" Her hand shot to his arm, clasping it tightly. "When did you see her? Is she well?"

In his own fervor to help Fia, Murdoch didn't realize the effect his revelation would have on the innkeeper. He softened his tone, "It was not long ago that I saw her and...she's better now."

"Better?" Annie tugged his arm. "What do you mean, 'better'?"

Murdoch was beginning to regret having started this, but it was far too late to retreat. "She's healed now; but she was savagely beaten."

"Beaten," Annie gasped. "Who? Who would do such a thing to that sweet lass?"

Murdoch covered her hand with his. "It doesn't matter now. Fia is better and, except grieving the loss of your friend Ross, she'll be fine."

Annie's mouth set in a stern line. "Then I was right; I told Martin that Fia loved him!"

Murdoch stared at her. "You told him that?"

Annie nodded vigorously, "He wouldn't listen to me; said he knew what he was doing and I'd make it worse if I interfered." Tears scalded her eyes knowing how bitterly Martin regretted his decision.

"Aye," Murdoch muttered sourly, "worse." Each was silent a moment, then Murdoch stood. "I need to be on my way, Madam, I'm sorry I've upset you; truly, that was not my intention. I was angry at Ross for not seeing what a delightful, strong, loyal and loving lass Fia is."

"Oh," Annie gave him a hard look, "Martin saw it; he didn't choose to pursue it and now it's too late with the wedding and all."

Sadly, Murdoch shook his head. "Then Ross is a bigger fool than I thought."

Martin cradled the baby in his arm and put the tip of his small finger at the child's lips to pacify him temporarily.

Squatting on the earthen floor, the father swiped his lank hair from his eyes and whined, "He cries so much."

"He's at my breast all the time," the new mother declared anxiously.

Martin gently responded, "Because he's hungry. But your baby has colic. He wants food, but he hurts. And, until he gets over it, he'll cry so much, he may drive you both mad."

Martin wrapped her baby in a clean cloth, and placed him back in her arms. "Now, you can make him more comfortable by walking with him, or gently rocking him. Movement will help. In the meantime, I want you to boil onions. Take the broth and add a couple of spoons of honey to it and feed it to your son. Is that a problem?" Martin asked.

Rising, the young mother shook her head. "I'll get started." She passed the babe to its father, picked up a small cauldron and went to fetch water.

"We never thought of colic. I guess, this being our first, and not being near anyone to ask.... We're grateful." Embarrassed, the young man stood and carried his son around the small room.

The mother's crooked smile lit the dingy croft as she reentered. "Thank God He brought you to our door; only He knows what we'd have done if you hadn't come along."

There was a strained silence and Martin realized they were likely waiting to see if he would demand payment for his advice. The tidy, shabby interior of their croft suggested they had little but pride. "Perhaps I lost my way because God wanted me to help your son." He rose. "Your bairn will improve, but it may take a little time. You must both be patient. Now, I have to be on my way. Since I'm sure I'm on the wrong road, you'd be doing me a great service if you could direct me to Jedburgh." Martin waited expectantly and saw the man's relief as he told Martin that he wasn't far lost. Martin left the couple in their tiny croft. He shivered suddenly, realizing that the child's continual squalling could have driven its parents to rash action. They were little more than children themselves, ignorant and easily panicked. It was a simple diagnosis, but an important thing he'd done for the new family. And he was surprised how good he felt at having helped them–as though another missing piece of him had been returned to its proper place.

From Odhar's back, Martin took a deep breath of the moist, sweetly scented air. He felt his senses reawakening. The weather had been exceptionally pleasant and, though it couldn't last much longer, Martin was grateful; the landscape offered little in the way of shelter. When he stopped at the end of the day, it was usually to bed down on the open moor. Martin frowned. It was at night, when he struggled for sleep, that thoughts of Fia and desire for her nearness haunted him ceaselessly. Nothing seemed to help, but he was thankful not to have suffered again the nightmare he'd had at Alex's. Kicking Odhar's sides, Martin urged the steed to a canter and let the wind clear his head of its cloying thoughts.

By the time the June sun was low on the horizon, Martin was nearing the ruin of Jedburgh Abbey, its pink sandstone walls glowing eerily in the fading light. Beyond the Abbey and across the river nestled the town, but it seemed unappealing compared to the solitude of the Abbey. Martin decided to spend the night right where he was and dismounted next to the Abbey's nave, noting that glass still survived in many of the windows. After tending Odhar and wondering what had become of Arthur, Martin picked up his saddlebags and strode between the majestic columns toward the west front of the building, admiring the fine rose window set high above the arch of a beautifully carved Norman doorway. Near that door, where it met the nave wall, was a sheltered place inviting him to take refuge for the night. This was the first time in years he'd been in a House of God; he hoped God wouldn't mind if he sought shelter there from the chill of the evening air.

No one was in sight who might object to his plans, so Martin spread his plaid on the grass, which now served as the Abbey floor, and sat with his back against the wall. Looking toward the bell tower, he imagined the missing roof back into place. It must have been magnificent–it still was, even in its current condition. A sudden noise caught his attention and Martin turned as Arthur loped toward him. "Ah, there you are," Martin chided. Reaching into his pack for some dried pork, he pulled the dirk from its sheath, cut off a chunk, and tossed it to his companion. "That's all for you, friend. You have to find the rest of your supper yourself."

Arthur snorted, picked up the meat and carried it a few paces before stopping to eat it. Martin turned the remainder over in his hand realizing, unexpectedly, that he was too tired to eat. Repacking the meat, and replacing the dirk, he hoped this meant that he'd sleep well.

Martin stretched out against the wall, covering himself with half the plaid. As he looked through the missing roof at wisps of clouds beginning to brush the night sky, he fingered the heavy cloth, thinking of his grandfather. Though the law forbade Scots to wear plaids since the '45, Martin could still seek comfort and warmth in its other function as a cover. "If I had offered this to Fia, I would never have lain with her molded against me," he mused, "never made that sweet memory." Martin recalled his glimpse of her body through the transparency of her sweat-soaked shift. He ached to cradle her against him, to explore every inch of her beauty and slide into her, gently, tenderly, coaxing her response to his love. Groaning, Martin clenched his fists. Certain now that it would be some time before sleep claimed him, he closed his eyes.

"Grandda?" Martin called desperately. His feet slipped in the mire beneath him and the icy rain stung as it struck. Between the sleet and the madness of the battle, Martin lost sight of his grandfather. Kneeling, he tried to stem the flow of blood from one Highlander's neck, fully aware that it was already too late. Frantically, his eyes darted among the straining, grunting men, but he didn't see Hugh. The ice pelted him, the noise adding to the din and confusion. All around him, Martin heard the clang of sword against targe, the crack of musket fire. Instinctively, he ducked as a shriek tore the air. "*Grandda*," he cried, as Hugh abruptly reeled past him. Martin watched as his grandfather collapsed. Cold fear clutched Martin's heart; *he* was supposed to be under Hugh's lifeless body. Crazed, he stumbled and slipped through the blood and muck to kneel at Hugh's side and was paralyzed by the horror before him. Hugh's black, vacant eyes stared through Martin, his hacked, bloody body sprawled over another: mangled, distorted, too familiar–Fia's.

Martin lurched backward, the scream tearing his throat, bringing him back to the broken Abbey and echoing through the drenching blackness that now engulfed him. Frantically, he clutched at the stone walls, eyes bulging wide in the streaming rain. Desperately, Martin gasped for breath then retched violently on the grass floor of the Abbey.

Chapter Thirteen

Martin plunged his face into its haggard reflection in the burn. The cold water jarred his nerves and he came up dripping and sputtering. Arthur and Odhar patiently waited while Martin wiped his face, still fighting to come awake. He lay back along the bank, a bluebonnet blossom fluttering gently beside his face. Closing his eyes, Martin slept only to awaken, startled and confused, minutes later. In the week since Jedburgh Abbey, he'd slept fitfully, never more than a few hours at a time and, sometimes–like now–hardly at all. Sitting up, Martin rubbed his aching neck. He had continued his journey, skirting Edinburgh where he crossed the Firth to Dunfermline, and headed north. But now he saw little, felt even less. The vision of Fia's mangled body on the field at Culloden tormented him endlessly. Her arm lay at a queer angle to her body; her dark curls were tangled and matted with blood from her swollen, slashed face. Martin dug the heels of his hands into his eyes, again trying to banish the image. "Why didn't Hugh protect her as he protected me?" he asked uselessly, then angrily growled, "This is torment."

Martin stood abruptly and swung onto Odhar's back. "Arthur, race with us," he commanded and kicked his mount into full gallop. The dog dashed beside them until they reached the edge of a village where Martin reined in. Arthur dodged around Odhar's hooves and Martin chuckled, "What, haven't you had enough? What would I do if you weren't here to make me laugh?" Arthur began to bark, over which another commotion caught Martin's attention. He stared over Odhar's ears toward the far end of the lane. In front of the forge churned a small sea of people and Martin picked out a woman's voice wailing hideously above the racket. Odhar leaped forward at the touch of Martin's heel and, moments later, he swung off the horse's back, fumbling for his medicines, nearly dropping them in his haste. Pushing his way to the side of a lad writhing in pain, Martin knelt. The sobbing woman cradled the youth's head against her breast and the crowd moved in all directions except to help the boy whose leg lay twisted absurdly just below the knee. "Do you have a physician?" Martin yelled above the woman's sobs and began removing the woolen stocking from the broken leg.

"No, Sir," came a faceless, raspy response. "You are a doctor?"

"Aye and I'll need help." Locating the wrinkled face that belonged to the voice, Martin asked, "Can you have someone look after this woman before she needs treatment too?"

The man nodded, "Duncan's mother." He motioned two women forward and they coaxed and pried the mother a short distance away. "Now, Sir, what do you need?"

Martin leaned over Duncan, smoothing the lad's hair from his face and laying a comforting hand on his arm. "I don't want you to worry, Duncan. My name is Martin. I'm going to take care of your leg, but I'll need your help."

The lad's anguish and fright shone clearly through his flowing tears, but he nodded bravely.

"Good. Right now, I want you to lie still." Turning to his helper, Martin ordered, "I need a sturdy bark or several lengths of wood to reach from Duncan's ankle to above his knee; and I'll need a bucket of clean, hot water."

The elder man dispatched more villagers to do Martin's bidding. "What else do you need, Sir?"

"A blanket and...is there any fresh comfrey? I need the root–clean!" Again people hastened to fetch the requested items. "One more thing," Martin added. "Someone tell me what happened." He removed a vial, linen cloth and small mortar and pestle from his medical supplies.

The man searched the remaining onlookers until his eyes lit on one person. "He'll have to tell you; he found Duncan."

Martin's gaze followed the man's crooked finger to the angular face of a man seated on a nearby barrel. The man returned Martin's stare with eyes so startlingly blue they seemed to leap from his pale face. A shiver crept Martin's spine. He felt something studying him intimately from behind those eyes. Martin tried to ignore a gnawing uneasiness and said to the man, "You don't look well. Are you injured also?" He tucked the blanket around Duncan from his shoulders to mid-thigh.

"I don't think so...just a bit shaken." He nodded his flaxen curls to Martin's left. "Duncan was repairing the axle on that cart. It slipped from the block and he couldn't get out of the way. It pinned his leg."

"And he," finished the amazed old man nodding at the man on the barrel, "lifted the cart so we could pull Duncan free."

As he crushed the comfrey root he'd been handed, Martin grunted, "No wonder you're shaken." When the root was a sticky pulp, Martin drained it through the linen and turned back to the lad. "Duncan, you won't believe this, but you're very lucky. There's a little damage to your skin right at the break, but it's minor, a scratch really. I'm going to clean it with the comfrey juice. I'll use the pulp to set the leg. Now, this may be a little uncomfortable; just try to relax if you can. It's important to set the bone before we move you and not risk a larger tear in your skin." Martin turned to the woman returning with a small cauldron of hot water. "Take half the leaves in that vial, crush them, and add them to the water."

"What is it?" The blue-eyed man left the barrel and knelt at the boy's head.

"Lovage. It's good for fighting infection. This really is a scratch but there's no sense in taking chances."

"My name's Simon MacLaren. Tell me when you're ready to straighten the bone."

Martin glanced up, then around. "Have we got the...ah, good." Martin wiped out the bark presented him and smiled apologetically at Duncan.

"You'll have to bear with me, lad. I'm going to lift your leg into the bark and then, Simon and I will have to set your bone in place. That will hurt but, as soon as we're finished, I'll give you something that will help you feel better. Are you ready?"

"Aye," Duncan grimaced bravely and Martin lifted his broken limb. When it rested in the splint, Martin nodded to Simon who reached over Duncan's shoulders to grasp his hands. With a steady, sure tug, Martin popped the leg bone into place. Duncan's howl set his mother to wailing again, and Simon thought the lad's grip would crush his fingers.

Simon spoke soothingly to Duncan as Martin quickly dressed the break, packing the splinted leg with the comfrey pulp. Martin took the steeping lovage, strained it, and handed it back to the woman who'd fetched the water. "See that he drinks this." Once more, Martin reached into his supplies and, this time, removed a vial of lettuce oil. It was old fashioned, but a good sedative and would work well for Duncan. He wouldn't use opiates anymore–not since Bridgid. "Give him this when he's finished the lovage tea." He patted Duncan's shoulder. "You did well, lad." Some townsmen fashioned a litter and bore Duncan to his home. Martin promised to look in on the lad later then turned his attention to Simon. "I'll see that shoulder now," Martin ordered, wiping his hands on a cloth handed him.

"My shoulder's fine," Simon assured.

"Probably so. I just want to find out whether that blood on your sleeve is yours–I doubt it's Duncan's."

"What blood?" Simon twisted until he found the blood high on his arm. He sat back down on his barrel and removed his waistcoat and shirt. A shallow tear showed on the back of his upper arm. "Now, how did I manage that?"

"Caught it on the cart, I imagine. Luckily, it's not bad. Just the same, I want to clean it and have you drink some lovage tea as well."

Simon sat patiently while Martin cleaned the cut, applied a lanolin ointment to it and tied a clean bandage on. As he put his shirt back on, Simon peered curiously at Martin who was packing his supplies. Could this man be the cousin for whom he'd been searching? The name was right, and the profession. The confusing thing was that, though Simon had never met his cousin, he was almost certain he'd seen this Martin before. As he pondered where, it came to him suddenly that it wasn't Martin he'd seen at all–it was his grandfather, Hugh Stewart. Simon fought to squelch his rising excitement. After all the time he'd spent looking for his cousin, Martin Ross had stumbled upon *him*. He had to play it smart; not scare the man off. "You'll need a place to stay the night, if you're going to check Duncan's progress. I was told there's a small tavern; I was headed there to find a room myself when I saw the accident." Simon hesitated, thinking the physician wasn't listening then continued, "I appreciate what you've done. Why don't you come along and let me buy you a meal."

Martin closed his medicine bag and replied, "Thank you, but that's not necessary. Like you, I was just passing by."

Simon grinned rakishly. "Since when do doctors not ask fees for their work?"

Martin frowned, thinking of Fia and the payment he'd extracted from her. He shook his head, banishing the thought for the time being. "You're right, since when?" He acquiesced, strapping his bag to Odhar's saddle. "A meal it is."

Simon noted that Martin didn't commit to staying at the tavern, but he was satisfied that he would at least have Martin's attention through supper.

Martin ordered hot water when they were seated, brewed more lovage and forced Simon, who shuddered as it went down, to drink it all. "Is it that bad?" Martin grimaced.

"To me it is," Simon answered and ordered mead to kill the flavor. "Haven't you ever had to drink that venom?"

"Aye, but I don't remember it being terrible. Maybe it's too strong; I haven't made it in a while."

"Oh, why's that?" Simon asked casually.

"No need to," came his simple reply.

Nodding, Simon nursed the drink placed before him. "That's much better."

"Your quick reaction when that cart fell on Duncan probably saved his leg, maybe his life."

"It's fortunate that I was there since no one else seemed capable of coming to his aid." Simon looked at his empty mug. "Besides I have a bad habit of playing the Good Samaritan whether people want me to or not."

"I'm not sure that's a bad thing. Young Duncan is sure to be glad you do."

Simon stared intently at Martin. "Seems to me the lad was twice blessed today. You were there to patch him up."

Martin shrugged. "I hope he'll be able to take the time to let the bone heal properly; I'd hate to see him end up crippled when it can be avoided."

"Duncan will be fine if he follows your advice. I've seen trained doctors and those in the field at work. You're trained–and good."

Martin asked, "Where have you been to see so much medicine being practiced in the field? Have you seen fighting?"

"Some," Simon admitted. "I've been working in America much of the past five years."

"You were a soldier?" Martin asked.

"I'm an actor."

Martin looked confused. "Not the kind of occupation which normally leads one into the pitch of battle."

Simon signaled for another mead. "Quite right, unless you stray from time to time to find out what it's all about."

Martin cocked his head. "It?"

"Aye, the French, the colonists, the Indians and, of course, His Majesty King George. Everyone has a role, everyone has a point of view, and everyone has something they want. The question is, who has the resources and is willing to fight hardest for 'it'."

Martin grinned at his companion as an innocuous looking mutton stew was placed before them. "You stray a lot don't you?"

A toothy smile split Simon's face. "That I do. I'm lucky that my profession gives me the chance to meet people and get into places others can't get near."

"What are you doing back in Scotland then? You've lost much of your brogue, but I know this is where you're from." Martin dipped bread into the hot stew and bit into it.

Elbows resting on the table and fingers laced above his bowl, Simon responded, "I'm looking up family members."

"You haven't seen them in five years?"

"Aye, and some I've never seen, just heard about." Simon picked up his fork. "Why don't you tell me something of yourself?"

Martin didn't look up, but something in the tone of Simon's voice vexed him. He hesitated then responded, "I don't talk much about myself."

Simon examined the contents of his bowl. "I don't want much, just a little. It helps keep the conversation going."

If Martin could shake his apprehension, he would enjoy talking to Simon–in fact he was, until the conversation had turned to him. "You're right, of course," Martin began, "and I was being ungracious."

"True," Simon agreed heartily.

The two men sized each other up, then Martin suddenly demanded, "What is it about me that makes you look as though you knew me?"

The corners of Simon's mouth turned up slowly. "Ah...now we get down to business."

His response set Martin's nerves on edge. "What 'business'?"

Simon leaned back in his chair. "I'll tell you. You remind me of a man I met once back in '44."

"I was a lad then," Martin stated the obvious.

"So was I."

Martin fidgeted in his seat. "You met him once, sixteen years ago, and remember him so well?" he asked suspiciously.

"He was a very impressive man, my great uncle; he died two years after our meeting. He was a Jacobite, so you may guess how he perished. His grandson supposedly favored him." Simon's face was carefully blank. "I was thinking perhaps you were his grandson; you have the same look. And I'm told the grandson went on to become a doctor, which you are."

Martin's heart thudded dangerously. He was almost afraid for Simon to continue. What did the man want? Was he more than he professed, a sheriff maybe? He prompted Simon warily, "A doctor?"

Simon crossed his arms over his chest and propped his boots on a vacant chair. "Aye, on Skye." He noted that while Martin's gaze fell briefly, there was no other outward sign to show what he was thinking. "Tragic story really," Simon continued. "My cousin was accused of two murders, his wife's and child's. His brother, it seems, was in love with his sister-in-law and, when she died, he maliciously drove the doctor away. As far as anyone knows, that brother never returned to Skye."

There was a roar in Martin's ears as panic surged through his body. When he was able to speak, he asked, "Why do you seek this cousin of yours?"

Simon sat up and leaned in. "Because, he was wronged. I don't think he knows that his good name's been restored. No one blames him now."

"How," Martin rasped, "how do you know this?"

"I was there not two months ago, on Skye. I saw the brother, Hugh. I don't know what he was back then but he's a rather pathetic drunk now. I talked to him as well as to others."

"And...?" Martin asked faintly.

"Hugh killed his brother's wife–by accident–but he killed her just the same. The doctor had dosed his wife with laudanum and left the bottle. Hugh couldn't bear her suffering and gave her all she begged for. His misery at her death and his panic when he realized it was at his hand, made him turn on his brother. He's eaten alive with guilt–looks twice his 30 years."

"Guilt for killing Bridgid," Martin muttered harshly, "none for what he did to his brother, I'll warrant."

Simon watched Martin's face flush and eyes brim with bitter tears. "You know your brother well, Martin Ross," Simon soothed. "But you're free."

The long repressed pain and betrayal crushed him and Martin was lost under its weight. He didn't know what to do or what to say. He wanted to flee, craving a stiff wind to lash his face or a hard rain to beat his skin numb–anything to quiet the rage and sorrow he'd swallowed unendingly for three years. Instead he clung, white-knuckled, to his chair. After long minutes struggling to ease his turmoil, Martin muttered, "What about the bairn?"

"When everyone calmed down–which I'm told took quite some time–they realized that the child's death was a natural one."

Martin drew a ragged breath and glared at Simon. "I...don't understand why you went to the trouble, or how it happens that we've met like this. But I thank God you cared enough, Simon. I'm grateful...beyond words."

Simon cleared the lump from his throat at the sight of his cousin so moved. "Actually I started my search," he said to Martin's bewildered look, "for selfish reasons. I wasn't sure what I'd find, but I remembered your grandfather talking about you...not the exact words, mind you, but he spoke highly of your character even as a lad, your eagerness to learn and a compassion he found unusual in one so young. I was in Philadelphia when I received word from my mother about your wife and child. What she described didn't fit the picture your grandfather had painted. I promised myself that, when I came home, I'd get to the truth. I thought your grandfather would want that."

"About the child," Martin began.

"I know it was Hugh's," said Simon. "That's why people so eagerly believed his story that you had murdered your family; a crime of passion. In the scheme of things, his adultery didn't seem so terrible."

"No," Martin agreed quietly, "I suppose not."

Simon scowled at his now tepid stew. "I'm going to order some hot food. I hope you'll stay for a time. I'd like to get to know you now that I've found you."

Martin nodded slowly, still in shock. "I'm not going anywhere. You go ahead and eat; I can't."

Simon got the maid to take away the bowl and bring him a replacement. She also delivered two more drinks. Simon pushed one toward Martin and hoisted his own. "To freedom," he offered.

Martin picked up his cup and touched it to Simon's. "To freedom," he echoed, "and eat fast. I'm anxious to know about you and how we're cousins."

"I promise to answer all your questions after I'm done. In the meantime, why don't you tell me what you've done with yourself all this time."

Martin nodded, putting his thoughts in order, and began, "I haven't practiced much medicine since I left home. I didn't want to be conspicuous in case someone was looking for me. I also live in a fairly isolated spot and don't see many people."

"But you're here today," Simon mumbled between bites. "Why's that?"

"Well, not long ago, I decided it was time to rejoin the world. Being cut off became...unbearable, even though, for a long time, it was all I wanted."

"So how did you pass the time?"

"I took up my grandfather's profession and have earned my way as a weaver."

"And is there a woman?"

Martin's eyes narrowed. "Why would you ask that?"

Simon looked at him, mildly surprised by the sharp edge to Martin's voice. "You're a man. Isolation or not, at some point, a man simply yearns for the attention of a woman."

Martin searched for the right words, then mumbled, "There was one...almost," as his thoughts turned to Fia.

Simon studied his cousin for a long moment, intrigued by his statement and Martin's obvious withdrawal at the thought. Finally, he waved a hand before Martin's eyes until his cousin refocused on him. "Are you all right?"

Embarrassed, Martin cleared his throat and nodded too eagerly. "Aye, sorry."

"No need to apologize." Simon pushed his empty bowl aside and decided it was time to change the subject–for now. "Did you want to check on Duncan tonight or in the morning?"

"Both. Do you want to come along?" Martin asked on impulse.

Simon smiled broadly. "I would, thanks." As the two set off for Duncan's, following directions the barmaid had given them, Simon told Martin that his grandmother was an Appin Stewart, sister to Martin's grandfather. "She always talked about Hugh in hushed tones; always in awe of him. My father said that Gram was compelled to publicly disapprove of Hugh's marriage to Meriel Campbell. And, because she did, she didn't see her brother until years later when he visited after his wife returned to the Campbells."

"I remember Hugh mentioning a sister–once. A MacLaren?" Simon nodded and Martin sighed. "I guess I know now why he never wanted to talk about her."

Simon glanced at his cousin's bleak expression. "Don't be too hard on my grandmother, Martin. She did what she had to do and spent years suffering for it."

Martin turned to him suddenly. "Is your grandmother still alive?"

"Aye." Simon brightened. "What are your plans, Martin?"

"My plans?"

"Aye. Where are you headed?"

"Wherever Odhar and Arthur take me." To Simon's quizzical expression, Martin explained, "My horse and dog."

"Why don't you all travel with me for a spell? I'll take you to meet Eleanor...your great aunt."

Martin stopped. "You will?"

"I will! Martin, I want you to come with me. I don't know how my revelation about your brother's deception may affect your future, but, right now, you're without a family of your own. Perhaps, you'd like to share mine."

Staring into Simon's earnest blue eyes, Martin stammered, "Si...Simon, your offer is truly generous. We are kin, but you don't know me."

"I know enough...I hope to learn more. I think we can become great friends. Now, what's your answer?"

Martin beamed and offered his hand which Simon clasped in his own. "That's settled then," Simon laughed.

"Aye," Martin agreed. "Now, let's see how Duncan fares."

"I think you've settled in nicely, Fia." Alayne perched on a stool in the curtained section of the shop watching Fia take the last stitches on a pair of embroidered pockets.

Fia smiled. "I feel good when I'm here. Believe me, I appreciate you making this so easy for me. I'm well aware that, if you were a different kind of person, my life here could be a living hell."

Alayne crossed her arms. "What kind of person have you decided I am? You've known me for only three weeks."

"You're strong, independent, fair and honest. I figured that out by the end of my first day. You're also nice, though that took until the end of my second day to decide."

"What happened on day three," Alayne asked with raised brows.

"That's when I decided I really enjoy your company." Fia had never heard Alayne laugh and was delighted with the throaty, musical tones.

Suddenly serious, Alayne angled close, careful not to block Fia's light. "I wanted you to fail, you know that."

Snipping the thread, Fia smoothed the finished pockets with her palms. "I know." She looked into Alayne's intense stare. "Are you sorry I didn't?"

"No. I'm surprised to find that I like having someone my age to talk to–and someone who doesn't tolerate me just because I married Muir Matheson."

Fia's expression clouded. "It's clear you and Aunt Kate aren't close, but is it really bad between you?"

Alayne shrugged. "Kate and I get on well enough; she likes to be in charge. That's fine here, it's her millinery. But outside the shop, I don't let her desires rule me and I don't want you to get between us. Kate and I have to work out our own troubles." Alayne rubbed her hands together, considering her next words. "I...I hope my relationship with your aunt won't keep us from becoming friends. Since you arrived, I'm reminded just how I've missed my old friends...and of course my family in the colonies."

Fia hesitated a long moment. "I think I understand something of what you feel. You see, I've spent the last eight years of my life with relatives who made sure my basic needs were met, but who didn't care about me. They wanted to rule my life. No, I won't interfere between you and Aunt Kate." Fia smiled warmly at Alayne. "And, I already consider you my friend. I've been alone too." Stretching her arms, Fia asked, "You haven't stayed at Aunt Kate's since I arrived. I'm not keeping you away, am I?"

Alayne shifted uncomfortably. "I've been a little reluctant; you're just getting acquainted really."

"I can do that whether you're there or not. Please don't let that stop you from staying. The upstairs room here can't be that comfortable."

"It's small, but it suits my needs most of the time."

"I'm not going to ask you everyday where you're going to spend the night," Fia promised, "just know that I'd welcome your company at Aunt Kate's."

Alayne's soft smile lit her face. "Thank you, Fia."

Fia grinned, "So, where are you spending the night?"

Alayne laughed unexpectedly. "At Kate's, where else?"

The two young women giggled and chatted all the way to Douglas Row and Kate's supper table. Kate was pleased, but finding their sudden exuberance a little overwhelming, finally shooed them into the drawing room so that she could have some peace while Flora cleared the table and prepared to leave for the night.

"Thank you, Flora," they called over their shoulders as they scampered out the door. The glowing peat fire cast flickering amber light on the two young women who discussed some clothes Fia wanted to make for herself after shop hours. "I need to be seen in more than two petticoats or I'm going to ruin the shop's reputation."

Nodding, Alayne added, "Besides, the one Kate let you alter doesn't really suit you."

Fia agreed. "I never liked myself in brown. In fact my least favorite sack dress was brown and I wore it to do my most dreaded tasks."

Alayne's interest piqued. "Really? What, for instance?"

Almost before Fia knew it, the story of her betrothal and near miss at the kirk had tumbled from her. Prompted by Alayne's inquisitive nature, Fia gave her details she'd left out when telling her aunt of the Forbes brothers and their alliance with Elizabeth and George Graham. "So if you ever hear the names of Struan or Andrew Forbes, be careful," Fia ended her tale.

"Sweet Jesus, no wonder you decided to come to Kate's. What despicable treatment."

"Ah, but there was money to be made," Fia sniped.

"And to marry without love...even Muir and I thought we were in love when we wed." Alayne shook her head sadly and, in the silence that followed, realized that Fia's thoughts were elsewhere. She touched Fia's shoulder. "What are you thinking? Is something wrong...something I said?"

Swallowing a knot of loneliness, Fia responded, "Marrying without love...is such a bleak prospect."

Curious, Alayne gently urged, "Have you found someone to love?"

"I have," Fia murmured, "but he's married now."

"Then try to let him go," Alayne sensibly urged.

Fia looked sidelong at her new friend. "I'm not sure it's a question of me letting go. I can't seem to separate him out. He's all those parts of me I barely knew were missing. I...," she couldn't finish and Alayne covered Fia's hand in hers.

"Just let it out, Fia," she spoke soothingly. "It'll help for a little while."

"Did crying help you when Muir disappeared?"

"I didn't cry. I didn't love him by then."

"Alayne what are you going to do? You can't live like this forever," Fia insisted.

"I don't intend to. In another few months, November to be exact, Muir will have been gone four years. I can have the marriage annulled on the grounds of malicious desertion. I know it sounds harsh. Please don't tell Kate; I will when the time is right."

"Of course I won't, and I don't think it sounds harsh. Surely she must realize how hard this has been on you."

Alayne shrugged.

Fia sighed shakily. "Aren't we a pair? I haven't told Aunt Kate about Martin, either. Since they're all I have, I guard my memories pretty selfishly."

"I can appreciate that. His name is Martin?" The corners of Alayne's mouth turned up a bit. "She won't find out about your Martin from me."

Their friendship firmly sealed by a pact of silence, the two women talked on into the night.

"Alayne," Fia called, "are you here?" There was no answer. In the month since she'd been working, Fia had never arrived to a darkened shop except when they'd arrived together after the night Alayne had stayed at Kate's. Parting the curtains, she found the workroom unlit and empty. "Alayne?" Still no answer and Fia's apprehension grew. The narrow stairs leading to the second floor were shrouded in murky light. She'd never been invited upstairs, but this was no time to stand on ceremony. Fia lifted her petticoat and carefully made her way to a small sitting room at the top which housed a chaise, two candle stands, a writing table and two wooden

chairs. No sign of Alayne. At a door separating the sitting room from what Fia presumed was the bed chamber, she called again, "Alayne, it's Fia." There was no response. "Forgive me," she muttered and gently pushed the door open. The acrid smell of vomit assailed her nose and Fia rushed to the bed where Alayne lay curled in a ball clutching her head. "Alayne!" Fia cried. "What's wrong? What's happened?"

With obvious effort, Alayne opened her eyes, and stared dully at Fia. "Sick..." she breathed, "the headache."

On her knees beside the pillow, Fia quietly repeated, "Your head aches?"

Alayne closed her eyes and nodded. "Do you want a doctor? What can I do to help?"

"No doctor. Ice...cold...."

Fia grimaced in frustration. "You're cold or something cold will help your head?"

"Head," she answered wretchedly.

"All right, I'll be right back." Fia sped to the ground floor and out the door, grabbing a pail as she went to the well. Drawing a bucket of water, she filled the pail and dashed back to Alayne's side. Soaking a cotton cloth in the water, Fia soothed, "I'm going to put a cloth on your forehead." As the cool cloth touched her skin, Alayne cringed. "I'm also going to bathe your arms and wrists." Fia wet her handkerchief and tenderly dabbed Alayne's arms. What is this all about, she fretted, wondering if Alayne often got such vicious headaches. She freshened the cloth on Alayne's forehead and whispered, "I'll be back in a few minutes."

Downstairs, Fia went through the motions of opening the shop. She would just have to keep checking on Alayne. Fia wondered whether her aunt knew anything of this but, unsure, Fia decided that her safest course of action was not to alert Aunt Kate. She knew she could handle the shop and, hopefully, Alayne would improve by afternoon when Aunt Kate planned to stop by.

Fia split the morning by running the shop and seeing to Alayne who slept most of the time. There were a fair number of customers, several who asked for Alayne for they didn't know Fia. She explained with her most ingratiating smile that Alayne was out on shop errands and that she was Kate Matheson's niece whom Alayne had trained. The explanation satisfied most, and only one person decided to return the next day and speak directly with Alayne. Fia prayed silently that Alayne would be up and about. When she closed the shop for her mid-day meal, Fia took some broth Flora had sent with her upstairs and was thrilled to see Alayne's eyes open. "You look awful," Fia said with relief, "but you're awake."

"I'm over the worst of it," she offered weakly.

"That's good to hear; I've been so worried." Balancing on the edge of the bed, Fia said, "I won't ask you to tell me about this now. You need rest and...do you feel like a little broth?"

"No, I can't eat." Alayne insisted.

"You lost whatever was in your stomach. I won't force you, but as soon as you feel up to it," she pulled over a stool and set the bowl on it, "swallow some of this."

Alayne managed a slight smile. "I promise. What time is it?"

"A little after one o'clock."

"Oh, no," Alayne's eyes grew wide with worry. "What about the shop? If Kate finds out we didn't open..."

Patting her friend's hand, Fia urged, "Lie quietly. I've been handling the shop and, so far, everything's gone well. Mr. Wallace will be back tomorrow to deal directly with you though. You will be better tomorrow won't you?" she asked anxiously.

"Aye, but has Kate been in?"

Fia shook her head. "She told me she'd be in this afternoon. I've told everyone who asked that you were on errands. I don't think that will work with Aunt Kate."

"No, it won't. Can you help me clean up?"

Fia stared aghast. "You don't seriously think you're coming downstairs?"

"I have to. Listen, it'll work. I'll rest in the workroom until she arrives. Then if she asks for me, you can fetch me."

"Alayne..." Fia began to protest then realized that what she suspected was true. "You've had headaches before and Aunt Kate doesn't know about them, does she?"

"No, she doesn't. I don't have them very often–never did until Muir disappeared. Usually, I feel them coming on–a knot at the back of my neck–and can treat them before they get bad. This one I didn't catch."

"I guess you didn't," Fia agreed. "Are you sure you can make it downstairs?"

"Not without your help. Please, Fia?"

"Then you eat a little while I get your clothes." Fia helped prop Alayne up on pillows and put the broth in her hands.

Nearly an hour later, Alayne was resting in a chair in the workroom, pillow behind her back, a blanket over her lap. After assuring herself that she'd done what she could for Alayne, Fia reopened the shop. She'd just sold an exquisite set of silver French shoe buckles to a gentleman for his lady's birthday when Kate swept in. While Kate stopped to speak to the man, Fia eased her way to the workroom and found Alayne asleep. She quickly roused her friend with a whispered, "Kate's just arrived." Helping Alayne to the doorway, she left her just inside so she wouldn't have far to walk if Kate called her. By the time the gentleman left, Fia was back behind the counter.

"Well, dear," Kate began taking off her gloves, "how is everything going today? It's turned so warm outside, you can't imagine." She removed her hat and laid it on a shelf behind the display case. Patting her hair into place, Kate glanced around. "Where's Alayne...in the back?"

"Aye. Did you need her?"

"In a few minutes. It's just that I ran into Mistress Dunbar and she said Alayne was at the market this morning. I wondered why since I told her I'd bring a list today of items I thought we needed."

"She wasn't gone long. There was a particular embroidery thread I needed to finish the neck handkerchief I promised would be ready today. She found it and I've finished."

"Oh, fine. And you got to practice minding the shop alone."

"For a short while. Alayne's teaching me carefully."

Kate nodded her approval. "You do need to learn the merchants, of course–who has the best buys and quality. But how to deal with the customers must be the first priority."

Emerging from behind the curtain, Alayne added, "I'll make sure Fia learns it all, Kate."

Kate spun to her daughter-in-law's voice. "There you are, dear. I was just praising your teaching methods."

Alayne mustered a smile. "Thank you. Fia makes it very easy."

"I brought my list," Kate bubbled, then quieted suddenly. "Alayne, are you well? You look dreadfully sallow." She reached for Alayne's face, but the young woman stepped aside.

"A little tired maybe, nothing more. Did I hear you say you had your marketing list ready?"

As the two women conferred, Fia finished arranging some new fans on a shelf nearby, keeping one ear on their conversation. The exchange went without mishap and Kate was soon on her way home. As the door closed behind her, Fia breathed a sigh of relief. Turning, she saw Alayne slump over the counter, exhausted from the effort to appear well. "You're going back to bed," Fia ordered.

"I'll be fine if you just get me back to the chair," Alayne protested. "I can rest there and you won't have to run up and down the stairs."

"Alayne, are you sure? I really don't mind."

Alayne assured, "The chair will be fine. And, Fia, thank you. This is the first time this has happened when I was supposed to be in the shop."

Fia helped her stand. "I was wondering how you'd kept this from Aunt Kate...and why."

Alayne leaned on Fia's arm responding, "She did see it once, the first time it happened, about two months after Muir disappeared. She nursed me through it, but her reaction was very strange. I believe she was afraid I'd die and leave her truly alone. I was the only family she thought she had left. When I recovered, she insisted I stay with her. You see, I'd already talked about leaving. But I felt sorry for her because she was alone–didn't know what had happened to her only child. For about four months I stayed. That was enough."

"Is that when you took over the upstairs room?" Fia asked as Alayne lowered herself into the chair.

"It was a compromise; I'm still under her roof this way."

"But not under her control?"

Alayne bobbed her head. "That's the way I see it. And I've never told her that I've suffered more headaches because it'll upset her."

"And that will upset you."

"Aye."

Fia tucked the blanket around her friend. "Thanks for telling me."

"I'll be fine tomorrow, you'll see," Alayne promised.

Fia strolled unhurriedly toward Kate's row house. The balmy evening air soothed her spirits, lifting tendrils of hair as it swirled gently around her. Breathing deeply, she caught a trace of roses, their sweet scent perfuming the night. How beautiful, she thought. Maybe the fragrant breeze was that much more comforting because of the hectic day just ending. Fia wasn't sure why but knew that, at this moment, she felt almost at peace. Her birthday had passed without fanfare–just a plate of thickly iced scones–over a month ago. And last week, she'd gotten a letter from Douglas Sutherland. He was taking the legal steps to transfer her inheritance and he assured her that, except for the expected confrontation with Andrew the day Fia had left, things had been quiet. In fact, he'd been told that Andrew and Struan had gone their separate ways on business trips. He wasn't sure what that meant, but would keep his ear to the ground for further news. And Murdoch had returned without incident. He'd shared with Douglas Fia's information about Andrew and his activities. Douglas ended his letter cautioning Fia to continue to be watchful. There was just no trusting either Forbes brother. But then, who knew that better than she?

Fia sighed to herself. What had she done to deserve friends like Douglas and Murdoch? Even with his somber warning, knowing that he was looking after her interests made her feel warm and protected. She looked up as a gull laughed overhead and flashed white on its way to the Firth. Fia's thoughts leaped to a morning she'd been chasing Arthur between the croft and burn while Martin cooled Odhar down after a bit of exercise. She'd been startled by the mournful screech of a golden eagle soaring above the woods. The bird was so close that Fia could hear the wind ruffle the tips of its feathers as it turned and floated on the cold air. Before she realized it, Martin was at her shoulder.

"Magnificent, isn't he?" he stared appreciatively at the bird.

"Aye, he is," she agreed. "Are there any others?"

"He had a mate; I haven't seen her for some time. I hope she's still alive. He's a young eagle and they mate for life."

Fia turned and caught an almost forlorn expression on his face; there was a definite sadness in his eyes. Impulsively, she rested her head against his shoulder for a moment. "You'll see her again."

Martin touched her hair tentatively. "Why do you think so?"

"You haven't killed her, and they don't have to go beyond these woods to hunt. I just don't think the chances of someone or something else having killed her are that great. I just feel it." She grinned ruefully. "I see I haven't convinced you."

Martin said wistfully, "So many things can happen, unexpected things. But, I hope you're right, Fia."

"Miss, watch out!" A brawny man yelled, yanking her out of the path of a fast moving cart.

Thoroughly shaken from her recollection, Fia thanked the man who'd saved her. "So much for feeling at peace." she scolded herself. She stood a moment collecting her scattered thoughts. Peace of mind had always eluded her with Martin. She'd experienced just about every other sensation when she was with him, but peace was impossible amidst the tumult of emotion his presence brought her. She found it frustrating that, after just those few weeks together, so many things reminded her of him. Fia looked west into the fiery umber of the setting sun and, as if to mock her, she envisioned Martin's hair shimmering in the glow of firelight. He was not fading in the least with time. Every detail seemed more acutely etched in her conscious thoughts now than a month ago. But then, Fia didn't really expect to forget him. She'd meant what she told Alayne; Fia couldn't tell where she began and he ended. Her thoughts made her ache with loneliness and, forcing them aside, Fia realized the evening was turning cool. She pulled her capuchin closer and hurried on her way.

Chapter Fourteen

"Should I ask him or shouldn't I?" Simon fretted silently as he pondered the reason for Martin's fitful sleeping habits. Since they'd left Duncan's village three days earlier, Simon had been awakened repeatedly by Martin's restlessness and his muttering. Ordinarily, he might not care. But now, Martin was asleep; Simon was wide awake and unhappy about it. He knew he only had to wait a few minutes and his cousin would rouse. "This time," Simon decided, "I will ask him."

A gasped breath, a jolt, and Martin sat upright, staring bleakly across the glowing embers into Simon's scowling face. "What?" Martin asked in sudden alarm.

"Are you going to tell me what's going on, Martin?" Simon demanded.

"Tell you what? I don't understand."

"I'm talking about why you can't sleep like a normal person, why you're so unsettled."

Groggy, Martin rubbed his forehead trying to rid his mind of the clinging vestiges of sleep. "Simon, I'm sorry. I'm keeping you awake; no wonder you glare at me."

Simon grimaced. "I didn't mean to glare; I want to know how I can help."

Martin shook his head. "I don't think you can. Maybe I should bed down away from the fire." He began to gather his things, but Simon stopped him with his next question.

"Has this anything to do with Fia?"

The silence stretched as Martin stared and tried to think, "How–?"

"You speak the name in your sleep." Simon noticed again the softening that crept over Martin's face as he looked away. "Ah," Simon said in recognition, "the one that was...almost."

Martin dropped his things and flopped back down on Hugh's plaid. He held out his hands in despair. "Simon, I have horrible dreams that she's dead. They're brutal dreams; scenes from my own life in which I'm powerless to protect her."

"Does she need protection?" Simon asked quietly.

Martin was bewildered. "I don't know, so why these nightmares?"

Simon shrugged. "I couldn't begin to guess; I know nothing about her except that you aren't with her, you're with me."

"Aye, and that's not likely to change." After a long pause, Martin began apologetically, "I know you sometimes find yourself in the middle of other people's muddles, but–"

"I'd love to hear about her," Simon assured, dragging his blanket closer to Martin. He crossed his legs, sat forward and stared into Martin's surprised face.

Unexpectedly, Martin howled with laughter, his pent-up unhappiness and exhaustion pouring forth at the sight of Simon's eagerness. When Martin's cackles began to choke him, Simon indignantly inquired, "Just what is so amusing?"

"I...I was about to...ask pardon for wanting to impose on you and talk about Fia. But you... you've been hoping, haven't you?"

A little hurt, Simon looked down at his clasped hands and atoned, "I can't help it. It's my nature." He shifted to face Martin and spoke earnestly, "I promise you that it's not idle curiosity. I'm at my best when I'm of use to others." He faltered, "Yet, if you'd rather not talk, I'd understand."

"No, you wouldn't." Martin clasped his cousin's shoulder. "But that's fine, Simon, because I really need to talk about Fia. I'm thankful you want to listen."

"A fortunate coincidence," Simon piped, reassured.

"You're a compassionate and generous fellow, Simon. That's rare. I'm going to enjoy having you for a cousin."

Simon gulped an unbidden lump from his throat. "I said we might be good friends."

Martin grinned. "And you were right. What in the...?" Arthur had ambled over and was collapsing with a grumbled huff between the two men. "I guess I disturbed him as well." Martin stroked the dog's long back.

"You can tell me about how you came to have this mongrel some other time. Right now," Simon urged, "I'd really like to hear about Fia."

Martin glanced at the fire and took a deep breath. "Just as the borrowed days were setting in, I found Fia lost in the woods. She was sick and I took her to my croft which was closer than Inverary, where she was headed, by quite a distance. Fia stayed with me for a few remarkable weeks while she recovered."

"Just the two of you?" Simon broke in.

"Aye," Martin rubbed his bearded cheek, "just Fia and me. While I liked her, I didn't always appreciate her intrusion in my carefully ordered life. We fought sometimes–mostly my fault–but we became quite adept at forgiving each other. In some ways, we were as close as two people could hope to be. And I fell in love, though I told myself the whole time it was happening that I didn't want to and shouldn't."

"Why did you think that?"

Martin responded bitterly, "Let's be honest. My instincts about women are questionable." His regret-filled eyes shone black in the firelight. "Once I admitted to myself that I loved Fia, I made up my mind to tell her. I went fishing that morning to give Fia some privacy for a bath." Martin paused, his expression darkening with pain. "When I returned, she was distant, withdrawn and, out of nowhere, told me she was betrothed and ready to leave. I tried to talk to her about it–I was frantic and unable to believe she would settle for a 'comfortable' marriage as she put it. But, she shut me out completely. So I took her to Inverary and watched her leave." Martin released a deep soughing breath. "It was a stormy and... unkind parting; again my fault."

Simon mulled the story over. "You think there was truly something special between you; that it wasn't one-sided?"

Vehemently, Martin declared, "I would swear to it. There were times I felt almost scorched by the air between us."

Simon prodded, "And when you fought?"

"Oddly, each disagreement broke through some barrier between us. Simon, I carried a great deal of anger and distrust because of Bridgid and my brother. Fia confused those feelings in me, and I confused her in turn. I resisted letting her get close at the very same time I was telling her some of my most guarded secrets."

"So did you tell her about Bridgid? Could that be why she changed so abruptly?"

"I never told her."

Simon considered his answer then surmised, "You never told her you loved her either."

Martin rested his head in his hands. "No. There seemed no real reason to."

"Where is she now, do you know?" Simon inquired.

Martin lifted his head but his eyes remained downcast. "I'm not sure. I think she's still in Glasgow; she's married now."

"How do you know that?"

"Her cousin, Elizabeth, told me that much."

"Glasgow, huh?" Simon remembered his brief encounter with Arabella, facing a brutish marriage that would pit her against a lecherous, murdering brother-in-law.

"What about Glasgow?" Martin asked, curious at the distant tone in Simon's voice.

"Oh, it just reminded me that, when I was looking for you, I met a lass in Glasgow–pretty, friendly–facing some rough times because of her own betrothal. I encouraged her to find a way to escape; I hope she did. And I hope your Fia hasn't regretted her choice. If she does, she has an unhappy future ahead of her."

"I truly want her to be happy," Martin vowed, "but dwelling on what might have been won't change things for either of us. Fia has set her path."

Silently, Simon studied his cousin, who held his hands out to the fire for warmth...or meager comfort. Fia may have set her path, Simon thought, but Martin's not finished with her yet–there's far too much emotion roiling about in him.

Martin cocked his head at Simon. "You've gone very quiet. Still thinking about the lass you found? Was she another distressed soul you just couldn't pass up?"

"I told you I have no control over that," Simon swore, but kept his other thoughts to himself.

"But distressed she was. When I first noticed her, she was being accosted on the street by her future brother-in-law."

"What do you mean 'accosted'?"

"He'd promised her that she'd never want for attention as a married woman."

The hairs on the back of Martin's neck prickled, and he whirled to see if someone was behind him.

"What's wrong?" Simon puzzled.

"I...I don't know. " Martin glanced at Arthur who hadn't stirred. "My imagination, I guess. Perhaps your friend's brother-in-law reminds me too much of my own brother."

"Except that, unlike Bridgid who wanted your brother, this lass wanted nothing to do with either man."

Martin grimaced. "Do you think she'll follow your advice and try to find a way out?"

Shrugging, Simon answered, "Who knows? I hope so. She seemed to have spirit, but it may cost her dearly. I wish I knew what became of her; I've thought of her often since we met."

"Maybe you can ask around the next time you're in Glasgow. What was her name?"

Simon looked sheepish. "I'd like to tell you, but I don't know. I called her Arabella after a character in a play. She seemed to like it–made her laugh, in fact."

"Perhaps she needed the laugh more than you needed to know her name," Martin concluded. "Simon, when do you expect we'll arrive at your home?"

"Tomorrow assuming the weather remains good. Are you looking forward to meeting Gram?"

"I am, though I admit to being a bit nervous."

"God's life, why?"

"Because, according to you, she loved my grandfather dearly. Except for Meriel and my mother, I've never met anyone else who felt anything but fear or grudging respect for Hugh."

Simon scratched his head. "I'm more concerned about how she's going to react to you. It might be quite a shock for her to see you–Hugh reincarnated."

"I hadn't considered that." Martin rubbed Arthur's ears. "She's not frail is she?"

"Good Lord, no. But then I haven't seen her in nearly five years." Simon shook his pale curls and dismissed the concern with, "We'll have to be careful how we break the news to her, that's all. And we'd better get some sleep," he glanced meaningfully at Martin, "because we have a long day ahead."

Martin placed his palm over his heart and promised, "I'll try my best." As they settled again, Martin leaned on his elbow. "Thanks for listening, Simon."

Simon twisted his head to look at his cousin. "I'd like to hear more sometime. If you love her, I'm sure I'd like her–even if she is misguided."

"Misguided?" Martin puzzled.

"Aye. She chose some lout over my cousin didn't she? I call that misguided." Martin chuckled as he lay back and Simon pronounced, "Good to hear you haven't lost your sense of humor, lad."

The millinery was unlocked when Fia arrived with Kate and she offered up a silent prayer of thanks when Alayne, true to her word, appeared fully recovered. "Good morning, Alayne," Kate addressed her daughter-in-law briskly.

"Kate, I'm surprised to see you so early. Is there a problem?" Alayne's questioning gaze shifted to Fia.

Fia smiled her greeting as Kate responded, "Nothing's wrong. I just thought this would be a good day for you to show Fia the Market. I want to work on the books, do a few other things here, so I can mind the shop while you two are out."

"That's a splendid idea," Alayne beamed, "an outing will do us good. We won't often have the chance to go together."

"No, not often," Kate agreed. "So you two run along, take whatever time you need; you have the list I gave you yesterday." Minutes later, the young women were enjoying the mild July morning as they ambled off High Street toward the Market.

"You haven't had a chance to see much of the town have you?" Alayne asked.

"No, but before you start pointing out all the sights, tell me that you're really fine and you don't just look it," Fia begged.

Alayne linked her arm through Fia's. "I swear, Fia, I'm completely well. I promise to catch the next headache before it gets to that stage."

"How?" Fia demanded. "You were totally incapacitated when I found you."

"By doing the same thing you did for me."

Puzzled, Fia asked, "Do you mean cold compresses?"

Alayne hesitated. "If I have no choice but, if I do, it's a bit more drastic than that. Same principle though."

Fia stopped abruptly and faced Alayne. "Please don't speak in riddles, you'll give *me* a headache. Are you going to tell me or not?"

Alayne's eyebrows arched in surprise. "Why is it so important?"

"It's important," Fia replied patiently, "because I saw what this headache does to you. I haven't a clue how quickly it comes over you, but I have to tell you, Alayne, it's frightening. If you need help again, I want to know what the best thing to do is."

Almost green in the sunlight, Alayne's eyes searched Fia's serious ones. Quietly, she apologized, "I didn't realize it was so bad from your perspective. Let's walk, Fia, and I'll tell you what I do." They picked up their pace and Alayne continued, "Southwest of town, about twenty minutes on horseback, there's a small glen where I played as a child. A burn runs through it and, at one point, there's a rock outcrop and small waterfall–just high enough for me to stand under up to here." She touched her collar bone. "I stay in the water until the knot in my neck disappears. It works quickly. Of course, if I don't have access to one of Kate's horses, I resort to water, or ice during the cold months." She laughed. "Fia, your mouth's open."

Fia was stunned. "Are you mad? You could catch your death doing that."

Alayne shrugged. "It works. It's much worse if I don't do it and the headache catches me. Besides," she dropped her voice to a whisper, "it's not the most bizarre thing I've ever done."

Fia stared at Alayne with a sudden new appreciation for her mettle. "I bet it's not. Sometime, you'll have to tell me."

"Aye, another time," Alayne promised. "Oh, Fia, I have a wonderful idea. Sunday, after services at the kirk, I'll take you out there. We'll take some food and make an afternoon of it. Kate will lend me a horse, I'm sure, and yours must need exercise."

"I think we should do it," Fia agreed enthusiastically. "It'll be good to ride Barley; the stable lad is on him more often than me."

"Good! Now, being out like this really is a treat–we should make the most of it."

They stood in the center of the lane in the shadow of the Cross that identified the Inverness Market and surveyed the scene before them. The street broadened down toward the river so that the rows of shops which lined it on either side framed the actual Market. From where she stood, Fia could see women with flat trays of goods, carts with awnings protecting everything from fish and vegetables to tools and herbs, and old women with nosegays made from heather and wildflowers filling baskets held in the crooks of their arms. As the flower-sellers walked, hawking their sweet-smelling wares, they spun wool or linen threads onto spindles never squandering a moment in which they could do something useful. Being a clear, painfully sunny morning, the Market was crowded and extremely noisy. There were dogs running loose with the children, and other dogs trying to keep their small flocks of sheep together amidst the chaos. Beyond this commotion, merchants who owned the shops fringing the street tried to compete by having young boys call to passersby about the wares inside.

Alayne took Fia to all of her trusted merchants and vendors and checked several new ones to see if there were better bargains or quality to be had. By the time their outing was ending, Fia was exhausted. "I'll never keep all these merchants straight." she cried, dodging a juggler. "Which vender has the beautiful silks, which one the sturdiest broadcloth; who makes and sells the finest threads...the lace dealer. My head is spinning."

"Oh, in time you'll sort them out." Alayne encouraged. "I'll help, don't worry." She glanced around to get her bearings. "There's one more stop I want to make. I always visit the printer's to see what the news is from America."

"Is it because your family's there?"

"That's why I went at first. I think sometimes that I'd like to go there–so many people I know have emigrated. And I'd like to see how my brothers and sister have grown. The youngest is twelve now." Her eyes danced, speculating on what they might be like.

"Do you miss them?" Fia asked.

"Now and then. They've been gone quite a while." Alayne glanced at her companion. "You never had brothers or sisters did you?"

Fia shook her head. "I always thought it would have been nice."

"Well, I'll tell you, Fia. Having you here is a bit like having a sister. Sisters share confidences, protect each other, are happy when good things happen to the other and feel pain when bad things happen."

"We've already done a good bit of that haven't we?"

"Aye. Of course, it helps when the sisters like each other." Alayne laughed her throaty laugh. "Come...to the printer."

Fia sat propped up, knees tucked under her chin, a lone candle burning steadily beside the bed. For hours, she'd been trying to sleep with no success. She thought about Alayne who seemed very brave and strong and independent–traits Fia admired. If she'd ever had such qualities herself, they seemed to have vanished in the sanctuary of Kate Matheson's home. She admired Alayne's ability to cope with her problems, to take setbacks in stride, but not let them rule her life. If nothing else, she found acceptable compromises to tide her over until ready to take on the next obstacle. In Fia's weary mind, she paled in comparison to Muir's wife. "Other people always have to get me out of scrapes and bad situations." She bemoaned, "Look at me now, I'm in hiding. Except for today, I've gone from Aunt Kate's, to the shop or the kirk–no farther. And, if I should forget to be cautious, Douglas reminds me in his letters, or Aunt Kate does." Fia shut her eyes hoping the sound of the rain spitting against the window would calm her. She ached for the comfort of Martin's embrace, knowing she had no right to be in his arms. The fact that she didn't deepened her despondency. She was annoyed that she wanted to turn to someone else for help–even Martin. He'd saved her from certain death when he found her and took her in; Simon MacLaren had given her the push to do what she had to for self-preservation. Douglas had helped her escape the chains of wedlock, and Murdoch had seen her safely to refuge with Aunt Kate.

Fia tossed the blankets aside, leapt from bed, and stood with her fingers gripping the window sill. She shook her head in denial. Surely things would look better in the morning. Her heart told her she'd taken what charge of her destiny she could. She hadn't been in Inverness long enough to know what direction her life would take next. Alayne had been living with her problem for nearly four years. Her self-assurance and confidence in her own abilities were part of that. "Her past haunts her just as mine haunts me. I just need to be patient; I need time, that's all." Fia had let the night confuse her with its empty, silent and gray hours. And, thinking back, she acknowledged the source of her sleeplessness. During the trip to Market, each time she looked at carders, people spinning yarn, selling dyed wool, or herbs and potions, Martin was beside her. She saw him sitting on the bench of his loom as clearly as the kiss he'd taken in payment for his medical services still burned her lips in memory. Rivulets of rain traced their path down the window pane as tears followed their course down Fia's cheeks. Would thoughts of Martin ever stop their nagging?

Two days later, Alayne and Fia approached Kate with their plan for an outing.

"I don't think it's a good idea, girls; the answer is no." Kate rose from the dining table.

Alayne's jaw dropped. "Why? You've never denied my request to ride before."

Kate wouldn't look at her daughter-in-law. "It would be unseemly on the Sabbath."

Arms crossed and eyes blazing green, Alayne forced calm into her voice. "I've been riding on the Sabbath before and it's never been a problem. What's the real reason," she challenged.

"The reason," Kate snapped, "is that you don't have horrible people hunting you. Fia does."

"But Aunt Kate," Fia stepped between the two women, "I can't stay inside forever. I want to live a normal life."

"Oh really?" Kate's eyebrows shot up. "And have you considered that you could be putting Alayne at risk by riding all over the country so you can feel like your life is 'normal'?"

Fia faltered and glanced at Alayne who chastised, "Don't do that to her, Kate. It's not fair to make her feel guilty and you know it."

Recovering her wits, Fia asked, "How is this different than Alayne showing me the Market on Wednesday?"

"There are plenty of people at Market who could help if–"

"Alayne is still at risk when she's with me," Fia persisted. "How is this different?"

Kate's mouth opened but no sound came out. She looked from one to the other, finally blurting, "I don't want anything to happen to either of you!"

Fia covered Kate's hands with her own. "Nothing will. But, Aunt Kate, I can't let those monsters make me a prisoner in this house or in the shop."

"Besides," Alayne added, "Fia can take some precautions, like she did when she came here. You know, disguise herself."

Kate's normally generous mouth was small, puckered with doubt. "Are you sure? I really think–"

"I'm sure," Fia comforted.

"As I am," Alayne echoed.

With an enormous, noisy sigh, Kate's shoulders slumped. "All right," she said meekly. "But you'd better come home safe or I'll never forgive you for siding against me like this."

The friends hugged her quickly, smothering their excitement for Kate's sake. After all, her concerns were not unfounded. But when Kate left the room, Alayne danced with glee all the way to the front door. "Sunday out; how delicious." She picked up her capuchin. "I'm going back to the shop. I don't think I should try Kate's patience any more tonight by staying here."

"Alayne, wait. I meant to mention earlier that I'm going to have to work late a few nights if I'm ever going to finish my new dress. I hope that's not a problem."

"No problem. Do you want help?"

Fia shook her head. "I just want to make sure I won't be in your way."

Alayne snickered. "I'll never hear you, you're so quiet in the workroom. Come any time."

"Are you sure?"

"Aye, any time at all. Just don't wake me up." Alayne waved goodbye, tossed her strawberry tresses, and disappeared into the limpid evening light.

For the next half-hour, Fia tried to read but, thrilled at the prospect of riding again, she couldn't concentrate. "I need something to do," she muttered.

Kate looked up from her needlework. "Did you say something, dear?"

"Aye, I can't seem to keep my mind on this book. It's still early and I'm too fidgety to read."

"Early?" Kate chuckled, "Why it's nearly eight-thirty."

"That's early enough," Fia said. "I'm going over to the shop and work on my dress."

Kate's hands dropped into her lap in exasperation. "What's gotten into you, Fia? First the outing with Alayne and now this."

Rising, Fia answered, "I'm restless, Aunt Kate. I don't expect you to understand completely, but I've been running and hiding for weeks. I've got all this energy eating at me and I thought I'd put it to good use on my new dress. I won't work on my own clothes during shop hours."

Kate looked wounded. "I thought you were happy living here."

Astonished, Fia stared at her aunt. "I never said I was unhappy, Aunt Kate. On the contrary, I'm very grateful and I enjoy your company. Haven't you ever felt uneasy and restless?"

Dropping her gaze, Kate mumbled, "I suppose so."

"I just need something to keep my hands busy." Fia dropped to her knees beside Kate's chair. "Aunt Kate, have I done something to make you think I'm unhappy?"

Kate's lip quivered slightly, but she remained dry-eyed. "No. It's just that having you here, reminds me of how lonely I am when you aren't around. I don't like living alone," she admitted. "I had gotten used to it, but I hate it."

"Would you prefer that I stay this evening?" Fia offered. If it would ease her aunt's loneliness, it was the least she could do; Kate had been kind and loving to her.

Sniffing, Kate shook her head and flashed a shaky smile. "No, dear, you run along. It's not like you won't be home later. You go on, but be careful."

Fia kissed Kate's cheek. Thank you, Aunt Kate."

It was well after ten o'clock when Fia lay her needle aside and stretched stiffly. "That's enough for tonight," she yawned as she admired her handiwork. The dress was coming along nicely. She'd chosen a soft bluish-gray broadcloth and planned a white quilted petticoat on which she intended to embroider a sprinkling of bluebonnet blossoms. As she imagined what the finished ensemble would look like, Fia noticed again that the color was very similar to that of the shirt she'd sewn for Martin. Closing her eyes she saw herself again measuring the cloth, feeling the warmth of his hard chest beneath her fingers, seeing the thin silvery scar from Culloden below his ribs, and remembered sadly that he'd reminded her she'd have to leave him. She wished she could cry enough tears to stop the hurt, but she doubted that many tears existed. Instead she rose, snuffed the candles and picked up her capuchin. Reaching for the door, Fia snatched her hand away as she realized the door was opening. Quickly, she flattened herself against the wall on the far side of a storage cupboard and, heart pounding like cannon-fire, Fia held her breath. Enough light seeped in to define a smallish man. He paused, head turning from side to side as his eyes adjusted to the interior light. Fia's throat tightened. For a moment, she considered throwing herself at the intruder then running. But Alayne was sleeping upstairs; Fia wouldn't leave her alone and vulnerable.

Without looking behind him, the trespasser swung the door closed, fumbled for, found and lit a candle. He raised it high, casting ominous shadows around the small workroom.

Fia's hand touched and closed around an ivory-topped walking stick which had been set aside for a customer. Quietly raising it above her head, she stepped forward to strike just as the man whirled and saw her. He cried out and the candle thudded to the floor cloaking them in darkness once more. Fia lowered the cane and, angry from fright, railed, "Alayne Matheson, what in God's name are you doing? I could have killed you!"

When Alayne found and relit the candle, she saw that the fury in Fia's eyes matched that in her voice. "You scared me," Alayne countered. "What are you doing here this time of night?"

Fia threw her wrap on the chair. "Working on my dress. Remember, you said anytime would be fine, just not to wake you up. You weren't even up there."

Removing her uncocked felt hat and the pin which held her hair in place, Alayne ran pale fingers through the heavy strands and glared at Fia. "All right, I did say that. I certainly didn't expect you to be here tonight."

"You said 'anytime'," Fia repeated.

"All right, all right," Alayne snapped peevishly, "that's what I said."

"Where on earth would you go dressed in breeches and frock coat?"

Alayne nearly growled, "Well, if it isn't 'little Kate'. Stop badgering me! I have every right to do whatever suits me."

If Alayne had hit her, Fia didn't think it would have hurt more. She had apparently stumbled onto forbidden ground. She had to respect Alayne's wishes. With a deep breath, she steadied her voice. "You're angry because I caught you. Don't worry, I won't ask about it again." Snatching up her wrap once more, Fia finished, "I'll be here as usual tomorrow morning."

The misty air stung her eyes even as it soothed her heated face. What was wrong with Alayne, Fia wondered. She realized that part of their anger with each other was because they'd each received a dreadful fright. But what of their friendship? If it was going to be conditional, Fia wanted to know what those conditions were. Her feelings bruised, she shuddered her disappointed. Alayne's friendship was important to her. Fia was wondering what it meant to Alayne when she heard light, fast footsteps behind her. She turned just as Alayne caught up with her and threw her arms around Fia's neck, tears streaming down her face.

"Don't go yet," she pleaded. "Don't be angry, please. Come back and talk to me. I didn't mean what I said."

"I wasn't being nosy, I just want to understand," Fia choked through her own tears.

"I know. Please come back."

Fia pried Alayne's arms from her neck and steered her back toward the shop where Fia suggested a glass of claret. Alayne was shaking badly and needed something to steady her. Upstairs, Fia poked the embers back to a small blaze, just enough to take away the night chill. Then she poured Alayne some wine and watched as her friend downed the glass then crept closer to the fire for comfort. Fia handed Alayne a blanket, which she clutched tightly, and sat facing her friend—waiting and worrying. This was a side of Alayne she'd never seen.

Out of the silence, Alayne's voice was small. "It's a long story."

"I have time," Fia assured.

"Could I have more claret?" Fia refilled the glass and handed it to Alayne, who set it down untouched. "This is about Muir," she began. "When he disappeared, I was certain he'd been spirited away by the King's Navy. Kate may have told you, he spent a great deal of time on the docks, drinking, gambling...whoring." She glanced up and caught the surprise on Fia's face. "You didn't know about the women, did you? No, I guess she wouldn't have mentioned it."

Fia shook her head. "No, I didn't know, I'm sorry."

"Don't be sorry, there was a reason for it. About four months after we were married, Muir came home disgustingly drunk, smelly...and amorous. I refused him and he tried to force me to perform my wifely 'duty'. That was the last time he tried. I cracked him over the head with a bottle of," she giggled, "claret. He bled like a pig. Kate heard the commotion and came running only to see her precious son bloody, filthy and stinking with his breeches around his ankles, and my shift shredded and my breasts covered with welts where he clawed me."

Fia cringed, Andrew's merciless beating flooding her memory, bringing bile into her throat. Swallowing hard, she forced herself to concentrate on what Alayne was saying.

"He never came to me after that night. He'd already found willing women who worked cheap to take my place." Alayne stopped. Looking suddenly embarrassed, she murmured, "Fia, I didn't intend to...this isn't what I was going to tell you."

"It's all right," Fia reassured her. "I'm glad you told me; it will help me put all this in perspective."

"Are you sure? He's your cousin, after all."

"He's your husband. I only knew him as a child. I hate that he was cruel to you; I wish I could undo that for your sake."

Alayne's smile wavered. "Thank you, I appreciate the thought."

"But why this?" Fia's hand swept wide indicating Alayne's appearance.

"It was but a few weeks after that night that Muir didn't come home. Not even Kate thought anything of it for a few days. Then we both became concerned and started asking around. Muir was tall but lean, not burly. I didn't think he'd stand a chance against anyone who wanted to carry him off...or do him in." Alayne looked apologetic. "He'd passed many personal notes that he couldn't make good on. Anyway, I was angry at being left with no husband, such as he was, and no freedom. I had nothing but a possessive mother-in-law who was, and still is, incapable of having an objective conversation about her son."

"He was her life for years," Fia reminded gently, "all she had."

"I know. I don't blame her for that. But, for a long time, Kate couldn't deal with me as a separate person." Alayne shook her head ruefully. "It's still difficult at times. Well, for my sake and for Kate's, I had to try to find out what became of Muir. And I couldn't go to the quay at night–the only time the people he gambled and drank with were around."

"You pretend to be a man so you can ask questions on the quay?" Fia interrupted, incredulous.

She nodded. "I used to go down whenever a new ship arrived in case he'd just run off. I only go now when the Navy ties up." Alayne hesitated. "At first, I was terrified and tried not to draw attention to myself. I never stay long. Over time, I've minimized the risks. And if I hear the slightest rumor that the King's recruiters are about, I come home. Let's face it, if they tried to enlist my services for the Navy, I would only have to reveal that I'm not a man at all."

"Aye, then they'd either escort you home, which I think unlikely, or they'd rape you and say they thought you were a whore because no decent woman would be on the quay at night, or dress as a man." Fia declared, eyes flashing. "I don't think you should take that risk. Did it ever occur to you that the danger you put yourself in is not worth finding out what happened to Muir?"

Alayne was startled at Fia's remark and simply said, "Wouldn't you want me to find out?"

"No," Fia spouted, "he hurt you enough, Alayne. The only good that could come from this is if you were to find that you're free of him and can get on with your life."

"By free you mean if he's dead?" Fia nodded and Alayne continued, "I never really wanted him dead Fia, you must believe me."

"I do."

"I know you're right, but this is something I'm driven to do. If I concentrate on the possibility of something horrible happening to me instead of what I'm doing, I'll fail and I'll be discovered."

Fia said, "Did anything unusual happen tonight?

Alayne frowned. "Someone I talked to thought he'd seen Muir about two years ago on a ship in Jamaica. He wasn't sure."

"Two years is a long time, Alayne," Fia said.

"Aye, but it wasn't a Navy ship." Alayne's rueful grin was lopsided. "That means he probably 'disappeared' willingly. I only have a few short months to go, Fia, and I'll be free. I didn't want to hear about Muir from anyone."

"In all this time, is this the first word you've had?" Alayne nodded quickly and Fia saw she was about to break down. "Alayne, if Muir was seen by this man–and the man wasn't sure it was him–if he's been gone so long and never contacted anyone, I wouldn't think he's interested in returning."

"Really?" Alayne sniffed.

"It seems reasonable, don't you think?" Fia encouraged.

"I...I suppose it does."

Fia suddenly changed the subject. "I...hesitate to ask but, do you do anything more outrageous than this? The waterfall cure for your headache now seems completely sane and natural."

A reluctant smirk tugged at Alayne's generous mouth; she sighed gratefully, knowing that Fia understood even if she did not accept her actions. She wiped her eyes on her sleeve. "I can't wait to be free, Fia. There'll be no more quayside visits, no more men's clothes, although they're quite comfortable, and I can look to the future."

Fia kissed Alayne's cheek and stood. "That will be a day I'll gladly help you celebrate. I have to go before Aunt Kate sends someone to look for me." She reached the top of the stairs and looked back. Alayne's hair hung about her shoulders like rivers of flowing honey. In the firelight, she looked content–for the moment. "Alayne, I hope you won't let your experience with Muir keep you from recognizing a truly loving, giving man when he appears."

"You're sure one will?" she joked.

"Quite sure, if you allow yourself to see him. You deserve someone who'll be wonderful to you."

"As do you, Fia."

Chapter Fifteen

Leaving Dingwall before daybreak, Simon led Martin almost due north until they came to the River Carron, then he turned west and followed its course up the strath, gentle hills rising on either side where it cut through, until they rounded a broad bend in the river an hour later. Rain had brought them to Simon's home a day after they'd hoped, but the late July sun blazed warmth on them now. Ahead, past several clumps of birch trees, stretched a small farm. A meadow lay before the snug-looking, lime-washed house, and a neat yard surrounded by stone outbuildings stood behind. Martin observed cattle and sheep dotting the green and purple hills beyond the tidy farm and inclined his head toward them. "Do they belong to your family?"

Simon proudly responded, "Everything to the tops of those hills beyond the river." Simon identified the spot with a nod then pointed to a young man in the yard. "That's my brother, Grant." To Martin, Grant appeared to be made of only arms and legs he was so lanky. Simon's full head of curls were repeated on his brother, but they were a nondescript brown, almost the color of Simon's dun gelding, Devenick. Breaking into a huge smile, Simon added, "And that beauty, is my sister, Mairi."

Martin dutifully moved his gaze to Mairi who stirred a steaming kettle not far from the rear of the house. She was striking with pale, straight hair splayed like a gossamer veil around her shoulders. Even from this distance, Martin detected what looked to be a secretive smile playing at her lips. "Are there any others?" he asked.

"Mairi was the last." Simon turned to Martin and offered, "Don't take this the wrong way, but Mairi's a ravishing tease; you don't need that."

"Simon, it took three years for Fia to come along and crack my shroud of bitterness. If there's ever another lass, it won't be in the foreseeable future." He cocked his head and grinned warmly. "Your sister, delectable as she may be, is safe from me."

"Ah, but are you safe from her, that's the question," Simon beamed in return. "Come, then, I'm anxious to be home!"

As the two men approached the yard, Arthur raced ahead into a gaggle of geese, scattering them honking in all directions.

"You mangy hound," Grant yelled, running toward the commotion. He shrieked, "Get away from—" and stopped short, seeing the horsemen. "Simon! Mairi, Simon's back!"

Simon leapt from his horse before it stopped and embraced Grant who was a head taller, but seemed half Simon's size. "I'm glad you haven't forgotten what your brother looks like." Simon exclaimed.

"And how could I not recognize you of all people? Look at you, Simon. America suits you."

"And you, Grant, you've grown so tall. I guess my days of tossing you into the Carron to cool down that temper of yours are over." The two laughed heartily until Simon was spun from Grant's grasp by his sister. Her arms locked so tightly around Simon's neck, they nearly severed his head from his shoulders.

"Simon, where have you been for so long? Why didn't you send word you were coming?" She laid her velvety cheek against his stubbly one and sighed contentedly. Suddenly she pulled back and flashed, "When was the last time you shaved?"

"Promise me you haven't turned into a nag." Simon ducked quickly, not quite missing the swipe of her hand across the top of his head.

"That's for your impertinence, big brother," she said haughtily, trying to stifle a grin.

Arms circling her tiny waist, Simon whirled her around exclaiming, "You haven't changed a bit."

Grant grumbled, "That's not what the Strathcarron lads would say...ow!" Grant gingerly rubbed the spot where Mairi's elbow stabbed his ribs.

"You're crude and impudent and jealous," she hissed, glaring.

Bemused by their terse exchange, Simon held up his hands to hush them. "Enough. You can tell me about this later. Look, I've brought a friend. Where is everyone?"

For the first time, Grant and Mairi really looked at their visitor, saying nothing as they scrutinized him. Grant found his tongue first responding, "They're around," and to Martin grumbled, "Your dog?"

"Aye, I apologize about the geese. Arthur seldom sees any and always forgets his manners when he does." Martin glanced around and, spotting the dog, whistled.

"He minds well enough now," Grant observed coolly as the dog sat at Odhar's side.

"Arthur has a mind of his own," Simon volunteered. "Mairi, what have you to say?"

Mairi approached slowly as Martin dismounted. Her clear, pale eyes only left his face to admire the lean strength apparent in his movements. Mairi dipped her curtsey to which Martin bowed in return. "What a pleasure to have a friend of Simon's stay with us. If there's anything I can do to help you feel welcome, I'd be delighted."

Simon rolled his eyes. The years of practice had only polished Mairi's technique. He was glad he'd warned Martin for he could see Mairi was already smitten with the idea of a new conquest. He toyed with telling her straight away who Martin was but he wanted to tell Gram first. After all, her's was the biggest risk in seeing Martin, and Simon couldn't predict how she would react. He stepped up, pried Mairi's hand from Martin's arm, where it now lingered, and grimaced, "That's enough, Mairi." He raised brows to Martin. "See?"

"Simon? Is that you son?" Peering around Mairi, Simon recognized his mother's scurrying figure, his father close on her heels. She wrapped her son in a huge hug while his father heartily pounded his back in welcome. When the kisses and exclamations began to subside, Simon said, "I've brought someone to meet you," and swiveled only to see Mairi slip her arm through Martin's and eye Simon triumphantly. Martin shifted his weight away from Mairi's body, but the lass simply leaned in and gazed at him appreciatively. "Mam, if you don't tell Mairi to leave Martin alone," Simon began then said, "oh, never mind. Let me start over. Where's Gram?"

"In the house," his father replied.

"She has to be here," Simon pronounced. "This has to be done just right."

"What are you going on about, son?" asked Simon's mother.

Martin interjected, "Simon is concerned that your mother may find meeting me to be...difficult."

Lachlan MacLaren studied the stranger. "Why should it bother..." His eyes narrowed in dawning recognition and his wife stifled a gasp of dismay as she, too, realized their visitor's identity. "Martin," Lachlan hissed. "You're Martin Ross, Hugh's grandson."

Mairi's arm fell from Martin's and, as she hastily withdrew to stand behind Grant, Martin felt a crushing sadness.

Lachlan glowered at his eldest son. "What were you thinking, Simon?"

Bristling at his father's rebuke, Simon answered, "I was thinking that I would very much like Martin to meet my family and his grandfather's sister. What I didn't think," Simon spat, "was that Martin would receive such a disgraceful welcome."

Martin submitted, "Simon, it's all right. Mr. MacLaren, Mistress, I understand your...reluctance to have me visit your home."

"You murdered your family," Grant blurted.

Furious, Simon cuffed his brother's ear. "By God, I'll pitch you in the Carron yet if you don't shut your mouth. Martin committed no crime. With my own ears I heard his brother confess that he, not Martin, was to blame." Simon glared at Grant. "You're too young to remember Hugh Stewart. I remember him as an honest man, loyal to what he believed in–loyal to the death. He worshiped his grandson and believed in Martin's strength of character; it made a deep impression on me. That's why I searched for Martin–"

"*Searched* for him?" his father questioned.

"Aye, so that I could tell him all know now of his innocence." Simon turned to the others. "Then I convinced him to come meet you because he's been denied the warmth of a loving family too long. I'd hoped there was enough love amongst you to include him." Only then did Simon feel the tug of Martin's restraining hand on his arm.

"Simon, they had no way of knowing." But Simon saw the sorrow in Martin's eyes and ached that his good intentions had caused his cousin further grief.

"He's right, son, we...we didn't know," his father reiterated.

"You should have put more faith in my judgment than you did." Temper simmering, his own feelings wounded as well, Simon was unwilling to let them atone so easily.

"It was a mistake for me to come," Martin said gathering Odhar's reins. "I lost one family, I won't damage another."

"Please, Martin," Jessie MacLaren began her plea, but Martin interrupted.

"I don't blame you for reacting as you did, believe me. This last week, while I've been enjoying Simon's company, I forgot how others see me. And because I forgot, you're fighting amongst yourselves and with a son you haven't seen in five years. That's the last thing I wanted; you can mend these rifts easier if I'm not here." Martin mounted Odhar, but Simon grabbed the bridle.

"Stay and meet Gram," Simon urged vehemently.

Martin shook his head. "No, this is better for all, Simon. I'll go back to Dingwall. Come see me in a few days; I'll take supper at the inn so you'll know where to find me." He reached down and grasped Simon's arm. "Thank you for giving my life back to me."

"Don't go, Martin," Simon entreated. "This is my fault; I handled it badly and caused this mess."

"You did not, Simon, you tried to help," Martin replied. "I just think it's best I be on my way." He straightened to leave, but stopped, staring over their heads at a slight figure crossing the yard behind the tense group. She moved unhesitatingly through her family members to stand next to Simon whose cheek she kissed warmly and received a bone-crushing hug in return. Her graying hair still held remnants of copper and, staring into eyes much like his own–and exactly like Hugh's–Martin dismounted.

The strength of her voice surprised him. "Martin Ross. I've waited many a year to meet you, lad." Eleanor MacLaren held open her arms and Martin nearly stumbled in his haste to feel them around him.

In the silence that accompanied their embrace, Jessie dabbed at her eyes with the corner of her apron. Simon wrapped his arm around her shoulders; his own eyes smarting from tears, and wondered what he would do if his family were suddenly stripped from him. At the thought, he shuddered violently and held his mother closer, his eyes darting from his father to Grant, to Mairi, and back to his cousin.

Eleanor finally held Martin away, studying his clear brown eyes and lazy copper curls. She patted his bearded cheek with fondness springing from familiarity. "Aye, you do look like my brother though, I think, a wee bit more handsome." She beamed at the speechless man then pivoted to face her kin. "Now, what's this uproar about? Surely you can extend hospitality to your own flesh and blood."

Lachlan stepped forward, "It was a misunderstanding, Mam, one I hope Martin will allow us to put behind us." He addressed Martin, "We would ask your forgiveness, man."

Not hesitating, Martin extended his hand which Lachlan took. "There's nothing to forgive."

"Then you'll stay?" Jessie asked hopefully.

Glimpsing the still cowering Mairi, Martin decided that if his presence in her home disturbed her, he had no business there. "It's a gracious offer, but no. Arthur and I are used to being on our own, and I think you should have time to get used to thinking of me as a cousin, not a murderer."

"Now look here, Martin," Simon began, but was interrupted by his grandmother.

"This subject is not open for debate; you'll stay, lad. If you'd be more comfortable in the byre with the animals, and away from the lot of us, so be it. But, I will not let you leave before we have the chance to become acquainted."

Lachlan looked relieved and chuckled self-consciously, "My mother has spoken."

"And no one, defies Eleanor," Jessie stated taking Martin's arm. She barked orders over her shoulder, "Grant, stable the horses. Mairi close you mouth–it's hanging open–and finish your chores. Martin," she said smiling from behind brilliant blue eyes, "welcome to our home. It was a rough beginning but, we'll try to make the rest of your stay more pleasant."

Mairi stroked her ginger tabby cat while guardedly watching the newcomer who sat with her brothers at Gram's feet. Her feelings were jumbled. Until today, they'd been ashamed to utter the name Martin Ross. When the family first received news of the tragedy, she and Grant had spent hours speculating about the fiend their cousin must be to have murdered his family. Grant thought maybe he took more after Gram's brother than anyone realized. He'd often whispered to Mairi tales of Hugh, the fierce warrior, a cruel-tempered man who'd broken Gram's heart. He made her swear not to discuss Hugh Stewart around Gram and, since he had died when Mairi was toddling about, she had no memory of the man. Grant's tales were all she knew of him. Mairi sighed quietly and focused on her cat. Through supper and now into the late evening, she listened to Martin and the family conversation. He didn't fit the monstrous picture she'd carried of him. In fact, he seemed almost gentle. His looks were appealing, his voice deep and resonant, his manner more animated as the evening wore on and he grew more comfortable with the family. Mairi liked what she saw–at least, she thought she did.

"And what might you be thinking?" Mairi hadn't noticed Simon leaving Gram's circle of admirers and his question startled her into giving a truthful answer.

"That Martin is not the ogre I'd imagined."

Simon gnawed his lip. "Are you thinking he's attractive or do you simply find him morbidly fascinating?" Mairi glared peevishly at him and Simon chided gently, "You behaved childishly today hiding behind Grant; and you've spent the night staring at Martin from across the room. Have pity, Mairi, he feels awkward enough. He's not a leper, don't treat him like one."

"Until a few hours ago, he was a killer," she whispered defensively.

"You know better now but have still stayed by yourself in the corner all night. Right or wrong, I'll offer you some brotherly advice. If you by chance find yourself drawn to him for whatever reason, don't mistake him for one of your simple, doting, doe-eyed farm lads. Martin's life in recent years has been unimaginably hard: his dignity and good name were stolen. He's a complex, cautious man and is just getting used to the fact that there's no price on his head."

Mairi was silent, trying to absorb what Simon was saying, then murmured, "It sounds to me like he might benefit from some affection and tenderness."

"You've a soft heart, Mairi, and you can offer those things to Martin–as a sister." Mairi nodded absently and Simon squeezed her hand.

As midnight approached, Mairi surprised Martin by offering to show him where he could bed down. With a lanthorn, she led the way to a warm corner of the byre where she helped him arrange some clean straw and offered a blanket.

"Thank you, Mairi, but I have Hugh's plaid."

"You'll have no fire tonight for extra warmth. I'll leave the blanket in case you change your mind."

"Maybe you're right." There was an awkward silence as Mairi sought the right words. She ran her hand along the worn beam at the edge of Martin's stall.

"Simon tells me I owe you an apology; I've been rude," she admitted.

"Simon is trying to smooth my way which, I've discovered, is typical of Simon. He's a truly good person. But, you don't need to tell me you're sorry for anything. My arrival shocked everyone."

"Except Gram," Mairi allowed.

"Aye, but does anything shock your grandmother?"

Mairi dug her toe into the straw. "Not that I ever saw. Martin, I am sorry. I should have realized myself that an apology was in order."

Martin smiled ruefully. "I'm not good at making or accepting apologies. Let's say no more about it. Tomorrow, we can start over...if you'd like." A dazzling smile graced her face and he could see why Simon had warned him about her. Mairi was charming in her directness and impulsive behavior. He imagined she caused fits among her suitors.

"Good night, Martin. I'm glad you're here." She left the glowing lanthorn, closing the door behind her.

Martin surveyed the small building, but saw little from the dim light the lanthorn provided: stone walls, six stalls with horses, including Odhar, one empty, and one for him. Arthur settled in noisily as Martin spread his plaid, then snuffed the lamp. The warmth and smell of the horses reminded him vividly of the day he'd driven Fia from his croft. He'd only gotten her out of the cold by inviting her into Odhar's byre and held her hand as they'd returned to his home. He twisted onto his side, the ache of loneliness tormenting him, the pressure of his desire unsettling.

Where was Fia? Did she ever long for him or even think about him? Martin squeezed shut his eyes to banish his thoughts. Tonight, please God, he didn't want to dream horrible dreams. He focused instead on becoming better acquainted with Simon's family. And Eleanor MacLaren... she was everything he might have expected of Hugh's sister. He was grateful for her easy acceptance and was already completely enchanted.

Alongside Alayne's mount, Barley pitched clumps of mud high in the air as he thundered down the road, and Fia's exhilarated laughter tore from her and was lost in their wake. The churning muscles of the animal, the urgent rhythm of its hooves enthralled Fia. She wanted the steed to run until they both dropped from exhaustion, but they were fast approaching the grove of beech and oak Alayne had told her to look for and knew they would soon rein in. Indeed, Alayne slowed her horse's pace considerably and called, "It's right through here." Ducking a low hanging limb, they descended a slope and rounded another into a miniature strath traversed by Alayne's burn. A short distance upstream was the little waterfall that emptied into a shallow pool rimmed by mossy banks that gave way shortly to the heath-covered rise of yet another hill.

"Alayne, what an enchanting place. I would have never expected to find such a haven so close to the road."

"I'd have been disappointed if you hadn't loved it."

Fia dismounted and gazed around in wonder. "How could I not think this splendid? Thank you for sharing it with me."

Alayne came over and linked her arm through Fia's. "If I can't share this spot with my dearest friend, then who?"

The day had grown hot enough that Fia joined Alayne in the burn. The water was cold but, with some splashing around, they soon warmed up and later lay in the sun, their shifts and hair drying in its heat. They munched gingerbread and cheese biscuits, talked and lazed into the afternoon.

"This is such a treat," Alayne sighed. "Normally, when I come here it's for one of those blasted headaches. It's rare when I can just enjoy the day."

Turning onto her stomach, Fia rested her chin on the back of her hand. "If we are very sweet to Aunt Kate, maybe we can change that," she suggested. Alayne grunted doubtfully but Fia continued, "Well, we should at least try."

"Agreed," Alayne spouted. "Still, let's not spend much effort on it just yet. Tomorrow is the first of August and within two weeks we should be busier than you can imagine at the shop."

Fia lifted her head, "Why?"

"Because the annual hunt balls are coming up in early autumn and before you know it, Hogmanny will be upon us. There will be lots of new clothes to make and refurbishing of last year's fashions to be done. Besides," Alayne added wrinkling her nose in disappointment, "by the time we get another free day, the weather won't be warm enough to play in the water."

"There must be other things we could do if we had an opportunity." Fia hesitated, grasping for an idea. "I know," she finally declared, "we could attend a play.

"A play?" Alayne gaped. "I've never been to a play in my life."

"Neither have I," Fia confided cheerily. "Why should that stop us? I think it would be fun."

Alayne shook her head. "Kate wouldn't allow it."

Fia laughed long and hard finally managing to gasp, "Since...since when has that stopped *you*? Besides, we could always ask Aunt Kate to accompany us."

"In that case, I'd rather not go!" Alayne declared, trying to stifle a grin. She began pulling on the rest of her clothes and Fia followed suit.

"Aunt Kate's not that unrelenting. We're here aren't we?"

"We had to work for it." Alayne added, "I'll tell you what would help. Kate needs a man in her life–and I don't mean some nice old fellow whose bed she heats with warm bricks."

Fia opened her mouth to respond, but could think of nothing to disagree with. A man in Aunt Kate's life would be nice–help keep her from brooding about Muir, which Fia suspected she did too much considering how long he'd been gone. But, traveling back to Inverness, her mind churned around Alayne's statement until she could stand it no longer and blurted, "Alayne, may I ask you something personal?"

Alayne answered, "Of course, what is it?"

"Is...is passion...with a man that you love...?"

"Exciting," Alayne supplied then continued, "satisfying, remarkable, fulfilling? It can be any or all of those things and more, Fia." Alayne halted her horse and studied her companion. "When you aren't in love, it can also be a chore that makes you seethe with resentment."

"It must have been painful when the love disappeared," Fia surmised.

Alayne nodded. "It was at first. I don't remember exactly when everything changed. I've wrestled with the questions why and how the loss of love can make the physical part of marriage so distasteful."

"Have you found any answers?" Fia asked.

"I discovered too late what kind of man Muir really was: selfish, dishonest, and uncaring. And I think what was left when the love died just couldn't make up the difference." Fia's stricken look tugged at Alayne's heart and she knew her friend was thinking of Martin Ross. Attempting to ease Fia's heartache, Alayne added, "I think lovers are responsible for making their love as grand as it can be–in every way. Muir and I, we weren't interested enough. I know it can be different. Perhaps someday...." her voice trailed off then Alayne chuckled ruefully. "Listen to me talk...the expert. Come, Kate will worry if we're much later. Fia," she finished, "your turn will come. I promise."

"It's uncanny," Eleanor said to Simon, seated beside her on the bench behind the house. "Martin is so like my brother, he even carries the same look in his eyes Hugh had after Meriel left him."

"What look is that?" Simon inquired curiously.

"It's hard to describe, dear; half lost...or...haunted and...half dead."

Simon shivered a bit. "Aren't you being a little dramatic, Gram?"

Patting his hand, Eleanor said, "You're the actor in the family, lad. I just tell you what I see."

"Well, I've seen him look sad but, I hadn't noticed any expression I would describe quite the way you just did," Simon admitted, scratching his smooth chin.

"Nor would you because you've never seen it. I assure you, it's there." Eleanor puzzled,"What causes that look in Martin...that sordid business with his wife?"

Simon shook his head. "I doubt it, Gram. That hurt him deeply, made him angry...and there's some bitterness certainly. Knowing as little about Martin as I do, I think I can still safely guess the source of that look. In simple terms, her name is Fia."

Eleanor perked up. "Fia you say? Really, Simon? What can you tell me about her?"

Simon smirked at his grandmother. "I just realized that I come by my penchant for mixing in other people's business quite naturally."

"Oh, so you think you get that deplorable tendency from me, do you?" she chuckled in return.

"I'm positive." Suddenly, Simon turned thoughtful and suggested, "Gram, this cuts to his core–you may want to leave it alone."

"I don't think so, lad. I did great wrong by Martin's grandfather. Perhaps I'm being given the opportunity to make some amends. Now," Eleanor insisted, "are you going to tell me what you know or not?"

With a deep breath, Simon related what little he could and apologized because, "It isn't much. I only learned of Fia a few days before we arrived." Simon focused dreamily on the emerald hillside. "I'll tell you something though, Gram. Someday, I want to be able to look at a woman with the devotion I see in Martin when he speaks of this woman. It's so intense...it's glorious and frightening at the same time."

Eleanor caressed her grandson's angular face with a gnarled hand. "Always, Simon, you've felt things more deeply, more acutely than anyone else. That ability has taken you places and led you to people no one else cared about. That's why you found Martin. His pain reached you."

Smiling indulgently, Simon said, "Gram, now you really are being fanciful. I didn't know Martin except through your brother's eyes–and that was a very long time ago."

Eleanor gently chided, "It was enough to cause you to seek him out. You know I'm right. That's who you are, Simon. I'm very proud to have you as my grandson. And I've no doubt, because of who you are, that you'll find the woman and love you seek. But, you must promise me that you won't let her slip away as Martin did. I never want you to know that kind of anguish!"

"Gram, if I'm fortunate enough to find her, nothing will come between us."

"You two look like conspirators." Grant walked briskly toward them and, without waiting for a response continued, "Martin seems a handy fellow. He fixed the calf right up–some sort of lotion."

Simon sighed. "He's a doctor, Grant. Of course he's 'handy' with a sick calf." He called past Grant as Martin ambled toward them, "You didn't make it drink that witch's brew did you?"

Martin laughed. "No, I felt bad enough for the poor thing." Wiping his hands on a rag, Martin continued, "It's a fairly severe irritation, but it should be fine before long–maybe a week. I flushed the eye with leek and Grant's promised to continue the treatment."

"Splendid." Eleanor smiled. "I'd like it if you sat with me a while, Martin. I believe Simon wanted to spend some time with his brother–and I'd like to spend some with you."

"I'd love to," Martin agreed, brightening.

Taking the hint, Simon rose just as Grant whined, "Can't it wait, Simon? I'd like to stay with Gram."

"You live with Gram. Right now, I want to talk to you. Come, I'll even help you with whatever your next chore is."

Grant grinned demonically. "Mucking out the stalls–you picked a good one."

Wrinkling his nose at the thought, Simon dutifully steered his brother toward the byre. "I'm glad to see you're getting along reasonably well with Martin."

Grant huffed, "It would be easier if everyone didn't treat him like a martyr."

Simon frowned. "I hadn't noticed that anyone does. I think the family is just trying to make up for the rough start when we arrived last week. Mairi has come around," he added hopefully.

"Mairi fawns over anything in breeches between fifteen and the grave," Grant sneered unkindly.

Simon hid his surprise at Grant's bitter tone. He'd always considered Mairi's avid appreciation of the lads one of her most endearing vices. "Aren't you being hard on Mairi, or have I missed something?"

Grant shrugged. "You haven't missed anything. And you said it yourself, she hasn't changed."

Simon decided not to pursue it but said, "Whatever your feelings are about how our sister behaves, don't hold it against Martin. Give it time, Grant. I think you'll enjoy his company."

"I'll reserve judgment, big brother," he snapped peevishly, "if you don't mind." They lapsed into silence, Simon's an uneasy one.

"*Are they close?*" Martin asked gazing after them. "It's difficult to tell."

"They share a brother's love. However, Grant does tend to try one's patience, especially when Simon's home. I believe Grant sees him as competition, odd as that sounds."

"Maybe it's understandable; Simon's very special." Martin paused before asking, "Any idea why Grant dislikes me?"

"He doesn't 'dislike' you, lad, he's a bit jealous, that's all. You've caused quite a stir since you arrived and Grant likes his share of attention–not easy in this family." Eleanor rested her hand on his arm. "You've won over everyone else, even Lachlan."

Martin covered her hand with his and spoke in a vibrant, almost urgent voice, "I can't describe to you how I feel being here among your family."

"It's your family too, Martin, and there's no need to explain," she soothed.

"But, when Simon asked if I wanted to meet you, I'd forgotten Hugh even had a–" He stopped, embarrassed.

"Didn't mention me often, did he," she said, guessing the end of his thought.

"I wasn't thinking when I said that," he apologized.

"Nor should you have to think about what you say with family," she replied firmly. "No harm's been done, Martin." Changing the subject, Eleanor said, "I couldn't be more pleased for you that this ugly matter with your wife turned out as it did."

Martin glanced in the direction of the byre. "If not for Simon, I would still be hiding. I owe him my life."

"You do know that your friendship is all Simon would ever ask in return?"

"Aye, I understand." Martin studied her wrinkled face and smiled. "And I am that, for as long as it suits him."

Eleanor rocked gently on the bench as she thought fondly of these two young men. "I believe," she began finally, "that Simon is the slightest bit envious of you."

"I beg your pardon?" Martin was certain he'd heard her incorrectly–the thought was ludicrous.

"I said envious. Apparently you have found something that Simon greatly desires." Confusion filled Martin's face. "Love, Martin." Martin straightened, his wariness returning, but Eleanor patted his knee reassuringly. "It's all right, lad. Simon told me about Fia."

Momentarily, Martin was speechless then blurted, "Why in God's name would he covet that kind of pain? He must have told you she's married."

"I'm not talking about the reality of your situation. What I'm referring to, Martin, is what you feel for the lass. That is what Simon hopes lies in his future."

"I hope he's smarter about it when his turn comes than I was," Martin vowed earnestly.

In a small voice, Eleanor said, "Well, he promised he'd try." The remark elicited a surprised laugh from Martin. Eleanor asked, "What are you planning to do, lad?"

"Planning to do?" he replied blankly. "About what?"

"Why about Fia, of course."

"I don't understand what you want me to say. Fia is someone else's wife–by choice."

"And you haven't been able to get her out of your thoughts," Eleanor declared.

"I suppose...it'll take time, but it's hardly relevant under the circumstances."

"Martin, if Fia were a mild flirtation, aye, time would take care of it. But she's not a passing fancy, is she?"

"I've been wrong before," Martin replied acidly.

Eleanor spoke sympathetically, "I'm sure you wish meddlers like me would stay out of your affairs, not stir emotions that barely rest as it is. But can you tell me I'm wrong?"

"No," he replied without hesitation. "I can't deny it–still it doesn't change what's happened."

"Neither will just thinking about it. You must take some action for your own peace of mind." When Martin didn't answer, Eleanor continued, "Even if you weren't of my brother's flesh, I'd still be fond of you, Martin, you're kind and gentle and good. That's why I'm interfering, offering you the benefit of my years on this earth. I've done good things–Lachlan and his family–you know about the bad." Martin nodded silently. "When I look at you, lad, I see you suffering as Hugh did ever after Meriel left him. Oh, I know he still saw her, but it wasn't the same. We managed to rend his family in two and I, God forgive me, was party to it. I can't undo what's done, Martin. But I don't want you to walk blindly down that same path, ending up bitter and alone."

"Eleanor, the circumstances are very different. And, if Grandfather was ever bitter, he never showed it to my grandmother or me."

"He never would. Hugh had more than his share of pride," she reminded him sharply, "more than his share."

In that instant, Martin realized that Eleanor was still suffering because Hugh was cast out and she had genuinely grieved over it. Martin hesitated, then confided, "Eleanor, I couldn't swear to you that your brother wasn't bitter, but I *know* he didn't end his days alone."

She waved his statement aside. "Of course not, he was with the rest of Prince Charlie's faithful."

"And with me," he offered soberly. "I was with him when he died, protecting me to the end."

Eleanor stared unmoving as she contemplated the implications of Martin's statement. Unexpectedly, long held tears flooded her cheeks and she rocked in silent agitation.

Beside her on the bench, Martin wrapped his arm around her bony shoulders and held tightly murmuring, "You can rest easy, Eleanor, Hugh was dearly loved and respected. He wasn't alone–ever."

From the well, a bewildered Mairi observed the peculiar scene before her. She motioned to her mother, and Jessie's brow furrowed with concern. In the twenty-seven years she's been married to Lachlan MacLaren, his mother had lived with them. Jessie had never seen her cry. "Wait here, Mairi." Jessie started across the yard in the direction of her mother-in-law, deftly dodging Mairi's cat along the way.

She liked Martin; he was personable and helpful and seemed to appreciate the smallest things done for him. However, if he was upsetting Eleanor, Jessie would not stand for it. By the time she reached them, Martin was offering Eleanor his handkerchief. He stood when he realized Jessie was near. She glanced from him to her mother-in-law. "Mither, what's wrong?"

Shaking her head, Eleanor wiped her eyes, responding, "Jessie, dear, things couldn't be better. Martin has...put my mind at ease over something that has nagged me for sixteen years."

"Then," Jessie prompted gently, "there's no reason for me to be alarmed?"

Eleanor held Jessie's work worn hand against her cheek. "No, daughter, everything's fine. I'm sorry if you were distressed."

"Then...these are tears of happiness." She studied Martin who looked as if he were personally awaiting the verdict on judgment day.

"I would never knowingly harm any of you," he stated emphatically.

"I must ask you to make allowances for my caution, Martin. I haven't known you long and Eleanor is very dear to me."

"You opened your home to me, Jessie. I can only be grateful to you for your kindness," he said.

Clearing her throat, Jessie smiled shakily, "Well, I must get back to the geese." She left them, feeling embarrassed, relieved, and unaccountably content all at once. Now if she could reassure Mairi that her grandmother was fine, and somehow shake Grant from his moodiness, maybe they could stop tip-toeing around this newly found cousin.

Watching Jessie, Martin realized that his arrival had not been easy for her. Eleanor had usurped Jessie's control over the household by daring them to accept him, and his relationship with her younger son was strained at best.

Eleanor again commanded his attention. "Martin, I want to say something to you and I want you to listen," she dabbed her eyes. "I don't want you to spend your days alone. Take some action that will ease your mind about Fia and let you get on with the business of living a full life. Do it soon. Your good name's been restored, you're young, and you have the gift of healing. You deserve happiness. Now, I'll say no more on the subject." She rose stiffly. "Excuse me, Martin, even an old woman like me has work to do." He bent to receive her kiss on his cheek. "Thank you. I can't remember the last time I so enjoyed a conversation."

The morning was gray and too brisk for mid-August. Martin sat on the bench by the house and carded wool, preparing it to be spun; Simon sat nearby oiling the wagon harness. "Simon, I need to ask you something."

Without looking up from his task, Simon replied, "Sounds serious."

"I hope not, it's your father. Is there something... physically wrong with him?"

Hand stopping in mid-stroke, Simon cast a sidelong glance at Martin. "Not that I'm aware of, why? What have you noticed?"

"Nothing specific," Martin hurriedly assured, "it's his behavior that makes me ask." To Simon's tentative expression, Martin responded, "Grant, Mairi, Jessie, Eleanor, you and even me to an extent, all seem to be occupied. There's always a task that needs doing. But Lachlan...he seldom joins in. Frequently, he's off after breakfast and–"

"We don't see him again till most everything else is done for the day," Simon acknowledged. Martin's voice reflected his relief. "Then you've noticed. Is it cause for concern?"

"Well, there's no cause for immediate concern." Simon shifted the weight of the harness and asked, "Do you remember your high praise for the whiskey we sampled after dinner yesterday?"

"Aye, it was excellent," Martin exclaimed. "Lachlan said it was a special...." Slowly his face filled with disbelief. "You don't mean...."

Simon nodded.

Martin whistled a sigh. "But he doesn't sell it does he?"

"No, thank God. He's been asked to but has always refused. Others in the strath do sell. The mere existence of the still could bring trouble." Simon lowered his voice as Mairi approached, "It's far too risky."

"There you two are." Mairi wrapped an arm around Simon's neck and pressed her cheek to his. Turning to Martin, Mairi said, "Mam wanted to know if you'd look at the calf again–she's not sure Grant's following your instructions."

"Of course, where's Grant?" he asked rising.

"At the MacRae's on an errand. I'll walk with you if that's all right."

They left Simon to his task and Mairi walked briskly to keep up with Martin's stride as they crossed the yard and stepped onto the hills flecked with grazing cattle and bleating sheep. Arthur trotted alongside, stopping now and then to investigate a blossom or rock.

Mairi maintained a steady stream of chatter which Martin listened to with fond amusement. Since their tentative start, Martin found himself elevated by Mairi to the status of third brother. Certainly he didn't warrant or receive the devoted hero-worship she bestowed on Simon, but he fancied himself a notch above her tolerance of the bull-headed Grant. Martin thoroughly enjoyed her change of attitude toward him and felt as if Mairi were indeed his sister. Aside from her beauty, she was an exceptional young woman with her candid manner, natural buoyancy and passion for nearly everything. His pride in her surprised him a bit and he felt the need to share it with her. "Simon and Grant are fortunate to have you as a sister," he said warmly.

"Why thank you, Martin, though I think sometimes Grant would disagree with you." She stooped to pick a primrose and twirled its pinkish blossom under her nose.

"I'm sure Grant only wants what's best for you," he began.

"And how would he know what's best for me?"

"No one but you can know that, Mairi. Maybe you're a bit high-spirited for his comfort."

"That's generous of you considering how Grant sulks and snipes at you," she said bluntly. "Truthfully, I've been too 'high-spirited' for Grant ever since Flora Buchanan spurned him near a year ago this past Beltane. He wanted desperately to marry her. Instead, she ran off with a pretty lad from Wick whom she barely knew. I'm sure he now thinks of me as the Flora Buchanan of Strathcarron, ready to run off and be wicked with any comely man who shows his face." She linked her arm in his and announced, "That means you, Cousin."

Martin grinned lopsidedly at the thought and said, "He's very protective of you; he doesn't trust me yet."

"Then he's a dolt. I would trust you with my life," she vowed emphatically.

"You're a much more open and accepting person, Mairi." Sheep ambled from their path and Martin continued, "All of your family want you to be content."

She frowned. "And what makes everyone think I'm not content?"

"That's not what I meant. May I ask you a question, Mairi?"

"Of course."

"Which of your suitors do you favor? I've seen three since I arrived."

"Oh, so that's what this is about." Mairi's brilliant smile dazzled him. "I'm fond of them all."

"That doesn't answer my question," Martin chided.

Mairi clasped her hands behind her back and asked, "Which one do you think, Cousin? Haven't you a guess? Physicians are supposed to be observant people."

"Aye, but love isn't normally looked upon as an illness. Besides, my judgment in matters of the heart is suspect." Mairi screwed her face into a frown and he laughed. "Give me a minute." Staring thoughtfully at the spongy turf beneath his feet, Martin suddenly stopped and turned to her. "It's young Rob!" Mairi's jaw slackened and she flushed heavily. "Ha! I'm right," Martin exclaimed, delightedly cackling until he realized Mairi was not laughing with him. "What is it Mairi? Am I wrong after all?"

"You aren't wrong, Martin. The question is, am I that transparent?"

"Certainly not. Do you think Rob would be such a miserable wretch if it were that easy to see how you feel?"

Mairi shrugged. "Perhaps not," then she teased, "it's a good thing I'm not the heartless wench Grant imagines. If you weren't my cousin, I might easily have turned my wiles on you." Martin opened his mouth to respond, but Mairi continued, "It's odd what's happened though."

Martin cocked his head. "What's happened?"

"Well, because I didn't flirt outrageously with you, or try to win your undying devotion, now, I have a friend. I don't have many friends. I've discovered that I'm happier than if you'd been just another conquest."

"And we can be friends as long as we live." He kissed her cheek and confided, "You'll make Rob a very happy man!"

She giggled, "Aye, I'll have to stop torturing poor Rob," and resumed walking toward the calf. "As long as we're talking about love," her lips twitched into an affectionate smile, "why has no woman captured you, Martin?" Instantly, she regretted the remark as his expression grew melancholy and she grabbed his hand. "I'm sorry. That was so thoughtless. It's just that you always knew you were innocent. Oh, that didn't come out right either."

"Mairi, it's all right." For a few moments, Martin struggled for the right words. "Someone did capture me, Mairi. But she's out of my reach–married now. By the time I could have told her I loved her, it was too late."

"Oh, Martin, it's never too late to tell someone that you love them. You simply have to tell her," she said fiercely and threw her arms tightly around him as if to absorb his pain.

Her gesture brought stinging tears to his eyes and he stroked her hair once. "Thank you for caring; it means a great deal to me." Pulling away gently, he admitted, "I've been thinking about telling her, even now when there's nothing to be gained except perhaps coming to terms with her marriage and moving on." He crooked a smile. "Did you know your grandmother gave me the same advice you just did?"

"No, I didn't. But, if two of us can see it, that should convince you." She glanced hopefully at Martin. "You will tell this woman–"

"Fia," Martin supplied.

"You will tell Fia, won't you?"

"I'll think about it," he promised.

Hands on hips, she prodded, "You've been thinking about it. Do it for Gram and me if not yourself. We want you to be happy too, Martin," she added anxiously, "just like I hope Rob and I will be."

Martin lay one hand on the calf's neck. "All right, you've convinced me. And as for you and your Rob, I've no doubt that you'll be happy, though you may need to tame that appreciative eye you have for the lads," he chuckled and Mairi joined in his laughter.

As they returned from examining the calf, Martin and Mairi were laughing, heavily flushed and slightly disheveled from a race halfway back to the farm. It was such an unexpected sight that all in the yard stopped to look in their direction; Simon, glad to see that Mairi was well past her doubts about Martin; Jessie grinning at her daughter's infectious laugh; but Grant, just returned from his errand, clamped his jaw which throbbed in fury. Before anyone could move, Grant lunged for Martin and knocked the air from him as they hit the ground hard. Martin struggled for breath, unable to fend off Grant's fists which brought blood spurting first from his nose, then over the bone of his cheek.

"Grant, what are you doing?" Mairi screamed, yanking desperately at her brother's arm.

Seething, Simon shoved mightily with a well placed boot on Grant's backside sending his younger brother sprawling. Mairi and Jessie dropped to Martin's side just as he gasped a huge gulp of air and began to cough. Jessie removed her neck handkerchief and put it to Martin's bloody face. "Are you badly hurt?" she inquired anxiously. The agitation in her voice seeped through, only Martin didn't know if she was angry with him or her son. He simply shook his head. "Good," she said with forced calm and turned to her daughter. "Mairi, see to his wounds."

"Aye, Mam, but Grant...." her voice trailed off to the look on Jessie's face. "Aye, Mam," she repeated helping Martin sit up and reaching out to calm the barking, growling, Arthur.

Grant was red-faced from anger and embarrassment at having been so easily dispatched by Simon who bellowed, "You'd better settle down and tell us what the Hell that was all about."

When Grant didn't answer, Jessie spoke slowly, deliberately, coldly.

"Aye, Grant, tell us what provoked that attack on your kinsman."

Grant shifted his spindly frame from foot to foot uncomfortably and pointed beyond his mother to where Martin was lurching to his feet. "It's him. He's had Mairi up in the pasture. You saw them, how they looked when they came back...blushing, laughing like lov–Oof!" he finished abruptly as Mairi flew at him with all the rage in her.

"How *dare* you?" she shrieked. "You're insinuating that Martin took advantage of me or that I encouraged it aren't you? *Aren't you?*" she screamed in his face. Jessie stepped forward but Simon stopped her. Grant was beginning to dig a hole so deep he might never climb out of it– and Simon had no intention of letting anyone stop him. He suspected Mairi was going to teach Grant a valuable lesson. Simon glanced at Martin who stood beside them feeling that he should intervene, but this was Mairi's fight–it was her honor Grant had besmirched. "I'm not surprised Martin would want to bed you," Grant shot back, "every other man in Strathcarron wants to, you tease them so cruelly." Grant shot a baleful look at Martin. "It's pretty obvious Martin took you up there for only one reason."

The crack of Mairi's fist on Grant's chin could be heard across the yard. "Shut your filthy mouth, Grant. Even if you can't bring yourself to trust Martin, you should know my teasing is harmless. And if you cared about me, you wouldn't make such accusations about the state of my virtue based on what you *think* is 'obvious'. I'm not Flora Buchanan! Stay out of my business and don't leap to foolish conclusions." She stalked to Martin's side.

Martin asked, "How's your hand?"

"Hurts like the devil," she admitted in hushed tones, "but it felt glorious while I was doing it."

"Soak it in cold water and I'll be in to check it," Martin suggested.

"What about you?"

"Bleeding's stopped," he replied.

"Good." Mairi left after receiving a wink of approval from Simon.

Martin turned to Grant. "And how's your chin?"

"Leave me alone," Grant grumbled, averting his gaze.

"A cold cloth wouldn't hurt," Martin said.

Jessie moved to stand beside Grant. "That will have to wait because my son and I need to talk." Taking Grant's arm, Jessie steered him to the byre from which Martin and Simon presently heard him being lectured to in loud, unforgiving tones.

Martin glanced at Simon who wasn't sure whether it was safe to open his mouth. At Martin's raised brow, however, he convulsed with laughter. "God's blood, Martin, you do make life exciting. For the world, I would not be Grant right now." Calming, Simon wiped his eyes. "I'm afraid I don't know what to say except I'm sorry. I don't know who Grant gets his quick fuse from, or his morbid ideas."

"A fascinating family you have," Martin noted.

"Are you sorry I brought you to meet them?" Simon asked sheepishly.

"I wouldn't have missed it," he exclaimed, touching his cheek gingerly.

"And you're really not hurt badly?"

"No permanent damage done. Let's see how Mairi's knuckles fare." He stopped and turned his most innocent expression on Simon. "You will chaperon won't you?" Simon chuckled and nodded.

Supper that evening was a sorry affair. Grant offering a sulking apology to both Martin and Mairi, and Mairi determined not to accept it. Lachlan's shame upon hearing the tale was apparent, and Jessie's annoyance with Grant simmered making her so short-tempered that Eleanor finally lay down her knife and rose at the foot of the table. "I don't know what's gotten into this family, but I want it to stop: the fights, the brooding, the distrust–all of it." She looked at each unresponsive relative in turn and decided desperate measures were in order. "If any of you is interested, there is some good news we can share tonight." All looked at her blankly. "Mairi's decided to accept Rob's proposal of marriage."

Mairi started, knocking over her cup. "Gram, you promised you wouldn't say anything."

"I know, dear, but between your excitement over Rob and your unhappiness with Grant, I made the promise to calm you. Now I find I can't keep my promise–not if it will help pull this family together. It is good news," her grandmother replied, gently touching Mairi's shoulder, "too good to keep to ourselves."

"Indeed, it is," Jessie and Lachlan chorused in relief and rose to hug their daughter.

"Mairi, this is splendid," Simon declared, grasping his sister's hand. "When did you decide? Does Rob know yet?"

Mairi responded loftily, "I haven't told Rob yet because I just decided earlier today when Martin and I went to see the *calf*." She discharged a malevolent look at Grant. "Martin helped me take a clear look at my suitors. I realized that I wasn't being fair to Rob or the others because it wasn't a contest. Rob is the man I want."

Her parents looked at each other in stunned silence. In one afternoon, their coquettish daughter had matured considerably. Lachlan cleared his throat. "Martin, I think we may all owe you a debt."

Martin was bewildered. "I'm afraid I don't understand."

Grant spoke bluntly, "He means none of us ever thought she'd make up her mind and you've forced her into it."

"*Grant!*" Lachlan thundered.

Almost imperceptibly, Martin straightened. "Grant, I need to say a few things to you, and I hope the rest of your family will forgive me. I know I'm an outsider here and that has caused some discord. I regret that. Yet, I feel that you are partially responsible." Grant started to protest but Martin ignored him. "I don't care whether you agree with me or even whether you like me. What I really want you to listen to, Grant, is this. I forced Mairi into nothing–not a compromising position, and not her decision about the man she loves. Mairi knows what she wants. You seem to give her no credit for being intelligent enough to make decisions about her own life. Don't keep making that mistake. You run a terrible risk of driving an insurmountable wedge between you. Now," he addressed Lachlan, "whatever you were thanking me for, I must tell you what your daughter did for me. I have some unfinished business in Glasgow which Mairi, along with Eleanor, have convinced me needs finishing." His gaze settled on Simon. "Unless there's a reason for me to delay, I'll be leaving tomorrow."

Surprised, Simon leaned forward, face mottled from shadows cast by the rush lights illuminating the table. "I'm going too then–for moral support."

Martin argued, "Be reasonable, Simon. You haven't seen your family in years. I'll go alone."

"I'll come back here and visit after we go to Glasgow, whether you return with me or not," Simon insisted.

"Simon, I appreciate your concern and I know your intentions are noble, but I can take care of myself."

"Of course you can," he conceded agreeably. "Maybe I'll just look up Arabella while you're taking care of your business." He raised his brows, daring Martin to argue the point further.

"Wait, lads, wait." Lachlan held up his hands for quiet. "Your bickering is making me dizzy. Martin, your reason for traveling to Glasgow is not my business. Still, it won't hurt if Simon accompanies you, will it?"

After a brief hesitation, Martin shook his head.

"Then it's settled." Lachlan pointed his finger at one, then the other of them. "But I want you both to return as soon as you can. Now, I only have one question remaining." Simon and Martin looked expectantly at Lachlan who begged, "Who in the world is Arabella?"

Keeping a brisk pace south, but mindful not to exhaust Arthur, Martin and Simon crossed the southern tip of the Black Isle and were just west of Inverness when Odhar's gait slowed. "Simon wait," Martin called and dismounted.

"Is there a problem?" Simon came back and leaned over Devenick's neck.

"Odhar's picked up a rock." Martin dislodged the stone, released Odhar's hoof and, taking the reins, walked him forward.

"He's limping," Simon observed.

"That he is." Anxiously, Martin patted Odhar's neck. "One more day won't make any difference, I guess. Feel like resting tomorrow in town?" he asked Simon.

"Why not? Anyway, I don't see that there's a choice." Simon dismounted and walked with Martin along the Beauly Firth into Inverness. Arthur was suddenly seized with energy and, darting between the horses, charged a wild swan paddling at water's edge and raced back, dripping wet, having sent the bird skyward. He shook his coat from head to tail-tip, splattering Simon who grumbled, "Is he doing this on purpose?"

Martin grinned. "Probably. After all, we're on his level now. He no longer has to chase after us."

The travelers stopped before the stone arches bridging the River Ness near the ruins of the castle Bonnie Prince Charles had destroyed before his defeat at Culloden. "I can't take Odhar any further," Martin apologized. "He needs to rest."

"I agree." Simon looked around. "You know the last time I was here, I thought I noticed an inn close to the bridge. Ah, there it is."

The innkeeper settled Martin and Simon into a stifling room with three other travelers. There was nothing appealing about the room except that the beds appeared to be clean. Unfortunately, they couldn't say the same for the rest of the inn. And, as they came down the narrow staircase, a rancid odor assailed. Without exchanging a word, the two friends made their way through the noisy, jostling crowd, nearly stumbling into the street when they reached the door.

"I suppose we should feel fortunate that we got a place to stay at all," Simon shrugged. "Do you think Odhar will be ready to travel tomorrow?"

Martin shook his head. "I'd like to rest him just to be sure. There's no hoof damage, but the flesh is a bit bruised. Since we have a long way to go, I'd just as soon not take chances. Anyway, take a look at that sky," he nodded westward. "Tomorrow could be really troublesome." He clapped a hand on Simon's shoulder. "It'll give us some time to explore Inverness. Who knows what we may discover?"

"The first thing I'd like to discover," Simon whined over a grumbling stomach, "is something to eat."

Alayne peered with difficulty through the shop window. "Why does it have to rain today," she groaned in dismay.

"Rain is an understatement. It's gotten much worse since I arrived. Listen," Fia said, "I haven't dried out yet. If you want me to go to Market in your place, I will."

Turning, Alayne smiled crookedly. "Thanks, but you went last week. "Besides," she said forcing herself to be cheery, "it'll probably lighten up after a bit."

Fia joined her and peered upward. "It doesn't look like it has any such intention. That sky looks like slate."

"Aren't you encouraging," Alayne pouted then sighed. "Complaining about it isn't going to get it done." She donned her mantle and pulled her hood close about her face. "I'll be back as soon as I can; have something hot waiting for me will you?"

Fia promised she would and, fighting a blast of wind and water, closed the door behind Alayne. Normally, Fia found an outing to Market to be a nice break from routine, but she certainly didn't envy Alayne's trip today. It was raw outside. And, because of the storm, they didn't expect many customers. That was all right though–she had plenty to do. Business had picked up just as Alayne had predicted.

Though Market was held only one day a week, the stalls, carts, and customers today bore little resemblance to the usually bustling scene. In the summer, even when the weather was foul, patrons enjoyed milling about and visiting, or bargaining just a little longer with the vendors to make marketing more a social occasion. But it was so miserable today, the sellers had covered their wares to protect them, and the few customers who were out were attracted to familiar faces rather than the goods offered. Alayne kept her head down and, holding her hood close under her chin, hoped to make short work of this outing.

Standing under a green awning, Simon looked out on the worsening weather that had forced him and Martin to abandon their plans to explore Inverness. Instead, they decided to do errands although, at this moment, Simon couldn't imagine why they hadn't decided to stretch their legs before the inn's smoky fire. Martin had headed off to replenish some of his medical supplies and Simon was in search of just the right gift to celebrate his mother's birthday. The problem was, he hadn't any ideas. Sighing, Simon resigned himself to his fate; he had another half hour before he was to meet Martin. Glancing around, the only carts within sight were covered making them useless as he sought a worthwhile idea. Annoyed, he tapped his booted foot and mumbled, "Maybe a shop would...be...better...." His voice trailed off as he spied a woman, frame slightly bent into the torrent, pass near him. Without thinking, Simon fell into step behind her, followed her to a shop, but did not enter after her. Instead, he watched through the distorting waves of the window pane as she shook rain from the folds of her mantle and lowered its hood. She laughed and chatted with the proprietor and, though Simon couldn't hear what was said, it was obvious they were well acquainted–so she was a regular customer. He stared at the young woman, intrigued by her good humor on a miserable day; her generous smile and the sunset-gold of her hair in the glow provided by the candles warmed him. Simon wished he could better see her. As she raised her hood and tucked her purchase into the crook of her elbow, Simon sprinted to the next storefront where, undetected, he might continue to observe her.

The shop bell tinkled brightly and Simon watched her glance skyward, shake her head and give the puddle at her feet wide berth as she picked her way swiftly to her next stop. Again, Simon strained to see into the dimly lit shop. This time, as she moved about the shop, he noted how proudly she held herself. Simon abruptly became aware that his pulse had quickened like a schoolboy's. He knew the cause was not his game of intrigue in following this unknown woman, but a desire to come face to face with her. The storm was worsening by the minute; perhaps he could offer assistance. The thought distracted Simon just long enough to startle him when she passed close enough for him to catch her tantalizing scent and a glimpse of her face.

Alayne clutched her purchases tightly as she hurried from the square. All she could think of now was getting back to the shop and whatever treat Fia would have awaiting her. A gust of wind reached under Alayne's mantle and whipped it wildly behind her. Gasping at the sudden attack, she turned from the blast and shifted her load so that she could better hold the edges of her mantle together. Taking a deep breath, Alayne whirled into the full force of the squall and ran headlong into an unseen object. Packages exploding from her grasp, Alayne staggered backward but strong hands gripped her upper arms keeping her from sinking into the muddy lane. When she landed again on her feet, Alayne found herself inches from a most beguiling face.

Neither moved for long seconds until he asked in melodious, spellbinding tones, "Did I hurt you?"

It took a few more moments for Alayne to find her own hesitant voice. "I'm not injured. You can let go of me now."

"I don't think so," Simon countered.

Alayne tilted her head slightly and her voice was little more than a whisper in the wind, "What do you mean?"

With the familiarity of a lover, Simon caressed her face, eyes drinking in details of her appearance. Simon felt shock jolt Alayne's body, and she quickly pulled away from him. "You...you shouldn't have done that," she insisted, glancing around.

But Simon heard no admonition in her voice. He bent quickly to gather her packages and give himself time to find his next words. When he straightened, the bundles cradled in one arm, Simon said, "Perhaps I shouldn't have, but I'm not sorry. I was planning to introduce myself, though not by knocking you over." His laugh was soft and easy. "I have to confess, I've followed you since I saw you enter the Market."

Confused, Alayne's eyes shifted from his penetrating stare. "Why?"

Simon shook his head. "I'm not certain, but it seemed my only choice. Seeing you for the first time on this horrid morning must be fate, because it is now a splendid morning."

Alayne knew she should be indignant and angry. After all, this man admitted stalking her, and had stroked her as though he had the right. But she only felt jittery–and fearful–not of him, but of what his touch and look had awakened in her. She could feel her body's quaking betrayal. To hide her bewilderment, Alayne grabbed her packages from him and held them rigidly. "I have to go," she insisted, hood fallen about her shoulders, and hair soaked to her skin. While his own plastered curls dripped rain in his eyes, Simon reached behind her and pulled the hood around her face. He felt her stiffen but overlooked it in his dread that she might disappear. "Come, have tea with me," he implored and, to her dubious expression urged, "something, anything! Please."

Alayne clamped her mouth shut so that her lips would not surrender to his request. She shook her head and was amazed to see the distress on his face as he sought for the words that would keep her with him. "At least tell me your name," he pleaded, "that's not too much to ask, is it?"

Swallowing hard, she murmured, "Alayne," and was rewarded with a smile so huge it seemed to cut his face in half.

"Alayne," he whispered just to hear it from his own lips; she was transfixed by its sound. Biting rain struck her full in the face shattering the spell. She had to escape before something happened she would truly regret.

Mustering all her courage, Alayne boldly stepped away from him. "I do have to leave now."

Simon reached for her, but she took another step away. "If now is not the time," he begged, "just tell me when I might see you again, Alayne."

"You can't." She forced her voice to remain cool. "You think meeting me this morning was fate?"

"Aye. And by your eyes I believe you know it to be true."

She began, "Believe what you like–"

"Simon," he interrupted, needing her to know his name.

Alayne began again, "Believe what you like, Simon, but you can't see me again. My mother-in-law would not approve." Before he could respond, Alayne hurried away as quickly as the slippery muck would allow. She did not look back, not wanting to see whether there was disappointment on his face or not. And because she did not look back, Alayne did not see Simon follow her.

Chapter Sixteen

Fia jumped as thunder crashed overhead. "Where is Alayne?" she mumbled nervously, straining to see through the wall of water tumbling from the blackened sky. It seemed that Alayne had left for the market hours ago but, when Fia glanced at the clock, she saw it had been just under an hour. Turning back to the window, she heaved a sigh of relief and threw open the door as Alayne reached its threshold. "Quick, get inside!" Fia yelled to be heard over the pounding rain. She pushed the door shut, wrenched the packages from Alayne's stiff fingers and carelessly tossed them on top of the display case. "Come to the back," she urged, but had to coax Alayne with an arm around her sodden shoulders. Once behind the curtain, Fia said, "I'll fetch your dressing gown. Here," she said placing a towel in Alayne's hand, "I'll be right back."

As Fia's footsteps faded up the stairs, Alayne hesitantly approached the window. Moving the drape slightly, she peered out and saw only the gale in full force. The sound of Fia's return cut into her daze and, releasing the curtain, Alayne moved away and began to disrobe. Everything had to come off for she was drenched and numb to the bone.

"Let me help with your stays," Fia said and deftly unlaced them for her. "When you're wrapped up, come over by the fire." Fia disappeared back up the stairs and, when she reentered the workroom, Alayne was bundled in the dressing gown, hands extended to capture the warmth from the peat fire. "Drink this," Fia commanded and placed a glass of sherry in Alayne's hand. "It should help."

Dutifully, Alayne downed the liquid and cringed as it burned her throat and sat like embers in her belly. "Thank you," she finally croaked, "I...I've never been out in weather like this."

"And I've never seen weather like this! Are you alright?"

"I'll be fine when the feeling returns to my body."

"You rest while I close and straighten up in the shop," Fia said and, as an afterthought added, "call if you need me." Alayne promised with a nod, and Fia left.

A violent shudder seized Alayne. She had lied to Fia. The longer her body stayed numb the better. She was afraid that, when the feeling returned, the fluttering ache she'd felt at Simon's touch still would be there to haunt her. *He* would haunt her. On the fringe of her thoughts, Alayne scolded herself for making a great deal out of nothing–a chance meeting, a fascinating face, a tender caress. But she knew it was anything but nothing. An incredible, unnerving thing had happened to her–his name was Simon. A loud moan escaped her and Alayne buried her face in her hands. A few moments later, Fia was before her and she studied her friend closely.

"Alayne, you'd tell me if something were amiss, wouldn't you?"

Alayne averted her gaze. "Nothing's wrong, it's just this horrid storm."

Fia stood back. "I think there's more." Alayne was silent and, reluctantly, Fia decided not to press further just now. "Is there anything more I can do? Would you rather rest upstairs?" Alayne shook her head and Fia stood. "All right then, maybe this will help," Fia said setting a saucer in Alayne's lap. "This was going to be your treat. I brought it with me this morning but, when you returned, you looked more in need of the sherry."

Alayne poked the seed cake and, with a lopsided grin said, "I'd forgotten you promised me something special."

"Actually, I promised you something hot, but I guess the sherry warmed you so I've kept my word."

Alayne opened her mouth to thank Fia, but nothing came out. Swallowing hard, she tried again. This time, it was a confession. "It was a man, Fia...following me at Market." Alayne began to shake again.

"A man?" Fia's heart stuttered then pounded in sudden terror. "What man?" she yelped, gripping the arm of Alayne's chair. "What did he do? What did he look like?"

Even in her fog, Alayne recognized Fia's panic and quickly gulped, "No, it wasn't Andrew or Struan," as she set aside the cake.

"But you've never seen them; are you certain?" Fia persisted anxiously.

"I'm sure." Alayne wiped her nose on her towel and said, "He was fair. You said the Forbes' were dark."

"Aye, dark." Fia's dread steadied somewhat, and she forced herself to ask calmly, "Do you want to tell me what happened?"

Alayne grimaced and blinked back tears of confusion. "I'm not totally sure. I was starting back; the storm was fierce, almost like it is now. I ran into this man...literally. He came out of nowhere and admitted he'd been following me."

"He said that?" Fia asked warily.

"It was so strange."

"Strange how?"

A strangled laugh escaped Alayne. "I recognized him...in here," she said, pressing her hand to her heart. "Yet, until today, I know I've never laid eyes on him. Sweet Jesus, right there, in the midst of that tempest, he just caressed my face as if it was the most natural thing in the world, as if we were..." She shook her head. "His touch was so...familiar. I don't understand it. He wanted to have tea with me, to see me again; he said our meeting was destiny." As Alayne spoke, her turmoil spiraled and Fia gripped her friend's hands.

"Did he hurt you?"

Alayne's voice sounded thin and high, "No, but what if someone saw what happened? I'm a married woman."

"Who hasn't seen her husband in nearly four years," Fia reminded.

"That doesn't matter, don't you see?"

Fia studied Alayne a long moment. "I see that this man has had a profound effect on you. Why don't you tell me what's really bothering you."

Alayne gaped in disbelief. "Truly, you don't understand?"

"I understand how it might be interpreted, but it could be explained." Fia puzzled, "I'm not sure I understand why you're so troubled." She hesitated before saying, "I have an opinion, if you're interested."

Alayne looked at her expectantly, almost afraid to hear what Fia had to say.

"You're shaken right now because the man was so mysteriously familiar. Maybe when he touched you," she said with a gentle smile, "it was because he also felt a special bond. You think your duty is to regret what happened because you're still another man's wife. But you can't." She paused briefly. "Alayne, you've been alone for so long and, this man, he's reached right into your soul. What would be shameful is to pretend it was nothing."

Alayne raked slender fingers through her damp hair. "Fia, I don't know; you make it sound... almost respectable. I'm only sure that I don't want anything to get in the way of my plans to rid myself legally of Muir."

"That I understand." Hesitating, Fia asked, "Did you agree to see him?"

"Fia," Alayne whimpered, "how could I do that?"

"Because you enjoyed his caress?"

"Be serious, Fia," Alayne cried indignantly.

Fia spoke gently, "Alayne, I am serious. You disguise yourself, searching for any shred of information on a husband who deserted you years ago. Can you not think of a way to discreetly see this man if the attraction is so strong? In November, you'll be a free woman. That's just over two months, Alayne. What do you really have to lose by seeing him again?"

"What do I have to gain?"

"Maybe nothing; perhaps everything. He wants to see you."

"I told him no," Alayne responded flatly, "he's gone."

"Are you sure?" Fia asked.

Embarrassed, Alayne mumbled, "I told him my mother-in-law wouldn't approve."

Fia smirked, "Well, you're right about that. But, considering how you and Kate get on, that alone should be incentive for you to seek him out." She hoped for, and was rewarded with a grudging smile from Alayne.

"It doesn't matter," Alayne murmured, "since bumping into him again isn't very likely."

Fia stood. "You should think about it though, so you'll know what you want to do the next time you stumble into each other."

"Do you really think that will happen?" Alayne asked, hesitant to hope for such a recurrence.

"If he felt anything of what you experienced today, I believe you'll see him again. And, Alayne, I'll help if I can, you need only ask. I'd dearly love to see you in love."

Peering into the gloom, Martin tramped through the mire searching for Simon. Thoroughly bedraggled, Arthur moped beside him. Though sorely tempted, Martin couldn't bring himself to return to the inn across the River Ness; he'd promised to meet Simon at Market. Someone tapped his shoulder and Martin whirled to see Simon smiling foolishly as wind blasted rain in his face.

"I'm late," Simon admitted.

"I noticed, but won't hold it against you for long if we can go back to the inn *now*." Simon nodded and as they neared the bridge, Martin inquired, "Where were you anyway?"

"Over on High Street at a millinery," Simon answered.

"Did you find a gift for Jessie?"

"Oh, I didn't go inside," Simon blinked raindrops from his lashes.

Martin was confused. "Then what were you doing?"

"I was following someone."

"Who?" Martin exclaimed, stopping so abruptly his feet nearly slid from under him in the muck.

"The most captivating woman," Simon answered dreamily. "I met her at Market; her name is Alayne. There's only one problem." He glanced sheepishly at Martin. "It seems she's married."

Martin rolled his eyes. "Only one problem." He took his cousin's elbow and propelled him onto the bridge. "The minute I have dry clothes on, I'll order up some hot mead for us and you can tell me more."

"I don't know if I can wait that long," Simon protested good-naturedly. But, thirty minutes later, the two men stretched their legs before the fire Simon had longed for earlier, with tankards of steaming mead warming their hands.

"So how did you meet this woman?" Martin prompted, noting Simon's expression immediately brighten.

"I was trying to decide where to look for Mam's gift when this young woman passed near me. I watched her go into a shop and she smiled at the proprietor, laughed with him and, when she lowered the hood of her mantle, Martin I got the oddest feeling that I was ordained to be there, at that moment in time, for the sole purpose of seeing her."

"Did you go in and introduce yourself?"

"Oh, no," Simon assured, "I wanted to savor simply watching her. I can't get over how radiant she was when everyone else I saw wore scowls and cursed the weather." Drawing a long sigh, Simon paused to reflect a moment.

Impatiently, Martin urged, "So how did you meet her?"

"I approached her from behind, intending to introduce myself, when a gust of wind made her spin and bump into me. Her parcels spewed everywhere."

"Off to an impressive start. I assume you gathered up her packages?"

"Of course, but not until after I caught her to keep her from landing in the mud. Martin, I tell you she snatched the very breath from me."

"Beautiful?" Martin asked.

"Stunning!"

"Then what happened?"

Simon frowned. "I asked her–nearly begged her–to spend some time with me, have tea, whatever. She refused; said her mother-in-law wouldn't like it. She has smoldering green eyes."

"The mother-in-law?" Martin piped, receiving a glower in return.

"Alayne!" Simon corrected. "Martin, what do you think?"

Martin drank from his tankard, and then rubbed his thumb along his mustache, wiping the lingering drops of mead before pronouncing, "You are definitely besotted."

"That much I already know," Simon asserted. "I mean what do you think about Alayne?"

Martin studied Simon's eager face and said, "She sounds intriguing. You don't think she was insulted by your desire to spend more time with her, do you? She didn't slap you or scream for help did she?"

"No, she didn't. I don't believe she was insulted," Simon rushed to agree. "That's a good sign don't you think?"

"Except that she's married," Martin added dutifully.

"Aye, married." Simon's lips pursed in a thoughtful pout.

Martin leaned his chin on the heel of his hand. "One thing that puzzles me," he said thoughtfully, "is why she said her mother-in-law wouldn't approve. Why didn't she say 'her husband'?"

Simon stared a moment at his cousin then, jumping up, he paced. "I never even thought about that."

"Simon, as you tell it, I'd say you were hardly thinking at all. You were acting purely on instinct," Martin surmised.

"True enough but, now that you've pointed it out, it is very strange. What do you suppose it means?" Simon pondered.

"It's difficult to say. Maybe her mother-in-law is more formidable than her husband–it's been known to happen. But you'll only get an answer from Alayne. Go see her tomorrow and ask her."

Simon's head snapped up. "What do you mean 'tomorrow'?"

Martin rubbed his eyes as a gust of acrid smoke from the sputtering fire billowed into the room. "Only a few months ago, I would have sworn an oath that what happened to you today was impossible–that you couldn't be so completely seized by any woman. But I know better now, and it will consume you, Simon, if you don't see Alayne soon and get some answers."

"I know where Alayne is; I'll give her a little time to think about me."

"You're sure she's going to think about you?" Martin smirked.

"Positive. Besides, Cousin," Simon exclaimed, waggling a finger at him, "you don't get rid of me that easily. I'm going with you. And there's still Arabella to find."

Martin's brows shot up in exaggerated surprise. "I would have thought Alayne had driven all thoughts of other women from your mind."

"All but Arabella." Simon frowned. "Her resolve I admired. Truthfully though, I doubt she was any match for that unctous bastard I saw her with." His scowl mellowed. "I'd like to find her, see how she fares. I'm sorry now that I didn't let her tell me her real name. No, Martin, I'm coming with you to Glasgow: to meet Fia, to look for my friend, to be there for you. After all, Inverness does lie on the path home and we did promise my father we'd return. I'll see Alayne on the way back to Strathcarron. And, truthfully," he hesitated, "I don't want to risk scaring her away."

In the morning, a fully recovered Odhar refused Martin's attempts to travel cautiously. He tugged at his bit, pranced and shook his lustrous black mane in frustration until Martin had no choice but to give him free rein. They were within sight of Glasgow by sundown the day after leaving Inverness and the closer they got, the quieter Martin became. He hoped he'd be grateful for Eleanor's and Mairi's counsel to make this trip. Martin supposed he would be–eventually. With luck, he would say his goodbyes to Fia, closing that chapter of his life and...and what? His thoughts refused to pass that point; he couldn't imagine what was left for him once he'd seen Fia in an attempt to move on.

"This looks like a good place to stay the night." Simon pointed to a copse of beeches across the road from the river. "Glasgow isn't more than a half hour's ride from here," he added, reining in.

"I'd prefer this to town," Martin admitted. "I can wash up in the river there and, with luck, look presentable when I see Fia."

Simon's gaze softened and his voice held a note of compassion. "Fine idea." Martin was trying hard to be matter-of-fact about it all, to keep his emotions controlled. "You know, Cousin," Simon continued, "I'm truly looking forward to meeting your Fia."

"She isn't mine," Martin said pointedly. "I'll introduce you if I can, but I can't promise."

Simon nodded. "We'll see how it all goes tomorrow."

In the morning, Martin stripped and bathed head to foot in the frigid river. And while he dried and dressed, Simon set out cheese, oatcakes and a little dried meat. When Martin sat down again, he asked, "Do I look...presentable?"

Simon surveyed the results of his cousin's work. The grit and sweat rinsed from Martin's hair had restored its shine. Martin had brushed the stains of traveling from his breeches and they were the brown-black of peat once again; he'd even wiped his boots. And from somewhere in the recesses of his saddlebags, Martin had produced a slightly wrinkled shirt, bluish-gray, not exactly like any Simon had ever seen. Around Martin's neck was a knotted handkerchief.

"Well?" Martin prompted testily.

"Patience," Simon snorted, "I'm taking stock of your efforts." Martin looked far younger than his twenty-seven years, hopeful and vulnerable, which caused a pang of sympathy to swell in Simon's chest. "Martin, you look grand. Where did you get that shirt; I like the cut."

Martin ran a hand gently down the front of the shirt, knowing the only other person ever to touch it was Fia. Quietly, he remarked, "Fia made it for me. I've been saving it for the right occasion."

"Then let's get on with it!" Simon enthusiastically thumped Martin between his shoulder blades.

Martin forced some food into his mouth, not really wanting it or tasting it, but after Simon had gone to the trouble, he thought it only polite. Besides, it was bad enough that he might make a huge fool of himself shortly–he didn't want Simon to know exactly how nervous he was. When they'd packed and mounted up, Martin whistled for Arthur to follow as he and Simon started the last leg to Glasgow.

Simon looked up as leaden clouds scuttled across the sky on a rising wind. A chill crept up his spine and a queer feeling gnawed his belly. He didn't put much store in premonitions so decided not to mention his sudden apprehension to Martin. Though the feeling stayed with Simon all the way into Glasgow, he simply offered, "Good luck," as Martin dismounted and approached the Graham's door.

Elizabeth wanted to soak in a hot bath, but she was too exhausted to heat the water and fill the tub herself–and there was no one else to do it for her. Her father wouldn't return from London for another two weeks and, last night, she'd dismissed Una until her mother, whom Elizabeth considered indecently old to be having another bairn, delivered her twelfth. Elizabeth, experiencing some discomfort herself over the last few days, was positive it would go away if she got that scatter-brained maid out from under foot. Why she'd started to feel better almost immediately. "I much prefer being alone," Elizabeth thought, "to suffering through that twit's fretting and hand-wringing all day." A smile stole over her face. The real reason for her improvement was Andrew, who had paid another visit yesterday evening and, this time, stayed all night. "I do miss him dreadfully when he's away," she sulked remembering the short treks he'd undertaken over the last few weeks. Every time he returned to Glasgow, he brought her little gifts and a bottle of some exotic wine. "Fruits of my labor," he laughingly called them, insisting that they toast each reunion and each keepsake as she opened it.

Immeasurably more important to Elizabeth than these trinkets, was the change she observed in Andrew. She recalled during his visit two weeks ago, he had asked after her health. Knowing him irate over her pregnancy, Elizabeth haughtily replied, "The babe and I are thriving!" Much to her surprise, his anger didn't flare at the mention of the child. Instead, Andrew only grumbled unintelligibly. When he returned at the end of that week, and they lay, damp limbs entangled, Andrew had inquired, "Is the bairn old enough yet for you to feel movement?"

Elizabeth pondered his interest and answered, "There has been some movement, why?"

Andrew placed her glass in her hand. "I find myself curious...interested in his growth."

Her pulse jumped at the prospect that Andrew might be having a change of heart, but she chose to respond playfully. "So, you're sure the bairn is a lad?" Andrew had simply smiled, kissed her, and asked her to drink with him to that prospect.

Several days ago when Andrew called on her again, arms overflowing with presents, he had barely deposited the bundles on the table before taking her hungrily; her own needs mirrored his.

"By my oath, the child makes you more voracious than ever before," he had grunted as he thrust into her, hands gripping her hips.

"That is a benefit we didn't count on," she had purred as he latched his mouth to her breast, shuddered into her, and fell away, panting. They drifted into a light slumber and, when Elizabeth

The Borrowed Days

woke, her discomfort had returned. It was not bad, but more noticeable than before. "It feels like cramps," she decided.

"Hm, what?" Andrew had mumbled as he stirred.

"Nothing, my love," she had assured. "I've just felt a little...off...these few days. I feel it again now."

Immediately alert, Andrew locked worried eyes on her face. "My dear, should you have the midwife examine you?"

Surprised and pleased at his concern, Elizabeth stroked his face, thumb lingering on the silvery scar. "Andrew, I'm fine and the babe is fine. It's perfectly normal when carrying a child to have days that simply aren't as good as others."

"My dear, I want you to be certain; take no chances with our son."

"Oh, Andrew, you do want our child! You've changed your mind; you called him 'our son'." Tears had gathered in her eyes and her voice trembled. "I love you so." She kissed him fervently and when she pulled back, his own eyes were moist.

"Each time we've been separated, I've thought more and more about you nurturing a new life inside you that we created together. It's...so humbling. Elizabeth, my heart has changed. To have a child with you...it is the most blessed gift you could ever give me."

She caressed his face. "Thank you, Andrew." They loved again, tenderly this time, drank to the babe's health and their own future. Finally, Andrew had to depart. "I'll see you again the day after tomorrow, my dear, but then, not for several weeks I'm afraid," he had apologized, then grinned. "When I return from that journey, I'll bring a special gift for the bairn."

And last night, Elizabeth was rewarded with passion that flowed throughout the dark hours. Andrew attended all her desires. She thrilled most as, more than once, Andrew spread his large hand over her slightly rounded belly and caressed it gently. That tender act had stirred her deeply and Elizabeth snuggled down into her bed going to great lengths to satisfy her lover.

Spent and perspiring, Andrew leaned across her and picked up his valise. He strode to her dressing table, produced a bottle of Madeira. Elizabeth heard him open it and pour two glasses while she lay back, admiring the breadth of his shoulders, strong hips and muscular thighs. He was vain about his body but, to Elizabeth, that meant Andrew would take pains to look this good for as long as he could–and the way he appeared pleased her enormously. Andrew returned with the wine and handed her a glass. He traced her lips with his thick finger. "This is a special bottle I brought for this occasion. When I leave again today, I don't want you to forget how important you are to me just because duty calls and I'm not here to remind you. Besides, it will relax you."

Elizabeth grinned wickedly, her fingers feathering his inner thigh. "It can't relax me any more than you already have."

Kissing her lightly, Andrew touched his glass to hers. "To you my dear Elizabeth, mother of my child."

Elizabeth's eyes glowed as they drank and Andrew whispered against her ear, "When you finish that, I have a special goodbye for you."

Elizabeth quickly downed her wine, handing the empty glass to Andrew who placed it on the bed table. On his knees between her legs, he grasped her hips and pulled her onto him. Leaning forward, he took the last small sip from his own glass and, placing his lips between her breasts, dribbled warm wine over her skin. Grinning at her, Andrew licked the wine from her in slow tantalizing strokes which he began to match with his movement inside her. "Oh," he feigned disappointment as he breathed against her neck, "there's no more wine."

"You've never needed wine before. You'll just have to make do," Elizabeth pulled his mouth to hers, but he broke the kiss quickly and concentrated on the rest of her willing body.

Later, as he dressed, Andrew would not bend to her pleas to stay longer. "I have to leave, my dear. One of my northern suppliers is causing problems. I have to deal with him now; it wouldn't do to let him think he can cheat me." At the dressing table, Andrew had poured her another glass of wine and brought it to her. "Remember when you drink this, Elizabeth that you belong to me."

She hugged herself tightly recalling his parting words, and now lay listening to her body, still humming with the pleasure Andrew had given her. Suddenly frowning, she realized through her haze of contentment that, beneath it all, the annoying cramps had returned.

Elizabeth rested a while longer then stretched languidly deciding, finally, that she should get out of bed and get a bite of breakfast; some tea at least. After all, it was nearly nine o'clock now. Quickly, Elizabeth brushed and tied her hair, pulled on her shift, a dark green petticoat, ivory waistcoat, slippers, and headed down the stairs. As she descended, she wondered when to tell her father about the bairn. Since she intended to raise the child with Andrew, now that he was looking forward to fatherhood, Elizabeth saw no reason to hide the child's existence any longer. In the entryway, Elizabeth stopped abruptly as another, stronger pain passed through her belly. She grimaced thinking the night too exciting for the babe, and scolded herself for having behaved so wantonly with Andrew. "We'll just have to learn to curb our passion for a time," she determined.

Making breakfast suddenly felt like too much work, so Elizabeth settled for a scone with clotted cream, and gulped scalding tea to rinse it down. "I think I'll have that bath after all," she said to herself and, as the pressure in her belly abated, she spoke to the child, "It may be soothing to us both." But before she could set a cauldron of water to heat, the knocker at the front door sounded. Grumbling irritably as she went to answer it, Elizabeth threw open the door and gaped. "Mr. Ross!"

With a small bow, Martin returned her greeting, "Miss Graham, may I speak with you?"

"Why...of course, won't you come in?" Elizabeth stepped aside for him to enter, self-consciously patting her already tidy hair into place. About to close the door, Elizabeth spied Simon and questioned, "Who is that?"

"My cousin, Simon."

Elizabeth looked at him distractedly. "Does he want to come in, too?"

"Not necessarily. My reason for disturbing you shouldn't take long," Martin replied.

"Then, please," she said, closing the door, "join me in the drawing room." Elizabeth lead the way, saying over her shoulder, "I'm very surprised to see you."

"I imagine so after my last visit," Martin responded dryly.

Ignoring his remark, Elizabeth sat on the edge of a pale yellow damask chair and indicated that Martin should sit facing her. When he was barely seated, Elizabeth asked, "Now then, what can I do for you today?"

"Tell me where I might find Fia. I assume the wedding trip is over."

Smiling with genuine pleasure, Elizabeth said, "I'd forgotten how direct you are Mr. Ross. Aye, everything's done. Apparently, they had a splendid time. With Struan's schedule, there was no time for the trip to the Continent they wanted. But to be quite honest with–" A gasp ended her response and Elizabeth clamped the edge of her chair with white-knuckled hands.

"What is it?" Martin leaned toward her as he watched the color drain from her face.

"A...a pain. It seems to be subsiding now." Slowly, Elizabeth eased her grasp a bit.

"Take a deep breath," Martin advised. "Are you faint?"

"No, I'm fine," she protested, but Martin noticed she took several deep breaths anyway. "I began to tell you," Elizabeth continued a bit unsteadily, "that I really don't know where my cousin is at the moment. Fia left, quite suddenly, on a trip."

"With...her hus...husband?" Martin nearly choked on the word.

Elizabeth answered truthfully, "Fia went alone. Struan is in Edinburgh, I imagine she went to join him." Hesitating a moment while studying Martin's troubled expression, Elizabeth almost felt sorry for him wasting his time pining after her trollop of a cousin. "Mr. Ross, if I might make a suggestion," she offered, "you should give Fia up. I know you told me once you were a friend, passing through, but frankly, Sir, I believe your feelings are not those of a mere friend. If I'm correct, you would be doing her a favor by leaving her alone. After all, she didn't choose you, did she?"

"You don't mince words either, Miss," Martin said with a blandness he did not feel. "I still consider Fia my friend, and I do want to see her."

Elizabeth's tight smile was indulgent. "But will she want to see you?"

Martin was considering her statement but never responded. Elizabeth cried out as her belly was gripped by pain. On his knees before her, Martin grasped her wrist seeking her pulse. "Tell me what's happening, Miss, where's your pain?" When she didn't answer him, Martin demanded, "Elizabeth, talk to me!"

His tone seeped through her agony and she railed against it. "How dare you raise you voice to me, you lout! First, you come begging for news of my simpleton cousin, now you demand

I answer idle questions about my body?" she seethed. Bottle of wine be damned; where was Andrew when she needed him? Why was she stuck with this... this Highlander, when Andrew should be with her? Elizabeth tore her wrist from Martin's grip and growled through clenched teeth, "Just what do you fancy yourself to be, a doctor?"

"I *am* a doctor; and you're a wretched patient, Miss. Now tell me what's happening," Martin ordered sternly.

Panting heavily as the pressure began to ease slightly, Elizabeth stared doubtfully at Martin. "Are you what you claim?" she asked, seeking assurance.

"I've always been direct with you," Martin reminded, glaring at her, "you said so yourself."

Despairing, Elizabeth surrendered. "I have this...cramping, here." She gingerly touched her belly.

"When did the pain start?"

"Not this bad before."

"And before?"

Elizabeth hesitated. "Cramping and discomfort for five... six days now."

Martin asked, "Have you eaten anything or done anything unusual? Elizabeth?" he prompted.

She struggled through her embarrassment to tell him, "My...my gentleman was here all night. We...didn't sleep much."

Martin fired questions at her. "Is that all? Anything else? Have you experienced any tenderness near your belly? Have you been ill?"

"I'm pregnant," Elizabeth blurted.

"Sweet Jesus," Martin muttered, then to Elizabeth, "Is your maid about? Anyone?" To her shaking head, Martin said, "Have you noticed any bleeding?"

Elizabeth's eyes grew round. "Bleeding?" she questioned in growing panic. "Why would I bleed?"

Martin took her hands and held her frightened gaze with his concerned one. "There could be bleeding if this is a problem with the bairn. Have you noticed any blood?"

"Just...a small amount," she admitted reluctantly.

"And how far along are you?"

"Five months," she whispered in a voice shrunken with dread.

"Tell me who your midwife is; I'll send Simon to fetch her."

Elizabeth shook her head frantically. "You take care of me."

Martin's jaw dropped. "Elizabeth, you don't mean that. You need someone who knows you and whom you trust."

"I trust you, *Doctor* Ross," she vowed, her voice suddenly icy. "I'm your link to Fia; you won't let me die."

"We'll have no talk of dying." Martin's voice reflected his exasperation, "and we're wasting time. Who is your midwife?"

"You are, Martin Ross."

They stared stubbornly at each other until Martin decided that to argue longer would serve no useful purpose. "I'll be right back; don't leave this chair."

He flung the door wide and called, "Simon, I need your help."

Hurrying over, Simon rattled, "I knew it! I've had a bad feeling all morning."

Martin's eyes widened in surprise. "Well your premonition is right. Elizabeth is ill."

Simon stopped short. "Elizabeth? What about Fia?"

Martin's face acutely reflected his disappointment. "Not here, and Elizabeth says she doesn't know where she is. But Simon, Elizabeth may be in real trouble." Simon entered and removed his coat while Martin called, "Arthur!" The dog nudged Martin's hand before sitting just inside the door as Martin bade, "Stay."

Quickly, Simon glanced around, noted the fine furnishings, then saw Elizabeth Graham, pinched and ghostly pale. He followed Martin into the drawing room and there was just enough time to be introduced before another wave of cramping made Elizabeth press her fist tightly to her mouth and fix frightened eyes on Martin.

"What's happening?" she cried frantically.

"Try very hard to stay calm, Elizabeth." Picking her up, Martin headed for the stairs. "Your room...which is it?"

"On the right, first one."

"Simon, find some toweling. There's no one here but us."

"Right!" Simon sprang into action while Martin safely deposited Elizabeth on the bed. He deftly removed her waistcoat and petticoat, speaking gently and reassuringly as he did so. "I know you're suffering, Elizabeth, and I also realize it would be unpleasant for you but, if I examined you, I might be able to better tell what's happening. Of course, I'll abide by your wishes."

She gaped at his impudence suggesting that he should actually.... Unable to finish the thought, Andrew's tender expression when admitting he longed for the child flashed from her memory to humble her pride. With a deep breath, Elizabeth swallowed her embarrassment and muttered, "If it will help."

Before she changed her mind, Martin rolled up his sleeves and performed a quick examination then covered Elizabeth with the linen sheet. "There is some bleeding. I know this will be difficult for you to do, but I want you to lie still and, please, try to relax." Martin dragged a chair up to the bed table and sat down. "Listen to me, Elizabeth. Simon and I will do everything we can to help you. It appears as though your body is preparing to deliver your bairn. I'm not sure why this is happening—you seem to be in good health. We'll have to work together, so I want this clear between us now—don't fight me. You'll do as I say, understood?"

She nodded.

He bit his lip then continued, "You need to know that, with the severity and frequency of your cramping, the best I can do may not be good enough. If these *are* birthing pains, making you comfortable is about all anyone can do."

Elizabeth's stricken expression cut Martin. "Are you telling me you can't stop them?" Her voice pitched high on the edge of terror, "I could be delivering my babe *now*?"

Martin calmly replied, "I wish I could give you the answer you want to hear but, Elizabeth, I do believe you are going to deliver."

She struggled to sit up. "Do you mean I'm going to lose my child?"

"Lie back Elizabeth." Martin placed his hands on her shoulders.

"Why, so I can miscarry in comfort?" she screeched, batting at his hands.

"So that you can rest. You'll need your strength for whatever lies ahead." With gentle hands, Martin pushed her firmly back into the pillows.

Just then, Simon entered briskly, arms loaded with towels which he placed on the end of the bed. "Can I do anything else?"

Martin motioned Simon aside. "Elizabeth's pregnant and I'm afraid she's about to give birth; it's far too early."

"Don't talk behind my back," Elizabeth harped.

Martin responded sternly, "I told you to relax, now stay quiet. I'm only telling Simon what you already know. We'll need his help and he has to know what we're dealing with."

"What kind of help?" Simon questioned warily.

"If I need more than one pair of hands, it will be yours—even if it's just to give Elizabeth something to hang on to."

"I'll do what I can, Martin, of course. What's gone wrong?"

Martin murmured, "I wish I knew. It could be any number of things but, whatever it is, it isn't obvious."

An agonized cry erupted from Elizabeth as a spasm tore her belly. Both men rushed to her, Simon grasping her hands and Martin coaxing her to breathe deeply until the pain lessened. To Simon, he said, "See if you can find some wine. There must be more where that came from," and pointed to Andrew's near empty bottle. "Elizabeth can finish this one first."

"No," Elizabeth protested in an unsteady voice, "it tastes funny; wine all tastes queer lately."

"It's to bolster your strength and take the edge off your pain; you will drink it." Martin insisted.

Simon sniffed the open bottle. "It doesn't smell spoiled." Reading the label, he added, "It's an unusual Madeira. Maybe a claret or port would do—something she's used to."

"Good idea." Martin nodded. "See what you can find, will you?" Simon eased himself from the room leaving Martin with the mute woman. "Elizabeth, is there anyone you'd like me to send for? Your gentleman might—"

"No! I don't want him to see me like this." Elizabeth shook her head in confusion. "Wait...

he...he's gone anyway. I forgot. He left town this morning...business."

"Anyone else?" Martin asked.

"No, no one." Elizabeth jerked her face to the window putting an end to the conversation.

Hours ago, doubt had vanished–Elizabeth was going to deliver her bairn and there was nothing to do but wait. How many more times, Martin wondered, would she squall the same question to which he could only respond, "I can't explain it Elizabeth. Miscarriages happen, so often for reasons no doctor or midwife can identify, much less explain."

Inwardly, Martin sighed as Elizabeth panted toward the end of another contraction. Dabbing her sopping brow with a cloth, he said, "It shouldn't be much longer, a couple of hours at most."

"All for nothing," she noted sourly. "I can't...can't accept...oh, God!" Elizabeth puffed and strained against the pressure in her belly.

"Breathe, Elizabeth," he urged, but she screamed instead. Grabbing at him, Elizabeth raked her nails the length of his forearm, drawing angry welts which quickly disappeared under his surfacing blood.

"Stop this now," she commanded. "I can't bear it!"

"It's almost over," Martin gasped from the pain, prying her nails from his wrist. "Simon!" he bellowed and Simon was there in an instant. "Help," he pleaded, "and watch her talons."

Simon paled at the sight of Martin's shredded arm, but bravely grasped Elizabeth's hands.

A short time later, when Elizabeth finally pushed the child from her body, Martin was tempted to let Simon whisk it from the room–but it wasn't his decision to make. "Elizabeth, do you want to see him?"

Drawing the back of her hand across her eyes, taking sweat and tears of exhaustion with it, Elizabeth said, "Him...a son? Andrew wanted a son." She clawed her still aching belly.

Martin exchanged a sympathetic look with Simon who waited nearby. "Elizabeth?" Martin asked gently.

A demonic scowl consumed her face. "Get it away from me," she snarled.

"As you wish." Martin wrapped the toweling over the child and motioning to Simon. He handed the small bundle to his cousin, murmured a few words to him and, after Simon took his leave, Martin turned his attention to dealing with the afterbirth and making his patient comfortable. When she was clean and settled, Martin said, "I'd like you to have a bit more wine, Elizabeth. It'll help you."

Without protest, she drank and, handing him the empty goblet said sluggishly, "Simon must have been right."

"About what?" Martin puzzled.

"This wine doesn't bother me. The ones Andrew brought, the exotic ones, all tasted odd."

"I guess he was right then," Martin agreed gently. "Now, you sleep. I'm going down to help Simon, and then I'll be back."

Nodding dumbly, Elizabeth closed her eyes and Martin descended the stairs, passed through the kitchen, and into the garden. In the dying light, he spotted Simon slouched on a bench amid the rain-wilted flowers. Sitting heavily beside him, Martin inquired, "Did you have any trouble?"

"No, the vicar baptised the bairn and said he'd see to its proper burial. I had to name the poor mite," Simon spoke too briskly, wiping his nose on his sleeve, not looking at his cousin.

Martin lifted his arm to touch Simon's shoulder, but saw it encrusted with his own blood, so instead offered, "I'm sorry you had to be involved in this at all." He rose and drew a bucket of water. In silence, the two men washed until the bucket was empty. It was nearly dark now and the early stars showered sparks overhead. Simon was profoundly heartened by their presence.

Martin's gaze followed Simon's skyward and he quietly asked, "Do you want to talk?"

Simon replied, "The night sky is comforting."

"Aye," Martin agreed, taking a cleansing breath.

Simon murmured in thick tones, "The bairn never had a chance to see it. He never even experienced one moment in which he was shown a mother's love." He knelt and buried his fingers deep into the comfort of Arthur's fur, for the hound had come to stand between them. Emotion rattled Simon's voice. "I was always affected when I saw men dying in battle; especially the many who were younger than I. So much was left undone; lives and opportunities stolen from them by untimely death. That was wasteful. This," he swallowed hard, "seems completely futile. That tiny babe waiting to be born, to go through all that pain, and never even have...a chance. It's...it's...how do you bear it?"

Martin crossed his arms and stared at a pebble he pushed with the toe of his boot. "Only one thing makes it bearable, Simon–when everything works right, and you hear the sweet cry of a new life." Martin continued, "I really am sorry, Simon. I should have realized–"

"No." Simon shook his head. "Martin please, it wasn't your fault. It's just...no experience I've had.... Anyway, I'm glad I was here to help you."

"As am I. Listen, I'm going to dress my arm then sit with Elizabeth for a bit. Why don't you get some sleep?"

Simon nodded. "I'll come in shortly."

Patting Simon's shoulder, Martin hesitantly left him searching the heavens for answers.

Chapter Seventeen

"You're exhausted, Martin," Simon whispered. "I'll stay with Elizabeth; go rest for a bit." Martin began to protest, but Simon insisted. "She's been sleeping for several hours and that's what you need to do."

"You're tired as well," Martin dutifully pointed out.

"No, I napped after leaving the garden; that will hold me for some time. Martin, please," Simon urged, prying his cousin from the chair.

In the dim hallway, Martin noted long-tailed paper birds splashing the walls in shades of yellow and green. The door closed quietly behind him and he sagged against it. God's life, what a horrible day. He forced visions of the aborted bairn aside along with Elizabeth's agonized screams and curses. They reminded him of Bridgid as nothing else ever could, and he was never as grateful as when Elizabeth had lapsed into the exhausted sleep which still enveloped her. He knew that Simon spoke the truth–he was spent, his energy drained, his wounded arm throbbed painfully. Raising weary eyes, Martin scrutinized one door after another down the corridor and strength surged back into his body. One of these rooms had been Fia's.

Striding directly across the hall, Martin flung wide the door. The feeble, ashen light from the window was useless, so he lifted the candle from the table at the top of the stairs and entered the room, and the next, then a third when he stopped short. Without question it was Fia's; Martin's heart fluttered to a faster beat. As if treading sacred ground, Martin examined everything he encountered with great care. Sitting at her dressing table, Martin fingered bottles she had touched, ribbons she had worn. Opening a small carved box, Martin found a thin silver band designed with Celtic knots, and a strip of cloth–the one Fia had borrowed from him to tie her voluminous curls. He lifted it, feeling its smoothness between trembling fingers. Did its place in the box mean that, somehow, it was special to her? Even as he hoped, despair washed over him. What did it matter if she kept the ribbon as a reminder? She'd married Forbes and had no further use for Martin except in a bit of cloth. Martin let it slip from his fingers, back into its cask.

Advancing to the wardrobe, he pulled the door open and held the candle high. A gnawing ache caught him as his eye fell on the deep blue traveling outfit. Setting the candle atop the wardrobe, Martin withdrew the dress, buried his face in the soft woolen folds, and breathed deeply. Her lingering scent catapulted him back to his croft, the darkness of early hours when he'd wakened to find Fia standing, pale and melancholy, in the middle of the room. What exquisite sweetness when he had held her, willing, in his arms. Martin clenched the garment against him as if she were wearing it now and savored the memory. Finally, his gaze rested on the high bed. Martin reluctantly replaced the dress, picked up the candle and approached, noting the embroidered spread and wondering if Fia had crafted it. Half expecting her bed to be where he felt the strongest pull to Fia, Martin was strangely disturbed that he felt nothing. On turning away, however, the window seat seemed to beckon. He set the candle down once more, doffed his boots and folded his lean frame into the seat's comforting pillows. From his new vantage point, Martin surveyed the shadows beyond reach of the taper's glow before facing the rivulets of rain staining the window. While the few personal articles he could connect with Fia made his heart cringe with painfully delicious memories, the rest of the belongings were meaningless and, momentarily, he felt empty. What he did not understand was why the room should look as though she still lived in it. Why were so many of her things still here?

The chimes of the tall clock in the entry sounded and Martin began to breathe easier. Seeping into his sluggish brain was Fia's fragrance, lightly resting on the pillows with him–hypnotic and soothing. Martin crossed his arms over his chest and, closing his eyes, Fia joined him. Tenderly, he stroked her hair, fingers traveling to her jaw, tilting her face, her lips to his kiss. A shiver coursed his body as he tasted her willingness and cradled her fluid body as it molded to his.... His eyes snapped open; he was alone again.

In the stillness of the early hours, Simon had long since given up reading the leather bound volume he'd plucked from a downstairs bookcase. He wanted to plan and dream of his next meeting with Alayne, but his mind was crammed instead with all that had happened since arriving in Glasgow. Truly he was glad to have been useful to Martin. The power that a physician had over the quality of people's lives intrigued him. In the colonies, Simon had seen all manner of doctors–the saints and the butchers treating victims of the French and their Indian allies. Never had he prepared himself to experience the emotional havoc caused by a miscarriage. Simon was proud of his cousin's ability to deal with it all.

"What are you smiling at?" Elizabeth croaked caustically.

Not realizing she'd woken, Simon started at the sound of her voice. "I was thinking how fortunate you are that Martin was here when you needed help."

"Fortunate," she rasped, "is your opinion." Elizabeth retreated into her own thoughts, but not for long. "Why are you here?"

"Watching you while Martin rests, which is what you should be doing," Simon suggested.

"I want to talk...and I meant, why are you in Glasgow? Is it that cousin of mine who brings you here as well?" she sniped.

Simon was surprised at the venom in her voice and, wary, kept his countenance blank. "I'm traveling with Martin, that's why I'm here."

Elizabeth sneered, "Ah, fortunately for me."

"Aye, as it turns out." Simon's forehead creased in annoyance but he kept his voice even. "Shall I fetch Martin? Are you feeling badly?"

"How do you think I'm feeling?" she snarled.

Simon rose. "I'll get Martin."

"No...not yet," she pleaded.

"Then I repeat, you should rest," Simon insisted.

"Just one question."

"Which is?" Simon asked skeptically.

"Why has he returned for her?"

"He stopped to pay his respects," Simon carefully replied.

Elizabeth frowned. "It's more than that."

"You're seeing only what you want to see," Simon replied. "Now try to sleep. If you aren't weary of this, I certainly am."

But Elizabeth ignored him, her face reddening with wrath. "Let me tell you about Fia. She ties men in knots until they're so befuddled they can't think except with their loins. And she feigns innocence so well; no man can resist a chaste, virtuous woman after all–not your besotted cousin, surely!" she spat.

Simon cringed at Elizabeth's raw hatred. There had to be a reason for it and only one came to mind. He stepped closer to her bed and asked, "Does the inability of men to resist Fia include your 'gentleman' friend? Is that why you only speak ill of your cousin?" The wounded expression, replaced quickly with loathing confirmed his guess was on target. Elizabeth's lover was at the center of her enmity toward Fia. Unexpected disquiet filled him. He realized that Elizabeth had not responded to his remark and, when he focused on her again, he felt a small pang of remorse for his words. It was evident that Elizabeth was struggling with her grief; perhaps her anger was fueled by her loss. For a moment, Simon thought to apologize then changed his mind. He didn't believe she'd accept sympathetic words. Miserably, he sat in his chair again and watched as Elizabeth stared unseeing at the canopy overhead.

Andrew stared blindly through his whiskey at the licking flames of the tavern fire. Damn Elizabeth! Why couldn't she have listened to reason? Why did she force him to resort to trickery? Did her pain mean that the oil was working? Fervently, he hoped so since he didn't know how much longer he could keep up this charade. Downing his glass, Andrew growled, "Another!" to the barmaid.

When a new glass was before him, Andrew scowled at it. "That crone of a midwife better have been telling me the truth," he mumbled. On a tip, Andrew had sought out the biddy's crumbling croft, and woven his tale of woe. "My wife and I have been so careful. Her physician said it was not safe for her to bear more children, that it would surely cost her life." He dropped his head sorrowfully. "But she has missed her flow, and I fear the worst." Andrew raised his tearful gaze to the sharp-featured woman. "Please, I beg you, help us. I could not bear to lose my beloved wife."

And, for the right coin, she did help, urging him to use the oil of pennyroyal most sparingly to bring on the missed flow. "More than a bit could kill the mother," she warned solemnly.

So a little more than the "safe" dosage would surely produce the outcome Andrew desired. Time was not on his side–he wanted to be done with the thought of fatherhood. Hoping Elizabeth's pains were a reaction to his remedy, he hastily retreated–but only as far as Dumbarton before the implications of what he was attempting weighed him down so that he could not go on. What if she did die? His eyes furtively searched the room as if someone might suspect his misdeed simply by looking at him. "I did the right thing," he assured himself, "and cleverly. Aye, soon everything will be back to normal."

Andrew gulped the contents of his glass and, licking whiskey and sweat from his upper lip, called again for whiskey. Other matters demanded his attention now. There really was trouble with one of his suppliers and he had to make an example of the scum to discourage others from challenging him. Beyond that, everything was ready for moving shipments on and off Fia's beach. He was anxious to begin this operation; the loss of Luce Bay as a transport site was costing him money.

"Fia's beach," he sneered coldly. "Where have you got yourself hidden you little harlot?" His hired men had turned up nothing in their search for her and, disgusted with their ineptitude, Andrew had dismissed them. He intended to renew the search personally once his newest operation was safely underway. Absently, rubbing the silvery scar, Andrew vowed afresh that when he found Fia, she would pay for her actions–repeatedly. "How I cherish the thought," he drooled in anticipation.

Kate opened the door to the polite but insistent knocking. An intrusion was the last thing she needed while trying to balance the shop's books. She envisioned one of her neighbors wanting to stay for a chat and herself spending the rest of the afternoon unwillingly playing hostess. The man who stood on her stoop, however, was a stranger. He was tall and lean, with a square jawed, intelligent face beneath neatly queued flaxen hair. "How may I help you, Sir?" Kate asked in a clear, strong voice.

The man removed his tricorne and replied, "Are you Mistress Katherine Matheson?"

"And if I am?" Even the soothing timbre of his voice would not make Kate reckless; people depended on her.

The caller smiled gently. "If you are Mistress Matheson, then I would say you are a kind and loving aunt and ask you to tell your niece, Fia, that her solicitor, Douglas Sutherland, wishes to see her."

Kate's pulse quickened a pace, but she feigned ignorance. "Douglas Sutherland?"

"I hired Murdoch Sinclair to deliver Fia into your safekeeping, which he did on the sixth of June last, posing as Fia's husband. I...believe you fainted in his arms."

Kate reddened but, for the first time smiled. "Do come in Mr. Sutherland, and welcome." Kate stepped back and Douglas followed her inside setting his tricorne on the entry table. "You understand Sir, that I must be careful who comes to my door."

"Indeed." Past Kate, on the desk in the drawing room, he saw papers spread wide. "I see I've interrupted you," he began his apology, but Kate cut him off.

"Don't give it another thought. I was working on the accounts for my millinery shop; it's been an exceptionally busy August. However," she assured him, "I can resume that later. In fact, I was thinking of making some tea. Would you join me? Or would you take some sherry, perhaps?"

"Tea would be fine, thank you."

"Please make yourself comfortable, Mr. Sutherland, I'll return in a few moments." Kate swept from the room, no longer annoyed by the interruption. On the contrary, she was surprisingly pleased. "Flora, I have a guest for tea," she announced.

"Aye, Mistress," came the maid's reply.

Douglas' gaze wandered the room as he gathered impressions of Katherine Matheson. He already knew she was a handsome woman, just as Murdoch had described: sparkling brown eyes, chestnut hair with traces of silver. The way her cheeks rounded when she smiled made his knees a little weak. Now he surveyed her drawing room and saw everything neatly in place, clean and polished, except the paper strewn desk. When she finished balancing her books, Douglas had no doubt that the books and her desk would be as tidy as the rest of the room. Touching a Chinese willow-ware bowl of flowers, Douglas felt a yearning for the little touches that women employed to turn a house into a home.

"Is something wrong, Mr. Sutherland?" Kate asked, Flora stepping past her bearing the tray which she placed on a small table. "Thank you, Flora."

Flora bobbed a curtsey and retreated with a sidelong glance at the guest.

"Nothing amiss, Mistress," Douglas assured her. "I was only lost in thought. Your flowers are lovely, as is the rest of the room."

"Thank you. The girls picked the flowers for me on their outing yesterday."

"The girls?" Douglas prompted.

"Aye, Fia and Alayne, my daughter-in-law." Kate poured tea and offered Douglas a plate with slices of heavy, sweet gingerbread on it. When she was settled, Kate said, "Fia is working at my shop Mr. Sutherland. Perhaps you'd like to go there after a bit."

"I would, thank you. And I'd be grateful if you would call me Douglas."

"If you return the favor and call me Kate. Fia lives here with me and has added much life to this otherwise empty house. She has spoken highly of you and with much fondness. I assume she knows nothing of your visit because she hasn't been dancing with excitement. She'll be overjoyed to see you again."

"And I, her. Tell me," Douglas hesitated, "do you think Fia has healed well?"

Kate spoke through pursed lips, "I assume you're referring to her emotional state because her face has been healed for some time."

"Aye," Douglas nodded, "she was much abused by those people."

Kate confided, "Murdoch's presence helped bolster her courage to tell me the details of what they put her through. I'm gratified to report that Fia appears to be fine now. In fact, sometimes I think I worry more about her than she does." Kate shook her head in amazement. "It must be because she's so young that she seems unaffected. And then, of course, there's Alayne."

"They've become friends?" Douglas asked hopeful.

"Oh, aye, firm friends." Kate's face clouded a bit.

"What is it you aren't telling me?" he asked alertly.

Kate chewed her lower lip thoughtfully. "Alayne can be headstrong. It's not that I think she's a bad influence, I only wonder sometimes if Fia may be a bit less careful than she ought because of her friendship with Alayne."

"Obviously, I've not met your daughter-in-law. My experience with Fia, however, is that she has a mind and will of her own. And I thank the good Lord for it; a lesser resolve might not have withstood what she has endured. More than anything though," Douglas finished, "I'm happy that Fia has a true friend in your daughter-in-law. And your son, how does he like having his cousin back in Inverness?"

Kate's stricken expression shot dread through Douglas. It was clear he had said something terribly wrong. He stood quickly and bowed slightly before her. "Please accept my humble apologies, Kate, I've deeply distressed you. It wasn't my intention."

Swallowing hard, Kate did not immediately look at Douglas but said, "Of course not. You couldn't have known that my son is no longer with us. Please, don't chastise yourself."

Douglas reseated himself, heavy with remorse at having caused this gracious woman pain. But Kate sensed his discomfort and sought to ease it.

"Fia has a good friend in Alayne, but none better than you and Murdoch." With a nod, Douglas acknowledged her compliment. Kate continued, "I suppose you'd like to go to the shop now?"

"If you'll direct me–"

"Nonsense," she interrupted, "I'll take you there. The day is really too beautiful not to go out." Kate rose and Douglas with her. "I'll get my wrap."

He followed her regal figure into the entryway and warmed to the thought of walking the Inverness streets with Kate Matheson on his arm. "Are you sure I should go to the shop? Will I keep Fia from her work?" he called after her.

"I assure you the work will be finished. There's still enough evening light that the girls tend to put in longer hours. Anyway, Fia would not forgive me for keeping you all to myself if she knew you were here."

Douglas returned Kate's smile and lay her wrap lightly over her shoulders, fingertips grazing the base of her neck in the process. He colored slightly as his blood pulsed more rapidly through his body. Douglas breathed deeply to clear his head. He needed to focus on Fia; it was she who brought him to Inverness. Even so, on the stoop, when Douglas offered his arm to Kate, and she accepted with a coquettish downswing of her lashes, Douglas felt as though he were twenty again.

"Only a half hour more and we can close up," Alayne grumbled.

"And lock all these people out for a few hours," Fia added. She flexed her hand tentatively before picking up her needle again. "When you told me three weeks ago that we were going to be busy, I had no idea. My hand has never gotten sore from sewing until now!"

"I have to admit, this surpasses even my expectations. People must be feeling wealthy this year." She paused looking dismayed.

"Alayne?"

"September won't be much better but, we still have October, November and half of December to get everyone ready for Hogmanny."

"Oh, Alayne please," Fia groaned, "let's don't think of that now. I can't bear it."

The bell on the shop door sounded and Alayne volunteered, "I'll get it," but stopped at the curtain separating the shop from the workroom. "Fia, will you look at this," Alayne whispered over her shoulder. "It's Kate on the arm of some dapper looking fellow."

"Let me see," Fia pushed her work aside, hopped up, and pulling the curtain a fraction farther open so she too might observe. The man's back was momentarily to her, but when he turned, Fia squealed in delight, *"Douglas!"* Running from the back room and straight into his embrace, she hugged him fiercely then stood back to look at him, hands clutching his. "Oh, Douglas, this is a glorious surprise. You look wonderful doesn't he look wonderful Aunt Kate? How good it is to see you!" Fia collapsed against his chest and squeezed again.

Douglas couldn't catch his breath from her exuberant greeting. "Fia, I'm...I'm overwhelmed." This time he held her back slightly, examining her intently. "And you lass, you have blossomed! I couldn't be happier." He planted a kiss on her cheek then spotted the young woman standing between the counters. "Ah, Fia tell me, is this your friend, Alayne?"

"Oh, forgive me." She turned to Alayne and motioned her forward. Alayne advanced as Fia performed introductions. "Alayne Matheson, my good friend, meet another dear friend, Douglas Sutherland."

As she dipped her curtsey, Alayne smiled somewhat awkwardly, feeling peculiarly out of place, but Douglas quickly won her over. "It is an unexpected pleasure, Mistress Matheson, to be counted in your company as Fia's friend. Your mother-in-law has told me that you two young ladies make quite a pair."

Alayne smiled wryly at his diplomatic summation of what she was sure was a more cryptic report by Kate. "I'm certain she did. And for that bit of tact, I must ask if you are still a solicitor or considering running for a seat in Parliament?"

Douglas laughed heartily. "The former, have no doubt." He turned his attention back to Fia. "Surely, you're wondering why I've come to Inverness."

Fia shifted from one foot to the other. "I'm a bit afraid to ask."

Resting a hand on her shoulder, Douglas assured, "Nothing bad. We need to discuss a few things, but as far as the troubles are concerned, everything's been quiet."

Fia breathed a sigh of relief, and Kate offered, "Would you like to return to the house, Fia?"

"It depends. Douglas, how long will you be here? I don't feel that I can leave just yet. Things have been so hectic."

"I saw that by the stack of paperwork on Kate's desk." Fia and Alayne exchanged swift glances at his use of Kate's given name. Douglas continued, "I'll be here several days so there'll be plenty of time." He turned to Kate. "If I may, I'll drop by later, after Fia's finished for the day."

"Fine, come to supper; you too, Alayne. Shall we say half past eight?"

The night faded into a dismal excuse for day, wet and gloom hanging like a pall over everything Martin could see from the window. He closed his eyes again, wishing for more sleep, knowing it was a wasted thought–his melancholy over not seeing Fia would not allow it. Slowly he sat up and rubbed his eyes, deciding to go in search of some water with which to wash.

Pulling on his boots, Martin headed for the door but stopped abruptly, catching a glimpse of himself in the mirror. He still had Fia's shirt on. Martin cursed his carelessness and quickly examined the shirt for damage. Miraculously, he saw only a few drops of dried blood, he guessed from his own arm, and sighed his relief before starting downstairs. He could wash those out.

Stepping into the soggy courtyard behind the house, Martin was nearly knocked over by Arthur's enthusiastic greeting. After spending a few minutes entertaining the hound by chasing him in circles, Martin huffed, "Enough for now, laddie. I'll get you something to eat shortly."

Martin drew water from the well and rubbed his face briskly with it, drew a second bucket, and carried it back into the kitchen. He poured some into a small bowl and placed it on the floor for Arthur who had followed him, dripping, into the house. He cut a chunk of cheese from the larder, ate some, and gave the rest to the dog. Simon had set the saddlebags in the entryway and Martin tucked Fia's shirt into the bag after scrounging his only clean one. Pulling it on as he ascended the stairs, he bumped into Simon at the top. "How's our patient?" Martin inquired and, at the irritated look on Simon's face asked, "What?"

"We have to talk before you see her, Martin." Simon motioned him away from the door and gave an account of what had transpired between him and Elizabeth in the early hours. "I tell you, Martin," Simon lamented, raking hair from his forehead in a futile gesture. "She's been ranting; I don't know where she found the strength to carry on so. And I didn't like what she was saying."

Martin frowned and offered, "Losing her child has to be very hard on her."

"You won't be so charitable when I tell you that there's something sinister about all this. Elizabeth sees some connection between her man and your Fia."

Martin studied him thoughtfully. "Did she say that?"

"Aye." Simon grasped his cousin's shoulder. "And she has no sense of gratitude whatsoever for your help."

"Simon, that's not unusual considering the bairn died. I can't make her appreciate what we did."

In growing frustration at Martin's empathy toward a woman Simon had begun to consider dangerous, Simon pressed, "Martin, she's going to goad you, and say things meant to hurt you. Elizabeth's guessed your feelings for Fia. I believe, wherever Fia is, she's better off away from Elizabeth's venom."

Martin assured, "I appreciate the warning, Simon, and your concern. Now," he concluded, "I've had my sleep, it's your turn."

"You'll get no argument from me." Simon went down to the room beside Fia's, removed his boots and, stretching across the bed, fell instantly into a fitful sleep.

In Elizabeth's room, Martin took up the vigil from the bedside chair. He was so lost in thought over his discussion with Simon that he scarcely heard Elizabeth's muffled request for water. He helped her sit up long enough to drink, then settled her again on her back.

"Have you had any more cramping?" Martin asked.

"No," she murmured.

Examining her briefly, Martin affirmed, "I see nothing out of the ordinary," and waited for her to speak, but in vain. Elizabeth lay unmoving, staring vacantly into the dimness of the room until exhaustion made her sleep again. Martin was glad she slept for she needed to regain her strength. Still, he was anxious to hear what she would say to him. Possibly, she'd been fishing for information with Simon and didn't intend to address her questions directly to him at all. When she next awoke, however, Elizabeth had more to say.

"Your lover is gone, Doctor."

Martin tensed, asking, "Who are you referring to Elizabeth?"

She looked at him with cold eyes. "Why can't you admit what Fia is to you?"

"Fia is not my lover, never has been," he said.

"But you love her..."

"Aye, I love her," he admitted, "not that it matters since she has made her choice by marrying Struan Forbes."

"Then why do you chase her," Elizabeth gritted. "Don't you know when you've lost?"

Martin rose and stood at the end of Elizabeth's bed. "I simply want to see that she's happy. What I fail to understand is why it's so important to you how I feel about Fia? Why do you delight in playing this cat and mouse game with me? I've done nothing but try to help you."

She ignored him and asked, "When will you and Simon be leaving?"

Head bowed, Martin sighed heavily. "If you improve steadily throughout the day, we'll be gone tomorrow, that is if you expect you're maid to return. You shouldn't be alone or get out of bed for at least a week." Martin offered, "Tell her you've had the gripe."

"Fine. But I would like to be alone now, if that's acceptable to you, Doctor," she sneered.

Martin wondered if that was all Elizabeth had to say about Fia. It appeared he'd have to wait to find out. "Of course. I'll check on you later but, if you need me, I'll be within hearing distance."

When Simon found him, the bedroom door was open so that he might hear if Elizabeth called. Simon had washed from his sleep and looked remarkably refreshed. Standing just inside the door, Simon glanced around with interest. "Is this Fia's room?" he inquired with a slightly befuddled look.

"Strange isn't it?" Martin replied with an affirming nod.

"Aye, it looks like she didn't take anything with her to her husband's home." He peaked inside the wardrobe. "Strange indeed!"

Swinging his feet to the floor, Martin clasped his hands over his head and stretched. "I thought the same thing; toiletries, jewelry, everything's here. And I don't think these are simply the belongings she left behind."

"I suppose Elizabeth still claims not to know Fia's whereabouts?"

"Elizabeth isn't telling me anything, she only wants her own questions answered. Right now she's resting. I told her that, if there are no setbacks and if someone is here to tend her, you and I will leave tomorrow."

"Tomorrow?" Simon's voice sparked with excitement and Martin smiled.

"Aye, so start practicing your speech for Alayne," he teased affectionately.

Simon rubbed his palms together in anticipation. "I just have to select the right words out of several thousand possibilities."

Elizabeth found she could not sleep. Something Martin had mentioned gnawed at her; had she eaten or drunk something tainted? The more Elizabeth thought about it, the more one notion stabbed at her, and the more apprehensive she became. Why had she found each of the wines Andrew presented her slightly disagreeable? He had so opposed her pregnancy that she had zealously embraced his declared change of heart. But was it really a change of heart, or had he pretended simply to gain her confidence while he assured he would have his own way? Her heart twisted viscously as it recognized the truth her mind fiercely resisted.

Unclenching her fist, Elizabeth absently smoothed the sheet she'd caught in her grip. The murmur of men's voices reached her and turned her agitated contemplation to Martin Ross. "What to do with the good Doctor," she mused. Now that...it...was all over, Elizabeth grudgingly admitted that he was not the rustic she'd originally determined, but accomplished, forthright... even kind. Didn't he deserve some kindness from her in return for his efforts? "Should I tell him Fia never married?" Elizabeth's stare hardened. "Shall I tell him to find her before Andrew does otherwise there may be nothing left he'll want?" Her hand flew to her mouth to stifle a sob. Before today, Elizabeth had convinced herself of many "truths" regarding Andrew, including that he had given up his search for Fia. Now, she doubted everything about him and, if he had dealt this harshly with Elizabeth herself for defying him and keeping the bairn, she didn't doubt he would humble Fia or kill her in the attempt. For him, it was a simple matter of pride. Fia had gotten the better of Andrew and Elizabeth knew now he would never abide that. "He'll want his revenge," she hissed, "for all that matters to Andrew is what Andrew desires. And he desires Fia." Fia had been trouble since the day she'd walked in the door: wanted to borrow books, wanted to ride the horses, wanted to share Elizabeth's tutor, was willing to go to London as Elizabeth's maid just so she could see the city. And for George Graham's kindness in taking the brat in, providing a roof over her head, food and clothing, Fia had repaid him with betrayal. She had refused a good marriage–a better match than she deserved! Fia was a traitor–just like Andrew. And she didn't deserve the devotion of a respectable man like Martin Ross–another poor bastard Fia had cast her spell upon. There was no other way to explain it. No, Elizabeth would not help that vile bitch ruin anyone else. "Never!" she flared.

In the late afternoon, at Elizabeth's request, Martin dispatched a note to the maid asking that she come round in the morning. The messenger returned with Una's agreement. "We'll leave early," Martin assured Elizabeth, "so as not to invite talk." Removing her supper tray, Martin descended to the kitchen leaving Simon at Elizabeth's bedside. Patiently, Simon waited for Elizabeth to speak and, when he was able to bear her silence no longer said, "You ought to help Martin; tell him what you know about Fia."

"This is not your affair," she answered sullenly.

Simon grinned perversely. "So, you do know something."

Elizabeth's jet eyes flashed her rancor. "I know that Fia is as deceitful, ungrateful and selfish a witch as ever breathed. Your cousin has been addled by her–him and every other man she decides to seduce. The Doctor doesn't deserve to be sullied by the likes of her." Elizabeth started, spotting Martin standing in the doorway, fists clenched. With an unexpected burst of hostility, Elizabeth bolted upright screeching, "And I don't know *where* the whore is!"

Simon hastily withdrew a step as Martin stormed to the end of the bed. "You're twisted, Elizabeth. You lived with Fia for years and don't know the first thing about her."

"Oh no, I don't know her," Elizabeth gritted sarcastically. "But because you bedded her, you think you do." Martin gripped the bedpost so tightly Simon expected it to split under the strain. Still, Elizabeth persisted, "I'll never understand why you men all want to worship between her legs–even Andrew can't leave her alone. And you, you pitifully blind fool, you think you're in love! If you had told me that when we'd first met, I could have spared you a great deal of suffering."

Martin spat, "If your love means so little to Andrew that he wants someone else, I pity you. But don't judge me by his standards."

"You are worse than a fool, you're an imbecile to have been duped by that shrew," Elizabeth scorned.

"If Fia ever needs me, I will do her bidding without question. And if by God's grace she ever carried my child, nothing would take me from her side."

Between Elizabeth's bitterness and Martin's rage, Simon gaped helplessly. And when Martin stalked from the room, he glowered, "Elizabeth, you're damned lucky Martin's the decent man he is."

Simon followed Martin's example and, as he was pulling shut the door Elizabeth screamed, "He needs to hear the truth!"

"Not your truth," Simon threw back at her as she dissolved into plaintive sobs of despair.

As they fetched the brandy, carrying it to the drawing room, Alayne whispered to Fia, "This has got to be the most pleasant evening I've ever spent in this house. Douglas has had such wondrous adventures in Calcutta, Bombay and the West Indies. He's seen and done so much–what an exciting fellow."

"I'd say that Aunt Kate agrees with you," Fia allowed. "She seems totally charmed."

Alayne's face lit up. "Douglas isn't really a confirmed bachelor is he?"

"He has been until now." Giggles barely restrained, the two young women entered, sat and served the brandy which Douglas declared superb.

Kate smoothed her petticoat and, without looking directly at him, blushed like a school girl. "I'm pleased you like it Douglas. I've saved it for a special occasion."

"And it has been a very special occasion," Douglas smiled into the amber liquid he swirled in his glass. A moment of comfortable silence passed between them, and Fia and Alayne exchanged looks of amazement at the flirting going on before their gladdened eyes.

Kate broke the spell gently. "Douglas, I think Alayne and I should leave you to speak to Fia.

You have only a few days in Inverness and much you want to accomplish, I'm sure. We can't allow our selfish enjoyment of your company to interfere."

"That's thoughtful of you, Kate. However, I can stay an extra day or two...if circumstances dictate."

Alayne rose and Douglas with her. "Kate's right. You and Fia need some privacy. Perhaps, since you've graced us with your company this evening, we've already set your schedule back by at least a day?" She smiled broadly at him, and he bowed his tall frame above her hand.

"Graciously said, my dear, and I thank you." He helped Kate rise, and the two women bade him and Fia goodnight.

Fia slipped from her seat and settled on the floor by the hearth. "So, what do you think of my aunt?"

"I think your aunt engaging; you, on the other hand are incorrigible. I've watched you and Alayne grinning and whispering. Don't get any ideas of playing matchmaker."

Reaching up to squeeze his hand, Fia said, "I have no ideas that I didn't see first in your eyes."

Self-consciously, Douglas cleared his throat. "I'm too old for such nonsense."

"*That*," Fia accused, "is nonsense. You enjoy each other's company; there's nothing wrong with that."

"No," he spoke fondly, "nothing wrong with that. Fia, you do look well. Are you?"

"Aye," she replied to the flames before her, "quite well. Aunt Kate and Alayne have been wonderful to me. I'm not afraid here; I work at the shop and enjoy it very much."

He touched her shoulder. "And are you happy?"

Surprised by his question, Fia searched his face. "Of course, why wouldn't I be?"

"I had a long talk with Murdoch when he returned. Telling me about Kate and the murder Forbes committed was not all he revealed."

"Oh," she murmured, her face mirroring her regret, "he told you about Martin." Douglas nodded and Fia rallied. "I'm happy, Douglas. I think of Martin more than I should, but, I hear time will take care of my disappointment."

"If you're fortunate," he said sympathetically.

She shrugged and changed the subject. "I can't thank you enough for arranging for Murdoch to bring me here, and for all you and Agnes did for me."

"Murdoch spoke warmly of you also and, as for Agnes and I, we were very pleased to thwart the Forbes brothers. Each has spent more time out of Glasgow than in since you left. Struan is mostly in Edinburgh and London; where Andrew is–that's hard to say. I have asked the authorities to watch for him. On your information, I told them that I suspected he may be involved with free traders."

"Good, but you should take no risks where Andrew is concerned," she stated emphatically. "What brought you to see me, Douglas?"

"Your father's estate has been settled. You are free to deal with the bank on your own behalf just as soon as you sign these letters." Pulling them from his pocket, Douglas handed them to Fia. "The deed to your land is in their safekeeping and, when I return the signed letters to the bank, my work on James' behalf will be complete."

There was a moment of silence as Fia fingered the documents. "I'd like to retain your services as my solicitor, Douglas."

"Lass, that's kind, but you'll be needing someone close to you, here in Inverness."

Shaking her head, Fia was adamant. "Kindness has nothing to do with it. Having a solicitor in Inverness might make sense to most people, but not to me. I trust you implicitly; I know no one here and want no referral. Douglas, please, say you'll do this for me," she pleaded. "And if nothing else will convince you, consider that this way, I know I'll see you again–at least now and then."

Sutherland leaned down and kissed Fia's forehead. "I only hope I continue to deserve the faith you've placed in me, my dear."

"I've never met anyone, anywhere, like Elizabeth Graham," Simon swore as they left Glasgow behind, "hateful, thankless, just plain cruel. And don't you say a word in her defense," he challenged Martin. "This goes far beyond losing her child and you know it."

"I've no wish to defend her," Martin pledged, "though I do feel sorry for her."

"So...*sorry*? Oh, please," Simon shook his head in disbelief, "don't tell me that."

"But I do," Martin insisted. "Elizabeth has had all the advantages in life anyone could desire: wealth, beauty, education. And look at her–she's wretched, consumed by jealousy and hate. Her life is pure misery and you'd see that clearly if you weren't so loyal to me. Her attacks aimed at Fia and me are clouding your judgment."

Reluctantly conceding, Simon said, "A valid argument though it still surprises me that you can be charitable toward Elizabeth, all things considered."

"Believe me, it's not charity. What a relief to be out of her poisonous presence."

"Now, on that point we agree totally!" Simon cheered.

Martin suddenly pulled himself tall on Odhar's back. "Simon?"

"Uh huh?"

"I feel like I've been locked in a cell for days."

Simon nodded. "That's exactly how I feel."

"Here we are, still talking like we're imprisoned. Look around–the day is beautiful!"

Simon did scan his surroundings. The air was still, sweet and lush with the promise of rain. "Why it feels like May, not the brink of autumn. I hadn't even noticed."

Martin grinned. "I have cobwebs in my head that only a good race will clear. Since the horses rested well in the stable you found, I think they may be itching for a run. Are you game?"

A smirk tugged Simon's mouth. "If you think that hulking beast of yours can outrun my Devenick, why we'll just have to show you how a real horse can race."

"A challenge Odhar and I gladly accept. Arthur, stand aside!" The dog scampered away at the wave of Martin's hand, and the race was on.

Chapter Eighteen

Documents signed, their business completed and legal responsibilities met, Douglas and Fia exited the stuffy bank building into the wisp of breeze that kept the morning comfortable. As they strolled, Douglas decided to broach a subject about which he'd been increasingly interested since hearing of Forbes' smuggling activities. "Let's talk about your property, Fia."

"What about it?" she returned expectantly.

Douglas tucked her hand into the crook of his arm and asked, "Have you ever seen it?"

"No, I've been too busy settling myself into life with Aunt Kate." She paused, a frown creasing her forehead before continuing, "and I doubt Aunt Kate would allow me to go so far from home on my own." A moment of silence stretched as they ambled onto High Street and the millinery came into view.

"I understand. Still, I was thinking that, since the property is now truly yours, perhaps your curiosity's been aroused. Honestly, I'm more than curious and, well, I'd be delighted to escort you there if you wanted to visit."

Fia studied him thoughtfully. "Truly, you're that interested?"

"I am."

Fia admitted, "Going there would be a less daunting prospect if it were with you. All right, Douglas, when shall we go?"

"Today?" Douglas piped hopefully. "It has to be in daylight when no smugglers will be about."

"Douglas, I'm sorry, I couldn't possibly go today. Aunt Kate has been an angel giving me this much time with you. And it's not fair to Alayne–there's so much work to do at the shop."

Shrugging, Douglas said, "A shame, I did want to see the tract myself."

Fia stopped abruptly and, beaming from ear to ear, wheeled to face him. "It's perfect, Douglas; stay until Sunday. The shop will be closed and, if the weather's nice, we can all ride up there: you, me, Alayne and Aunt Kate. We could pack a light dinner. Oh, Douglas," she pleaded, "please say you'll stay."

Indulgently, Douglas replied, "My dear, that's two more days; Agnes is expecting me back by Tuesday evening."

"Agnes has worked for you long enough to know that you can't always control your schedule. She probably won't even begin to fret until Wednesday night at the earliest."

Douglas raised his brows. "And you're so sure about that?"

Fia whined, "I don't mean it personally, Douglas, it's just that it would be so lovely if you would stay. We'll have such a grand time. Please? If not for me," she said, grinning mischievously, "for Aunt Kate?"

"Now, lass, don't start that again."

"Then agree to my plan and I'll not mention how nicely you and Aunt Kate get on, or how you blush in each other's company, or–"

"All right," Douglas cried, "you win; I surrender. But I won't forget this piece of blackmail, my dear." He waggled a finger at her then secured her hand once more in the bend of his elbow. "We'd best go tell the others–and the weather had better be perfect!"

When Sunday arrived, all agreed they couldn't have ordered a more exceptional day. Warm for early September, the sky's blue was so intense it made their eyes ache. Fia and Alayne urged their mounts to race each other, Douglas' mount and, once, even Kate's mare. Finally, taking pity on their steeds, the young women affected a more leisurely pace until they reached their destination.

Standing on a knoll that swept down to the meadow-like, stunted grasses of the machair and to the crescent of sandy beach beyond, tears pricked Fia's eyes. This was her land; a gift from her father. Turning to her companions, she proclaimed, "It's so beautiful!"

"It's so...unprotected," Kate grimaced. "A good storm would sweep you into the sea."

Alayne tugged Fia's sleeve. "I think we should explore a bit before we eat. Kate, Douglas, will you join us?"

Kate's hand waved the invitation away. "I'll stay and set out the food."

Douglas wouldn't hear of it. "Come along with us for a few minutes, Kate, then I'll help you." For Douglas, she acquiesced easily, and the four made their way down to the shore.

Fia and Alayne quickly shed their boots and hose and taunted the lapping waves with their toes. Douglas glanced up then down the beach until something caught his eye and, with Kate's hand on his arm, they strolled toward a narrow ledge that partially obscured what he assumed was a cave entrance. Reaching it, Douglas remarked, "Stay here will you, Kate? I want to have a look around."

For a brief moment, she clung to him. "This is what that beast Forbes wanted?"

"Aye, a cave is a useful tool for any smuggler; on a sand bottom beach, it couldn't be more ideal." He stared into the gaping blackness and said, "I'll return shortly." When he reemerged, Fia stood at the entrance craning her neck to see into the shadows beyond. To her questioning look, Douglas replied, "The cave isn't terribly deep."

"Any sign of...activity?" Fia asked anxiously.

"I saw none, but the tide reaches to the back and would erase any footprints left behind. As for other signs," he added, scratching his head, "it's pretty dark in there, even once your eyes adjust to the light, so I can't be sure."

"I'm going to look around," Fia determined. "Alayne, do you want to join me?"

Alayne was beside her before Kate could open her mouth to protest; Douglas steered Kate away. "We'll see you back on the knoll," he said. "I don't know about the rest of you, but I'm getting hungry."

The two women were disappointed to discover the cave dank and boring. In no time, they re-crossed the machair then climbed the bank to join Douglas and Kate for a leisurely meal. As they prepared to leave though, the wind rose rather quickly to a persistent whine. The foursome began a hurried retreat suspecting the weather would turn bad long before they completed the ride home. They angled south-west, away from the now churning sea, to increase their chances of finding shelter should they need it. When the storm broke, they found themselves on a scrubby moor. "There's a croft just over there," Alayne shouted over the rising maelstrom.

Following Alayne to the heavily thatched stone house, Fia leapt from Barley's back, tossed the reins over a post and pounded on the door to no avail. Testing the latch, she pushed the door wide to a cold hearth. "No one's here," she called and motioned her companions inside.

They tumbled in with the blowing rain and Fia slammed the door behind them. The women shook wet skirts and hair while Douglas searched the small room until he found peat bricks and lit a fire. Thoughtfully, Kate had snatched up what food remained and, as the rain battered the croft with no sign of abatement, all were grateful she'd done so.

"It'll be dark in another hour." Douglas snapped shut his pocket watch.

Besieged by guilt, Fia apologized, "This is my fault, Douglas; I talked you into staying. Now Agnes really will be anxious about you."

"Now, lass, I'll be just a few hours later than planned arriving home," he assuaged.

"We can't travel in the dark," Kate worried.

"No, we can't," Douglas agreed, "but as soon as it's light, we'll push on. With any luck, the storm will be over by then."

Alayne ran fingers through her tangled hair. "Thank God we have this dry croft in which to wait."

"Amen," Kate whispered.

Fia woke in darkness. Had someone shouted? She called softly to the others, receiving as response the steady breathing of people in restful slumber. In vain, she listened for a voice and gradually realized that silence now loomed where the pounding, then patter of rain had been. She began to close her eyes again, then bolted upright. She did hear a voice: plaintive, mournful.

Quietly, Fia rose and peered through the small window into a spectral world of swirling vapor. She saw no one–heard nothing. Fia opened the door enough to slip through, and closed it silently. She guessed the croft's owner had probably returned and was shaken at seeing the strange horses. Cautiously, she greeted, "Hello? We don't mean any harm; we just took refuge from the storm."

Not receiving a response, Fia ventured to the drystone wall a few paces from the snug croft. Through the stillness, vague metallic clinks and clangs drifted to her ears. The noises reminded her of a smith's forge, yet she'd never heard anything quite like them before. Drawn by the sounds, Fia passed the wall and timidly walked onto the moor. It was difficult to decide where the clamor emanated from; Fia thought to her left but, as she went that direction, the noise remained distant. Another sound reached her–the faint skirl of bagpipes. Fia had not heard those stirring strains since her childhood–not since playing them had been banned because the English called them "instruments of war."

The heavy mists closed in, obscuring her view of the croft where her friends slept. The heath rose gradually beneath her feet for a few paces, then retreated to the lower, spongy terrain. Stopping, Fia extended upturned palms to sleet just beginning to fall. She knew it was foolhardy not to return to the croft. "I'm going to get lost and wander around the moor all night," she mumbled. The hairs on her arms prickled so intensely that Fia rubbed them vigorously. Abruptly, she realized she couldn't go back; instinct told her to wait...but for what?

A shrill cry pierced the air turning Fia rigid with fear. Men scurried around her in the icy mist; some wearing plaids, some clad only in their knee-length shirts, others dressed in uniforms. They performed a macabre dance with swords, targes, pistols and muskets, their drab figures lunging and dipping, twisting and stumbling, unmindful of her presence.

Fia's terror mounted with the dawning knowledge that the men waged a battle–but what battle? They weren't at war. Yet, those were the King's troops and Scots who had not fought each other since...since... Violently quaking, Fia croaked, "Impossible!" A scream tore her throat as the men drew nearer and she clapped her hands over her ears to drown the grating din of weapon against weapon, the surprised gasps and shrieks when weapons struck flesh.

Staggering toward her out of the murk was a man, shaggy beard and hair matted, eyes bleak and empty of life. Fia took root at the edge of the rise and gaped at him, his sword dragging the ground at the end of a mangled arm. He was within inches when Fia recognized him, and fainted dead away.

Douglas and Alayne burst through the door, Kate shoving from behind. "Where's Fia? That scream, I know that was Fia!" she squalled, tugging on Alayne's arm.

"Kate, stop it," Alayne shrugged off her grip and veered toward Douglas. "We should split up and search–"

"The fog is too thick for us to separate," he fervently interrupted, "it's too easy to get lost."

"It's clearing," Alayne insisted, pointing skyward. "Look, the moon! I'll be all right; you take Kate with you–please." Without waiting for a reaction, Alayne forged ahead leaving the clammy mist coiling in her wake.

Minutes seemed an eternity before Alayne bellowed, "Here, over here!" Waving her arms frantically in the dimness until the others spied her, Alayne dropped to her knees on the sodden field, hands flying over Fia's limbs assuring that nothing was broken.

Kate sank to the ground and gathered Fia's limp body to her, murmuring, "You're safe Fia; it's Aunt Kate, dear."

"Any sign of blood?" Douglas questioned, to which Alayne shook her head.

"There are no injuries as far as I can tell." Alayne leaned over to study a large stone near where Fia's head had lain. "We're fortunate she didn't strike her head on that marker. We'd better get her inside."

Douglas wrested Fia from Kate's grip. Carefully, he tread the slippery heath and, once in the croft, he lay her near the peat fire. Having nothing to wrap her in for warmth, he briskly rubbed Fia's arms.

Unexpectedly, Fia's head lolled to one side, her face contorted. "Mar..Martin? N...no...not... not Martin," she babbled.

"Martin," Kate inquired, looking from Douglas to Alayne, "Who is Martin?"

Alayne glanced away knowing she should tell Kate–not wanting to break her promise to Fia. Her jaw dropped in surprise when Douglas solved her dilemma.

"Martin is the man Fia loves, Kate." He tapped Fia's cheek hoping to help revive her.

"The man she loves?" Kate echoed in astonishment, scrutinizing Alayne. "What do you know about this?"

Straightening her shoulders, Alayne said, "I know that Fia loves him and longs for him more than she admits." Alayne didn't appreciate Kate's tone and resolved to tell her no more.

Swiftly, Fia sat up, startling each by crying out, "*Martin*?" Head twisting, eyes expectantly darting to see into all corners of the croft, she settled her uncertain gaze on the circle of concerned faces hovering about her. She gripped her head between her hands and demanded, "Did you see him? Did you see Hugh?"

With an accusing glower, Kate grilled Alayne, "And who is Hugh?"

"I don't know," Alayne snapped. "Can we please concentrate on Fia?"

"Quite right," Douglas agreed. "Fia, dear, we are the only ones here: Kate, Alayne and I. We saw no one else on the moor where we found you. Can you tell us what happened; who is this Hugh?"

Waves of giddiness engulfed Fia's head and she slumped back to the floor, hugging herself against the trembling that racked her body. "Where are we?" she finally asked.

"Back in the croft," Kate responded.

"No, no, where are we? What is this place?" Fia pressed to be understood.

"Fia, don't you know? This is Culloden," Alayne furnished the answer and watched Fia's little remaining color bleed to pasty white.

"That's enough." Kate took charge. "You're exhausted, cold and wet. Morning will be time enough for all the questions to be answered. You need to sleep; it will be light soon."

Without protest, Fia lapsed into silence; the others lay down, but no one slept.

It was a slow, blissfully uneventful ride back to Inverness. All the while, Fia scarcely uttered a word. She protested loudly though when Kate insisted she be put to bed. Fia's objections were overruled and, when she was tucked up, Douglas came to perch beside her.

"I hate to leave you like this, my dear," he spoke ruefully, "and there are so many things I'd like to ask you."

Grasping his fingers, as much to comfort herself as him, Fia assured, "You're leaving me in excellent hands; and I know you have to go–would have days ago if not for my foolish idea to have an outing."

"The idea was a good one, Fia. What matters now, though, is how you fare."

"I'm feeling silly, bundled up like some invalid. You have my word–I'll be back in the shop tomorrow. Oh," she cried, sitting up suddenly, "the shop! It's Monday, isn't it?"

"Aye, but don't fret, lass. Alayne has gone to the shop–reluctantly; her concern is for you."

Remorseful, Fia said, "I've caused you all such worry; I'm so sorry."

"Of course we worry, but there's no need to apologize. We love you and want you to be well. Your dream has taken quite a toll."

Fia looked up in surprise. "Dream? Douglas, I wasn't dreaming–at least, not all of it was a dream. Somebody called out and woke me. I thought it must be the person who owned the croft. At first, I saw no one; then there were men–clansmen and...soldiers, a lot of them. They fought desperately–slashing, killing each other. Their screams would curdle blood." Fia wrung her hands, desperately seeking the right words. "One man reeled toward me and I...I thought it was Martin." Her voice broke into huge sobs and Douglas held her, patting her back to sooth her. He caught Kate's reflection in the dressing table mirror and beckoned her in.

"It wasn't Martin though was it, lass?" he asked gently.

"N...no," she stuttered, fighting to regain her composure. "It was his grandfather, Hugh."

"How could that be, dear?" Kate stood beside them. "There was no one there."

"It *was* Hugh," Fia insisted vehemently. "He died at Culloden protecting Martin. And Martin told me he looked very like him."

"Fia," Kate entreated, "you're exhausted. Why don't you try to sleep."

Instead, Fia scrambled to her knees. "Don't you see? The battle was waged again last night for me. I don't know why, but only I woke and saw it, *heard it*." She read doubt in Kate's expression, interest in Douglas' and continued. "Where exactly did you find me?" Her questions grew more urgent with her heightened agitation.

Kate responded indulgently, "On the field at Culloden."

"On the edge of a clan burial mound," Douglas added recalling the rock Alayne had discovered behind Fia's prone body.

"Which clan was it, Douglas?" Fia held her breath.

"Alayne said it was the Stewarts of Appin."

Fia released her breath and closed her eyes in a moment of grateful relief. "Hugh," she finished triumphantly, "was an Appin Stewart."

Each stared at her trying to comprehend what she had said. Douglas mused, "So, when you thought you saw Martin, you realized it was really Hugh?"

"Aye." Fia lay back, exhilarated and exhausted at once.

Kate tucked the covers around her again and said, "You're safe now, dear. No more vile nightmares."

Fia rose to her elbow and fixed stern eyes on her aunt. "Please don't say that again. It was not a dream–of any kind. If you don't believe me, I can't make you. But I did not imagine this Aunt Kate. I know what I witnessed, only I don't know why."

Douglas tried to relieve the tension. "We are all shaken by your experience, Fia. It's strange and complicated and will take time to understand."

"Of course," Kate hesitated, "Douglas is right. Fia, I'm sorry."

Fia squeezed Kate's hand, and smiled her gratitude to Douglas who leaned over and kissed her cheek.

"Thank you for sharing with me what happened," he said. "I'd have gone mad trying to guess. Now I must go; Agnes will be frantic." Rising, Douglas faced Kate and asked, "Will you see me out?"

Chin raised a notch, Kate led the way to the entry hall where she blurted, "You must think me callous and unfeeling."

Surprised, Douglas studied her wild, challenging eyes. "Hardly that, Kate," he replied. "Skeptical. But who wouldn't be if they'd never seen phantoms before?"

With a bitter twist of her mouth, Kate charged, "My phantoms have always been too real."

"Kate," Douglas soothed, "you're a sensitive woman trying to steer two headstrong young ladies in what you believe is the right direction; trying to protect them from hurt such as you have suffered. There's nothing wrong with that." His lips drew into a sympathetic smile. "You love them. All they want is your trust and respect, and to love you in return."

"This talk of seeing ghosts, I can't accept; I'm too set in my ways," she grumbled.

"Not so set that you can't bend a bit. You and Fia are of the same stock; look how resilient she is."

"She's young," Kate muttered and Douglas boldly cupped her chin in his hand.

"And you are younger than you let on; you hide your youth behind a veneer of propriety."

"I...I'm a businesswoman, respected in this town," she countered, shaken by his touch.

"You've earned that respect, Kate; you've worked hard. But it's difficult–no man has helped you in a man's world. You've been widowed many years."

"My son–"

"Aye, you had to be mother and father to him. But your son vanished long ago, Kate." Douglas persisted, "I've glimpsed the vibrant, exciting woman you try to hide behind your business and behind the loss of your son. Don't do it, please." He released her chin and raised her hand to his lips. "I've said more than I should. Goodbye, dear Kate. Please think about what I've said." Picking up his tricorne, Douglas pulled the door open.

"Douglas, wait," Kate called tentatively, "I...hope to see you again. You're always welcome in my home." Impulsively, Kate stretched on tiptoe to kiss his smooth cheek.

"I think that's a very promising start," he beamed leaving a becoming blush staining Kate's cheeks.

"Simon, you don't have to put on a brave face for my benefit," Martin insisted. "I know how disappointed you must be. You had no time to look for Arabella in Glasgow, and now this."

"Who could have known Elizabeth would require all our time and attention?" Letting go a frown, Simon admitted, "I really did want to get here before the shop closed." He jiggled the unyielding latch once again.

"Matheson Mantua Makers and Millinery." Against the glare of the setting sun, Martin framed his face with his hands and peered in the window. "Some beautiful fabrics."

"The beauty of the cloth pales next to Alayne," Simon waxed.

With a grunt, Martin turned and leaned on the shop's pink granite facade, crossed his arms and smirked, "If that wasn't a line from one of your plays, I can't wait to meet this woman. She must be exceptional."

"I haven't exaggerated one bit," Simon promised and, in disappointment repeated, "I so hoped to see her today."

Martin clapped Simon's shoulder. "I feel bad for you, but pity me–I have the onerous task of keeping you occupied until tomorrow. Come, let's find lodging and something to eat."

In the morning when the men returned, they were met pleasantly, if somewhat formally, by the proprietress who introduced herself as Katherine Matheson.

Martin who had tucked the cloths from his loom under his arm when they'd set out, busied himself studying miniatures of people he didn't know, assuming they were samples produced by local artists. Meanwhile, Simon began his interrogation.

"Excuse me, Mistress Matheson, but there's a young woman who works here–"

"That's right," Kate replied, instantly wondering if he was looking for Fia.

Simon continued, "Alayne?"

Kate straightened almost imperceptibly. "I would be pleased to assist you."

"Alayne does work here?" he persisted.

"She does," Kate replied frostily.

"Do you expect her today?" While Simon wanted to appear casual, the tightness in his voice betrayed him.

"I do not. Again, Sir, may I be of assistance?" Kate asked, her narrowing eyes reflecting a mounting wariness.

Taking a different tack, Simon said, "I told Alayne last week that I might want to discuss an idea I had with her. I promised I would see her again regardless...to let her know what I decided," he added hastily.

Kate's patience and even temper were quickly disappearing. "Alayne is caring for my niece who had an accident at Culloden. I'm not sure when she'll be returning. Do you wish to come back or may I tell her of your decision?"

When the name "Culloden" reached his ears, Martin turned his full attention to the conversation.

"Thank you," Simon replied, "but I will return to speak with Alayne myself."

"About your 'idea'?" Kate prompted skeptically.

"A birthday gift for Simon's mother," Martin intervened. "My cousin is a very special woman. She happens to have similar coloring to Alayne which is why Simon wants to deal personally with her."

Kate looked from one man to the other. They were physically very different, each pleasant enough to look at though the dark one was a bit unkempt. Still, Simon's interest in Alayne was troubling, and their explanation did not sway her. "Why do you presume to address Alayne by her given name?" she asked bluntly.

With an ill-concealed start, Simon realized belatedly who this woman was. "Perhaps your daughter-in-law was concerned that having two Mistress Mathesons in the same millinery might be confusing. Forgive me, I did not mean to give offense." Kate's expression relaxed a fraction, and Simon silently thanked God for letting him remember Alayne's warning about her mother-in-law. "I will return another time."

"I think that would be prudent," Kate encouraged.

"Before we go," Martin said, "might I inquire, is your niece recovering sufficiently from her accident?"

At Kate's scowl, Simon offered, "Professional interest–my cousin is a doctor."

Kate's surprise was so blatant that Martin was embarrassed by her scrutiny. Finally, she answered, "It's kind of you to ask. I'm sure she'll be fine; she suffered a dreadful fright."

"It's a truly frightening place," Martin replied. "May I offer my hope for her full and swift recovery? We'll take our leave now, thank you." Martin inclined his head and edged Simon toward the door, but Kate stopped them with a question.

The Borrowed Days

"May I ask, Sir, about the cloth you carry?"

Martin returned to the counter where she stood. "I was taking them down to the shops."

Puzzled, she further inquired, "To sell, or did you want something made?"

"I intend to sell them. While, Simon speaks the truth, I am a doctor, lately I've done more weaving." Martin looked into her now curious eyes, colored very much like his own. "I see it isn't the kind of cloth you stock, but would you care to see it?"

Kate fingered the edges that protruded from the leather wrapping and nodded.

As Martin unrolled the leather and arranged the two cloths for Kate's inspection, Simon stood to the side in grateful amazement. The woman's business instincts had taken over and shifted the attention from him and what he knew was a blundered attempt to obtain information about Alayne.

"This is a fine, close weave," she marveled, "strong colors."

"Lichen, broom, and heather here," Martin explained, pointing to the brown, yellow and green in one cloth, "and alder bark, iris, water lilies and rocket here."

Kate studied the black, grey, pale blue and rich yellow of the second cloth. "Lovely, Sir, truly."

"Thank you, Mistress." Martin began to fold the wools when Kate stopped him with a touch on his forearm. He glanced questioningly at her.

"I would like to buy them, if we can agree on a price."

Martin's face lit in pleasant surprise. "I'm sure we can agree on a fair amount. There are two falls of cloth, six ells or 21 feet each."

"I'll give you the going rate, one merk for each ell. That would be, we'll say eight pounds?"

"As I said, Mistress, a fair price," Martin replied.

After receiving his coins, both he and Simon bowed their farewells and neither spoke again until the shop was out of sight. Martin exclaimed, "I did unexpectedly well, but you...Simon, she was not happy with your questions."

Worried, Simon tugged at the collar of his shirt with an agitated hand. "No, she wasn't. God's life, I hope I said nothing that will cause Alayne trouble."

"You were vague enough, I think."

Clenching and unclenching his fist, Simon looked over his shoulder in the direction of the millinery. "I hope that will do. Mistress Matheson seemed overly cautious."

Martin's brow wrinkled in thought. "It could be she's edgy over the niece's accident, but I doubt it. More likely, she perceived you as a threat of some kind to her son."

"Why? Simon flailed his arms. "Why should she jump to a conclusion like that?"

"Because it's true," Martin replied earnestly. "I said you were vague Simon, I didn't say you were subtle. When I stepped into the conversation I was hoping to ease some of the tension. I was starting to think it might become nasty."

Simon glanced at his cousin. "I do appreciate your help; you distracted her completely with your beautiful cloth."

"A nice surprise, I must admit. And, I can use the money." Martin smoothed his beard. "The point now is, how are you going to see Alayne without running afoul of her mother-in-law?"

"I've made it difficult, haven't I?" Simon muttered dejectedly.

Martin agreed, "You haven't helped." He threw his arm around Simon's slumped shoulders. "Let's walk: we'll work on a plan."

"Aye," Simon heaved a sigh, "then you can buy me a large whiskey to numb some of Mistress Matheson's sting."

Fia refused to stay in bed past mid-morning and Alayne, recognizing her friend's stubborn will, agreed to let her rise. "Don't you dare tell Kate I gave in so easily," Alayne threatened, "or she'll have my hide."

"Would I snitch on so agreeable a guard?" Fia answered, gleefully tossing the covers aside.

Alayne's thoughtful gaze followed Fia to the wardrobe where she pulled out a dove gray broadcloth petticoat. As Fia reached for a wine and white striped waistcoat, Alayne blurted, "How did it feel when you thought you saw Martin on the moor?"

Fia dropped her gaze to the petticoat she held. "My heart leaped so far up my throat I thought I'd choke on it," she whispered and sat heavily on the bed. "Kate doesn't believe me, what I saw."

"And why would she? Kate believes in what she can touch with her hand or see with her own eyes."

"Douglas understands, I think," Fia mused, tilted her head and finished, "and I believe you do."

"Certainly I do," Alayne said, a touch indignantly. "That's why I'm not fighting to keep you in bed. You aren't sick, just suffering a terrible shock." Hesitating, Alayne added, "I didn't tell her...about Martin, I mean. And I knew nothing of Hugh."

"I never thought to mention him. Martin told me about his grandfather but, afterward, he was sorry he'd shared the story."

"So Martin was really there during the battle?" Alayne shivered to Fia's nod. "Now you have a glimpse of how ghastly that must have been–how utterly terrifying. I can hardly imagine." Her train of thought shifted. "By the way, you didn't tell me Douglas knew about Martin."

"Murdoch told him." Fia squeezed her hand. "Thank you, for not speaking to Kate. I suppose I should, though she hasn't asked me about him yet."

"In time she will–believe me," Alayne promised, then warned, "maybe even tonight."

That night, however, Kate had other things on her mind. She had put away the lovely plaids she had purchased until she could decide on some special use for them. Plaids were still used sparingly since the British had banned them after Culloden. And, later, as she approached her home, the conversation that had transpired with the man, Simon, began to repeat itself in her head. By the time she sat down to supper, she was once more suspicious and provoked. Not a word passed her lips about Fia being up and dressed–she barely asked how her niece felt. Stress marred Kate's face and her manner was stilted.

"What happened at the shop today, Kate?" Alayne asked when she could no longer stand the strain.

"Interesting that *you*," Kate paused her reply for emphasis, "should ask."

Alayne sat back in her chair. "I don't understand; why wouldn't I ask?"

"An acquaintance of yours visited the shop today, fairly insistent on seeing you. It seems you are the only person who can help him."

A nervous knot began to weigh in Alayne's belly; though no sign of it showed outwardly. "Are you going to tell me who it was?"

Kate's eyes became slits as she assessed her daughter-in-law. "Simon," was all she said.

Alayne gripped the seat of her chair, but she blinked only once before asking, "Simon who?"

"I didn't catch his last name," Kate's brittle reply crackled.

Alayne's tone was cool and remote. "Then what did he want, Kate, and why are you so irritated?"

Kate's chin lifted as she accusingly asked, "How well do you know him?"

"Aunt Kate," Fia exclaimed, "how can Alayne answer that? We aren't sure who he is yet."

With difficulty, Kate tore her eyes from Alayne long enough to acknowledge Fia's remark. "Perhaps, I am moving too quickly." Her glower returned to Alayne. "He said he had talked to you about doing some work."

"Did he say what kind of work?" Alayne prompted stiffly.

"His companion said a birthday present for this 'Simon's' mother and something about you being of a similar coloring."

Alayne knew she was going to have to respond to Kate with something besides questions. Still, not knowing what had passed between Kate and Simon, she had to be careful. "Did this man have blue eyes and flaxen hair?"

"Aye." A slow, triumphant smile crossed Kate's face.

Alayne remarked, "I remember him now. He didn't give me much information about what he wanted. I assumed, when he reached a decision, he'd come to the shop."

"You never mentioned him," Kate sniffed.

"But she did, Aunt Kate," Fia broke in, "to me, the day of that horrible storm."

"Aye," Alayne picked up the tale. "I thought one of the shopkeepers must have pointed me out to him at Market."

Tapping the table cloth as if it would jog some memory, Fia said, "I remember you were upset when you returned; he'd startled you and kept you standing out in that wretched weather."

"I excused myself as soon as I could." Alayne shook her head. "I don't think I've ever been so drenched."

The two women had successfully taken over the conversation and left Kate trying to absorb the events they cryptically described. Finally, Fia turned to her aunt and said, "I'm sorry Aunt Kate. Did you finish telling us what the fellow wanted?"

Kate tried swallowing the last traces of her suspicions and replied, "A gift for his mother–that's all I know–that and that he seemed determined to see Alayne."

Alayne shrugged. "If he was so insistent, it's too bad I wasn't there to help him. It might have meant good money for the shop."

"He said he'd return," Kate scrutinized her daughter-in-law for reaction but was unrewarded–Alayne only lifted a noncommittal brow.

In the late hours, Kate paced her room, working herself into a reproachful frenzy remembering her last conversation with Douglas. His understanding words, compared to how she'd reacted to the day's events, made her feel ashamed. "Why am I so eager to think the worst of Alayne," she berated herself, "just to preserve Muir's memory untarnished?" The thought of sullying her son's reputation was almost enough to make Kate cry–he'd accomplished the task well enough on his own. Why if he hadn't disappeared, Alayne probably would have followed her family to America long ago, he treated her so callously. If she were being fair, Kate would give Alayne more credit. She had faithfully stayed by Kate and, until tonight, Kate had never acknowledged it–even to herself.

There was a knock and, upon Kate's beckoning, Fia entered. "I thought you might like to talk, Aunt Kate."

Eyes averted, Kate asked, "About what?"

Arm wrapped around the bedpost, Fia rested her cheek against its cool smoothness. "About what it is that's bothering you. What angered you so about a customer looking for Alayne?"

Kate blurted, "I'm not at all sure what that customer really wanted."

With care, Fia said, "Why would you think he wanted anything other than a gift for his mother?"

As she dropped into her chair, Kate's eyes glittered. "He was clearly disappointed when I told him she wasn't there. I'm not imagining it," she added sternly.

"However this 'Simon' acted, Alayne is not to blame," Fia insisted, then tread onto dangerous ground. "Aunt Kate, is it this man's behavior that upsets you or a fear that, at some point, Alayne may find and love a man who isn't Muir?"

Kate rubbed her arms, warming them against an inner chill. "I am very fond of Alayne," she began and hurried on, "I'm sure she wouldn't believe that though. Muir, he wasn't good to her, he had...unsavory friends and...a compulsive nature. Still, he's my son and I love him."

"Of course you love him, but he's been gone almost four years. Alayne has so much to give to a man who will appreciate and love her."

Kate dabbed her nose with a lace-edged handkerchief. "Aye, he'll be a lucky man. She's been extremely loyal to me–and she barely even likes me."

"Aunt Kate, that simply isn't so. You both bear wounds made by Muir; they still fester." Fia left the post and knelt beside Kate's chair. "Go talk to her, Aunt Kate."

"It's too late; she's asleep."

Shaking her head, Fia pulled Kate from the chair. "It's not 10:30 yet and, if I know Alayne, she'll be awake fretting–much like you."

Kate searched her niece's face. "I'll talk with her now, but don't think I'm through with you, young lady. You owe me an explanation about Martin."

"Some other time," Fia agreed. "It's far more important that you and Alayne understand each other."

Fia watched Kate rap on the door then enter Alayne's room. Instead of returning to bed, Fia picked up her mantle and left the house to sit, knees tucked under her chin, on the front stoop. The night was quiet except the rattle of leaves shivering on a nearby tree as a north wind ushered in the autumn. "Four years for Alayne, four months for me," she murmured. Fia could not dispel the emptiness which seemed increasingly acute since her experience at Culloden. Eyes closed, she breathed deeply, Martin's and Hugh's faces mingling before her–then Hugh's was gone. Fia recounted Martin's features, his coloring and expressions in exasperating detail. Momentarily,

Fia watched threads of clouds crossing the sky snuffing stars on their journey. Lowering her head to her knees, Fia shed lonely, scalding tears.

Alayne stood brushing her hair, back to her mother-in-law. "What is it now, Kate?" she asked with impatience. "I should think there's little more to say this evening."

"You're wrong, Alayne," Kate began timorously, "I...I do have something to say."

Carefully, Alayne lay her brush on her dresser and turned to face her mother-in-law. "Then get on with it."

Hands clenched before her, Kate stammered, "I w...want to apologize for having so readily jumped to unfounded conclusions."

"Fia sent you, didn't she?" Alayne accused mildly.

"She urged me not to put off my apology," admitted Kate, "and she was correct. Alayne, I truly bear you no ill. We don't agree on everything, I suppose our age difference and our individual relationships to my son are responsible for much of that. Still, you have always been dependable and dedicated to the shop. More importantly, you...you've stayed by me through the most difficult time of my life, and I haven't always responded kindly or with understanding."

Alayne spoke no words, but her narrowed eyes betrayed her misgivings.

A deep breath, and Kate continued, "About this 'Simon', I realize now that you cannot be held accountable for his actions."

"He's a potential customer. I don't understand why whatever he did or said should anger you," ventured Alayne.

"That's the point, my dear, they shouldn't have. As I think back with...a clearer mind, nothing he said was so contemptible."

Alayne extended her palms, exasperated. "Then I don't understand what happened, Kate."

"Since you became my daughter-in-law, your life has not been as...uncomplicated...as it should have been."

"That's a point, I won't argue," Alayne declared.

"But you're still my son's wife. I have never seen another man, even a customer, show such interest in you. I...I didn't enjoy it." Alayne opened her mouth to speak, but Kate rushed on. "Oh, I know that isn't fair of me. Someday, someone else will come along and capture your fancy, you're far too young for it to be otherwise."

"I am–so are you, Kate," Alayne offered and Kate gulped her surprise, fleetingly thinking of Douglas. "Neither one of us needs to live for the past."

"True," Kate agreed in a sad voice, "if only the past were easier to forget."

For the first time, Alayne approached the older woman. "First, Kate, you have to try, then you'll have to work very hard at it."

"But, Alayne, should I forget?" Kate asked the younger woman, and Alayne shook her head.

"Just remember that it is the past, Kate–it's over," Alayne emphasized, encircling Kate's shoulders with her arm.

Kate bestowed a tiny smile on her daughter-in-law. "Thank you, Alayne, for standing by me–it hasn't been easy, I know. And I am honestly sorry for being so hasty in my judgments and so quick to lay blame."

Alayne nodded. "All right, Kate. Let's promise though, to try to remember this talk, whatever the future brings."

In a rare moment, Kate kissed her daughter-in-law's cheek, patted the other and, bidding her goodnight, left with a fragile truce between them.

Leaving Martin just stirring, Simon rose early and stationed himself along High Street to watch for Alayne's arrival. At half past seven, his belly lurched; she was approaching alone. "I'll give her ten minutes," he murmured excitedly. "Ten minutes," he promised, pacing the edge of the road. "Ten minutes," he pledged, crossing the street. "Ten minutes," he exclaimed as he walked through the door not a minute behind her.

Startled at the sound of the door opening and closing, Alayne hurriedly dropped her mantle. Parting the curtains, she stepped into the shop, her smile of greeting turning to a gasp at the sight of Simon's wild, golden halo and penetrating eyes. "How did you find me?" she demanded in a whisper.

"By God, you are a beautiful woman," Simon vowed.

Alayne gripped the edge of the display case for support and did her best to insist, "You've no...no right to speak to me like that."

"I'm obliged to speak the truth."

Ignoring his remark, Alayne repeated, "I want to know how you found me."

Simon sauntered the distance between them. "The day we met, I followed you. Where's the Grand Inquisitor?"

"I warned you about my mother-in-law," Alayne replied loftily. "Did you come about the gift for your mother?"

Simon waved her question aside. "It was a ruse."

"So you have no business here," Alayne deduced.

Leaning toward her over the counter, Simon said, "My mother does have a birthday coming up, but you know that's not why I'm here."

"I only know that I can help you with a gift for your mother," Alayne insisted.

Simon apologized, "I hope my visit caused you no trouble."

Alayne avoided his fascinating face. "It was difficult, not knowing what you'd said to Kate, but I got through it." She proceeded to the end of the counter. "We offer a variety of neck handkerchiefs. I don't know what kind of woman you mother is, but these are always useful."

"She's not a fancy woman. My mother works hard and dresses plainly except on the Sabbath. Her name is Jessie. What would you recommend?"

Sifting quickly through the choices, Alayne displayed one across her palms for his inspection. "Simple, elegant–embroidery sounds like it would suit her better than lace."

Simon slipped his hands under the handkerchief and grazed Alayne's before she pulled away. "Are you afraid of me, Alayne?"

Through chattering teeth she insisted, "I'm not afraid. But you seem to forget that I am a married woman; you are far too familiar in your actions."

"I don't find the fact that you're married discouraging."

"Really?" She mustered her most impervious tone to ask, "Then are you a peacock who amuses himself spoiling women's reputations?"

"N...no!" Simon cried indignantly. "The reason I don't find your marriage discouraging is because you have yet to speak a word about your husband. There's something wrong with that. And until I find out what that problem is, I feel no need to remind myself of your state of wedded bliss."

For a charged moment, Alayne's voice failed her. "You're guessing," she squeaked.

Simon studied her intently and finally declared, "But I guessed correctly. Where is your husband, dear lady?" he asked gently.

"Do you want the handkerchief?" she persisted.

"Aye, and an answer to a simple question. Where is your husband?" Simon repeated.

Alayne snatched up the gift. "I'll be right back." She disappeared behind the curtains to wrap his purchase. Briefly clutching her knotted belly, Alayne packaged the handkerchief and turned to spy Simon standing at the parted curtains.

"Alayne, I don't mean to frighten or offend you. Upon my word, I mean you no ill. I want a chance to know you better. That isn't much to ask, is it?"

"Haven't you heard m...me?" she choked in disbelief. "I have a husband."

"Aye, I've heard you but, my instinct tells me that something is very wrong. Please, Alayne, tell me about your husband," Simon begged, but she was stubbornly silent. "All right," he stepped back, "I'll start. Your husband is an incredibly fortunate fellow to have so loyal a woman devoted to him."

Tears of shame burned Alayne's averted eyes.

Simon waited patiently.

"Not so fortunate," she finally admitted, "he vanished several years ago."

A flutter of hope beat in Simon's chest. "Vanished? How?"

Rubbing her head as if the effort to remember hurt, Alayne answered, "We don't know if he was pressed into naval service or...just left."

Simon memorized the proud angle at which she held her head, the uncertainty in her hazel eyes, her sumptuous mouth. "I can't imagine a fool big enough to purposely leave a woman like you."

She barked a laugh. "There's a good possibility one exists."

"You've looked for him? Asked about him?" Simon questioned.

Hesitantly, Alayne confirmed, "I've made inquiries."

"And you've found nothing."

"Nothing," she conceded.

"How long will you wait, Alayne?" Simon asked softly.

"The required time–that's all," came her frank reply.

"Then, for that time, can we be...friends?"

Alayne's surprised gawk displayed her skepticism and Simon laughed. "Friends for now, at least. It's a place to start."

One side of her mouth tugged into a smile. "Thank you for your honesty," and the smile disappeared with her next words. "But I'll do nothing to cast doubt on my reputation. It's not possible for us to be friends."

"It is possible," he offered hopefully, "in the company of others."

She studied him intently. "What do you mean?"

"Chaperons," he suggested, "trusted friends in public places."

Feeling her resolve weakening, Alayne said, "Please go back into the shop–it wouldn't do to have someone see you behind the counter."

Simon immediately left, not willing to risk the minute ground his instincts told him he'd gained. When she joined him with the gift, Simon asked, "Will you think about my suggestion?" His eager expression melted all but a tiny core of her remaining resolve. "I'll consider it."

The breadth of his delighted smile unexpectedly produced a shy one from Alayne. "I'm leaving for Strathcarron to see my family. When I return, I'll come here–and pray Mistress Matheson is somewhere else. We can observe any propriety that makes you comfortable." Counting out coins for the handkerchief, Simon's fingers lightly touched her palm as he passed her the payment; he thought she shivered.

"I only said I'd consider it," she reminded him sternly to which he flashed a smile in return.

In the middle of a perfectly sound slumber on the first night of their return trip to Strathcarron, Simon's eyes popped open in horror. He had dreamed pieces of an appalling puzzle and shuddered at the grisly prospect that they might actually fit together. A quick glance across the last of the fire revealed that Martin slept soundly, head resting on the arm scarred by Elizabeth's nails. Andrew was the name Elizabeth gave her lover, the man she said was also bewitched by Fia. And the man with the scar, who'd threatened Arabella at Market, he was called Andrew. "A fluke–a flimsy happenstance," he insisted silently, hoping to convince himself. "Is it really possible that Arabella and Fia are the same person? I won't upset Martin with absurd speculation," Simon determined. "I won't mention it at all," he muttered, and slept no more that night.

The next day, the last of their journey to the MacLaren farm, dawned steely and dry. Simon was uncharacteristically quiet still thinking, Martin assumed, about Alayne. "I'm sorry I didn't get to meet Alayne–or see her for that matter." Martin's statement was met with stony silence. "What ails you, Cousin?" he questioned in concern.

"Nothing," Simon responded too quickly to which Martin halted Odhar's stride. He stared at Simon. Simon squeezed shut his eyes. "I must be losing the skills of my trade," he muttered, "first, Katherine Matheson, now you."

Shaking his head, Martin demanded, "Simon, make sense will you."

In short temper, Simon flared, "I seem to have suddenly become transparent. An actor worth his salt should be able to keep his thoughts from others."

Thinking himself a worthy confidant, Martin was surprised by Simon's outburst. "You know I wouldn't force you to tell me anything you preferred to keep to yourself. It's just...you're acting so oddly."

"I know, I know. Martin, please forgive me," Simon atoned, torn now by doubt as to whether he had any right to withhold his fears about Fia from Martin. He kicked Devenick back into a walk while pondering his dilemma.

Martin kept pace on Odhar and said nothing. Not since he and Simon met had there been any hint that the other's counsel was not appreciated. Martin was shocked to realize how much Simon's choice to shut him out hurt. While he didn't understand the sudden change, he had to respect it. After all, it wasn't but a short time ago that he hadn't wanted anyone prying into his thoughts–even when he shared them of his own volition. Hadn't doing so caused him to fight with Fia?

Lunging out, Simon grabbed Odhar's bridle jerking him, once more, to a halt.

Arthur stopped too, and sat to rest.

At Simon's mercurial behavior, Martin said, "What's going on here, Simon, have I done something amiss?"

The battle was over. The musings which had rumbled in Simon's head half the night commanded–for good or ill–that he voice them. "God knows, Martin, I wish it were as simple as you doing something amiss. I don't even want to share this with you–it's only guesswork–I've no idea if there's anything to it."

Baffled and a bit alarmed, Martin urged, "Go on."

"It's...something strange that happened when we were with Elizabeth made me wonder."

"Wonder what?"

"Andrew–wasn't that the name of Elizabeth's lover?" Simon tasted sweat above his lip and felt his face flame with the fear of what he might unleash by asking these few questions.

"You know it was Andrew, why?" Martin glanced at his cousin, saw the change in him and asked again, "Why?" concern furrowing his brow.

In a moment of panic, Simon tried to back away. "I have bits of information that should be unrelated, but don't seem to be. This is conjecture, Martin; the possibility that I'm totally wrong is very good."

"Whatever your 'theory' is, Simon, you'd better share it with me before I go mad."

"Honestly, I must be–have *got* to be wrong about this."

"Wrong about *what?*" Martin's spiraling dread did nothing to calm Simon.

"Elizabeth said Andrew was bewitched by Fia. When I met Arabella, the man pestering her, his name...was also Andrew."

Martin's heart raced. "Are you telling me that you think Arabella might...might really be Fia?"

"God help me, Martin, it came together and woke me in the night. And what's worse, this morning, more seems to fit together: Elizabeth's unreasonable hatred of Fia; I told you I thought it had something to do with Elizabeth's lover."

Martin's breathing was shallow with dread. "Describe Arabella."

Hesitantly, Simon said, "About half a head shorter than me, soft laugh, eyes the color of the sea on a gray day, dark curls half down her back," he watched Martin turn ghastly pale, "a small mouth but generous smi–"

"What is it?" Martin rasped painfully at Simon's broken description.

Excitedly, Simon remembered, "Arabella carried some sadness for a man she loved, but said he was married. How could that have been your Fia?"

"You describe her so perfectly, how could it not?"

"But you aren't married," Simon reminded.

"Maybe she was referring to another man," Martin offered through clenched teeth.

Simon returned, "The woman you described to me is not that conniving. Come, Martin," he urged plaintively, "I'm sure now that I must be wrong."

Martin reminded, "Fia surprised me once before about her marriage to Forbes, another man might have existed all along."

Vexed, Simon flushed. "You don't believe that. It would be convenient if it were the truth; you think it would make it easier to forget her. Well it won't! Did she ever mention this Forbes having a brother?" Martin shook his head. "There, you see?" Simon finished. "My theory must be wrong."

Staring past the top of Odhar's head, Martin stated, "No matter what I want, forgetting her is not possible. You describe her perfectly–"

"Brown hair and gray eyes are common enough, Martin," Simon broke in.

"Perfectly," Martin reiterated. "Now, it's even more imperative that I find her...somehow. If Fia is your Arabella, and Elizabeth's faithless lover Andrew wants–"

Simon's face blanched and, noting his cousin's reaction, Martin seized on it demanding, "What is it? Tell me what you know–Simon, you must."

Simon woefully responded, "I remember something Arabella said to me," he hesitated, sickened by the implications of his next words for all concerned. "She told me that she had witnessed Andrew commit murder–on the Inverary road." He rushed on, "Martin, forgive me, I should not have brought this up at all–not when we are so helpless, not knowing where she is."

"When I first saw Fia, she begged me not to kill her; thought I was the man who murdered a passenger she was traveling with along the Inverary Road." After an interminable lapse of seconds while he labored to breathe, Martin finally gasped, "Until I find her, pray that her husband cares enough to protect her. It may be her only hope."

Chapter Nineteen

Still in her mantle, Fia stood in the door to the workroom and stared at Alayne who sat beside the hearth. "Simon was here this morning?"

Alayne nodded. "He walked in right behind me, and he'll return again–whether I want him to or not," she added dutifully, though not convincingly.

"You do want him to don't you?" Fia hung her mantle by the back door.

"Fia, you know how I feel about it," Alayne reminded. "I have to be careful; nothing is more important than ridding myself of this sham of a marriage. I won't jeopardize that by giving anyone an excuse to question my actions."

"Did you explain this to Simon?" Fia asked.

"I did; he seemed to understand." Alayne glanced away and began bouncing one knee in a nervous motion.

"And...?" Fia prompted.

"He...he'd still like to see me...as a friend."

Fia swallowed a pleased smile and kept her tone light. "Would that suit you?" And to Alayne's silence she continued, "Don't you like him, or find him attractive?"

"He's a comely man, no doubt. And what little I know, I don't dislike," Alayne responded before frowning. "Didn't we have this discussion the day of the storm?"

"You're right; we've had this conversation before." Fia picked up a case of brass pins and a frock coat she'd been working. Unexpectedly, she offered, "All day, every day, I regret that I never told Martin I loved him. I never gave him the chance to tell me about Jean MacNab, her importance to him. Maybe if I had, I could begin to forget. How can I convince you...if you believe this man is special, even to be a friend, think long and hard before you send him away. As I said before, if you can put on men's clothing to search for a husband you care nothing about, can't you give this man enough of your time to find out if you could care for him? There must be a way."

Pensive for a long moment, Alayne ventured, "Trusted friends in public places?" To Fia's quizzical look, Alayne responded, "Simon's idea."

Eyes sparkling with intrigue, Fia agreed, "A fine idea. I'm available to go with you anywhere, anytime you want to see him–and I know you want to see him."

"I'm not certain," Alayne hedged.

"God's blood, why aren't you? I, for one, can't wait to meet him."

"You could have today if not for Kate. I thought she would never stop fussing and let you out of the house."

"I'm out now and plan to be here to meet Simon the next time. And what will you tell him then?"

"That I'd like to be...friends," Alayne allowed herself a moment to dream, "at least for now."

Fia grinned, happy to realize that Alayne had turned the corner of her trepidation. She began pinning pieces of the coat.

Her decision made, Alayne chattered happily and the day passed quickly. She declined to accompany Fia back to Kate's for the night. "I don't want to risk ruining this mood."

"I'll tell Aunt Kate he returned; try to smooth it over."

Alayne hugged her friend. "Thank you, Fia. What would I do without you?"

"Probably bolt! This man sounds very interested in your future–a future you'll be starting in less than two months. Remember, I'm available if you need me." Fia returned the hug and made her way home, whipped by a stiffening September breeze.

Fia decided not to wait and see if Kate asked so, over supper, said, "That fellow, Simon, came back to the shop today."

"You saw him?" Kate's interest perked.

"I apparently only missed him by minutes. He bought his mother an embroidered handkerchief and left." Pausing for effect, Fia added, "He did apologize for any difficulty he may have caused; he sensed your disapproval of his request to deal with Alayne."

"I think Alayne and I resolved that last night." She reached over and laid a hand on Fia's. "Thank you, dear, for recommending I talk with Alayne–it cleared the air on a few things."

"I'm so glad, Aunt Kate."

"Now," Kate said setting her napkin aside, "what about you, Fia?"

"What about me?"

"Don't feign ignorance with me; I'm talking about this 'Martin'. I'd like to hear about him."

Fia fidgeted with the linen ruff covering her elbow. "There's not much to tell, Aunt Kate. Martin is part of the past now."

"You don't expect me to believe that, surely?"

"Do you see him here?" Fia replied brusquely. "Have you ever known me to communicate with him or even mention him? I'm telling you that part of my life is done."

Kate contemplated Fia's denial and knew it to be false, at least in her niece's heart. She took a different tack. "If you say you have moved on, I accept that. But he was very important to you–you love...d him. I want to know what kind of man touched you so deeply, Fia. Who had that good fortune and let it slip through his fingers. Please, dear, I'm not making this request lightly. I realize there must still be pain."

Fia searched her aunt's face and, with trembling voice said, "The memories are precious to me–there are so few."

"Sharing those memories will not make you lose them, Fia; they'll still be yours. You shared them before and they still belong to you. Fia, please, I don't plan to pass judgment on you or Martin."

Fia acquiesced though, in the telling, she kept much to herself. Still, Kate gleaned plenty from the alternating anguish and radiance that transformed Fia's face. "I know four months is not much time to have passed," Fia finally sniffed, "but I don't know why I ache more for him now than I did when we parted."

"Unfortunately, I have no answer for you, dear." Kate took her niece's hands in her own. "I wish I could ease your sorrow. Martin sounds very special–a compelling man. So many women never meet a man such as you've described–someone who really cares for them–and it's clear to me that he cared for you. Often a man is just looking for a woman to run his house and bear his children. Even though he's gone, Fia, you're more fortunate than most."

Fia nodded. "I know. I still see him as clearly as if he'd just walked into the room." She searched Kate's benevolent face for its comfort and wisdom. "Part of me is waiting for all of that to fade because people say that happens over time. What really terrifies me though, Aunt Kate, is that it will."

"*I understand your* anxiety and your eagerness to start looking, Martin. Just give me a day or two in Strathcarron then I'll go with you anywhere you want to search for Fia."

Shaking his head, Martin said, "You have a life of your own to live, Simon. I don't expect you to keep roaming the countryside with me."

"Martin," Simon protested, "there's a woman out there who may need our help. If Fia is indeed Arabella, I'm involved in this for her sake as well as for yours."

As they forded the River Carron, Martin proclaimed, "What about Alayne? I don't want you to risk–"

"Let me worry about Alayne. The smartest thing I can do where she's concerned is to move slowly. She's anxious about ending her marriage. I didn't realize the circumstances and certainly don't want to make things difficult for her."

Martin suggested, "Perhaps there's a way you can help her through this, though 'how' is a good question."

"Maybe...I'd like to. I need to find out more about it first; I've caused enough upset charging in as I have." Simon sighed and changed the subject. "We'll be home in half an hour."

Martin sensed that, for a change, Simon might need his support, and he wanted to be there for him. Besides, as much as it pained him to contemplate, Martin thought it unlikely that Fia's situation–whatever it was–would change in the next several days. "I'll stay a day or so." He conceded, "It'll be good to see your family again. There's something very comforting about the closeness you share."

Grinning ruefully, Simon reminded, "And then there's Grant. Try not to annoy him this time will you, Martin?"

Soon the lime-washed farmhouse came into view and Martin spied Lachlan on the hill beyond. "There's your father," he said nodding in the general direction.

"He must be returning from his still," Simon guessed. "Ah, there's Mam. I hope she likes her birthday gift."

"And why wouldn't she," Martin teased, "the fair Alayne picked it out, didn't she?"

Hesitantly, Simon said, "I'd appreciate it, Martin, if you wouldn't mention Alayne just yet."

"Whatever you wish," Martin promised with a raised brow.

"It's just, well there isn't anything really to tell," Simon explained.

"Aye, she's yet to agree to see you," Martin obligingly pointed out.

"She will," he responded, voice more confident than his heart.

Their homecoming was a cheery one and Mairi was a whirlwind of news. She'd given Rob her answer to his proposal the day after the two men had left for Glasgow. "We plan to wed on the eve of St. Martin. We thought since everyone would be feasting anyway before winter begins, that it would be perfect. And," she smiled shyly, "since it was Martin who brought me to my senses, it seemed fitting. You don't mind do you, Martin?"

Martin could barely speak he was so touched by her gesture. "Whatever day you wed, Mairi, will be a joyous one. But I thank you just the same."

Jessie looked uncertain. "We'll have to make you a dress. Mine served me for Sabbath for many years."

Simon suddenly sat up very straight. "I'll have Mairi's dress made; it shall be my gift." His family turned to gawk at him as Mairi flung her arms around his neck and Martin guessed Simon's plan.

"That's very generous, dear," Eleanor acknowledged. "Are you sure you know what you're getting into?"

"Martin and I will take her to Inverness, to the shop your neck handkerchief came from, Mam. Aye," Simon's eyes sought Martin's as Mairi danced gleefully around the croft.

In the byre, as Martin and Arthur were settling for the night, Simon paid a visit and asked, "What do you think of my idea?"

Rising on one elbow, Martin said, "I think it's generous, ingenious and dangerous."

Simon's brows drew into a frown. "Dangerous, how?"

"If you seriously don't want people to know about Alayne, do you think you can keep Mairi from noticing your interest in her? Your sister may be delirious with excitement, but she's a perceptive young woman."

"You're right, I'll have to be on my guard," his cousin acknowledged and left, bidding Martin good night.

Despite the long day, Martin lay staring into the dark, listening to Arthur's soft, snuffling breathing and the sounds of the horses shifting in their stalls. His heart ached and his belly was leaden. He was deathly afraid for Fia's safety. "I'd give anything to know her life was the comfortable one she sought," he sighed, "for, at least, I'd know she was safe." Tears of remorse stung his moss-brown eyes. "I could have kept her safe," he swore to himself. "Why didn't I tell her how much I loved her, yearned to be her husband?" Martin choked back his pain. "God's life, why didn't I try harder to keep her with me?"

Early the next morning, Mairi set out for Rob's, clamoring to share her news about Simon's wedding gift. Jessie decided to accompany her and visit Rob's mother, Alice. At the farm, Lachlan cornered Simon and Grant to repair a segment of drystone wall close to the river. Martin carded and spun wool with Eleanor, passing the time with idle chatter until she paused to stretch her gnarled fingers.

"You've said nothing about your trip, lad. We're all anxious to hear about it," she encouraged.

"And you're all too polite to ask," Martin submitted, then smirked, "I was sure Mairi would demand all the details."

It was Eleanor's turn to chuckle. "Ordinarily she would but, aside from being in a tizzy about marrying Rob, she was also forbidden to bring up the subject. Jessie and I felt it important to let you tell us in your own time."

"But now you're asking."

"Aye," she nodded sheepishly. "I'm in part responsible for you going to Glasgow; my curiosity is ripe. Since you've been so quiet though, I doubt my prayers have been answered."

Martin laid his carders in the basket at his feet and drew his hand across his mouth and down his beard. "If you prayed I'd find Fia, I didn't. Her cousin doesn't seem to know where she is."

Pursing her lips, Eleanor said, "That's strange don't you think?"

"Not really, since Elizabeth has no love for Fia." Martin hesitated before adding, "But Simon thinks that his friend Arabella may actually be Fia."

Eleanor started. "I remember he mentioned the name at dinner the night before you left. Still, why would he think they were the same person?"

"It's a complicated story, Eleanor," Martin promised.

"I'd like to hear it, lad." Eleanor suggested, "if you feel up to it."

Martin carefully shared the clues that Simon had put together with no mention of Elizabeth's plight.

Eleanor listened intently, punctuating his narrative with an occasional gasp or disbelieving shake of her head. "Tis no wonder you said nothing when you arrived yesterday. But, do you think this is your Fia?"

"Until I find her, there's still doubt. But Eleanor, listening to what Simon has pieced together, in my heart, I know it's true. Elizabeth's lover Andrew, if he's the man who threatened Arabella, would be Fia's brother-in-law. He could...see her any time he wished. I simply have to find her. When we leave tomorrow with Mairi, I'll part with her and Simon in Inverness and return to Glasgow."

"Why go to Glasgow? Elizabeth will tell you nothing–you know that."

"That's why I'm going to Forbes' office–*he* shouldn't be difficult to locate." Martin covered her hand with his. "I'd like to leave Arthur here. I'll be traveling fast and I've run the poor laddie ragged as it is."

Eleanor's eyes sought the dog, snoozing beside Martin's bench, muzzle resting on Martin's foot. "You can try, Martin, but I'm not at all sure he'll be willing to be left behind." Just then, she caught sight of Grant crossing the yard toward them. "Grant looks in a foul mood; what eats at that grandson of mine?"

"Gram," Grant acknowledged, then addressed Martin. "Pap wants to know if you'll see the lamb. I told him it's healed–but you're the physician."

"Eleanor, excuse me," Martin rose and faced his cousin. "Where's the lamb?"

Grant sniffed haughtily, "Follow me; I doubt you could find him alone."

As Grant turned away, Eleanor started to rebuke her grandson but Martin's upheld palm stopped her as he followed his irascible cousin toward the browning hillside. After examining the lamb, he pronounced, "You did a fine job, Grant. If it happens again, you can cure any animal on the farm."

Grudgingly, Grant accepted Martin's praise then, shuffling his feet, finally blurted, "How long will you be staying this time?"

Martin narrowed his eyes, but answered coolly. "I thought you knew. Tomorrow, we return to Inverness with Mairi, then you won't need to fret about me for a bit."

Forcing a laugh, Grant swaggered, "I don't worry about you, Cousin."

"All right then...Cousin...when I leave, you'll have to find another target for your nasty disposition. Your frustrations and your pettiness are starting to annoy me."

"A...annoy *you*?" Grant choked in disbelief.

"Aye. Whatever the cause of your discontent, whether it be the lass that jilted you or your sister's playful nature, I'm tired of your grousing. I prefer doing nothing to upset Jessie or Eleanor, but if you keep up this nonsense, I won't be caught off guard again. Have I made my intentions clear enough?"

"You think you can just move in and make my family yours," Grant sputtered angrily, "after your own threw you out."

"So that's what this is all about," Martin declared. "Happily for me, the rest of the MacLarens have bigger hearts than you, Grant. They love you as they always have and will. Still, they have room to accept me; I've not replaced anyone in their affections."

Grant shifted his gangly frame and accused, "Ever since you arrived, all they do is yell at me or punish me, yet you say they love me."

Martin stopped and faced the younger man. "Aye, they love you, though they probably don't understand this animosity you bear me any better than I did until just now. It frustrates them and perhaps that's why you keep getting punished. They're confused, and you're so angry you won't explain it to them. I might have guessed, but I thought it was about Mairi or the bitterness she told me you suffered over the love you lost."

Grant turned his glare away and muttered, "Mairi doesn't know what she's talking about."

"Maybe not; she was also at a loss to explain your hostility." Martin stared at the toe of his boot, wondering if sharing his own pain would help Grant. It was worth a try. "Still, if it was true, and the lass in question still holds your heart, I understand that kind of pain–it grips me as well."

Casting a sidelong glance at Martin, Grant reticently asked, "Are you speaking of this 'Fia' I've heard mentioned?"

"I am. When Simon and I traveled to Glasgow, I was trying to find her; I foolishly let her leave me without telling her that I loved her."

"You did something as stupid as that?" Grant mocked.

Martin checked a flash of annoyance. "Grant, no one ever said I was perfect, least of all me. I made that mistake and regret it with all my heart. It's too late to set things straight between us; she has a husband now."

"Then...why are you looking for her?" Grant mused.

"Because I need to see her, to know if she's well, to try to settle the past and move on if I can." Martin shifted his weight and asked, "Did you ever tell your lass how you felt?"

"No," Grant admitted reluctantly.

"You see, we have a common bond, Grant; we've made the same mistake. There's one difference though, I'm older and should have known better. But I was hiding behind my past. I let my marriage to Bridgid and her death cloud my judgment with Fia, just as you let it influence your opinion of me when I arrived." Martin shook his head. "I wouldn't want you to repeat my mistake."

Thoughtful for a long moment, Grant said, "Do you mean if someone else should come into my life, I shouldn't let what happened stand in my way."

Smiling, Martin acknowledged, "You understand."

With a sheepish grin, Grant asked, "Did you find her–Fia?"

Martin's face clouded. "Sadly, no. I'm no closer to seeing her now than I was before."

"I'm sorry, Martin, and not just because you didn't find her."

Martin nodded. "Can we try to put the past behind us, Grant? I'd like to."

"You would? After all my posturing and ranting?" At Martin's reassuring nod, Grant tenuously extended his hand.

Even in her state of rapture, Mairi noticed a subtle difference in how Grant and Martin behaved toward each other that evening, and Eleanor took Martin aside to say in wonder, "Whatever you did, lad, I congratulate you."

"We found some common ground; it's a beginning," said Martin, optimistically.

Mairi professed being too excited to sleep that night, but had to be roused in the early hours just the same. After breaking the fast, the trio mounted up, Jessie issuing last minute instructions to her daughter. "Mind your brother and Martin. Inverness is a big place; don't let it frighten you, and don't get separated–"

"Mam, enough," Simon laughed, "we'll take care of her."

"You have our word on it," Martin added and, to Grant, who held Arthur, requested, "Take good care of him for me."

Over the squirming, whimpering hound, Grant proclaimed, "If I can hang onto him, we'll take care of each other."

"Arthur stay," Martin commanded as he turned Odhar south and touched his sides with boot heels. Until Martin and his companions were almost to the rise, Arthur moved no muscle. Suddenly, without warning, he tore from Grant's grasp and sped after his master. Barking furiously, Arthur caught them at the top of the hillock and at full run, leaped from the ground to Odhar's back where Martin barely caught him in time to keep him from falling off the other side. In no time, Martin was damp from frantic face-licking and, while Mairi laughed hysterically, Simon waved to Grant and yelled, "We'll take him along!"

Arthur refused to get down, taking no chances on being left behind. Instead he settled across the saddle resting his rump against one of Martin's thighs, his front paws on the other. Even when they cantered, he somehow maintained his perch.

"This is ridiculous," Martin exclaimed. "Am I going to have to make a sling to carry you?"

"Oh, Martin, I think he's so clever," Mairi chirped and received a mock scowl in return. When they finally stopped for a bit of food, Arthur decided it was safe and left his throne atop Odhar's back.

Not only was traveling to Inverness a new experience for Mairi, sleeping outside was also. Beneath her blankets, she shivered with anticipation at what awaited her in town. However, with her bed placed between her brother's and her cousin's near the fire, in the chilled darkness, Mairi felt secure and content. By mid-day, as they traveled the shoreline of the Beauly Firth, Mairi discovered that Martin was leaving them to return to Glasgow. "Martin, you can't go yet," she whined prettily, "I was counting on both of you to help me with my dress."

Martin chortled, "Believe me, lass, the ladies at the shop will be infinitely more helpful than either Simon or I. Besides, my leaving is only temporary; I'll catch up with you."

Simon added, "I plan to keep you incredibly busy anyway."

"I suppose...if it's important...," Mairi pouted.

"It is," Martin replied, "but so is your wedding dress. You have my word, I'll return as quickly as I can." He leaned over and kissed her cheek, rode around her to grasp Simon's hand and confirmed, "You'll be at the 'White Rose'?"

"Aye, and Martin," Simon added, "take care."

With a nod, and a last wink at Mairi, Martin wheeled Odhar south, whistled to Arthur, and was on his way.

Simon decided to wait until morning to take his sister to Matheson's Millinery; it was more important that he secure lodging at the agreed upon inn. Further, Mairi was making herself dizzy trying to take in all the unfamiliar sights and sounds of the town. Simon thought giving her a little time to adjust would be useful. "Once we're settled," Simon offered, "we'll do some exploring. Would you like that?"

"Oh Simon, I would," she returned ecstatically, "there's so much to see here." Concern clouded her face. "What about the millinery?"

"First thing tomorrow we'll go to the shop; that'll be time enough." With that promise, her expression cleared and she was, once more, her sparkling self.

By the time Simon finished introducing Mairi to Inverness, she still had vitality to spare–his feet hurt. Simon fully expected his sister to pound on his door at first light but, if Simon had worried about arriving at the millinery too early, he needn't have bothered. Mairi, concerned at looking too provincial, took her time dressing and grooming herself.

They skirted the crowded Market, Simon's glance darting here and there in search of Alayne's face. What if she wasn't at the shop and he was forced to deal again with that dragon Alayne called her mother-in-law? He shrugged it off with a quick prayer that things might go his way today, and coaxed Mairi away from a cart full of delectable looking sweets. "Remember, we just ate," he reminded playfully.

Indeed, Simon was crestfallen when it was Katherine Matheson behind the shop counter discussing with a new client the details of ordering a snuff box from London.

Spotting Simon as he entered, a shadow flickered across her face until her glare settled on the pretty young woman on his arm.

Mustering his most sincere smile and nod, Simon greeted, "Mistress Matheson," and led Mairi to the front of the shop where she could examine more closely the silks, brocades, and materials he couldn't name. To Mairi he said, "We'll wait to be helped but, in the meantime, why don't you look at some of these.

In the workroom, Alayne heard the melodious lilt of Simon's voice, quickly composed herself, and entered the shop. The sight of Mairi nearly knocked the breath from her and she rasped,

"Didn't your mother care for her gift?"

With a brief bow and lingering eyes, Simon assured Alayne that the handkerchief pleased his mother. "So much so," he added, "that I have a more complicated project I'd like to discuss."

"My wedding dress!" Mairi blurted, looking lovingly at her brother.

Alayne's pleasant smile turned frosty. "Wedding dress?"

Hugging Simon's arm, Mairi prattled, "Aye, I'm so excited and Simon is such a dear to bring me to Inverness to have my beautiful gown made. He wants me to look stunning in it," she giggled.

Assessing the girl's creamy skin, huge eyes and lovely shape, Alayne was surprised by a stabbing ache of remorse for her budding fantasies about Simon. She fought her regrets, rallying to say, "I can't imagine you looking anything less than stunning."

Cocking her head, Mairi ceased her blathering to smile warmly at Alayne. "That was a kind thing to say, thank you."

"I meant it; your betrothed is a lucky man."

Simon squeezed Mairi's hand between his and said, "I assure you, her betrothed agrees with you."

Alayne spun away to face the bolts of fabric piled high above her and momentarily imagined them falling and burying her alive. She shook from the vision and said stiffly, "Did you have something specific in mind?" Why hadn't Fia returned from Market, she thought peevishly. Why couldn't she have been here to wait on them instead?

"Did you hear me, Alayne?"

Alayne's head jerked toward Kate's voice. "Oh, Kate, I'm sorry, what did you say?"

"I asked if you needed my help now that Mr. Ogilvy has gone."

Shaking her head, Alayne said, "Not right now, thank you. We are going to be talking fabrics, color and style for a bit. This young woman–"

"Mairi," Simon obligingly supplied.

"Mairi," Alayne said with a steadying breath, "needs a wedding dress."

Kate turned a delighted face to the bride-to-be. "I overheard and, may I say, you'll make a lovely bride."

"Thank you, Mistress," Mairi accepted the compliment gleefully, thrilled at being the object of so much flattering attention.

Kate then faced Simon. "Perhaps you have other errands and would like to return later for, Mairi?" But Mairi clutched Simon's arm.

"Oh, no," she cried, "Simon has to help me."

Simon smiled tenderly at his sister. "I wouldn't dream of going anywhere. However," he glanced from Kate to Alayne and added, "you have my word, I'll stay out of your way."

Alayne's resolve to appear unaffected was about to desert her. In desperation, she suggested to Mairi, "It would really be best to surprise Simon and I think his presence would only distract us." To Simon, she said, "You'd be doing the young lady a great service if you'd leave her here and come back in say, two hours."

Simon's eyes searched hers briefly, but saw they were silent. Finally, he relented. "If you think it's best for Mairi."

Mairi's eyes grew round with alarm at the thought of being left alone; Simon kissed her cheek and assured, "You'll scarcely know I'm gone before I return for you." He bowed and left the shop.

"If you're sure you don't need me," Kate said, "I'd like to pay Mistress Hays a visit."

"You go on, Kate, and please tell her I hope she feels better soon." When Kate was gone, Alayne turned her attention to Mairi. "First, tell me when you plan to marry."

"The eve of St. Martin," Mairi eagerly supplied.

"All right, we have barely two months and, for November, you'll want something warm," Alayne began.

"And something I can wear on the Sabbath," Mairi added, "and not too expensive. Simon was generous to offer to pay for my dress, but I won't take advantage of him."

Alayne smiled in spite of herself at Mairi's directness and demeanor. "I'm sure we can come up with something to make you both happy."

"And I have to look stunning!" Mairi cheerfully reminded.

Alayne brought chairs to the front room and they were deep in discussion when the curtain parted and Fia stuck her head in. Looking up from some sample sketches, Alayne declared with relief, "There you are; was the Market crowded?"

Fia looked from one woman to the other. "Aye, and I had trouble matching the embroidery threads because Mr. Ramsey wasn't there today. What are you doing?"

Alayne rolled her eyes. "Forgive my manners, Mairi, this is Fia, Kate's niece. She works here with me. Fia, this is Mairi; we are creating her wedding dress."

Fia's eyes lit. "How lovely, Mairi. When are you to wed?"

"November 11," Alayne supplied abruptly. "Simon brought her to us."

"Do you know Simon also?" Mairi asked Fia, who gripped the curtain behind her and shook her head, fearing her voice would fail her. "Well, you'll meet him when he comes to pick me up. He's so wonderful to do this."

"I...I'll just take off my mantle and help if you'd like."

Alayne insisted, "I wouldn't have it any other way."

Fia had trouble collecting her scattered thoughts but hurried anyway, certain that helping make the wedding gown for Simon's bride was a blow to Alayne. She chastised herself for having encouraged Alayne so forcefully to give Simon a chance. "How far have you gotten?" she asked returning to the shop.

"Mairi does not want a sack back gown and I was about to say that a quilted silk satin petticoat would dress up the plainer open robe style quite nicely," Alayne responded.

Fia nodded. "Indeed it would." She leaned over the sketches and rifled through them until she could point to an example. "Like this, Mairi."

The three bantered ideas about until Mairi finally held her hands up. "Wait, please, I'm getting confused."

Fia laughed, "And no wonder. Why don't we stop for now and measure you? You come to the back with me and Alayne will follow with some fabrics for you to look at."

When Alayne was alone, she covered her face with her hands and took deep breaths to stave off her disappointment. She was glad for these few solitary moments to collect her thoughts.

Stripped to her linen shift and stays, Mairi tried not to squirm while Fia measured, but her good intentions fled as she spied the fabrics in Alayne's arms. She rushed over, leaving Fia measuring air and extolled reverently, "These are exquisite." Clasping her hands together to keep from fingering the cloths, Mairi reluctantly asked, "Are they expensive?"

"No, these are reasonably priced, Mairi; I know you want to spare Simon's purse," Alayne replied dutifully.

"The yellow one, may I see it?" Mairi gasped as Alayne set the others down and displayed the pale ribbed silk.

"It's a lovely color for you," Fia came to stand beside them.

Mairi held it against her lithe frame. "Do you really think so? Do you think Simon will like this?"

"Undoubtedly," Fia stepped in to answer, "how could he not?"

Mairi anguished, "But will Rob love me in this, that's the real question."

There was a long silence as Fia and Alayne exchanged bewildered glances over Mairi's bowed head. "Who," Alayne finally questioned, "is Rob?"

"The man I'm marrying, of course!" Looking from one to the other, Mairi's hand flew to her mouth as she realized, "I never told you his name, did I? Isn't that just like me to get carried away like that. Why you probably thought I was marrying Simon." She burst into peals of laughter at the thought. "Imagine that," she gasped for breath.

"What's wrong with Simon?" Alayne asked a tad defensively.

"No...nothing," Mairi stuttered regaining her composure, "I'd marry him in a minute if he weren't my brother."

Alayne's voice quickened, "Brother?"

"Aye, my oldest brother," Mairi confirmed, turning her attention back to the silk.

Fia's smile of relief nearly lit the room whereas Alayne looked as though she'd been slapped. Fia sought to keep Mairi's attention on anything but Alayne. "Let's get back to work here, Mairi. When your brother returns, he'll want to see some progress."

The three threw themselves into the design of Mairi's dress with lighthearted abandon and when the two hours were nearly up, the decisions had been made. Fia heard the shop bell and excused herself to answer it. She was back quickly looking so disturbed that Alayne and Mairi both stopped to ask what was wrong.

"Aunt Kate has sent a messenger to ask me to bring the embroidered muff Mistress Hays ordered around to her house–she forgot to take it with her."

"Now?" Alayne asked in disappointment.

"Unfortunately," Fia responded, "I was looking forward to meeting Mairi's generous brother." Shrugging a smile, Fia said, "I'm sorry, Mairi, maybe when you return for the gown I'll have that pleasure." Throwing her mantle round her shoulders, and grabbing the muff from the top of the storage shelves, Fia bade an exasperated goodbye. As she trudged down the street, she was beginning to think she'd never meet this mystery man.

Not ten minutes later, Simon reappeared at the shop and had hardly set foot in the door when Mairi wrapped his neck in her grateful arms. "What a wonderful gown I'm going to have," she enthused then, remembering he was buying it, added, "that is if you approve it, of course."

"And why wouldn't I approve?" He beamed at her then turned his appreciative gaze on Alayne. "What have you concocted for my captivating sister?"

"Oh, let me tell him, Alayne, please?"

"Certainly, it's your gown after all," Alayne obliged, not taking her eyes from Simon.

Simon listened attentively as Mairi showed him the ribbed silk and described the matching stomacher, cream silk satin petticoat that would be quilted, and the lace trimmed linen bodice and sleeve linings. "Mairi, Rob will be struck dumb you'll be so beautiful," he swore.

"Simon," Mairi laughed, "do you know that they thought I was going to marry you? I forgot to tell them about Rob until Alayne brought out this lovely silk."

One look at Alayne's face and Simon realized it was true. He found himself breathless as though he'd been hit in the stomach. What must she think of him? Recovering, he apologized, "Alayne, I'm so sorry, it didn't even dawn on me that you would think–"

Alayne shook her head. "It doesn't matter."

Momentarily forgetting Mairi, Simon stood close beside Alayne. "It matters a great deal if it affects what we've already discussed. I'm very serious about that."

"Serious about what?" Mairi chimed. "You can't be serious about anything today, dear brother," she exclaimed. "Alayne, I forgot to tell him about the crowning touch to my gown."

"You did indeed," Alayne agreed.

"My gown will be embroidered with garlands of bluebonnets, bright blue ones...not too many...just sort of a trimming."

"I can't wait to see it," Simon declared. "How long will this take?"

"We can have the gown done in about ten days," Alayne told him, "but the embroidery will add another three to four weeks of time–it's just the two of us working."

"So, around the end of October then?" Simon asked and, to Alayne's nod, he crossed his arms. "You know, Mistress Kate doesn't strike me as the kind to work in the shop all day."

Alayne said, "She seldom does."

Simon mused, "Then who will help you with the gown?"

"Mistress Kate's niece," Alayne responded.

"Aye," Mairi said, "the embroidery was her idea; she and Alayne both agree the design will add a simple elegance to my gown."

"I'd like to meet her; the two of you have obviously pleased Mairi enormously. Is she here?"

Pursing her lips, Mairi frowned. "No, her aunt has her on an errand."

The little bell heralded the opening door and a young woman entered. "Miss MacGregor, how good to see you," Alayne exclaimed. "I'll be right with you." To Mairi she instructed, "If you want to, you may return in two to three weeks, Mairi; the gown will be ready for you to try on. I won't expect to see you before then." She opened the door for them, received an appreciative hug from Mairi, and exchanged a carefully reserved look with Simon. As she was closing the door behind him, Simon stopped her and asked in a low voice, "I'd like to speak with you, Alayne, just tell me when and where–please."

Alayne's gaze flitted from his face to her waiting customer, but she said nothing.

"I'll come back here if that's what you want."

"No...you have no reason to return until Mairi's dress is ready. She sucked in a deep breath and, before changing her mind blurted, "Tomorrow, I'll be at the Castle ruins, about seven in the evening."

"Thank you. I promise you won't regret it."

Closing the door after him, Alayne leaned against it wondering if that were true. Shaking herself from her musings, Alayne addressed Miss MacGregor. "Now then, what may I do for you today?"

The next evening, Simon left Mairi soaking in a hot bath having made her promise not to leave her room until he returned. Quickly, he rode the street which followed the River Ness until the Castle ruin came into view. There was no sign of Alayne; it was nearly seven o'clock.

Simon urged Devenick down to the end of the fortress away from the river, then half the length of the back wall where he dismounted, looping the reins over a scrubby sapling. Quickly, he walked the remaining length of wall, turning the corner at the far end. His pulse quickened until he neared the corner closest to the river and Alayne appeared before him. The urge to encircle her waist and lift her high off the ground almost overwhelmed him, he was so elated. Instead, Simon jammed his hands deep into the pockets of his frock coat. The gesture was not lost on Alayne.

"I'm on time aren't I?" she asked.

"Aye, and thank you for meeting me."

"I said I would," Alayne reminded, "but it was a rash promise–I can't stay long."

"I understand it wasn't an easy decision." Simon indicated a good sized, flattish stone. "As long as you're here, why don't you sit down?"

Alayne did just that and looked at him expectantly.

"You must believe I'm sorry for the misunderstanding about Mairi. It was foolish of me not to have realized–"

"That's over and done," Alayne interrupted with a shrug.

"And forgiven?" he queried optimistically.

"What is there to forgive? There is nothing between us, Simon, except the prospect of friendship. You owe me nothing."

"I will always owe you the truth, Alayne," he stated and, noting her upturned mouth asked, "Why do you smile so?"

"A man always wanting to be truthful with me...how I would enjoy that," she sighed.

Tentatively, Simon sat beside her and quietly asked, "It was not so with your husband?"

Staring into the evening sky, Alayne's smile faded. "No, it wasn't."

Simon closed his eyes against an array of imagined wrongs committed by Alayne's husband and Alayne stole a glance at his profile finding his nearness intoxicating. At length, she said, "I confess to being...somewhat disappointed when I believed you'd brought your bride to us." Gripping her hands together tightly, Alayne continued, "The fact that it mattered to me made me realize that I've already become careless, and that simply won't do."

"Yet here you are," he declared softly.

Alayne looked surprised. "I...I felt I owed you an explanation. After all, I said I'd consider... becoming friends."

Gently shaking his head, Simon denied her reasoning. "You're less afraid of being seen with me than you imagine or you wouldn't have come here tonight." His hand boldly covered her clasped ones. "For now, I would be content to be some small part–any part–of your life. What should that part be Alayne–not in two months, or next year, but right now."

Knowing that her hand in his belied her words, still she lacked the will to remove it. "I have no right to ask anything from you, Simon. I'm a married woman," she repeated.

"Only by the ring on your finger," he insisted and she was silent. "You intend to end the marriage; you speak as though that will happen soon. What will you do then? You'll need all your friends, I dare say." Simon watched her struggle with her thoughts before asking, "Will we be friends, or would you really rather I simply went away–at least until your marriage is ended?"

Alayne's voice tensed, "I've no business being with you, no business at all. Agitated, she withdrew her hand from his and stood leaning against a relatively intact piece of the Castle wall.

Simon rose with her and said, "I'm asking to spend a bit of time in your company, Alayne. What's so evil about giving a man who thinks you are exquisite the opportunity to bask in your presence?"

Hot tears sprang to her eyes but Alayne refused to let them fall. "Don't you hear a word I say?" she whispered tremulously. "I'm not free to encourage any man to pay attention to me."

"I don't need encouragement!" Simon's fists pressed his chest for emphasis. "This is what I want, and what I hoped you might as well. But you haven't answered me, Alayne." He slowly crossed the few steps until he stood so close that her petticoat brushed his legs. In the encroaching dusk, Simon could still make out her features but not the color of her eyes. "Do you want me to go away? Just tell me what you honestly want."

Everything about him conspired against her: the intensity of his expression, the smell of his skin, the nearness of his taut body–her own longing even betrayed her. Without a word, Alayne edged the corner through a breach in the wall where she'd awaited Simon's arrival. "If you want honesty," she whispered in frustration when Simon followed her inside, "you shall have it. I don't want to be friends–I don't want to take a chance that I'll come to care for you." She bit her lip, tasting blood, and glowered at him. "I'm afraid, Simon, afraid of making the same mistake and suffering the same anguish! There, are you satisfied? Is that honest enough for you?" Trying to push past him, Simon's arm shot out to block her path.

"No it's not–you left out something critical," he asserted. Holding her face gently but firmly with both hands, Simon declared, "You already care for me–at least a little." Alayne began to sputter denial but he stopped her with a finger to her lips. "Yesterday, at the shop, your face told me how disappointed you were thinking I was marrying Mairi; it wasn't because you thought I'd been callous or cruel in bringing my bride to you. Lass, I don't pretend to know the Hell you've endured because of your husband. I am not your husband; I'm Simon MacLaren–I beg you not to confuse the two."

Tears blurred her vision, but Alayne heard the reverence of his request in Simon's soft, reassuring voice. Unexpectedly, she collapsed against his chest convulsed with sobs she had swallowed for years. Simon swaddled her in his arms, stroked her hair and cooed comforting sounds to help calm her. When Alayne finally spoke, it was almost dark inside and outside the gap in the wall. The darkness gave her courage.

"She'll do it...my friend, Kate's niece. She'll help us."

Simon tightened his grip on Alayne and momentarily lay his cheek against her hair. "Thank you, lass," he basked a moment in the warmth of her decision.

Raising her face to his, Alayne could only see a partial outline of his unruly locks. "I hope you are still thankful once you get to know me; we aren't off to a good beginning."

"But it is a beginning."

Chapter Twenty

"*Martin! You've only* been gone two days. How could you possibly have gotten back so quickly?" Simon asked in surprise as Mairi raced through the public room to engulf her cousin in a welcoming embrace.

"There was no reason to stay–and every reason to return. So," he urged Mairi after disentangling himself, "tell me all about your dress."

Mairi catapulted into a detailed description of the gown. Simon thought Martin's attention was elsewhere for most of the account but, when Mairi finished, his enthusiastic response made Simon doubt his assessment.

Mairi excused herself saying, "I want to freshen up before supper; Simon and I visited so many shops today. Now, in case you two are wondering, I'm famished, so don't go anywhere. I'll be back shortly."

As she disappeared, Martin and Simon looked at each other. "Well," Simon asked impatiently, "what happened?"

Martin rubbed his neck hoping to ease the tension that gripped it. "I easily found Forbes' office. The clerk who works there said Struan had gone to Edinburgh–"

"We already knew that from Elizabeth," Simon interrupted.

Martin's eyes reflected his gnawing concern. "The man had no idea if Struan was returning directly to Glasgow or if he had business elsewhere."

"I'm sorry, Martin." Simon frowned and asked, "Were you able to find out anything useful at all?"

"I wish I could say no, but Struan does have a brother named Andrew, who has a pronounced scar from the left corner of his mouth down to his chin. The clerk says Andrew also has quite a temper–he'd run afoul of it himself."

Simon grimaced. "It's as bad as we feared. Is there any news of Fia though?"

"I decided not to mention her at all. If the clerk reports my visit and questions, I don't want either Forbes to think Fia is involved."

"Wise decision, but now what will you do?"

"Accompany you and Mairi home while I try to think where to look next." Martin gazed wistfully into the tavern's flickering fire. "Did I tell you that Fia once lived in Inverness?"

"No, I didn't know that," Simon admitted.

"She left when she was eight; her parents drowned in the Moray Firth. If I knew what kind of work her father did after moving here, or had ever heard her mother's family name, maybe this would be the place to look."

"It's a shame she never told you," Simon sighed.

Shaking his head, Martin cut his eyes to his cousin. "That's enough about my miserable failure. Tell me, were you more fortunate with Alayne? Did you even get the chance to speak to her with Mairi about?"

"Not really–that is not until I left Mairi upstairs bathing last night and met Alayne at the Castle ruins. By the way, Mairi doesn't know anything about Alayne, yet."

"I won't say a word, but tell me what Alayne said," Martin urged. "I can't help but think it's promising that she met with you at the Castle."

Simon recounted the events of the past two days. "First she misunderstood and thought I was to be Mairi's husband." To Martin's incredulous gape, Simon assured, "It's true! Once we straightened that out and she agreed to meet me, she said again that she wanted only to end her marriage. She feels she needs to be above reproach to ensure that happens."

"It's hard to fault her for that," Martin reasoned.

"And I don't, honestly," Simon assured. "Though she gave me no details, I fear her husband was...unkind to her. I told her I would help in any way I could, even if it meant going away until her marriage was dissolved."

"Considering how you feel, that can't have been easy. And it's just like you to put her needs first. So how did she respond to that?"

Simon beamed his pleasure. "That Kate's niece had agreed to help us. Isn't that wonderful?"

Martin's expression softened. "Aye, Simon, it is. And when will you see her next?"

"On Wednesday at Market." Simon twitched a nervous grin and rubbed his hands together in delicious anticipation.

The next morning, soupy fog surrounded the trio as they left Inverness. Following the shore of Beauly Firth, the only sounds that reached them were those made by the hooves of their own mounts–not even the gulls cried.

"This is positively dreary," Mairi sulked after the first hour of plodding single file. "I'm so damp from this fog I think I could wring out my skirts and get a full cup of water."

"When the sun climbs, the fog will burn off," Simon assured.

"What sun?" Mairi moaned with a dramatic sweep of one arm. "And wouldn't we be drier if we traveled away from the strand, even a wee bit?"

"Possibly," Martin replied from his place in line behind her, "but we'd also risk getting lost. If we follow the coast, we know we're headed in the right direction, even if it isn't the most direct route."

"We'll make up the time when the weather clears and we can see where we're going," Simon added, "So stop fuss–whoa!" Devenick suddenly shied away from the water and Simon reined him in. "What's the trouble, laddie?" He leaned over to pat the horse's neck reassuringly only to have the animal dance sideways again.

"Simon, what is it?" Martin called.

"I don't know. Look around, do you see any–" Arthur's barking cut into Simon's instruction, but before Simon could react, Martin was off Odhar, had snatched up his medicines and run to Arthur's side.

"Mairi, stay on your horse; Simon, there's a man here," Martin reported.

Dismounting, Simon tossed Devenick's reins to Mairi and knelt beside Martin who was hunting the pulse point under the man's jaw.

"He's still alive, barely."

"By the way he's dressed," Simon pointed out, "I'd say he's off a ship."

"I think you're right. Help me turn him over." The two men rolled the sailor onto his back only to be met by a pulpy mass that once was his face. Mairi's shocked cry sliced the stillness and Martin shifted quickly to block her view. He stripped off his coat and laid it over the man, tucking it around him for warmth.

"Sweet Jesus, what do you suppose happened to him?" Simon mumbled.

"Let's see if we can find out. God's blood, I wish the light was better." Martin leaned in close to the sailor's face seeking the source of his disfigurement and spoke to the man. "We're here to help you. Can you tell us who you are and what happened to you?" His questions were met by silence; Martin repeated them and, this time, got lucky.

"Co...Connor," the injured man gasped.

"Your name is Connor?" Martin verified and the man gave the slightest nod. "How were you injured?"

Connor struggled to form words through a mouth almost invisible in his raw, distended face. "Beat...thro..own over."

"You were beaten and thrown overboard?" Simon queried.

"Dead," Connor gurgled.

"They thought you were dead," Martin muttered extracting a bottle of comfrey juice from his supplies. "I'm a doctor, I'm going to try to clean your wounds."

"No...use," Connor hissed, "get...him...."

"The man who beat you?" Martin asked and, at the flutter of Connor's eyelids inquired, "Who is he?"

"Trader...Gordon," Connor sighed his last breath.

In the silence that followed, Mairi whimpered, "Is he dead?"

188

Simon rose quickly and came to the side of her mount. "Aye, Mairi, he died, poor soul."

"What happened?"

"Someone beat him to death," Martin supplied, then retrieved his coat and threw it over Odhar's saddle. "He said this 'Gordon' was a trader, I suppose he meant free trader."

"A smuggler?" Mairi's eyes grew wide. "Do you really think so?"

"A reasonable guess," her brother responded.

Looking from one man to the other, Mairi begged, "What do we do now?"

"We'll put him on Odhar and take him to Beauly, that's the closest place we can leave him." Martin went back to the body and Simon followed. They awkwardly lifted and deposited it across Odhar's back.

"I'll double with Mairi, you take Devenick," Simon offered Martin.

It was after mid-day before they were able to leave Beauly. The Sheriff had been summoned to examine Connor's body; the cabinet maker was brought to build a coffin; questions were asked and answers provided as best they could. No one Martin or Simon spoke with in the burgh recognized the man. When Simon mentioned the possibility of a smuggler named 'Gordon' being involved, the only response was that there were no excise men or King's troops nearby to whom they could report the news.

By the time Martin and Simon picked Mairi up at the Sheriff's house where his wife had kept her company, the day mercifully had turned sunny. They left the burgh quickly, eager to put the unpleasant incident behind them. After a long mind-clearing canter, Mairi reluctantly asked Martin, "Where's your coat?"

"I left it for Connor to be buried in. He had nothing and, quite honestly, I didn't want it back."

"Still, that was good of you," she praised gently before turning her attention elsewhere. "I'll be glad to get home."

"Won't we all," Simon agreed.

The following day, the bedraggled little troop finally entered the familiar yard in Strathcarron. Martin helped Mairi from her saddle. She was so exhausted he wasn't sure she could stand without help. Jessie glimpsed them first and hurried over, her excited greeting dying on her lips as she beheld her ashen daughter, eyes made larger by the dark circles under them. "In God's name, what happened?" she cried. "Mairi? Simon? Martin? Someone answer me!" Jessie pulled Mairi into her arms and stroked the girl's hair.

"I'm only tired, Mam, really," Mairi insisted with a weak smile.

"You're going straight to bed–and you," she turned her glare on the two men, "I will talk with you directly–you were supposed to take care of her."

"Mam, it's not their fault," Mairi protested, "they took wonderful care of me."

"Not by the looks of you."

Mairi ceased objecting and the two women disappeared into the farmhouse. Simon nodded toward the byre. "We might as well stable the horses." They led the animals into the dark interior of the stone building and it was there that Jessie found them–Martin stretched in the straw that served as his bed and Simon propped against the wall, head back, eyes closed. Only Arthur raised his head in welcome, beating his thick tail on the floor.

Jessie contemplated the scene before her and her ire subsided. "Obviously, Mairi is not the only one who suffered on this trip," she declared.

Martin pulled himself up and Simon drew his knees close to his chest, resting his arms atop them. "Everything went well, Mam, until we left Inverness to return home," Simon began. "Mairi's going to have a lovely dress in which to be married."

"I'm glad to hear it," she replied caustically. "Your sister was so tired she didn't even mention it; that tells me quite a bit."

Simon went on, "We started back in a bad fog and stumbled upon a man who'd been beaten and nearly drowned. The man died within minutes of our finding him and we had no choice but to take him to Beauly and answer a great many questions for the Sheriff. We spared Mairi what we could." Simon pressed the heels of his hands to his forehead and Martin continued the story.

"We left in the afternoon and wanted to make up some of the lost time so pushed on longer than perhaps was wise. Even with the angelica tea I brewed to help her, Mairi slept very little last night–she kept seeing Connor, the dead man, whenever she closed her eyes. Then early this morning came a drenching rain. It's been a miserable, ugly trip, Jessie, but now that she's back home, Mairi should be fine in a few days."

"I see." Jessie reached down to lay a caressing hand on her son's golden head and asked, "And what of you lads, are you all right?"

Simon took his mother's hand and held it against his cheek. "Aye, Mam."

"Martin?" Jessie prompted.

He nodded. "Tired, that's all."

"Rest up then and, when you get hungry, come to the house. With luck, Mairi will sleep through supper and, maybe, through the night."

Weary eyes sought Jessie's face. "I doubt it," Martin prophesied.

It was late when Martin finally trudged to the farmhouse and, as predicted, Mairi was awake. She sat before the fire with the ginger cat in her lap, hypnotically stroking its fur. With a mumbled greeting to the others, Martin approached and crouched before her. His hand touched the cat's fur then entwined Mairi's fingers causing her glazed eyes to flicker and focus on his comely face.

"Did you rest, lass?" he asked.

"Some," she responded with a small smile.

"I'll brew you more tea before you go to bed tonight."

"Do you know what I really want?" she asked.

"No," Martin admitted, "what do you want, Mairi?"

Her mouth quivered. "I want to see Rob."

Eleanor approached to stand beside her. "We'll send for him in the morning. In the meantime, Martin's tea will do you good."

"Thank you, Gram. Please don't worry, I'll be fine."

"I know, sweet," her grandmother replied. "You've had quite a trip and quite a shock. You're strong though."

Loving tears shone in Mairi's eyes as she bestowed a shimmering smile on Eleanor. "Like you, Gram."

The family sat at the table for some time after Mairi retired, her belly warmed and mind dulled by the angelica tea. Martin found he wasn't really hungry and settled for a cheese biscuit and ale; Simon had eaten earlier.

In low tones, Lachlan, Jessie, Eleanor and Grant were given the details of the journey including Martin's trek back to Glasgow. Only one topic was not discussed except in connection with Mairi's wedding dress–Alayne.

"I'll leave at first light to fetch Rob," Grant volunteered.

"Good lad," Lachlan said approvingly and, to Martin added, "What are your plans now?"

Thoughtfully, Martin rubbed his beard. "I'd like to stay, rest myself and Arthur, keep an eye on Mairi until Monday. Then, I'll head back to Inverness."

"Why?" Grant inquired.

"Frankly, it's about the only place I can think of to begin searching for Fia. If she has relatives still there, perhaps they know how I can find her."

Eleanor turned to Simon. "And I suppose you'll be leaving with him."

"You know me well, Gram," he said patting her worn hand.

She sized him up and smirked, "It's more than your need to be useful, lad," and to the inquisitive tilt of his head added, "something about this woman making Mairi's dress...Alayne."

Stunned, Simon could only sputter, "Wha...I don't...what do you mean?"

Jessie, Lachlan and Grant all turned to observe the exchange as Eleanor stated, "Your tone, your face...they take on a tenderness when you speak of her."

"Oh, Gram," Simon self-consciously pushed away from the table and scoffed, "stop it. They'll think you're serious."

"You think I'm not?"

Simon's mouth opened, but he was too flustered for words.

"I don't hear a denial," Eleanor purred and turned to Jessie, "do you, Daughter?"

"Why, no, I don't," Jessie replied in wonder. "Son, is she right? Is there something you aren't telling us?"

Simon's scowl cut to Martin who shrugged, palms upturned in denial of any role in Simon's being found out. He examined the eager anticipation in the faces around the table and grimaced.

"I only met Alayne when Martin and I were traveling to Glasgow. She sold me your birthday gift, Mam."

"Helped pick it out," Martin supplied, lips twitching to hold back his smile. He was enjoying watching Simon squirm.

"You aren't being helpful, Cousin," Simon fumed.

Jessie swallowed a pleased grin and said, "Well, she has excellent taste," belatedly adding, "the handkerchief too. I hope you told her how much I liked it."

"I told her. And, I thought she could make Mairi a fine wedding dress."

"Is that all?" Lachlan asked.

"For now," Simon offered. "I do like her, and...hope to know her better." He arched his brow in his grandmother's direction. "Satisfied?"

A slow smile split Eleanor's face as she echoed, "For now."

Alayne stoked the workroom fire against the mid-September chill and ended her recounting of her meeting at the Castle. "I did try to make it clear when I spoke to him, Fia, about Muir. I spared the sordid details but," she said in wonder, "he...seemed to understand."

"There was no reason to dwell on Muir's contemptible behavior." Fia sympathized, "Still, I'm glad Simon understood–he has a lot at stake." Alayne looked at her blankly and Fia emphasized, "You, Alayne, his interest in you is what he has at stake."

Hesitantly, Alayne admitted, "I told him you would help us."

Excitement lit Fia's face. "So, I will finally meet this wonderfully persistent fellow!"

"At Market, Wednesday," Alayne promised, brightening considerably.

Fia rose and took Alayne's hand. "I have something to show you, come with me." Fia led Alayne to the mirror used by customers during fittings. "Look," she entreated, "can you see the change already?"

"Fia, don't be silly." Still, Alayne studied her reflection and unexpectedly blushed.

"There, you see? You've made a good decision, Alayne, a good decision," she emphasized. "Already it has taken the strain from your face and, I dare say, having his arms about you–"

"I was crying hysterically," Alayne reminded.

"It doesn't matter, don't you see?" Fia sanctioned. "He was there when you needed him, and he was caring. Some would have tried to press the advantage while you were in tears."

"What an incurable romantic you are, Fia," Alayne stated hugging her friend. "And I'm so glad."

"And nothing will keep me from Market next week," Fia promised. "Now, I'll fetch the silk satin so we can begin work on Mairi's petticoat."

In the front of the shop, reaching high for the fabric bolt, Fia heard the jingle of the shop bell behind her. "I'll be with you in just a moment," she called.

"You dare keep your husband waiting?" demanded the familiar, deep tones.

Fia started, clutched the fabric and whirled. "*Murdoch!*" she cried and, dropping the bolt on the counter, ran to him and was swept into his bear-like embrace. It was in this position Alayne found them as she rushed from the workroom in response to Fia's squeal.

They abruptly stood apart, clutching hands and laughing their pleasure at the sight of one another. Murdoch planted a quick kiss on Fia's cheek, then spun her around to get a good look at her. "God's life, it's marvelous to see you."

"Oh, Murdoch," she declared, absorbing the details of his appearance, "How wonderful that you've come to visit!" Her voice caught in her throat and she put her arms around him and hugged him once more.

From the curtained door, Alayne crossed her arms and offered, "I think you made it clear how pleased you are, Fia."

"Alayne, come quickly," Fia dragged Murdoch forward and they met in the middle of the shop. "This is Murdoch Sinclair, the man who brought me to Inverness."

"I gathered this was Murdoch." She dipped her curtsey and declared, "I'm pleased to finally meet you, Mr. Sinclair. Fia has spoken of you often and with great affection. Welcome back to Inverness."

"Thank you, Mistress." He bowed then addressed her with twinkling gray eyes, "I hope you will excuse my enthusiasm; I've missed Fia."

"I find your 'enthusiasm' charming," Alayne assured him.

"Murdoch, what brings you here? Are you on an errand for Douglas?" Fia questioned.

"Not exactly for Douglas, though he was concerned about you after that night on the moor. He told me all about his visit."

Fia squirmed at the reminder, "I'm fine, please believe me."

"So you came to check on Fia yourself, Mr. Sinclair?" Alayne asked assessing his tall, broad frame and agreeable face.

"Murdoch, please. Aye, I thought it would ease Douglas' mind; it also gave me the perfect excuse to come check on my lady wife–number two."

"How are Elspeth and the children?" Fia inquired.

"All fine and, we have another bairn on the way." Murdoch's chest puffed with pride.

Fia lay a hand on his arm. "How exciting for you both; when is the babe due?"

"Early spring, in March we think. The little ones are eager to see the newest family member."

"No more eager than you, I'll wager. And Agnes, was she terribly upset that Douglas was delayed in his return?"

"My sister got over it quickly enough."

Fia inquired, "Can you stay and chat for a while?"

"I have business to attend to, but I plan to be in town for a few days," he replied noncommittally.

"Splendid," she said, "come to the back and sit with us. We're beginning work on a wedding gown. It'll give us a chance to catch up."

Murdoch glanced at Alayne. "No, I don't want to interrupt your work."

"Nonsense," Alayne argued. "You won't interrupt a thing, and Fia will be crushed if you leave so soon. Besides, I've wanted to meet you since I first heard about you. Heavens, you even won over my mother-in-law, Kate–not an easy task. Really, Murdoch, I wish you'd stay."

Murdoch bowed slightly. "That's very kind, thank you."

"And you will lodge at Aunt Kate's," Fia added.

Murdoch chuckled, "Don't you think we should ask your aunt first, Fia?"

"She would have it no other way," Fia teased. "Don't forget, she did swoon in your arms."

Murdoch grimaced and, as he followed the women to the back room, remarked, "Speaking of swooning, will you two please tell me what happened between Douglas and Mistress Matheson?"

Alayne and Fia halted so abruptly that Murdoch bumped into them. The two women exchanged smug expressions of triumph and linked their arms in Murdoch's. "Gladly," Fia chortled, "if you'll tell us what made you ask."

That evening, Murdoch was warmly greeted by Kate who would hear no excuses. "As long as you're in Inverness, you stay as our guest," she assured him warmly.

The night was surprisingly mild and, after supper, Fia and Murdoch walked Alayne to the shop, ambling back, enjoying the silken air. "I like Alayne," Murdoch said, "she's got a wry humor and easy way about her that's very becoming."

"She's been a good friend to me; she could have made my life miserable," Fia admitted.

Murdoch asked, "Did I tell you how lovely you are without bruises all over your face?" To her slightly startled look, he reminded her, "This is the first time I've ever seen you in your normal colors."

"I guess it is at that," she agreed sedately.

Murdoch apologized, "I didn't intend to remind you of that repugnant business with the Forbes brothers. It was my clumsy way of telling you that you look remarkable: happy, well... maybe even content–but I doubt that."

Fia barked a laugh, "Murdoch, you might as well be my husband as well as you know me."

"I'll always be your second choice," he vowed.

"And I yours," she returned, studying his silhouette in the darkness. "Aunt Kate and Alayne have been so supportive and protective–just as you and Douglas have been. I'm a very fortunate woman."

"And I say you were overdue for people to fuss over you and appreciate the engaging woman you are."

"That still makes me blessed."

"True enough. What about love, Fia?"

She faltered a step and answered, "I'm still in it, if that's what you mean."

"Aye, that's what I mean. No word or sign of Martin?"

"Even if he cared to look, Murdoch, he wouldn't know where to find me," she stated flatly.

"I guess I just hoped."

"And just think, Alayne calls *me* an incurable romantic."

Murdoch tugged the stock at his neck as though it choked him. "I have a small confession to make, lass."

"A confession?" she inquired, interest piqued. "To me? What could you possibly confess to me?"

"After I left you here in June, I returned to Glasgow by way of Inveraray."

Fia staggered to a halt. "You did what?"

"You heard me, Fia, I traveled to Inveraray." Murdoch sighed. "I had this grand idea that, somehow, I might help you by finding Martin Ross and telling him to his face what a dolt he was for giving you up."

Voice barely a whisper, Fia demanded, "Tell me you didn't do that, Murdoch."

"I didn't," he confirmed, then grumbled, "but not because I changed my mind about it! Ross made a grave mistake when he scorned you."

Eyes tearing at Murdoch's loyalty, Fia lightly touched his cheek. "Your concern for me... Murdoch, I'm so grateful. I told you though, Martin chose Jean MacNab. He knew and loved her before I ever came along. We can't blame him for loving someone else any more than I can blame him because I still love him."

Murdoch clasped her hand in his. "I love Elspeth as much as a man can love a woman–it didn't stop me from seeing how extraordinary you are, Fia."

"All men aren't as perceptive as you, Murdoch," she bantered lightly.

"Fia," he insisted, "I'm serious."

"I know, but what would you have me do? Martin didn't see in me what you do or, if he did, it apparently couldn't compare to Jean MacNab's favors." Her companion grumbled and Fia insisted, "Now stop. Tell me what happened in Inveraray; I am interested, you know."

"I looked up Annie MacAuley thinking she would lead me to Ross."

"Annie," Fia's tone softened with affection, "how was she?"

"Fine, protective of Ross. She wouldn't tell me where he lived, said he was traveling anyway."

"Wedding trip, I suppose," Fia murmured.

"That she didn't say. I told her I knew you."

Head snapping up, Fia exclaimed, "You didn't tell her where I was did you?"

"No, lass," Murdoch replied, "but I did tell her that Ross was a fool to let you go. Would you like to know what she told me?"

She gulped tentatively. "I...I suppose so."

"She said she told Ross that you loved him."

"*What?*" Fia gasped.

"He told her that she shouldn't meddle; he knew what he was doing and any interference from her would make things worse."

"I'm sure he believed it." Fia wiped spilling tears from her cheeks. "We'd better get back to Aunt Kate's before she worries."

Aggrieved because he'd reopened her wounds, Murdoch asked her pardon. "If I was wrong to go, forgive me lass. Even though my intentions were good, sometimes that's not good enough."

Fia soothed, "You weren't wrong to go, Murdoch. I thank God he has granted me so fine a friend as you. If you ever need my assistance, I pray I'll be there for you."

By the time Rob departed for home in the early afternoon on the Sabbath, Mairi was almost her old self. Martin and Simon were greatly relieved to see her improvement. They didn't want to return to Inverness leaving Mairi behind, still shaken from the encounter with Connor. They planned to leave on the morrow.

The chores were done and the family just sitting down for a light supper when Arthur began to bark furiously. "Is he after the geese again?" Grant smirked.

"I don't know," Martin sighed, rising to investigate. He stepped into the yard and immediately saw Arthur over near the goose pen. "Aye, it's the geese. Go ahead while the meal is hot; I'll be right back."

As he crossed the yard, Martin wagged his head at the hound who pranced and sniffed, darted and dodged at an unseen foe. Unable to detect the cause of the ruckus, Martin began to worry that Arthur might actually have injured one of the birds. "Arthur, stop!" he called and was surprised that the dog raced to his side. As he bent to chastise Arthur, the hound bounded back to the pen. Hastening his stride, Martin finally saw the source of Arthur's spasm. He ran the last few steps and dove to his knees beside Rob. He spied blood in the dirt. Martin carefully turned the lad face up. "Rob...*Rob!*"

Eyes flickering open, Rob clutched the front of Martin's waistcoat. "My father," he gasped for breath, "killed. Mam..." his eyes teared and he could not continue.

"Take your time, Rob, we'll help all we can. Let me look at your arm." Martin ripped the sleeve where the blood stained scarlet and saw, gratefully, that the shot had missed the bone. With a strip of cloth from the tattered shirt, Martin tied it round the wound. "Can you walk if I help you stand?"

"Aye...aye, I can walk."

"Good lad." Martin assisting, Rob stood. "Lean on me now; I'm going to call for help." With that slim warning, Martin bellowed for the MacLarens who came crashing out the door in their haste to respond to his anxious cry.

"Rob!" Mairi screamed and dashed to desperately wrap her arms around him as Lachlan and Grant rushed to support the wounded man.

Martin wrested the reluctant Mairi aside and firmly grasped her shoulders. "Pay attention to me, Mairi. Rob is injured but he'll be fine–I promise you that."

Mairi tore huge, tear-filled eyes from Rob. When she saw reassurance in Martin's face, she calmed somewhat. "H...how can I help him?"

With an approving nod, Martin let her go. "I need a large bowl of hot water, toweling and a blanket."

Mairi sprinted back to the house and had gathered what Martin requested by the time the men had settled Rob on one of the beds.

Lachlan plied the lad with whiskey so Martin could extract the ball. When that was accomplished, Martin cleaned and dressed the wound.

At last, Rob roused himself enough to beg, "You have to go to the farm. Pap's dead." He drew a shuddering breath and spilled, "I don't know if Mam's bad hurt or...or...I don't know."

Lachlan ordered his sons to saddle three horses and, when they had jumped to carry out his orders, Lachlan asked, "What happened to you and what of your brother?"

Rob shook his shaggy coal-colored hair, "I didn't see Geddes. When I reached the farm, Mam screamed. I ran toward the croft just as Pap was pushed out the door and fell. A man followed him and, my father begged, but the man killed him. Mam yanked at the man's arm and he struck her."

"And you, Rob?" Jessie prompted.

Rob shivered and Mairi quickly tucked a blanket around him. "When he hit Mam, I yelled. His eyes were cold, evil; he raised his other pistol and shot. I ran here."

"All right," Martin propped a pillow behind him. "You rest awhile in the care of these ladies and do as they tell you. We'll check your family."

Struggling to sit up, Rob bawled, "I'm going with you!"

"No, and don't argue," Martin threatened. "You've suffered physical and emotional shock. You rest quietly and we'll be back soon."

Simon and Grant reentered proclaiming the mounts ready. Lachlan ordered, "Grant, you're the best shot in the family; you stay here in case there's trouble."

"Aye," Grant immediately went to the corner or the room, picked up and began loading the two muskets that rested there.

Issuing last minute instructions to Mairi to get some lovage tea down Rob and to keep him warm, Martin followed the others outside and strapped his medicine bag to Odhar's saddle. The three men mounted and urged the horses from the yard at a gallop.

At the pace they kept, it took about fifteen minutes to reach their destination. As the horses skidded to a halt in the yard, Martin spied Rob's father sprawled on his back, just beyond the croft door. He was beside him in a flash.

"Alice?" Lachlan yelled. "Alice, it's Lachlan MacLaren, we've come to help!" Without a pause, he passed his old friend, Magnus, seeing that Martin was closing the man's empty eyes, and entered the croft in search of Rob's mother. Martin entered behind him.

"Simon's gone to search for Geddes," Martin offered and knelt beside him where Alice sat slumped just inside the door.

"Good," Lachlan nodded. "Alice, it's Lachlan. This is my cousin, Martin. He's a doctor and will help you."

Alice raised glassy eyes to him and asked, "Magnus?"

Lachlan gingerly pushed a thick lock of graying hair from her forehead and lamented, "I'm sorry, Alice, Magnus is dead."

A mournful wail swelled within the woman and she clamped her hand to her mouth trying to still it. Lachlan patted her heaving shoulders in a vain attempt to bring her comfort.

Martin pressed, "Mistress, how badly are you injured?"

With effort, she straightened somewhat, studied him, and turned to Lachlan to implore, "Rob...Geddes...where are they?"

"Rob came to us, and that's how we knew there was trouble. He's still there. Simon is outside searching for Geddes."

"He was at the s...still. Go after him Lachlan," she pleaded, tears continuing to spill. "I'll be all right with your cousin."

Lachlan looked uncertain but Martin urged, "Do as she asks," and he left.

Rob's mother was a painfully thin woman and her balance unsteady. He found a kettle containing water and hung it on a pot chain over the fire. "Now, Mistress, let me look at you." Blood dyed the hair on one side of her head crimson. It trickled down her face and neck from the center of a huge lump, confirming that she'd been hit hard. Martin pressed a cloth to her head and, upon examination found no other wounds. When he had cleaned the cut, and dabbed it with a lanolin and lovage ointment to protect it from infection, Martin said, "You should lie down and rest; I'll see if I'm needed elsewhere. Will you be all right alone for a few minutes?"

Her fingers closed around the raw scars on his arm and she asked in a quavering voice, "Geddes?"

"We'll find him." Covering her hand with his Martin said, "I wish I could do more to help than bandage you."

The elfin woman bit her lip, nodded bravely, and Martin reemerged from the croft just in time to witness Simon and Lachlan place Geddes, throat slashed into a grotesque grin, next to his father. Lachlan submitted, "Geddes was at the still, just as Alice predicted. Where is she?"

"Resting. Do you want me to break it to her?"

Lachlan shook his head. "No, I'll handle that task–but thank you."

Martin knelt beside Simon who crouched, knuckles pressed against his mouth, at Magnus' side. There was no need, but Martin checked for Geddes' pulse. A shuddering howl from Alice roused shivers in both men and, furious, Simon flashed, "What monster did this?"

"God knows," Martin replied, "but between Alice and Rob, we might get a good description of him."

Simon grimaced, "Is Alice hurt badly?"

"Her body will heal more quickly than her heart; it's going to be a long journey for her." Martin paused before asking, "Have you ever heard of anything like this happening in the Strath before?"

With an irate toss of his head, Simon snorted, "Never!"

At the door, Alice appeared leaning heavily on Lachlan. Upon seeing Geddes, she pitched forward and gathered her dead kin under her trembling arms and howled.

The men stood awkwardly for a few moments before Martin squatted beside the distraught woman. "It's little comfort, Mistress, but their deaths were quick."

Lachlan touched Alice's shoulder. "The lads will get the cart; we'll take them home to prepare them for burial."

"No," she said flatly, "I will prepare them. I was part of Magnus–I gave birth to Geddes."

"Alice, please let us help," Lachlan begged, wishing Jessie was with him to help persuade her.

"You can, Lachlan. Tell the Reverend I will bury them in the morning. And send Rob home."

Martin insisted on staying to help Alice prepare her husband and son for burial while the others did her bidding. Simon rode to the kirk in search of the minister and Lachlan left to fetch Rob.

Shortly after sunrise on Monday morning, Magnus and his son were laid to rest amidst a small, silent contingent of family and neighbors. The little crowd had witnessed death before– that brought about by illness, old age, childbirth, or the rigors of their frequently hard life. But this was different–a barbarous act committed by an intruder in their glen. And when Alice named the murderer, several of her friends paled and pressed their mouths into grim lines, for they knew him. They did business with him as Magnus had; he bought their illegally made whiskey and, until now, he'd been a fair man to trade with. Alice spoke to the tense group of men surrounding her after the prayers had been spoken. "I knew about him, but had never seen him until yesterday when he came to accuse Magnus of cheating him. But he didn't cheat," Alice cried in her dead husband's defense. "Magnus called the man 'Gordon'."

"Gordon?" Simon repeated, immediately thinking of Connor and the 'Gordon' who'd beaten him. "Do you know if this 'Gordon' is a smuggler?"

A neighbor affirmed, "We supposed that's why he bought our whiskey."

"Can you describe him for us, any of you?" Simon implored.

Again the neighbor obliged. "He's about Lachlan's height, not heavy but strongly built. His hair's almost black."

"And his eyes are cold as ice," Alice added emphatically, "just like his voice."

"Anything else you can think of?" Simon prompted warily.

"One more thing," Alice supplied, "a thick scar from his chin to the corner of his mouth–left side."

Glowering, Simon asked, "A scar?"

Jessie, who had come to take Alice from the interrogation, scolded, "Don't make her repeat herself. Can't you see how hard this is for her?"

"Mam, you don't understand," Simon said. "I don't want to make this harder for Alice, but she has described a man I've seen and know to be dangerous." He faced Alice once more. "Do you have any idea where he was going when he left?"

"To Hell I hope!" she declared angrily.

"Maybe Inverness," Rob suggested quickly. "Pap...he told me once that Gordon was frequently there."

"That makes sense if, indeed, he's a smuggler," Simon acknowledged.

"Simon and I are leaving for Inverness this afternoon," Martin announced. "We'll search for him and alert the Dingwall and Inverness authorities as well."

"Excuse me, Simon," Mairi said, lightly touching her brother's arm. "Before the two of you leave, there's something else to be done."

"What, lass?" Simon puzzled.

"The Reverend has agreed to marry Rob and me today. You can't leave before I'm wed."

"Mairi, *no*," Jessie cried in dismay, "don't make this day of sorrow your wedding day."

Taking Jessie's hands, Mairi assured, "We'll make this a happier day. Rob needs me, Mam, so does his mam. I can't stay without being married, you know that. Besides," she lowered her gaze and continued shyly, "I'm ready to become Rob's wife. I want to share every day with him, the good and the bad that comes with it. I don't want to wait any longer."

Alice touched the girl's face. "You have raised a generous and thoughtful daughter, Jessie, Lachlan."

"We're p...proud of her," Lachlan choked.

Mairi faced her brother. "I'm sorry about the dress, Simon."

"No need to be sorry," Simon declared, "you shall have the dress regardless." With a quick, silent embrace, Mairi thanked him.

The ceremony was brief and, despite the circumstances, Mairi glowed. Rob gazed at her adoringly throughout, and Jessie dabbed at her eyes. When Mairi and Rob were pronounced husband and wife, Jessie embraced Alice who fiercely returned it, and the two shed hopeful tears for the future of their youngest offspring.

Mairi's prediction had been correct. The joy she and Rob shared dispelled much of the grimness of the morning. As the MacLarens prepared to return home, Martin and Simon turned their sights toward Inverness. Mairi hugged and kissed her brother and hugged her cousin. "God speed," she said, a quiver in her voice. "I don't know when I can return to try on my gown but, when you explain things, I know Alayne and Fia will understand."

Martin stared at her, stupefied. "Did...did you say...Fia?"

Blankly, Mairi returned his gaze. "Aye, Mistress Kate's niece." In the next instant, Martin's interest dawned on her and she hurriedly assured, "Oh, Martin, it couldn't be *your* Fia; she lives in Glasgow."

Blood roared in his ears and Martin croaked, "Fia lived in Inverness as a child."

Rattled, Mairi sputtered, "She...she'd c...come up to here," she indicated his chin, "on you," she paused. "She's dark-haired, slender–in a pleasing way. A little older than me...*Martin!*" She clamped her arms around him, having seen the pain of recognition engulf his face. "Forgive me. I never dreamed that Fia...oh Martin!"

Simon, who'd been distracted, noticed the strange exchange and demanded, "What's wrong here?"

Mairi turned tearful eyes on her brother. "Martin thinks I've found his Fia; I didn't say anything because it didn't occur to me that...I'm so sorry, Martin," she sobbed, burying her face against his chest.

"Hush now, Mairi," Martin smoothed her hair, scarcely able to draw breath, "there's nothing to forgive. I believe you have found her for me; I'm in your debt."

"She's in Inverness?" Simon clamored.

Martin nodded. "She's at the millinery; she's Mistress Kate's niece." Simon sucked in a gasp and Martin took Mairi's hands. "We have to leave now. Don't fret, it'll work out somehow. One last thing lass; new gown or no new gown, you are a beautiful and courageous bride and I wish you only great happiness." He kissed her cheek, mounted Odhar and asked Grant to pass Arthur up. With the hound settled firmly across the saddle, the two men silently turned their mounts east. Simon, still considering the latest bit of information dropped on him, shuddered. Fia was in Inverness which meant the chances were more than fair that Andrew Forbes was there also– and Andrew Forbes fit the description of Magnus and Geddes Ramsay's killer. Simon's head pounded. Not even the prospect of seeing Alayne could ease his aching brow.

Chapter Twenty-One

Martin was lost in thought which, for once, didn't bother the usually gregarious Simon. They rode until darkness made it dangerous for the horses then found a hillock near which to make camp, still more than a day out of Inverness. Half a day's travel had been lost today due to the funeral and Mairi's wedding; each man desperately wanted to make up the time.

Simon slept fitfully that night and Martin's sleep was cruel, shaded by uneasiness that pervaded all his dreams. As the iron gray of night faded into the first purple hues of day, the two packed their meager belongings, Martin whistled for Arthur, and they resumed their journey with knotted nerves cramping their bellies.

Patiently, Fia stood beside Alayne as she feigned interest in a pair of shears offered by one of the Market merchants. For the third time in an hour, Alayne started to claim she'd waited long enough and, once again, uttered no sound.

"Let's go back to the Market cross, Alayne. If you said you'd meet him there, you shouldn't chance missing him," Fia reasoned.

An injured pout pursed Alayne's full lips. "I can see the cross from here."

"But Simon may not see you," Fia insisted. "What if he thinks you've left?"

"You forget, he knows where to find me," she answered grudgingly.

Fia sensed Alayne's bruised pride and fledgling doubts about Simon's intention then quickly brightened. "Well, at least Murdoch's found us." She flashed a grateful smile in his direction.

"Ladies, have you finished your errands?" He glanced from one to the other and realized there was no evidence of any buying. "It doesn't look like you've even started. What will Kate say?"

"Good question; what will Aunt Kate say? We badgered her to allow us both to come today," Fia admitted. "Alayne, one of us has to do the errands."

Alayne fidgeted, wringing her hands till her knuckles blanched. "All right, but hurry please. I'll...wait at the cross."

Fia snatched Murdoch's hand and the two were off, leaving Alayne ambling back to linger next to the Market cross. Long minutes dragged by and her color heightened as she perceived passers-by gawking. "Probably wondering what I'm selling," she grumbled.

At long last, from behind her, Simon's voice reached her ear. "Forgive me, Alayne, I was detained in Strathcarron."

Her relief and pleasure knowing he'd kept his promise were short-lived as indignity took over and she blurted, "People are staring at me I've been here so long."

"I'm truly sorry and will explain everything," Simon repented glancing around. "You weren't supposed to be alone though. Where's your friend?"

"Someone had to actually run the errands we used as an excuse for being here," she explained in exasperation.

Equally frustrated, Simon asked, "Is she coming back?"

Suddenly wary, Alayne asked, "Why are you so interested–"

"Simon MacLaren, is it really you?" an intruding voice trilled.

Simon whirled and cried, "Arabella!" He gripped her hands so tightly Fia nearly cringed.

"Arabella?" Alayne's puzzlement was evident, but Simon asked for confirmation instead.

"You're Alayne's friend?" He eyed the solid, gray-eyed man beside her–the one carrying her bundles in a basket over his arm.

"Aye. Simon how glorious! Alayne's description sounded like you but I couldn't believe such a coincidence. Alayne," she explained, "this is Simon, the actor I told you I met in Glasgow."

"Actor?" Alayne repeated.

Murdoch frowned. "You mean that time Andrew hounded you at Market?"

"The very same." Fia paused and tilted her head thoughtfully, smile fading. "Simon, you look...unwell. Have you been ill?"

Before Simon could answer, Murdoch stiffened, quickly pulling Fia closer. "There's a man over there staring at you." He nodded over her head. "Do you know him, the one with the black hound?"

"Black...hound?" Fia's heart stuttered. She reeled and beheld Martin, beard bushier and hair flowing around his shoulders, crouching to restrain the wriggling Arthur. "Martin," she uttered in a soft breath. Eyes locked on Martin's, her knees wobbled and she stepped back against Murdoch, who steadied her with a hand on her waist.

"Martin Ross?" Alayne cried and gaped at the man she never believed she'd lay eyes on.

A mighty lunge tore Arthur from Martin's grasp and he raced to greet Fia. The sudden commotion diverted Fia's attention and she knelt on trembling limbs to rumple the dog's thick ruff and return his affectionate greeting with a choking hug around his neck. Over Arthur's wagging body, Fia again sought Martin's face. She shrank at the anger that flooded it now and despair overwhelmed her. "Alayne, Simon, I'm sorry," she muttered and, grasping Murdoch's outstretched hands, pulled herself up. "I'll be more helpful...next time you meet," she raggedly promised.

Simon pleaded, "Fia wait!"

She did not notice his use of her real name but, to Murdoch beseeched, "Take me away from here."

Murdoch's furious expression challenged Martin but, for Fia, he swallowed his ire. "Alayne are you coming?"

"Aye. Simon, you know where to find me," she tendered, and the three melted into the crowd. Martin whistled sharply for Arthur who was happily following Fia.

Walking the ten paces to his cousin's side, Simon declared, "What a disaster."

For a moment, Martin's anger drained. "We found her, Simon."

Ever to the point, Simon added, "And her husband, it would seem."

Martin pressed his lips together tightly. "He...he seemed considerate toward her...didn't he?"

"Aye," Simon agreed warily, before Martin's rage fired.

"That *swine*! How dare he bring her here, mix her up in his brother's sordid business."

Hopefully, Simon suggested, "Maybe she's visiting her aunt and that's all."

"I wish I believed it was that simple." Martin ground his knuckles into his palm. "Mairi said she's working at the millinery and if that's the case–"

"That would mean she's been here for some time," Simon deduced. "Martin, you'll have to talk to her to find out for sure."

"Talk to her?" The idea startled Martin. "Look how she reacted when she saw me. She cringed, couldn't leave quickly enough. She wants nothing to do with me, Simon."

Simon gripped Martin's shoulder. "She'll talk to you, why wouldn't she?"

"Because when I kissed her goodbye, she accused me of calling her a whore and I didn't bother to correct her. Didn't I tell you that?"

By this time a few curious onlookers, hearing his comments, gathered to hear more. Simon urged the small crowd to scatter and led Martin to the horses. Arthur trailed behind, displaying new interest in every woman they passed like one of them might be Fia.

"Where are we going?" Martin finally asked when Odhar's reins were thrust into his hand.

"To the inn," Simon replied. "Fia will need time to recover from the shock of seeing you again. You and I need to decide how to find Andrew and, I don't know about you, but a whiskey or three would suit me just fine."

Murdoch steered Fia home leaving Alayne to return to the shop and explain it all to Kate. Once inside the house, Fia stood staring out the window while Murdoch poured them each a glass of claret.

"Come sit here, lass." He urged her to a chair near the hearth.

Listless but obedient, Fia took the chair. "He despises me, Murdoch; did you see the hostility? Annie shouldn't have told him how I felt–it just confirmed what he suspected anyway."

"Fia," Murdoch comforted, "loving the man shouldn't cause him to bear you any ill will.

Believe me, any normal man would be flattered–they just wouldn't have handled it as witlessly as he did."

Miserable, she whined, "Then why did he look at me like that?"

Murdoch calmly ventured, "To be honest, I thought his wrath was aimed at me; he wanted to rip my heart out."

Fia stared. "Why would you think that? He doesn't even know you."

"I can't explain it. I only know what I saw. Besides," Murdoch snarled, "I wanted to tear out his heart for the grief he's caused you!"

She pressed his hand between hers. "Murdoch, you mustn't be angry at Martin for following his heart."

The front door crashed open and Kate burst through, Alayne crowding behind her to bang it shut. Murdoch gave up the foot stool to Kate and took his stance behind Fia's chair.

"Fia, are you all right?" Kate demanded.

"A bit shaken is all, Aunt Kate," Fia assured.

"Did you speak to him? Do you know what he's doing here?"

"I saw him, Aunt Kate–he saw me–that's all there was to it. He didn't seem particularly... happy...to see me."

"On the other hand, the hound was thrilled." Murdoch's wry little joke succeeded in rousing a reluctant grin from Fia.

"Ah, but Arthur and I have always gotten along," she confided.

Kate stood, hands clasped primly before her. "This has been a great shock to you, dear, you should rest."

Alayne rolled her eyes declaring, "Napping is not the answer to all of life's upsets, Kate."

"Alayne's right," Fia affirmed. "Besides, Murdoch has to leave in the morning. I won't waste a moment of time alone in my room."

"Where you can think," Alayne added, "and drive yourself mad."

A pang of guilt suddenly engulfed Fia. "Alayne, I'm sorry, for ruining our outing I mean."

The corners of Alayne's mouth lifted sympathetically. "I know what you mean. And God's life, don't apologize, there'll be other outings."

The afternoon and evening passed quietly and pleasantly enough considering how the day had begun. As always, Flora's meal was sumptuous–only Fia couldn't taste what little she ate. Until she was in her room, Fia fought to keep Martin beyond the fringe of her conscious thoughts. Now, sitting by the window, a blanket wrapped around her, it was a different story. Thoughts of him battered her. Her heart had leaped to her throat upon seeing him again, then plunged to her belly as his beloved face twisted with fury. Why was he so horribly angry with her? Had Jean said something that ignited his wrath? Fia stood and splayed her fingers across the cold window pane. The half-moon winked at her. In the cloudless night, she glimpsed dancing ribbons of light threading their way across the northern sky. "What brings him to Inverness? If I see him again, what can I say that might soothe him?" she wondered in vain. Weary to the bone, Fia crawled into bed and forced herself to study the embers of the fire until her eyelids drooped and a foul sleep claimed her.

It wrenched Fia to bid Murdoch farewell. Alayne had said her goodbyes last evening before returning to the rooms over the shop and Kate, after wishing him Godspeed at breakfast, had thoughtfully left Fia alone with him. They stood at the door, hands clasped. Tears stung Fia's eyes and spilled over as she forced a smile. Murdoch gathered her in his huge embrace and whispered, "I know, lass; I'll miss you as well. I wish I didn't have to go now."

Reluctantly, Fia stood away, wiping her damp cheeks. "Everything will work out, Murdoch. Give my love to Douglas and Agnes and, if I don't see you before, send word when the bairn arrives. I'm eager to know if you've a new son or daughter."

"I promise. And you, take care of yourself–you look tired this morning," he observed with concern.

"As Alayne predicted, I've been thinking too much. But I promise I will positively pamper myself," she swore with forced gaiety, "so don't worry." She hugged him once more, kissed him lightly, and waved till he was out of sight.

The dawn was cold, crisp and crackled with anticipation of the day to come. Martin refused breakfast. He'd tossed half the night and sat alone in the tap room the other half. "If I eat, it won't stay down," he assured Simon.

"Some mead then," Simon urged, "it can't hurt."

Martin grimaced, his belly lurching at the idea. "I'm a doctor–I know what I'm doing."

"Normally, I'd say that's true. Today, I'm not certain." He stopped pushing though, realizing he wasn't all that hungry either.

As they trudged toward High Street, Simon spouted, "Anxious as I am to explain my late arrival to Alayne, I think you should have a couple of minutes alone in the shop before I come in. I'd hate a repeat of the confusion we caused at Market yesterday."

Martin conceded, "That's generous, Simon, thank you." When they reached the shop, he entered alone while Simon waited nearby.

As the bell sounded, Alayne raised her eyes to look past her customer. She sucked in a surprised breath and surveyed Martin Ross as he approached: smallish frame, broad-shouldered and sinewy, burnished hair and engaging face. His nut-brown eyes were hypnotic and she blinked to break their spell. "I'll be with you shortly, Sir." Martin nodded and it took all Alayne's effort to concentrate on completing her business with Mr. Leslie. When the man left some minutes later, Alayne turned to Martin. "May I help you?" she inquired stiffly.

"Good day, Mistress Matheson, I'm Martin Ross, a friend of Fia's."

"Friend? One would hardly have gathered so the way you glowered at her yesterday." Alayne chastised, before biting her lip to keep from saying more.

"I admit I was...out of sorts–but not with Fia. Is she here?"

Brows drawn into a frown, Alayne wondered, "How did you know she'd be...." Her voice trailed off as Simon opened the door. "I see," she said flatly.

"I'm afraid you don't, Mistress," Martin explained. "It was Mairi who told me Fia worked here. She is here isn't she?" he repeated anxiously.

Alayne blinked from Simon back to Martin. "Wait here," she mumbled, disappearing into the workroom where Fia stood, icy hands clenched before her.

"You heard?" Alayne questioned in a low voice.

Fia focused on Alayne's flustered expression. "He's here."

"With Simon; he's mixed up in this. Will you see Martin?"

"Things between us can hardly get worse," she muttered and nodded quickly before she could change her mind.

Alayne embraced her for luck and suggested, "Wait for him upstairs." As she began to return to the shop, Fia grabbed her hand.

"I know you were uneasy yesterday, but let Simon explain what delayed him before you make any rash decisions."

A blush stained Alayne's cheeks. "Don't be concerned, I promise I will. Now go."

Fia nodded and climbed the stairs while Alayne reentered the front room.

"Fia has agreed to see you, Mr. Ross," she said in starched tones, but softened a bit observing his relief. "You'll find her in the sitting room upstairs."

"Thank you." Martin disappeared through the curtains, and Alayne turned to Simon.

"Fia made me promise to hear you out," she stated awkwardly.

"Bless the lass," Simon murmured and stood across the counter from Alayne. "I'm sure you doubted your wisdom in waiting for us at Market."

"I was only expecting you–and I admit I was getting...discouraged...and annoyed at perhaps having misplaced my trust." She rushed on, "Fia told me about meeting you in Glasgow, how you came to her aid, and that you're an actor."

"All true," Simon assured her.

Alayne dropped her eyes. "It just makes me realize I know little about you otherwise."

"I'll tell you anything you want to know," he offered.

"There's so much," she murmured, "but, right now, I have to ask how you know Martin Ross? That the two of you should come here together–it's unsettling."

"Martin is my cousin. When I met Fia I was looking for him–even mentioned him to her though not by name. I certainly never suspected she would know him. At that time, I hadn't even met him. After I found him, I took him to meet my family. Then we brought Mairi to Inverness, to you, to have her wedding dress made."

"Martin wasn't with you," she puzzled.

"No, he went on to Glasgow looking for Fia."

"Really?" she asked skeptically.

"Really," Simon assured. "He's been three times to Glasgow searching for her, but she seemed to have dropped from the face of the earth–until Mairi mentioned her."

"But, surely that must have been days ago."

"It was Monday morning, after her wedding."

Alayne gaped. "Her wedding? But I thought St. Martin's eve–"

"Circumstances change, Alayne," Simon stated. "Her husband, Rob, suffered a terrible loss on Sunday. In fact, we all did."

Bewildered, Alayne asked, "What kind of loss?"

"Rob's father and brother were murdered."

"*Murdered?*" she exclaimed aghast.

Simon nodded. "Rob's mother was injured as well, and Rob shot in the arm. He managed to get to our farm to summon help. Mairi decided her place was with Rob so, after the funeral, the Vicar married them."

Alayne pressed her hand to her throat but said nothing, her senses reeling.

Simon continued, "I'm sorry she won't be married in the dress you're making, though I still want her to have it."

"Bother the dress! What a brave woman, your sister."

He responded simply, "She loves him."

Dangerously close to tears, Alayne's glittering eyes rested easily on Simon's angular features. "I...could see that when she spoke briefly of him."

Simon boldly wove his fingers with hers. "I'm sorry everything went wrong yesterday." He felt a slight pressure on his hand before Alayne withdrew from his grip.

"I think your cousin may be with Fia for some time. I'll get you a chair–if you'd like to wait with me."

Never had Simon wanted to kiss a woman so much. His gaze caressed her lips with such familiarity that Alayne's face grew hot. Then he answered, "Almost nothing...would give me more pleasure."

His pounding heart threatening to burst, Martin approached the stairs through the sanctuary of the workroom and ascended to discover Fia silhouetted by dim light filtering through a small window. For an interminable moment, neither moved, then Fia's soft tones floated to him. "After yesterday, I didn't think you'd want to see me again."

"Not see you?" Martin was incredulous and his voice cracked as he announced, "I...I've been searching for you."

She doubted he had, but offered, "I guess I wasn't easy to find."

Martin stepped toward her, but Fia moved away. Her only hope of not making a complete fool of herself was to keep distance between them.

Abruptly he stopped, but consumed the details of her appearance like a starving man his first meal: the curls framing her sweet face; eyes dark and wary; slender figure; and small, soft mouth. "God's life, I've missed the sight of you," he declared in hushed tones.

"You," Fia's voice thinned, "you look fine, Martin–perhaps a bit tired."

Martin twisted his bonnet in his hands. "I didn't sleep well last night."

"No," Fia replied, remembering her own miserable night. "Tell me, how did you find me?"

"Mairi told me you were here."

She looked at him blankly.

"Mairi MacLaren, Simon's sister," he explained in the silence.

Momentarily confused, Fia finally realized the Mairi he spoke of. "Simon's sister, of course. How do you know them? How would she know who I am?" She eased forward and sat.

In response, Martin poised on the edge of the chair across from her. "I told her about you some time back but, when she met you, she didn't realize you were the same woman. Mairi, Simon and I are kin–cousins actually."

"I didn't realize you had kin except your brother."

"Simon and I met only a short time ago. Before that, I didn't know he and Mairi existed. Their grandmother is Hugh's sister."

At the mention of his grandfather, a shiver coursed through Fia. Martin leaned forward and asked, "Is something wrong?"

"No," she assured in a less than convincing tone. Fia found his nearness agonizing. She fidgeted with her fingers, straightened her skirts and glanced at him in snatches. "Why are you here?" she almost whimpered. "Why have you been trying to find me–wasn't our parting hard enough?"

Infected by her agitation, Martin rose to pace the small room. "We had harsh words before the chaise carried you from Inveraray. I'm sorry; that was the last thing I wanted. But I searched...I needed to see for myself if you were content...happy," he finished woodenly.

Fia puzzled, "I don't understand. The look on your face yesterday didn't show interest in my well-being. It was anger–anger identical to when you stormed into Annie's that morning and asked payment for services rendered. Why are you really here, Martin?"

"That is the reason I set out to find you. However," he added swallowing hard, "on Sunday, something happened and, it's the reason I reacted as I did yesterday." Martin returned to his seat, elbows braced on his knees, fingers woven before him. He took a cleansing breath and began, "Two murders have been committed–possibly three–by a man Simon says you know."

"Murders? Someone I know?" she repeated warily.

"Aye. The man you were with yesterday–"

"Murdoch would never hurt anyone!" she interrupted brusquely, surging to her friend's defense.

Baffled, Martin blinked. "Murdoch?" he asked. "That man was not Struan Forbes?"

"Certainly not," she said indignantly.

"Then...Struan is not in Inverness?"

"I pray not."

It was Martin's turn to stare. "You don't know?"

"What's Struan got to do with this?" she demanded.

Martin drew his hand over his mouth and down his bearded chin in a familiar gesture that twisted Fia's belly. "Yesterday, I thought this man 'Murdoch' was Struan. I was infuriated thinking he'd dragged you to Inverness and into this squalid mess."

"What mess? Murder? Martin, I'm lost. Struan is too cowardly to commit murder."

Martin stared at her. "Perhaps, but Andrew Forbes isn't. Simon says he fits the description of the murderer and, when we spotted you yesterday with a man we believed to be Struan, Simon and I took it as evidence that Andrew was probably in Inverness."

Fia's pallor bled stark white and she shrank against the back of the chair. Martin was so unnerved by the change that he reached for her hand, but she snatched it away. If he touched her, she would unravel.

Martin forced himself to continue. "The two men we believe he killed in Strathcarron made whiskey illegally and sold it to a man who calls himself 'Gordon'. The men in the Strath believe 'Gordon' used it in smuggling operations, probably out of Inverness."

"And you thought I could lead you to Andrew, is that it?"

"I thought you might be in danger," he asserted sternly before softening his tone. "There's more. The men he killed were Magnus and Geddes Ramsay, father and brother to Mairi's Rob."

Fia groaned, crushing her knuckles against her mouth. "Mairi, is she all right?"

"Aye, she wed Rob Monday morning after the funeral. That's why Simon was late meeting Alayne."

A terrifying thought struck her and, wide-eyed, she hissed, "You aren't going after Andrew?"

"Simon and I have alerted the sheriffs in Dingwall and here in Inverness but, aye, we're looking for him as well."

"*No*," she cried, clamping down on his wrist and begging, "you mustn't! He *is* a killer. Martin, he's the robber who killed the man on the post chaise and sent me stumbling into your path. He told me then he was a smuggler. You have to stay away from him–and so must Simon!" she commanded immovably.

Lightly, Martin touched her fingers. "I can't do that."

Fia twisted away, rising in the same movement and desperately shrieked, "I know what he's capable of."

With deadly calm, Martin promised, "If he's touched you, I'll send him to Hell."

His tone sent cold shivers through her and Fia abruptly quieted realizing that anything she might tell him could inflame his determination. Fia returned to her chair but wouldn't look at him. "I beseech you, Martin, stay clear of Andrew."

Her pale, graceful features and obvious fear for his safety plucked at his heart. "I believe you've answered my question," he murmured.

"What question?" she asked, distractedly.

"Whether or not you're content–you aren't," he observed.

Fia rallied a bit. "Most of the time I'm fine."

"And when you aren't?"

"I'm thinking about you." The truth slipped out before Fia realized it, and she bit her lip hard. Martin could scarcely draw breath. "You...think of me?"

It struck Fia that she could afford to tell him the truth. She'd already lost him to Jean, so what was the harm? Emboldened by that realization, she confessed, "Aye, about the weeks spent at your croft, about how we parted but, mostly, I just think about you." She plunged deeper, hoping to find some healing when she finished. "Did you believe Annie when she told you that I loved you?"

Bewildered, Martin asked, "How did you know about that?"

"Murdoch went looking for you; Annie told him."

"Did you send Murdoch?" he asked, mouth parched.

Fia shook her head. "Murdoch went of his own accord. But you haven't answered my question, Martin. Did you believe her?"

"I wouldn't let myself believe her," he said, then struggled in silence for several moments. "I couldn't bear the thought that you might love me, yet chose a man with whom you would be 'comfortable'."

Fia wondered why it could possibly matter who she chose under the circumstances. Dully, she asked, "What about Jean?"

Martin started. "Jean?"

"MacNab," Fia supplied.

An icy wave of apprehension swept him. "What do you know of Jean?"

Her relentless gaze boring through Martin's heart, Fia revealed, "She paid you a visit one day, the day you were fishing on Loch Awe."

Martin surveyed the room, seeing nothing and hearing only his own labored breath. Finally, he whispered, "You spoke to Jean?"

"Aye," Fia replied. "She arrived just as I finished my bath...and told me of your plans to marry."

"She told you we were marrying?" he demanded in shocked disbelief.

"And made it abundantly clear," Fia paused, battling the tremor that shook her words, "how very close the two of you were."

Martin flushed heavily as he imagined how Jean might have explained their relationship. "No wonder everything changed between us that day," he lamented, sick at heart, "and small wonder you hate me so."

Calmly, Fia stated, "I've never hated you, Martin; I just had to leave–I had to."

"Fia, I...I don't know what to say except...how very sorry I am."

"So am I, Martin." She straightened and continued, "If that's all–"

"No, there's something else." Martin considered his words while Fia waited. "Should I have believed Annie?"

Fia simply murmured, "Annie doesn't lie."

For a long moment, Martin focused on her slippers which peeked from beneath her petticoat. When he spoke, Fia heard sorrow in his voice. "Did Annie tell Murdoch...that I loved you?"

Fia's voice failed her; she shook her head.

"Because I should have told you myself," he grieved. "I loved you then, Fia–I love you still."

Fia's shocked and anguished eyes joined his until she could no longer bear the truth and regret they mirrored. "You'd be...better go," she choked.

He stepped behind her chair and stopped. Tentatively, he reached out but withdrew his hand without touching her.

It took all her willpower, but Fia sat unmoving.

Simon and Alayne jumped as Martin's hurried footsteps penetrated their conversation. He burst through the curtains, the turmoil on his face silencing them both. Brusquely, Martin nodded to Alayne. "Simon, I'll see you later at the inn."

Simon recovered enough to ask, "Don't you want me to come with you?"

Martin looked from one to the other. "No, I want you to spend as much time with this lady as she'll allow," he insisted.

"Simon and I can meet another time; I do have work to do." Alayne was surprised that a wave of sympathy for Martin swelled in her chest. "Besides, I should see to Fia."

Martin struggled to appear calm, his stricken eyes betraying him. "I would be...be grateful for whatever comfort you can give her," he stuttered and fled the shop.

Simon turned to Alayne. "I'll be here tomorrow." Lips brushing her fingertips, he grabbed his tricorne and sped after his cousin.

Face thunderous, Martin trod down the lane, agitatedly vowing, "I'll see her again; I won't lose her twice!"

"What of her husband?" Simon reminded matching his cousin's stride.

"That hasn't stopped you," Martin answered testily then came to an abrupt halt, momentarily burying his face in his palms. "Forgive me, Simon. I had no cause to say that; there's no parallel between your situation and mine."

"You're overwrought, nothing more," Simon instantly forgave.

Hands spread in despair, Martin told him, "Fia loved me, Simon."

"Then what happened? Why did she turn to Forbes?"

"Jean MacNab." Martin scowled.

"Another woman?" Simon's confusion was evident. "I don't recall you mentioning a Jean MacNab. Who is she and what's her part in this?"

Martin irritably pushed his long locks from his face. "Jean...I must speak to Jean."

"No you won't," Simon declared, "your disappointment is too raw. You'll say something you may regret later. Come then, tell me–who is Jean?"

"A widow near Inveraray with whom I shared a bed from time to time. Over Jean's objections, I ended our liaison and, only hours later, I found Fia. The day I left the croft to fish, the day I finally admitted to myself that I was in love, Jean paid a visit." Knuckles white, Martin continued harshly, "According to Fia, Jean left no doubt about the intimacy of our relationship."

"So that's it," Simon murmured, but Martin corrected him.

"Only part of it. Jean told Fia I was marrying her. That's what led Fia to speak of Forbes. Maybe it would never have come up otherwise. Under those circumstances, it's no surprise Fia reacted as she did." Martin rubbed the heel of his hand over his eyes. "And I was too stubborn–"

"Enough, Martin, don't berate yourself further. What about Forbes? Does he know of his brother's deeds? Did you discuss that at all?"

"The man with her at Market was some fellow named Murdoch. When I spoke of Andrew, it was clear that she's terrified of him. When I mentioned he might be here, her reaction was frightening. She said she knows what he's capable of and she pleaded with me to avoid him at all costs–you too."

Cautiously, Simon asked, "What did you tell her?"

"That we couldn't."

"I'm sure she didn't like that answer."

"No, she didn't."

"Her point is well-taken though; we should be on our guard with this demon. I've been thinking about our search; we should start at the quay where we can keep eyes and ears open about ships and people."

Martin nodded his agreement. "I think we should split up. We aren't known around here. If we show ourselves together, it may arouse suspicion. Why don't I go down tonight, I need something to do."

Simon viewed him skeptically. "Are you sure? Don't you have enough to think about after your meeting with Fia?"

"My point exactly." Martin managed a lopsided grin. "I have a question for you. Have you explained what happened in Strathcarron to Alayne? I've been so preoccupied with Fia, I've not given you a moment to tell me. You weren't talking when I came downstairs."

"You scared us into silence when you charged in like a wild boar," Simon declared, only half-joking. "We spoke at length; she understands why I was delayed and what my relationship is to you. I told her that Mairi is now Mistress Ramsay and why. I was actually talking to her about some of my time touring the colonies when you came in. Her family is there so she's very interested."

The 'White Rose' crept within sight over a slight rise in the road. Martin grimaced. "I don't know about you, but I don't want to go in there with so much daylight left."

"Me neither," Simon agreed. "Let's get the horses and go exploring."

"Fine, and you can tell me more about Alayne as we go. She's a striking woman, Simon."

"I'm surprised you noticed considering how viciously she glared at you."

"But when you came near, just before I went upstairs, I saw a softness that stole over her expression—though not her voice, I admit," Martin sighed.

The door closing behind Simon sent Alayne scrambling toward the workroom and Fia though her flight was checked when the bell above the door jingled and she pivoted, smile frozen to her face, to greet a customer instead. To Alayne, Miss Buchanan took far too long to examine the shop's small stock of fans and finally to select the delicate carved ivory with gilt trim that had first caught her eye. The delighted young woman paid for her purchase, and Alayne patiently closed the door after she strolled out. A short dash placed her behind the curtains where she stopped abruptly, spying Fia working on the open robe that would have been part of Mairi's wedding gown. Cautiously, Alayne called, "Fia?"

Fia raised a carefully composed face in response.

Puzzled, Alayne said, "By looking at you, I'd swear you were taking this better than Martin Ross." She approached and bent to more closely study her friend. "Are you?"

Fia's poise crumbled as her glance darted from Alayne.

"Oh, Fia, cry if you need to," Alayne urged wrapping her friend in a comforting embrace, "it's only me that will hear."

Fia's body heaved with silent sobs Alayne found particularly disconcerting. The bell sounded again and Alayne's head jerked up. She drew away and pressed a handkerchief into Fia's hand. "God's teeth," she cursed in profound annoyance. "I'll be right back."

In Alayne's absence, Fia tried with little success to calm down. She felt a fool; she felt cheated. For a fleeting moment, she berated herself. If she had only confessed her desire to Martin after her encounter with Jean, perhaps briefly, she could have found the closeness with him she so craved. The idea brought a bitter laugh. With Jean's image and painful words fresh in her mind, tearing her heart, she lamented, "How could I have lain with Martin that night?"

"Fia?" Alayne prompted.

Alayne's voice hauled her back to the present and a ragged sigh escaped Fia's soul. "Martin's going after Andrew—he and Simon."

"Andrew...Forbes? Why?" Alayne gaped.

"Didn't Simon tell you about the murders?"

"Aye, but what...?" Alayne pulled a harsh breath. "*Andrew?*"

Fia nodded. "Simon saw him with me in Glasgow, remember? The killer's description is a perfect fit. I...begged Martin to stay away from him, to keep Simon away as well. He won't listen."

"I'll talk to Simon," Alayne promised.

"I hope you are more persuasive," she muttered.

Alayne sought to sooth Fia's jangled nerves. "Martin had a great deal on his mind, Fia. After all, it wasn't easy for him to see you again either." To Fia's quizzical look, Alayne added, "He looked devastated."

"He said he should have told me he loved me. He says...he still does."

"I believe him," Alayne vowed.

Fia turned a hopeless gaze on her. "What does it matter? He's married."

"Did you ask about Jean?"

"I did. Martin clearly had no idea that I'd met her. He was shocked that she told me of their marriage plans."

Alayne dragged a stool near and balanced on it. "Simon told me Martin was searching for you. What about that?"

Fia rubbed her forehead. "He wanted to assure himself that I was...happy. Then Sunday, Andrew became a factor and Martin says he was worried about me."

"I'm sure that's true," Alayne stated.

"That's why he looked so hostile yesterday."

"I don't think I understand," Alayne hedged.

"He thought Murdoch was Struan. He was outraged that Struan had brought me to Inverness right into the middle of Andrew's sordid business."

Alayne rolled her eyes. "My God, Fia, how incredibly confused this has become."

"Aye, well," Fia announced as she picked up her needle, "I think now that Martin's curiosity about my well-being is satisfied, I won't see much of him."

Alayne reached out and stopped Fia in mid-stitch. "I know that's not what you want; aren't you just bracing yourself against further disappointment?"

"And what if I am?" Fia defended. "Simply looking at him makes me ache." Fia raked the back of her hand under her dripping nose.

Quietly, Alayne declared, "I think I can understand that. Still, I know he'll be back–you know it too."

Stubbornly, Fia determined, "He's made his commitment to Jean; I won't be the cause of him dishonoring that promise."

In the early hours after a long, dank night on the quay, Martin reported to Simon in a hushed voice, "Gordon doesn't appear to be in Inverness–yet."

"How do you know that and what do you mean by 'yet'?" Simon whispered loudly over the men snoring in the bed next to theirs.

"A vile looking character at a tavern called the 'Albatross' was telling Connor's story to the man sharing his table–that is Connor's story up until he was thrown overboard. Seems Connor crossed a free trader with no tolerance for cheating, at least not in others."

"Was the name 'Gordon' mentioned?"

"No," Martin replied with a quick shake of his head, "still the man said he'd heard the trader mention business with a supplier, which certainly could have been Magnus Ramsay, then some personal matters he had to attend in the south."

"How did this fellow know all this?" Simon asked.

"His companion asked the same question," Martin replied. "The talkative one said that the trader was having trouble filling out a crew for his ship. Talk of his actions had made the rounds along the quay and, among the toughs who crew these boats, our 'friend' has apparently over-stepped their code of honor."

Simon acknowledged, "You've done remarkably well, Martin."

"It was my third stop and I was fortunate–the man was well into his cups and gave far more information than he would have if I'd been asking questions."

"Still, that information buys us some time to establish ourselves here."

Martin looked uncomfortable. "Simon, I can't afford to stay here indefinitely, at the 'White Rose' I mean. Arthur and I will set up outside of town. I can meet you here each day and we'll continue to look for Forbes."

"Nonsense, I'll move out with you. Lodging at an inn is too conspicuous. Besides, if I don't start spending more wisely, I'm going to have to go back to acting sooner than I planned."

Martin cocked his head. "Why not?"

Baffled, Simon asked, "Why not what?"

"Find an acting job. There must be a troupe or a theater you can join while here. It's a perfect reason for you to be residing temporarily in Inverness. No one would suspect you had any other motive for being here."

Simon peered intently at him. "Why didn't you think of this before? It's perfect. I'll start making inquiries today."

Martin dipped a nod in agreement. "Simon, could you spare me for a few days?"

Simon guessed, "You're going to see Jean MacNab."

"Try to understand, I must know what happened. I can't ask Fia any more about it–that was what changed everything. It hurts her–I can see that."

"Oh, I understand," Simon said. "Go on then, but try to remember when you speak to her that Jean must have strong feelings for you to have done what she did."

Martin carefully responded, "I appreciate what you're saying to me, Simon, and I'll try to hear her out. But it won't be easy considering the damage she's caused with her lies. Now, I'm going to offer you a piece of advice."

Simon cocked his head. "And what would that be?"

"That you consider saving your sympathy for innocents like Alayne and Fia who rightly deserve it," Martin began, "and don't waste it on those who purposely deceive."

For a long moment, Simon considered his cousin's comment, so long in fact, Martin wondered if he'd made a mistake in speaking. Finally, Simon nodded his agreement. "You're right. What I need to concentrate on is Alayne and what's best for her, be it making inquiries about her husband or, God forbid, leaving her alone until her marriage is over."

Sympathetically, Martin said, "I know that would be hard for you to do; you're quite fond of her aren't you?"

"Aye. She tries to wear such a brave face. Marriage to Katherine Matheson's son was a mistake, one she pays for each day. Now that she's so close to being free, she's very vulnerable."

"You'll need to tread carefully."

Simon conceded, "Whatever my feelings and needs, they're second to hers." Simon clamped a hand on Martin's shoulder. "I owe you thanks for reminding me of what is truly important. I've spent too many years following my instincts, regardless of who was involved or whether my assistance was wanted."

"Lucky for me," Martin emphasized.

"And me, in your case," Simon grinned.

"Will you watch over Fia while I'm gone?" Martin asked, already sure of the answer.

"Gladly."

Chapter Twenty-Two

Bleary-eyed, Simon trudged up to the Castle ruins. With his back to the wall beside the nook where he'd held Alayne, he sank to the ground to wait. The September sun was still too low to provide any warmth, so he huddled within his frock coat and spoke his thoughts to the absent woman. "We'll have to make other arrangements, lass. I can't keep coming to the millinery." He grimaced, envisioning Katherine Matheson's disapproving scowl. "Neither can I keep you from your work." His sigh instantly turned to vapor and, pulling his coat more tightly about his wiry body, his musings turned slightly to Fia and her promise to help Alayne see him. "But, is she still willing to do that after yesterday?" A twinge of guilt made him shift uncomfortably. Martin had found his love; Simon was grateful for that no matter what it meant for him. He yawned and shook his head hoping to clear the wisps of slumber clawing at it. Half the night, he and Martin had talked and now, Martin was on his way to Inveraray to confront Jean MacNab about her deception.

With a start, Simon awoke, surprised to see the sun well overhead and a large ewe staring at him while she made quick work of a mouthful of grass. "You might have woken me sooner," he chided the sheep and rose. After dusting the back of his breeches, Simon began his walk to the High Street shop.

Upon opening the door, only Fia's drawn face met him. Neither was sure what greeting the other would find acceptable so they stood unmoving. Finally, Fia came around the display counter, slipped her hands into his and kissed Simon's cheek. His relief transformed his uncertain expression and he muttered, "Thank you."

"Now I understand why Alayne was so torn about you."

His lopsided grin split his face. "You were on my side, I hope."

"Long before I knew it was you," Fia confirmed. "I want Alayne to have someone special in her life, even as a good friend. And," she encouraged, "I already know you're someone special."

"But can I convince Alayne?"

"I don't doubt it but, if I may offer some advice, patience is your strongest ally now, and support the most important thing you give her. In November, Alayne can request that her marriage be dissolved and the closer that day gets, the more single-minded and anxious she's becoming." Fia cautioned, "Aunt Kate knows nothing of Alayne's intentions." Her eyes warmed with delight. "I'm so glad it's you, Simon."

Briefly, Simon cupped Fia's chin in his hand. "Who could have guessed from that chance meeting in Glasgow, our lives would become so entwined?"

"Certainly not I," Fia assured and flustered, "I...I'm so sorry...for you all...about the Ramsays, and Andrew's part in causing their deaths."

"You sound as though you think it's your fault, Fia. It's not, you know; this has nothing to do with you. The bastard's pure evil–there's no other explanation."

Her voice tightened with fear. "That's why I'm begging you, don't go looking for him–leave his punishment to the authorities."

Simon shook his head. "I can't do that Fia, I'm sorry. The monster must be stopped before he hurts anyone else. If it helps, I can tell you that, at the moment, he isn't in Inverness. Martin found that out at a tavern last night."

Fia nodded, unconvinced, and Simon eyed her curiously. "Don't you want to ask me about Martin?"

Mouth suddenly dry, Fia swallowed hard and asked, "Is he...will I see him today?"

"Not today, lass. Martin left this morning for Inveraray."

"Inver–" she blurted then dropped her eyes. "I see."

"He's coming back, Fia."

Distractedly, Fia said, "Martin told me you're kin–cousins, I believe."

"That's true. Do you remember when I told you about the cousin I was looking for?"

Fia searched her memory."Of course, the one who was wrong...ly...," her voice trailed off and she stared. "Martin?" she whispered incredulously. "He's the man accused of murdering his wife and child...but that's preposterous! He's incapable of such malice."

Simon's expression softened at her leap to Martin's defense. "You're right, Fia. But I think it was a highly emotional time for all involved–no one was thinking clearly."

"And...he's lived with that injustice for how long?"

"Three years."

She glanced away, trying to hide her confusion as she cast back over her time with Martin and her inability to understand his swift mood changes. No wonder. Her focus swung back to Simon. "What did you just say?"

"I said, he loves you," he repeated gently.

"Is that supposed to make me feel better? Like my own, his declaration is a bit late, don't you think?" she asked tersely.

"No one knows better than Martin how...untimely it is. Still, it happens to be true," Simon maintained.

"It's hardly relevant any...." Her voice trailed off as the shop bell chimed. Expecting Alayne, the two were instead greeted by Kate's suspicious glower.

"I thought you weren't coming back until your sister's gown was ready for fitting!" she declared bluntly.

Fia felt Simon bristle and said, "Aunt Kate, I'd like to formally introduce you to Simon MacLaren. I didn't realize before that I knew Mairi's brother; Simon and I met in Glasgow."

"Do you expect me to believe you actually know this man?" Kate challenged, and Fia's frayed emotions surfaced to meet her aunt's surliness.

"That's what I said, Aunt Kate," Fia snapped. "Not only is Simon my friend, but he's also a good customer in your shop."

Kate flushed crimson, stung by her niece's unexpected rebuke and, her feelings bruised, stumbled through her peculiar version of an apology. "Sir, a...friend of Fia's is always...a welcome customer in my shop."

"Aunt Kate!" Fia cried in exasperation.

The door opened once more and all swung toward Alayne who studied the flushed, tense group. "Have I interrupted something?" she inquired, unexpectedly causing Fia a fit of jittery laughter.

When she recovered, Fia gasped, "What do you think?"

"My guess is that I have. "

Kate ignored her daughter-in-law, turned to her niece and clucked, "I think you need a rest. This woeful business of seeing that man at Market has distressed you."

Sobered by her aunt's observation, and feeling it best to free him from Kate's scrutiny, Fia turned to Simon. "Will you walk me home?" She glanced from Kate to Alayne before resting her eyes once more on Simon. "I doubt there's more to accomplish here today."

While Simon and Alayne each craved a word with the other, they were grateful for Fia's diversion.

"With your aunt's leave, I'll happily accompany you." He arched a questioning brow in Kate's direction and, receiving a curt nod, asked Fia, "Do you have a wrap?"

Alayne volunteered, "I'll fetch it, Fia," and disappeared into the workroom returning shortly with the mantle across her arm. As she held it out, Simon took it, purposely brushing her forearm under the mantle's folds. He dropped it across Fia's shoulders, opened the door, and bowed to the Matheson women. "Ladies, good day."

Kate watched hawk-like as Simon and Fia ambled down the street. Suddenly, she spun thinking to catch Alayne staring after them as well; she was disappointed. Her daughter-in-law was removing her own cloak, her back to the door as though nothing unusual had occurred. "That man is trouble," she grumbled, "he wants something."

Alayne pursed her lips. "Does it matter what he wants, Kate?"

"Of course it does, he's disruptive!" she retorted. "He keeps coming back here, but for what?"

"A handkerchief for his mother, a wedding gown for his sister–he's a customer, Kate."

"It's an excuse, I can feel it."

"A very expensive excuse wouldn't you say?" Alayne responded dryly.

"That's right, make light of it. What of this supposed 'friendship' with Fia? She says she knows him from Glasgow. Why has she never spoken of him?" Kate demanded.

Alayne tarried at the curtain and fought to keep her voice even. "Fia mentioned him to me quite some time ago. They met at Market one day when she was being pestered by Andrew Forbes. Mr. MacLaren saw what was happening and came to her aid. She thinks highly of him; I see no reason to doubt her judgment–or her word." With that, Alayne entered the workroom, flung her mantle at the peg on the wall, grabbed her shears and began ripping a seam in a petticoat she was bringing up to the latest fashion.

Face tinged with resentment, Kate shoved aside the curtain and entered after her. "You seem to know a great deal about Fia and her friends that I don't."

Alayne dropped her hands into her lap replying, "Did it never occur to you that, as much as Fia loves and respects you, she opens up to me because we have a great deal in common?"

"And just what are all these things you have in common that lead her to confide in you?" Kate prodded irritably.

Alayne shoved the petticoat aside and stood before her mother-in-law. "Fia and I are close in age, born in the same town, derive the same pleasure from creating things with our hands." Kate's pout deepened and Alayne stepped closer. "We both thrill to the thundering gallop of a horse beneath us, we enjoy an adventure. We're both related to you, and we've both been disappointed by the thing we crave most–love. The difference is, I'm suspicious of it, and she hasn't experienced enough of it to be that smart."

Kate sputtered angrily, "Surely...you couldn't...Muir is not to blame for your...your dissatisfaction...your failure at love."

Green eyes blazed darkly as Alayne replied, "I never laid all the blame on your son. But he was the one who took all I gave and threw it in my face; he tossed it onto the street each time he took a whore to him; and he laughed at me each time you condoned his behavior."

"*Don't say that!*" Kate screeched, hand flashing out to connect resoundingly with Alayne's cheek. Tears smarted Alayne's eyes but she was immovable. "You know I'm right," she hissed, "we've discussed it before. But what bothers you now is this sick competition for Fia's affection you imagine exists. Kate, you're pathetic. She's not here to replace Muir, to give you a second chance. You don't know your niece well enough to realize that Fia has a boundless capacity for caring: for me, Murdoch, Douglas, Martin, Simon–you. There's room for everyone." Alayne's hand crept to the back of her neck as she felt its muscles knotting. "I'm going out; I won't return to the shop today. Mistress Hays' petticoat will have to wait."

Cheeks awash with tears of denial, regret and self-pity, Kate watched the door slam behind her daughter-in-law.

Fia and Simon had barely stepped inside Kate's row house when they heard a commotion. Alayne thrust the door wide, eyes wild with misery. She went straight to Fia begging, "Let me borrow Barley."

"Alayne, what is it?" Alarmed, Fia grasped her friend's arms. "What's happened?

"Nothing." Alayne kept her eyes from Simon's face, but Simon came close.

"Something is dreadfully wrong. Tell me...." He bent to get a better look at her face. "That witch struck you!" he seethed as she jerked away.

"Leave me alone, *please*." And clutching the back of her neck, Alayne focused with difficulty on Fia. "Barley?"

"Aye, take him and go now," she urged, realizing what was happening

"Wait, Alayne, let me help," Simon pleaded starting after her, but Fia's hand shot out to seize his coat. He turned in exasperation, trying to shake Fia's hold. "What are you doing?"

"Let her go," Fia said calmly, "trust me."

Simon glanced in dismay between Fia and Alayne's back as she disappeared through the kitchen entrance. Back to Fia, he asked in bewilderment, "Why didn't you let me try to help her?"

"I will, Simon, but first listen to me." Fia loosed his coat and smoothed it absently. "At times, if something bad happens, or Alayne is upset, she suffers from horrible headaches."

Impatiently, Simon asked, "What are you talking about?"

"Hush and I'll tell you," Fia instructed. "She's getting one of those headaches now. You saw her rubbing her neck?" To Simon's brusque nod, Fia added, "Only one thing seems to help her– if she catches it quickly enough. There's a glen with a burn and a waterfall south of Inverness well hidden off the Loch road. That's where she's going–to let that icy water beat her numb–and that's where you'll find her."

Simon's gratitude spilled in a huge hug. "Tell me exactly how to find this glen."

All clothing save her shift littering the ground nearby, Alayne stood under the tumbling, healing water. She leaned against the rock at her back, closed her eyes and tried to clear her mind of Kate's hateful jealousy and blind love for the son who had deserted them both. Alayne thanked God that her love for Muir had died within weeks of their marriage–if she had continued to love him, she might have ended like Kate. "Stop thinking," she silently commanded and, running her hands down her body, scooped water near her knees and drew it to her throbbing cheek.

Her body stiffened sensing she was no longer alone. Simon stood on the bank not much farther than the length of three arms from her. Acutely aware of the transparent state of her shift, Alayne nevertheless stood unmoving, surprised that, beneath her foul mood, she felt a sweet current flow through her, roused by Simon's presence and stare. "How long have you been watching me?" she asked.

He blinked and replied, "It'll never be long enough. You are exquisite, lass, but I knew that before seeing you in your sopping shift." He struggled to doff his boots, stripped his coat and shirt before entering the frigid water. Sloshing through the distance between them, his bold perusal further stirred Alayne's blood.

Eyes closed, Alayne rested her head once more against the rock and stretched slowly, letting the light and water play off her body. She shuddered involuntarily as Simon's lips touched hers. "Do you want to love me, Simon?" she asked in a breathy whisper.

"In truth, I do, lass," he admitted, hands sliding up her back, bringing their bodies closer. "You deserve to be loved, treasured." He looked into her fierce, defiant eyes and recognized there was more at play than mutual attraction. It took all the strength he could muster to say, "But you must want me too."

"I do," Alayne vowed too quickly, "I want you *now*."

His finger twirled a tendril of hair beside her damaged cheek. "You want me now because you're injured, angry, disenchanted–maybe all three. When we love, Alayne, it will not be for revenge, or to prove something to anyone but you and me–that we want meant to be together."

Alayne gaped at him in disbelief. "You're...you're turning me down? What kind of man are you?" A hard shove of her hand sent Simon staggering several paces. "You say you like what you see?" she railed, reached down and pulled her shift over her head to stand naked before him. "What do you say now?"

"A...Alayne," he choked, "please listen to what I'm saying to you."

She moved to press against him. "Your body doesn't want to turn me away, I feel it."

One hand behind her head, Simon's mouth sought hers and was met eagerly.

With fingers laced through his blond curls, Alayne encouraged his lips to travel where they would, their warmth and the heat of his hands bringing her to life. She was jarred to her core when he abruptly wrenched from her and demanded, "Look at me." She was nearly lost in the depths of his eyes. "I don't...don't just want your body. I want all of you; I will wait forever for all of you, Alayne."

In a swift, embarrassed motion, Alayne plucked her shift from the water, pushed passed Simon, nearly toppling him, and lunged onto the shore. A tug brought her shift over her head but it clung maddeningly to her skin as she struggled to cover herself.

"Alayne, I'm not trying to vex or humiliate you," Simon stood close behind her now.

"No, I don't suppose you are," she muttered, shaking as the rising wind nipped her dripping body.

"Lass," he begged, "stay with me awhile."

"Why, so we can talk? I'm cold, I want to go back," she insisted.

Simon's eyes widened as an idea struck him. "Have I scared you? Are you're running from me?"

Alayne whirled to face him, so burdened by emotion she could barely speak. "Aye, you...you frighten me. Any normal man would gladly take what I just offered you. But to h...hear your prattle, one would think you were asking for...love–love from the heart, from the soul."

"In truth, isn't that what we all want?"

Misery etched her face. "I don't know what truth is when it comes to love, Simon. Muir swore his love before the vicar and half of Inverness. Before the month was out, he was whoring down on the quay."

Simon gently rubbed her shoulders. "That was Muir, not me. Don't compare us, Alayne, I've told you that before. You'll find me a much different man–one who won't abuse you, one who will defend you and would be fiercely proud one day if, God willing, you grew to love me." He steadied her face, forcing her to look at him. "And don't think, for one foolish moment, that I don't crave you; everything in me cries out for you. But I've tried very hard to give you what is most important to you now, my friendship and my strength to draw upon. Being inside you now, is not worth the risk of having nothing of you later."

A heart-rending sob escaped her and Alayne clung tightly to him. He drew her to the ground and wrapped her securely in his embrace to warm and comfort her–and himself.

After Simon's departure, Fia anxiously paced the entry way waiting for Kate to come home. Though tempted, she didn't go to the shop to confront her aunt for fear of creating a scene in front of customers. But she was unprepared when Kate trudged in like a beaten warrior. The face Kate raised to Fia looked a full ten years older. "My God, Aunt Kate, what happened?"

Kate's dull eyes were matched by her voice. "How could it have gotten so out of hand?" She let go her mantle and Fia caught it before it hit the floor. Listlessly wandering into the drawing room, Kate collapsed into her favorite chair and, when Fia drew a chair up before her, Kate blurted, "*How*?"

"What got out of hand?" Fia asked.

"Alayne defending that...man...." her voice trailed off.

Through tight lips, Fia guessed, "Simon MacLaren?" and Kate nodded. "Surely, Alayne saying a good word on Simon's behalf isn't the problem."

Kate whispered, "It just started it. We disagreed about...Muir. Alayne said things I...I couldn't accept."

"Couldn't or wouldn't, Aunt Kate? Were they true?"

With a shuddering sigh, Kate admitted, "Aye, they were true; I just couldn't bear to hear them uttered. And we had words...about you."

Fia started. "Me?"

Limply, Kate waved her hand before her face. "Alayne knows things about you that I don't. I suppose, envy describes my feelings. Muir never confided in me; the fact that you don't either reminds me of my failings with him."

Fia asked quietly, "Why did you hit her, Aunt Kate?"

"She said I condoned Muir's lewd behavior–and God help me, she's right, I did, by turning a blind eye." Kate wailed piteously into her hands.

She knew she ought to, but Fia couldn't bring herself to offer comfort. "If you knew Alayne was telling the truth, why did you strike her?" she hounded.

"Because I was in so much pain. Ever since she fled the shop, I've gone over and over everything she said–everything I did or didn't do where my son was concerned. I was a doting, protective, blind mother; it didn't help Muir and it hurt Alayne. I hurt her again today." She turned desperate eyes on Fia, "Will I ever stop hurting her?"

Fia's brows drew down sharply. "Only you can answer that Aunt Kate. Can you stop hurting Alayne now that you admit the truth about Muir?"

Kate sniffed into her handkerchief. "Even if I could, would Alayne ever forgive me? How can I look her in the eye after today?"

"I don't know if she'll forgive you. As far as facing her, tell her what you've told me. Be honest with her. Even if she can't forgive the past, you don't have to cause her pain in the future." Fia dropped her gaze. "And as for me, I love you Aunt Kate; I don't intend to shut you out. You've been loving and good to me. But Alayne is what I imagine a sister to be, and we spend a great deal of time together as I imagine you and my mother once did. Besides, you have enough on your mind without suffering all my chatter." At last, Fia rested a hand on Kate's. "I'll make you some tea and bring it to your room; I told Flora to go home. You need to rest quietly and decide what you want to say to Alayne in the morning. I'll bring you a dram of whiskey as well."

Kate looked at her uncertainly. "Do you hate me for what I've done, Fia?"

"Hate you? No. Oddly enough, I'm glad you've been forced to face things you've been hiding from all these years. I honestly hope it's going to help, Aunt Kate. Now, go on to your room, I'll be along shortly."

Kate had drifted into an exhausted sleep within minutes of drinking Fia's bracing tea, and Fia settled in the kitchen to await Alayne's return.

On the edge of town, Alayne assured Simon that he could count on Fia to see her safely back to the millinery. He looked confused.

"Why would you return to the shop at this time of night?"

"Most of the time, it's where I live."

"Alone?" he asked disconcerted.

"Aye."

"I didn't know." Simon took a deep breath. "You haven't said yet; may I see you again?"

Alayne blushed and was thankful for the dusk that hid it. "I would think you'd seen as much of me today as there is to see."

His hand covered hers on Barley's reins. "A most beautiful sight it was." Then he muttered, "God help me if presented again with that temptation."

Alayne brought his fingers to her cheek and rubbed them. With that, she was gone, leaving his hopeful heart leaping in her wake, but with no plans to meet.

The last bloody hues of twilight had tapered to violet when Alayne returned Barley to his byre. Simon, who followed at a discreet distance on Devenick, watched as, true to Alayne's prediction, Fia stole from the house to greet her return. Still, disquiet worried Simon's belly. Fia may take care of Alayne but, with Forbes possibly nearby, Simon watched until Fia returned to the Douglas Row house. With a cleansing breath, he decided to seek out the Inverness theater–there was bound to be at least one. "Tonight's as good as any to plead my case for a job."

"*Andrew, come in*," George Graham offered behind the most courageous face he could muster.

"Graham," Andrew acknowledged gruffly, brushing trickling rain from his coat and tracking mud through to the drawing room where it dropped in clods from his boots. "What is wrong with that daughter of yours? Why didn't she answer my summons?"

Sweat popping out on his upper lip, George placated, "Elizabeth took ill when I was in Edinburgh and you were away. She's still weak, Andrew, and shouldn't be leaving the house in weather like this." He gestured vaguely upward receiving a glare from his guest in return.

"Perhaps," Andrew suggested haughtily, "now that I've come to *her*, she'll find the strength to grant me a few minutes."

George's trepidation was momentarily overcome by annoyance and he snapped, "You might show some concern, Andrew, since you claim to be much taken with Elizabeth."

Andrew realized he was on the verge of crossing the line of Graham's tolerance and immediately laid a hand on George's shoulder. Remorse thickening his voice, Andrew soothed, "You're right, of course; I do care deeply for Elizabeth. Foolishly, I've let less important concerns cloud my judgment. Forgive me, George. How does she fare?"

Somewhat mollified, George mumbled, "Better, but she mopes in her room–in fact, seldom leaves her room at all."

"I would very much like to see her," Andrew requested glibly. "Could you send your maid up with a message?"

George nodded and called Una. When the maid scrambled in and dipped her curtsey, George ordered, "Tell Miss Elizabeth that Mr. Forbes is in the drawing room and wishes to see her."

"Aye, Sir." She bobbed again and scurried up the stairs.

George found small talk with Andrew excruciating, but he was exhilarated enough about the potential profits from their joint smuggling enterprise to make an attempt. "I take it tis business kept you busy in my absence."

Andrew sprawled onto the chaise and admitted, "I've traveled a great deal on business. No doubt, Elizabeth told you."

"No," George shook his head, "when I returned home, she told me you were away. Except for that, she's scarcely mentioned you."

A thunderous look rumbled across Andrew's face, but he forced a smirk. "My, she has been ill. Well, Graham, the new ship handles well; it's one of your best, I'll wager, and she's fast. I had a bit of difficulty with one of your crew; I dismissed him. Also, I took another look at your niece's land. I'm more convinced than ever that it's perfect for our needs."

"Except it doesn't belong to us," George reminded.

"Not a concern. As your beautiful daughter so aptly stated, we don't need Fia to have use of her land." Andrew kept his tone light, but resentment towards Fia made his bile sour.

"True...true. So, everything is in order then?" George asked stroking his side-whiskers in greedy anticipation.

"There was one other problem, but I resolved it."

The tone of Andrew's voice made George cringe, and cold dread inched up his spine. Straightaway, he decided he did not want to know more about this other 'problem'. "Then we... we can begin operations immediately," George concluded hopefully, and Andrew shot an indulgent glance in his direction.

"Already underway," was his reply.

"Excellent, Andrew, simply–Elizabeth, my pet. How good it is to see you up and about." Her father bustled to her side and planted a relieved kiss on her cheek.

"Thank you, Father." Elizabeth was pale but otherwise looked no worse for her experience.

Andrew pulled his bulk easily from the chaise and glided to her in two long steps to raise her fingers to his lips in a lingering kiss. "My dearest, George told me that you've been ailing. Please tell me you are recovered and," he paused to emphasize, "that everything is well."

"Fully recovered," she responded, extracting her hand from his. "It's good of you to ask." Elizabeth passed him noting the flickering confusion in his eyes. Of course, he didn't expect everything to be well, so she didn't mind in the least letting him stew. Elizabeth settled herself in a chair and arranged her skirts before politely asking, "And how was your trip, Andrew?"

"Successful." Wary of what her formality denoted, Andrew declared, "You don't seem pleased to see me."

Before Elizabeth could respond, George stepped beside her and rested a hand protectively on the back of the chair. "Really, Andrew, you shouldn't expect too much. Too much excitement after being indisposed, even that of seeing you, is not good for her."

Andrew eyed the reticent twosome, bewildered. As the silence drew out though, irritation pricked his temper. He summoned an even tone to inquire, "Graham, would it be possible for me to speak to Elizabeth in private?"

"If that is what she wishes," was his surprising reply.

With teeth gritted, Andrew asked, "Elizabeth?"

The young woman rose and took her father's arm. "I'm a bit unsteady, Andrew. Forgive me, but I really must return to my room and rest."

George bravely escorted his daughter past the malevolent glare of his guest and business partner, stopping at the bottom of the stairs. "Perhaps you'll call some other time, Andrew. Show yourself out, will you?"

On the stoop, Andrew clenched and unclenched his fists, fuming at having been summarily dismissed. Had that old fool forgotten with whom he was dealing? And had he gone soft himself to let Graham get away with such behavior?

Into the street he stepped and, for a few moments, Andrew stood, immensely vexed and unable to decide his next move. Finally, he strode to his horse, put one foot in the stirrup and halted as the door swung wide and George appeared on the threshold. Andrew sneered, removing his foot from the stirrup, knowing the old man and his daughter had come to their senses. "Well?" Andrew demanded, fully expecting to be invited back inside.

Graham cleared his throat. "Elizabeth wants to know why you didn't bring her a special bottle of wine this time?"

The unexpected query and realization that he may have erred grievously, rattled Andrew's composure and, turning back to his horse, Andrew mounted quickly. Ashamed of his reaction, Andrew snarled, "I forgot," then urged his mount away.

By the time he had stabled his horse, Andrew was thinking more clearly, though his annoyance was still ripe. He had many questions and few answers. Heavily, he scaled the stairs, jerked off his boots, and flopped on the bed, hands clasped behind his neck. "What game is she playing?" he murmured of Elizabeth. He was reasonably confident that the pennyroyal had done its job, though that was not the impression Elizabeth wanted to give.

An ugly frown marred Andrew's dark features as he admitted fully his one mistake. "I should have gone there loaded with gifts," he chided and his frown turned to concern. "Why did she ask only about the wine?" A shake of his head, and his supreme self-confidence dismissed a stabbing disquiet. "Elizabeth would never guess my hand in her 'illness'; her hunger for me would not allow it."

Jean's heart leapt to the sound of Martin's excited greeting and, flinging the door wide, she was instantly gathered into his arms, her lips crushed against his. When they parted long enough to savor the sight of each other, tears welled in Martin's eyes.

"This is where I truly belong, in the arms of my beloved." Again, he pulled her tightly to him and drank in her fragrance.

Jean rained kisses on his cheeks, his eyes and forehead. "I've been lost without you. Never did I think we'd be parted this long."

"It'll never happen again." In a swift motion, Martin swept her up and, whirled her around until she laughed, giddy and breathless.

"Lie with me now, here before the fire. His face blurred as it came close to hers and Fia's eyes flew open. Violently, her body quaked and she labored for breath, waiting to recognize her surroundings.

The darkness and her nightmare confused her briefly then, with a moan, Fia buried her face in her pillow, smothering the same sobs she had muffled the previous night. Why did her memory have to be so perfect when it came to Jean MacNab? For once, couldn't it fail completely so that her visage and her importance to Martin wasn't made so painfully clear?

Fia left the bed knowing she wouldn't go back to sleep. She pushed her arms into the sleeves of her dressing gown and wandered through the gloomy house finding solace in no room or thought. Eventually, Fia returned to her room, splashed water on her face and dressed. Her work was all she could turn to and she stepped from the house into crisp autumn air. The sky barely brightening, Fia began the hike to High Street.

There were more cats about than people. Her heart nearly stopped as she narrowly missed stepping on one that scampered past her feet with a startled yowl. Once she calmed, Fia glanced around. "On the wrong road," she chided and continued, "pay more attention to what you're doing." Exhausted and nauseous, she tried to concentrate on her path to the shop. If she felt better, Fia would have had to laugh at herself. "Imagine," she mumbled, "thinking that speaking to Martin might let me move on with my life–how naive, how foolish, how like me when it comes to Martin."

Finally, the millinery stood before her and Fia fumbled in her pocket for the key. As she inserted it in the lock, she abruptly froze, the hairs on her neck tingling. Fia whirled, eyes immediately locking on a figure poised before the wigmaker's shop across the lane. It was a man, yet shadows obstructed his identity. He seemed content to study her, for he didn't move.

Fia thought to call Simon's name but, with a chill racing her backbone, she hurriedly entered the shop and locked the door behind her. She backed away, into the murky interior until she could observe the man without being seen in return. Fia waited a full ten minutes until, with long, loping strides, the man withdrew.

Anyone she knew would have greeted her. Only someone unknown would behave as the man outside had, scrutinizing the shop in total, insolent silence. "Or someone who means harm." Fia's blood raced dread throughout her body; her knees buckled and she hit the floor whimpering fear into the hand clamped to her mouth.

Chapter Twenty-Three

Alayne was unusually quiet about her trip to the glen and Fia, distracted, respected the silence. She sensed that something significant had occurred when Simon had ridden after her friend Alayne's expressions and few uttered words seemed to shift with the hour from contentment to agitation, despair to joy. Finally, and reluctantly, Fia intruded on Alayne's thoughts with a subject that could not be ignored.

"I need to talk to you about Aunt Kate."

Without looking up Alayne snipped a thread from the stomacher of Mairi's gown. "Talk all you'd like, Fia, but don't expect me to listen."

Glumly, Fia sighed. "All right, but I hope you *will* listen. I do have some idea of what you're feeling."

"Do you?" Alayne fixed a doubting gaze on the other woman.

"Aye," Fia declared, "humiliated, infuriated, unappreciated, betrayed and just plain sick of the whole bloody mess."

A lopsided grin cracked Alayne's stoic face. "That's very close, but you forgot 'unforgiving.' So, don't waste your breath pleading Kate's case."

"I don't intend to; she can do that herself if she can work up the courage." Fia hesitated at Alayne's obvious surprise. "Aunt Kate hasn't determined yet how she can ever hope to ask your forgiveness."

"I shouldn't wonder," Alayne grumbled.

Fia remeasured fabric for the back panel of the bodice. "What I wanted to say was that I have never seen Aunt Kate look as frail, or behave as despairingly as when she arrived home yesterday evening. She must ask your pardon. I do know she regrets what she did. I only ask you to hear her out when she comes to you. If it's not in your heart to forgive her, so be it."

"Is that all?" Alayne asked skeptically.

Grimly, Fia responded, "No. I will say, I was shocked to find out that I had become part of the problem between you."

"And I'm surprised she told you that," admitted Alayne.

"I never dreamed our friendship would make matters worse for you. For that, I'm sorry."

"It isn't your fault. Kate's very possessive; that's evident in the way, despite all she knows to be true, she clings to the portrait of 'Saint' Muir her memory has painted. I believe she sees you as her chance for redemption."

A chill shuddered Fia's frame and her expression clouded.

Her needle poised in mid-air, Alayne vigilantly asked, "What is it, Fia?"

"Something that happened early this morning; I've been reluctant to mention it."

"Something with Kate? Whatever it is, I can see you're disturbed by it."

"Not Kate." Absently, Fia straightened the ruffle at her elbow. "You know I came to the shop earlier this morning than usual."

"Because you couldn't sleep," Alayne supplied.

"When I started to unlock the door," Fia resumed, "I realized I wasn't the only person about. There was a man, lurking in front of Mr. Hanley's wig shop."

Alayne caught her breath. "Are you certain? Did he speak to you?"

Fia shook her head. "He said nothing, but he was definitely watching. I let myself in and locked the door behind me. It was a long time before he retreated. In truth, I was frightened." She paused. "I realize I've had little sleep and I'm distracted this morning, I even took a wrong turn coming here. But I did not imagine this man. If his intentions were respectable, I can't help but think he would have addressed me."

"I agree," Alayne declared frowning. "Could you see him?"

"Not really. He was tall and slim. It was fairly dark; I certainly didn't recognize him." Fia hesitated before dutifully adding, "Alayne, I don't want to make more out of this than it warrants."

"You aren't, you're being cautious," she assured, "and not without good reason." Alayne set the stomacher aside. "It's probably wise for you not to go about alone for a time."

"How can I do that?" Fia protested. "You and Aunt Kate can't spend your days accompanying me everywhere I go. It isn't fair to either one of you."

"Aren't you forgetting Simon? He'll help."

Fia graced Alayne with small, appreciative smile. "I know he would, but I'd rather he not stay in Inverness indefinitely if it means he's searching for Andrew. I want him to stay only if he's here for you. Besides, according to Simon, Martin has discovered that Andrew is not in Inverness, not yet anyway."

"At least that's good news. Now, what of Martin?" Alayne suggested.

"He has returned home to his wife," Fia stated flatly, taking Alayne aback.

"He...what do you mean he's gone home to her?"

"Simon told me yesterday when he came to the shop–Martin heard at some tavern on the quay that Andrew is not here, then he left for Inveraray."

Alayne demanded, "Is that all? Didn't Simon tell you anything else?"

"About Martin?"

Alayne blanched and stammered, "Aye."

Fia rubbed her forehead which was beginning to pound. "Simon also said that Martin would be back and that...that he knew Martin loved me."

Alayne rose and rested a hand on Fia's shoulder. "I know he loves you. I saw the torture on his face when he came downstairs after speaking to you–that look still makes me shiver. And, if Simon says Martin will return, I've no doubt he will."

"I believe him. But, whether Martin returns or not, whether he loves me or not," Fia resolved, "it doesn't change the fact that he married Jean."

"No, it doesn't," Alayne said sadly. "Well, to the immediate problem, Kate and I will help protect you without question–this man could be Andrew's spy. And, we'll ask Simon for help; I believe we can depend on him," Alayne determined, and Fia smiled at Alayne's inclusion of herself as one who could rely on Simon.

"*Mam!*" *Donald called*, racing through the crowded taproom.

His mother appeared quickly, heart fluttering with apprehension. Had something dire happened or would she scold him for disturbing her patrons? Annie snatched him by the sleeve and bent toward him. "Hush now, what is it, lad?"

"It's...it's...Martin!" he blurted.

Abruptly, Annie straightened. "Martin? Are you sure?"

Donald nodded eagerly and tugged her by the hand as he retraced his path to the door. "Not by the bridge, Mam," he corrected as she looked toward Inveraray Castle, "from the north."

And, indeed, there he was. Annie's eye caught movement as Arthur shot toward Donald, nearly trouncing him in his excitement at seeing the lad again. The hound's yips blended with Donald's giggles as the two wrestled and rolled in the lane.

Her delight at seeing Martin again shone from her face and she wordlessly enfolded his lean body in her arms the moment his feet touched the ground. It seemed to her that he clung more tightly than usual and, immediately, she worried. "Ah, Martin," she released him to arms' length and spoke soft words, "we've been lonely for the sight of you. Where have you been," she pouted, "and why didn't you write as you promised?"

For a long moment, Martin studied her then embraced her again, his grip tight.

"Mar...Martin...Martin, please!" Annie gulped air as he relinquished his hold.

"I missed you, Annie." He smiled a nervous smile and said, "A good deal has happened. I hope, in time, you'll forgive me for failing to send word."

Narrowly, she eyed him. "It will depend on what you tell me."

Martin grinned and turned to Donald. "No greeting for me, lad, only for my dog?"

Donald leaped from the ground into Martin's arms, a cloud of road grime bursting around them as their bodies met. Martin spun the boy around while Annie coughed and waved the dust away from her face.

"You two ruffians," she said, clearing her throat, "clean up, then come in for some mutton stew." Annie left Martin chasing Donald to the well, returning inside to prepare a place for her favorite men to sup. While stacking fresh oatcakes on a platter, Annie promised herself that she would not bring up the subject of Fia Graham. Nearly five months ago, she had bade him safe journey as he rode away trying to forget the lass. From the look of him, he suffered still.

Fondly, Annie listened to Martin and Donald banter between bites of their meal. Martin told him about prescribing a potion of onions and honey for a bairn with colic. Donald's nose wrinkled in disgust.

"Maybe you'll like this story better," Martin offered. "I rode into a small burgh in the south where a lad, not quite as young as you, had broken his leg."

"Did you give him onions, too?" Donald piped.

Martin chuckled, "No, it was a different treatment I gave him. But, the best part of this story is that I met the man who came to the lad's aid. He turned out to be my cousin, Simon."

Annie started. "Truly? I didn't realize you had family, Martin."

"It surprised me as well. His grandmother is my Great Aunt. Simon took me to his home and I met his whole family, the aunt, her son and his wife, and Simon's brother and sister." Martin's gaze grew distant for a moment. "Very special people," he murmured then focused again on Annie, "and they've opened their home to me."

"I'm so pleased for you, Martin."

"Why's your hair so long?" Donald broke in. "And your beard looks like a cuckoo's nest."

"Donald!" Annie forced a stern tone.

Martin laughed heartily. "Leave it to you, laddie. Except for bathing, I've not had cause to pay much attention to my grooming. I guess you're telling me I need to neaten up a bit."

Donald nodded eagerly before pointing to the red streaks scarring Martin's arm. "What happened there?"

Exasperated, Annie was about to chide him for his inexhaustible curiosity, but abruptly changed her mind when she noticed the marks herself.

Casually, Martin unrolled his sleeve covering the scrapes and answered, "Another patient did that to me. She was in great pain; it was an accident."

Before Donald could ask yet another question, Annie stepped in. "You take your bowl and Martin's to the kitchen, please. Say goodnight to Martin and I'll tuck you in later, Darlin'."

"Will you be here in the morning?" the boy asked Martin.

"Indeed I will."

Donald flung his arms around Martin's neck in a strangling hug, kissed his mother's cheek, and balanced the bowls precariously into the kitchen.

"I have almost as many questions for you as Donald," Annie confided, "but I'll bide my time while you tell me what else you've been up to." Momentarily, she dropped her gaze. "And I have something to tell you...about a visitor."

"A burly fellow named Murdoch?" Martin offered and Annie's jaw sagged.

"How did you know that?"

"I saw him on Wednesday."

She leaned closer. "You saw him four days ago? Where? You know he's a friend of Fia's," her voice trailed off, her private promise already broken.

"When I saw the gentleman, Fia was with him."

Her eyes grew round and her ability to speak momentarily deserted her. Finally, Annie whispered, "So you saw Fia. Is she well? Were you able to speak with her?"

Martin drank over-long of his ale before answering. "I saw and spoke with her Thursday morning and she's in good health."

"A doctor's answer," Annie snorted, before cutting to the question most concerning her. "And you? How do you fare now that you've come face to face with the lass again?"

"Not as well as I'd like, but I understand things now which baffled me before."

Bewildered, Annie said, "What things?"

"Why Fia said nothing of being promised to someone until the day I left her alone; why she turned distant after we shared a rare closeness; why she preferred marrying someone she didn't love–"

"To the man she *did* love," Annie broke in, sadness swelling her voice.

Martin's eyes glistened. "You were right, Annie."

"The lass admitted her love for you?"

With a nod, Martin added, "And I finally told her what I should have months ago."

Annie's hand covered her friend's. "Martin, I wish I could turn time back for you both."

At her sympathetic suggestion, Martin soothed, "A lovely idea, but there was a force at work I wasn't aware of." His expression hardened as he explained, "Jean paid a visit the day Fia was alone at the croft. She lied to Fia, announcing that she and I were marrying; that was the day Fia told me of her intention to wed Forbes. When I spoke with her in Inverness, Fia said, after Jean's visit, she just couldn't bear to stay with me."

Annie's eyes searched his face. "So you've come to see Jean."

"If you ever decide to sell the inn, Annie, I believe you have a future as a seer."

"Saying you intend to see Jean is not foretelling the future, lad, that would involve a bit of guesswork." She bit her lip. "What will you say to her?"

"I'm not sure. Annie, I have to know what happened that day."

"Didn't Fia tell you?"

Martin shook his head. "No details really and, considering everything, I couldn't bring myself to question her about it."

Annie's face etched with concern. "Jean's cost you so much, Martin, won't you think twice about confronting her?"

"I've no choice; I owe it to Fia. But I promise you, everything will be fine. Now," he forced a change in the topic, "could I borrow some shears? As Donald so truthfully pointed out, I've turned into a wooly sort of beast. I need to trim up."

Reluctantly, Annie rose and Martin, knowing she worried still, stood and kissed her smooth, pink cheek. "It will be all right," he repeated.

Annie pursed her lips, then softened her sulk. "Let's get those shears."

"*It's a start,*" Simon told himself, rather pleased that the theater troupe had agreed to take him on, even though it was in a small way, and one not always appreciated by the audience clamoring for the play. He would begin this very night with the prologue to the play, and dramatic recitations between scenes. In fact, Simon was grateful to squeeze in one night of work before the Sabbath when no performances would be held. Luckily, his stage experience in the colonies enabled him to begin with virtually no rehearsal–he simply had to decide what he wanted to quote.

Simon stood on the bridge staring into the shallow Ness beneath, pondering a different body of water. His focus blurred at the memory of the suppleness of Alayne's skin to his touch, the warmth stemming from her body, even in the frigid pool. He moaned softly. "God's life," he murmured, noting the increasing pressure in his loins, "I'll have to control myself better than this." He almost laughed aloud thinking, "How much more control could I have shown than when Alayne stood naked and willing in my arms–and I insisted on waiting?" But his most vivid recollection was the desperation and anger in her eyes–emotions which had nothing to do with him. Simon was grateful to have been able to keep himself from taking advantage of Alayne's moment of weakness–he would never have forgiven himself, and neither would she when her thoughts had cleared.

"If only I could find a way to invite Alayne and Fia to come for the performance." But after yesterday's uproar with Kate Matheson, Simon decided it was prudent to remain scarce. His belly lurched as an uneasy thought came to him, that Alayne might misread his absence believing it, in some fashion, connected to what occurred in the glen. Simon's longing to see and reassure her made him briefly reconsider visiting the millinery. Finally, he decided on a different course, and briskly started back to the theater.

Late in the afternoon, a lad of about twelve entered the shop and Fia looked up from her stitching and bestowed a welcoming smile. "How may I help you, Sir?"

Timidly, the boy returned her greeting and advanced to where she sat, halting momentarily when Alayne appeared at the curtained doorway. His hand extended, the lad said, "If you please, Miss, I am delivering playbills for tonight's performance and would kindly urge your attendance." He passed the bill to Fia who stood to take it from him. The lad swept a wide, dramatic bow to which the women could only respond with their most sincere curtseys.

"Why haven't we seen you before?" Alayne inquired.

"I was hired especially for this performance," he replied, "and now I must leave." With another bow, the lad departed leaving Alayne and Fia baffled in his wake.

"Can you imagine what that was about?"

Alayne shrugged. "Maybe if we read the playbill, the answer will be there." They bent heads over the paper and read it over carefully, then read it again.

"I still don't under–wait!" Alayne exclaimed. "Look at this sentence. 'Recitations by renowned actor recently in America.' That has to be–"

"Simon!" they declared in unison.

"*Did you have* trouble getting out of the house?" Alayne asked with trepidation.

"If you mean Aunt Kate," Fia said, "no. I saw her briefly when I told her where we were going, but it seemed not to trouble her."

"That, in itself, is odd," Alayne declared.

Fia pulled her mantle close against the October chill and picked up her pace. "I must confess feeling guilty about going to the theater when Aunt Kate is suffering."

"This will sound callous, I realize, but Kate is responsible for her own suffering. She couldn't bring herself to come to the shop to see me today, and that delay will only make it harder for her."

Fia nodded agreement. "But I still feel badly about it."

Alayne slipped her arm through her friend's. "Tonight, just try to enjoy yourself. I plan to."

"You're right. Since I first met Simon, I've wished to see him on stage." Fia shook off her gloom. "Tonight I predict, we are in for a treat."

The women reached the theater too late to claim seats in the unadorned boxes a level above the simple wooden stage. There, they might have enjoyed the evening relatively undisturbed by other patrons. Instead, they positioned themselves on a bench five rows from the stage and found themselves jostled by last minute arrivals and unable to hear each other for the boisterous crowd. The soft glow of the many lanthorns at the edge of the stage provided light for the coming performance. When the first player made his entrance, his features were startlingly distinct behind make-up designed to exaggerate and make those features visible to those in the back of the room. His image was also pleasantly familiar–it was Simon.

For several moments, while individuals in the audience noticed his presence and quieted somewhat, Simon stood unmoving. At last, he spread his arms wide, and his voice rang eloquently and unobstructed to every ear. "Dear Ladies and Gentlemen, patrons all. This night we present for your pleasure and, we sincerely hope your approval, a tale of greed, romance, virtue, innocence and redemption. We present "The Beaux' Stratagem," Mr. Farquhar's comedy of manners." There was polite applause, and Simon strolled to stage right, took up his stance, and began the prologue.

"When strife disturbs, or sloth corrupts an age,
Keen satire is the business of the stage.
When the Plain-Dealer writ, he lashed those crimes,
Which then infested most the modish times:
But now, when faction sleeps, and sloth is fled,
And all our youth in active fields are bred;
When, through Great Britain's fair extensive round,
The trumps of fame the notes of UNION sound;"

When reference to the Act of Union which brought Scotland under England's parliamentary government was made, a smattering of hisses and disgruntled curses could be heard. Simon missed not a beat, finishing his lines without further interruption, and stepping aside as the curtain was drawn back the first Act began.

While it was an intriguing farce, Alayne and Fia each found it difficult to patiently wait for Simon's next appearance. There were five Acts in all, so he returned for three recitations, each in marked contrast to the performance underway, each providing him an opportunity to show his versatility. Fia was enchanted and Alayne was moved perilously close to tears by unexpected pride in him. She chanced a sidelong glance at Fia who, if she noticed Alayne's reaction, did not let on.

Simon and his two guests were gratified that he seemed to please the assembly immensely. The applause heaped on him finally dwindled into the beginning of Act V and, at the end of the play, Alayne and Fia adeptly elbowed their way to the door, glancing back at the curtain call before stepping into the chilling air where they took up a stance from which they could easily spy Simon emerging from the theater.

Most of the crowd had dispersed by the time Simon appeared, clean of the garish make-up, a smile of triumph splitting his face. "You received my message, I see."

Alayne hung back, suddenly timid, but Fia snatched up his hands and kissed both cheeks. "Simon, you were wonderful, utterly inspiring!"

"Many thanks, Fia. Still, I hope you will both have the opportunity to see me in a full performance," he stated.

Alayne offered her hand sedately, but her eyes shone when she congratulated him. "When did the troupe employ you? You said nothing of this earlier."

"I sought them out yesterday evening, after a delightful stop along the Loch road. I decided it was time I began to earn some money, and what better place than here in Inverness?"

The dim glow of the street lamp hid Alayne's blush at his reference to the glen.

"Aye, what better place."

Fia was apprehensive. As long as he remained in Inverness, Simon would not be swayed from seeking Andrew Forbes. She did not speak of it, only vehemently hoped that between courting Alayne and earning a living, Simon would be too busy to continue his search.

The door to Jean MacNab's croft swung wide and Martin stood uneasily in the doorway studying the picture Jean made: flaming hair knotted loosely at the nape of her neck, flour mottling her arms as she kneaded dough. The whole way from the 'Rowan and Thistle', Martin tried to convince himself that Jean had done her worst for the best reason–she loved him. He had failed.

Jean glanced up and jumped at finding his narrow gaze focused on her. "Martin!" she exclaimed, heart thudding. She had both anticipated and dreaded the day she would see him again. It had been easy for her to discover that Martin's 'guest' had left soon after their encounter. And Jean also knew that Martin had left Inveraray, though unsure as to why. Now he was back; she hoped...prayed he had returned to her.

Despite Martin's dour expression, Jean chanced an alluring smile and, wiping her hands slowly on her apron, approached with the familiar, flouncing swing of her hips she always saved for him. Her fingers walked his chest until they met behind his neck. "You've been away too long– but you're here now, and I've missed you." Her lips sought his but he turned aside. Undeterred, she rested her hands on his chest. Martin's hands closed around her wrists.

"I think not, Jean." His severe tone foretold her fate.

She forced a lighthearted laugh. "What...what are you doing?" she asked, trying to shake free from his grip. "Let go of me,"

Martin freed her and she stumbled back a step. Panting her apprehension, Jean nervously smoothed her hair and summoned an indignant air. "Just what brings you to my door if not to enjoy me once again?"

Contempt rang in Martin's voice. "I've come to hear your confession, Jean."

The woman blanched but kept her voice even. "Since when did you become a priest?"

"The kirk no more condones a lie than the old church does."

Jean feigned surprise. "Lie? And what lie are you accusing me of telling?"

"Stalling will not help you, and it won't change what you did."

Blankly, Jean looked at him, reluctant to give up, eager to postpone the inevitable.

Martin's temper flared at her maddening silence. "You came to my croft after I told you not to, told you I would no longer see you, and lied to Fia Graham, told her that you and I were to marry."

"I did say that," she admitted with a lift of her chin. "What of it?" she added as if it was of no consequence.

Through clenched teeth, Martin gritted, "Why did you lie to her?"

"It wasn't a lie, my love. At the time, I fully intended to marry you," she explained.

"Jean, if you believed that after my last visit here, you sadly deluded yourself."

Stung from his rejection, Jean rebelled charging, "No, Martin, you're the one who suffers delusions. You talk as though you meant something to her. If that scrawny trollop wanted you as I want you, nothing I said would have kept her from you. Yet, she never challenged me; I'll wager she didn't think my visit important enough even to mention to you. And if, by chance, she did fancy you, she obviously didn't have the backbone to put up a fight. She left you. I fought for you, Martin; I want you, I love you. What are you to that simpering, skinny child whom you've mistaken for a real woman?"

Jaw tight, Martin retorted, "I was warned, but made a mistake coming to you. I thought I'd at least hear the truth if I asked you for it. I was wrong. Apparently, you are incapable of recognizing truth, Jean, at least when it interferes with your own desires. You've perverted what really happened to suit yourself. You may want me, Jean, but you don't love me. Your distorted defense of your actions proves that."

"I *do* love you, you *can't* doubt that," she pleaded, throwing her arms around him. "I battled for you, Martin, the only way I knew how. What else would you have me do?"

"Recognize the *truth*," he yelled, wrenching from her grasp. "Your motives don't justify what you did–the pain you have caused, not just to Fia or me, but to yourself by your refusal to accept the simple truth." Mouth set in a grim line, Martin moved to the door. "Goodbye, Jean. That's all that remains to be said."

"That...that can't be all, Martin, please. I...I'm *sorry*," she whined.

He stalked through the still open door, swung into Odhar's saddle and, with a sharp whistle to Arthur, didn't look back.

Before returning to the "Rowan and Thistle," Martin made the trek to his croft. Astride Odhar, he sat mutely staring at the dwelling, loneliness threatening to overwhelm him. For a moment, he imagined Fia standing at the door, laughing while he chased Arthur around the yard. When the vision became too painful, he dismounted and trudged inside, going straight to the trunk without looking right or left, refusing to allow his memories to goad him further.

Martin dug through the contents of the trunk and pulled out three additional pieces of cloth he'd woven. To Arthur, Martin absently commented, "I have no idea how long it will be before we return; still, I surely will need more money." Martin grimaced. He had only one cloth left after these were gone and each day that passed was one he did not work to support himself. There were no vegetables, nothing for the winter to come. Still, Martin hadn't a moment's doubt that he had chosen his course correctly. He had rediscovered the fulfillment of practicing medicine, gained a fine friend who gave him back his freedom and favored him with a new family. Martin's jittery hand covered his mouth and stroked the length of his beard. "And I saw Fia again," he murmured, her winsome image ripe in his mind's eye.

Emotion clogged his throat and Martin dropped the lid of the trunk, crammed the woolens under his arm and closed the door behind him.

"I must be losing my touch," Annie declared with an exasperated shake of her head. "You're not going to listen to me at all are you, lad?"

Martin protested, "Annie, it isn't that I've stopped taking your advice–"

"Tell me when you started," Annie declared with a snort.

"Simon is waiting for me. I've stayed these past two nights, talked myself out, and made all the repairs I could for you."

She cuffed his arm in mild displeasure. "You know, Martin, it's not because of the labor you do here that I don't want you to return to Inverness."

"Aye, I know that. You want me to remain here so that I won't be pained each time I see Fia." She nodded passionately. "Annie, I don't even know if she'll still be there when I return."

"And if she is, what good will it do you?" Annie demanded.

"None except that, if Andrew Forbes shows his face in Inverness, I'll be there to help protect her."

Annie implored, "She has a husband to protect her, Martin, don't run afoul of him; Fia could get hurt again–or you could."

The Borrowed Days

Martin tilted his head and studied her. "What do you mean 'Fia could get hurt again'?"

Annie swallowed hard and squeaked, "I...I thought you knew."

"Knew what?" his voice tightened.

"Murdoch Sinclair told me...told me she was badly beaten," she finished in a rush.

Martin dragged a harsh breath. "Who", he demanded rigidly, "who beat her?"

Her head shaking her denial, Annie said, "He didn't tell me, Martin," then blurted, "and I wish I hadn't told you! I've just made things worse."

Tears of fright pooled in Annie's eyes. When Martin saw them, he struggled to quell his outrage, hoping to ease her concern. "No, you haven't; you've just confirmed what I already sensed. Fia needs my protection. Her hus...Forbes can't or won't protect her."

Martin glanced over the choppy waters of Loch Fyne and back to his worried friend. "Now I've got to be on my way, Annie. I've caused Fia a great deal of misery; I will be as careful with her now as I know how to be. Regardless," Martin finished, "Simon needs my help, and I promised it to him."

Annie saw from the set of his jaw that the time for pleading was done; she could not stop his return north. Impulsively, she asked him to wait, flew into the inn and returned after a few short minutes with a bundle in her hands.

"What have you there?" Martin asked, curious.

Annie shook the material out into the shape of a greatcoat. "I noticed your coat is gone. It'll soon be too cold for you to go without something to cover you. This was my husband's and does no good folded in a trunk. Take it, lad, and please–*please*–promise me you'll take care of yourself."

Martin noted tears again glistening in her eyes and, gently removing the heavy nutmeg colored greatcoat from her clutch, he wrapped her in a grateful embrace. "Thank you, Annie. No one could ever want a finer friend than you." With a kiss to her cheek, Martin fastened the coat to Odhar's saddle, mounted and, with Arthur in step, began his journey back to Inverness.

Chapter Twenty-Four

The tiny corner of Glasgow visible from the Forbes' drawing room window revealed a drab landscape. Incessant rain transformed stone houses to the color of pitch, and turned the lane into a quagmire. By three days, Struan was overdue to return from London. Andrew didn't doubt that the weather caused the delay, still he chafed with impatience.

"What am I to do with my dear brother?" he muttered. Struan had become little more than an irritation. His laziness and penchant for the hunt and silly games incensed Andrew. If Struan were capable of recognizing that there were appropriate times for leisure, earned after some hard work, Andrew would have been more tolerant of his brother's foppishness. But Struan always preferred a romp and it surprised Andrew that his brother ever accomplished anything useful. "Can't put it off any longer," Andrew grumbled.

His back now turned to the panes, Andrew surveyed the familiar room, his gaze coming to rest on his mother's spinet. Since being spurned by the Grahams yesterday, Andrew had contemplated the predicament he was now in. How should he play his hand? Elizabeth was no longer with child, of that, he had convinced himself. Still, he had to proceed as though she were, at least until she confessed otherwise. Then, he would grieve with her over their loss. A snarl consumed Andrew's swarthy face.

"God in heaven," Struan declared from the doorway, "I believe Satan himself stands before me!"

Andrew's head snapped to his brother's voice. "What in Hell took you so long?" Andrew growled at the water-logged visage.

"Ah, I was right," Struan quipped sarcastically, dashing rain from his sleeves with gloved hands. "I missed you as well, dear Brother and, if you must know, I've been traveling mucky roads and fording swollen burns for days now. So, kindly be civil–my mood isn't gentle either." With that, he carelessly tossed his dripping coat over the chaise and headed for the brandy decanter. "What has you in such a swivet?" Struan asked, gulped the liquor and refilled his goblet.

"None of your business," responded Andrew with studied control.

"Then, I'll warrant it's the fair Elizabeth," Struan concluded before flopping his gaunt body into a chair.

Through gritted teeth, Andrew growled, "How Elizabeth fares does not concern you."

"Well, I pray you handle her better than you did Fia–what a mess you made of that."

Menacingly, his eyes narrowed and Andrew observed, "My, you are enjoying yourself greatly at my expense. Is there a particular reason for your foolhardiness, or are you just being your usual insipid self?"

Struan glared in return. "I was enjoying myself in London, immensely I might add. I did not appreciate being summoned back to Glasgow."

Andrew swept Struan's booted feet from the stool on which they rested. "Time for play is over, you leech," he snarled. "Even Graham works harder than you do and he's an old man. If you expect to share the profits from this venture, then pull your weight. You've had it too easy; your slothful days are finished."

Struan leapt to his feet, angrily sputtering, "Do you think my life has been easy living under your tyrannical thumb, being at your beck and call, never being given credit for any contribution I make? Except for mother, you've only cared about two things in your life–money and yourself."

"Stop whining, it makes you look like a weasel," Andrew advised, already tiring of his brother's tirade. "And stop being so self-righteous, it doesn't suit you."

"You're a boor and a brute," Struan accused, poking a finger at Andrew's chest, "a churlish lout. Why a woman like Elizabeth would give you a second nod, I'll never understand."

Faster than Struan could comprehend, Andrew had grasped the offending digit. "It's because I give her such intense pleasure, you sniveling runt," he replied, smiling, and snapped Struan's finger as though it were a twig.

Howling in agony, Struan lurched around the room, clutching his hand. His eyes flashed raw pain and hatred at Andrew. *"Why did you do that?"* he screeched.

In a long stride, Andrew came nose to nose with his whimpering sibling. "To remind you," he mocked, "just who you are. You seem to forget your place, Struan. The next time you jab me, I'll break them all."

Struan knew Andrew's promise was sincere—his throbbing finger left no doubt. At this moment, he wanted nothing more than to escape his brother's presence. "I need to have a physician set this bone," he half declared, half suggested.

"There will be time enough when we've finished talking," Andrew replied, nodding to the chair. "Take your seat."

Reluctantly, Struan sat, still clasping his hand, afraid that it would hurt more if he let go of it. "All right, Andrew," he submitted glumly, "what is it you need me to do?"

Silently, Andrew strolled to the window and back. "I should stay away from the north for a time."

"What happened?" Struan ventured.

"Let us say I was looking out for the business. Our first shipment is due shortly; you need to get to Inverness. I want you to oversee the first landing."

"What?" Struan gasped, momentarily forgetting his pain. "I've never supervised a landing, only seen two. Why now?"

"Don't be dull-witted. I've told you. I need to stay away, and you need to do some of the work. You must go to Inverness."

Struan protested, "But the landing is east of Inverness; you could easily take care of it."

"No, dear brother," Andrew hissed, "you get to share in the danger as well as the riches. You'll need to know the landing site like it was made for you: the shoreline and cave, and the routes to distribute the bounty. I'll provide you with the name of your contact in Inverness. Now, while you meditate on all that," he advised, shooting Struan a disgusted look, "go get your finger straightened out."

Struan's shock was so great that, for a long moment, he failed to move. Then, overwhelmed, he darted past his brother, forgetting his coat. From the stoop where Struan stood in the soaking rain, Andrew's derisive laughter reached through his fear and spurred him away.

From her room above the workshop, Alayne heard the door open and close. "Fia, I'm late," she called out. "Give me just a few minutes." She tugged a tangle through her rose gold hair and nearly dropped the comb when her visitor spoke.

"You aren't late, Alayne," Kate explained at the top of the stairs. "I left Fia at the house. She'll join us at the kirk for services."

Alayne whirled to face her. "You left Fia alone? Didn't she tell you about..." Her voice trailed off as she beheld Kate's sickly pallor, her spiritless eyes rimmed by sooty smudges.

"Tell me what?" Kate prompted feebly.

Alayne swiftly decided the woman could shoulder no more worry. "It can wait. Sit down, Kate, you look...tired."

Kate crossed the room and eased herself onto a chair. After a deep breath, she exclaimed, "You know why I've come."

"I hope I do," Alayne answered evasively.

"You...you may never find it in your heart to forgive me, Alayne. I've tried to place myself in your position, and I'm not sure I could be that generous." Kate's thoughts seemed to stray briefly before she roused herself to continue. "I had no right to strike you, no right to be envious of your closeness to Fia. After a great deal of soul searching," she said, palm pressed to her chest as though trying to grasp that soul, "I've concluded that I can no longer delude myself about my son. I may or may not have been able to influence the kind of man Muir grew to be but, the fact is," she choked, "he w...was a rogue, wicked; it is time for me to accept it." Her voice dissolved to a tremulous whisper, "Even if it tears me apart."

Alayne pulled the other chair close and perched on the edge. "I think it's a wise decision,

Kate. Each time you and I argue over Muir, it's a longer, more difficult road back for us. In your heart, you have always known of Muir's failings. Still, as his mother, I'm sure it has to be hard for you to accept." Kate nodded listlessly and Alayne took a bracing breath. "In November, I will ask for my freedom on the grounds of malicious desertion. Not knowing for certain whether Muir lives, I've no choice. I pray you will understand and support my decision but, support it or not, that is my intention. I wanted you to know."

Haunted eyes searched her daughter-in-law's, but Kate finally relented, "Of course, you must. It's the only sensible thing left to do, and it can't hurt me worse than my son's disappearance has." She stood slowly and smoothed her skirts. "Will you walk with me to the kirk?"

Alayne stood next to her. "I will. And, Kate," she said, "thank you."

Fia was relieved to see the two women together and after the service, they returned to Kate's home. The older woman kissed both her niece and daughter-in-law before dragging herself up the stairs to rest in her room.

Her eyes following her aunt, Fia murmured, "I'm sending for Douglas if she doesn't soon improve."

"Don't you think she will now that she and I have cleared the air between us?" Alayne frowned.

"I hope so, but she looks so worn. And you heard her coughing during the sermon."

"How long has she been doing that?" Alayne asked.

"Just since last night," Fia admitted. "I heard her after I returned from the theater."

"Well, Douglas can't cure her cough, but he could certainly lift her spirits." Alayne offered, "I'll send for him–just in case there is anyone paying attention to who corresponds with our Mr. Sutherland."

In the clearing canopied by birch and elm limbs, Elizabeth saw standing stones. Large rock cairns loomed before her, so massive, Elizabeth could not see over or around them. The sky was dark but held a strange greenish hue that made her quake. Fidgeting and glancing nervously about, she spied him. A man crouched by the yawning blackness that served as the opening into one of the cairns. She wanted to call his name–needed to warn him–but his name wouldn't come to her lips. Panic racing through her, Elizabeth stumbled into a run and, as she neared him, the coppery-brown of his long, loose hair and beard became clearer, and his face revealed intense, desperate eyes. Thunder roared at her back, heaving her body forward, pain blinding her just when she thought–

A jolt brought Elizabeth upright from the depth of her feather mattress. "That face," she gasped, "that man, how could it be? Martin Ross?" She leapt to the floor, taking the coverlet with her and wrapped it around her shaking body. To the window and back she paced. It was the same dream she'd had in June after Fia had run off, the day after she'd met Ross and decided him a fool. Why would he now appear in her dream when another man had been there before? Why was she so anxious to warn him? About what? And the thunder, the pain.... Impatiently, Elizabeth swiped strands of tousled hair from her face, confessing to herself what she knew instinctively–that the man in her dream had always been Martin Ross. Why, she couldn't say; it frightened and befuddled her.

The sound of her father's heavy tread on the stairs fought its way into her consciousness and Elizabeth threw the door open even as he raised his fist to knock.

Startled, George saw the distressed look on his daughter's face. He circled her shoulders with his arm. "Whatever is the matter, my dear, have you had a relapse?"

"No, Father," Elizabeth rasped, "only a bad dream."

"Can I help in any way?" he asked sympathetically.

She flashed him a shaky smile and assured, "No, thank you. I'll be fine in a bit. I...I just woke up."

George took her hand and led her to the window seat. "I came up to tell you that Andrew has sent a messenger to say that he intends to visit this morning." He noted a sour look cross her face and asked gently, "Shall I send word that you won't be receiving visitors today?"

She considered her father's question and her conviction that Andrew had caused her to lose the bairn. And she wondered again about the bizarre circumstance of her dream. Elizabeth began to feel the blood surging through her limbs, strength returning–not only to her body, but also to her mind. "Today, I'll see Andrew," she determined.

The hall clock had just completed its tenth strike of the chime when Andrew knocked. Una stood aside for him to enter, a brisk breeze whipping crumbling October leaves into the entryway behind him. "I'll take your hat, Sir and, if you'll wait in there, I'll fetch Miss Elizabeth."

Andrew relinquished his tricorne and sauntered into the drawing room Una had indicated, barely aware of the swishing of the maid's petticoat as she went to fetch her mistress. He wiped a bead of sweat from his upper lip, annoyed that any sign of his nervousness should manifest itself.

Before long, "Andrew, " Elizabeth welcomed in a pleasant tone.

He spun to her greeting. "Oh, my dearest," he declared, hastening to her side, lifting her fingers to his lips, "how marvelous to see you looking so much better. I feared when I last visited that you were far more indisposed than you or George let on."

"I was quite ill for a short time." Elizabeth smiled without warmth and eased her hand from his. "Sit, please. May I have Una fetch wine?"

"No, no," he protested, "I only want to see and speak with you. To hear from your sweet lips that you are truly recovered and that all is well."

Elizabeth squared her shoulders. "I am recovered, and your concern is most reassuring."

"And...?" he prompted tenuously.

"And all is not well, I fear." Elizabeth crossed to stand before the window and stared into the cobbled street. "Your son is no more." But then, she thought bitterly, he knew that already.

With what he determined was just the right amount of disbelief in his voice, Andrew protested, "N...no. I...I didn't hear you correctly." He waited a moment in her silence then stepped quickly behind her and, with hands on her shoulders, spun her to face him. "Tell me I didn't hear you correctly. Our son...our son...gone?"

Elizabeth gaped in fascination, never having realized how cold his pale eyes were; their blue reminded her of ice–like the blood in his veins. "It was a boy, and I lost him shortly after you left on your last trip. That's why I've been ill."

Andrew shoved the knuckles of both meaty fists against his mouth and raised a stricken look to her detached one. In a fluid movement, his arms were around her, cradling her to him, rocking her. "Oh, my darling, how you've suffered. It's no wonder you had little tolerance for me when I last visited. I was far away when you needed me the most."

"It's just as well you weren't here, Andrew. I would have been unhappy to have you see me writhing in agony as I fought to keep our son." She left him to sit.

He found her description to be repulsive. However, Andrew kept his expression appropriately sorrowful. "How did you survive this alone? I mean with just your maid."

Momentarily, Elizabeth's gaze narrowed. "What an interesting question...how did I survive... alone. Truth be told, I didn't. Una wasn't here though; I was tended by a doctor and his assistant."

"Doctor?" Andrew queried, swallowing with difficulty. "What doctor?"

"You don't know him. He did his best."

"How fortunate he was here to care for you. Was he able to tell you why...why this happened?"

Elizabeth studied her lover's face. "You look pallid, Andrew. Is it the shock, do you think?"

Andrew flailed his arms and yelped, "Of course I'm in shock! I believed I was to be a father; we were to share a child. Elizabeth, I wanted that more than anything."

She watched his performance with growing impatience. How dare he profess desire to be father to the bairn? "Food or drink," she announced.

"What?"

"Food or drink...that was the doctor's diagnosis as to what caused the miscarriage–tainted food or drink."

Andrew paced. "Preposterous. How could that be? Your 'doctor' obviously didn't know what he was talking about." Andrew turned on her. "Who was this doctor that I would not know him?"

"A friend of the family and you don't know him," she repeated.

Andrew did not like the turn this conversation had taken. Elizabeth was too close to the truth. A cutting fear surfaced that, if he didn't distract her quickly with some mighty gesture, she might guess his role in her loss after all. He turned and fell to his knees before her, surprising her.

"Elizabeth," he entreated, "I came here today with one intention. The grievous fact that our child has been lost will not deter me." His large hands engulfed her delicate ones. "Marry me, Elizabeth. We were put on this earth to bring joy into each other's lives, and to see each other through our misfortunes. I will not let you endure another calamity, no matter how vast or even how trivial, without me." His hands squeezed hers. "Say you'll be my wife."

Elizabeth noted the ardent tone of his plea, but it did not mask the lack of emotion in those cold eyes, eyes that she realized mirrored her own. Slowly, a semblance of a smile creased her mouth. "Indeed, Andrew, I will marry you."

He was inordinately pleased with himself. Andrew knew he could postpone the actual wedding indefinitely but, she had accepted him. Elizabeth believed him innocent of all wrongdoing–she must or she would have rejected his proposal outright. He stifled a chuckle and puffed out his deep chest, "I couldn't be more gratified, my sweet."

The sitting room had grown too small. Alayne circled it once again, chafing her hands in discontent and impatience. "Momentous," she determined, "is the word that describes this Sabbath." Early in the day, there had been Kate's visit and her glum declaration that, at long last, she accepted Muir for what he was, though Alayne would have chosen stronger words to describe her husband than 'wicked' and 'rogue'. Then, not half an hour ago, Alayne had penned a note to Douglas Sutherland asking him to come to Inverness. Briefly, her lips curled in pleasant memory. Alayne liked Douglas for his good sense, his easy way of commanding a situation, and the twinkle that often tweaked his soulful eyes.

Now, Alayne needed to do something for herself. Without further thought, she crossed to the trunk that held the men's clothing she dressed in to visit the quay-side taverns. "Only a few weeks more," she whispered, belly churning, unsure what awaited her when she left the shop. Quickly, she dressed, descended the stairs, snuffed the candle and closed the workroom door behind her, locking it securely. Before reaching High Street, she stooped and smeared dirt on her face and the backs of her hands, then was on her way.

Alayne breathed deep the bracing breeze and pondered the night before. Her chest swelled when she remembered Simon's flawless performance. Her enchantment with him had spiraled when he readily agreed to help ensure Fia's safety from the mysterious stranger. And when Simon had parted from her at the shop to walk Fia home, his proper bow over Alayne's hand had become an exquisitely intimate moment between them when, in the dark, Simon had turned her palm up and pressed his warm lips against her flesh. Memories of his lips elsewhere on her body flooded her with heated pleasure and quickened her heartbeat in a way that she hadn't experienced except with him. Clearing her thoughts, Alayne made her way cautiously toward the waterfront taverns.

Down by the quay, dampness seeped into the air and her teeth began to chatter. The dank smell of lines and furled sails was unusually disagreeable and Alayne hesitated before the entrance to the first tavern she reached. "This doesn't feel right," she confessed uneasily and, without hesitation, decided to return home. She whirled, so deep in her own thoughts that she failed to hear the boisterous gang of men approaching from behind. They paid no heed to the slight lad in their path and, like a wave, carried Alayne inside and deposited her, unceremoniously, next to a crude bar.

Swiftly, Alayne straightened her cap over her hair and eased from the bar, seeking a more obscure spot from which to view the crowded room. But, if she hoped to remain unnoticed, Alayne's good fortune had deserted her.

"Will you order, lad, or stand like a trapped hare, shaking in the corner?"

Alayne's head snapped to the gruff voice of the man who leaned toward her over the rough, scarred planks upon which he served his customers. His pendulous belly was barely contained behind a dingy apron; his stubbly chin glistened with sweat. Alayne realized with a sinking heart that, in her hasty departure from the shop, she had forgotten to bring a few coins. Normally, she would easily bluff her way out of this, but her confidence was shaken; Fia's warning that she could get into deep trouble repeated in her mind.

"Well?" the man barked impatiently and belched.

"S...sir," she tremulously responded, "I was only looking for my brother. Mam would skin me if she knew I took a drink."

The man squinted suspiciously. "Your mam, huh? Why does she send you down here at all if she worries so about you?"

"My brother, Sir, she wants me to find him and bring him home."

"What's this brother of yours look like?"

Alayne felt her composure returning and took a small step forward. "Tall," she said, "thin, blond, smooth face and blue eyes. He's twenty-four."

"Aren't you forgetting something?"

Eyes darting around the room, Alayne brought her gaze back to him. "Like what?"

"His name, laddie, what's your brother's name?"

"Oh," she breathed relief. "Muir, his name is Muir."

Unexpectedly, the man turned toward the rest of the taproom and called out, "Anyone here seen a thin, yellow-haired fellow named Muir?"

Alayne, tried to back into her spot away from the bar but, like a flash, the lumpish man grabbed her arm making her wince. This was not the kind of attention she wanted. Always before, she had managed to make her inquiries without bringing undue notice to herself. Now she felt half the patrons staring at her. With all her might she tried to wrench her arm from the oaf's grasp, but without success.

"This lad here is looking for his brother. His mam sent him." His head tipped back in a gap-toothed cackle and several nearby men joined him. One approached Alayne on unsteady legs, and taking her face roughly in one massive paw, tilted it so she looked into his.

"You're a sweet looking lad," he declared in breath stinking of whiskey and stale tobacco. "Do you l...look like your mam, without a woman's tender parts of course?"

Alayne twisted her chin from his grip. "I favor my father," she spat.

"Pity," said the man, rubbing his bleary eyes, "for I would have you take me to your mam, so I could take her mind off her lost son." He rubbed his groin hard, leaving no doubt as to his meaning and, sickened, Alayne fought rising panic.

"Have you seen my brother?" she demanded.

He pitched toward her, barely catching himself with a hand on his friend's shoulder. "Never," he vowed and threw his arm around Alayne's neck. Alayne tried to back away from him but he staggered along, hold never slackening. "You *are* a pretty lad. Perhaps you'd be more interested than your mam in keeping me company for a bit." The man's companions guffawed and their din made Alayne tremble.

"*Alan!*" came a sharp call and, dumbly, Alayne watched as Simon elbowed his way through the small crowd surrounding her. "How many times have I told you, no matter what Mam asks, never, *never* come to the quay alone. See the mess you're in now?"

Nearly swooning with relief, Alayne recognized Simon's very real apprehension. Dutifully, she hung her head. "I'm sorry, I was just doing as I was told."

"Say, lad, who is this?" the man behind the bar asked.

"Can't be the lad's brother," drunk sniggered. "He said 'tall'."

"To a younger brother, I am tall." Simon explained patiently, but not so patiently returned the drunkard's shove, at the same time extricating Alayne from the lecher's grip. "The lad meant no harm; I'll take him home now." Simon thrust Alayne in front of him and tossed a coin onto the bar. "Buy him a consolation drink," he instructed and kept moving.

Alayne was afraid to look back once Simon had pushed her out the door. She was grateful to be leaving the wretched place, but feared seeing condemnation on her rescuer's face. To their good fortune, the reeking drunk was too indisposed to give chase; he only stumbled over a choice curse.

Outside, Alayne stopped in relief, but Simon placed his palm between her shoulder blades and forced her to fall into step. Well away from the quay, he had said nothing. She tried to steal a glance at him, but the darkness prevented her reading his expression. Nearer the shop, the silence had grown ominous and Alayne began to fear the worst until, with a jolt, she realized his body shook. He was *laughing* at her! Anger and embarrassment flared and she twisted away from him. "Just what do you think you're doing, hustling me through the streets like this?" she accused.

"We won't talk here," Simon ordered.

Alayne thrust her finger toward the ground and demanded, "Here!"

Simon ignored her and marched the remaining distance to the back entrance of the shop giving Alayne no choice but to follow. When she grudgingly caught up to him, he said, "In there."

"What arrogance," she silently fumed, unlocking the door. Before she could speak again, Simon passed her and knelt at the hearth to stir the embers into a small flame. Cross-legged, he sat before the pitiful blaze and stared into it.

Confused by his odd behavior, Alayne closed and latched the door, tossed her cap and coat aside and stood uncertainly at arm's length from Simon. Finally, she mustered enough indignity to charge, "What was it you thought so funny?"

Slowly, Simon shook his head. "Nothing," he murmured, and in a stronger voice repeated, "nothing." Suddenly he turned pained, angry eyes to her. "How dare you?" he exclaimed.

"M...me?" Alayne sputtered aghast. "What do you mean–"

"How dare you put yourself in danger for that mangy bastard you call a husband? Don't you know that any one of those men could have–would have gladly eaten you alive?"

Belatedly, the thought seeped in that rage, not mirth had caused the quaking Alayne had discerned in him. "I...I was looking for evidence that Muir–"

"Not *good* enough!" Simon shouted, cutting her off. He lunged to his feet, glaring at her. "Simon, I–"

"To risk your very life, Alayne–for what?"

Alayne began to bristle. "I'd have been all right," she defended. "It's not the first time I've been there."

"Oh, I've no doubt you've done this before, you're so headstrong. But this time it would have ended badly. If I hadn't been there–"

"Is that what this is about?" she cried. "If you hadn't been there to step in and save me–"

"That's not the point," Simon ground his fist into his palm. "Alayne, you only have days to go–days out of four years. What made you go to the tavern tonight? Why now? You're so close!"

Hands clenched before her, Alayne said, "I doubt you'd understand."

"I'm willing to listen," he promised bluntly.

"Kate came today and apologized. She said she's ready to accept that Muir is gone and that she will not stand in the way of my action to dissolve the marriage. It was such a significant turnaround I...felt as though I owed myself one last search for anyone who might know something." She gulped and averted her gaze. "When I got there, things felt...wrong," she admitted. "I was about to go home when those men shoved me through the en–"

Simon smothered her words with his mouth, hard and desperate against hers and Alayne stood stupefied in his arms. Finally, he tore his lips from hers to bury his face in her flowing hair. "Don't ever," he panted, "risk yourself like that again. I will ask anyone whatever you wish. But nothing bad should ever happen to you again on account of Muir Matheson." He held her face in his hands. "Tell me you agree–promise me, please, Alayne."

His eyes glistened with unshed tears and she gently stroked his golden curls, searching his face in wonder. "You were truly afraid," she whispered.

"Promise me," he answered, clutching her ever tighter.

"I promise." Alayne rested her cheek against his and felt his body trembling once more. She found herself trying to blink back her own tears. With his thumb, he gently wiped the tear that tracked through the grime on her cheek. "Only days," he whispered, a small smile tugging his mouth.

She grasped his hand and kissed it. "Forgive me, Simon, and thank you for being there when I needed you."

"I'll always try to be." It was hard to tear himself away from her warmth, but Simon knew if he stayed longer, he would have difficulty resisting her nearness. "It's best I go now."

Alayne nodded. "Will I see you soon?"

"You tell me when and where."

Bones rattling in the chill, Struan hugged himself to stave off the cold, and swayed awkwardly from side to side on the back of his plodding horse. "Why should Andrew have the right to decide how I live my life?" he groused, remembering the 'talk' the two of them had just prior to his departure for Inverness.

The Borrowed Days

"Seek out Thomas Gray when you arrive. Inevitably, you'll find him in some tavern on the quay. The old man's a sot," Andrew had said, "but trustworthy. He'll give you the routes and tell you who will pack out the goods and the timing of the tides so that the unloading can be safely done. He'll also arrange a decoy–just in case troops or excise men are spotted." Andrew cut Struan a disdainful look. "I suppose you can find your way to Fia's strand?"

"I can," Struan shot back and reminded, "I scouted it for you the first time."

"Ah, so you did," Andrew smirked.

Struan's mount staggered and Struan kept his seat only with great difficulty and much cursing. Supremely annoyed, Struan swatted the horse's muscular neck and conjured the image of Andrew's irksome countenance once more. "Always, Andrew demeans me," Struan griped, kicking his steed into a half-hearted trot, "and I'm damned tired of it."

232

Chapter Twenty-Five

Alayne seemed to float through the millinery in a euphoric trance that Fia envied. She didn't doubt Simon was the cause of that blissful mood and it was plain that her early reservations had not kept Alayne from growing closer to him. Who could blame her? Simon was the opposite of all she'd heard about Muir. And there was no doubt in Fia's mind that he was more than smitten with her friend.

"You're staring at me, Fia," Alayne pointed out good-naturedly.

With a start, Fia assured, "I didn't intend to; I'm pleased to see you looking so...pleased."

Alayne chuckled. "Do I?"

Fia nodded. "May I attribute some of that to Simon?"

Dreamily, Alayne replied, "He cares what happens to me, Fia, truly cares."

Somewhat surprised, Fia asked, "Didn't you already know that?"

Alayne rearranged some sachets in a china bowl on the display counter, taking the time to breathe deeply of the top two. "I conveniently made myself deny it...until last night."

"Last night?"

"Aye." Alayne turned sparkling eyes on her companion. "He came to my rescue down at the tavern—"

"Oh, Alayne," Fia interrupted brusquely, "you went searching for Muir last night?"

"I did. And your prediction was beginning to come true; a very insistent drunkard was getting too friendly. But, Simon was there to help me." She glanced at the floor and added dutifully, "He was furious with me".

"I'm not surprised; he should be."

Impulsively, Alayne scooped Fia's hands between her own. "I scared him, Fia, because it could have ended very badly for me and he was livid that I was searching for Muir at all so close to my bid for freedom. He made me promise not to do it again."

"Well, I hope you keep your promise to Simon. Obviously you didn't listen when I advised you not to do it again." Fia chided.

Alayne looked sheepish. "You're cross because I didn't heed your advice."

"I am. What if Simon hadn't been there? I've told you, the thought of you alone on the quay scares me nearly to death." Fia took a calming breath and added, "I'm very grateful he was and that you're safe." She withdrew her hands, picked up her embroidery needle, and changed the subject. "I should be able to finish decorating Mairi's gown by tomorrow."

"I should have taken your advice to heart," Alayne apologized. "And I'm sorry if I've run on about Simon."

"You should never apologize for that. I couldn't be happier that the two of you are drawn to each other. Remember, I'm the one who urged you to give him a chance." Belatedly, it dawned on Fia that her lack of enthusiasm was giving her friend the wrong impression. She lay down the threads and smiled meekly. "I'm the one who should beg your pardon for being so dour. I'm just a bit cross this morning. Truly Alayne, no one deserves to be happy more than you. And you know how I feel about Simon."

"There's nothing to forgive," Alayne swore. "And you deserve to be happy, too."

Fia forced a smile and went on with her work.

When Alayne and Fia parted that evening at Kate's, Fia realized her head had begun to ache and she felt restless and apprehensive. She looked forward to the distraction of dinner with her aunt, but was disappointed when Kate came down for supper and spoke scarcely a handful of words to her.

"Aunt Kate," Fia probed, "are you feeling better today?"

Kate cast an impervious look. "I'm fine, why?"

"You're very quiet. I thought after you and Alayne settled your differences–"

"Is that what we did?" she snapped peevishly.

"I...I thought so," Fia stammered.

"You thought wrong. I gave in."

"Aunt Kate, I don't under–"

"I'm going to my room, Fia," Kate cut her off, rising in the same moment.

Stunned, Fia sat unmoving for some time, wondering what offense she'd committed for her aunt to treat her as she might an unwelcome stranger. That night, she slept badly, the pang of Kate's rebuke eating at her, and thoughts of Martin with Jean nearly impossible to banish.

A nearly steady stream of customers wandered in and out of the millinery Tuesday morning, but Alayne's attention was often on Fia who scarcely spoke, didn't smile. In the early afternoon, the shop was quiet and, in that quiet, Fia found herself fighting a moroseness clinging to her like a shroud. When Kate entered the shop in the late afternoon for a brief visit, Fia's mood did not lighten.

"Did the rose silk arrive from Paris?" Kate inquired, abruptly.

"Yesterday, Aunt Kate," Fia responded, snipping several loose threads. Carefully, she smoothed the completed open robe over the dress form.

Kate stood before it. "Is that Mairi MacLaren's wedding gown?"

"Not anymore," Fia replied dully, "it's just a dress."

Alayne objected, "It's still her wedding gown–and Fia has just finished it."

"Well, on that last point, I assume you two agree," Kate declared caustically. Into their silence, she grilled, "Where is the silk? I'd like to inspect it."

"I'll fetch it," Fia offered.

Alayne turned eagerly from the older woman's moodiness, and knelt to open a cupboard she rarely had need to enter.

"Kate, where did these come from?" She extracted two plaids and held them for her mother-in-law's identification.

"I bought them a short time back," replied Kate, relaxing slightly. "Pretty, aren't they?"

Alayne fingered the soft, colorful plaids and marveled, "They're exquisitely made, but not what we normally stock."

"I agree. But, I was so impressed when I saw them, I had to purchase them."

"Why do you have them stored away like this?" Alayne puzzled.

With a shrug, Kate answered, "I'd hoped to find some special use for them at some point."

"Fia, come see these," Alayne called and, to Kate, asked, "Where did you buy them?"

"Right here," Kate responded. "A man came into the shop with them under his arm." Kate relieved Fia of the bolt of silk and continued, "The man who sold them to me accompanied Mr. MacLaren that first day he came to the shop looking for you."

Alayne's head turned to Fia who, saying nothing, stretched a tentative hand past Kate. Alayne relinquished the cloths and Fia clutched them protectively, as if they were woven of gossamer.

Kate's confused expression prompted Alayne to ask, "A copper-haired, bearded fellow with a resonant voice?"

"You...describe him as though you know him," Kate pondered suspiciously.

Alayne nodded. "That was Fia's Martin."

Astounded, Kate demanded of her niece, "Your Martin?"

At last finding her voice, Fia quietly corrected, "Not mine." The woolens now clutched against her breast, Fia slowly passed through the curtains into the workroom and sank onto a stool by the hearth. She stared at the plaids, caressing their softness over and over. Her finger traced the blocks and rectangles of color that created their patterns. Before it dropped from her chin, Fia caught a slow tear and winced, her belly twisting at the memory of fashioning Martin's shirt. She hadn't wanted to cry on that cloth either.

The urge to wrap herself in Martin's plaids nearly overwhelmed her. Wouldn't their warmth be akin to the warmth of his embrace? Could the strength of his weave equal that of his arms? And the feel of the wool would surely give comfort. But could it compare to the exquisite touch of Martin's skin on her own? Fia strangled a cry as more memories crowded round: waking on the floor in his arms; sharing a desperate embrace during the snowy night when emotions hung thick and were denied; his tender kiss to her palm.

Fia's blood pulsed heatedly through her; she raged at the unbidden rush of passion. "Why can't I just leave Martin to his wife and forget him?"she railed silently. Suddenly, the woolens no longer gave solace–they stung. The images they evoked were too hurtful. She dropped the offending cloths, grabbed her mantle, and rushed into the raw autumn dusk.

Fia was glad the weather was harsh for it matched her turmoil. The wind bit her face and chafed her hands as she gripped the mantle about her. With no place to go, Fia haunted the streets, up and down, past the Market green, deserted today, awaiting the bustle tomorrow when vendors would be plentiful. The bridges appeared and disappeared: the castle ruins, the kirk, the Cathedral. Then the theater loomed before her and Fia stumbled to a halt. Her eyes searched the unadorned facade; she wondered where Simon was? Against bitter tears, Fia squeezed shut her eyes. Now, even Simon reminded her of Martin, and Fia knew that his loyalty would be to his cousin, not to their own brief friendship. "As it should be," her numbed mind conceded. Fia felt once more the crushing weight of being alone. Martin had Jean and Simon; Simon and Alayne had each other. Aunt Kate had grown distant and, when Douglas arrived, it would be to see to Kate's needs–that's why they'd sent for him. There would be no time for her disappointments, her futile longings. Fia's shoulders sagged despairingly, and she moved on, oblivious that some-one called to her. She trudged only a short distance farther when a hand on her elbow startled her so she yelped, jerked away, and clamped her hands to her mouth before recognizing Simon.

Alarmed, he apologized profusely, "My God, Fia, I didn't mean to frighten you so!" Simon swiftly noted her distress. "Something is dreadfully wrong; what is it? How can I help?"

"You can't," she responded with a terse shake of her head. Fia turned to leave, but Simon stopped her.

"Wait a moment," he urged, "you aren't supposed to go about alone, yet here you are. Now something has driven you out. Please, tell me what troubles you."

Fia glared past his vibrant blue eyes and concerned expression, then offered a stiff, contrite smile. "Feeling sorry for myself, if you must know."

Simon's brows drew down in bewilderment. "I find that hard to believe."

"Believe what you'd like; it's of no consequence."

"Why would you say that?" he asked.

"Because it's true."

Simon rubbed his neck and pondered what could have put Fia in this perverse mood, quite unlike her from his experience. "Does Alayne know where you are, does your aunt?"

She would not look at him.

"They'll be very worried," he declared, sure he could count on her desire not to want to upset those she loved.

"I'm not ready to go back," Fia stubbornly stated and tugged at the neck of her mantle as though it choked her.

"Then, may I send word that you're with me? You can stay in the theater, watch the perfor-mance if you'd like. I'll take you home later," he added carefully, "when you're ready." She appeared to be struggling inwardly and, though Simon feared she might bolt, he stepped forward and wrapped her in a concerned embrace.

Unyielding and tense in his arms, Fia found her tumultuous emotions finally touched by his silent strength. She inched her arms around his back, holding tightly, saying nothing more.

Alayne pressed a coin into the lad's palm and swung shut the door, Simon's note clutched in her fist. Immediately after Fia had entered the workroom, customers had arrived at the shop; Kate had gone home. Left alone to serve her clients, Alayne fumed at Kate's lack of sensitivity to Fia's distress. By the time Alayne had more than a moment to check, Fia had disappeared; Martin's cloths on the floor wrenched Alayne with worry; she scooped them up and put them back where she'd found them. For the next two hours, Alayne frantically paced the shop, loath to leave in search of her friend, sure that it would be worse if Fia returned and the millinery was empty. Thank God Simon's note arrived when it did. It brought Alayne a small measure of relief–along with additional anxiety. "Fia safe at the theater," it had read. "But I'm concerned. She won't talk to me. I'll bring her home when she's ready. Simon."

Unwilling to wait and intent on going to Fia, Alayne closed the shop and snatched up her mantle just as another knock sounded at the workroom door. She marched to answer it, annoyed at the interruption to her plan. Alayne lifted the latch and there, in the whipping wind, stood Martin Ross.

Her surprise obvious, Alayne stuttered, "Wh...what may I do for you, Dr. Ross?"

Martin noted apologetically, "You're just leaving, I'll not keep you. I was looking for Simon, he...he's not where I expected to meet him. I thought perhaps you might know–"

"I do. Come with me," she ordered, recovering her composure and stepping into the night with him.

"Where are we headed?" Martin asked.

"To the theater," Alayne answered. "Simon has gotten a job during your absence."

"That's good news; he said he might." To make conversation, he added, "I've never seen him on stage."

Alayne set a brisk pace and Martin fell into step at her side, Arthur at his. "You might get your chance sooner than you think. But there's a more important reason to go to the theater this evening." Alayne's step faltered and she cut him a sharp look, remembering the contents of Simon's note. Alayne stopped suddenly and glared at Martin. "It's you," she accused.

Martin turned a wary eye on her. "I don't understand, Mistress."

"Fia won't talk to Simon because of you," returned Alayne.

"Forgive me, I still don't–"

"Fia," Alayne broke in brusquely, "is with Simon. I found the plaids you sold Kate. When Fia saw them, she ran off. Simon found her but says she won't talk to him. She's fond of Simon, values his friendship. But he's your cousin." Alayne pressed her palms to her temples. "Why am I taking you to her? You'll only cause her more misery."

Martin's voice thickened with remorse. "I'm the only one who can help her," he stressed, "because I'm the cause of so much of her grief. Please," he implored, "let me come with you. If you don't, I'll follow anyway."

Alayne had been moved by the anguish she'd seen on Martin's face the day he'd spoken with Fia at the shop. And now, beholding his near-tortured expression, she quaked. "There is something terribly, terribly wrong here," she swore, "that the two of you should need each other so desperately and not discover it until too late."

"I'm begging you," he repeated in a strained whisper.

"Come," she resolved, "we're wasting time." The two did not speak again until they entered the theater where the performance was about to begin.

"Is it too late to search backstage for Simon?" Martin entreated.

"Aye," Alayne responded, "let's look for seats up front. If Fia is in the audience, we should be able to spot her."

Martin followed Alayne forward, all the while looking right and left, while Alayne craned her neck to peer into the boxes above. Seeing nothing, they squeezed onto a crowded bench and sat uneasily on its edge, their gazes continuing to roam the hall.

Simon appeared on stage in his garish make-up and Martin gaped at the sight of him. Once more, Simon intoned a welcome to the patrons and recited the prologue to "The Beaux' Stratagem". While his eyes adjusted to the light, Simon could not see past the edge of the stage. It was upon his arrival prior to Act Two that he spied Alayne, and nearly forgot his lines when he recognized Martin sitting at her side. He could do nothing until his next interlude on stage and, for that, he chose a purposeful passage from Macbeth:

> "Foul whisp'rings are abroad. Unnatural deeds
> Do breed unnatural troubles. Infected minds
> To their deaf pillows will discharge their secrets.
> More needs she the divine than the physician.
> God, God forgive us all! Look after her;
>
> Remove from her the means of all annoyance,
> And still keep eyes upon her. So good night.
> My mind she has mated, and amazed my sight.
> I think, but dare not speak."

Simon's glance toward the box closest to the stage was followed by the anxious stares of Martin and Alayne. As the play dragged on, the shadows in the box separated into vague shapes and there, pressed deep into the corner most hidden from view, was a woman. Martin started to rise, but Alayne clamped a hand on his arm, pulled him down with all her strength and whispered severely, "No! Your presence will be enough of a shock; I won't have you barging into the balcony unannounced."

Martin squirmed under her restraint, but held his peace. If Fia were truly distressed, he–more than anyone–had to use caution. Chest heaving, he glared unseeing at the actors before him and laced his fingers tightly with Alayne's.

The move startled Alayne. She stole a look at him and was nearly overcome by his misery. With hope of reassurance, she squeezed his hand and cast him a slim smile."We'll take care of her, Martin, I promise."

He could not respond except with a stiff nod. The words Simon had spoken came back to him. "More needs she the divine than the physician...Remove from her the means of all annoyance, And still keep eyes upon her...." Was he being literal, telling Martin to stay away from her? That God was her only comfort now? "When will this cursed play end?" he spat and, again, felt the sustaining pressure of Alayne's fingers.

Before the curtain call, Alayne elbowed through the crowd to the narrow stairs that led to the balcony boxes, Martin close on her heels. As they fought their way up the steps, the pair drew annoyed oaths from the people descending. Near the box where Fia sat, Simon hurriedly appeared, still in full make-up, finger pressed to his lips. He motioned them out of hearing distance, grasped Martin's hand in quick greeting and, in the now deserted passageway, openly kissed Alayne.

"You got my message," he spoke in a low voice.

"How is..." both Martin and Alayne began, then stopped and glanced self-consciously at each other.

But Simon had his own questions. "What happened to her? Did she see you earlier?" he asked Martin, almost accusingly.

"No," Martin assured firmly.

Quickly, Alayne explained, "Martin arrived just after your note did. Simon, Fia's not been herself since yesterday: distracted, silent and feeling...I'm not sure what," she admitted her muddle. "Then she saw some cloth which Martin made and sold to Kate, and fled." She grasped Simon's hand. "I was so relieved to get your note, Simon; I had no idea where she'd gone."

He sighed heavily. "She's waiting for me to take off this paint and come get her." To Martin, he said, "I don't know what seeing you will do to her."

Alayne searched her bag and extracted the key to the shop. She held it up to Martin. "I'm going to her; you go back to the shop and wait."

His first instinct was to argue; he wanted to see Fia now. Instead, Martin choked, "Are you sure you trust me to see her at all?"

"I don't really know you, so how can I trust you?" Alayne declared. "But Simon says you love Fia; I trust him."

Martin took the key and, in an instant, had disappeared.

Simon stared at Alayne. "Thank you for your faith in me; it isn't misplaced."

Alayne squeezed his hand, relieved that Fia was safe, but anxious about her state of mind. She scrutinized his face. "You had better hurry and take off that make-up. I'll wait with Fia."

Simon bounded away to do her bidding, and Alayne brushed aside the curtain covering the opening to the box and stepped in. "Fia?"

After a moment, Fia quietly responded, "I've caused you to worry; I'm sorry."

Alayne pulled up a wooden chair and sat facing her friend. "Aye, I was worried sick. That isn't important now, but you are. Will you tell what made you disappear that way? I know seeing those woolens must have brought painful memories, still, I can't help but feel it's more than that."

"Memories...remorse and regrets." She drew a ragged breath and spoke quietly. "All this time, I've tried hard not to brood over Martin so that I could get through each day. I didn't want my unhappiness to become a burden to others."

Alayne protested, "Fia, you aren't a bur–"

"You'd never tell me if I was," she interrupted glancing at her friend, "and I thank you for it. The point is, Alayne, I couldn't fight it anymore. I feel empty except for the loneliness and envy that torment me. I've been sitting here thinking about the kindness and friendship you and others have shown me–like what Simon did for me today. I'm so ashamed of my actions." Fia's head drooped from exhaustion.

Alayne wrapped an arm around her shoulders. "Fia, you've been brave for months now, trying to hide your feelings and your disappointment, but you don't have to bear it alone."

"That's why we're here," Simon assured from the doorway.

Fia looked up, reached for his hand and said, "Thank you for taking me in, Simon."

"Friends do no less for each other, lass." He brushed hair from her face. "Are you a bit better now?"

Fia nodded and swiped the back of her hand under her drippy nose. "A bit, aye. This dark corner has been a haven."

Over Fia's head, Simon and Alayne exchanged a worried look. Simon knelt before her. "There's something you need to know," he began.

"What's that?" Fia sniffed.

"Alayne didn't come to the theater alone tonight, lass," Simon spoke gently, "Martin came too."

Fia's hands clutched her belly in a vain attempt to still its sudden, violent lurch.

Hurriedly, Alayne added, "He desperately wanted to come to you here; Simon and I thought better of it though."

Fia's voice was barely audible. "Where is he now?"

"I gave him my key to the shop," Alayne responded and flinched when Fia leapt from her seat, toppling her chair.

"Take me home," Fia implored, wringing her hands. "I can't...can't see–"

"Of course, we'll take you straight to your aunt's," Simon interrupted. "Right now."

He wrapped Fia's mantle around her and escorted the two women out into the near-deserted street. They held tightly to their wraps and to each other against the cold, gusting wind. In unspoken agreement, they skirted the millinery and arrived at Kate's door, teeth chattering, noses and cheeks blushed with the cold. On the stoop, Alayne said, "I'll be in shortly, Fia."

"You're staying the night?" Fia asked and, to Alayne's nod, Fia turned to Simon and pressed one hand against his cheek. "I'm blessed to have you as my friend," she vowed and disappeared beyond the door.

Alayne stepped closer to Simon. "I don't want to leave her."

"Of course not," Simon agreed. "I'll go to Martin."

"And what will you tell him?" she inquired with a frown.

Simon looked surprised. "The truth; Fia couldn't bear to see him now." His brows drew together. "He'll take it hard, but he'll want what's best for her. Shall I bring your key in the morning?"

Alayne laid a hand on his arm. "Anytime tomorrow is fine."

His gaze lingered on her face and softened with affection. "Are you sure, lass?"

"I'm quite sure." A smirk played the corner of her mouth. "Only don't tell my mother-in-law I gave you the key."

Inside, Alayne found Fia in her room facing the cold hearth. In silence, Alayne lit the peat fire and invited her friend to come closer.

Fia's feet were leaden. Still, she dragged herself over and sank to the floor, dropping her mantle where she sat and, after a long moment, Fia offered, "You don't need to stay with me, Alayne."

"I don't mind."

"But I'll be fine," Fia insisted half-heartedly.

"Aye, you will," Alayne agreed, "but probably not tonight."

Tears slid down Fia's cheeks and she doggedly wiped them away. "Why is he back?"

Alayne shrugged. "I only know Martin came to the shop looking for Simon...and he was very upset when I told him what caused you to disappear. Do you know what you'll do when he asks to see you? He will, you know," Alayne predicted.

"He shouldn't...he has a wife. It just wouldn't make sense," Fia argued. "His return has nothing to do with me."

"My guess is that it has almost everything to do with you," declared Alayne. "I think you know it."

Fia's shaky hands lifted heavy curls from her neck, giving her a moment to think. Finally, she nodded. "About what I will say, truthfully, I don't know. If the time comes–"

"When the time comes," Alayne interjected.

"All right, *when* the time comes that Martin wants to see me," she paused a long moment, voice cracking as she finished, "I...I don't know, Alayne." Fia hid her anguish behind her hands.

Arthur barked Simon's arrival and, in the weak glow of the candle, Simon squinted. Martin emerged from the darkness like a phantom, his strained voice floating to his cousin. "Tell me, how is she?"

With a shake of his head, Simon offered, "I'm not sure. She appeared a wee bit better than when I found her earlier today. Then we told her you were here and wanted to see her and her upset returned," Simon answered grimly. "She insisted on going to Mistress Matheson's." Simon's fingers squeezed his cousin's shoulder. "Fia said she couldn't see you. I'm sorry, Martin."

Martin swallowed hard and dropped his gaze.

"Perhaps tomorrow...." Simon offered, but Martin shook his head.

"I don't want to force–"

"Of course not," agreed Simon. "Are you staying in Inverness? What should I tell her if she asks?"

Martin answered, "I promised you I'd help locate Andrew Forbes, and I will."

"What about Jean MacNab? Did you finish your business with her?"

"I've no reason to return to Inveraray," Martin assured. "Just tell Fia that I'd like to speak with her, if and when she's willing. I'm not going anywhere."

The two men left no trace of their presence in the shop and, the next morning, Alayne found herself doubting they'd been there at all. But at dusk, when she was preparing to close for the day, Simon hesitantly entered. His gaze swept the room and came to rest, along with a soft smile, on Alayne. "I'm returning your key," he said, holding it in his fingertips.

She bustled toward him, plucked it up and used it to lock the door. "Where have you been all day?" Alayne quietly demanded. "Fia's been on pins and needles, unsure as to whether Martin would walk through that door. Truthfully, so have I."

"I couldn't decide when to come–whether it would make a difference. I'm sorry." He glanced around. "Is Fia here?"

"I am," Fia answered, passing through the curtained doorway. Glancing around, Fia asked, "Is Martin gone again?"

"Not gone, only waiting until you decide that he may see you, whenever that might be."

"What does he want?" she pleaded.

"To speak with you. What he wants to say, I can't be certain, though I know he's worried for you and regrets that his return has caused you even more pain."

Fia's battered emotions betrayed her into craving solace where she had received it only once before–in Martin's arms. "No comfort there," she silently reminded herself before weakly nodding. "Tell him I'll see him tonight, Simon–here."

Alayne frowned. "Are you sure, Fia? Isn't tonight awfully soon?"

"I'm not sure at all," Fia wavered. "Still, I don't think it's going to help either of us to postpone it. I'm anxious enough now."

Simon's sympathetic voice soothed, "I'll tell him. Will an hour suit?"

Before she changed her mind, Fia agreed, "One hour."

When Simon had gone, Alayne asked, "Shall I be here or not?" But she already knew the answer.

"This I have to do on my own," Fia confirmed, voice shaking. "Stay until he arrives though... please?"

"As long as you want me to." Alayne hugged Fia. "How will you get back to Kate's tonight?"

"I won't," she answered bluntly. "I'll stay here if you've no objection; no one needs to fetch me."

Alayne wasn't happy with the idea of leaving Fia alone at the shop but nodded knowing Fia had all she could deal with facing her in just one hour. She had no intention of adding to that burden. "Just be sure to lock the door."

Exactly one hour later, Alayne opened the workroom door to the short, loud rapping. In the dark, she could scarcely see Martin and did not see Simon take his stance a short distance away. Before inviting him in, Alayne wrapped her mantle around herself and stepped across the threshold to stand beside him."Fia's waiting." The tone of her voice clearly betrayed her concern. Alayne raised her hood and stated, "You'd better go in now," and watched him do her bidding as Arthur settled by the stoop.

Simon's voice cut blessedly through the night, "I'm here for you, lass," and Alayne rushed to him, grasping his hands.

"Oh, Simon," Alayne fretted, "I'm afraid for them both. Is it a mistake leaving them alone? "

Simon consoled, "Only they can decide that. Come," he urged, "let me walk you to Kate's."

She tucked her hand into the crook of his arm. "Only if you take me the long way; I'm not eager to leave you tonight, Simon."

"Nor I, you," he assured covering her hand with his.

For a few moments when Alayne opened the door, Fia let the worktable support her while she fought panic. What could she possibly say to Martin that hadn't been said already? How could she resist his nearness with no one at hand to help bolster her courage? Fia closed her eyes, trying to calm herself, to tap her own frail resolve. And when she opened them, he stood before her, his heated perusal taking her breath.

Fia finally whispered into the silence, "Why did you want to see me again? Do you delight in tormenting me?"

"I take no delight in tormenting or being tormented," he responded quietly.

"Then I ask you again, why did you wish to see me? Why return to Inverness at all? I've begged you not to continue your search for Andrew; he's dangerous, a man with no conscience."

"I'm sorry I can't heed that advice. I made a promise to Simon and his family. And for me, there's another reason now to deal with Andrew Forbes. Simon told me of the threats Forbes made against you at Market. And your friend Murdoch told Annie you'd been beaten–I can guess by whom. Fia, I'll not let him hurt you again."

Warily, Fia left the security of the table and circled toward the bottom of the stairs. "I would think you had better ways to spend your time than trying to protect me."

"If there are better ways, they escape me." His thoughts shifted. "Will you tell me what happened yesterday?"

"No," she staunchly replied.

Undaunted, he advanced, stopping only when he saw her go rigid. "Alayne told me about the woolens." Fia averted her gaze, and Martin proceeded, "I didn't realize when I sold them that you were in Inverness, much less that you were Mistress Matheson's niece."

"How could you know?" Fia allowed.

"If they upset–"

"An unexpected surprise," she insisted too quickly, "that's all." Fia tried unsuccessfully to swallow the dryness in her throat, her racing heart leaving her light-headed. "Martin, I...I think this was a mistake. I'm sorry to have wasted your time having you come here." When she moved toward the door to open it, Martin's hand closed around her's bringing her to a standstill.

"I won't let Forbes hurt you," he repeated earnestly, "and who knows better than I what hurting you means?"

With difficulty, Fia forced her next words. "Martin, go home; go back to Inveraray where your life awaits you."

"My life stands before me," he declared ardently, weaving his fingers tightly with hers. "You're my love, my passion, my longing. I will protect you; I'll never be far away."

Her voice shook at his declaration and touch. "What you're saying makes no sense; it's not possible. Now, I've asked you to leave, Martin, please." Fia tried to extract her hand, but Martin used the action to draw her against him, his free hand at the small of her back.

On the verge of desperation, he ardently whispered, "It can't be impossible, lass, for I can't lose you again–I couldn't bear it." His mouth covered hers and she whimpered at the touch, knowing his kiss didn't belong to her. But tonight it did, she reasoned, and responded eagerly, their long withheld hunger threatening to drown them both. Martin kissed her mouth, cheeks, eyes, then traveled to the soft hollow of her throat.

Fia's heart raced to his touch; he filled her arms so perfectly, fit against her so beguilingly. She pushed the greatcoat from his shoulders and began to pull his shirt from his breeches. But, when her hands touched his bare skin, he jerked back violently.

Abruptly abandoned, Fia cried in bewilderment, "What...what's wrong?"

Martin reeled from her, his arms hugging his chest. "God's blood! I swore...I swore to protect you, promised I'd never hurt you again. Now I'm putting you in danger. Sweet Jesus, I can't do this."

Fia strained to command her tumbling emotions long enough to understand–but she didn't understand. "What do you mean?"

"We aren't free to do as we wish, Fia. Choices were made and, blessed Lord help me, I won't make matters worse again by surrendering to a moment of weakness."

Fia's head snapped as if she'd been slapped. "A moment of weakness?"

Martin ran his hands through his burnished curls. "Ruining your good name is one mistake–an immense one–I won't add to the ones I've already made."

Fia's belly twisted at his rejection and she blinked in disbelief at this new nightmare. Back at Martin's croft, she might have accepted being rebuffed. Now, when she loved and needed him so completely and desperately, acceptance was impossible. Fiercely, she scowled at him. "My good name? What of your own, Martin?"

Surprised by her tone, Martin demanded, "Mine doesn't matter. You understand what I'm saying, don't you? You agree with me, don't you?"

"No, I *don't*!" she railed. "You are my only love–the other half of my life's blood. If you believe this is a weak moment–a mistake–you're the *only* one who believes it. And I know all too well how easily you deem something a mistake after you've done it." Fia growled, "This talk is over. It's time for you to go, Martin." She swept his coat from the floor and shoved it at his chest.

"Fia–"

"*Now!*" she screeched. "I don't have a yard or byre to escape to this time–*you'll* have to leave."

Stung and befuddled by her rebuke, Martin bounded across the room and slammed the door in his wake.

Fia cast a crumbling look of defiance after him and hastily retreated upstairs. She grabbed up the iron, angrily jabbing and prodding the hearth embers to a blaze, but gleaned no warmth from the flames. The chill she felt might have been the October air, but more likely it was her now certain knowledge that she could never hope to be joined with Martin. Dejectedly, she puzzled Martin's bewildering declaration of love–and immediate dismissal. He had called her his life, said he would always be near–but how? Jean would not stand for him being absent long, Fia was sure of that. And what did it really matter to him to be near her? He might love her, but he didn't *want* her–that was clear enough.

Desolate, anger crumbling into despair, Fia feverishly undressed. Stealing a blanket from the bed in the back room, Fia enshrouded her shift-clad body, and curled on the floor before the flames. She squeezed shut her eyes, trying to force calm. What came instead, was memory of her resolution of months back–if she could know once the man she truly loved, she might live her life in some peace. "There's no peace to be had now–not ever," she lamented.

On the stoop, Arthur greeted Martin's anguish with a wag of his tail and a soulful look. Martin bent to scratch his head but ended doubled over in almost physical pain from having ripped himself from Fia's embrace. He closed his eyes, tilted his head back and opened them again to glimpse black clouds raging across a blacker sky. It took all his force of concentration to calm down and gather enough of his wits to try to sort through what Fia had said–to remember what he had said. When he did, Martin groaned and buried his face in his hands. How much easier it had been to remedy her fever five months past than to make her understand that he only wanted to do what was right now because he had done everything wrong before. Martin drew a deep breath, the air stinging his lungs, clearing his mind. He knew what he had to do. God had been merciful enough to let him find Fia again; he would somehow make things right with her.

He settled Arthur and, reentering the workshop, Martin closed the door behind him and retraced the path he'd fled minutes before. While deciding how best to attempt to repair this newest injury, he would await Alayne's return and ensure that Fia was not alone. The soft glow at the top of the stairs revealed Fia's presence above.

Martin crouched against the wall on the stairway landing: strained, rigid and pale. "This must be what it's like to go mad," he thought, reason and emotions colliding dangerously. Fia was just up the steps and no physical barrier stood between them, though everything else did–including himself. The workroom remained still, serene from all appearances.

Unaware of how much time passed, or whether he had dozed off, Martin started, suddenly alert. Had she called his name, or had he imagined it as he had countless times when alone? He unfolded and stretched his lean body, and again he listened. The meager firelight now created a pale half-moon in the upper doorway. Finally, he recognized the disturbing sound floating toward him. Swiftly, Martin took the stairs and, stumbling into the room, he beheld Fia's contorted body reduced to a tight ball under a blanket. Her sobs were scarcely louder than he had heard from the landing, but they intensified his ache, his belly cramping with remorse at her sorrow and his cause of it once again. Martin rushed to her, knelt and pressed near, trying to brush damp, clinging curls from her half-covered face.

"Lass, please," he begged, "you're breaking my heart."

Fia jolted upright, wild-eyed, face wet, and clumsily pushed herself beyond his reach, clutching the blanket to her. "What are you doing?" she accused harshly. "I told you to leave."

"I couldn't," Martin said without apology. "Fia, I can't just disappear now that I've found you again."

"Why not? You s...say you love me but you don't want to be with me. What I want doesn't matter to you. Just go."

"Lis–"

"No *you* listen," she demanded. Pale knuckles squeezing a fistful of blanket, Fia continued, "You embrace and kiss me, bringing to life the desire I fought all these months to quell. Then you thrust me away, and I tell you to go–but you won't. I know you've come back for Andrew, though I've begged you not to. So what is it that you really expect from me now?" she begged, dashing tears aside with her palms.

Martin swallowed hard. "I think I under–"

"No," she cried. "You couldn't *possibly* understand. Your very presence torments me. Your touch scorches and the sight of your face wounds my heart."

"But I *do* understand, lass. Don't you know that those same reasons are why I can't stay away from you? I came back tonight because I refuse to let my pride and stupidity wrench you from me again. You are a part of my life that I can't live without and, somehow, we have to come to an understanding, find some acceptable compromise, no matter how paltry. Fia, no man could desire more than to love you and be blessed with your love in return–even if it has to be from a distance."

Fia fumed, "It didn't *have* to be from a distance; that was *your* choice. When I realized I loved you," she confessed, "I made a selfish decision. My path had been chosen for me but, more than anything in my life, I wanted the memory of sharing love with the man I chose and I would have asked you to lie with me except for Jean. Tonight, I might finally have had that, but you stole it from me."

Stricken with remorse at hearing the simple, detestable truth spoken aloud, tears pooled in Martin's eyes. He cast his gaze away and sought, in vain, words to end their torment.

Fia saw and shared his pained struggle and, in the silence, drew a bracing breath to murmur, "I don't want to fight with you, Martin. I'm tired of hurting, and I don't want to hurt you either." She admitted in a trembling sigh, "I'm sick at heart from missing you". Martin, you're a fair and honorable man, which is why you keep trying to fix what's wrong between us. God knows it would be easier on both of us if I were as honorable. But downstairs, when you touched me, I prayed you would break your vows and spend this night with me so that I would have that memory to live on."

Martin stared at her, scarcely breathing. "Fia, I don't understand. What vows would I be breaking?"

"M...Martin," she choked in sudden fluster, "I beg you...I speak of your marriage vows."

His bewildered gaze met her sorrowful one. "Fia, my...my wife is long dead. Simon told you about that, didn't he?"

"Your present wife," Fia stressed heatedly, his puzzlement not yet apparent to her agitated mind.

"And, who is...Jean?" he asked cautiously.

"Of course," Fia flustered miserably. "I spoke to you about it the last time you were here. You went home to her the very next day."

Martin's heart lurched precariously and he crept closer. "I returned to Inveraray to tell Jean what I thought of her and her despicable lies. Fia," he confessed, "I never intended to, and never did marry Jean. That was finished before I met you. There's still the question of your vows though. When I spoke of putting you in danger, protecting your good name, I meant because of your marriage to Struan Forbes."

Bewildered, Fia narrowed her gaze and edged toward him slightly. "What are you talking about, Martin?"

"The first time I sought you out in Glasgow, Elizabeth told me–"

"*Elizabeth!*" she gasped. "You met Elizabeth?"

"I did. Simon and I both told you I searched for you."

"When? What did Elizabeth say to you?" Fia was so close now that her sweet breath caressed his face.

Martin searched the depths of her sea-gray eyes. "That it was your wedding day," he admitted bitterly.

"You were there? You spoke with her that day?"

"Aye," he lamented.

"And did you see her again?" Fia demanded.

"One other time."

"Did she tell you then about my wedding?"

"She told me about your...your wedding trip. Fia, this is agony." He begged, "Just tell me–"

"I've said no vows," she adamantly asserted, fingers losing their grip on the blanket to grasp his hands. "Elizabeth lied to you, Martin. There was no wedding, no wedding trip. I ran away. I would have no one once you were lost to me." She bit into her lip to stop it's quivering, her stricken eyes boring his shocked ones, each trying to comprehend what the other had revealed.

"My God," Martin murmured, fingers tightening on hers, "is this the truth? You're not Mistress Forbes?"

Fia winced hearing him utter that dreaded title. Still, she assured, "I am no man's wife, Martin. And you–"

"I have no wife." He tentatively touched her face. "You...you're free?"

Fia nodded dumbly, burgeoning hope in her expression. "As free as you are." Fear that he would be ripped from her again drove Fia to press herself against him.

Invaded by the same dread, Martin fiercely returned her clinging embrace. They clutched each other in desperate silence, afraid to believe what they'd just confessed. At length, he tremulously whispered, "There's nothing to keep us apart, lass...nothing." he pressed his lips to hers– incredulous at first–then compelling and reckless to her eager response.

They rose together to their knees and kissed hungrily. Martin's hands seared her skin through the linen of her shift and his caress of her bare thigh and hip jolted Fia with unexpected and intense pleasure.

She impatiently pushed Martin's shirt from his body and began to fumble with the buttons on the fall of his breeches. "I would see all of you Martin–now."

Quickly Martin shed the rest of his clothing and stood before her awed inspection. It was evident that she was pleased with his taut body and undisguised desire in the catch of her breath and the heat of her admiring stare. She reached up her hands and caught his to pull him back to her.

"Love me," she whispered.

Martin knelt in her embrace and gathering the hem of her shift, pulled it over her head. His hungry gaze devoured the sight of her delicate curves and the porcelain smoothness of her skin.

"You are more beautiful than I even imagined," he choked, happily drowning in his emotions.

They fell back onto the crumpled blanket, reveling in the scent and taste of each other. Martin's kisses and loving hands traced exquisite, urgent paths over her breasts, across her belly and between her thighs, eliciting whimpers and moans from her.

Just as his touch brought heightened excitement, the hard, sculptured smoothness of him under her own hands caused a barrage of unfamiliar, rousing sensations to waken and radiate through Fia in waves.

Their need for each other had been too great for too long and, at Fia's urging, Martin slid into her. The two melded in a motion so poignantly sweet, each cried out. Now her breath mingled with his; their eyes shut out all but each other. "I love you, my Fia."

Fia responded by drawing his mouth to hers and moved with him until his desire shuddered to climax.

The lovers lay silently in each others arms, drowsy, comfortably damp, and reluctant to break the spell. Each had imagined and yearned, but neither had realistically hoped to fulfill their love. Fia caressed his bearded cheek as she had often wished to do. Her fingers touched wetness and she rose up to taste the tears on his cheeks–tears that matched her own–before kissing his lips once more.

He clasped her so hard she thought he might pull her inside him–and the thought was rapturous. Martin lay facing Fia, his eyes seeking an answer before he even asked the question. "Be my wife, Fia. You bring such joy to my heart, and contentment to my soul."

Hands gliding over the warm, smooth skin of his back, she promised, "From the moment I nearly toppled you from Odhar's back, I was yours. I'll have no other for my husband."

Though their clench made it delightfully difficult to breathe, still they managed to rain urgent, ecstatic kisses over each other. When they parted long enough to gasp for air, Fia's eyes shone brilliantly and she declared, "With all that I am, I love you."

His voice choked with emotion. "You've never said it before–not straight out. You just told me that Annie didn't lie."

"And she didn't," Fia swore, and pressed her lips to his in a kiss that promised as many more as he might ever desire.

Chapter Twenty-Six

His horse plodding along, Struan slouched in the saddle, by no means in a rush to reach Inverness. The broken finger pained him, the throbbing made worse by his anger and humiliation that his own brother was responsible. Struan was beginning to consider leaving Andrew behind and striking out on his own. "Families are supposed to stand together not threaten and abuse each other," he grumbled to his mount. "And Andrew would try the patience of a saint. Why should I subject myself to his brutality?" Struan silently pondered what had thrust Andrew over the edge. He was not just sharp-tongued and greedy for fine things anymore, but truly evil. A woman had bested Andrew Struan nodded sagely to himself. "My own intended," he sneered and belated remembered that Fia Graham had made a fool of him as well. Who would have thought it? Aye, revenge now drove his brother, and Struan was certain that Andrew would somehow rid himself of his shame–and perhaps Fia–if it took his final breath. Meanwhile, it was business as usual–well, not quite as usual. Unhappily, Struan glanced at the splinted digit and shifted the reins to rest more comfortably in his uninjured hand.

At an inn not a two-hour journey ahead of Struan, Douglas Sutherland rested his bruised body; his steed had thrown him as a badger darted into its path. Fortunately, Douglas had discovered no serious injuries, but he had aches aplenty. Another day's travel would see him at Kate Matheson's yet, at this moment, he was not at all sure how he would manage another day on horseback.

The voice of the innkeeper disrupted his thoughts. "Bath's ready, Sir, up in your room," the man offered, showing gaps where three teeth used to lodge in his mouth. He was more than pleased to draw a bath for this lanky traveler who had paid him well. "Let me offer a hand, Sir," the man fawned, taking Douglas by the arm and helping him rise from the bench and shuffle toward the stairs.

When Douglas placed a hand on the newel post, he gently waved the man away. "I can make it from here, thank you."

"As you say, Sir," the man replied. "I'll send someone up later to empty the tub and bring you a bite to eat."

Douglas nodded his thanks and cautiously pulled himself up, one step at a time. When he finally eased himself into the hot water, he leaned back his head and closed his eyes. "Ah, Kate," he sighed, "I hope you'll understand my delay." He silently thanked God that his horse hadn't been injured. If it were at all possible, he would ride on tomorrow. "If only this bath will ease my stiffness," he prayed.

When Douglas had secured the last bit of warmth from the water, he emerged to cloak himself in the comfort of his dressing gown. He wanted to sleep but knew, if he lay down now, his muscles would pain him again in short order. At a leisurely pace, he walked around and around the tiny room until he thought he'd fall asleep standing up.

A knock on the door drew his grateful attention and Douglas opened it to a mussed, flustered young woman bearing a tray. After bobbing a curtsey, she entered.

"I'll put your supper on the table, Sir," she offered, and proceeded to do just that.

Douglas then watched her unabashedly straighten her rumpled bodice and smooth her petticoat which had stuck upon her hip at an odd angle.

The lass caught his astonished stare and, embarrassed, murmured, "Beg pardon, Sir. A man arrived a bit ago and made a grab for...well, nearly made me drop your supper. I'd have had to pay for it too!" she exclaimed indignantly. "When I go down, I'll be using the back stairs, you may be certain." She stepped toward the door. "Bruce will be up later for the tub."

"Fine, thank you." Douglas shut the door behind her and scratched his head thinking it shameful what a serving girl often had to endure. The young woman's comment was quickly forgotten, however, as Douglas realized he was famished. He wolfed chunks of mutton and potatoes, some sliced cheese and scones, happily washing it all down with a passable claret. For a long minute, he leaned back in his chair hands folded over his flat belly, and closed his eyes. The food lifted his spirits considerably and Douglas began to see hope for continuing his journey in the morning.

The sound of boots stomping the stairs and loud agitated voices disturbed his reverie. Douglas cocked his head toward the door. One of the voices had a familiar tone but, at its raised pitch, Douglas couldn't identify it. Clearly, there was a disagreement in progress. The sudden thud of a body against the wall outside his door brought Douglas to his feet. His limbs balked at the swiftness of his rising and he winced, steadying himself before opening the door. Face to face, Douglas stood with Struan Forbes, whose hands were closing around a young man's neck.

Upon seeing Douglas, Struan faltered and pushed the man away in annoyance. "Good Lord," Struan snarled, "you never know who's going to show up in these flea-infested pits."

"Odd," Douglas replied dryly, "I was thinking much the same thing."

"Clever, Sutherland," Struan jeered.

Douglas bowed slightly. "Why thank you, Forbes," he said, ignoring the churlish curl of Struan's thin lips. "Tell me," Douglas continued, "what unpleasantness causes you to create a disturbance at my door?"

Struan puffed himself up and answered, "None of your concern, Sutherland."

"Ah, but it is," Douglas disagreed, "if this lad's name is Bruce." He pointed at two buckets on the hallway floor and addressed the dark-eyed youth. "Are you Bruce, and have you come to empty my tub?"

"Aye, Sir," the lad admitted, dipping his head in assent.

"Splendid, I've been expecting you. Come in." Douglas stepped aside but, as the young man would enter, Struan grabbed him by the stock of his shirt.

"We haven't finished our business, laddie," he threatened.

Emboldened by Douglas' presence, Bruce corrected, "We have, Sir, unless you paw my sister again." With that, he shook off Struan's hold and entered Douglas' room.

His brows drawing down, Douglas glared at Struan.

"What?" Struan demanded, uneasily.

"I'm just reminded of what a loathsome boor you are, Forbes."

Coloring, Struan exclaimed, "That's slanderous."

"That is my considered opinion." Douglas shut the door in Struan's purplish face and turned to Bruce.

"Take as long as you want to empty the tub–and be careful while that man is here."

Filling a leather bucket, the youth grunted, "He's a bad one then; I thought as much."

A sudden dread brought a low gasp from Douglas and Bruce straightened in response.

"Sir, is something wrong?"

Douglas leaned heavily against the mantle and stared into the flames. "I pray not. But it just occurred to me that Forbes may be following me."

"But if that were so, Sir, why did he let you see him tonight?"

"Forbes isn't stupid. It just could be his colossal arrogance that makes him careless." He struck a thoughtful pose, chin between his thumb and forefinger. "Bruce, would you like to earn a little extra money?"

"Pardon, Sir?"

"Extra money," Douglas repeated and hurriedly added, "for information, nothing more sinister."

Bruce asked, "How would I get this information you need?"

"Only by observing when Forbes leaves and by what road," responded the older man.

"Would it help to know where he's bound?"

"Indeed," Douglas said, "but he mustn't know I'm interested. A young woman's life may depend on it."

Mention of a woman in danger clouded Bruce's face with memory of his sister in Forbes' clutch. "I'll do it for nothing, Sir," the young man enthusiastically vowed.

With an understanding smile, Douglas insisted, "A noble gesture, Bruce, but unacceptable. This is important to me and I will pay you." Douglas extended his hand. "Do we have a bargain?"

Bruce set down the full bucket, wiped his hand on his breeches and placed it in Douglas' firm grasp. "Done, Sir."

As the sun next rose, Bruce tapped on Douglas' door. Though he'd been awake nearly a full hour already, Douglas had not been able to rid himself of the aching stiffness resulting from yesterday's spill.

"Morning, Sir." Bruce bobbed his head.

"Bruce," Douglas greeted in return. "What news have you?"

"I wasn't able to get close enough to him to find out where he's going. He kept his eye on me all night. But he left by the Inverness road; I came straight up to tell you."

That fact alone was enough to cause Douglas great concern. "So he's just departed then?"

"About five minutes ago, Sir."

"Well done, Bruce. Have my mare saddled and brought round will you? I'll have some oat cakes and be on my way. Oh, and Bruce," Douglas said pressing a few coins into the young man's palm, "my thanks."

The last vestiges of night were diluted by the golden pinks of the late October morn when Douglas gritted his teeth and mounted up. He held his horse to a walk as he left the inn. Though the lumbering pace of his horse best suited his bruises, Douglas was anxious to reach Kate Matheson's. "I must caution Fia before it's too late," he fussed, knowing that he should travel faster but that, if he did, he might very well come upon Forbes in route.

The roan mare tossed her mane and danced forward a bit, apparently not understanding why she couldn't stretch her legs in a canter. Still, Douglas tightened the reins to settle her, stroked her neck and cooed, "I understand your frustration, my pet, but we have no choice."

Martin had awakened in the night with a jolt that roused his slumbering lover. Fia returned his anxious stare with a drowsy smile and, in silent agreement they tightened their hold on one another. When he again looked in her eyes, Martin saw the grogginess lifting.

Whispering, Fia said, "I can see and feel you. But are you here or is this my dream?"

Happy to reassure her, Martin's lips lingered on hers. "I'm very real, my love."

As she studied his features in the near darkness, tears shimmered in her eyes. "Thank you for coming back to me when I told you to leave. Because of you, all the forces that sought to keep us apart failed. In truth, two people could not be more blessed."

"You give me too much credit–I had no choice but to come back to you. Perhaps God was testing us; together we will discover what it means to be loved completely."

"Completely," Fia reiterated, arching to meet his kiss.

When the kiss ended, Martin was puzzled by the disconcerted look on her face. "What is it, lass?"

Shyly, Fia asked, "I wondered if...well...is it too soon to couple again?"

A delighted grin split Martin's face. "I'm so glad you asked!" His mouth sought hers again, ardently, and when she was breathless, moved to her throat and breast which he teased with a willing tongue until Fia's hands gently urged his teasing lower. She roused again to the wondrous sensations assaulting her body, and felt an overwhelming need to know Martin's body as intimately. Softly, she called, "Martin?"

In response, Martin ascended her body, strategically placing sensuous kisses until he was face to face with her again. Fia uttered no further words but urged him onto his back, rose over him and began her own rousing journey of discovery. At one point, Fia rocked back to her knees and her gaze passionately swept his taut frame and came back to rest in the heat of his eyes.

"You are beautiful," she whispered admiring him. "I always thought so: your face, the ease and grace with which you move, your form. But now that I see you, I have proof."

"You forget my temper, my moodiness; neither is so beautiful."

"There were reasons for–"

"None good enough," he swore. Martin sat swiftly and took her hands, solemnly kissing one palm, then the other. "A strange choice of words you use to describe me. You who kneel here, glorious in the curve of your breast and hip, skin smooth, flushed and perfect, and with a face as hauntingly lovely before me as when I thought you lost to me forever." His fingers feathered her thigh. "Like silk," he whispered, huskily.

Fia covered his fingers with hers and guided them into the moist warmth nearby. "And eager to take you inside me again," she pledged.

His fingers curled upward momentarily, and then gripped her hips to position himself better to satisfy them both.

Fia eased onto him with a glorious shudder. Slowly, they moved together, eyes locked. As their gyrations increased, breath came in short gasps and loving, urgent words melted into kisses.

Martin rolled Fia on her back; her legs wrapped his narrow hips and her arms, his back as she met each thrust driving him deeper inside until his body trembled with spasms of ecstasy. After a long moment, pierced only by the sound of their panting, Martin rolled to his side, taking Fia with him to prolong their oneness. His fingers caressed her damp face and he kissed her deeply. When his lips left hers, he chuckled quietly, "I thought I heard you purr, lass."

Fia blushed, but her expression was replete with love. "There's nothing wrong with your hearing." She sighed contentedly. "Is it wrong of me to never want to leave this point in time?"

"Not wrong, in fact, it's an idea I wholly support." Martin murmured against her ear. "In the morning though, the world will crowd in on us whether or not we want it to; we can't seclude ourselves here."

"We can at your croft," she suggested hopefully.

"Aye," he agreed, "and I long for the day when we can return there. But I promised Simon—"

"I know, I know," she rushed to quiet him, not wanting the name of Andrew Forbes uttered in their paradise.

Martin's arms tightened protectively; he believed he guessed her thoughts. "I promise you, my love, we'll return to the croft as soon as possible. In the meantime, this night—these moments—these will always be ours. I pray they are just a taste of a lifetime of moments we were born to share."

"Have no doubt, Martin, this is just the beginning." Contentedly, Fia snuggled her body against his and Martin pulled the blanket around them again.

After a few seconds of silence, Fia asked, "Do all men and women...fit together as superbly as we do?"

"No," came his blunt reply.

An uncomfortable feeling engulfed Fia. "That was thoughtless of me," she atoned. "You were married before, and I know it ended tragically. Forgive me."

He turned on his side and propped himself on one elbow to look at her. "How much do you know?"

"Only that your wife and child died and you were unjustly blamed. Simon told me that of his cousin when we first met."

"Do you want me to tell you about it?" he asked, quietly.

"Only if it's important to you; I feel no need to pry."

"It isn't prying. I know this wasn't true six months ago, Fia, but there's nothing I want to hide from you ever again, and nothing you should ever apologize for...not to me." Martin shifted to bring her closer. "My brother introduced me to Bridgid who was already his lover; he was married. The child was his, not mine, and Bridgid told me this as she was delivering her son, who was stillborn. That and her relationship with my brother is why everyone was so quick to brand me a murderer when she overdosed on laudanum."

"Because you'd been betrayed?" Fia asked, her sadness for him clear in her voice.

Martin nodded. "In the confusion and grief, it probably seemed a reasonable conclusion. Simon discovered that it was my brother who gave her the dose that killed her. It was, of course, an accident, but it has ruined him. So it did end tragically, but not for me. My innocence has been reestablished, and I have you beside me. What more could I ask?"

Fia's heart wrenched at his revelation. She caressed his face. "What horrible injustice you've endured. I feel so naive, so inexperienced in the world when I think of what you've suffered, Martin."

"Oh, lass," he said with a tender smile, "you *are* naive, in an admirably optimistic sort of way. What amazes me is that you maintained that guile through the loss of your parents, the cold-hearted disinterest of your uncle, the horrifying death of a good friend, and the wretched lies of two women who would keep you from me." Martin paused. "Inexperienced, Fia? Not you."

"Still," she said more happily, "I've now had the experience I craved the most, that of loving the man I would choose to spend my life with."

He grinned down at her. "Your inexperience didn't show there, my sweet."

Fia laughed. "Thank you, love." After a moment's silence, Fia said, "May I ask one more question?"

"Of course, lass," he replied.

"How did this happen?" she touched his scarred forearm.

Martin's body tightened slightly and Fia burbled, "If you'd rather not tell me–"

"I told you I want no secrets between us again. It's just that this isn't my secret. I received the scratches from a patient in great distress during a miscarriage. It was an accident."

"Oh, Martin, how awful," she lamented and kissed his wounded arm tenderly. "How long ago did it happen?"

Hesitating, Martin admitted, "The second time I searched for you in Glasgow."

Slowly, Fia turned her body toward him, trying to read his expression. Suddenly, a jolt brought her upright. "It was Elizabeth, wasn't it?"

"It isn't my secret to divulge," he repeated, though his gaze slid from hers.

A flash of anger at Elizabeth quickly gave way to regret. "I'm so sorry, Martin, how many ways she has hurt you."

"But I have everything I ever wanted in you, Fia. Elizabeth has nothing." He cradled her face in his hands and drew her down for his kiss. She molded her body to his and Martin reached round her and cupped the roundness of her breast in his hand while planting a moist kiss on the back of her neck. "I believe I'm ready for a bit more sleep." Just before drifting off, he felt her hand cover his, pressing it more firmly to her contented heart.

There was that immense black dog trying to stare Alayne down. "So, Arthur," Alayne addressed the shaggy hound, "can I assume your master is still in there?"

Arthur cocked his head and his tail swept the ground once in reserved greeting.

Alayne took this as a good sign, passed by the dog offering one timid pat on his broad head, and reached the door unscathed. Upon discovering the door unlocked, Alayne frowned. The ever-present possibility that a Forbes would discover Fia's whereabouts had made her cautious. That Martin might be within was the only thing that quelled Alayne's apprehension. But once inside the workroom, she saw no evidence to support her hope that he'd remained. She raised her eyes to the top of the stairs. "Do I dare go up?" she pondered quietly. "Perhaps not," she wavered, now standing at the bottom of the steps. But Alayne worried. Fia had been so anxious about meeting Martin–just needing it to be over with. What if it had gone badly? But, if it had gone badly, why would Martin's dog still be on the stoop? Only if Martin was upstairs, she answered her own question and smiled to herself. It must have gone well, very well. And if that is the case, Martin and Fia...

She knew she shouldn't, but Alayne hoisted her petticoat and took the steps lightly, halting at the top to survey the scene before her. In the dimness, a tangle of limbs, blanket and strewn clothing sorted itself out and she discerned Fia's head nestled against Martin's chest. He lay on his side, Fia gathered to him in a shielding embrace. With a start, Alayne noticed Martin staring at her. He put a finger to his lips signifying that Fia still slept.

Mortified at being caught intruding on the aftermath of their intimacy, Alayne decided to leave as gracefully as possible–quickly. She was surprised when Martin motioned her over. Alayne reluctantly minced her way nearer his face and knelt.

Martin lifted her hand and squeezed it. "Thank you, Alayne," he whispered, "for helping to make this possible."

His radiant expression made her redden and sputter, "You...you could have used the bed."

"Loving Fia would have been no more remarkable in a bed."

His bluntness made her parry, "But, perhaps more comfortable."

With a lopsided grin, Martin said, "A simple 'you're welcome' would suffice."

Alayne looked doubtful. "Do I have your word, she's all right? Because–"

Alayne caught her breath as Fia shifted slightly.

Martin pulled the blanket closer around Fia's shoulders. "On my love for this woman, we're both grand!"

Alayne released the breath she'd been holding. "Then...you're welcome–with all my heart, you're welcome. I'll give you your well-deserved privacy now. By the way, I think it'll be a slow morning–one person can handle the shop for some time."

"Bless you," he proclaimed, listening to the muted swish of her gown fading down the stairs. He snuggled against Fia, marveling at the feel of her against him.

Fia struggled to open her eyes and beheld Martin's face inches from hers. "What are you thinking?" she asked sleepily.

His hand tenderly brushed her cheek. "I'm thinking that, never again do I wish to forget any detail of how you look, or feel, or smell, or taste."

Fia nestled her fingers in the soft hair on his chest and asked intently, "Was there a time when you wanted to forget?"

"Every time missing you seemed unbearable," he replied honestly.

"And what if I promise to be with you always and never let you have a moment to forget?"

"I will be forever thankful to God for creating such a generous woman as you."

Her gaze warmed to his. "There is, of course, one stipulation," she teased, running her hand down his chest, over his hard belly, till her fingers reached and closed on their mark.

"And what, pray tell, is that?" he asked with quickened breath.

"That you make the same promise to me."

"You could never ask anything easier of me, lass."

"And I could never want for anything harder than this," she said with a grin and a light squeeze of her hand.

Martin smiled broadly, thrilled that she was so comfortable with his body and their intimacy.

Fia flipped over to lay on her stomach and Martin kneaded her back. "Do you suppose," she mumbled into the blanket beneath her, "we should wash up and go down to the shop?"

Offhandedly, Martin replied, "Alayne said not to hurry."

Scrambling to sit up, Fia flustered, "What do you mean Alayne said not to hurry?"

"Well, I'm not sure she knew whether or not I was here but, while you were asleep, she came upstairs. Fia, she needed to know you were all right."

Fia relaxed slightly. "And did you tell her?"

"I did indeed; I also thanked her. I feel I owe her a great deal."

"Alayne has been a wonderful friend to me." Fia frowned slightly. "Sometimes, she worries me. Her relationship with Aunt Kate is so tenuous and, in just a few weeks, she's going to have her marriage to Muir ended."

"Then I pray she'll let Simon love her; I'm sure he does."

"It's what I hope also. I've seen how Simon looks at her, how he treats her and is protective of her." Fia smiled. "I know she cares for him, and she certainly deserves happiness. While Alayne seldom lets on, I think these four years have often been miserable ones for her. Thank God she's strong."

Martin suggested. "Why don't we make ourselves more presentable, then go thank Alayne properly–in a bit."

Fia feigned ignorance. "Why not now?"

"Because you don't strike me as a woman who starts something and doesn't finish it," he replied.

"Oh? And what did I start that I've not finished?" she asked innocently.

He cast the blanket aside to reveal his plight. "You started this!"

She sensuously stretched till her full length rested on top of him. "And I'm delighted to see this through."

With the morning light streaming through the workshop windows, Martin saw the yellow ribbed silk gown that Mairi was to have worn on her wedding day. He halted, staring at its luminescence in the otherwise drab room. "How very beautiful," he remarked, almost wistfully.

Fia slipped her arm around his waist. "A shame it wasn't ready when she needed it."

"Who could have predicted the course her plans would take," he offered. "Still, it will look lovely on her when she finally gets to wear it."

"I agree. Now, perhaps we should greet Alayne."

But Martin hung back, looking suddenly uncomfortable. "I think it would be better if I see to Arthur and Odhar; they probably think I've deserted them." To her quizzical look, Martin continued, "There are a few errands I have also, errands that can't wait. You go on and I'll see Alayne again later."

Quite perplexed, Fia was unsure whether he was suddenly embarrassed or whether he had a deeper concern. "If that's what you wish, though I don't see the difference between a few minutes now or later."

His fingers cupped her chin. "The difference, lass, is that I think you may wish a few minutes alone with your closest friend." Before she could respond, he kissed her deeply. "And make no mistake, I will return before long."

"I'll hold you to that promise, Martin Ross."

With a last quick kiss, Martin stepped outside to be greeted by Arthur's exuberant barking.

Fia stood looking after him and shivered once. She never wanted to let him out of her sight again for fear that someone would yet find a way to keep them apart. Still, she knew that keeping him with her day and night was impossible, so she vowed to do her best not to dwell on it or let the worry cloud any moment she spent with him.

Fia glanced at the curtain leading to the shop and realized that Martin was correct–she did want some time alone with Alayne. So much had happened since last night; so much was different this morning.

In the shop, Alayne was alone. The soft rustle of the curtain drew her attention to Fia's radiant blush. Alayne beamed broadly as she thrust aside her stitching and rose to catch her friend in a warm embrace. "I'm so very happy and pleased for you–and for Martin." She drew back, each woman with tears in her eyes.

"Me too," Fia exuded. "Thank you so much, Alayne. You and Simon each helped make this possible."

"Oh, I think it was meant to be; simply a question of where and when. But, for whatever part I had in it, it's one of the best things I've ever done." Alayne sat again. "I heard the dog bark. Does that mean Martin's gone?"

Fia nodded and pulled a chair close, seating herself. "He has errands to see to. I thought perhaps he was a bit shy about facing you even though he saw you earlier."

A pale red stained Alayne's skin. "Fia, I apologize for intruding on your privacy–my curiosity got the better of me."

"It's all right. That's not why he left. He thought I'd like to spend some time with you. I suspect he might want the same with Simon."

Alayne fidgeted slightly, her curiosity again gripping her. "So, do you want to tell me what happened...and how you're going to deal with his wife?"

With a smile that almost lit the room, Fia grabbed up Alayne's hands and revealed, "He doesn't have a wife!"

"What?" Alayne almost fell from her stool. "What do you mean he–"

"–she doesn't have a husband?" Simon asked in shock, nearly spilling his tankard.

Martin explained, "Elizabeth lied to me–just as Jean lied to Fia."

Head shaking in disbelief, Simon mulled, "My God, the power others can wield over our destinies. It's a miracle that last night occurred at all."

"A miracle is just how I would describe it, Simon," Martin declared. "The sweetest, most stirring miracle I could ever imagine."

Simon cleared his throat. "So...I realize you were, um...preoccupied last night but, have you any plans yet?"

"None except to marry her as quickly as possible."

"How can I help?" Simon asked.

Martin beamed at his cousin. "I can always rely on you."

"I would hope so, as I know I can count on you."

"Aye," Martin agreed, "and last night hasn't changed that. You can help me by meeting me at the shop in about two hours; we must make plans for the revelry."

"You want me to help you celebrate?" Simon asked, confused.

"Of course, we have plans to make for tomorrow. Remember, it's All Hallows Eve. I intend that it be the most memorable ever. Now," Martin finished, "wish me luck."

"Good luck," Simon obliged. "Why?"

"I need to pay a call on Mistress Kate."

"You what?" Simon asked, hoping he'd misheard.

"About marrying her niece."

Leaping from his taproom bench, Simon cried, "Have you lost your wits? What if she says no?"

Martin stood and clapped Simon's shoulder. "Never fear, Cousin. I'm not going to ask her, I'm going to tell her–as a courtesy." He walked to the door, but Simon stopped him before he opened it.

"Martin?"

"Aye?"

"May God bless you both in your happiness."

Martin gulped the sudden lump in his throat, silently embraced Simon, and left.

Not long after that parting, Kate Matheson opened her door to Martin's tap. There was an audible gasp as Kate recognized the man on her stoop and exclaimed, "You're Martin Ross!"

"I am, Mistress. I'd like to talk with you...about Fia."

"Is she hurt?" Kate's voice tightened in fear.

"Fia is quite well, I assure you," Martin responded earnestly.

She sighed her relief then studied him with narrowed eyes until, finally, she responded coolly, "Come in then."

"My thanks," he replied, bade Arthur stay, and followed her inside. Not waiting for an invitation, he swung his greatcoat from his shoulders and hung it by the door, perching his bonnet atop it. The day had turned cold and he silently thanked Annie for her generosity.

Kate clasped her hands primly before her waist. "Well, you'd better come sit." Her offer had a reluctant ring, still she led the way to the drawing room and motioned him to an upholstered chair.

"After you, Mistress," Martin insisted and, when she had settled, chose a wooden chair for himself.

Nervousness made Kate impatient and she flared, "The colossal impudence you have, Sir, to trifle with my niece. She is extremely vulnerable. Surely, you are aware of the...fondness she feels toward you."

"I am. Mistress," he explained, "normally, I would let you speak all that's on your mind first; it seems you have some carefully chosen words you'd like me to hear."

"Indeed, I do," Kate confirmed.

"I believe you might regret some of those words if you speak them now. There are facts of which I doubt you're aware, and perceptions that bear correcting. Also, I'd like to tell you of the purpose for my visit."

"Very well," Kate conceded, though not graciously, evidenced by her pouting tone.

"Fia and I spoke at length last night and realized that each was laboring under a gross misunderstanding that the other was married."

"That's foolish," Kate barked indignantly. "Fia's never been married. She's as chaste as the day God brought her into the world."

Martin dropped his gaze, but could not disguise the blissful flush of his skin.

The silence that followed lay heavily between them. When Martin did look at her, it was to see that Kate's coloring matched his own, for she fully understood the implication of his reaction to her declaration. At last, he continued, "You may believe it foolish, Mistress, but it's true nevertheless. What is important is that we have uncovered the truth–that each of us is free–and we have rediscovered each other."

"You...you aren't married?" she inquired skeptically.

"Not yet," he replied quietly.

Kate's voice trembled, "Is this all you've come to tell me?"

"No," Martin assured. "I've come to tell you that I love Fia, as she loves me, and that, as soon as she will, I'll arrange for the local curate to preside over our handfasting–"

"Handfasting?" Kate cried, sitting forward in her chair. "Fia should be wed in the kirk! How could you profess to love her and offer her less? The marriage will be imperfect, incomplete without the wedding service."

"We will be legally married. We'll take the oath as is the custom of the church, before witnesses."

"Surely Fia has not agreed to this. She'll want a service."

Martin patiently replied, "I have yet to ask her what she prefers. However," he rushed on as Kate threatened to interrupt again, "tell me, Mistress, if you would encourage your niece to wed in the kirk when you know as well as I that banns would have to be read two Sabbaths in a row? Her name would be publicly announced and anyone who hears it will know they can find her in that same kirk on the third Sunday for the marriage service. Do you really wish to leave her that vulnerable with men the likes of Forbes eager to know her whereabouts? I will not allow it."

Kate's voice softened slightly, "I hadn't thought that far."

"You haven't had time," he allowed.

"I simply assumed any young woman would prefer to wed in the eyes of God, not by a curate," Kate finished.

"Quite possibly, you're right. I believe though that Fia will be satisfied with handfasting."

Kate pried with a note of hope, "Do you have witnesses?"

"Witnesses won't be a problem. Again, though, I must talk to Fia. You should know that I'm not a strong believer in the kirk, that it's the path to salvation. I do believe that God would approve of living a useful and loving life. And I believe God has brought Fia and I together, in the same place, to give us the chance to have what I truly believe was ordained, a life as husband and wife. Be at peace to know, however, that I will never stand in Fia's way to worship as she pleases."

Kate nodded then asked, "What of her tocher?" To Martin's bemused look, she tried again. "Her dowry?"

"I have no interest in anything Fia can bring to me except herself. Besides," Martin paused, "I have little to offer her other than myself. She shall have a third of my land, though; it's as much of a terce as the law allows me to give her."

Kate grudgingly found herself being won over by his honesty and single-minded desire to make Fia his own. "You only have to make such a gift to your bride if you receive one," she felt bound to point out.

"I will provide for her future under any circumstances," Martin stated.

Kate restrained herself from pointing out that Fia's inheritance alone could keep them both comfortable and stared at the man before her, not sure what to say. She had been shocked that he had come to her home; reluctant and apprehensive to hear what he had to say. By Fia's deeds, if not legally, she was certainly now this man's wife. That was disappointing, but Kate was forced to admit that Fia had made it clear to her how much she loved Martin Ross. Now he was here, declaring those same feelings for Fia. He didn't have to come to her; she was no legal guardian to her niece. And while Kate could wish for more faith from him in the power of the kirk, she doubted she could ask for anyone who would love Fia more, or protect her to his last breath as she believed this man would.

She stood so suddenly that Martin jumped up with her. Without a word, Kate went to the table which held the sherry and glasses. After filling two, she returned and offered one to Martin. "Fia is a sweet, unaffected young woman who has led an often unhappy life. I know my niece loves you; I know she will make you happy. I charge you to love her, protect her and keep her as content as is within your power–as you believe ordained." She clinked the edge of her goblet to his. "To your marriage, Martin Ross."

Martin was so stunned he could barely drink with her. When he lowered his glass, he raised her hand and bowed over it. "You have my sworn oath."

Kate swallowed hard. "Can...should I expect Fia to come home tonight?"

His expression softened a bit, but Martin shook his head. "I imagine she'll soon visit though." With that, he placed his goblet on the table, bowed again and, in the front hall, swung his greatcoat round him, picked up his bonnet, and closed the door in his wake.

"Arthur, come," he called, leaning down to ruffle the dog's thick fur then quickening his pace. Kate's last question left a nagging uneasiness in him. She owned the shop, but there was no reason to think she would continue to let them stay there indefinitely. In fact, he realized belatedly, Kate probably didn't know that he and Fia were at the shop. Martin rounded the far corner of the block where the shop sat, thinking hard about where, in Inverness, he and Fia might live until this whole ugly business with Forbes was concluded. He couldn't leave until he and Simon had things well in hand. As Martin pondered this new question, he stepped into the lane to cross to the other side. Arthur's unexpected bump into his legs, set Martin on his backside inches from the nervous, dancing hooves of a horse he'd not even noticed.

"You simpleton," berated the horseman, "watch where you tread or see if I don't let my horse trample you the next time!"

Martin pulled himself upright, any thought of apology for his own carelessness gone. Motionless, he stood glaring intensely at the reed-thin, lank-haired, colorless rider whose eyes set so close they almost crossed.

The man's unflinching glower made Struan uneasy as he tried to size him up. Decidedly, the ruffian was not tall, and he looked slight, but the greatcoat could be deceiving as to his true stature. As was his custom, Struan determined to bluff his way clear of actual confrontation and glanced furtively at the few people who had stopped to watch the commotion. He addressed them haughtily. "This Highland toad tried to unseat me by alarming my horse. Now he presents this threatening posture. Someone fetch the sheriff, and be quick about it so I can be on my way." Struan's hope to scare the man off by threatening the law had no visible effect–either on the man or the small crowd, for no one moved. Searching the crowd again, Struan trembled slightly; they looked none to happy with him. Through his disquiet, he heard the black dog's low, menacing growl and grinned his evil as he swiped out at Arthur's head with his riding crop.

In the next instant, Struan was looking at the fleecy sky, Martin's knee planted on his chest, the crop on the ground several feet away.

"A bit of advice, you *lowland* prick," Martin offered ominously. "Never insult Highlanders, particularly when you're in the Highlands; they don't take it well. And don't inflict harm on animals. Most are smarter than you, I dare say, and all have long memories for people who treat them cruelly. Now get up and be on your way." In a fluid motion, Martin had set Struan on his feet and thrust him toward his horse.

Hesitantly, Struan bent with outstretched hand for his crop, but a bystander's large boot pressed the stick into the dirt, and the owner's gruff voice offered, "I don't think you'll be needing this. And you should heed this man's advice."

Panic rising in Struan's chest, he whipped around, mounted his horse and spurred it to a gallop and away from the throng.

Amid pats on the back and words of support for his action, Martin knelt to inspect Arthur. With relief, he discovered that the rider had poor aim and Arthur was unscathed. As he straightened, Martin noticed Simon approaching and strode to meet his cousin.

"Why the gathering, Martin?" Simon asked and Martin obliged with a brief recounting of the incident. Simon vowed, "I would have given a great deal to see you put the louse on his back."

Martin grinned despite himself. "I must admit, it was satisfying."

"If you're ready to go to the millinery, perhaps Arthur should stay out of sight while we're there," Simon suggested. "We wouldn't want that fellow prowling about causing more trouble."

"You're right. He's bound to remember his anger with me–once his knees stop shaking. I had intended to see the curate," Martin noted, "I guess I'll do that in the morning." He picked up the pace, Simon falling in beside him. In response to Simon's request, Martin offered an accounting of his conversation with Kate and they soon found themselves at the shop. "I'll take Arthur round back; it's where I left Odhar. Oh, and Simon," Martin called as Simon reached for the door latch, "perhaps we shouldn't mention this to Fia. I don't want anything as trifling as this to intrude on her happiness."

"Agreed." Simon entered, just in time to see the only customer paying for the purchase of some French lace.

Alayne smiled in his direction. "I'll be with you shortly, Sir."

Martin entered through the workroom door and had scarcely closed it when Fia was in his arms, her kiss reaching up to his. The folds of his greatcoat covered her slender form as it arched against his in longing. She was gratified to feel the response of his body pressing her belly.

"I've missed you so," she breathed against his lips.

"And I've sorely yearned for this moment since I left you," he assured.

Fia stepped back and slipped his coat from him and hung it up. "I don't remember this coat."

"It was a gift from Annie; it belonged to her husband," he explained. "She knew I needed one and didn't want it to go to waste."

Fia smiled. "How like her to think of others. Did you get your errands done, Martin?"

Before he could answer, Simon's voice rang out from beyond the curtain. "Is it safe to enter?"

Fia turned to respond, but her words were stifled by a giggle of pleasure as Martin pulled her against him and planted eager, nibbling lips against her neck.

Simon repeated his request and, this time, Martin answered by holding the curtain aside. "Aye, it's safe for now."

Simon stood back for Alayne to enter and followed close behind her. This was the first time he'd seen Fia since she and Martin had...worked things out. He was stunned. Slowly, he approached and reached for her hand. "How truly beautiful love has made you, Fia." Her color deepened, her eyes shone and she carried herself with a confidence he could only attribute to someone who knew that she was loved and adored beyond measure.

Momentarily speechless, Fia hugged him tightly before finding her voice to say, "Thank you, and thank your cousin."

Alayne, observing this exchange, conceded that Simon was right. Fia was resplendent, transformed by having found Martin and by consummating their love. Alayne felt a pang of envy for she had never found that with Muir, not even when she thought they loved one another. She almost laughed thinking of the times she had counseled Fia on love. Quickly, she pushed her thoughts, and the envy, aside. Soon, she thought, I'll be free to follow my own heart. Alayne shifted her gaze to Simon's golden head and rested her hand on her belly to still its abrupt fluttering.

Chapter Twenty-Seven

Weary to the bone and flayed by a stinging rain, Douglas dismounted before Kate's row house. The darkness, having long since obscured his vision, seemed this night to have risen from the ground, not descended from the sky. Now that he was safely arrived, he allowed himself to shiver at the strangeness of it, and the contrast to the soft glow of many candles which touched the stoop invitingly when Kate opened the door.

"Douglas Sutherland!" she exclaimed, mightily surprised for the second time that day. Kate stood aside and urged him in before he could muster a reply.

"You must get these wet things off," she commanded. "Go stand by the fire in the drawing room while I fetch you dry clothes." Again, without waiting for a reply, she was off.

Douglas doffed his cloak and tricorne, and had barely reached the glowing peat bricks to soak in their deliciously earthy warmth, when Kate returned.

"These were my son's," Kate offered, holding up breeches, hose and a shirt. "He was tall and slender, as you are."

"Th...thank you, my d...dear Kate," he chattered his gratitude and, without thinking, removed his waistcoat and began to pull his shirt from his breeches.

Watching his actions, Kate belatedly handed him a towel. "I...almost forgot; you'll need this."

Douglas flushed heavily and, reaching for the towel, held it to his chest. "My apologies, Kate."

Kate colored slightly and pulled her eyes from his murmuring, "None necessary. Flora's gone for the day but I'll heat some soup while you finish changing." With that, she again left the room.

The last spoonful of bracing broth in him, Douglas leaned back in his chair, warm and content–except for the leftover aches from the previous day. From his hooded gaze, he watched Kate and imagined that this might be their home, she his wife, and that they shared an evening in quiet talk with promise of later pleasures in her demure smile.

"Douglas," Kate repeated, "is something amiss?"

Startled from his fantasy, he blurted, "It's lovely to be with you again."

Kate's flush swiftly returned. "Is that really what you were thinking?" she gently prompted.

Douglas dropped his gaze. "Aye," he responded, deciding it too forward to be more specific.

"I'm very glad to see you again as well," she offered.

He stood awkwardly, sucking in his breath at the pain.

"Douglas, what happened to you?" Kate asked, concerned by his obvious discomfort.

"My mare was frightened by a badger yesterday and I landed on the ground. I am better," he hastened to assure, "but I must be on my way while my legs can still carry me."

Kate rose swiftly. "Leave? Where will you go at this time of night?"

"One of the taverns; I must find lodgings. I'll be staying in town for a few days." His voice softened and he added, "I'd like to see you again while I'm here."

"Of course you'll see me while you're in Inverness; much has happened since you were last here. But the only thing you need do now is stable your horse. You'll lodge here for as long as you need."

After an awkward hesitation, Douglas replied, "If I may speak frankly, my thoughts earlier about being happy to see you were...well, not quite so general. They were nothing shameful," he hastened to add. "I...simply would not want you to be uncomfortable."

Kate stared at him, not sure she understood what Douglas was trying to tell her. However, the sudden pounding of her heart, and the tickling in her belly relayed the inference clearly. The second time she attempted to speak, she managed, "I'll not hear of you staying elsewhere. Besides, if it eases your mind, Alayne will be here shortly."

"And what of Fia?"

"There is news–good news–where Fia is concerned. But to hear all details, you must promise to stay." Expectantly, she awaited his reply.

Douglas didn't want to go. He had, after all, come to Inverness specifically to see Kate. And now that he was in her presence, he was struck again by the proud bearing of her graceful figure, her still radiant beauty and doe-like eyes. "I'll stay Kate, with great pleasure. Let me tend my mare and then you must tell me what I've missed."

By the time Douglas returned, Kate had brewed tea, laced it with whiskey and drawn two chairs before the fire. Upon seeing this, Douglas paused to absorb the cozy sight. Almost shyly, he smiled his appreciation.

"I thought you might need something to take any remaining chill from you," said Kate.

"It doesn't surprise me that you have put my needs first," he praised. Yet he noted a fleeting expression of unhappiness cross her features and remembered that he was here because Fia and Alayne thought she needed him. "Come," Douglas urged, taking her hand and leading her to a chair. "Sit with me and tell me how you've been since we were last together."

Somewhat flustered and flattered by his attentiveness, Kate began, "I've tried to take your advice Douglas, to bend a bit, and try to let go of Muir. It was good advice, but I haven't been terribly successful. However, what is truly important now is what has happened to our Fia."

Her hand on his arm and her open expression warmed him more than the whiskey. "You said... this is good news?" Douglas asked.

"Exceedingly good news," she promised.

"Has it to do with Martin Ross? Murdoch reported that he'd been seen in Inverness."

Kate nodded. "Fia and Martin have...reconciled their differences. It seems he has no wife after all. Just today, he came to tell me he plans for them to be handfasted as soon as Fia is willing."

"That is splendid news!" Douglas beamed. "It looks like I've arrived just in time to witness."

Kate fiddled self-consciously with the lace at her elbow. "I know nothing of their plans for witnesses, but I'm certain Fia will want you there."

"And, if you would do me the honor," he inclined his head toward her and finished, "I will escort you."

"I...I'm not sure there'll be a need," Kate reluctantly admitted.

"Whyever not?" Douglas asked, perplexed.

"The last time I saw Fia, I was in a foul, self-indulgent mood. I wasn't mean to her, I would never be that. Still, I was curt, absorbed in too many memories." Kate rose and began to pace, clearly agitated. "In just two weeks, my son will have been gone four years. Alayne and I worked out our differences over him not long ago. Then she told me she planned to end her marriage to him on the grounds of malicious desertion. The more I thought about that, the less I liked it. It's...it's selfish!"

Douglas dabbed the napkin to his mouth, patiently folded and placed it near his teacup, leaned back in his chair and gazed at her doubtfully. "Do you really mean that, Kate?"

"I...I do!" she insisted and, as an afterthought asked, "Why wouldn't I mean it?"

"Because by your own account, Alayne has never been selfish. She has remained with you, worked for you; in many ways, she really has been your daughter. What is selfish is expecting her to put her life on a shelf forever. Alayne is intelligent, pretty, talented, and has good business sense. Don't you think she deserves a full life with the love of some good man? With God's blessing, she might raise her own family."

Kate pressed her handkerchief to her nose and mumbled, "I suppose so."

Douglas continued, "Isn't part of this your own fear, dear Kate of being left alone?"

She sucked a startled breath, as if his accusation had been a blow to her belly.

Douglas wanted to comfort her somehow, but his experience with women was limited. He surely didn't wish to further offend her, so he remained where he sat, and waited.

Three quick steps Kate took toward him, an angry denial on her lips. Yet she stopped short and collapsed into her chair, her ire crumbling. A ragged sigh escaped in her words, "How do you always manage to cut to the heart of my feelings? Is this some special talent solicitors have?"

"I seem only to have this 'talent' as you call it, where you're concerned, Kate."

"It's very disconcerting," she tried to rally, dabbing at her eyes now.

Douglas smiled ruefully. "I'm sorry if it distresses you. Here," he offered, picking up the pot, "have more tea."

"No." Kate waved it away. "Any more whiskey and I never will stop this sniveling."

From the entry way, they heard Alayne's arrival. Kate shrugged and grinned at Douglas before calling out, "In here, Alayne."

"What wretched weather," Alayne declared. "I hope it clears up before tomorrow night or Hallowe'en will be–Douglas!" She beamed at the sight of him and hurried forward to take his hands and kiss his cheek. "How wonderful to see you. Oh, your timing couldn't be better." She turned to Kate. "You told him?" Turning back to Douglas, she rushed on, "Did she tell you about Fia?"

"Kate told me and I couldn't be more delighted," Douglas declared.

"And wait till you meet Martin; wait till you see the change in Fia–it's amazing." She looked suddenly serious. "I hope you haven't come to Inverness strictly on business."

"No," he assured, "in fact, I have only one piece of business to attend to." Douglas glanced down at Kate. "This is much more a visit for the pleasure of it."

"Ah, good...good." Alayne urged, "Please, sit down. I would join you both for a moment except," she mumbled while exaggerating a yawn, "I'm really very sleepy. Will you excuse me until breakfast?" Belatedly, Alayne asked, "You are staying here aren't you?"

"He is," Kate responded.

"Lovely. Well, I'm off to bed," she announced and whirled through the doorway, disappearing immediately.

Kate and Douglas sat a moment in stunned silence then Douglas turned to his companion. "She didn't seem sleepy to me."

"Nor me," Kate readily agreed. She rose and, approaching the bottom of the staircase, gazed into the emptiness above. "She seemed...preoccupied. I wonder what's behind it?"

Kate's assessment was accurate for, upstairs, Alayne undressed until just her shift covered her lithe form and went about the rest of her bedtime preparations as if she meant to retire. Faced with actually climbing into bed, however, Alayne turned away. She flung a shawl about her and crouched near the hearth, soon deep in thought.

So Douglas had answered their plea for help. Alayne hugged her knees, recalling how snug a scene Kate and Douglas made sharing tea in the drawing room. "Maybe his presence will help improve Kate's disposition," Alayne hoped. Now she could spare no more time for thoughts of them. Her musings drifted back the last few hours, first to the small shop serving modest fare where the four friends had supped, then back to the workshop. Here Martin had proposed they observe All Hallow's Eve together.

"This should be a very special celebration," Martin announced.

Simon teased, "I wonder if you would have been so eager two days ago."

"What does it matter?" he retorted, "I am now."

"And what say you, Fia?" Simon goaded a bit more.

She shifted an inch closer to Martin. "I say that I have a great deal to celebrate, and I'm ready."

"So, Simon, do you think you can help with our disguises?" Martin inquired.

Simon bowed from the waist. "At your command, my Lord." He turned to Alayne. "And what guise might I find for you?"

"Whatever you believe suits me, Simon," she responded, and immediately noted the gleam in his eye. "What are you thinking?" she demanded.

"That there must be an infinite number of choices. As to what suits you best, that will be difficult to decide."

Alayne allowed, "I trust your judgment implicitly," and shifted subjects. "What about a bonfire? They usually have several in town, down at Market for instance."

"We can visit more than one, can't we?" Fia asked.

"Aye," Martin replied, "and we should, though I was also wondering if we might not have one of our own as well."

Alayne seized the notion. "Why not?"

"The question," Martin said, scratching his beard, "is where?"

"Alayne's glen!" Simon piped. "Martin's never seen it."

"You have a glen?" Martin asked.

"Just a figure of speech," she said. "But it wouldn't do. It would be difficult to see in the dark."

Fia added, "It's too far to go to the glen that late at night. Besides, all manner of tricksters are about on Hallowe'en. I wouldn't want to come upon any that far from town."

"Are you sure it's not the fairies and spirits that concern you, my love?" Martin smiled, but abruptly ceased when Fia's face drained of blood and she stared at him.

"Lass, what is it?" he begged, alarmed.

Her voice nowhere to be found, Fia turned her face from his. How could she tell Martin what had happened to her on Culloden Moor? That she'd seen his beloved grandfather as clearly as she saw Martin beside her? Even if he believed her, how would he feel about it?

Belatedly, Alayne realized what was distressing Fia and thought to help by explaining, "It was that night on the Moor, Martin."

Martin whirled. "What did you say?"

"That night on Cul–"

"No," Fia broke into Alayne's explanation. "I'll tell him...later." She glanced at Martin again and forced cheer into her voice. "What about the Castle ruins? Couldn't we build our bonfire there?"

Puzzled by this exchange, Simon sought to ease the tension and agreed, "Fine with me." Besides, he had lovely memories of time spent at the Castle with Alayne.

Alayne also readily agreed that the Castle would be ideal. The three of them chattered on, anticipating the reverie to come.

Only Martin was quiet. Some memory nagged the corner of his mind. Clearly, Alayne was about to refer to Culloden Moor. A night on Culloden... "That's it!" he cried, jumping up and startling the others. "Kate said her niece was recovering from an accident on Culloden Moor." Martin clutched Fia's hand in his. "That was you. Why were you in that mournful place? What happened to make you look at me so strangely?"

"I...I," Fia stuttered, her eyes darting to each of her companions in turn. She could not bring herself to say more.

Alayne encouraged, "It'll be fine, Fia. You know what you saw."

Fia's heart beat faster and her breathing shallowed. Finally, with her gaze on Martin's anxious eyes, she admitted, "I thought you had come to me on the Moor. But it wasn't you, it was your grandfather."

Martin paled as Fia had, the memory of his dream at Jedburgh Abbey jarring him. Hugh had covered Fia's dead, mangled body. He fixed a penetrating glare on her. "Fia, what do you mean Hugh came to you?"

"On the Moor, amidst the fighting. I believe...think...he was trying to protect me," she offered. Martin croaked, "From what?"

Her eyes widened. "From the troops. They were all rushing about madly, brandishing broadswords and pistols, slipping about in the sleet and muck." She studied him a moment. "He looked so like you."

Martin's face twisted with grief, and he crushed Fia against him, feeling again the dreaded possibility of losing her.

Simon wasn't sure what was happening, but knew he and Alayne needed to give them time alone. "Alayne and I will be on our way now."

"There's no need," Fia and Martin mumbled at once.

"No, he's right," Alayne agreed. "Besides, I would like some time alone with Simon."

Simon glanced at her, unsure whether she spoke the truth or was simply trying to withdraw gracefully. As soon as they were outside in the rain, he quietly asked, "Did you mean what you said, about wanting to spend time with me?"

In the darkness, she came close enough so that he could see the answer on her face.

Tenderly, Simon smiled. He reached inside her hood, tilted her face upward and, with his eyes wide-open, pressed his lips to hers.

Alayne returned his kiss, slipping her arms beneath his cloak and around his waist. She felt her own heart quicken its pace and the rain no longer seemed as cold.

Reluctantly, Simon removed his mouth from her moist, sweet one. "I will see you home while I'm still thinking straight," he whispered unevenly. "Oh, Alayne. Every part of me longs for you. We don't have much longer to wait now, then you'll not need to fear or regret any word or feeling you have for me."

Alayne raised his hand and pressed it to her cheek. "I don't fear or regret them now. I just have to be patient."

"I hope you know how important your happiness is to me."

"You've made that abundantly clear." She hesitated, then added, "Do you have some idea how much I care for you, Simon? My situation hasn't allowed me to be–"

"Shh." He rested a finger on her lips. "I have an idea that you trust me, that you are, at the least, fond of me and, at the most, well, I look forward to the time when you are free to tell me in great detail."

Simon had tucked her hand into the crook of his arm and brought her to the door of Kate's house. There was a peaceful silence between them, one that swelled within Alayne as she readily admitted to herself for the first time, that Simon was indeed very important to her. She hesitated in his presence to even think the word 'love'. Now, alone in front of her own fire, the truth came easily to her.

When Simon and Alayne left the workroom, Martin whistled Arthur inside then locked the door. The dog trotted to Fia who obliged with a quick rubdown with toweling until Martin came to settle him by the hearth.

Silently, Fia lead the way upstairs, unsure about Martin's frame of mind. He must be shocked at her revelation, maybe annoyed that she hadn't told him sooner though, in truth, when had there been time? She took a deep breath and queried, "What would you like to know?"

Martin faced her, his hands resting on the back of a chair. "Everything. Why were you on the moor; what happened there?"

"Kate, Alayne, Douglas and I–"

"Who's Douglas?" Martin interrupted.

"Douglas Sutherland. He was my father's solicitor and friend and is the same to me now. It was with his help that I escaped the kirk the day I was to wed Struan. Douglas also hired Murdoch Sinclair to bring me safely to Inverness."

"Then I owe him a large debt," Martin declared solemnly. "Go on, lass," he encouraged.

"The four of us rode out to see some land near Nairn that Father had bequeathed me–beautiful land with a sand beach and large, but rather shallow cave–both useful for Forbes' smuggling operations and, as it turns out, the reason I was promised to Struan."

"For your land?" Martin asked.

Fia nodded. "It seems everyone but I was to profit from the illicit trade on my land." She noticed Martin's knuckles pale as his hold on the chair tightened, but continued. "When we started back home we were trying to outrun a sudden squall. It broke just as we neared a deserted stone croft surrounded by a low drystone wall. At the time, I didn't know we were at Culloden."

Martin could say nothing as the chill of memory shot up his backbone.

"Well, we were wet so Douglas built a fire. Before long we slept; the storm was still blowing hard at that point. I awoke later thinking I'd heard someone call out. I heard it a second time and, with the others still asleep, I went outside. The storm had stopped though the mist was thick. No one was there, but I heard other noises, metal clinking and clanging, so I went looking for the source. It began to sleet and the heath quickly became mucky under my feet."

The hairs on the back of Martin's neck prickled as she described the conditions he'd experienced during the battle.

"I wanted to go back to the croft but couldn't move. Suddenly, there were men all around me, in plaids, shirts, the King's uniform, slashing and stabbing at each other; the occasional crack of gunfire." Fia hugged herself and rocked back and forth at the memory. "There were agonized screams...and cries of triumph. And, out of the mist and sleet, a man came at me, the life gone from his eyes, hair and beard plastered with wet and blood, sword arm dangling, half-severed." She raised a stricken face to his and swore, "At first I thought it was you; I fainted."

Martin strode to the window and stared into the dense blackness. "What happened then?" he strained.

"When...when I awoke, three anxious faces hovered over me. I quickly realized what and who

I'd seen. I asked and Alayne told me they'd found me on the grave of the Appin Stewarts. If I'd had doubts, I didn't then; it was your grandfather."

Across half the room, Fia heard Martin suck in a ragged breath. She didn't know what to do or say. Lamely, she ended her story. "At daybreak, they brought me back to Aunt Kate's and put me to bed for the rest of the day."

Dizziness swept Martin and he braced himself against the window sill. He had no doubt that Fia had seen Hugh. His own terrifying dream of his grandfather and Fia still haunted him though Martin had prayed it was symbolic only of the fact that he believed Fia gone forever from his life. Now, accepting that she had come face to face with Hugh and survived provided some comfort and slight hope that perhaps the worst was over for both of them. Perhaps Hugh's appearance portended nothing sinister at all. But Martin couldn't be certain; there was still so much danger lurking for Fia. No, Martin determined, Hugh was warning him, showing him the way; what he needed to do for Fia, and what he had to do about Forbes to keep Fia safe. Of one thing he was certain. Martin would never tell Fia of his own, horrifying dream.

Martin's prolonged silence made Fia nervous. When she could stand it no longer, Fia rose, walked purposefully to where Martin still stood staring into the night. She slipped her arms around him, splaying her fingers across his chest and resting her cheek against his back.

Immediately, Martin's hands covered hers and, through his back, she heard his deep, rumbled, "Oh, my love."

Fia released the breath she'd been holding. "You aren't angry?" she whispered.

He pulled his erect frame even straighter and faced her. "Angry?" he asked, bewildered. "How could I be?"

"Your grandfather–"

He clutched her tightly, cutting off the rest of her words. "Hugh was protecting you when I couldn't. I only wish I could be sure from what."

"From the soldiers, what else?" It was Fia's turn to be confused.

Martin framed her face between his hands and tilted it to search her eyes. "It could have been as simple as protecting you from wandering around in the dark over unfamiliar land, or he might have been warning us to be vigilant. He must know about us for, by saving you, he has saved me all over again. I must do whatever it takes to keep you safe."

She started to speak, but he stopped her with a gentle, lingering kiss. "You think I'm reading too much into this incident," Martin guessed. "But Grandfather tried to teach me something valuable by every action he took. This was no exception." For several seconds, he scrutinized her. "Come, sit here." He led her to the chair that had supported him minutes ago and she obediently sat. One by one, Martin removed his boots, hose, waistcoat, shirt and, finally, his breeches. Sleek and golden in the firelight, he stood naked before her.

Fia's first instinct was to shed her own clothes and join him, yet something restrained her. She sensed some special significance to Martin's actions. This was not last night when he had stripped at her request so that she could admire for the first time his sinewy shape. Looking at him now, she realized anew that she would never tire of gazing upon or touching his fine body and her eyes drank in every detail of his form while she waited.

His silence stretched on and, still, she waited.

When his resonant tones broke the stillness, it was with a tremor that revealed a struggle with his emotions. "Last night we made love. And while you gave yourself freely and lovingly, I held something back." Martin crossed to her and, taking her hand, placed her palm against his heart.

Fia could feel its strong, sure beat pushing back on her fingers, but it didn't soothe her worry over what he would say next.

"My heart, you already own. My mind is consumed with you, so that must be yours as well. Without you, I am crippled so my soul, my very essence, you can also claim."

Tears stabbed Fia's eyes. "What are you telling me, Martin?"she whispered, voice trembling.

"I pulled away from you once when you touched me. I'll never do that again. What I denied you once, I freely give you now."

"D...denied me?"

Martin locked his intense gaze on her puzzled one. He guided her left hand over his ribs until it came to rest on the thin silvery scar; his mark of honor from the Battle of Culloden.

As she realized what Martin had done, Fia's hand pressed harder against him, she gulped air as though she could not get enough, and tears spilled freely down her face. In awed wonder, Fia's finger traced the length of the scar, faintly visible in the light of the fire. Overcome, she could not speak, but she rose and kissed him fiercely. His hands held her hips against his and Fia felt the pulsing blood stir her in response to his growing desire.

"Get me out of these clothes," she demanded, and Martin obliged, freeing her body in short order.

As she tossed her shift aside, Martin spread the blanket and waited on his knees. She knelt and pressed her body to his. "You'll never regret entrusting yourself to me, Martin." Again, she fingered the scar, while urging him onto his back. She bent forward and touched the scar with her lips, rested her cheek against it for a moment, then rose over him to kiss his mouth, deep and demanding, claiming all his future kisses.

Driven, in part, by memory of his old nightmare, Martin clung to Fia. And he was jolted afresh at how easily they could have missed finding each other again, discovering the truth. A lifetime together was almost lost. But God had intervened–He knew their paths lay together.

The ardor of their love making reflected the emotional pitch of their fears and their determination to conquer them. The teasing, tantalizing play of the early morning hours was gone and now there was hardly space for air between their bodies. Words were unnecessary; their communication, silent and instinctive. The tenderness with which Martin slipped into her was a measure of the infinite care he intended to lavish on her. He would never knowingly hurt her again–in any way. As he neared his own release, Martin heard Fia's breathing shallow and felt her body quiver. Fia cried out as her desire peaked and rolled through her in delicious waves.

Her head tucked under his chin, Martin held her tightly. Eventually, Fia heard the soft crooning sounds he was making. With the heel of her hand, she dragged tears of elation from her cheeks and softly asked, "Did I...was that...?"

Martin gazed blissfully on her dampened face. "You did indeed, my beloved."

She smiled her rapture, and pressed her cheek to his. "I could never have imagined...how glorious a feeling."

His thumb wiped a missed trace of tear. "You are so beautiful," he vowed solemnly.

"Because you make me so." She sighed contentedly as he kissed the hollow of her throat "Will it happen again?" she queried hopefully.

"I'm fairly certain it will." Martin smiled, reached for the blanket and drew it around them. "And I'll be right with you to help all I can."

Fia curled against him. "I can hardly wait."

Martin laughed sleepily, kissed her once again and, when he next awoke, Fia was studying him.

"Is something wrong?" he mumbled.

"No," she assured, and stated, "I never tire of looking at you."

"I'm not sure why," he yawned. "Handsome, I'm not."

"Seeking a few compliments?"

"No," he protested, "It's just that...I'm very...ordinary."

"Whoever told you that lied," Fia swore.

Martin wove his fingers in her lush hair."Would it be all right with you if we had this conversation when I'm really awake and can defend my point of view?"

She shook her head. "Your opinion in this matter doesn't count. Still, we can discuss it later if you like. There's something else I want to talk to you about."

"Now?"

"Aye, now."

Martin dutifully sat up, rubbed his eyes and said, "Sit here, love." He indicated his lap and Fia crawled onto it pulling the blanket around them both. "What is it you want to talk about?"

Fia stared into the fire.

"Lass?" Martin prodded.

She roused from her thoughts and declared, "I've never loved anyone else, but I know what I feel for you, and how you make me feel, is for life, maybe many lives." She slipped her arms around his neck, promptly dislodging the blanket. "I'm so overwhelmed with your gift to me, Martin. How can I make you understand how very much I love you? Even when we were apart, with no hope, I loved you more each day. I didn't think it was fair at all that you should so consume my thoughts and leave me so despondent, craving your presence. What was happening made me doubt my faith...all that had gone wrong, all my despair. But what I felt for you, only got stronger. And I realize now that my love for you, Martin, is my faith. And I will always believe in its power and grace, and its ability to sustain me. Make me your wife, Martin. I want to...*need* to call you 'husband' for, in my soul, that is what you are."

Martin's embrace tightened and he whispered against her lips, "I thought I was clear that I would have it no other way than to be your husband," Martin declared emphatically. "You tell me when we can wed–it can't be soon enough to my way of thinking." He urged, "Lie with me; I have news to share." When they faced each other, blanket momentarily cast aside, Martin apologized, "The talk about Hugh surprised me so that I didn't tell you what I did today."

"And what was that?"

"I paid a visit to your aunt."

Fia's brows lifted in surprise. "You went to see Aunt Kate? Why?"

"To tell her that, as soon as you would, I intended to marry you."

"You did that?" Fia whispered in awe.

Martin nodded. "I did. I meant to visit the curate to arrange for him to preside over our handfasting, but I was... delayed, so came here instead."

Fia grinned and teased, "So you don't think me too brazen, formally asking you to be my husband?"

"Oh, no, my love," he assured, "I'm honored!"

Her hand resting on his chest, Fia eased her leg between his. "I don't much fancy being married on Hallowe'en."

"Not tomorrow then," Martin lamented.

"All Saints Day?" she suggested.

The corners of Martin's mouth turned upward in pleasure. "The day after tomorrow then." He sealed the date with a kiss, then, wavering, he asked, "Do you mind not being married in the kirk?"

"That would take three weeks," she exclaimed, "far too long."

"Kate was concerned that you'd be disappointed," he admitted.

"We'd be no more married than we will by handfast," Fia declared. "Besides, as I said, my faith is in our love. God provided that, not the kirk."

"God's life, you humble me, Sweetheart." He kissed her, then suggested, "I believe Kate would like to be at the handfasting."

Fia snuggled closer. "And I would like her to be there."

"That reminds me of a problem we need to deal with," Martin said.

"What problem?" Fia yawned.

"I don't think we can continue to live here indefinitely. There's no adequate way to prepare meals and, if Kate finds Arthur sleeping downstairs, she won't be thrilled."

Fia chuckled. "No, I suppose not. But we have your croft. I see no reason–" Abruptly, Fia stopped and looked at him with narrowed, comprehending eyes. "This is about Andrew Forbes. You think we need a place to stay until you and Simon find and deal with him."

Martin opened his mouth to respond, but Fia sat up and away from him, wrapping her arms around her drawn-up knees and turning her thoughts inward.

He stretched out a hand, but stopped short of touching her. The barrier that had just sprung up between them hurt. Yet, if she shrank from his touch...no, that he couldn't bear.

On his knees behind her, Martin studied her pale skin and the narrowing of her waist below her long dark hair. No, he wouldn't let the barrier stand a second longer. His arms encircled her shoulders and he rested his chin so that his cheek touched hers. "Don't shut me out, lass."

Fia's hands pressed his arms harder against her. "Why must you do this? You know that Andrew is a dangerous man."

"He is indeed," Martin agreed. "He's too dangerous to let remain free to wreak his devastation. And I gave my word to Simon." To her silent trembling, Martin gently added, "Do you think I would choose to let you live the rest of your life in fear?"

"My fear is of losing you!" Fia blurted.

"I will not let that happen," Martin adamantly promised.

"If it were all within your power...you can't control–"

"Do you trust me, lass?" he interrupted. "Do you believe in the power of my devotion to you and the love we share?"

Fia gulped and nodded fervently. "I do."

"Then trust me when I promise you that I will spend a long, full life worshiping you. No one will deny me the right to prove each day, my love for you. Dealing with Forbes may be rough, yet justice will be done. And we'll be together and content beyond measure when it is." He caressed her cheek; trailed his fingers lightly over her lips and down her breast. "We'll talk about a place to stay later. Right now, a kiss would be heavenly."

Without hesitation, Fia turned and pressed her lips to his in a soft, lingering kiss. Silently, she determined to conquer her fear because she did believe in, and completely trust, Martin. And she had eminent faith now in their destiny to be together. With her decision, her mouth became hungry, demanding, and Martin readily responded, his hands touching and igniting her skin.

They lay down, each exploring, bestowing tender caresses and words. Their love-making was more deliberate this time, a complete blending which quenched emotional as well as physical desires. The only problem festering between them was in the open and resolved. Now, their loving and responsive movements brought another level of satisfaction neither had expected. They panted and strained and gloried in it before succumbing to a sleep of peace.

The quay was miserably cold and dank, fetid. The persistent deluge made Simon long to be back in the inviting comfort of Alayne's gaze. This was one of the few times he would allow himself to consciously believe a future with Alayne lay before him. His ecstatic grin was dashed by a gust blowing rain straight in his flushed face. "What I wouldn't give not to be here tonight," Simon lamented. But he reminded himself, without real regret, that he was doing a favor for Martin, and vividly recalled their brief banter.

"Really, Simon," Martin had valiantly insisted, "it's my turn to scour the harbor taverns for news."

"Oh no, Cousin. I'll not have Fia's wrath upon me by taking you from her charms so soon." Martin's voice wavered, "She would understand."

"She would not!" Simon had declared. "Martin, I truly appreciate your willingness, but let's not waste time arguing when we both know the outcome."

"All right, then," Martin had conceded readily. "But I will make it up to you."

"I'll see that you do," Simon promised with a bit of mischief in his eyes.

"I will indeed," Simon murmured to himself, stepping into a dimly lit, smoky taproom. He found an unclaimed copy of Tuesday's "Edinburgh Evening Current" and took it to a table near the wide hearth where he sat, hoping to dry out. The barmaid took his order for Atholl Brose while he draped his cloak backward over the chair to let the rain drip to the floor. A glance about told him he was a bit early for there were few men present.

"Your drink, Sir," the barmaid announced. She leaned close to him, placing the brew of honey, oatmeal and whiskey before him.

He purposely ignored the slight pressure of her breast against his upper arm, and sipped the drink gratefully. "Thank you, Miss, it's just what I need on this foul night."

"Call if you decide there's anything else you need on this foul night," she crooned, straightening slowly.

With the barest of nods, Simon dismissed her and her suggestion, and picked up the newspaper. "Ah," he murmured, "this is news London's been waiting a long time for." He scanned the report of the September 8 surrender of Montreal, Detroit, Mackinaw, and all other French possessions in Canada. Governor Vaudreuil, and the assembled Canadian forces, had fallen before General Amherst, whose collective British forces were too strong to be resisted. Simon thought he should feel good about the victory–he did, at least for the men whose lives would now be spared. But the French were still busy stirring trouble among the Indians in the northern colonies.

Though leafing through the other three pages produced nothing else of particular interest, Simon kept the paper before him as if studying it. It was an excuse to sit, listen and observe without appearing overly interested in any one thing going on. He pondered the task given him to disguise his dearest friends on the morrow. Some fancy masks borrowed from the theater might do to keep the spirits of the dead from recognizing the four, though the living spirits seemed much more frightening now. If he couldn't decide on suitable masks, he would suggest they blacken their faces with ashes as the Druids did to protect themselves from the occult. Simon smirked as the thought came to him that neither Alayne nor Fia would likely enjoy sooting their fair skins. His thoughts and table were suddenly jostled. Simon looked up into the watery eyes of a tallish man with slightly rounded shoulders, limp black hair and a long hand complete with splinted finger quickly laid down and withdrawn again in an attempt to steady himself against the rocking table.

"My apology," the man offered without sincerity.

Simon wanted no attention drawn to himself. "No apology necessary." He watched the fellow stumble away and concluded that this was not the first tavern he'd visited this night. His eyes turned back to the "Current", Simon stared blankly at the page and listened to the progress of the tipsy man as he made his way to a table that suited him.

The man bellowed for the maid and, when she responded, he roughly pulled her to his lap. She protested feebly until his free hand slapped a coin on the table before her. "This is yours for some information," the man proposed in a curt voice, much clearer than Simon would have expected given his inability to walk straight.

"And what would you be needing to know?" the barmaid responded, eyeing the coin.

"Thomas Gray...do you know him? Does he come here?"

"Aye, I know him. He's a regular, should be in before long. Is that all you want?"

"For now," the man said, but his hand stopped hers from picking up the coin. Instead, he gathered the coin between his fingers and slipped it down between her breasts. "I may need something later."

She giggled and rose. "Shall I point Thomas out when he arrives?"

With a mock bow, the man said, "I would be grateful." The wench started to leave, but he drew her back to his lap. "Perhaps later you'd consider showing me a proper welcome to town."

"Have you had no proper welcome, Sir?" she flirted, pressing a bit closer to his chest.

"Indeed not!" The man declared. "In fact, only hours ago, I was accosted by some lout whose cur tried to tangle with my stallion."

"Oh," she cooed, "were you hurt? Is that what happened to your finger?"

The man snorted, "That is a recent injury. No, I trounced him soundly."

At that remark, Simon spewed his drink and began coughing. The barmaid whisked herself to his side and pounded his back until he waved her off and croaked, "Thank you." Simon dabbed his watering eyes and blew his nose before noticing the man hovering over him.

"Was it something I said?" he snarled menacingly.

Simon covered his mouth with his handkerchief until his smirk was under control. At last, he replied, "Aye, Sir, to think you have been treated so shabbily in a town I have always found most welcoming. I'll luck, Sir."

Reassured that his word had not been doubted, nor his plight found amusing, he puffed out his chest and indicated the chair across from Simon. "May I?"

Simon nodded his assent and watched the man slouch into the chair. So this was the man Martin had encountered. In five minutes, he'd shown himself a pompous, lying, letch. A conversation with him might be an interesting way to wile the time. "You've just arrived today, then?" Simon asked, brimming innocent interest.

"By way of an inn where I ran into another disagreeable sort, though I knew this one. He's a petty solicitor who has been a thorn in my family's side of late."

"Bad luck again," Simon ventured, quickly realizing he only needed a few words to elicit many from the man.

"Bad luck indeed! This whole trip is a bad idea if you ask me." He turned and signaled the maid for another whiskey.

"This is business then?" Simon prompted and was startled by the sudden narrowing of the man's limpid gaze and the air of caution that descended almost visibly.

"What do you know of my business?"

"I assure you, Sir, I know nothing of your reason for being here. I merely said 'business' because you've not recounted any pleasurable experience yet."

The man's guard relaxed slightly and when the maid set his order before him, he grabbed her once again. "The night's not over yet; there may still be pleasure to come." He tried, with little success, to fondle her bottom through her petticoats, and the maid danced away toward another table where customers called for her. He threw back his head and emptied half his drink. "Speaking of pleasure," he queried, catching a dribble of whiskey on his finger and sucking it loudly back into his mouth, "is the grouse hunting good here?"

Simon shrugged. "I couldn't say; I'm not from Inverness."

"Oh, where then?"

"I've been in the colonies a long time." Instinctively, Simon was cautious with his information.

"I heard that Montreal is ours at last," the man exclaimed, wiping his hands on the barmaid's apron as she passed by.

Simon held up the paper. "Just read it myself." He tossed it just short of the man's glass. "And where do you hail from?"

"What business is it of yours?"

"The same business it is when you ask it of me," Simon coolly responded. "Idle curiosity–at least that's my intent."

"Again, my apologies, Sir," he grumbled and tripped over his lie, "Edinburgh."

Deliberately, Simon fingered the side of his glass. "By your accent, I'd have surmised further west."

"Ha! Good thing you don't earn your keep by making such guesses–or do you?"

"No, I don't," Simon replied. "However, accents are a...hobby...you might say."

"Hobby?" The man poked his nose disdainfully higher. "Grouse hunting. Now that's a hobby that's worth its while."

Simon's amusement with this character had vanished with the man's boorish behavior and he offered a strained grin as his only response. He prepared to excuse himself when the barmaid stopped beside them and addressed his companion.

"He's here, Sir, Thomas Gray. Over there."

Without hesitation, he rose, thanked her with a whispered promise that caused her to twitter, and glanced at Simon. "Maybe, I'll see you again..." He waited in vain for Simon to supply a name.

Simon answered, "Perhaps so, I'm here from time to time."

The man bowed stiffly and hustled over to the table of a stocky man with ruddy complexion and gray curls popping out from under a well-worn shapeless hat.

Involuntarily, Simon shivered at the sight of the two together. What a strange, disagreeable fellow for he and Martin both to have encountered in one day. He honestly hoped he would not run into him again.

Chapter Twenty-Eight

Although no one had actually informed Kate, Alayne was certain her mother-in-law knew that Fia and Martin were staying at the millinery. After all, why else would Alayne spend more than one night in a row at Kate's? She had been a bit apprehensive about having Kate and Douglas arrive at the shop so early in the morning, but had failed to talk them out of accompanying her. Douglas was impatient to see Fia and meet Martin.

Kate said nothing, yet was anxious about her next encounter with Fia. She had serious doubts as to whether her niece would be happy to see her. But she hid her concerns behind Douglas' eagerness, and insisted on going along.

To Alayne's relief, Fia was downstairs sweeping the shop when they arrived, readying it for the day's business.

Martin was perched on a stool near the curtained workroom door, blowing a sweet tune on a tin whistle. He ceased the moment he realized he and Fia were no longer alone.

Upon seeing their visitor, Fia dropped the broom. *"Douglas!"* she exclaimed her excitement, and wrapped him in a welcoming embrace, then stepped back to view him better, her hand in his. "I've missed you; it's so wonderful that you're here. There's someone I very much want you to meet." Fia reached out her other hand and Martin advanced to take it, bringing the two men face to face.

Unexpectedly silenced by overwhelming emotions, Fia couldn't perform the introductions. Douglas stepped in. "You're Martin Ross," he beamed. "I couldn't be more delighted to meet you."

Bowing, Martin said, "And you must be Douglas Sutherland." He returned a smile of honest pleasure and extended his free hand. "I am forever in your debt for saving Fia from the Forbes brothers."

Douglas took the offered hand. "Believe me when I say I've never performed a deed with more satisfaction." He studied Martin a moment, then fixed his gaze on Fia's radiant guise and proclaimed, "I never thought to see Fia so captivated. Murdoch told me you were in Inverness," he added, turning back to Martin. "But not until my arrival last night did I learn how well everything was working out for the two of you."

"It is, indeed," Martin agreed.

Finally locating her voice, Fia added, "The timing of your visit couldn't be better, Douglas."

"Oh? And why is that?" he asked, eyes twinkling mischievously.

"Because this means you can attend our handfast tomorrow. You and Aunt Kate must be two of our witnesses."

Douglas embraced Fia afresh. "It would be my honor and great joy," he assured her and, again, clasped Martin's hand.

"Aunt Kate?" Fia prompted.

Kate flushed with relief. She quickly stepped forward and hugged her niece. "Of course, my dear, I would be honored. And I hope you will have the ceremony in my home."

Enthusiastically, Fia gushed, "Thank you, we would love that."

Kate, unsure of how to suitably congratulate Martin, hesitated before extending her hand. Martin took it and kissed her cheek, which caused Kate's blush to spread down her throat to the neckline of her gown.

With some small embarrassment, Kate fanned her heated face in a deliberately casual fashion and asked, "What did you mean by 'two of your witnesses'?"

Martin responded, "Fia meant that we also want Alayne and Simon to witness our joining." He reached for Alayne's hand and pulled her into the circle.

Douglas sensed Kate stiffen and, without show, tucked her hand into the bend of his arm and patted it lightly, an act which succeeded in delivering its unspoken message.

Kate lifted her chin almost imperceptibly. "Of course you want them to share in your happiness. Fia and Alayne have grown so close." She glanced at Martin and stated, "And Simon is your cousin."

"As well as my closest friend," Martin added, the coolness of her tone not escaping his note. "Did you know that without him, I may never have found Fia again? He put the pieces together that led me back to her."

"No," Kate admitted, "I didn't know. For that alone he should be at your side," she vowed enthusiastically.

Fia eased toward her aunt. "Martin...Douglas, if you two will excuse us, there's a matter I need to discuss with Aunt Kate and Alayne."

Martin was pleased at this windfall which would give him the opportunity to finish some business. "Fine, lass. Perhaps Mr. Sutherland would care to accompany me to the curate's so that I can fix a time for the handfasting."

"I'd be happy to—on two conditions," Douglas said. "First, you must call me Douglas."

"Douglas." Martin agreed, prompting, "And second?"

A solemn mien stole over Douglas who turned to Fia. "I have some news."

"What...what is it, Douglas?" Fia stammered with sudden foreboding.

"On my way here, I spent the night at an inn, where I came across Struan Forbes."

Fia's lips clamped in a grim line, her fists clenched. She gradually became aware of Martin's supporting hands on her shoulders. She hissed her uneasiness, "Is Struan in Inverness?"

"I honestly don't know. What I do know is that he left at daybreak yesterday on the Inverness road." Douglas stumbled through his apology. "My dear I loath bringing even a hint of trouble into your life, especially when you are so happy. But I had to warn you in case that walking dunghill is indeed in town."

Fia could only nod; her appreciation and dread mingled.

However, Martin slipped one arm round her waist and inclined his head toward Douglas. "We're grateful for the information and the advantage of knowing we should be even more vigilant." Martin's glance took in Kate and Alayne, gripped in chilled silence. "Give me a moment with Fia, Douglas then we'll see the curate." Martin guided Fia through the curtains. Once standing in the workshop, Martin pulled his lover into a strong and comforting embrace.

Fia nestled into his clasp and fought to still her racing heart. She hated that Struan had the ability to affect her life so dramatically just because it was *possible* that he had come to Inverness. Did this news mean she'd have to look over her shoulder and around every corner before feeling safe doing even the most mundane tasks? Would it make her new life ugly by turning each day into an ordeal? "No," she muttered indignantly.

"Lass?"

"Tonight is All Hallows Eve; tomorrow I become your wife. I won't let Struan ruin that, won't give him that power over us. We've waited and suffered enough."

Martin saw resolve in her expression and her strength of will rebound. "You make me very proud. You are a courageous and determined woman. This man, Forbes—he'll never best you; he'll never triumph over us." Martin's face glowed with admiration. "We must take care and can because of Douglas' warning. If we do, Fia, we'll outlast Forbes, his brother, and anyone else who attempts to harm you and come between us."

Adoringly, Fia studied his comely face; her hands stroked the length of his back.

"Tomorrow is our wedding day," she beamed at him.

Martin lowered his head and their kiss was long and stirring. At its end, Fia rested a hand on his chest and suggested, "We've kept everyone waiting. You should take Douglas and see the curate now."

"Aye." Martin's mouth curved in a warm smile and the two reemerged into the shop where Douglas, Kate and Alayne stood exactly where they'd left them.

Her hand in Martin's, Fia reassured, "It's fine, truly." Almost collectively, the little group let out a sigh of hope that Fia's prophecy would prove correct.

Shortly after, the two men stepped out into the street and, as she watched them, Fia thought they made as interesting a pair in their differences as Martin and Simon did. Douglas was long and fair. His straight hair neatly queued, he dressed in fashionable mantle, frock-coat and breeches. Sinewy and taut, Martin was a half-head shorter, his loose chestnut hair and beard flowed fiery in the sunlight; his simple, serviceable clothing hidden by his oversized greatcoat.

Fia turned to her companions and asked with pride, "Aren't they exceptional men?"

"Undeniably," Alayne agreed, glanced at her mother-in-law and queried, "What say you, Kate?"

"Decidedly remarkable," was Kate's honest answer, bringing gratified looks from both young women. "Now, Fia," Kate asked, returning to business, "What did you want to discuss with Alayne and me?"

Fia beamed, "My wedding dress, what else?"

As they stepped out the front door, Martin turned to Douglas. "I look forward to becoming better acquainted, Douglas. While we're alone, though, I'd like to ask your help on several things."

"I'll assist if I can, Martin. What kind of help do you require?" Douglas asked.

"First, legal." Martin replied. "After we see the curate, I'd like to divert to some quiet place so that you might draw up the document needed for me to gift Fia with a third of my land."

Douglas stopped. "Are you sure?"

"I am."

His fingers rubbing his smooth chin thoughtfully, Douglas asked, "May I speak bluntly?"

Martin nodded curtly, not expecting or understanding Douglas' hesitation.

"Fia doesn't need your land."

Exasperated, Martin said, "I know she's better situated than I, still–"

"Perhaps I was too blunt," Douglas interrupted, "for that's not my true point, and I actually know nothing of your situation."

Confused, Martin asked, "What is your point, Douglas?"

"How much do you know about Forbes and this smuggling business?"

"Everything Fia has told me."

Douglas continued, "Then you must realize that, even without a marriage to Struan, there's nothing to keep them from illegally using Fia's land."

Martin admitted, "I hadn't thought about it but I understand. So?"

"I've alerted the authorities about our suspicions; that is the only course open to us at this time. But if anything were to happen with smuggling operations on that land and, God forbid, Fia were implicated, she could lose everything she has, including her freedom and your land– if you give it to her."

Indignantly, Martin defended, "No one would believe that of Fia. Anyone can see she's not devious just by looking at her."

Douglas put a restraining finger to his lips as Martin's voice had grown louder and was attracting a curious glance or two. "Believe me, Martin, no one can tell a person's honesty by looks. You and I know Fia; we know her to be truthful. Others don't. And the Forbes's are an insidious pair; the Grahams as well for that matter."

"But–"

"Others don't know her," Douglas reiterated. "There are four reasonably well-respected members of the Glasgow society who would undoubtedly swear against her–two in her own family. You must see how much weight that would carry."

"You've warned the authorities," Martin reminded.

"I have," Douglas repeated, "but Fia knows nothing of these possibilities. I didn't want to upset her more than she was already o..ver..." Douglas trailed off and he cut his eyes from Martin's.

Martin stared a moment, then nodded his belated understanding that Douglas referred to his own role in the heartache Fia had endured. His dejected look caused Douglas to grasp Martin's shoulder and state, "My best advice is to protect your land. Perhaps in some...ceremonial rather than legal way, you can share it with her. I can see how much this means to you."

"Once more, I am in your debt."

Douglas' lips curved upward. "See to it that Fia is as happy as your wife as she is today, and you will more than repay any debt you think owed me. Now, how else can I serve you?"

"Struan Forbes," Martin replied. "Tell me about him–everything you can think of. I don't even know what the man looks like. How can I help protect Fia if I don't know our enemy?"

Martin looked around suddenly as if expecting to see someone he knew. As though on cue, Arthur appeared at his side.

Douglas stood stone still, staring down suspiciously as the big black dog sniffed his boot. "Do you know this hound?" he asked.

Martin dropped to one knee and ruffled the fur at Arthur's neck. "Aye, Arthur's mine. He was on the stoop behind the millinery; must have heard me."

Douglas stretched out one hand to make Arthur's acquaintance and, taking the touch of wet nose leather as a positive sign, gingerly scratched the dog's head. Straightening, Douglas asked Martin, "Shouldn't we be on our way? We can talk as we go."

Martin cracked a smile and agreed, "Aye, we should." The three continued the errand together, Douglas profiling Struan Forbes for Martin's benefit.

"Forbes is a solicitor, I'm ashamed to say, though not considered a very good one by his peers in Glasgow. He works mostly out of Edinburgh these days. He's a pompous, insufferable braggart, and he's a bully. I believe it's intended to hide a rather milksop and cowardly personality. He has an eye for women but, seemingly, not much luck with them."

"Thank God," Martin murmured.

"Aye, thank the good Lord," Douglas seconded. "Struan has always been in Andrew's shadow, Andrew being stronger physically and in the mind. Struan is far better at amusing himself; I'm told by some colleagues that he loves the hunt."

Martin inquired, "Why was it Struan, not Andrew, who was to wed Fia?"

"Though not an innocent, I believe Struan was a pawn in Andrew's plans just as Fia was. Andrew is involved with Elizabeth Graham who will inherit her father's estate. I'm certain Andrew never considered a match between himself and Fia." Noting a change in Martin's demeanor, Douglas cocked his head. "The attachment between Elizabeth and Andrew doesn't seem to surprise you. I assume Fia mentioned it."

"She did. But in my encounters with Elizabeth–two of them," he offered in response to Douglas' raised brows, "the depth of her connection with Andrew Forbes became clear."

"I bet those encounters were fascinating," Douglas concluded.

"Fascinating and unsettling," Martin affirmed. "Elizabeth bears Fia a great deal of animosity. I believe much of it is caused by what Elizabeth perceives to be Andrew's interest in Fia, on a very personal level. When Simon met Fia, though he didn't know her by that name, she was being accosted by Andrew Forbes. My cousin didn't make the connection until much later after seeing first-hand that Elizabeth has no love for Fia."

Douglas nodded. "Then jealousy is behind Elizabeth's ire."

"Aye, unfortunately for my Fia."

The endearment did not escape Douglas and he smiled his increasing belief and satisfaction that Martin was all Fia believed him to be. He shook his head to bring his thoughts back. "Ah, I was about to describe how Struan Forbes looks."

"Good," Martin encouraged.

"He's between you and I in height; he's wan, sallow-skinned, and appears more so for the blackness of his wilted hair. Gaunt, with almost colorless blue eyes set very close. He's not a pretty fellow by anyone's standards."

Martin's gait gradually slowed as he pondered the familiarity of Douglas' description. When he had matched the image with his memory, Martin came to a halt, glowering at his companion.

Douglas also stopped and returned the glare with rising trepidation. "You've seen this man," he correctly guessed.

"I have, yesterday late in the afternoon. But for Arthur, Forbes' steed would have ridden me down. My God," Martin swore. "That stinking piece of filth was what they'd have had Fia marry? There is no justice."

"Ah, but there is," Douglas disagreed, "for Fia is about to marry you, Martin. With you, I judge she will be cherished and loved as much as anyone has a right to be. And if anyone has that right–"

"It's Fia," Martin finished.

"Come," Douglas urged. "You have errands. Now that we know for sure Struan is here, it will be easier for us to locate him and watch his every move."

Martin and Douglas tried once to return to the millinery only to be turned away at the door after a brief exchange with Kate and Alayne.

"I don't understand why I can't see Fia," Martin complained. "Just tell her I've returned."

Kate tipped her head to the side and, with a coy smile offered, "It's not that simple, Martin. Fia is to be married tomorrow."

His brows drew down. "I know that."

Patiently, Kate continued, "And because you all intend to join in the Hallowe'en revelry, that leaves very little time for her to prepare."

"Prepare what?" he demanded with some frustration.

Over Kate's shoulder, Alayne peeked out the door. "Martin, just as you have tasked Simon with finding our guises this evening, Kate and I are helping Fia with her guise for tomorrow."

Martin stared uncomprehendingly.

Alayne grinned at his stubborn inability to understand their teasing. "My, my...love certainly has addled your brain."

Finally, Douglas' tap on his shoulder broke Martin's trance. "I believe the ladies are referring to Fia's wedding dress."

Martin closed his eyes, shook his head in embarrassment and finally questioned in an oddly guilty tone, "Her dress?"

"Of course; like Simon had made for Mairi." No sooner had she uttered the words, did Alayne bite her lip with regret. Before she could speak again, Kate stepped in.

"That's correct, Martin, and Fia's gown shall be my gift to her."

Martin began his protest, "Mistress—"

"No argument." Kate cut him off with a casual wave of her hand. "Now off you go; we have work to do." She reached into her pocket and pressed a key into Douglas' palm. "If you want to go back to the house, just let yourself in. I'm not certain when I'll be there myself." With that, Kate closed the door and faced Alayne's admiring stare.

"Well done, Kate," Alayne praised. "Martin would lay down his life for Fia, but I don't think he can easily afford the dress he would like to provide his bride."

In a rare moment of closeness, Kate twined her arm with Alayne's. "I think he'll be happily surprised when he sees that he's had a great deal to do with the making of this gown."

On the stoop, Martin blinked dazedly at the door before he frowned and shifted a disgruntled gaze to Douglas, who laughed aloud.

Martin touched his chest with his open palm. "I should pay for Fia's wedding gown."

Douglas shook his head and swallowed a last chuckle. "Martin, you don't want to deny Kate the pleasure of doing for Fia what Fia's own mother would have if she were able."

With a resigned sigh, Martin turned from the door. "You're right, of course."

"And what of your own clothes?" Douglas ventured.

"My clothes?"

"Aye, what will you wear to your wedding?"

Color crept up Martin's neck and began staining his face. "I...I will have my breeches laundered in the morning, and my waistcoat brushed—my frockcoat is gone," he added belatedly. "I'll wear the shirt Fia made me." He straightened his shoulders, determined to look his best for his bride.

Douglas watched Martin closely. It was obvious from their very brief acquaintance that Martin was a proud man and Douglas wasn't sure how he would react to any interference. Still, he felt the need to try, so cleared his throat. "Martin, would you allow me, as an old friend of Fia's father, to outfit you with new breeches and frockcoat?" He held up his hand as Martin's expression clouded and hurriedly continued, "Fia is very dear to me—as near to a daughter as I will ever have. It would give me enormous pleasure to do this." Douglas half expected a polite but firm refusal of his offer. He was surprised then when Martin lowered his eyes and remained silent.

Martin shoved his hands deep into the pockets of his greatcoat and began walking; Douglas and Arthur fell in on either side of him. Finally, in a tight, clear voice, Martin responded, "It's against my nature to accept such an offer."

Douglas held his tongue, hoping Martin's tone implied his decision wasn't final.

"I...I don't want to embarrass Fia by looking too...worn."

Douglas vowed, "I don't believe you're capable of causing Fia embarrassment. Martin," he reiterated, "it would give me great pleasure to do this."

Martin raised repentant eyes to Douglas. "Even my pride has its price. With thanks, I accept your gracious offer. But," he hastened to add, "I will repay you."

Douglas beamed, happy with Martin's assent, not willing to quibble over later payment. "Fine, then let's be off, as Kate suggested, but in search of a tailor."

It was nearly twilight when the two men returned and ventured another rap on the door. Once again Kate answered; this time, she swung the door wide. "Come in and warm yourselves, gentlemen. Fia and Alayne should return momentarily."

Douglas and Martin entered, the latter inquiring, "Where are they?"

"They've taken Fia's dress to my house." Kate looked from one to the other, her gaze lingering on Douglas.

Knowing what the response would be, still Martin felt compelled to offer, "Why don't the two of you join us in our All Hallows celebration. I'm sure Simon could find two more disguises with little effort."

Before Kate could answer, Douglas said, "Thank you for the invitation, Martin. I hope this doesn't give offense, but I was rather looking forward to sharing a quiet evening with Kate before her fire."

"I can't think of a better way to spend any evening." Kate's comment set Douglas' heart to fluttering and she turned to Martin and touched his arm. "I too thank you for thinking to include us. We should start home now. You four enjoy yourselves and we'll see you tomorrow?"

"At five o'clock," Martin supplied.

"Tomorrow evening then, if not before," she concluded. "I'll just fetch my mantle."

A short time later, alone in the workroom, Martin wished he weren't. His mind spinning, he began to pace. Twice today, he'd been innocently reminded that he barely earned enough to support himself. At his croft, he could provide and grow what he and Fia would need to be comfortable. Or he could practice medicine again. But how would he manage for them in Inverness until this business with Forbes was settled? "I must sell my cloths at the earliest opportunity," he muttered, wandering upstairs where he felt closer to Fia. "I can't begin to guess how long it will take to find Forbes."

His pondering leapt to his most immediate concern. Now that he had proof Struan was in town, Martin knew Fia shouldn't stay. Discovery was too big a risk, but how could he convince her to go elsewhere? A shudder of revulsion toward Forbes shook Martin's frame and he felt suddenly cold. Kneeling at the hearth, he stirred the fire until blue flames licked the corners of the peat bricks. He scrutinized them until his focus blurred, and his memories drifted back to other fires in another hearth. There was Fia, her exquisite shape veiled by her damp shift after her fever had broken. Again, Martin saw her face, framed radiantly by the fire's glow as she stirred their supper; he remembered her enthusiastic dancing to tunes blown on his whistle for their meager Beltane celebration. And with a pang of regret, Martin recalled the sad countenance she'd turned to him when he'd questioned her past, forcing from Fia her tale of loneliness and misuse at the hands of her uncle and cousin–a bleak tale she'd revealed with more composure than he believed he would have if the circumstances were his.

As Martin thought about it now, he believed Fia had shared with him everything that night, all except the monstrous prospect of impending marriage to Struan Forbes. And where is the other Forbes? She didn't know him then except as an unnamed murderer along the coach road. Andrew Forbes, who he was certain was the one who beat her, tried to use her for his own gain, would brutally bed her against her will–rape her.

An anguished moan escaped Martin; searing fear for Fia filled him. After several deep breaths forced him to focus, he made a promise to himself. "I don't know how but I will keep Fia from harm at the hands of Struan and Andrew Forbes, the Grahams, or anyone else who would dare threaten her. By any means I can, I'll protect her." He barely heard the door open and close below. He called down to Fia and, in response, Fia answered him and climbed to the top where he welcomed her with loving arms.

She gave him a long, lingering kiss at length asking, "What time tomorrow will I become your wife?"

"Five o'clock," Martin swore. "I only wish it were sooner."

For a moment, she studied him. "Is something amiss? Something I don't know about?"

Martin shook his head. "Nothing new. I've been thinking about how badly you've been treated since you went to live with your uncle–how he plotted to give you to ghouls who would use you and abuse you for the rest of your life."

"Martin, that is the past," she attempted to soothe.

"It isn't, that's the point. I'm positive Struan Forbes is here, just as Douglas suspected."

Fia's grip on him tightened reassuringly. "As long as we're together, Martin, I'm not afraid."

"I am!" he declared. "You're in peril as long as you stay here."

Visibly, Fia stiffened, anticipating what he would say next. Her determined gaze captured his anxious one. "I'm not leaving."

"I need to make sure you're safe, Fia. I had a dispute with Struan Forbes yesterday–only I didn't know it was him until I asked Douglas for a physical description."

"You did what? What happened?" She shuddered at the thought that they'd come face to face.

Martin recounted the episode and added, "Simon and I agreed there was no reason to let the incident upset us all, that's why I didn't mention it. Arthur and I are fine. But if I had realized that sniveling carrion...." His voice trailed off and he swallowed hard. "I don't want to be separated from you–"

"You won't be," she broke in. "I've told you, I won't leave."

He pleaded, "Fia, I can't be with you every minute, and I'll worry every minute I'm not with you."

"You don't need to. Most of the day, I'm here at the shop. I still have Alayne and Aunt Kate close; I don't ever need to be alone."

"They would be no match for either Forbes brother. Be reasonable."

Fiercely, she declared, "Reason has nothing to do with it, Martin. This is about love and time stolen from us. I won't leave you. There's no room for fear or doubt, sadness or regrets, only for love and devotion–that's the least of what I will bring to you as your wife."

Torn, yet not prepared to give in, Martin searched her face for some hint of weakening he could prey on. At length, seeing none, he sighed his resignation, "I so cherish you, Fia. To have found you at all was a wonder; to have found you again and unraveled that which kept us apart is a true miracle. Your love is a gift from God." His kiss was intimate, searching and full of promise for the life they would share.

"Then God will watch over us, Martin, never fear. Now, Alayne is downstairs waiting. Let's sit with her until Simon arrives."

"We must tell them about Struan."

"Right away," Fia agreed.

"Why is it," Kate asked her companion, "that everything Martin and Fia do ends up thrusting Simon MacLaren together with my daughter-in-law?"

With infinite patience, Douglas inquired, "Will you feel differently about MacLaren when Alayne is no longer legally wed to you son?"

"How I feel won't matter," Kate responded caustically, "Alayne will be a free woman." Standing at water's edge, Kate stared into the shallows of the River Ness.

Douglas watched the turmoil playing on her face and wondered if Kate really could ever forgive what she almost certainly viewed as Alayne's betrayal. She'd made progress in that battle, he acknowledged, inch by tiny inch. Still, the thought that she might not forgive weighed him with sadness.

Kate broke the stillness, her expression relaxing ever so slightly. "Alayne has some feelings for MacLaren, of that I'm certain. Yet, I have to admit, whatever her involvement, she's been discreet; I'd have heard about it otherwise," she assured herself more than Douglas.

He remained silent, believing there was nothing he could say to sway her that he hadn't uttered before. The afternoon was lengthening, the light fading and, though no one was near them, he could sense the excitement brewing–people anticipating a night of All Hallows revelry. It would be dark very soon and while he thought of suggesting they return to her home, he said nothing. When Douglas again focussed on Kate, he was startled to find her face inches from his.

"You're tired of my tirades," she pronounced insightfully and, before he could respond, admitted, "So am I. No desire of mine will bring my son back, and I truly do want Alayne to be

The Borrowed Days

happy. As you've reminded me more than once, she's been my daughter. It's time that I put her needs before my own. So," she promised him with dark, sober eyes, "I'll not chastise her, nor interfere again. Alayne will find that I'll support her in every way I can."

Douglas stared at her, tears pricking his eyelids. Was this proclamation sincere he wondered, and found his answer in her serene expression. "Thanks be to God, Kate!" he murmured and, before thinking twice, framed her face between his long fingers and kissed her soundly. A stabbing doubt for the welcome of his kiss caused Douglas to falter and step from her stuttering, "I...I...can't imagine...."

Even in the gloaming, Kate saw the uncertainty flood his face. Purposefully, she stepped forward to fill the space he'd just vacated. "I hope you don't intend to apologize," she whispered and lightly graced his cheek with her palm.

They stood close for a time, tingling with warmth neither had experienced in far too long.

"*I think this* an appropriate choice," Simon declared, holding out an ornate mask of an owl and a cloak patterned like brown speckled wings.

Martin took the feathered visage from his cousin's hand and held it before his face. "How do I look?"

"Infinitely wiser," Simon grinned his response.

"To think of the years I spent in study believing that would make me wiser," Martin joked, lowering the mask and relieving Simon of the cloak. "All right then, what have you chosen for yourself?"

Simon brought forth his own furred guise for inspection. "Why the cunning fox, of course. After all, I had to think of so many suitable disguises."

"Indeed, you did," Martin sympathized and changed the subject. "Simon, I need to talk to you about the man I had the row with yesterday."

"Oh," Simon interjected excitedly, "I had an exchange with him last night at one of the quayside taverns. What an odious fellow."

"You did?" Martin exclaimed, shocked. "Odious is an appropriate description–that was Struan Forbes."

Simon's astonished eyes questioned what he'd heard and found confirmation in Martin's dour expression. "Struan Forbes? How did you–"

"From Douglas Sutherland, Fia's solicitor."

Confused, Simon asked, "When did you receive word from him?"

"Today. He arrived last night and accompanied Kate and Alayne here early this morning. It was on his description that I realized who had nearly brought Arthur and I to harm." Martin perched on a stool near the worktable. "Fia and Alayne know, and I suppose Douglas has informed Kate. Tell me though, what happened last night? How did you know it was the same man?"

Simon relived the encounter for Martin's benefit and added, "Now that I know who he is, I think he may have given us some unexpected help in our search for Andrew."

"Which is?"

"This Thomas Gray he was so eager to contact," Simon stated with satisfaction.

Martin agreed, "Of course. We must find out more about Mr. Gray, and quickly."

"Aye, but it will have to wait," pronounced Simon as a sound on the steps lifted both men's eyes upward. "The ladies return."

Simon had disguised both women in men's garb, mindful of protecting Alayne's reputation and Fia's identity. Alayne descended first as Shakespeare's Hamlet. Her silken hair was imprisoned under a soft-crowned hat with a small brim. She wore a long-sleeved shirt, woolen doublet, and hose which displayed her lithe legs from mid-thigh to her round-toed leather shoes. Both men gaped at the transformation which was completed by a large turnip lanthorn carved to resemble a human skull, and held in the palm of her hand. At first, Alayne had balked at carrying it, but realized quickly that she would take creepy delight in toting the 'skull' around on this particular night.

"Are you sure the theater troop knows you borrowed this costume?" she asked, stepping into the room.

Susan M. Walls

Simon reassured, "They know," and took her measure with longing in his eye. "Superb, don't you think, Martin?"

"Absolutely," he declared with enthusiasm. "I do hope you have a cloak for her in case she gets cold." He gestured in the direction of Alayne's legs. "Have no fear," Simon said, "I've provided everything. And here's Fia."

Martin turned to the stairs where Fia stood in her jester's costume: half blue and half yellow, the tunic's colors reversed from those of the breeches. Her own hair-covering came to two drooping points on either side of her head; bells were sewn onto each point. Her stockings were blue wool and her face was painted white with a garish black smile and brows on it.

"Well?" she inquired to the silence around her.

Simon beamed his satisfaction. "No one would ever recognize you, Fia. It's a triumph!"

Martin continued to stare until Fia could no longer stand his silence.

"Say something, Martin," she pleaded.

"I've never seen breeches look so good!" he obliged.

The paint could not hide Fia's blush of delight. She walked close and, standing before him, murmured her thanks for his praise and caressed his bearded cheek.

Alayne and Simon each looked away from the intimate moment and their eyes caught and held. In a low voice, Simon declared, "I've seen breeches look that good." He stepped closer and dropped his voice. "I love what I see whenever I look at you, Alayne. Every moment we share, is one I treasure. In two weeks, with your permission, I intend to show you how much you mean to me."

Alayne's hand stole against her fluttering belly. Bravely she returned his stare and, in a daring whisper inquired, "Will you have a change of heart if I again offer you what I did at the glen?"

Simon could scarcely breathe his promise, "My heart will not change; I cared for you and wanted you then. My answer will be different, I assure you." Distantly, he heard Martin clear his throat and glanced expectantly at his cousin.

"Come," Martin urged. "The sun has set; the bonfires will already be lit."

"Aye, I suppose so," Simon sighed, reluctant to give up this private moment with Alayne. His cheerful self returned as he added with dramatic flair, "We must be near the fires if we're to avoid the thundering horses of the witches' Hallowmas ride. "Here," he offered, handing another turnip lanthorn to Martin. "You'll need this to keep the demons away!"

Indeed, as they left the shop, the glow of bonfires began filtering the darkened sky and the four were joined by an excited Arthur. Fia tied a length of gathered yellow broadcloth around the dog's neck and he pranced beside them looking much like a silly, overgrown flower. When they stepped onto High Street, they were promptly swallowed up by guisers and revelers surging their way to Market and a number of faint-hearted folk who hurried on their way, fearing and wanting no part of the pagan side of this celebration.

The throngs crowded the lanes, laughing, chattering, chasing each other and squealing their excitement when caught. Some older folk seemed very solemn; Martin surmised they celebrated the Samhain, the Celtic feast of the dead, and would be giving thanks to the gods for the safe return of their livestock from summer grazing. Being the season of the earth's decay, many would petition those same gods for a renewal of the crops for the coming year. "On this one night," Martin pronounced, "the past, present and future all come together."

"They do for a fact," Alayne agreed, pointing to the shop fronts lining the Market. There, young folk were trying their hand at various means to divine information about their future spouses–a favorite Hallowe'en pastime. The four watched and listened as several methods of augury were plied.

Fia, who had never been allowed by George Graham to observe Hallowe'en in this manner, began spewing questions. "What are they doing with the kale?"

"You can tell much about your future spouse by pulling a kale stalk," Alayne offered.

"Such as…" Fia prompted.

"By the size, you tell his or her stature," she obliged. "And, by the taste, whether your spouse's temperament will be sweet or sour."

"Careful," Simon warned as several children careened into their path. Arthur's bark sent the little ones shrieking in different directions.

The bonfire roared, flames stretching upward, sparks exploding beyond where flames reached.

They watched the milling crowd, some with faces chalked with ashes, some masked like creatures, recognizable and not. And there were those who simply covered their eyes and nose with strips of material with holes in them to allow them to see their way.

The friends passed seers who coaxed all manner of folk into having their fortunes and futures told. On a few occasions, the friends watched as blindfolded diviners reached to place a hand in one of three bowls.

"Now, this one I can tell you about," Martin offered. "If the diviner's fingers reach into the bowl of clear water, the man is destined to wed a virgin. The bowl with sooted water means the spouse will be a widow, or at least a woman who is no longer virginal. If the diviner's hand rests in the empty bowl, bachelorhood is what lies ahead." Each completed prophecy drew moans and cheers from participants and spectators alike.

The scenes were repeated at other bonfires they visited. By unspoken agreement, no one urged another to have their futures told. Instead, they contented themselves with eavesdropping on omens given to others, and delighting in the antics of revelers around them.

Near the third bonfire, was a fiddler whose bow coaxed lively jigs and reels for those who wanted to dance. In unison, Martin dove into a jig with Fia, and Simon swung Alayne into the dance right behind them. Between giggles, misplaced footing and keeping pace with the fiddler, they were soon breathless. When Fia could speak, she exclaimed, "I wish you had your whistle, Martin; I would love to dance again to your tunes."

Simon turned surprise on his cousin. "Is that right, Martin? You play a whistle?"

"He was playing this morning," Alayne confirmed, "though I heard little of it."

"He used to play the fiddle as well," Fia chimed proudly.

"Really?" Simon exclaimed, glancing at his cousin. "I had no idea."

"It's been a very long time since I touched a fiddle," Martin assured and, turning to Fia, caught her chin gently between thumb and forefinger. "Later, I'll play for your pleasure."

"On that enticing promise, I think it's time to head up to the Castle and light our own fire," Fia finally suggested.

"I stored some wood and peat up there this morning," Simon announced.

"No wonder you were nowhere to be seen today," Martin remarked, amazed. "You thought of everything!"

"What about food?" Alayne asked. "I'm starving. It must be all this excitement."

Fia added, "And the fact that we had no supper." She turned to Martin. "Could we take along some apples?"

"Aye, we'll buy a few. They're plentiful enough on this night," he stated, glancing at several wooden tubs half-full of water where apples sank and reappeared under people's attempts to capture the elusive fruit with their teeth.

After they'd bought their apples, they began their trek to the Castle, Arthur trotting ahead of them. As they neared the opening in the wall where Simon and Alayne once had taken refuge, Simon suggested, "The ground gets very uneven here, watch your footing."

In response, Martin shifted the food and grasped Fia's hand in his. "You're cold, lass," he observed.

"Not for long. I'll soon have a fire to sit by, and your arms around me."

Alayne overheard Fia's response and turned thoughtful about her earlier exchange with Simon. Simon had never been specific about a future with her. "My own fault," she admitted silently, always having shunned such conversation because she was still married. Alayne cast Simon a sidelong glance, his strong profile stark in the moonlight. A pang of longing struck her forcefully, stealing her breath. Yet, she wondered if she'd made a mistake reminding him about the glen. "What if that's all he thinks I want from him," she worried. "He doesn't know I've grown to love him."

Alayne's shoulders drooped and her pace slackened so noticeably that Fia wondered if she were feeling ill.

"Here we are," Simon announced triumphantly.

Fia wasted no time. "Why don't you and Martin light the fire and excuse us for a few moments." She plucked up Alayne's hand and led her, unresisting, down to the end of the wall and just around the corner. Arthur was at their heels.

"Is there a problem?" Alayne asked dully.

"You tell me," Fia insisted. "You suddenly seem to have lost your enthusiasm."

Alayne rubbed her forehead with a gloved hand. "At the shop, Simon and I...we were talking about what might happen in two weeks. I said something I'm not sure I should have." She muttered almost apologetically, "I think he loves me."

"I'm sure of it!" Fia smiled behind the painted grin. "In two weeks, you'll be free to follow your heart at last." Fia bent to more closely scrutinize Alayne's face. "Do you know where your heart will lead?"

Alayne nodded. "I haven't told Simon that...that I love him. I *do* love him, Fia. Who would have believed it possible?"

"I would...Martin would...and I'm certain Simon hopes for it."

Alayne worriedly bit her lip. "I believe Simon might think all I'm interested in is...is...."

"Tell him of your feelings," Fia urged. "Tell him this night, then there will be no doubt in your mind what he believes."

A familiar voice drifted across the frosty air. "There are two lonely gents nearby who crave sharing a fire with two willing women– if they're the right women."

Alayne cast a doubtful look Fia's way, but her friend only nodded encouragement. Straightening her shoulders and swallowing hard, Alayne answered Simon's invitation. "How fortunate it is for the two gents that those very women are here. We're ravenous though and you said nothing of the food we brought," she continued lightly as she rounded the corner and slipped her hand into Simon's. "Is food part of the offer?"

"It is." He led her to a cozy spot between the wall and the blaze.

Fia and Arthur stood at the corner of the wall as Martin advanced. Fia's heart swelled with pride as she glimpsed his beloved countenance, no longer owl-like. God could not have been kinder to her than to allow her to share love with such a magnificent man. As he stopped before her, Fia fervently wished that her face wasn't covered in paint.

His breath caressed her skin as he asked, "What are you thinking that causes you to frown so?"

"How inconvenient a disguise is when it means smearing your handsome face with paint if I kiss you."

"But it has kept you nicely hidden which is–"

"Don't tell me it's more important keeping hidden than kissing you," she interrupted.

Martin slipped his arms around her back and whispered against her ear, "Only when in public, never at any other time."

"I'll accept that." Fia turned in his arms and wriggled her back against him until his cloak covered them both. "Are you warm? Can we stay like this for a while?"

"Well, it isn't as warm as my greatcoat but, with you under here with me, it'll do nicely." Behind her, Martin grinned. "We can give Simon and Alayne some time alone as well." Martin kissed the nape of her neck sending shivers of anticipation coursing through her. Resting his chin on her shoulder, Martin's gaze followed hers to Arthur's sweeping tail and yellow ruff. "Do you think Arthur has any idea how ridiculous he looks?" he smirked.

"I think he looks quite cavalier!"

Simon sat close at Alayne's side, his finger curling a lock of pale hair that had escaped the small brown hat. "Why do you think those two are staying from the fire?" he asked idly.

"They want time alone together. I imagine they must savor every moment, especially since there are still forces at work that would keep them apart." Alayne's smile was shaky. "Also, they probably think we'd appreciate time alone."

"What an inspirational idea." Simon pressed the curl against his cheek.

Alayne looked discomfited and, noting it, Simon lightly touched her hand. "What is it that bothers you, Alayne?"

With a deep breath, Alayne struggled to divulge her heart. "Simon, you've been considerate, kind and patient ever since we met."

Simon's heart began to pound and his belly to churn. These were words that, if strung together in a play, often meant a woman was trying to rid herself of an unwanted suitor. Had his own exuberance for her distorted his belief that she liked him? He was so despondent at that possibility Simon barely heard the rest of Alayne's thoughts as she spoke them.

"Your honesty and warmth and loyalty are so unfailingly genuine. I...I never expected to find all those things in one man, not after my experience with Muir."

Simon had gone so pale and listless, Alayne began to waver. "I tried to resist though everything about you draws me closer. Your nearness steals my very breath. Simon, I realize–to my surprise, I confess–that I've come to trust you...implicitly, and also...also, that I love you," she rushed to finish before her lagging confidence failed her altogether.

He stared at Alayne uncomprehending, then his mouth dropped open.

In the ensuing silence which Alayne found intolerable, she strove to explain further, assuming he needed it or he'd have spoken."S...since I'm still not free, I realize I'm being unfair, doing what I always ask you n...not to do. I haven't the right. And about what I said earlier about the glen, I shouldn't–"

Simon's astounded kiss sliced through her explanation. His arms encircling her, pulling her hard against him, told her clearly that he needed no further explanation, he understood.

When he broke their kiss, Simon lay his forehead against hers, panting through tears of happiness. His lips again found hers and when he looked into her moist eyes, Simon knew she'd spoken the truth. "I have prayed for your love," he choked, petting her cheek, her hand. "Now you've given it to me and honored me with your trust, which I believe may have been more difficult for you to bestow. Alayne, my love, you'll never regret it, I promise you."

She fervently returned his embrace then her lips joined his and captured his very soul.

Chapter Twenty-Nine

"You're making me nervous, Forbes," snarled Thomas Gray, pausing on his approach to the strand. "Stop twitching."

"I'm not *twitching*," Struan snapped peevishly. This whole business is not to my liking."

"Then in the name of all that's Holy, why are you here?"

Struan's head slumped forward as he grudgingly confessed, "It was Andrew's idea."

"Gordon," Gray harshly reminded, only to have the correction dismissed by the shrug of Struan's shoulders. The ruddy-faced Gray studied Struan through narrowed eyes trying to imagine how he and Andrew might really be brothers. Thomas had known Andrew for many years and respected his flair for business, though not all his methods used to accomplish the job. Andrew was as heartless as this one was feckless. Now, Gray doubted for the first time his partner's wisdom in insisting on a more active role for his younger brother.

"What are you staring at?" Struan snarled.

"Nothing."

"Then let's get on with this. It's creepy being out here tonight."

"Surely you don't believe in witches and fairies?" Gray grunted a laugh at Struan's hasty scan of the horizon and promptly lost interest in coddling this dullard. "All Hallows Eve is perfect for our business. Almost everyone is busy with their merry-making; they stay in town and away from us. Now, enough talk. There's work to be done and men, women and children waiting to do it."

Gray handed one of two lanthorns he carried to Struan. "Carry this...and don't light it until I tell you."

"How will this help?" Struan whined impatience. "Aren't we too far from the landing site?

"That's why we don't light them yet. It's to signal the ship once we see her."

"And if there's more than one ship, how will you know which ship is the right one?"

Thomas growled, "By God you ask a lot of stupid questions."

Struan huffed, "Gordon sent me here to learn; your job is to teach me. Now, answer me."

Gray clamped his jaw angrily and gritted, "In the first place, if there's more than one ship, nothing at all will happen tonight. But if there's only one, the signal will be all sails furled except the main topsail."

"After that?" Struan prompted.

"You just wait and watch–and learn. Teaching you doesn't mean I have to tell you everything. Keep your eyes and ears open."

Together, the two men trudged across the machair to Fia's strand and under the cliff where the cave gaped black and foreboding. As they neared it, Struan discovered people waiting quietly in the shadows, hands stroking the pack horses to quiet them, or checking rope slings which would secure tobacco bales and kegs of rum and brandy across the horses' backs. Just inside the cave, Struan glimpsed the bows of two boats and, directly above on the cliff, a crouched figure kept watch–not on the sea, but landward.

In a pale whisper, Struan asked, "What of excise men?"

"Our spies know where they are."

"If that's true," complained Struan, pointing to the figure on the cliff, "what is he doing?"

"Keeping his eyes open; a little extra care is a good thing," Gray barked. "Now stand back against the cliff, shut your mouth and wait."

And wait they did for what, to Struan, seemed hours. In reality, it was no more than twenty minutes till word came that the ship had been sighted. Gray and Struan lit the lanthorns and Gray held them both high then low, raised them aloft once again before snuffing them and setting them on the sand.

A short time later, the hidden boats were ordered into the water. Again, it seemed an eternity until the dinghies, riding low, arrived back at water's edge. Struan observed as the waiting workers disengaged from the shadows and the men, women, and several children Gray had mentioned, quickly ferried the cargo off the beach or directly onto the waiting horses. The moment a horse had two packs secured on its back, it was led away to one of several secretive places where the contraband would be stored. Struan didn't know where those storage places were and he didn't care. He shuddered at the eerie silence. With his estimated forty workers and nearly as many pack animals scurrying around, almost all he could hear was the slap of small waves on the sides of the boats. Apprehensively, he glanced behind him and was somewhat relieved to see the sentry still atop the cliff. Unsure whether the fact that it was Hallowe'en made a difference, from this night of experience as a smuggler, Struan knew he hated it and would try very hard not to do it ever again.

Exhausted and exhilarated at the same time, Fia wove her fingers with Martin's to begin the walk back to town. Behind her, she could hear Alayne's hopeful protest, "It simply can't be that late, can it?"

Simon reassured, "It can and it is, lass. I hate to be the one to tell you so." His voice was so mellow and rich with devotion it made Fia sigh. Simon and Alayne had confessed to their dearest friends that they had, at last, declared their love for one another, and their announcement was met with crushing hugs and joyful kisses all around–despite Fia's painted face. She was struck by both the awed shyness that seemed to have consumed Alayne where Simon was concerned and the pride and elation that glowed Simon's face brighter than the firelight.

They chatted and laughed as Arthur lead the way down toward the still boisterous scene being played out below the Castle ruins. As they approached the Market, Martin stepped beside Simon and asked, "Why don't you stay in the workroom tonight. There's no reason for you to go elsewhere."

"I wouldn't dream of it," Simon insisted, "not on the night before you wed."

Fia echoed, "Really, Simon, you should."

"No," he said, raising a hand to emphasize, "You're both very thoughtful; I appreciate it more than you know. However, with so much going on I haven't even mentioned that I moved into a small room at the theater."

Alayne responded with surprise, "The theater? Where? Is there even a hearth there?"

"In the corner of the dressing room is a small fire and I have the place to myself–the entire theater, I mean." He looked from one to the other as they viewed him with uncertainty. "I assure you all, it's fine. I come and go as I please, which is very useful."

Alayne shivered. "Are you certain, Simon?" There was something about him being alone in that place that made her uneasy.

He stopped, wrapped her shoulders with one arm and pulled her close. "I am." Reluctantly, he released her, realizing there were other people milling about. "I'll walk you to Kate's." Simon turned to Martin. "Where shall I meet you tomorrow?"

"Come to the millinery," Martin replied. "Fia is going over to her aunt's at about three o'clock; you and I can go over shortly before five."

The couples hugged each other once more and went their separate ways; Simon and Alayne set out for Douglas Row; Martin and Fia, with Arthur trotting along side, turned toward the millinery.

At the foot of High Street, Arthur darted forward to lead the way; Fia and Martin quickened their pace to follow. They didn't speak, knowing there would be time for tender discussion when they once again lingered in each other's arms, damp and appeased from loving. Their silence was so comfortable that Fia was nearly jolted from her feet when she spied a familiar figure striding toward her.

Instantly alert, Martin placed himself almost squarely in front of her. "Who is it?" came his harsh whisper.

She hesitated, her heart pinching painfully at his reaction–his need to protect her. Anger and fear were a powerful combination.

"Lass, tell me," he begged.

Fia curled her fingers round his arm. "Not Forbes," she quickly assured. "That man coming toward us, his face blacked by ashes–the man wearing the knit cap."

The man was almost upon them; Martin nodded his recognition.

"He was watching the shop that morning I arrived early because I couldn't sleep. It was before you and I–"

"Aye, Simon told me." From the corner of his eye, Martin watched the man pass by, seemingly unaware of their presence. At the same time, Fia moved up beside Martin and turned her head to observe further as the man melted into the darkness. She shivered and, with a gentle hand at her elbow, Martin urged, "Let's hurry; we aren't far from the millinery."

"No we aren't," Fia observed thoughtfully.

Shortly after, they entered the workroom with Arthur, who'd been waiting at the door and, while Martin locked up behind them, Fia relieved the dog of his costume. Delighted, he shook vigorously from nose to tail tip.

Martin turned to Fia. "You don't know the man, do you?"

Her perplexed response was, "I don't think so, yet, I'm certain he's the same man I saw that morning."

"How can you tell in the dark, lass? His face was covered in ashes."

"By his walk. I would recognize that loose, indolent gait anywhere; I believe it's burned into my memory."

Martin speculated, "He could be someone Forbes has sent to locate you but, if that were the case, and Forbes knew where you were, he'd have taken some action by now."

"I'm sure you're right, though why else would someone watch the millinery? He was only a few blocks away tonight. Could it have been coincidence?"

"Perhaps," Martin replied, his voice lacking conviction. "You don't believe it is, do you?"

"No," she declared through clenched jaw. "It seems that, each time we let our guard down, we are abruptly reminded to take nothing for granted."

"Nor should we," Martin responded in a calming tone.

"Of course not," Fia agreed, then abruptly announced, "There's no sense standing here all night trying to guess who he is or what he wants."

Martin agreed. "True...it doesn't help us. Anyway, for now, I believe there's no danger; he showed no sign of recognition."

Fia nodded before raising her face to his. "Nothing would please me more at this point than to rid myself of this disguise and show you how very much I want to be your wife." She gently rested her hand on his chest, her ire drained and her gaze warming to the love reflected in his eyes. "And since I want to be your wife more than I've wanted anything in my life, does that tell you something about the kind of night awaiting you?"

A mischievous grin tugged the corners of her mouth and Martin's breathing quickened. "I'll bring water up so you can wash off that paint."

Fia shook her head. "It's already up there; I just need to take all this off." Her hand swept head to toe of her jester's guise before she admitted in a conspiring whisper, "I may need help."

"I'll assist in every way you can think of, and then I'll try to think of some more."

"I'll hold you to that promise," she laughed and scampered before him up the stairs.

Alayne lay abed in her room at Kate's house, unable to sleep, unable to quit her thoughts of Simon or quell the trembling in parts of her body which had lain dormant too long. His attentiveness and touch this night held such promise for happiness that she could scarce believe her good fortune. Without Fia's encouragement, Alayne knew she would have turned her back on Simon's resolute courtship. Allowing another man a prominent role in her life had been all but unthinkable to her when Simon first appeared. Yet his eloquent persistence broke through her resolve. How glad she was.

A shiver abruptly coursed through her. The temptation to compare Simon with Muir was great, but Alayne resisted, knowing Muir could not win on any level of comparison she could conjure. With great certainty Alayne knew that Muir represented darkness and despair, pain and rancor. Simon was the sun–elation, rapture and fulfillment. More than that, she did not need to define.

On her side, hugging the spare pillow against her body, Alayne relished the stirring of her blood that accompanied Simon's presence; her face flamed heat in the darkness as she pushed one thigh over the pillow and allowed herself to imagine how much pleasure it would give her to feel Simon's hardness against her and inside her. With a moan, Alayne flipped to her back and covered her face with the conspiring pillow. "This kind of thinking will not help me sleep," she declared in the silence and strove to shift her thoughts. They settled on Kate and Douglas. She liked Douglas very much, and it had become obvious that Douglas and Kate liked each other somewhat more than very much. Fleetingly, Alayne wondered how they had spent their evening. Flora undoubtedly went home directly after supper which left Kate alone with her guest for hours. "I hope they made good use of the time," she chortled, then thought, "if not for Martin and Fia, who knows if Simon would have ever come to Inverness, or Douglas either. And if neither Simon nor Douglas had come to Inverness, Kate and I would still be lonely and miserable with each other. That's two things I have to thank them for." Nodding her satisfaction with her assessment, Alayne snuggled down, determined to find sleep before the sun rose again.

Douglas absorbed the play of light and shadows on Kate's face, which tilted delicately toward the sun's warmth, her eyes closed, a hint of a smile on her lips. That he could see her thus first thing upon rising every morning would, he believed, fulfill his fantasies. A fluttering in his stomach–nervousness or adoration, he wasn't quite sure which–caused him to shift, and that caused Kate to turn her head and look at him.

"It's a lovely morning, Douglas." Kate's voice rippled over him like the finest silk.

"A splendid day for a wedding," he rejoined, advancing to the window where she stood.

"Indeed," she agreed, never taking her eyes from his pleasing face. "Did you sleep well?"

Douglas flushed slightly and admitted, "After a time. And you?"

She glanced at her hands, and tried in vain to suppress a grin. "After a time."

"Ah, Kate," he said wistfully, taking her fingers lightly in his, "this morning you look like Fia's sister rather than her aunt." It was true. She glowed–signs of old hurts and disappointments faded.

His expression confirmed the truth of his words and Kate squeezed his fingers in thanks.

At the doorway, Flora cleared her throat. "I heard Mr. Sutherland come down, Mistress. Will you be wanting breakfast now?"

Without fuss, Kate retrieved her hand and attempted a somewhat formal tone, answering, "Fine, Flora. We'll be in momentarily."

Flora bobbed a curtsey and retreated.

Kate fumbled for an appropriate apology. "Flora is a discreet soul, you needn't worry about gossip."

"Because your hand was in mine or because we spent an entire evening alone together?" When she didn't respond, Douglas tilted his head and questioned, "Are you worried?"

For a moment, Kate considered his question. Finally, she answered truthfully, "I don't believe I am."

A smile split Douglas' lean countenance. "Then neither am I!" He offered his arm. "Shall we?"

Douglas settled Kate, then himself at the dining table, while Flora brought their meal. "This looks delicious, Flora," he offered. "You're a fine cook."

"Thank you, Sir." She bit the grin tempting her lips, but the lure was too great and she offered, "I hope you'll be here for many more meals, Mr. Sutherland," before hurriedly escaping to the kitchen.

Douglas and Kate exchanged a surprised look, unsure how they should react. Suddenly, they burst into laughter, arrested only when tears trailed from their eyes. It was in this state that Alayne found them and smugly concluded that their evening must have gone very well indeed! She determined then and there to require only a scone and some tea and be on her way to the millinery.

"*You should have* seen them together," Alayne declared. "I may as well not have been there for all they noticed. I was amazed–and charmed."

Fia was pleased at her friend's report. "I can't wait to see this myself."

"Well, I've no doubt you will this afternoon–that is if you can see anything but Martin!" Alayne leaned over and hugged Fia hard. "Speaking of your husband-to-be, where is he?"

"Gone to speak with Simon and run some errand he won't tell me about," she forced a playful pout.

"Wedding related I'd wager. But why's he gone to see Simon? Didn't Martin ask him to come here just before five o'clock?"

Fia nodded and confirmed, "He did but, after we left you last night, something disturbing happened."

Sobering quickly, Alayne asked, "What?"

"Do you remember the morning the man watched the shop from across the street?"

Alayne's expression began to cloud. "I do."

"I saw him again, not three blocks from here."

"You've no doubt?"

"None. He just walked past us, showed no interest. It shocked me to see him again though, I can tell you."

"What could he possibly want?" Alayne wondered.

Fia's mouth set in a grim line. "I wish I knew. By appearances, it would seem he wanted nothing. Still, he was so close to the shop, I can't but think it odd."

By half past two, Martin returned with a bundle under his arm and a beaming face. "Not long now, my love." he declared and kissed Fia soundly. "Alayne, you are radiant today," he added with satisfaction as his glance lit on her.

"I needn't tell you why, I'm sure," Alayne responded gaily.

"Well, if I weren't sure," he teased, "all I'd have to do is tell you that Simon has that same sort of glow about him."

She smiled broadly her thanks, and then turned to Fia. "Are you ready to leave for Kate's?"

Fia kissed Martin one more time. "I am now."

From the doorway, Martin's serene face glowed as golden as the light of the tapers filling the parlor. His enchanted gaze swept the scene slowly, memorizing the look and feel of the room where he would make Fia his wife. The tall-backed upholstered chairs provided a comfortable refinement; the highly polished mahogany candle tables and desk added a cordial welcome. Kate was so extravagant with the candles, all newly lit, that Martin was stunned. Their shimmering warmth reflected in their silver and brass holders the bases of which were surrounded by fir boughs, green and lush. More greenery was on the mantle along with a vase of the last of the autumn gentians, their dull red and purple blossoms somehow radiant in the setting.

Kate stepped beside Martin and touched a hand to his shoulder. "You are a very handsome husband-to-be, Martin," she proclaimed then nodded to Simon. "Mr. MacLaren".

Simon executed a bow in response.

"Thank you, Mistress," Martin sighed and nodded toward the room. "And thank you for this."

Simon agreed that the room was lovely then told Martin, "You look quite dignified…and a little nervous."

Martin grinned and mentally took stock of his appearance to reassure himself that he looked his best for his bride. He'd trimmed close his beard, and his unruly curls were, well, still a bit unruly. Though he was to be married in these clothes, Martin was conscious when Douglas purchased them of their need to be serviceable far beyond this day. The new frock coat and breeches were deep blue, wool broadcloth which contrasted the dusky shade of the shirt Fia had made when she was at his croft. The only decoration on the suit was pewter buttons. The effect was simple though elegant when combined with the white silk stockings and white embroidered waistcoat which had been Martin's only true indulgence. He hadn't planned to let Douglas purchase a waistcoat at all–he was doing enough already. However, the man who ordered it had refused it when finished–a discrepancy on the price. It fit Martin reasonably well and the tailor made them a good deal to take it off his hands. Martin looked down at his feet encased in black, silver-buckled shoes borrowed from Simon. "I can't remember the last time I wore something other than boots."

"Lucky I had them with me, and that they're a decent fit," Simon grinned.

While Simon chattered on, distracting Martin's thoughts, Kate studied him—for the first time with some measure of objectivity. He didn't look like his cousin, except perhaps in stature and the curl of his hair. She could accept that Simon was attractive in a different way. He smiled readily which, in some, would seem insincere. Yet in Simon, Kate surmised it reflected a natural state of ebullience and was quite genuine. It contrasted noticeably, she thought, to Martin's usually solemn expression. But Kate also allowed that she had never seen a face so transformed as Martin's when happiness exploded in his smile.

Simon's infectious laughter drew Kate's thoughts back to him. She now knew he'd helped Martin in his search for Fia—had insisted upon it, in fact. That spoke favorably of his concern for others, as did his befriending of Fia back in the Glasgow Market. And his purchase of a wedding gown for his sister spoke of his generosity. Kate fidgeted with the uncomfortable memory that she had believed the gown a ruse to ingratiate himself with Alayne. Perhaps there was something to that but, as Fia had pointed out at the time, it was a very expensive means by which to do so. Kate conceded now that there was a more noble reason to his actions.

She further surveyed Simon's appearance. He had donned a dark plum, ribbed silk frock coat trimmed with gilt edging. His breeches matched and topped cream-colored silk stockings. The lace rippling at his throat and wrists reminded her of the foam on a storm-tossed sea; he cut quite a figure. Kate surprised Simon and Martin, as well as Douglas, who had just entered, by telling Simon, "You look splendid as well, Mr. MacLaren."

Simon stuttered his shock, "H...how very kind, Mistress Matheson. I thank you." He executed a neat bow and, when he rose, he was beaming.

Douglas' chest swelled with pride at Kate's words. He knew she meant them or would never have spoken. It seemed that, indeed, she had come to terms with Simon MacLaren. "Well," Douglas interjected happily, "You, I surmise, are Martin's cousin, Simon." Douglas held out his hand which Simon grasped heartily.

"I am. You are Mr. Sutherland."

"Douglas, please," he insisted.

"It is an honor, Douglas," Simon bowed slightly, feeling somewhat light-headed still from Kate's compliment.

Douglas suggested, "Why don't you and I get better acquainted, while we await the curate's arrival? I'd like to see what Flora is up to in the dining room. Shall we?" He extended his hand toward the entry way in invitation.

"I'm right behind you," Simon answered, and the two crossed the front hall and into the room where they would adjourn for the wedding feast. They conversed over the beautiful table and bounty of food that Flora had set.

"I've heard much about you, Douglas," Simon began, "your kindnesses to Fia, to Martin. What a good friend they have in you."

"Your praise is generous, Simon." Douglas leaned toward the table and inhaled the delicious sent of warm saffron cake. "I assure you, whatever I do for Fia and her Martin gives me great satisfaction. Her father, James, and I were very close."

Simon nodded, adding, "And now, you and Fia are close."

Douglas returned his smile with genuine liking and nodded. "I've heard a great deal about you as well."

Next to a platter heaped with slices of pork, Simon hesitated a moment. "From Mistress Matheson?" he queried before chuckling, "And you can still say it's a pleasure to meet me?"

"Oh, not all I've gleaned has been from Kate and almost none of it bad—especially of late. Truly."

"Thank the Lord," Simon grinned, popping a sugared walnut-half from a plate of mince pies into his mouth.

"Here," barked Flora, with forced sternness, "there'll be no more of that, Mr. MacLaren."

With repentant voice and twinkling eye, Simon atoned, "My apologies Miss Flora. I confess I could not resist that tempting morsel. I'll not do it again."

She smirked her forgiveness and placed a silver bowl burdened with plump raspberries, and a sauce boat filled with thick, sweet cream on the table. "I'll take off your hand if you touch these!"

Simon and Douglas both gazed at the bowl in awe. "Where did you find these beautiful berries this time of year?" Douglas demanded.

Flora lifted her chin slightly higher in the air. "I've got my secrets–and that's what they'll stay." With that, she retreated to the kitchen.

Simon gestured to Douglas. "I think we'd better return to the drawing room," he suggested. "There's too much temptation here."

The two were passing through the entry when there was a rap on the door. Douglas chimed, "I'll answer it, Kate." As expected, it was the curate, a tallish man with a shock of white hair on his head and on the point of his chin. His brows were still nearly jet black giving him an almost sinister appearance. Douglas led him into the drawing room where Martin stepped forward to clasp his hand and introduce him to Kate.

"Welcome, Mr. Findlay," Kate spoke warmly. "You will make this a most happy occasion for us all."

"I'll do my best, Mistress," he said with a gracious smile and incline of his head. "Is the bride nearly ready?"

"She is," Alayne announced from the drawing room doorway and came forward to dip her curtsey before the curate, the folds of her pale green watered-silk gown dancing around her ankles. "We heard you arrive," she explained, adding with a wink at Martin, "and we have an eager bride-to-be."

Laughter erupted and died out almost as quickly when they realized Martin had gone silent, gaping at the entrance where Alayne had appeared moments ago. Their eyes followed his and beheld Fia, luminous and ethereal in the soft glow of the tapers. Her familiar embroidered white-damask stomacher and petticoat were magically transformed by the new gown she, Alayne and Kate had made yesterday. It had deep pleats sewn close down the back, hugging Fia's striking figure and enhancing her proud bearing. The sleeves ended in graceful flounces over sheer ruffles that matched the bodice trim. But most amazing to Martin, the gown was made of his own cloth, the pale blue plaid accented with dove gray, yellow and a touch of black that he'd sold to Kate that first day in her shop. The women had drawn the sides up which gave them a slightly puffy appearance and further softened the muted pattern. To make a wedding gown using his plaid–the effect was stunning.

Tears sprang to Martin's eyes as he stepped forward, swept her hands into his and held them to his lips.

Her own gaze shimmered as she studied him in awe. The suit of clothes was perfect for him and with…the shirt she'd made. She gulped, "How is it possible, that each time I see you, you are more handsome than the last?"

"It must be the magic that steals my breath every time you walk into a room," he responded, lightly caressing her cheek where her hair was pulled back and held by a mother-of-pearl comb borrowed from Kate who approached them now.

"It's time, if you're–"

"Aye!" Martin and Fia chorused together, and the company smirked delightedly at the couple's eagerness.

They took places by the fire; Alayne and Simon to their left, Kate and Douglas to their right. Each couple stood close together, happy to be witnessing the long awaited joining, happy to be near each other. Flora stood just behind Kate.

Fia held no flowers, but held Martin's hands instead. Mr. Findlay spoke a few welcoming words then asked Martin to repeat after him, "I, Martin, take thou, Fia, to my spoused wife, as the law of the Holy Kirk shows and thereto I plight thou my troth." Martin said them, but found them to be dispassionate and stiff–not at all reflective of what he felt for Fia. With a frown, he turned to the curate. "Mr. Findlay, may I say something else?"

Agreeably, the curate replied, "I don't see why not."

Satisfied, Martin again faced his bride, her hands still firmly grasped in his. "The words I spoke now, Fia, were official, without emotion or warmth. They aren't enough. The wisdom of the law has just recognized our destiny to be husband and wife. In the sight of the rest of the world, we now belong together, though words of law could not make me feel any more acutely the respect and love I bear you. If there's a limit to how much love two people can share, each time I look at you, lass, I know we've not reached that limit. All that I am…all that I own…is yours, now and ever after."

Fia lowered her head a moment, emotion threatening her ability to speak. "H...how am I supposed to say my own vows?" she lovingly complained.

With Mr. Findlay's help, she got through the same formal words, then spent a long moment studying Martin's tender expression, his eyes dark with the passion of loving her, before she began. "For the remainder of my life, I will consider myself the most beloved and fortunate of women. Many times, my love, have we discussed the circumstances that brought us together not once, but twice. Fate or God's will, be they the same entity or different, has blessed me with your love," she paused and swept her gaze quickly round the room, "and blessed us with the best of friends to share in our happiness. My heart is so full; I thank God every day that he brought our very different paths to the same point to share a love so beautiful and profound. I have never been happier than at this moment–and this is just the beginning. There'll be no more borrowed days, my love, they all belong to us."

Martin brought her hands once more to his lips and kissed them, his eyes drinking her in.

They shared an elated, somewhat nervous kiss, tears spilling freely. Each tried to speak, each failed. Instead they settled for a bone-crushing embrace, their faces buried against each other.

Their embrace was promptly shattered by Simon thumping Martin's back in congratulations and Alayne and Kate spinning Fia away so they could hug her, then they moved on to clasp Martin. Douglas pumped Martin's hand, embraced Fia, and there was relieved and enthusiastic laughter all around.

Kate stood back and wiped her eyes watching elatedly the scene before her.

Douglas came to stand at her side, a catch in his voice as he said, "I feel as though I've just married off a daughter."

Ever so briefly, Kate's cheek brushed his shoulder, and she teased lightly, "Then you must feel that you now have a son."

Douglas chuckled. "Now that you say so, my dear, I believe I actually do!"

Tucking her handkerchief away, Kate announced, "Flora has outdone herself with the marriage feast. Let's not disappoint her. Mr. Findlay, you'll join us?"

The curate bowed and accepted, "My pleasure, Mistress Matheson." He offered his arm to Kate who stood aside so that Martin and Fia could lead the way to the fully laden table.

A whole poached salmon occupied the last platter to be placed on the table, sitting between bowls of pickled beetroot and potatoes with leeks.

"Oh, Flora," Fia praised, upon seeing the repast set for them, "you are wonderful to do all this for us."

"It was my pleasure, Mistress Ross," she answered, a sparkle in her eye.

Fia caught her breath and turned to Martin. "Mistress Ross," she repeated.

"I trust it sounded as perfectly fitting to you as it did to me."

"Aye," she replied, face aglow, "it was perfect."

"All right, you two," Alayne inserted her voice into the exchange. "Let's not let Flora's efforts go to waste."

Simon, at Alayne's side, agreed and furthered, "There are toasts to be drunk as well."

The small, jubilant gathering fell upon the food and drink with zeal, insisting that Flora partake as well, which she did enthusiastically. In between bites and conversation, Douglas and Simon each offered a toast to Martin and Fia, and the couple drank from the quaich as tradition decreed. The two-handled, silver bowl was a gift from Alayne and Simon.

"Speaking of future," Douglas asked, "have you decided where you will live?"

Kate intervened, "They can continue to stay at the shop as long as they like," which removed any remaining doubt as to whether or not she knew where Fia had been spending her nights.

"That's generous of you Aunt Kate, but not fair to Alayne." Fia glanced at her friend, resplendent in the green silk that set off her reddish-yellow hair and the green in her eyes. Alayne's skin was prettily flushed; Fia attributed it to Simon's nearness and the tenderness in his eyes when he turned them on her. "Martin and I just took over the sleeping quarters at the shop. Alayne never said a word except that she was happy for us."

Martin added, "We need to give it back to her–with our gratitude." He reached to grasp Alayne's hand in thanks.

Alayne's throat tightened, but she offered, "There's no hurry."

"No," Kate suggested, "no hurry. I've enjoyed having Alayne stay here."

Alayne's gaze swung to Kate. From her expression, Alayne believed Kate's words to be sincere. A smile touched Alayne's mouth and she simply said, "Thank you, Kate," before shifting her gaze to Douglas, wondering his role in Kate's mellowing.

"Nevertheless," Martin continued, "tomorrow, we will look for temporary lodgings."

"Temporary?" Kate queried.

Simon submitted, "Once Martin and I finish some business in Inverness, I believe he and Fia intend to return to Martin's home in Argyll."

"And what do you intend to do then, Mr. MacLaren?" asked Mr. Findlay who had, until that moment, busied himself testing every dish of food on the table.

Simon's eye caught Alayne's, and then he turned back to the curate. "I'm uncertain at this moment, though I have some definite ideas."

Martin said, "At least Simon's employed here. I'm not. Tomorrow I must seek a buyer for…" Suddenly uncomfortable, he glanced at Kate before finishing, "some things I brought with me from my home. The coin will help tide us over."

But Kate noticed his hesitancy and correctly guessed, "You have more cloth? Bring it to me".

Martin's color rose slightly. "I wouldn't feel right about it, Mistress. Just because I married your niece–"

"I'll hear none of that," Kate declared. "Your work is exquisite. If it weren't, I'd never have bought the other cloths from you–including the one that your wife wears so regally. Besides," she sniffed, "I would take it as a personal affront if you took your material to one of my competitors without letting me see it first."

Martin bowed his defeat. "Then I shall bring them to you, with my thanks."

"That reminds me," Kate smiled at Simon. "We still have your sister Mairi's gown stored at the shop."

"Aye," Simon acknowledged, "I will take it to her as soon as I can. She'll be thrilled with it."

"Thank Fia and Alayne," Kate graciously conceded.

"I do, I assure you, Mistress," Simon vowed, resting his gaze contentedly upon Alayne.

Mr. Findlay questioned, "Is there anyone you will be informing of your marriage, Mr. Ross… family perhaps?"

Martin replied quietly, "Simon's family is the only family I have left, Mr. Findlay, and I'm anxious not just to tell them, but to have them meet Fia. Aside from that, there are two very close friends who will not forgive me easily if I'm remiss in telling them."

"Annie and Alex," Fia supplied. "Someday, I'd like to meet Alex," she said, turning to the others to explain, "Martin's teacher and mentor during his medical studies." She grasped Martin's hand, but turned to Douglas. "And, of course, I need to tell Murdoch and Agnes."

"Oh, aye," Alayne chimed, "Murdoch must know."

Douglas offered, "Fia, I would be pleased to deliver a letter to Murdoch and inform Agnes upon my return."

"Thank you, Douglas. I'll make sure you have one before you leave–"

"Which we hope won't be too soon," Simon voiced everyone's opinion.

With an incline of his head, Douglas acknowledged the friendship and good will surrounding him.

Mr. Findlay set his empty plate on the sideboard. "This has been most enjoyable; but now I must be on my way." He shook Martin's outstretched hand, and then nodded at Fia. "My best wishes to you both."

"Thank you, Sir," Fia responded. "I'll see you out."

"No, Mistress Ross," Flora piped, "you stay with your husband and guests. Mr. Findlay, if you'll follow me." As Flora lead the curate to the door, the others began to pair off for a few minutes of intimate conversation.

"How long do you think you'll stay, Douglas?" Kate asked, raising her face to better look into his gentle eyes.

"I can't say, Kate. There is still some business I need attend here in Inverness. Yet I can assure you of one thing–when I do leave, not knowing when I may see you again will steal my sleep at night."

Her expression serious, Kate studied him mercilessly before offering, "Douglas Sutherland, you may see me whenever you wish." And to the look of bliss enveloping his countenance, she added, "Who knows? If I were invited, I might even visit Glasgow sometime."

Douglas leaned close and whispered, "I would issue you an invitation I hope you could not resist, were we but alone."

Kate pursed her lips in a pert challenge, tilted her head to one side and replied, "Perhaps there will be a moment later for me to receive such an entreaty."

"Would you look at that," Fia murmured in astonishment, "they're *flirting*–in front of all of us."

Martin shook his head. "I hate to disagree with you, my love, but I think they're past flirtation."

Fia stared a moment longer, then turned to her husband, an enormous smile filling her face. "I believe you're right. This is grand!"

"Aye," he replied, warmly. "But still not as grand as you are, lass." He slipped his arms around her slender waist. "I don't think I can ever tell you what this day means to me."

"We have the rest of our lives for you to try," she declared.

"Seriously, Fia, to see you in a gown of my cloth, that you would do that for me..."

"It never occurred to me to do otherwise. Just as you wear the shirt I fashioned for you, my gown was tribute to you and my love for you. Besides, there isn't finer or more handsome cloth in all Britain than that which you make, and I'd not marry you in anything less than the best. But you must tell me where did you find such a striking suit? And when?"

"You may thank our good friend Douglas. I hesitated but his argument was a good one and I gave in on the promise to repay him." He smiled gently at her. "I wanted to look like I was worthy of you." Martin kissed her willing mouth, after which, he asked, heatedly, "How much longer are we obliged to stay?" causing Fia to laugh.

Alayne looked longingly from Martin and Fia to Simon. "I wish..." she began and trailed off, forlorn.

"So do I," Simon immediately picked up the thought. "It won't be long, sweet Alayne. And, if you had any doubt about what I said earlier, I know precisely what I intend to do when this sordid Forbes business is resolved."

Her eyes burned into his. "It had better include me."

"It does, lass. It involves you and me and no one else–at least not in the beginning."

She looked at him, slightly puzzled.

"I hope it includes children, Alayne. You and I will make beautiful bairns."

"A...a family?" Alayne queried shakily.

"After taking you as my wife, a family is what I want most in this world." Simon hesitated, unsure what was going on behind Alayne's precarious expression. "We haven't spoken about it," he admitted, "still–Alayne, I'm sorry, I didn't think–"

"Girls or boys?"

Simon started. "Pardon?"

Recovered, Alayne repeated her question, "Girls or boys? Which would you want?"

Stunned into silence, Simon clenched and unclenched his fists at his sides. Finally, he said, "Both!" and rushed on to whisper, "Do you know how difficult it is not to take you in my arms right now, even in front of Kate? How truly hard it is?"

Nodding vehemently her understanding, she dropped her gaze from his piercing one and agreed, "It is hard."

Simon gaped at her a moment before uttering a surprised, "Alayne!"

She gasped, realizing that she was staring at the front of his breeches. Her face blushed crimson as she remembered her last words, and Alayne quickly looked away as Flora entered, carrying an almond cake, iced with a sweet, buttery glaze.

All groaned when they saw it and began claiming that they had no room left for such a magnificent creation. She glanced up as the door knocker sounded, and stood helplessly looking between the entry hall and her full hands.

In need of a brief escape, Alayne waved the maid's worry aside. "I'll see who's at the door Flora, just save me a piece of cake. I'll find room for it somewhere!"

The sounds of the joyful gathering accompanied Alayne softly into the entry hall where she stopped a brief moment to bask in the sensations they evoked in her. She realized that, for the first time since her family had emigrated to America, she felt as though she had a real family, one that loved her and loved each other–totally and unselfishly. Alayne was deeply moved by the revelation.

With contentment etched on her face as though it had always been there, Alayne opened the door to stare, unspeaking, at the man outside. In refusal to believe her eyes, Alayne blinked rapidly. Finally, her hand jerked to her mouth to silence the ragged gasp that ripped into her before spewing out in a stifled cry of despair. From her toes, through her legs, to her shoulders, Alayne's entire body set to trembling fiercely, her pounding, coursing blood the only thing keeping her on her feet.

Observing her upset, Alayne's husband asked, "You did miss me then?"

Alayne fumbled to shut the door before he could enter, but the madness invading her mind and body refused her attempt.

Muir Matheson summoned a concerned guise and sauntered through the doorway. "My dear Alayne, I know my arrival is a stunning surprise. No doubt, you've thought me long dead." He awaited some word in response and received only the sight of color draining her face to a stark pallor. He closed the door in her stead and turned to her again. "I see you are distressed; perhaps my little quip made things worse, but I hardly know how to greet you after so long. Almost four years."

Almost...almost. The word rumbled dully in Alayne's mind for what seemed an eternity before other words began seeping through her numbness.

"...plenty of time to talk, I know you'll want to hear everything that has befallen me. First, I must see Mither. I hear voices...is she in there?" he finished, pointing to the room beyond her.

Still without words, Alayne turned her shock from her husband. Unsure whether she could place one foot before the other, Alayne reached out a hand, dragged her way along the wall, and felt rather than saw her way back to the dining room. Her fingers edged around the door jam and pulled her body into the room, where she sagged heavily against the wall.

For a fleeting second, Simon's glance caught Alayne's. She turned her tortured expression from him. The grayness of her skin and her defeated posture caused him to drop his glass. Before it even reached the floor, splintering into tiny, jagged shards, he had darted round the table toward her.

The sound of the shattering glass caused an immediate chorus of questions, turning heads, and shifting eyes, each person hoping to discover the problem.

As Simon reached the end of the table, he came to an abrupt halt nearly doubling over as though struck. No one had to tell him who the rangy, yellow-haired man now standing beside Alayne was. His stomach lurched violently and, looking back at Alayne, he wanted to howl his anguish. More than ever, she needed him, and now, he couldn't go to her.

As the roaring in his ears subsided, Simon realized that Martin had gone to Alayne and was supporting her with one arm round her waist and her left hand clenched in his. "My God, my God," Simon muttered brokenly–for Alayne and for himself. Only then did he realize the pressure of Fia's hand on his own arm. He turned blindly toward her.

"Have courage Simon," she begged quietly, "for Alayne's sake."

Valiantly, he struggled to compose himself and his attention shifted once more to Muir Matheson, now in the incredulous vise of his mother's embrace. Simon watched Kate take her son's face between her palms, tears gushing from her relieved eyes. He saw her lips move, but he heard nothing she said, nor did he wish to. Simon looked at the floor–the only place he could escape the wreckage around him.

Chapter Thirty

Simon prowled the workroom at the millinery while Fia stood by, feeling helpless. "Martin will be here soon to tell us how Alayne fares," she offered, hoping to soothe.

"I'm thankful Martin can be with her," he responded curtly.

Fia bit her lower lip. "I don't know how you managed to get through that horror at Aunt Kate's, Simon, but I'm very proud of you."

"I don't want you to be proud of me, Fia," he snarled. "I want Alayne! I want Matheson to go back where he came from! I want him to go to the *Devil*!" Simon grasped his head in his hands, then reached out and pulled Fia into his agonized grip. "I'm sorry, so sorry," he atoned. "You're the last person to whom I'd ever want to raise my voice. Forgive me, Fia, it's just...just..."

"Nothing to forgive," she assured. "I have a fair idea what you suffer."

Simon released her slowly and sank onto the floor where he'd stood. "Why?" he pleaded the answer he sought. "Why did he have to return now, when there were only two weeks...two short weeks in four long years for Alayne? Matheson couldn't have timed wreaking this havoc better if he'd planned it."

Fia squatted beside him. "It's a grotesque twist of fate. Simon, I'll do everything in my power to see Alayne through this."

He glared at her and asked bitterly, "See her through what? Matheson has returned."

"Alayne must be reeling, but she's never let anyone keep her from what is important to her. She loves you, Simon. She'll find a way."

"Then why did she turn from me?" Simon spewed his pain. "No. If he wasn't dead before, Matheson isn't likely to die now. So what hope is there?"

The door swung open and Martin entered with Arthur and a gusting wind at his heels. Closing the door, he made his way to his wife and cousin, who both leapt to their feet.

"How is she?" Simon demanded.

"She's traumatized. I stayed with her until she drifted off though it seemed a restless sleep." Martin studied Simon's crestfallen countenance and promised, "I'll see her first thing in the morning."

"I appreciate it," Simon responded listlessly.

Martin and Fia exchanged a worried glance. "What about you?" he asked Simon.

"If Alayne is well, then I'll get on," Simon shrugged.

Tired, Martin rubbed his bearded face. "Truthfully, it may take some time."

Fia rested a hand on his arm. "Should you have left her tonight, Martin?"

"It'll be all right, my love." Martin stroked Fia's hair.

"Will you tell us what happened?" Fia asked, moving away to fill two glasses with whiskey. She gave a glass to each man. While Martin turned his glass between his palms, Simon gulped the burning liquid and wiped his mouth on the back of his hand.

Martin handed Fia into a chair and sat on the floor leaning against her legs. "I took Alayne to her room; Kate came with me and helped get her into something warm."

Simon's voice dripped sarcasm, "Kate could tear herself from her precious son?"

"Kate is understandably elated at having her son return from the dead, so to speak. But she didn't hesitate to come to Alayne's aid," Martin answered honestly.

Fia urged, "We can discuss Kate later. What of Alayne?"

"She was rigid as a stone when Kate and I finally got her under the blankets. Her eyes wouldn't focus on anything but empty space." Martin finished his whiskey. "At one point, while I was alone with Alayne, I heard Muir outside the door talking, rather loudly, with his mother. That was the only time I saw Alayne react. She pulled herself into a tight ball and glowered hate so fierce that it should have burned Muir right through the door."

Simon clutched his belly and leaned forward. "Did...did she speak at all?"

"No," Martin replied. "I left the room and told Matheson he would have to be quiet or get away from the door."

"I bet he didn't care for that," Fia guessed.

"He didn't, that's a fact. He insisted Alayne was his wife and he had every right to see her, see for himself how she was."

"Surely he didn't think anyone would believe he was worried," Simon snorted derisively.

"On the contrary, I actually think he did if he played it right. Anyway, I told him I was her physician and he wouldn't see her until I deemed her well enough. Kate supported me, which I can tell you came as a welcome surprise." Martin closed his weary eyes a moment. "When I returned to Alayne, her hand crept from under the blanket and clutched mine. I simply spoke to her until she slept."

With impatient hand, Simon dashed wetness from his eyes. "And what's to keep this...this... wretch away from her tonight?" Simon demanded.

"Douglas. He's stationing himself outside Alayne's door–after Kate's gone to bed." To Simon's frown, Martin rushed on, "Alayne will be all right until Kate retires. Douglas is in a precarious position. We all suspect strongly that Douglas and Kate have become close but, after all, we are talking about Kate's son. She may not appreciate Douglas' actions."

Fia leaned toward Simon. "Martin's right."

Simon nodded and lamented, "You have to help her, Martin...help Alayne, I can't."

"You have my word," his cousin responded. "I'll be there for her."

Simon swallowed with difficulty and stared first at one then the other of them. "'Tis a poor wedding night you've waited for," he said apologetically.

Martin blurted, "Who waited?" which brought a slim shadow of a smile from his cousin, and a blush to Fia's cheeks.

Recovering quickly, Fia offered, "Our handfast was perfect–that's what we waited for. As Martin said, we've had our wedding night. Now," she rose and finished, "I'll get some blankets."

Startled, Simon gushed, "No! I'll not stay here tonight."

"Indeed, you will," Fia insisted.

He shook his head stubbornly. "I'll do nothing to disrupt your night further."

"*You've* done *nothing* to disrupt our night," Martin declared. "I agree with Fia." He raised his hands to ward off further disagreement. "As your doctor, I prescribe it."

"Be reasonable, both of you. Tomorrow, I'll have to work and it'll be you, Martin, who has to go down to the quay. Take advantage of what's left of the night. God's life, I'm a grown man– I'll manage."

"We love you, Simon," Martin said. "We just don't want you to be alone."

"I'll have to be alone sometime; it might as well be tonight." Simon smiled ruefully. "Don't you remember, Cousin? It doesn't get any easier over time to be without the woman you love."

His words struck Martin to silence. He could only nod the truth Simon had spoken.

Fia's eyes teared for she understood all too well, and ached for what lay ahead for Alayne and Simon. "You're right, Simon," she trembled, and hugged him hard. "We'll see you tomorrow?"

"I'd better be careful about coming around," he replied.

Martin stepped up to clasp his arms about Simon's shoulders. "Nonsense, you are my cousin, and now, Fia's. Come tomorrow afternoon. By then, I'll know something."

Simon eased toward the door, bending to give Arthur a quick scratch between the ears on his way out. When the door was closed behind him, he sagged against it, his body shaking with anguish. Drawing several ragged breaths, Simon pushed himself from the stoop and stumbled into the street heading toward the quay.

Before leaving for the handfasting, Martin had carried the feather tick from the bed in the back room and spread it on the floor before the fire. He was loath to give up lying hearthside with Fia, but thought it time to add some comfort to their nights.

Silently, they sat together on the tick; their wedding costumes put carefully aside. Their skin cast golden by the firelight, Martin sat behind his wife who leaned against him, loving and needing to feel his arms around her. Martin had obligingly slid one arm across her breasts, one across her belly, and held tight. Fia's cheek rested against his in the continuing stillness. At length, she confessed, "What happened tonight is so alarming, shocking."

"Aye," offered Martin, "it's a hard thing to accept that we can't always control our own fate." He nuzzled her hair. "Think of how many incidents beyond your control conspired to set you in my path just as the borrowed days were setting in?"

Fia nodded. "There were many."

"And those that brought us to the same town and to this night?"

Fia squeezed his arms even tighter around her. "Are you saying Muir's return may not be the end for Simon and Alayne?"

"I pray it isn't," Martin's voice shook slightly and he spread his fingers low over her belly.

Fia stirred under his touch and turned to straddled his lap and wrap her arms around his neck. Her eyes revealed to Martin a mixture of emotions: contentment, love...and fear. "No one will take you from me," Fia swore.

Martin stroked her face, fighting his own dread of ever losing her again. "Never as long as I breathe, lass," he agreed. His mouth covered her's, his arms slid around her back and pressed her needy body against his own.

Douglas pondered his predicament, and the suddenness with which one's whole life could change. Yesterday, he and Kate had been close. Yet he feared that, when she discovered his role in preventing her beloved son from pestering his stricken wife, Kate would likely be offended and their closeness finished

"A high price to pay," he muttered sadly, but was resigned that his choice had been the only right one. There was no one else to ensure that Muir would allow Alayne the time required for her to recover from the shock of his reappearance. Plainly, it couldn't be Simon. His own distress was clear, and his apparent commitment to Alayne...well, it just wouldn't be appropriate for him to stay. Kate wouldn't see the need to protect Alayne, and Martin had a new bride.... Douglas shook his head at the sorry ending to such a beautiful celebration.

Uncomfortable, Douglas shifted in the chair he'd carried from his bedroom to Alayne's door. He'd been awake most of this long night–a night interrupted only once, when Muir had paid a visit.

As he stole quietly through the hall, Muir had gasped in surprise at coming upon Douglas in the gloom. "What are you doing here?" Muir snapped, cross at having been foiled. His butter-colored hair shone like a halo in the light of the candle on the table across the hall.

Douglas had the uneasy sensation that the halo didn't fit and responded, "I'm ensuring Alayne gets a much-needed rest."

"Well, I aim to see her; she's my wife."

"Lower your voice, please," Douglas warned, mildly. "I'm sure you want to see her, but it won't be tonight. Her doctor has so ordered."

With studied sincerity on his smooth face, Muir coaxed, "Would you please help me understand something? Is the doctor my cousin's new husband, or is he the relative of that sickly looking fellow hanging onto Fia–the one with the pale hair? Of course, that would make *him* her new husband. Oh, that might well account for why he looked so wretched. He certainly didn't look up to performing his wedding night duties."

So this was who Muir was, one to play games, one to defame strangers. Steadily, Douglas obliged, "Fia is married to the doctor. There were introductions made, Muir."

"Oh, aye," Muir agreed emphatically. "It's just hard to remember so many new names and faces when presented all at one time. Why I didn't even know my dear Cousin Fia. Take you, for instance," he began, with a gleam in his eye, visible even in the murk. "The way you hovered over my mother, I thought surely I was about to meet my new father."

Douglas refused to be drawn out on this personal matter, instead answering, "Your assumption was wrong."

"Aye. Imagine my surprise to find you're just the solicitor." Undaunted, Muir continued, "Answer for me then, if you will, Mr. Solicitor, who was that other fellow?"

Douglas replied simply, "He is the doctor's cousin, and a witness to the handfasting."

"Ah, the handfasting," he sighed, raising his eyes toward Heaven. "If I'd arrived home sooner, I could have witnessed also. Such bad luck."

"Indeed," Douglas dryly responded. "However, considering the chaos your return caused, an earlier arrival might have ruined the celebration entirely. On such an occasion, the joyful couple should be at the center of attention, don't you think?"

Muir's velvety voice slid effortlessly into his agreed, "Absolutely. I'm just sorry I missed it. I've missed so much these past years, you know."

"No doubt," Douglas uttered and continued, "Your mother is beside herself with happiness at your return."

Muir's brow furrowed deeply as he quipped, "Did you expect less?"

With a shake of his head, Douglas said, "Just an observation."

"Aye, well, rather an obvious one." Muir shifted his gaze to Alayne's door. "Do you think, once she's over the surprise, my wife will be pleased at my return?"

"I can't speak for Alayne."

Muir shifted a challenging glance to Douglas. "But you have an opinion, surely."

"My opinion about how or if Alayne will adjust is irrelevant. However, my opinion on this conversation is that it's finished. You must be tired after your long absence–"

"You mean 'journey'," Muir corrected.

"No," Douglas assured, "I meant what I said. I don't know where you came from. But I do know that you should return to your bed, for you won't enter this room on this night."

Rigid, Muir stood glaring down the slope of his nose at Douglas' calm, upturned face. Gradually, his expression relaxed into a smirk. "I suppose one more night won't bring the end of the world." He turned from Douglas and strode down the hall, his gait loose like his joints were only barely wired together. Over his shoulder, Muir called, "We'll talk again; this was fun."

In the middle of the night, and now as the grey light of dawn snuck across the carpeted hall, Douglas doubted that he would enjoy talking to Muir again.

"Douglas...*Douglas*!" Kate's calling interrupted his reverie. "What's going on? What are you doing out here?"

He rose to his feet and stretched, trying to compose his greeting to her. The plain truth won out. "I spent the night here to ensure Alayne was not disturbed."

Kate appeared perplexed. "Just who would you think might trouble her?"

"Your son. Martin wanted Alayne to get complete rest and I took on the task."

Ruffling, Kate admonished, "Then after spending an uncomfortable night in a chair for no reason, I hope you're satisfied that my son is more sensitive than that. After all, you know I spoke with him myself to ease his fears for her. He respects his wife's need to adjust to his return."

Already prepared to accept her wrath, Douglas only responded, "Alayne was not disturbed."

Kate studied his drawn face a moment, lifted her chin and coolly offered, "Breakfast is ready in five minutes."

Douglas bowed slightly, picked up the chair and returned to his room to change his shirt and splash water on his face. He saw no need to hurt Kate unnecessarily by telling her she was mistaken–and she might choose not to believe him if he did. A deep melancholy attacked him. All progress Kate had made recently in her relationship with Alayne and toward accepting her son's weaknesses instead of denying them seemed to have disappeared that quickly, that simply, when Muir had walked through the door. Her defenses had risen again, before Kate even knew where her son had been for nearly four years, what he'd done, or why he'd never managed to contact her. Douglas feared the Kate he'd glimpsed might be buried and lost again, this time, with no hope of reemergence.

Douglas turned to the door then put his back to it again. When he descended the stairs, his bag was in his hand. He saw Flora, looking peaked herself from the events of the previous evening.

She glanced at his bag, at his face, and her eyes turned sad, though her mouth gave a slim smile. "We'll miss you, Mr. Sutherland," Flora offered sincerely.

"Thank you, Flora, you're very kind." Douglas set the bag on the floor. "Is Mistress Kate about?"

"I'll get her for you, Sir." She bobbed a curtsey and retreated to the dining room from which Kate almost immediately emerged.

She looked pinched around the mouth yet held her head high and her carriage straight. "Flora tells me you're leaving?"

"I believe I must, Kate. You have your son back and you'll want to get to know him again."

"And, by that you mean...?"

"Only that, after all this time, it'll be an adjustment for you. As much as I'll regret not spending time with you, it wouldn't be wise for me to stay. I'm afraid I would interfere. That is not my right and you wouldn't forgive me for it if I did, even if it were unintentional."

Kate wanted to question further his reasons for leaving, but her pride prevented it. "You're always...always welcome here, Douglas."

He wanted to say that he'd never doubted it...until Muir walked into the house. Instead, Douglas chose, "Thank you, Kate. I hope that will always be true." He studied her face, eyes lingering on her lips. "You still have an open invitation to come to Glasgow–anytime you wish." He reached for her hand, raised it to his lips and let them linger a moment on her graceful fingers. When the door closed behind him, Kate stood in astounded silence. Minutes later, wiping tears from her cheeks, she trudged, head bowed, back to the dining room.

Simon moved stiffly on his pallet; his head hurt, his eyes stung and–to his immense surprise–his heart continued to thud dully behind his ribs. For a moment, he thought the sourness in his throat was from the whiskey he'd drunk at the tavern. But he thrust suddenly toward the chamber pot and retched until there was nothing left to come up. Weak, Simon sat catching his breath before rinsing his mouth with water and adding it to the contents of the pot, which he turned from in disgust.

Flopping back on his pallet, Simon closed his eyes and thought back, not to the moment when Matheson had appeared, nor to the memory of Martin and Fia valiantly attempting to comfort him–those were too painful. Instead, Simon thought of the tavern.

He'd arrived at the door yesterday evening, unsure as to how he'd gotten there. Within were Thomas Gray and the friendly barmaid, who was planted on Struan Forbes' lap. Simon glared at the man Fia was to have married and his belly churned with anger. He fought the bile clawing upward in his throat and hastily made his way to a table a respectable distance away. Simon sat, ordered his first whiskey, and forced himself to do what he was there to do–find a way to avenge the wrongs done by Andrew Forbes. Simon licked his lips which had suddenly gone dry. He realized with a jolt, that the thought of revenge could be an intoxicating one and, right now, the need for revenge seemed to fill him.

Simon tossed back his drink, signaled for a second and, rather than hide behind a paper, simply stared into the fire. From the other table, he picked out bits of conversation, sorted through them, and saved or discarded them as interest dictated.

"For God's sake," Gray cursed irritably. "If you want to bed the wench, take her upstairs. Don't do it in front of me. We've business to finish if you're leaving tomorrow."

"What a crotchety old geezer you are, Thomas," Struan sneered. "You don't mind a little tickle now do you, Betty?"

As he buried his face in her ample cleavage, the maid let out a delighted squeal. Even so, Struan carelessly pushed her aside saying, "But, as Thomas says, there is business to tend to, my dear." He tossed her a coin and winked at her the promise of more to follow. Struan turned his attention and watery gaze to Gray. "I don't know why you have to be so thoroughly unpleasant."

Menacingly, Gray leaned in and hissed, "Your brother sent you to me to learn the business. So far, all you've learned is how willing Miss Betty is to have you play cock to her hen."

His face fixed with a snide grin, Struan declared, "I find Betty's willingness to play extremely useful to have learned." Struan thrust his pallid countenance into Gray's and loudly growled, "And as for my brother, *Gordon* sent me here only because he has to stay out of sight after his folly up north; you know that perfectly well."

Thomas Gray slowly slouched back in his chair, his eyes narrowed, brow furrowed in thought. His mute scrutiny made Struan nervous; at last he risked looking away as he ordered another drink. The silence dragged until Struan could no longer abide it. "What's the matter?"

Gray hesitated answering, apparently seeking the right words.

Simon strained to hear what Gray would say. He was surprised and captivated by the obvious friction between the two men; it was not what he expected.

"Your brother has, I fear, misjudged your interest in this enterprise."

"Nothing but the profit interests me. How it all gets done is of no consequence," Struan haughtily announced.

Slowly, Gray nodded. "I will recommend to Gordon that he involve you no further."

Simon tensed at the implication of those words to Struan's future well-being. However, the prophecy seemed to escape Struan who, looking pleasantly astonished, responded, "I'd be ever so grateful to you, Gray. And, now that we've settled that, I believe I'll stay on a few days, see if I can find something in this unrefined little town you call 'home' to amuse me."

In a smooth voice, Gray offered, "Grousing, perhaps?"

Struan beamed, "Indeed, that would suit me well!"

With a slight incline of his head, Gray said, "I'll be happy to show you one or two of my favorite spots."

"Thoroughly decent of you, Gray," Struan admitted, slapping the older man on the back. "You aren't such a boor after all."

Dropping a few coins onto the table, Simon departed. He'd heard critical information–and believed he'd heard Struan's death sentence delivered. Clearly, Thomas Gray saw Struan as a danger to their smuggling operation. His cavalier attitude was far too careless to be tolerated. He was only puzzled by Gray's interest in keeping Struan in Inverness a while longer. Perhaps Martin would have some ideas about that.

The rumbling of his belly broke into Simon's thoughts, forcefully reminding him it was empty. Yet thought of putting food into it only increased its uneasiness and made him want to retch again. His gaze wandered the room aimlessly, from the tables cluttered with face paints and rags, to the small cracked mirror everyone fought over to check their appearance before going on-stage. He spied the costume rack and there, on the end closest him, was Alayne's Hamlet garb. Simon stared, conjuring the memory of how she looked in it. With effort, Simon tore his gaze away and gasped for breath, confronting again the question that threatened him with madness, "Does she still want me now that he's back?" In the stillness, Simon threw his arm across his eyes to block everything from sight. "I need to know," he moaned. "I need an answer."

Abruptly, he stood, searching about for his breeches. But when he had them in hand, Simon let them fall limply to his side. After all, he had no place to go for the answer. Standing by the cold hearth, Simon recalled the fire at the Castle ruins on Hallowe'en. How perfectly right it felt to share the fire's warmth with Alayne at his side. Clearly now, he saw her elation in the light of the flickering flames as they spoke of their love. At that moment, Simon knew the answer to his question. Alayne wasn't rejecting him in favor of her long lost husband. On the contrary, it was her own anguish at what Muir's return might portend that forced her to turn from Simon. No, now more than ever, Alayne needed his strength. "And she'll have it, by God," he vowed. "Matheson can't expect to reappear after all this time and pick up as though nothing has happened." His face set with determination, Simon thrust one leg then the other into his breeches.

"*Douglas,*" *Fia exclaimed* in surprise. "It's so early, what's happened? Is...Alayne..." Her voice faded upon spying his valise.

"May I come in?" he requested in a weary voice.

"Of course," she said, stepping aside for him to enter. "You look exhausted."

"I am rather tired, and I haven't seen Alayne this morning, but she was not disturbed during the night."

"Why are you leaving?" she asked, feeling she already knew the answer.

"I simply felt it best." Douglas rested the valise on the floor and continued, "Kate is already shielding her son. I saw no reason to jeopardize the bond we were building by staying, maybe forcing her into a position where she would have to choose between us."

Fia nodded her understanding and asked, skeptically, "So all was quiet last night?"

"Not exactly, Muir did try to see his wife. I dissuaded him. Still, Kate is less than pleased with me after learning I'd spent the night outside Alayne's door."

"But, if Muir tried to–"

"I didn't tell Kate," Douglas admitted.

"Why not?"

"Because, Fia, I can't and won't compete with him. If Muir denies what I tell Kate, she *will* choose."

Fia squeezed his hand. "I'm so sorry Douglas, for you and for Aunt Kate."

Ruefully, he replied, "As am I."

"Douglas, good morning," Martin called, reaching the bottom of the stairs.

"Not so good, Martin," Douglas replied.

Martin's quick glance took in the man's haggard appearance and his bag. "You're leaving."

"I am. Kate has her son back. If I don't leave now, I believe, in very short order, my welcome will come to an end."

"He's already coming between you," Martin acknowledged sympathetically. "Douglas, I'm sorry to have asked you to watch over Alayne. I hope–"

"That's only a small part of the problem. Besides, I'd have sat up for her even if you hadn't suggested it. There's something about Muir.... Well, enough of that. If my actions offended Kate, better I know it now." He rubbed his face vigorously with his hands as though trying to revive himself. "I'll be heading home today."

"Douglas," Fia insisted, "you should go upstairs and sleep for a bit–you were up all night. Can I bring you anything?"

The temptation to refuse Fia's offer quickly dissipated as Douglas realized he was, indeed, spent. "I hate to impose..."

"Nonsense," Martin assured, "follow me."

Martin picked up Douglas' bag and, as they disappeared up the stairs, Fia heard Douglas comment, "I hope Kate won't mind that I rest here. I gave her no warning I was leaving."

"How could you?" Fia murmured, moving through the curtained doorway leading to the shop.

Martin returned, came straight to her, and they wrapped their arms about each other. Fia tucked her head under his chin. "I love you," she whispered fiercely, and his grip tightened.

"And I, you," he responded, kissing the top of her head. "It's astonishing the speed with which Muir has come between Douglas and Kate."

"It's vile," Fia swore. "Whatever is going to happen now?"

He cupped her face in his hands and his nut-brown eyes explored hers. "God alone knows, lass, but we will face it, and everything to come, together."

Fia drank in his kiss trying, as she always did, to memorize the taste and scent of him. When she was heady with the sensations, she felt a stab of guilt that she should know such joy when her dearest friends were in misery. Reluctantly, she eased herself from his embrace and stood still a moment to force calm into her veins. Somewhat sheepishly, Fia eyed him and beheld Martin smiling his enchantment.

"How wonderful it is," he whispered, "that you want me as much as I crave you."

"Even now, with everything happening?"

"Especially now," he assured, fingers caressing her throat.

"I'm glad you don't want me to pretend otherwise."

"My love, you should never hide your desires or needs from me. Whatever they are, I'll always do what is in my power to fulfill them."

"You've already fulfilled my greatest wish, Husband," she promised, pressing her palm to his. "Now tell me, when do you plan to see Alayne?"

"I'll leave right away and, before I return, I'll begin making inquiries for some place for us to live."

"Good. It's important that Alayne move back here as soon–" Fia stopped as the workshop door opened and Alayne stepped into the room, a few flakes of snow powdering her shoulders and uncovered hair.

The three stared at each other, Martin and Fia shocked to see her, Alayne's face blank, but her glance darting between them. As one, the three moved together in a comforting clutch and, when they parted, each tried to compose themselves. Martin spoke first, questioning, "Why are you out of bed?"

"I couldn't stay there a moment longer," Alayne answered, surrendering her mantle to Fia, who hung it beside the door.

"Did you have trouble getting out?" Fia queried.

Alayne shook her head. "No one saw me."

Fia returned, "Aunt Kate doesn't know you're here?"

"No," Alayne affirmed. "From my window, I saw Douglas leave. I remember hearing his voice sometime during the night."

"Talking to Muir," Martin stated.

"Aye. It was listening to him, sitting there, defending my need for privacy that roused me from my trance. I owe Douglas a great deal. Now he's gone."

"Not quite," Martin revealed. "He's upstairs asleep."

"Here?"

"Aye, he was so worn after last night we doubt he could have stayed upright in his saddle this morning," Fia explained.

"Then he *is* leaving," Alayne said.

"He is," Martin confirmed.

Alayne's face clouded and she sighed raggedly. "At least I'll be able to thank him." For a long moment, she stared at the floor, eyes welling with fat tears which tumbled down her face when she tried to blink them away. "Simon," she whispered, tremulously, "How's Simon?"

"Suffering, as you are," Martin answered bluntly.

She jerked her eyes to his. "Where?" she demanded.

"At the theater; he's promised to come here later," he added hurriedly.

Alayne looked uncertain. "Don't you think I should go to him?"

"It's your decision," Martin stated. "But I wouldn't want Kate to arrive demanding to know where you are. I think that would make things harder for you and for him."

Alayne's shoulders slumped.

Martin added, sympathetically, "I know how much you want to see Simon."

"I *need* to see Simon," Alayne fervently declared.

"What will you say to him?" Fia asked. "If you haven't seen Aunt Kate this morning, I assume you've not spoken with Muir at all."

Alayne spoke harshly, "What have I to say to Muir except that I should never have married him, and I've paid for my mistake many times over. I still intend to divorce Muir. *That's* what I'll tell Simon."

Martin scratched his beard thoughtfully. "That raises another concern." Both women looked to him expectantly, and he continued, "Where will you live? When you arrived, Fia and I were talking about you returning to the shop. Yet, I doubt Kate will allow you to remain here if you're divorcing her son. It's even possible she won't allow you to continue to work here."

Alayne paled and her voice faltered, "I...I hadn't thought about that. The shop has...has been my life for so long." After a moment, she straightened her shoulders and rallied, "I'll find some place to go."

"Martin, can you look for lodgings big enough to house Alayne as well?" Fia suggested.

"I'll do my best," Martin readily agreed.

"That's kind, truly," Alayne said, hesitantly, "but I couldn't intrude on your privacy."

"We'll have plenty of privacy, never fear," Fia assured, and received Martin's concurring nod.

"Your offer is very tempting," she admitted. "I'd have only a little money to contribute and, if Kate dismisses me..."

"That should be the least of your worries," Fia surmised. "Any other millinery in Inverness would love to snatch you up."

Martin left the two women in discussion and put on his greatcoat and woolen bonnet. "I'll be on my way; it's time for you to open the shop anyway."

"Before you go," Alayne offered, "I also want to thank you for your help last night, and your friendship and support. If we do end up sharing quarters, I'll try not to get in the way. You are just wed, after all," Alayne asserted. "And I'll look for a job as–"

"Alayne," Martin kindly interrupted, "don't worry about anything but how to extricate yourself from your marriage. Everything else will fall into place as it's meant to."

"*Good morning, Mither*," Muir greeted from the doorway. "It's wonderful to wake up in my own house." He approached Kate, whose face lit upon seeing him.

"Oh, Son, it's so good to have you home again. This is the day for which I long prayed. I'm ashamed to say, of late, I'd nearly given up hope." Kate tilted her face to receive his kiss on her cheek.

As he sat opposite her, Muir exclaimed, "Well, you can hardly be blamed for that. I've been gone a very long time."

"You have indeed," Kate agreed, unable to take her eyes from his slim form and innocent face. "Will you tell me what befell you? I've imagined such horrible things," her tear-thickened voice trembled.

"Mither," he soothed, reaching across to stroke her hand briefly, "don't be sad, I'm home now." He picked up his spoon and ladled porridge into his mouth, stuffing a chunk of scone in behind it. "This is good," he mumbled, "been a long time."

Kate's brow immediately drew down in concern. "Were you not fed properly, Muir? You do look a bit thin."

"I've not always been well fed. His Majesty's Navy is not generally acknowledged for its fine treatment of its crews."

"Oh!" Kate gasped. "You *were* stolen from me by the press gangs."

Muir's hypnotic voice fed his mother's assumption. "So you guessed that was what occurred?"

"It was my first thought," she rushed to assure. "Alayne's as well."

"Forgive me Mither, but I rather doubt that of Alayne."

"Why do you doubt it?"

Muir carefully dabbed his mouth on his napkin before answering in silken tones, "I believe her first thought was, 'Thank God, he's gone'."

"Son!" Kate cried. "How could you think that?"

"Oh, Mither, let's admit that my behavior toward my wife was not altogether...kind. I have had many hours to contemplate how wretchedly I sometimes behaved towards her, many months to regret it, and the desperate sadness of thinking I might never be able to tell her how sorry I am and to beg her forgiveness." He dashed a perfectly timed tear from his cheek and implored his mother, "Dare I hope she can forgive me?"

With a cry, Kate leapt from her chair, bent before him and circled his shoulders with crushing arms. "How could she not forgive you? Surely you have suffered enough for any ill treatment of her."

Muir patted his mother's back and shrugged from her grip. His eyes, dry now, sought hers as he beseeched, "Do you think it would be all right for me to see her now? The solicitor wouldn't let me see her last night."

Kate stiffened slightly. "You...tried to see Alayne last night?"

Sensing he'd made an error, Muir grasped her hands between his own. "I know it was wrong! I'd promised you faithfully but, dear Mither, I have anguished so, remembering the injury I'd done Alayne. On top of that, my return was such a shock to her I...I couldn't bear the wait."

"At least you admit it was wrong," she allowed, and added, "I'll see if Alayne is awake. You finish your breakfast."

Kate left him at the table and climbed the stairs, one hand over the vague uneasiness in her belly. "Why didn't Douglas tell me?" she mused. "Why did he not defend himself?" The thought brought her up short. "Defend himself?" her mind repeated. An unbidden ache filled her as she realized why he must have felt it necessary to leave. Her joy at having her son back had already biased her thinking–and maybe cost her Douglas' good will.

Upon reaching Alayne's door, Kate knocked gently, still lamenting Douglas' departure. She rapped again, thinking she'd not heard Alayne's response, then guardedly opened the door on the empty room.

"*I'll be happy* when this fitted bodice is finished," Alayne remarked with a forced air of indifference. "Afterward, I can help you."

Fia heard the strain in her friend's voice but did not comment on it. "That would be fine, though I may finish shelving these new fabrics before you complete the bodice. Why Miss Duncan wanted such intricate work on chintz, I'll never know."

"Well, that's Miss Duncan. It doesn't matter what you tell her about how delicate the material is, that the embroidery will certainly outlast it; she knows better. The painted chintz would have looked very pretty–certainly better than this piece will look with all its stitchery."

Fia stopped what she was doing and came closer to inspect Alayne's work. "Perfectly beautiful, as always. Miss Duncan may not know how to pick fabric, but she certainly knows how to make the most of it."

Susan M. Walls

"Why, thank you, Mistress Ross," Alayne grinned at her companion who flushed with happiness.

"It's a splendid name and I'll never tire of hearing it spoken."

Alayne put her needle down. "No, I wouldn't think you would. Your Martin is as fine a man as you always believed, and he loves you deeply."

"I'm very fortunate," Fia agreed, "and won't forget it. May we talk about you now?"

"What more is there to discuss?"

"How and when you will proceed to divorce Muir, for instance."

Alayne stared at a length of silk that Fia had just removed from its wrapping. "Lovely color," she commented, then returned her gaze to Fia's. "I won't ask Douglas' involvement, I promise you that."

"My involvement in what, my dear?" Douglas inquired, entering from between the parted curtains.

The women looked up with a start. Alayne pushed her sewing aside, stood, and impulsively hugged him.

"Thank you, Douglas, for being there for me last night. I have some idea what it may have cost you–for that, I'm truly sorry."

"Anything I've lost was not caused by my guarding you last night, but by your husband's reappearance. It has reawakened Kate's protective instincts and perhaps blinded her to what appear to be flaws in Muir's character." He took a deep breath and patted her hand. "I'm very surprised to see you here."

"I seemed to have surprised everyone," Alayne admitted, "though, as I told Fia and Martin, it was hearing you outside my door turning Muir aside that started me thinking again. I'm glad you came here. I wanted to thank you myself and thought I'd missed my opportunity when I saw you leave this morning."

"You look more rested, Douglas," Fia asserted.

"I do feel better, though I didn't sleep as well as I thought I would. Too much to think about, I suppose." He turned to Alayne again. "Now, what was it you weren't going to involve me in?"

Alayne backed away from him. Now that he was before her, the temptation to lean on him for assistance was great. With some effort, she squared her shoulders and replied, "My divorce."

Astonished, Douglas' eyebrows rose. "You intend to divorce Matheson?"

"I do. But I will not put you in a position to which Kate will object. That wouldn't be fair to either of you."

Douglas' gaze softened. "Your concern for me, and for Kate, does you great credit. However, if you wish me to help–"

"No!" Alayne stated, with an emphatic shake of her head.

"Could I recommend a solicitor here in Inverness?"

Alayne refused to look at him, feeling herself weaken.

Fia said "Alayne, you need the name of someone you can trust." She turned to ask, "Douglas, is there a solicitor in Inverness who has experience handling divorce? It's such a rare thing."

Douglas cast Fia a tender look. "Aye. His name is William Francis and he's located on Bank Street. You're a good friend, Fia," he said, and kissed her forehead.

"You're both good friends," Alayne smiled her gratitude.

Douglas said, "It's time I took my leave, though I would like to say farewell to Martin."

"Then stay a while longer," Fia urged.

"No, it's better that Kate not find me still here when–" He broke off his sentence as the shop door opened and Kate walked in, her son behind her. Upon seeing Douglas, Kate stopped abruptly and Muir stumbled into her.

The three shop occupants steeled for what they assumed would be a difficult, if not ugly, confrontation.

"You're still here," Kate remarked to Douglas, a hint of relief in her voice.

"I beg your forgiveness, Mistress. I came to say my goodbyes to Fia and Martin; they offered me a place to rest before I journeyed home."

"There...there's nothing to forgive," she said in a small, somewhat melancholy voice. "You are always welcome in my home or shop."

Muir watched the exchange through hooded eyes, noting with interest more of what he'd only

299

glimpsed the evening before. There was some...attachment...between his mother and this man–an attachment he was sure he didn't like. It was bound to cause trouble for him.

"Mither, can we not attend our true reason for being here? My wife."

Muir took only one step toward Alayne when she rose to a threatening posture and called, "Stand where you are."

"Or you'll do what?" he mocked, unwisely advancing another step.

Alayne snatched up the heavy shears they used to cut fabric and stood in silent promise of what she would do.

"Muir," his mother commanded, "keep your distance. And you, Alayne, put those down. This goes too far. It's a poor start to renewing your relationship."

"Is that what he wants?" Alayne huffed, laying the shears on the counter with a thud. "It isn't possible."

"But Alayne," Kate began ardently, "you must understand. He was pressed into His Majesty's–"

"Aunt Kate," interrupted Fia, "Muir needs to speak for himself."

Kate answered testily, "Fia, this is none of your business."

"Nor yours," Fia reminded calmly, which brought Kate up short.

"Douglas?" Kate sought his support, but Douglas averted his gaze and returned to the workroom. His action made her heart constrict painfully. He obviously agreed with Fia. "Excuse me," she mumbled and followed through the curtained door.

Fia moved toward the curtain as well; Alayne stopped her.

"Don't leave me alone with him," she stated more than asked.

Muir turned his velvety tones on his cousin, "I assure you, Fia, Alayne will be unharmed."

"I'm sure she will be," Fia agreed and walked back to the counter where she resumed unwrapping bolts of material.

Displeased at Fia's decision to stay, Muir frowned, marring his smooth, boyish face. "You can trust me, Cousin."

"My friend has asked me to stay, and I will," Fia responded.

Muir's glower deepened; he turned back to Alayne. "Are you angry with me?" he asked, absurdly.

"For leaving or for coming back?" she answered snidely.

Muir defended, "I had no choice in the leaving."

"So you say."

"Why should you doubt me?" he blustered.

"I know you too well."

"Four years can change a man," he vowed earnestly.

"If it were four years, we wouldn't be having this conversation," she stated and, before he had the opportunity to question what she meant, Alayne continued, "Why did you never get word to me or to your mother?"

"The Navy is loath to let its conscripts go ashore for fear they will desert."

Alayne shook her head. "Someone could have carried a letter ashore. Try again."

Frustrated, Muir tossed his flaxen hair and snapped, "It's not as simple a matter as you think."

"Perhaps. Then why don't you tell me how you come to be here now."

Muir became oddly animated as he explained, "A bit over a week ago my ship moored in Plymouth. We'd been caught in a monstrous squall on the crossing and limped into port needing repairs. I was assigned to accompany the foretopman to the sailmaker. He was a friend and turned his back. Here I am."

Alayne's skepticism of his too-glib tale was apparent as she sneered, "Dangerous move for the foretopman."

"He was a very good friend," Muir said sincerely.

"And a fool if he risked himself for *you*," Alayne spat.

Fia ceased her pretense of work and stared as her cousin's face reddened and his mouth clenched into a thin, angry line. But when he spoke again, his voice was unruffled and buttery in its placid pitch. "My dearest Alayne, I don't expect in one day that you'll forget all that has happened–all I have had part in that has caused you pain. But I beg you, try to open your mind and heart, just a little, to hear objectively what I'm telling you. What I've told you is reasonable.

You don't want it to be, so you don't hear it that way."

Alayne's eyes were hard. "You say what you've told me is reasonable. I accept that. What I don't accept is that it happened to you."

"It was not my fault," he insisted.

"Nor mine," Alayne countered. "I simply don't believe you."

Muir's fists closed and he took one step toward his wife, but Fia rushed to Alayne's side before Alayne could again seek her shears. Immediately, Muir stopped and swung his glower to his cousin. "What are you gawking at?" he harped.

Fia bit her lip yet, unmoved, simply turned her gaze to the counter before her.

Muir growled and stormed past Alayne through the curtained doorway.

When Kate proceeded into the workroom, she both hoped and dreaded that Douglas was waiting for her on the other side. Instead, the empty room brought a pang of bitter disappointment. She cast a longing look at the stairs, now certain he'd retreated up them to avoid her. She didn't blame him.

Voices reached her from the shop and, while she knew she shouldn't, Kate listened. In Muir's words and tone, Kate heard contriteness, impatience, a plea for sympathy; in Alayne's she heard doubt, coldness, and firm resolve. "Son," she said morosely, "you are wasting your breath."

"You're right, you know," Douglas offered from behind her.

Kate whirled in surprise, her heart catching in her throat at the sight of him standing, once more, with valise in hand. "Oh, Douglas," she began, "I'm so sorry about this morning. Why didn't you tell me?"

Douglas set down his bag and his long fingers wrapped around his tricorne. "I'm surprised Muir did."

"He's just so...so eager to make amends with Alayne."

"Then perhaps you would do them both a service by convincing your son that, as you said, he's wasting his breath."

"Fia is right, I shouldn't interfere. They have to work this out together," she stated, with small hope.

Douglas stepped closer. "Work *what* out, Kate? There's nothing left for them. That was true before he disappeared. Surely—"

"But it was not his fault," she burst.

"Whose fault it was is immaterial," Douglas responded benevolently. "It doesn't change the fact that, whatever emotion or feeling caused them to wed no longer exists." He lay his hat on the worktable. "Kate, look at Alayne. You must know she cares deeply for Simon."

His mention of Simon drew fire to Kate's eyes and ice to her voice. "Simon?" she hissed. "If not for him, Alayne would not be making Muir suffer now. She would hear him out without judging first. And why is everyone concerned only about Alayne? My son was kidnapped and made to serve in the Royal Navy. Pity him living in those wretched conditions all these years."

"I do pity your son anything he has suffered, but he's fine now. Alayne is twice-over a victim, first robbed of her husband, now robbed of the chance for new happiness—to move on with a life that has been fixed in time these many years." He came closer, placing his hands lightly at her elbows. "You mustn't blame Simon for what has long been dead, nor for caring for Alayne. You love her, Kate. Don't blindly discount her needs and her pain because you've been fortunate enough to have your son restored to you. I beg you." Douglas drew her hands to his lips.

"Please...please don't leave, Douglas," Kate implored. "How will I manage to make sense of things, to see all sides without your wisdom?"

"If I believed it would do more good than harm, I would gladly stay. Dear Kate, you need time alone to reestablish your bond with your son. Muir must be a changed man; you're a changed woman. I've been privileged to witness some of those changes."

Her palms now pressed against his chest, tears shimmering her eyes, Kate readily admitted, "I will miss you terribly. I've gotten quite spoiled; I so prefer being with you than to being without you." She tilted her face and stood on tiptoe, touching her lips to his, prompting Douglas to pull her within the circle of his long arms.

"Well, how cozy," Muir sneered from the curtain, his expression decidedly ugly.

Kate broke from Douglas, her face flaming.

"How humiliating to find my mother being pawed by the night watch."

Douglas fought an almost overwhelming urge to slap Muir till his head spun, and gritted, "What manner of man are you to purposely embarrass your mother?"

"I believe it is being caught love-making that has caused her to color so...becomingly, not a thing I've said." Coldly, Muir continued, "At least one of the Mathesons has a lover; I have a wife who no longer loves me."

At his sides, Douglas' fists clenched white. "You didn't really expect to return after all these years to find everything as you left it."

"Why am I discussing this with you?" he dismissed. "My wife and mother are not your concern, Mr. Solicitor."

"Muir!" his mother finally snapped. "Speak civilly to Mr. Sutherland, please. He is a dear friend."

Muir stuck his face in Douglas'. "Oh," Muir chuckled obscenely, "I believe he's a *very* dear friend, Mither."

"You go too far," Douglas warned.

"She's my mother," the younger man taunted. "It's my duty to see no one takes advantage of her."

"Kate is too strong a woman to let anyone take advantage of her," Douglas countered.

"Then I don't know how you slipped through her defenses and into her bed."

Douglas grabbed the stock of Muir's shirt, constricting it and nearly wrenching the man from his feet. "You accuse your mother as if she were a common trollop. You call that protecting her?" The muscle in Douglas' jaw twitched violently and his eyes gleamed like cold steel. "She has done nothing to earn such disrespect and you will apologize now!"

Kate was so staggered by the escalating war of words, that she stood, dumbfounded. Now, with Muir struggling to free himself from Douglas' clench, she tore her rooted feet forward and pressed, "Let him go, please, Douglas! There have been changes since Muir left–he has adjustments to make, too."

Fia and Alayne tumbled into the room, drawn by the raised, agitated voices. They were amazed at the scene before them and Douglas' response to Kate.

"You were never the doxy your son has compared you too. *That* hasn't changed."

"I know, I know. He's upset. He's never seen me show affection to any man but his father." Gently, Kate tugged at Douglas' arm.

"Your husband has been dead many years," Douglas complained. "If that is your son's problem, then he has a great deal of maturing yet to do." Without ceremony, Douglas released Muir who staggered to regain his footing and fill his deprived chest with air.

Douglas turned to Kate. "You are owed a very large and sincere apology from your son. If you don't–"

"*Douglas*," Fia called out, leaping forward just in time to catch the brunt of Muir's thrusting fist as he swung at Douglas.

"*Fia!*" Alayne howled, and dove to the side of her crumpled friend.

"Dear God," Douglas lamented, dropping beside the stricken woman as did Kate.

"I...I..." Muir looked from his mother to Douglas to Alayne. "Why did she do that? She shouldn't have gotten in the way."

With Douglas' handkerchief, Alayne dabbed the blood from a small gash along Fia's cheek and accused, "This is what you *always* do, Muir. You hurt people! And it doesn't matter whether it's intentional or not, because you don't care either way, as long as you get what you want."

"Alayne, that's not true. This was an accident. I came back to make amends. I never wanted–"

"You're wasting your words." Alayne responded with an odd gleam in her eye. "When Martin returns, you'll have to answer to him–and he'll believe you no more than I do. You want to make amends, you say? So you accuse your own mother of loose behavior? You strike out at someone who has been good to her because you can't stand the thought of her finding some happiness that doesn't revolve around you."

Fia stirred, her head wobbling back and forth as she tried to clear it.

As Douglas bent to ask Fia how she fared, Muir fell to his knees beside her and gathered her hands in his. "Oh, Cousin, forgive me! I didn't intend for you to be injured. If only you hadn't jumped in front of me."

302

"You see?" Alayne shot at Kate. "Even in his apology, he blames her, not himself." Alayne batted at Muir's hands. "Get away from her, you've done enough."

He sat away a few inches and glared at his wife, who suddenly smiled a triumphant smile. "What–?" Abruptly, Muir was thrust aside. Staggered, he glimpsed his cousin's husband as he knelt, examined Fia's cheek and spoke softly to her, receiving her nod in return. Martin kissed his wife's forehead, then stood and turned to Muir.

For a brief moment, Muir was pleased to note that Martin was shorter than he. Yet the pleasure was short-lived as Martin thrust him against the wall, holding him there easily in a powerful grip, and Muir found himself gaping at Martin's incensed, thunderous visage. Greatly alarmed, it began to dawn on Muir that Martin was not someone to be taken lightly. "M...Martin," Muir began. "Let me assure–"

"You could have nothing to say to me that would justify why you struck my wife. You are a coward to have done so and an utter fool if you think you can talk your way clear of blame."

"But, it w...wasn't my fault!" Muir exclaimed.

Martin's hand closed round Muir's neck with such force that Muir's head cracked sharply against the wall. "I believe I've heard enough," Martin stated. With deadly calm in his voice, he continued, "I'll say this once; you listen. If you ever touch my wife again, harm her in any way, it will be the last thing you do." He abruptly released Muir, who toppled to the floor, and turned away.

Vaguely, Kate's in-drawn breath resounded in the room and, astonished, Muir staggered to his feet sputtering, "It...it was an accident." He looked around at the stone-like faces that met him and cried again, "It was an accident!"

Kate stepped forward but did not lay a hand on her son, partially for fear of embarrassment if he withdrew from her touch. "It was an accident, but your intention was to hurt Douglas. It was a mistake to bring you straight here to see Alayne. We should have taken the time to talk first about things that have changed in our lives these four years. I believe that could have prevented many misunderstandings and the injury to Fia." She glanced at the group, including Fia, now sitting upright, Douglas' arm supporting her, Martin tending her wound. "I'm sorry. I only knew how important it was to Muir to speak with Alayne, to try to make her understand how...sorry he was...about..." Her voice trailed off for there was nothing more she could say.

Alayne stood up and approached Kate, taking the woman's hands in her own. "It isn't for you to be sorry, Kate. But I will tell you now, and put an end to any wish your son may have of reconciliation. I will seek a divorce at the earliest opportunity." She felt Kate stiffen, yet her mother-in-laws hands remained in her own, which Alayne took as acceptance. "Thank you, Kate, for not fighting me on this."

"Well, she *should* fight you," Muir blurted. "You haven't given me a chance, Alayne."

"You don't deserve a chance," she responded harshly. "I hope you can rebuild your life; I hope you can show nothing but love and respect for your mother. But there is nothing between us Muir; that was true even before you left."

"I didn't leave," he protested, "I was taken."

"It doesn't matter," Alayne stated, "that's the point."

Muir looked from one to the other. In Douglas and Martin, he saw disgust and anger; on Alayne's face, there was nothing. His mother showed an abundance of sadness and pain. And from Fia...Fia. This was *her* fault. If she hadn't gotten in his way... Muir's eyes narrowed as he scrutinized his cousin and her look, in return, was one of confusion. He turned on his heels and strode across the room and out the door, slamming it in his wake.

Kate began to cry softly and Alayne and Douglas took her to the hearth, sat her in a chair and tried to comfort her.

Martin's attention leapt back to his wife, for her body had gone suddenly rigid. "What is it, lass?" he inquired, uneasily, thinking there was some other injury he hadn't seen.

Fia gaped at the door behind her departed cousin and immediately her body shuddered violently. "Oh, God," she murmured, so low that, over Kate's tears, no one but Martin heard her.

Afraid now, he grasped her hands, his face a bare inch from hers. "Fia, tell me what's wrong," he begged.

Her eyes, filled with dread, finally focused on his.

Martin abandoned her hands and crushed her against him to drive out whatever horror plagued her. "Please, my love, please tell me."

"It's him," she choked. "That walk, I'll never forget that walk."

Her meaning beginning to seep through, Martin abruptly pulled away to look at her face again. "Are you telling me...are you sure that–"

She nodded furiously. "Muir is the man Hallowe'en night; the man watching the shop–"

"Weeks ago," Martin finished her thought.

"What does it mean, Martin?" she anguished, and he drew her again into his comforting grip.

"I don't know, Fia. I only know we'd better find out quickly."

Chapter Thirty-One

"*Your motives were* noble, my love, but Douglas can take care of himself," Martin assuaged as he swabbed Fia's cut more thoroughly.

"I wasn't thinking," admitted Fia, cringing at her husband's tender ministrations to her bruised cheek.

"If Muir wasn't so cowardly trying to attack Douglas from behind, this wouldn't have happened at all," Martin reminded.

Fia frowned. "Think how happy we'd all still be if Muir hadn't returned." She waited for a pang of guilt for having uttered such a thought, but none came. "Why did he reveal himself now? Why not when he first arrived in Inverness?"

"I wish I had the answer, Sweetheart," Martin evoked. "It might make it easier when we tell Alayne and Kate."

"How?" she implored. "How can we do that without breaking Aunt Kate's heart? How much more disappointment can Alayne stand?"

Martin enveloped her hands in his. "If you're certain it was Muir, we have no choice. I believe Kate has glimpsed the man her son has become; her heart must be wounded already. We can't condone his lie; she has the right to know."

Reluctantly, Fia sighed, "It will be very hard." Her eyes sought his. "Truthfully, I'm every bit as worried about Alayne's reaction."

"Knowing this won't change things for her. She'll still seek a divorce."

"But don't you see? Muir must have known his four years were almost up."

Martin cocked his head thoughtfully. "You're right. That's very likely."

"Oh, Martin," she anguished. "Alayne is so hurt and angry. To have been so close to her freedom–to a life with Simon–and have it stolen from her in so calculated a manner." Emotion trembled Fia's voice causing Martin to pull her from the chair, sit down and ease her onto his lap. He held her while the tension and pain of the morning flowed with her tears.

Like Alayne, Martin was angry. He was angry at Muir for all the trouble he had caused in less than one day, and at himself for not being at the shop to keep Fia safe. Martin's belly churned with concern and remorse since he'd found her crumpled on the floor of the workroom. And he sensed a continued threat connected with the return of Alayne's husband. A chill down his spine strengthened his determination. Simon would understand if he left Inverness long enough to take Fia somewhere safe. He would be more focused, more useful to his cousin in dealing with Struan and Andrew Forbes. Martin roused from his thoughts realizing Fia no longer cried and her glare pierced him with such intensity–like she knew his thoughts.

Indeed, she did. "Do you remember what I said last night? That was not an idle promise. We stay together."

"And what happens the next time I'm not with you, and the next?" he demanded.

"You'll just have to stay with me," she resolved.

"I'm not jesting," he promised, with mild frustration.

"Neither am I," she stated. "Martin, what happened today was an accident; Muir didn't intend to hurt me. I will not leave unless it is with you. That's the end of it." She pressed her lips to his in a lingering, sweet kiss, then vowed, "To be so cherished by the man I love more than life, I'm the most fortunate woman in the world."

He buried his face against her neck and held her silently, for nothing but inadequate words came to him.

Surprised to find Muir home, Kate had tried to reason with him and now, she sighed her frustration with her son. "You keep ignoring advice and plunging ahead as you please. You all but threatened Alayne–"

"Threatened *her*? She's the one who waved scissors at me."

"And that was every bit as wrong on her part, but you didn't listen when she told you to stay away. Son, she doesn't love you, she doesn't want you back."

"I'm her husband."

"You heard her; she intends to divorce you," Kate reminded.

"Divorce *me*?" After a moment's hesitation, Muir began to chuckle and, before long, cackled in genuine malicious delight.

Stunned and confused by his reaction, Kate stood with her mouth agape.

"And just what," he asked, gasping for breath, "what grounds will she use?"

Kate's brow furrowed with worry, unable to account for his odd behavior. "Muir–"

"*What grounds?*" he roared, causing her to jump.

A fleeting fear shivered her, then, indignant that her own son should elicit such a reaction, Kate steeled her body, hardened her eyes and voice to respond, "I don't know and, if I did, I'm not sure I'd tell you."

It was Muir's turn to gawk. "Why are you against me?" he cried.

"I'm not. I'm trying to help you," she snapped. "I don't deserve to be growled at, and I refuse to accept such behavior from you. Now, I want you to tell me, have you been ill?"

"Why would you think that?" Muir puzzled, exasperated.

"You're acting so unpredictably–one moment you are sweet and loving, the next menacing. This is not the Muir I remember."

He turned on his heel to leave then whirled to face her. "Four years of hard living can change a man, Mither. You realize that my homecoming has been somewhat less enthusiastic than I'd hoped. I'd like nothing more than to pick up my old life, but you and Alayne are making it very difficult."

Remorse squeezed Kate's heart. "Son, I realize this must frustrate you. I'm sure you've suffered, but your old life is gone. You need to try to determine what your life should be now and that will take time and patience. We must learn how we've changed and build from there. We can't go back."

"Drivel," he rumbled. "You speak to me as if I were still a toddling child. I'm a grown man who has a wife–she is still my wife–and she will be my wife until I say it's finished."

"Dear, have you heard a word I–"

"I've heard all your words, Mither, I simply don't accept them." He stalked out the door, calling over his shoulder, "I won't be home for supper."

Muir fumed, storming down Douglas Row kicking up slush left in the wake of the morning snow. "Why did I ever bother to show myself?" he groused under his breath, all the while knowing the better question to be, why wasn't he prepared for the reception he'd received? His clandestine observation of the shop had shown him that his wife still worked there. His hope had been that Alayne would have long since disappeared; he was more than displeased she'd not done so. There was no one with whom he wanted to share his mother's money; certainly he didn't care to waste it on, "My wife," he finished the thought aloud. No, he had plans for that money.

Muir had returned to Inverness when Thomas Gray told him that, if he could scrape up the money to "invest", he would be able to double it on one or two of the shipments taking place before the end of the year. That was when the traders could demand the highest prices. People were willing to pay dearly to have special gifts and spirits to celebrate the Yule and Hogmanay.

Muir's clear blue eyes focused narrowly as he pondered how to talk his mother into parting with a tidy sum. "If Alayne had taken me back–or even treated me kindly–Mither would have granted me anything," he grumbled. Yet, Alayne had rejected him. Not only that, his cousin had made his situation almost unbearable. She was an enormous bother he hadn't figured on. He hadn't even known who she was when he'd first seen her, much less the colossal trouble she'd cause. And what's more, Fia's husband was now threatening to kill him. For all this abuse he was suffering, his own mother not only turned on him, but also presented another impediment he couldn't have foreseen–her attachment to that slug of a solicitor. The only good thing that had happened since his return was Sutherland's departure. "What did I ever do to deserve such wretched treatment?" he complained.

Muir chafed at the thought of not being able to amass a small fortune on these next shipments. He'd struggled for some time after joining up with Thomas Gray because, thoughtlessly, Muir had fled Inverness with little in his pocket. But his years as Gray's agent in the Indies had managed to make him a reasonably comfortable living. If he failed now to avail himself of his mother's money, he had to think of something else, something lucrative. Otherwise, he might just as well have stayed away from Douglas Row.

Muir's pace faltered briefly as a new thought flitted into his consciousness. Just what was his cousin doing in Inverness? What had brought her back from Glasgow? It was Glasgow, wasn't it, where her uncle lived? From the time she'd gone away until the time he had, Fia had never visited, never contacted his mother, not as far as he knew. Muir pondered the implications, but could make nothing of it. Still, he decided to keep the question around, just in case it should prove useful.

"Maybe I should pay my dear cousin a visit," he mused. "Apologize again...aye." In any case, it might prove an interesting diversion till something profitable came his way. Fia was clearly close to his wife. If he played his hand wisely, why Fia might even tell him how Alayne planned to go about divorcing him. Alayne couldn't use desertion because Muir had reappeared in time to prevent that. He chuckled his satisfaction at that stroke of brilliance. "The only other grounds for divorce she...can't...prove." Muir stopped in his tracks as a scheme of revenge crowded his mind. Revenge because Alayne was still here, still clinging to his mother, still holding herself apart from him. "I am yet her husband," he gloated, "but perhaps not for long." Whistling his pleasure with himself, Muir set his fluid gait in motion again in the direction of the quay.

Fia woke to Martin's anxious scrutiny. "What...what is it?" she questioned worriedly.

He stroked her hair and bent to kiss her. "I should have throttled him for striking you. Your cheek is purple, where it isn't bruised blue or brown."

"I think you left no doubt how you felt, Martin, and my cheek will heal." She snuggled closer to his warmth. "We have more pressing problems where Muir is concerned. How will I tell Aunt Kate and Alayne about his deceit?"

"*We'll* tell them, lass," he corrected, resting his cheek on her forehead. "We just will. No amount of planning will help, I'm afraid. Now, listen. I haven't had a chance to tell you that I found rooms for us, though they won't be ready till mid-month. There's little available so we'll have to make do." He felt her forehead pucker into a frown and urged, "What are you thinking?"

"That I should ask Aunt Kate if we can stay in my old room so that Alayne can move back here. In fact," she added, "Alayne should be here now."

Martin was loath to give up having his wife all to himself; still, there was no question Fia was right. "It's early, my sweet. You've only napped briefly. Perhaps we should speak with Alayne first."

Fia's love-softened gaze carefully searched his face. She recognized his sacrifice of their privacy; she felt it too. Yet his regard for Alayne's well-being was genuine and–if possible– she loved him all the more for it. Her kiss told him so. When she rose, patting and pulling her hair into presentable order, she stopped abruptly and turned to Martin inquiring, "Do you think Alayne will be safe here by herself?"

"I think so but, again, we need to ask Alayne how she feels about it."

Together, they descended the steps to the now deserted workroom. They heard voices, which Fia quickly deduced was a customer speaking with Alayne. Once the client had departed, she and Martin entered the shop.

Upon seeing her injured friend, Alayne crossed the room and hugged Fia. "How are you feeling?" she asked, concern etching her face.

"Better, really," Fia assured with a smile that faded too quickly. "Martin and I do need to speak with you though."

Alayne glanced warily from one to the other and observed, "By the looks of you, I may not want to hear what you're going to say."

"In part, that's true," Martin candidly replied. "First is to tell you I found rooms for us, however, they aren't available until mid-November."

A resigned sigh escaped Alayne. "So I stay with Kate."

"Not necessarily," Martin continued. "If she'll have us, Fia and I are prepared to move to Kate's so you can have your quarters here until the rooms are ready. Our only concern is that you feel safe wherever you are."

"Safe?" Alayne questioned. "I can lock the door anywhere."

"Then you should be here, out from under Muir's scrutiny," Fia said and Martin nodded agreement.

Alayne studied her friends' earnest expressions and simply said, "Thank you both." Suddenly, she straightened. "Wait...there's more you have to tell me. Something I may not like?"

Fia took Alayne's hands. "There's no good way to tell you this. Muir has been in Inverness for some time now."

Alayne's face was blank. "I...I don't understand."

Martin explained, "Just this morning, Fia recognized Muir as the same man she saw lurking outside the shop and on All Hallows Eve."

Her heart pounded so hard Alayne could scarcely hear her own words. "Are you...are you sure?"

With a regretful nod, Fia answered, "I wish I had even a shred of doubt."

Alayne leaned heavily on the counter, her expression agitated. "That means that he planned this, timed it just so," she concluded in a small, brittle voice.

"It would appear that way," Martin agreed.

After a moment, Alayne lifted her gaze. "Why would he do that? I'm at a complete loss to think of any reason–any excuse–for such behavior. He's alive, in Inverness, spying on the shop and doesn't make himself known? God's life, what is he plotting?" Alayne closed her eyes, covered her mouth with her hand, and moaned softly. "Poor Simon. I could have spared him if I'd known."

"Spared him what?" Fia asked, perplexed.

"The embarrassment of having declared my love when I should have known it was impossible."

"It isn't impossible," Fia countered. "The fact that Muir has returned doesn't change how you and Simon feel about each other."

Martin urged. "Don't give up, Alayne. You haven't spoken with the solicitor yet."

"That's right," Fia chimed in. "Talk to the solicitor before–what's that?" she asked, then realized, "Someone's at the workroom door."

"It must be Simon," Martin said, glancing at the clock on the nearby shelf.

He and Fia both looked expectantly at Alayne, who appeared about to be sick, but who moved into the back room to answer the knock.

Upon opening the door, Alayne and Simon stared at each other cautiously, and such was his entry into the room. Alayne closed the door and turned to face him. Simon hesitated a long moment before extending his arms to her. Without thought, Alayne delivered herself into them and was immediately wrapped in their healing embrace. Tight was their clasp, and they both choked on unshed tears.

"I thought–" they started simultaneously.

"You first–" they continued.

Simon's kiss was passionate, desperate.

"I...I was so afraid..." she finally gulped.

"So was I," he admitted.

"But not...not now," Alayne vowed, "Not when you hold me."

Simon stroked her hair and assured. "No, my love, not now."

They basked silently in their joy at being together even knowing how much stood between them, how much had to be resolved.

Finally, Alayne led him to the hearth and they sat facing each other, fingers entwined.

"How did you fare last night?" Simon inquired.

"Well enough. I came here early, shortly after Douglas arrived in fact. He risked his relationship with Kate to protect me, you know."

Simon nodded, stroking her cheek.

"I'm so grateful to him for that," she confessed.

"As I am." Tentatively, Simon asked, "Have...have you seen anyone else?"

Almost apologetically, Alayne responded, "Later in the morning, Muir and Kate arrived. It got ugly, I must admit," she said ruefully.

Alert, Simon straightened, demanding, "Ugly in what way?"

She cast her eyes to the hearth and responded, "Well, though I asked him to stay away from me, Muir wouldn't. So, I threatened him with the shears. Kate chastised us both and left poor Fia to keep order between us while she went, I think, to try to repair the damage between her and Douglas."

"I hold Fia in exceedingly high regard," Simon declared, then continued, "but what could she have done if Muir persisted?"

Alayne shrugged for she had no answer.

"Where was Martin during all this?" Simon queried a little unnerved at what he was hearing. "Why didn't Kate turn to him for help?"

"He'd left before all this happened to go look for new lodgings for us."

"Us?" Simon puzzled. "You mean him and Fia."

"And me," Alayne responded, "until I can divorce Muir."

Simon stared wide-eyed then his gaze softened. "You told him...divorce?" To Alayne's nod, he queried, "What was Kate's reaction?"

"Silence. I had warned her of my plan before and she said she would support me. I'm so thankful that I don't have to fight her as well as her son."

Simon raised each of her hands to his lips. "You are courageous, lass. I'm so proud of the woman you are."

"I love you, Simon," she explained simply. "I want to be your wife."

Tears once more stung his eyes as they searched hers. "You would marry me?" he said in wonder. Though he'd longed to, Simon had never asked her. Always he had tried to respect Alayne's reluctance to make any commitment–even of her feelings–while she was still married.

She lay her palm against his chest. "When you ask me, Simon, that will be my answer," she promised.

Simon pulled her against him and gently rocked her. "Then I promise you, I'll ask you at the first possible moment you can freely give me that very response."

She pressed eager lips to his mouth and her blood stirred to his response, strengthening her determination to seek out, first thing in the morning, the solicitor Douglas had named. Alayne's sleek fingers touched Simon's hair and her brow furrowed. "There's something else you must know."

"What is it?" he urged.

"Just before you arrived, Fia and Martin were telling me that Muir has been in Inverness at least several weeks–the man Fia saw watching the shop and saw again on Hallowe'en."

"*What?*" he gasped.

"She's positive," Alayne assured. "Perhaps knowing it was Muir will help me get the divorce. Simon, you...you realize, this won't be easy."

"I'll help you however I might," he stated earnestly.

Alayne smiled tenderly. "I love you so, Simon. I can never tell you how much I regret Muir's return." Her smile crumbled into a bitter confession, "How I hate him for what he's done."

Simon framed her face between his hands. "We will defeat him, Alayne. You and I together will be a formidable force against Muir. I promise you, we'll beat him."

For a long moment, she contemplated what he said, studied his face, then responded in a clear, strong voice, "I believe you, Simon."

Martin, Fia and Alayne walked briskly toward the Douglas Row house of Kate Matheson. The wind was rising, yet there was no cloud to be seen in the turquoise-blue sky. Only the sliver of new moon, lying heavily on its side, was visible above the fiery horizon.

Each silently prayed that Muir was not at his mother's home. Kate would need time to react to his deceit and compose herself.

"If only we knew what his reason was for concealing himself," Fia murmured their collective thought.

"Would it make a difference, do you think?"Alayne asked.

Martin replied, "We will never know for sure."

They reached Kate's door and entered leaving Arthur just outside. Taking off their wraps, the trio noticed Kate at her desk, quill poised as if to write, but she made no movement. A sound behind them made Alayne turn to Flora's welcome.

"It's raw out," she observed. "Would you like some tea to rid you of the chill?"

"Oh that's thoughtful, Flora," Alayne answered.

Just then, Fia turned and Flora blurted, "Mistress Ross, what happened to your face?"

Fia replied lightly. "It was an accident, Flora. My husband has fixed me up quite well. Please don't be concerned."

Kate turned to Flora's bellow and saw only Martin looking her way. She half expected him to rush in and accuse her of fault for what Muir had done to Fia. Would she blame him if he did? No. But what she found instead was great sympathy in his eyes and Kate discovered she didn't care much for that reaction either. Rising, she invited, "Come in. I didn't hear you arrive."

"You were preoccupied," Martin said, executing a small bow. "I've Fia and Alayne with me. Is your son here?"

Kate steadied her gaze, but her voice faltered, "No, M...Muir is not here."

Martin moved toward her. "Before the ladies come in, I want to thank you, once again, for yesterday. I could never have imagined such a lovely setting in which to marry Fia. The only thing more beautiful was my bride. I appreciate your kindness more than I can tell you."

Momentarily speechless, Kate at last replied, "It was truly my pleasure, Martin. It just seems so long ago already. Oh," she added as an afterthought, "do remember I want your cloths as we discussed."

He nodded. "I'll leave them at the shop for your approval, with my thanks."

At that moment, the two young women entered. Fia paused, wondering what had occurred between her husband and her aunt who still stood close together. If it was important, she knew Martin would share it with her later. "Flora is bringing tea, Kate," Alayne said. "I hope you don't mind."

"I would welcome it, Alayne." Kate crossed the room to her niece and hugged her. "I'm so sorry that you were injured, Fia. I'd undo the deed if I could."

"Aunt Kate, it wasn't your fault. And I'll be fine, won't I, Martin?" Fia called over her aunt's shoulder.

"You will, lass," he confirmed.

"There, you see?" Fia held Kate away to better see her. "You have my personal physician's word. If you have the time though, we really must speak with you.

Kate's nervous glance skittered among the three. "Of course, I have the time. But first, I have something for you Fia. I was going to give it to you yesterday after the celebration of your handfasting but, well, that wasn't possible." Kate went back to her desk and pulled a package wrapped in cloth from one of the drawers. She handed it to Fia. "You're a married woman now; you'll be needing this. I admit I will miss seeing your lovely hair though."

Martin looked confused, but when Fia opened the wrapping, he understood. An embroidered, linen kertch rested inside.

"Oh, Aunt Kate, it's stunning," Fia exclaimed.

Martin added wistfully, "It is, indeed. Now I understand why you'll miss seeing Fia's hair."

Kate bestowed a gentle smile on him. "She need not wear this in private, of course, but should otherwise. I thought, not knowing who might be looking for Fia, they'd likely not look for an obviously married woman."

Martin praised, "You're right, Mistress. This may very well help conceal her."

Just then, Flora entered with the promised tea.

"Set it here please, Flora," Kate said, indicating a round table near one of the upholstered chairs. "That will be all, thank you. The rest of you please sit. You wanted to speak with me."

Kate poured the tea and asked them to help themselves to the gingerbread Flora had provided. However, none could bring themselves to eat, and this polite refusal of the delicious, dark cake made Kate fidget. She was certain now that something unpleasant was about to happen. Her own cup, untouched on the table, Kate sat back and clenched her hands in her lap till the knuckles paled. "All right," she prompted, "you'd better tell me what's on your minds."

"Two things, Aunt Kate," Fia replied. "If it suits you, Alayne will be moving back to the shop and Martin and I will move into my old room tonight."

Alayne added, "I think it's for the best, Kate."

Kate gazed sadly at her daughter-in-law. "I suppose it's the reasonable thing to do, but I'll miss you Alayne. Please believe me."

Unprepared for the lump of regret that leapt into her throat, Alayne leaned over and squeezed Kate's clasped hands. "Th..thank you, Kate. I do believe you."

A small smile appeared then, and Kate said to Fia and Martin, "And I welcome you both for as long as you want to stay."

"Thank you, Mistress," Martin said, "but we expect it won't be for long. I've located rooms here in town that should be available in about two weeks."

"Oh," she responded in a small voice. "Well, if that doesn't work out for you...."

"That's kind of you," Martin conceded.

"You...you said there were two things," reminded Kate. "What was the other?"

Hesitant, Fia began, "Do you remember not long ago, I found a man watching your shop?"

Kate's brow wrinkled slightly. "Of course."

"Martin and I saw him again on All Hallows Eve."

Her belly beginning to flutter from a growing alarm, Kate prompted, "And what has that to do with me?"

Fia blurted, "I realized this morning that the man was Muir." Kate flushed heavily and, before she could ask, Fia offered, "I'm certain Aunt Kate. I'm so sorry."

"But...but that...that would mean...my son has been home and not...not come to see me...or Alayne. You must be...mistaken," she finished painfully, hopefully.

Fia shook her head. "I'm not; I wish I were."

As Kate rose and began a restless pacing, her high color faded and her pallor became chalky. "How could that be?" she said more to herself than to the others. "*Why* would that be? What possible reason could my son have for not making it known to us that he was alive and well?"

"We've asked ourselves that same question, Mistress," Martin said in soothing tones. "We need to find out."

Kate turned suddenly to her daughter-in-law. "Alayne?" she asked almost accusingly.

Alayne's instinct was to snap back at the tone of Kate's question, but she conquered the urge. "I had no idea he was here. Surely you can't doubt that."

"No...you're right, I can't." Kate's palms went to her face, fingertips beginning to knead her temples. "I'm afraid I don't know when Muir will be back; he said not to wait supper for him."

Alayne bit her tongue once more, but Fia said, "Martin and I will walk Alayne back and pick up our things. I should be here when you talk to Muir, Aunt Kate."

"We should be here," Martin firmly corrected.

Kate shook her head. "It's better for me to speak with him alone."

"But I'm the one who saw him, not you," Fia protested. "If I'm here when you confront him, it will be harder for him to deny the truth."

Martin added, "Though I would prefer it otherwise, I have to agree with Fia."

Alayne stood, bringing the debate to an end by stating, "If you're going to be sure you're here when he returns, we need to act quickly." She approached Kate. "I'm sorry, Kate; you deserve better from your son. Thank you though for understanding my need to move back to the shop."

Kate nodded, but turned away and said to no one in particular, "I'll see you later then."

"*So, have you* come up with the money yet?" Thomas Gray blandly inquired.

Muir shook his head in sharp response.

"Time's running out, lad," the older man advised. "There may be one more opportunity after this one. Profits won't be as great after Hogmanay; folks won't be indulging their pleasures for a while."

"I understand that," was Muir's petulant response. "I've run into trouble."

"Not altogether unexpected I would think. It's been many a year you've been 'dead' shall we say?" Gray frowned. "When you told me you still had a mother here with money and no one to spend it on, I thought you a fortunate fellow. But your mother is more than surprised at your return isn't she?" he guessed, hoisting his tankard to his mouth.

"Aye," Muir grumbled, "and so's my wife."

Thomas spewed ale in surprise. "Wife?" he said, wiping droplets from his chin. "You still have a wife? No wonder you have troubles, and no wonder you so eagerly volunteered to sail off to the Indies in the first place. A wife!" Thomas held his jiggling belly as his chuckle rumbled into a roar.

"Enough!" Muir hotly decreed before lowering his voice. "Is there no other way I can earn a share in this shipment?"

Gray blotted the corners of his tearing eyes with his sleeve and, when he lowered his arm from his face, the joviality was gone, replaced by a shrewd intensity that took Muir aback. "Might be," Gray offered cryptically. "Man of your talents, there might be a way."

Just as Muir would have asked for details, the door swung wide and a tallish, scarecrow-thin man with stringy black hair and close, pale eyes appeared. Muir heard his companion's low groan and surmised that this must be Gordon's brother.

Struan swayed slightly and blinked into the gloom in which the lone rush lamp shed near-futile light. "What are you doing in this hole," Struan demanded, "and, who is he?" He pointed a bony finger at Muir's golden head.

"Why this is the man atop the cliff," Thomas replied glibly. "He's one of those who keeps us all alive by sounding a timely warning."

Struan's glare was blurred by drink and he plopped heavily into a vacant chair. Ignoring Muir, he inquired, "Why aren't you in the taproom? That's where all the excitement is."

"Sometimes," Gray spoke slowly, "it's better to discuss your business in private. Besides, you look and smell as though you already drank your way through the taproom."

With a shake of his head, Struan assured, "There's plenty left. And Betty's down there."

Muir snickered. "I doubt you'd be much use to Betty this night."

Struan lurched from his chair and grabbed Muir's collar more quickly and firmly than Muir or Gray would have given him credit for in his condition. "I could out-service you with any whore of your choosing."

Thomas reached up casually and wrapped his hand around Struan's wrist. "No harm meant by the lad. I was just about to ask him to guide your grouse-hunting. No sense losing a perfectly good guide over a jest."

"He doesn't look like he could find his way off the quay much less to a good spot for fowling," Struan observed with a loud belch.

"But you don't want to take that chance, do you? He's lived here most of his life, knows the area." Thomas appeased, "Sit down, now. I'll fetch a bottle and we'll talk it over. What do you say?"

Struan studied the mute newcomer and slowly reclaimed his chair. "Aye, we'll talk–over a bottle."

It was well after midnight when Muir made a stumbled entrance into his mother's home. Through bloodshot eyes, he barely registered surprise to see wavering light emanating from the drawing room. Inwardly, he groaned his annoyance that his mother had apparently stayed up to "welcome" him home. "I'll just tell her it's too late and I'm too drunk to hear her lecture," he mumbled, tossing his coat at a peg on the wall and ignoring it as it missed and fell to the floor. In a loud voice, Muir proclaimed, "All right, Mither. It really wasn't necessary for you to wait up for–" He stopped short as he spied not only his mother, but also Fia and Martin; the latter glowered darkly at him.

"Come in, Son," Kate invited in a flat voice. "We've been waiting for you."

Muir hesitated, uncertain how much trouble he was in. The fact that the three were waiting at this late hour, probably didn't bode well. He arranged a contrite expression. "If this is about your cheek, Fia, I really am sorry. I intended to seek you out in the morning to apologize once more."

"It's not Fia's cheek," Martin stated, "though you certainly owe her an apology."

"Indeed," Kate agreed.

Worry began to fire Muir's impatience. "Then what's the problem?"

"Son, why don't you sit down?" Kate urged.

"I believe I like it right where I am, Mither."

312

Susan M. Walls

"Fine," she said, and stood also, unwilling to be drawn into a petty squabble. "Muir, why didn't you tell me that you returned to Inverness some weeks ago?"

Her son's jaw dropped and he sputtered, "I...I...What are you saying? Weeks ago? Why that's preposterous! Why would I ever do such a thing?"

"That's precisely what we'd all like to know," Martin responded.

Muir shifted restlessly from one foot to the other as though unable to decide which way to bolt. "It's absurd," he rallied. "Who told you this?" he blustered.

"Before you deny it outright," Fia intervened, "no one told us that you were here. I saw you– twice. I just didn't know until this morning that it was you."

"That's...you must be mistaken."

"I'm not," she replied bluntly.

Trapped, Muir stood silently, his sculptured lips disappearing in a tight line of suppressed rage, bright eyes suddenly murky and hard. Damn his cousin. *Damn* her. Twice she'd managed to cast him in disreputable light–all in one day. He wouldn't abide that.

As Muir leveled his murderous glower at Fia, the hair on Martin's neck bristled. In a fluid motion, he rose from the chair and placed himself between his wife and her cousin.

Martin's sudden appearance in Muir's line of vision broke the spell and Muir turned to his mother whose cheeks were wet with tears. "Don't cry, Mither," he urged, mustering his most endearing look. "It is true; you...you just took me by surprise."

"Think how surprised I was," she protested, mopping her eyes. "Why did you not show your-self?"

To compose his story, Muir briefly hung his head then said, "I've been away a long time, un-able to come home. I didn't know what to expect when I returned: had you and Alayne moved on with you lives; did you think me dead; did you still grieve for me? I didn't even know for certain that you would still be here. I had to see for myself where things stood. I...I felt it would be wrong of me just to barge in and disrupt your lives if you'd already gone on as though I never existed."

Fia now stood at Martin's side, her hand clasped with his. "And why did that process take weeks?"

Smoothly, Muir responded, "I know very few people in Inverness any more and, to my cha-grin, those I still know are not people with whom I expect my mother and wife to associate. They wouldn't be able to tell me what I wanted to know." His eyes steeled once more. "In other words, Cousin, it took time to study the situation." He turned to Kate and challenged, "Well, Mither?"

Kate cast her eyes to the floor and nodded sadly.

Fia felt Martin's body tense to Kate's easy acceptance of Muir's explanation. She was baffled as well.

"Good!" Muir gloated his victory. "Now that that's settled, you two," he waggled his finger at Martin and Fia, "can slink back to wherever it is you bed down and let Mither and I enjoy some peace."

"That would be here," came Martin's retort. To Muir's mystified expression, he elaborated, "We are 'bedding down' here."

"What? Are you suggesting that I have to see you first thing tomorrow morning?"

"Exactly so," Martin assured him.

In distaste, Muir's expression soured and he announced, "I won't be breaking the fast with you, Mither. My belly's not that strong." With that, he turned on his heel and took the stairs two at a time, pleased with his performance, that he'd gotten the upper hand. Still, he seethed resent-ment at Fia's continued interference; neither was he happy with that menacing husband of hers. As he kicked off his shoes and flopped onto the bed, Muir decided that the task of getting even with Fia Graham Ross needed pursuing. "In the morn," he decided with a yawn. "I should have plenty of time to dwell on what to do about my cousin when I take that churl Forbes fowling." Without leaving the bed, Muir wriggled out of his clothes and dreamed of how to triple the money he would earn from that hunt on the next shipment.

"*Don't look at* me that way," Kate begged as Fia and Martin turned questioning gazes on her.

"Aunt Kate," Fia explained, "we simply want to understand."

"Then listen to me. No," Kate offered, voice quavering, "I don't believe he's telling us the entire truth. Yet it's the story he's given us and we must accept it. We can't disprove it and it has allowed him to save his pride a bit." She held up her hand to stave off argument. "Restoring his pride is important–I saw the venom in his eyes when he looked at you, Fia. Martin, you saw it," she accused, seeking support.

"Aye," Martin allowed, "as clearly as daylight."

Kate continued, "It's better that he thinks we believe him. I'm not saying he would harm you intentionally–"

"But we won't take that chance by boxing him in," Martin said, finishing her thought, pleased that Kate was not blind to Muir's ire. "You're reasoning is sound, Mistress," Martin praised. "Thank you. I know this can't be easy for you."

"It isn't. I love my son," Kate replied simply. "Goodnight to you both."

Fia kissed her aunt's cheek and watched her dejected retreat up the stairs. "She looks twenty years older than she did this morning," Fia observed.

Martin slipped his arm around Fia's waist. "Come, Sweetheart," he entreated, "it's very late, and I desperately need the feel of you against me."

Arthur greeted them when they entered their bedroom where he'd been put on their return to Kate's. He settled again before the fire and, a short time later, Fia curled spoon-like against her husband's taut body. His warmth quickly dispelled the chill from the sheets and her skin, but did nothing for his own apprehension. Fia roused from near sleep, realizing his body remained tight with worry. She turned in his arms and, in the faint light, saw his eyes gleam darkly.

"How selfish of me," she murmured her apology. "I'm snug and safe tucked up against you, and ready to drift off."

"And what's selfish about that?" he asked, his hand caressing her back. "I want you safe and snug."

"You're still anxious. I've been taking from you what I need without giving back what you need."

He opened his mouth to speak, but only a somewhat strangled sound emerged.

Fia rose up on one elbow and confessed, "I know what I'd like to give you more than anything."

"I only need you, my love," he declared, "nothing else."

She moved her fingers to his sculpted chest, stirred by the strong beat of his heart beneath. "You have me, Martin, and always will. I want to give you a child."

The thought clearly startled him and Fia bit her lip thinking she'd made a mistake telling him what was in her heart. Maybe it was the memory of the child he thought was his. The idea settled a hollow ache high behind her ribs.

Martin tenderly guided her head to rest against his neck and blinked back tears.

After a time of silence, Fia's muffled voice asked, "Martin? Are you displeased?" She felt him swallow hard.

"No, lass. Creating and bringing our bairn into the world–I can think of no greater joy."

"Then tell me what you're thinking." Fia pleaded, knowing something troubled him.

Martin spoke quietly. "To have found you again, become your husband, to have you return so completely the love I bear you, is more good fortune than I've had in the rest of my life."

"Are you trying to tell me that you fear the odds may be against us now? That our blessings might not last long enough for us to bear a child together?" she implored staring up at him with anxious eyes.

"I can't help but sense our happiness is tenuous," Martin reluctantly confessed, tightening his hold on her. "It was bad enough to have Forbes wishing you harm. Now there's Muir; I don't trust him. I want no one to hurt you ever again."

She whispered, "I know, and you'll never fully appreciate how it touches me knowing you'd do anything in your power to ensure it. You're accustomed to fending for yourself, Martin, and now you're burdened with worry for me."

"You're not a burden," he stated emphatically.

"I am if you fret so," Fia disagreed. "We're together now and can't let fear rob us of our happiness or the right to live as we wish. Remember, Martin, we're not alone in our fight against Andrew. Together with Simon, we'll prevail. And I'll keep my distance from Muir–give him no reason to harbor ill will against me."

"It may be too late for that."

"His displeasure will fade now that Kate's accepted his explanation and we're forced to. How can I convince you?"

"You can't," he responded.

She sighed raggedly. "Then what are we to do, my love?"

In the silence that hung heavily upon her question, Martin grappled with his anxiety. Not knowing if or when her enemies would strike sometimes threatened to cripple Martin. He now knew Struan's quick temper first hand. Andrew had beaten Fia once, and Martin had seen for himself what she had not–the ghoul's handiwork at the shore of Beauly Firth as well as on Rob's family. Martin prayed Fia was correct that Muir's wrath would settle. But Andrew Forbes? Struan? There would be no night Martin breathed easy until their fates were sealed.

Martin felt Fia shudder her misery. Guilt of a different kind invaded him. Somehow, he had to bridle his concern so that it didn't interfere with their joy as it was doing now. He wondered fleetingly if he shared any of Simon's skill as an actor, but decided not even to try deceiving Fia. Into the stillness Martin offered, "I'll try very hard to keep my concerns reasonable and not invent trouble where there is none. I don't think I can promise more than that, Fia."

She raised her face to his. "I can't ask more than that you try. Thank you, Martin." Fia pressed her cheek to his, then squirmed her way into a sitting position. "Now, how should we deal with your immediate problem?"

"What is that?" Martin questioned.

"You're very tense. Roll onto your belly."

"Come back under the covers," he commanded, "the heat of that fire will not keep you warm."

Leaning forward, Fia kissed the hollow of his throat and urged, "If you do as I ask, I won't be up here very long."

In the meager firelight, he could make out the shape of her before him and reached a hand to lightly stroke the curve of her breast. "Turning my face to the pillow when I might gaze at you is no choice, lass. I like it where I am; you're so splendid to look at."

Martin's touch shimmered heat through her and Fia speedily abandoned her original plan. Instead she drew one leg over him and positioned herself astride him. Placing her mouth against his ear, she confided, "I would have started trying to ease your strain at your neck and shoulders. But I think this approach may work better." Her mouth closed on his and her breasts rubbed against his chest and were, in turn, tickled by his fine reddish fur.

His fingers caressed her hips and slid to the slippery warmth between her thighs. Breathlessly, he reminded, "We do have an unfinished piece of business, lass."

"Which is?"

"Our bairn. If you aren't pregnant already, I'd say we're ready to try again. Would you agree?"

"Aye, as often as it takes and more," she assured and eased herself onto him. Her liquid gaze mirrored the desire in his own eyes and as they swayed together, they rolled until she was under him, legs locked around his waist.

When their pitch became fevered, their lips clenched and bodies tensed in a shuddering climax that left them spent and whimpering softly in each other's embrace.

Alayne wrapped her mantle around her and left the shop with Martin as escort. In the paltry warmth of the morning sun, she insisted, "I can see the solicitor alone."

"I realize that," he assured with a contented smile. "I'm just walking with you."

From the corner of her eye, Alayne studied him. He was quiet and serious as he often was, however, there was something different in Martin's demeanor today. "So, are you going to tell me what's happened?" She now watched him shrewdly. "I get the distinct impression that, inside, you are grinning from ear to ear."

"Am I?" he responded.

"You are and you know it well," Alayne replied. "Let me guess–something to do with Fia. It's just so obvious this morning that you are completely in love. It looks good on you, Martin."

He stopped to look at her, seeing sincerity in her expression. "Thank you, Alayne. It feels good, too," he confided. "We talked last night about having a bairn."

"Just talked?" she questioned teasingly.

Martin blushed furiously and Alayne swallowed a grin. She reached a tentative hand and touched the sleeve of his greatcoat. "I'm sorry, I shouldn't tease you."

"Well," he finally offered, "we talked also," and laughed with genuine mirth.

"You should laugh more often," she said, liking the transformation it brought in him and continued walking.

"I intend to," he promised, then abruptly ceased. "Fia and I didn't want you to have to visit the solicitor alone. Fortunately, Kate came in today so I could be with you."

"I understand; I'm grateful for your company. I don't mind telling you, this makes me nervous. If I didn't stand to gain so much, I doubt I could go through with it."

"You could. You're a strong-minded woman; that has served you well."

Alayne proclaimed, "What a nice compliment. Not many men appreciate a woman who stands for herself."

"Then they're fools and I feel blessed for I know several such extraordinary women, including my own sweet wife," he finished, halting. "This is it, William Francis, Solicitor. I'll wait here."

Alayne hung back a bit, suddenly cautious, as if the name on the sign would bite her. "No, please. At least wait inside for me, Martin."

Noting her disquiet, Martin agreed, "As you wish. Shall I knock?"

With a shake of her head, Alayne stretched out her arm and lifted the brass knocker. "I need to do this myself."

A distinguished looking fellow with black hair and heavy eyebrows to match answered, introducing himself as William Francis. "May I be of assistance?"

"I hope so, Sir, for I need your help. My name is Alayne Matheson."

Mr. Francis raised the massive brows in recognition. "Douglas Sutherland said you might pay me a visit. Come in, please." He eyed Martin somewhat dubiously. "I take it this is not your husband."

"Oh, no," Alayne rapidly assured, "he is the husband of my dearest friend. May I introduce Dr. Martin Ross?"

"I'm pleased to make your acquaintance, Dr. Ross."

"And I, yours, Sir. It sounds as though Douglas spoke to you of the nature of Mistress Matheson's business."

"He did, as he was leaving Inverness," Francis responded. "Mistress, will you follow me to my office?"

Alayne nodded. "Martin may wait here?"

"Of course, though you'll be more comfortable in the library, Doctor."

Martin nodded his thanks and the solicitor guided Alayne to his office.

Seated before William Francis' smallish ivory inlaid mahogany desk, Alayne poured out her story of her marriage to Muir, his disappearance, her search for him, his sudden reappearance two nights earlier, and his deceit about his return. "I had planned to divorce him on grounds of desertion, which I could have done within these two weeks," she acidly confided. "I assume that option is no longer open to me."

"I'm afraid not, even though his long absence did create an irregular marriage," the solicitor said, sympathy in his eyes. "May I ask, if your husband was cruel to you upon occasion as you have stated, why did you make the effort to search for him?"

Alayne straightened her shoulders. "When I married Muir, Mr. Francis, I fancied myself in love, though that was over by the time he disappeared. However, his mother grieved enormously and, frankly, I wanted to know whether I was free to move on with my life."

"And have you," he asked, "moved on with your life?"

Something in his tone forced her gaze to narrow slightly. "Why?"

He folded his hands before him. "How much do you know about divorce, Mistress?"

"I know very little, which is why I've come to you. I need to know how I can proceed now that Muir has returned."

"There are only two grounds for divorce existing in Scotland."

Alayne hesitated. "Only two?"

"I'm afraid so. The first you know well, the second may be difficult for you to prove. It's adultery."

"How...how can I prove adultery? I don't even know where he's been all this time. Before he disappeared, I knew there were other women. He looked and smelled of it. Still I've no proof."

"Even if you could prove it, there would be other considerations of property and land to settle. But, in the end, you would be as though widowed, free to wed again."

Agitated, Alayne stood and paced. "I support myself so that would not change; he doesn't provide protection—he hasn't been here. And, thank the Lord, there are no children." She stopped suddenly and faced the solemn man asking again, "Wait. Why did you ask me if I'd moved on with my life?"

He sighed and looked at his folded hands. "Because, Mistress, if there is a chance that your husband can prove that you—"

"I've not committed adultery!" Alayne declared forcefully.

"Part of me is happy to hear you say that because any settlement you brought to the marriage would be forfeited to your husband, as would property, if there were any."

"There's no property."

"And," he hesitated, "any man named by your husband as co-respondent in the divorce suit, you would be forbidden by law to marry."

Alayne's flushed skin drained of color as the solicitor's words rang in her head—forbidden by law to marry.

Mr. Francis rose, alarmed at her sudden paling. When she came from her daze, he was helping her back into the seat. "May I get you a brandy?"

She shook her head.

He gazed down on her shock with sympathy. "There is someone?" he prodded gently.

Alayne looked up at him with dry eyes and quivering mouth. "Someone...someone I love. There is no one with whom I've committed adultery. What part of you is not happy to hear that I have remained faithful?"

"The part of me that says, with no proof of adultery on your husband's part, you stand little chance of having the Commissary Court in Edinburgh grant you a divorce."

Panic began to steal her breath. "Isn't...isn't there somewhere else..."

"No, my dear. All divorce cases are heard by the Commissary Court. There are so few cases that no one has seen fit to require making concessions to ease the process. If you want to pursue it, we will have to travel to Edinburgh."

"Is there a basis on which to pursue my petition?" she asked with scant hope.

"I can try to appeal to them for leniency on the desertion grounds, or even that, as a man, the urges of nature make it an unnatural thing to expect he has been faithful to his marriage vows during so long an absence."

"Do you think there's any chance they will listen to such arguments?"

"I hope so, for I've nothing else to offer you, Mistress. If I may say so, men are known frequently to be vain about their prowess, we can pray these judges won't be the exception and that they'll believe in the probability that Mr. Matheson committed adultery."

Martin heard the door to Mr. Francis' office open and emerged from the library, abashed at the expression on Alayne's face. Over her head, the solicitor offered him only a grim look. Without glancing at him, Alayne stood for Martin to drape her mantle over her shoulders.

Mr. Francis opened the front door saying, "We should go soon, Mistress. Send word when you are ready to leave for Edinburgh."

Chapter Thirty-Two

Muir was astounded at the pompous arrogance of his charge. Nothing had gone smoothly since he'd called for Struan nearly three hours earlier. First, Struan kept him waiting while he break-fasted. Next, Struan argued with the stable hand over the manner in which his horse had been groomed. Now he was turning sullen and whiny, claiming that the moor they traversed did not look suitable for grouse. Muir knew it would be an extremely long day. "If I don't earn my share of the profits with this sacrifice," he thought, "there is no God."

"How much farther is it?" Forbes called out for the third time. "This nag's jogging makes my head and ass hurt."

"What's the difference?" Muir muttered under his breath.

"What was that?" Struan turned his head to hear his guide better.

Muir twisted in his saddle. "Not far. We'll stop just over that ridge," he announced, finger poking the air toward their destination, "then walk a bit so the horses won't scare the birds. Why grouse anyway?" Muir asked. "They aren't a popular game–too strong a flavor."

"It's an acquired taste," Struan sniffed. "Stuffed with a little butter and whortleberries to bring out the flavor, wrapped with fat bacon to keep it from drying out when you roast it, a bit of rowan jelly on the side, and you have a delectable meal. Take my word for it."

"I will," Muir replied, unconvinced.

A few minutes later Muir reined his horse, slid his nimble form from its back, knelt, and hobbled its forelegs in the treeless landscape. He followed suit with Struan's mount, which shook violently as soon as Struan had dismounted. "Aye, good riddance", Muir mused in silent empa-thy with the animal.

With spare powder and shot, and a length of rope with which to truss any birds Forbes might kill, Muir led Struan, carrying his own fowling piece, onto the moor by a path even less discern-able than the one they'd arrived on.

Struan experienced a brief bout of cold dread as he looked across the expanse of moor that stretched as far as he could see. The land all looked the same to him–uninviting and unforgiv-ing. He experienced a twinge of grudging appreciation for a guide who knew his way through the heath.

"Here," whispered Muir abruptly.

"'Here' looks no different than anywhere else," Struan grumbled, his appreciation forgotten. "Why here?"

Muir cut him a scathing look. "Because *here* is where your birds are. There's a slip of a burn at the bottom of that hillock. It's rockier and the heath is less dense."

Struan looked around suspicious of the landscape changes he could not detect with his own eye. He had the uncomfortable feeling that the only bird involved in this outing would be a wild goose. His displeasure and uneasiness roiled and he swung to face his guide and thundered, "I'm no man's fool, Math–"

Several plump grouse thrust themselves from hiding with a furious flapping of wings. They were not far from where the two men stood–twenty to thirty feet. Mouth agape, Struan stared after them.

Muir put a hand to his forehead and rubbed hard, not sure whether to laugh or be vexed. In-stead, he perched on a rock, the rounded top of which peaked from the heather.

Mortified, Struan muttered, "What...what are you doing?" his normally sallow face, flushed.

Hands clasped around one knee, Muir explained, "You hardly need me to help find the birds. You're quite adept at it."

Struan's countenance darkened and he blustered, "Get out there you insolent prick and find me more birds."

"If there are any birds left," Muir retorted, "find them yourself! You're too rash for me to want to step anywhere into your line of fire."

"Mr. Gray will hear of your conduct, don't think he won't," Struan threatened.

Slowly, Muir rose from his rock and approached to within inches of Struan who, he could see, was struggling to overcome the urge to step back. "You can tell Thomas whatever you'd like," Muir sneered. "I agreed to guide you, not grovel. I've done my job," he announced, dangling the shot and powder horn from his fingers. "I'm going home."

With that, Muir dropped his burden and began the walk back to his horse. He had almost reached it when Struan recovered from his stupor.

"Wait, Matheson. *Wait!*" he hollered, prompting another startled grouse to take wing, momentarily distracting him. But Struan recovered quickly and screeched, "You can't just leave me here."

"Can't I?" Muir tossed back, removing the hobble from his horse.

Disbelieving, Struan gawked at Muir who, with a shake of his pale head, determined Struan to be unworthy of more wasted time. He vaulted into the saddle, turned the horse back toward Inverness, and kicked it into motion.

The full force of his potential plight finally dawned and Struan swiftly grabbed the dropped horn and shot, and bolted for his own mount. Acutely, he was aware of Muir's rapidly retreating figure. Hastily, he stowed his gear, unhobbled his horse and, once in the saddle, pursued his guide at full gallop.

Up ahead, Muir's smooth brow was marred by a frown of concern that he'd been foolhardy. What if Gray was angry with him for not keeping Forbes happy and occupied? His wide mouth curled in an ugly pout. No matter how obnoxious Forbes was, Muir was certain Gray would expect him to endure it. A glance over his shoulder revealed Struan's horse closing the distance between them. Longingly, he turned his gaze back toward Inverness. Then, with a resigned sigh and a muttered, "Hell," Muir reined in and waited.

Struan's breathing was labored by the time he'd caught up. "What...what's the matter now?" he inquired warily.

"I've had a change of heart," Muir remarked. "The day's barely begun and I know other areas ripe with birds." He observed a flicker of interest touch the gaunt man's face. "If you'll be civil to me," continued Muir, "I'll take you."

To Struan's silence, Muir fidgeted, finally deciding truth would be the most convincing explanation he could offer. With a shrug of his broad, lean shoulders Muir said, "I could use the money. But, I'm not desperate and I don't appreciate being treated like your minion. Now, would you like to go after birds or not?"

Struan's close-set eyes had narrowed almost to the point of disappearing. After some moments, he nodded sharply. "Lead the way, Matheson."

With a return nod, Muir turned east once more.

"*There's no point* in putting it off," Alayne declared miserably. She'd spent a sleepless night weighing options she felt weren't options at all. "If the Commissary Court doesn't grant me a divorce, I might as well know sooner than later–waiting won't change their decision."

"I didn't realize how few options there were," Fia commiserated.

"You never had reason to want to know. I did, but I wasn't prepared," grumbled Alayne. "I felt sure there must be something besides desertion and adultery on which to base a divorce. I just thought I hadn't heard about it because almost no one gets divorced." She rested her elbows on the table, her head in her slender hands.

Fia's heart ached for Alayne's dilemma and she glanced helplessly at Martin who leaned against the edge of the workroom table at which the women sat.

His return gaze offered no encouragement.

"So when will you travel to Edinburgh?" Fia asked glumly, regretting her inability to offer an idea that would ensure Alayne's quest was a success.

Alayne swiped a hand under her nose as she raised red-rimmed eyes. "Five days from today if Mr. Francis is available then." Restless, the young woman rose and wandered the room. "Since Muir returned, I've gotten nothing accomplished here, and I faithfully promised Mr. Ingram that

I'd complete his wife's new gown this week." She dragged one hand across a bolt of brocade lying at the far end of the table and grimaced at its prickly stiffness.

"Could Fia finish it for you?" Martin inquired with hope of speeding the departure of Alayne's trip. But Alayne shook her head.

"Normally, she could," Alayne responded. "However, Mr. Ingram has a particular affinity for my needlework."

Fia added, "Of all the dressmakers Mistress Ingram has ever used, Alayne's is the only work both Ingrams agree on."

"Well," Martin sighed, "five days then. Shall I drop around to ask Mr. Francis if that's convenient?"

Alayne bestowed him a grateful look. "I'd appreciate it, Martin. Thank you."

He pushed away from the table. "I'll do it now, and leave the two of you to your sewing."

As Alayne stepped into the shop, Fia walked her husband to the door where he shrugged into his greatcoat. She handed him his bonnet and they stared at one another a long moment before sharing a bone-breaking embrace.

"You'll go with her?" Fia questioned softly as though it were a statement of fact.

"I don't want to leave you," he whispered vehemently. "Remember what we said about not spending nights apart?"

"Of course I remember," she assured. "There's no real choice though, Martin, is there? We can't send Simon though he would gladly go. There's no one else and I need to tend the shop."

Again, Martin sighed. "Very practical; my desire to stay has little to do with being practical."

She clung to him again and mumbled into the front of his coat, "I'm being 'practical', as you put it, because I think it's the only way I can bear your leaving me. Martin, if Alayne is not granted a divorce, she'll be in sore need of someone to be with her who'll see her safely home. Not just a solicitor she barely knows but someone who cares about her."

He rested his cheek against her hair savoring its lush softness. "Aye," he murmured, "I know. It just doesn't help me feel better about being separated from you."

Fia nodded her understanding. "Do...do you think you'll be gone long?" she asked.

"No but, God help me, it'll seem like it."

Her hands gently captured his face, mere inches from her own. Fia caught her breath marveling again at the excessive good fortune that had brought Martin into her life. This captivating man with his vital presence, warm and generous heart, was her husband–her life's companion. She smiled at him, mouth trembling. "I never think I can love you more than I already do, Martin," she declared, "and every day, you prove me wrong."

Martin wasn't taking any chances leaving Fia unprotected. After visiting the solicitor and obtaining his agreement to Alayne's proposed journey to Edinburgh, he headed straight for the theater hoping to locate and speak with Simon. He easily found the dressing room his cousin was using for lodgings. The strain of the few days since Muir's return was apparent in Simon's pallor and in his greeting. "What are you doing here?" he bluntly inquired upon opening the door to that room.

Martin's brows registered his surprise. "I need to speak with you; I need a favor."

"You want me to continue the watch on the quay," Simon concluded.

With a shake of his head Martin replied, "No. In fact, I'll be taking the next four nights."

Wary, Simon narrowed his gaze. "What's this about?"

Glancing around, Martin spied no one else in the smallish room. He brought his gaze to rest again on his cousin. "May I come in, Simon?"

As though suddenly waking, Simon's head snapped back and he quickly stepped aside. "Forgive me, Martin. I...I've quite forgotten my manners."

Once inside, Martin faced him. "It's all right; it's me. Is there anything I can do for you?"

"You can tell me how Alayne is."

Martin drew a deep breath knowing the answer to this question would cause Simon further dismay. Yet he had to answer. "Alayne is busy finishing a gown for a very particular customer."

"And?" Simon urged.

"She's striving to finish in the next few days because, on the fifth day, she leaves for Edinburgh to seek a divorce."

A hopeful flicker in Simon's eye died in response to Martin's cautious expression. "And?" he prompted again, this time reluctantly.

"The solicitor wasn't very encouraging. He's going to try everything he can but it sounds as though there's little hope."

"Why?" Simon demanded, palms spread as though Martin could lay his answer in them.

"Desertion can't be grounds for divorce because Muir came back."

"I thought as much. What aren't you telling me?" he entreated.

"God's life, Simon, this isn't easy," Martin protested, swiping his bonnet from his head in frustration. "The only other grounds for divorce is adultery," he blurted. "And Alayne can't prove Muir has been unfaithful." To Simon's stunned silence, Martin said, "It could be worse, Simon."

Simon stared at his cousin, his belly leaden with fear. "What do you mean?"

"If it were Alayne's fidelity that was challenged, even if the Commissary Court granted the divorce, Alayne would be forbidden to marry any man with whom she supposedly committed adultery." He stood silently while his cousin struggled with the possible implications.

Simon turned and trudged to his pallet where he collapsed, face covered by his hands. "Bloody Christ," he finally spat raising his eyes to Martin's. "What's left? What are we to hope for...no divorce? She stays married or she lies about her own fidelity and ruins her reputation," he determined, disgusted and frustrated. Simon emitted a strangled sound and surmised, "There *is* no hope, not for Alayne." "

"There will be no one to question Alayne's conduct but I had to tell you everything. I know you want to marry Alayne. The solicitor told her there is a slim possibility the case would go in her favor. *That* is the hope we have to cling to," Martin offered in a mostly vain attempt to bolster Simon's spirits.

Simon roused himself standing to ask, "Is the favor you need...has it to do with Alayne? Is that why you are telling me all this and not her?"

Grim, Martin nodded. "Truthfully, she doesn't know I'm here. Fia has asked, and I agreed, to travel to Edinburgh with Alayne."

Simon tensed. "I thought that's what you were about to say."

"You do see I'm the only reasonable choice," Martin stated and watched the muscles in Simon's cheek work into a knot over his clenched jaw.

"Aye." The word barely escaped Simon's lips. Abruptly, he plunged his fist down in a thundering crash that sent bottles and jars of face paint leaping and flying from the dressing table beside his pallet. "I hate this. Martin, there is nothing—nothing—I can give Alayne that's of help. I can't even go to Edinburgh with her, to be there to comfort and support her."

"With God's help there'll be many years for you to comfort Alayne," Martin replied quietly.

"But what about now?" he huffed and turned his back to Martin. "Should I tell her I'm loaning her my cousin's company for that's all I have to offer?"

"And what's wrong with that if circumstances have made it the truth?" Martin returned then added gravely, "You won't want to hear this, but it would be better if you don't see her now." To Simon's biting glare, Martin stated, "Oh, aye, you could talk to her, kiss her, touch her, soothe her a bit, help calm her anxiety. But that's dangerous. The best way you can help her now—the only safe way, Simon, is to stay away. Alayne's trying to be very matter-of-fact about it all. I know it's a mask yet her fright and sorrow at the possibilities facing her aren't hidden too deeply. Seeing you might unleash all she's holding on to."

Simon stared at the disarray his fist had created on the table top: jumbled piles of leaking, oozing and broken containers. What he saw was exactly what his insides felt like. He drew a shaky breath. "There's nothing I wouldn't do for Alayne," he told Martin.

"I know," Martin said. "More importantly, Alayne knows."

"I can't remember if I've ever felt so totally helpless."

"But not for long," Martin encouraged. "No matter how bleak things seem, remember, a lifetime with her is the reward if all goes well."

Simon rubbed his face hard with both hands, and guessed, "So, you'll care for my beloved whilst I look after yours in your absence. Is that the favor?"

"Aye. You know," Martin added, "I'll help Alayne in any way I can."

With a nod Simon said, "And Fia and I will be waiting anxiously for the two of you to return."

The Borrowed Days

Martin rested a hand on his cousin's shoulder and squeezed it lightly. "May I tell Alayne I spoke with you?"

"Aye, and...tell her...tell her...." Simon's voice caught and he gulped his foreboding.

"I will," Martin promised, perched his bonnet on his head and reached for the door latch. Simon stopped him. "What is it, Simon?" he asked gently.

"No matter what happens in Edinburgh, don't let Alayne ever doubt that it makes the slightest bit of difference in the love I bear her. We'll work through whatever fate is handed us."

Martin nodded. "I'll be sure to tell her."

Perhaps a little trip to Inverness would cheer his bride-to-be, thought Andrew. Elizabeth made all the appropriate noises of eagerness to wed, but the passion they had shared had not returned since her miscarriage. In fact, there had been no intimacy between them at all. Andrew ground his fist into his palm to get his mind off his rising desire. That certainly wasn't a consequence he'd foreseen of his use of the pennyroyal oil. Andrew impatiently tugged at the front of his breeches, intent on taming his need by force. He realized the gesture was futile and determined that, if Elizabeth was unresponsive today, he would find someone else with whom to relieve his immediate urge.

Elizabeth watched Andrew's approach from her bedroom window. Not that she'd been looking for him–far from it. She'd been remembering the return of her dream: the standing stones, the large round cairns, the mute grove of trees. And there again, haunting her, was Martin Ross. This time, kneeling by one of the cairns, Martin turned toward her, his eyes wide, mouth opened to speak. He reached out one hand a split second before the thunder cracked and the pain nearly blinded her.

Elizabeth shook her head to clear it. She wasn't a believer in omens yet she knew many people who were. Still, after having the almost identical dream this third time, Elizabeth found it more disturbing than curious. When Andrew rode into her line of sight, Elizabeth's dark musings were shattered and she scowled. Not long ago, when some innocence still existed in her world, Elizabeth knew her heart would have leapt in anticipation upon seeing him arrive. Her glower deepened and she rubbed her palms down her skirt as though wiping dirt from them. Andrew had robbed her of the only innocence she had still believed in–her child.

"Let him wait," she snapped, hearing Una admit Andrew into the house.

Nearly half an hour after Andrew's arrival, Elizabeth swept majestically into the drawing room. She recognized the impatience and displeasure in his eyes and dipped her own lashes in coquettish fashion to hide the loathing in her own until she could control her expression to suit her purpose.

"I wasn't prepared to receive you, Andrew," she offered as explanation for keeping him waiting. "I was not dressed."

His stride toward her was as rapid as his quickened breath. "You needn't have dressed for me, my dear," he whispered suggestively–a suggestion Elizabeth purposely misunderstood.

"I can't very well parade around in my shift, Andrew." Before he could respond, Elizabeth moved away saying, "I'm surprised to see you. To what do I owe this visit?"

Andrew swallowed his frustration and announced his business. "I've heard from Thomas Gray. There's trouble I need to deal with now."

"What kind of trouble?" she asked.

"Struan. It made me wonder if you might not enjoy a trip to Inverness. It hasn't the attraction of Edinburgh, I realize. Still, it might prove an interesting diversion for a few days." His eyes narrowed as he contemplated the chances that there would be anything interesting about traveling to Inverness with Elizabeth in her current mood.

"Inverness?" she asked. "How would you suggest I spend my time while you and Mr. Gray are deciding Struan's fate?"

"There are things worthy of your attention, surely," Andrew stated, searching his memory for some recollection of the town that did not include taverns or brothels. "Ah," he said, finally. "There is a theater, and several lovely tea shops."

Elizabeth flicked imaginary dust from the mantle, avoiding Andrew's face. "You'll be on the quay with Mr. Gray. Who do you expect will accompany me to the tea shops and theater?"

She was making this damnably difficult. "I will escort you when I can, of course. And when

322

I cannot, I promise I will find someone eminently suitable to take my place." Andrew drew near, stopping only when his chest pressed her shoulder blades. He inclined his head to whisper against her ear, "We can be absent from your father's prying eyes." Andrew's fingers lightly traced a path up her arm. "We can plan our wedding and our future," he continued, lightly stroking the full-curved side of her breast as his hand reached her upper arm. "And...we can mourn our loss together, privately as befits parents robbed of their joy. We can begin to heal each other," he finished, palm closing round that same breast.

For a long moment while she forced herself to endure his touch, Elizabeth considered Andrew's proposition. It was only short weeks ago, she had sought eagerly his bold use of her body–had reveled in it. A trip to Inverness? Perhaps this was the opportunity she needed. If she were with him day and night–could stand to be with him–some reasonable way to exact revenge was bound to present itself.

Her mind made up, Elizabeth forced her pale lips into a smile and turned to face her betrothed. "It sounds exactly like what I need. When do we leave?"

The millinery was black as pitch save for a lone rush lamp and the pallid orange glow from the hearth. The wind had risen to a near constant whine and Simon's hair whipped about his face, partially obscuring his vision. He quickly glanced toward the street, thinking he'd caught a glimpse of something or someone in the writhing shadows of buffeted tree limbs and branches. He saw nothing there.

He rapped loudly on the door, fearing both that he'd lose his resolve and that the announcement of his arrival would be swallowed by the soughing wind if he did otherwise. Before he could lift his hand again, the workroom door opened. Alayne stood, mouth agape in surprise. She stepped aside for him to enter, the flame of the lamp guttering wildly for those short seconds before the door closed behind him.

"Martin told me–"

"That you wouldn't be seeing me before you left for Edinburgh," Simon offered. "That was what we agreed to, aye. Alayne," he apologized, "forgive me. I had to see you, tell you myself that, given the right, I would be nowhere but at your side through all of this."

She stepped close to him and her voice wavered slightly, "I know Martin told you what the solicitor said."

Simon choked, "He did. I'm grateful Martin will be with you...as I cannot."

"You are always with me," Alayne promised.

Simon's heart pounded with Alayne's nearness and his hand twitched at his side as he fought the urge to crush her against him. He took a step backward. "I should go. It was a risk to come here at all," he gulped miserably. "I'm afraid to touch you; I want you so very much."

"What a quandary," Alayne lamented. "All my care about appearances for the sake of propriety–"

"For your independence," Simon vehemently corrected. "There is no better reason, lass. Perhaps it's that alone that should sustain us now."

Tempting fate, Alayne set her lips lightly to his. She told herself it was a kiss of promise for their future but, when she stepped into it, she was instantly and acutely aware of him with every sense she possessed. The contour of his body, the muscles, toned and hard under his clothing, and his passion swelling against her belly watered her knees and ignited fire throughout her.

Their mutual cries of need and despair extinguished in the hunger of their kiss and it was the crash of a shutter blown loose by the whipping wind that caused them to leap apart, shaken and quaking.

They stared at each other, panting, trying to regain some semblance of control. Finally, Simon muttered, "We can't."

Alayne's teeth tugged her lower lip. "Would anyone ever know if we came together this night?"

"We would."

The bang of the shutter again staggered the pair and Alayne's reserve failed. "Simon, I'm near dying for want of you," she swore. "I love you. I belong with you...to you."

"And I love you, ache for you. But what I want more than anything is you–for the rest of my life. Alayne, we can't risk that–we just can't."

Alayne collapsed to the floor in a heap, a sob ripped from her throat. She knew he was right, also that she could rely on him to hold them both in check. Further, and with shame, Alayne admitted it was unfair of her to take none of the responsibility. Simon was an honorable man, and he loved her. He'd let no harm come to her even if she would cause it herself. "I'm so sorry," she atoned for the burden he bore for them both.

Simon knelt beside her, stroking her hair and murmuring comforting noises he hoped would help. Simon knew that she not only understood, but agreed with him. He sat down and drew her head onto his shoulder where she wept quietly.

"Only a few more days, my love," he encouraged, "then no one can ever say that we don't belong together. Hold to that thought, Alayne; hold tight to it, as I will."

"We talked only a little," Muir reported to Thomas Gray, over a late whiskey at the tavern. "Didn't want to scare the birds, you know," he continued. "Not that it would've made much difference. I doubt his conversation would have been very stimulating."

Gray smirked. "Found our Mr. Forbes to be a charming fellow, aye?"

Muir's laugh rumbled in his chest but never escaped his lips. "I earned a part of the profit I think," he ventured, waiting to see what reaction it evoked.

Between his rough, stubby fingers, Gray turned his glass. "Let's say," he began, "you've made a good start. Gordon may have other tasks for you to carry out."

"But the man was an insufferable bore, downright insolent," Muir argued.

Thomas cast him a withering look. "Surely, lad, you don't think enduring a few hours of that clod worthy of a sizable share off the next run? I'd be laughed off the quay if anyone got wind I'd rewarded you just for that."

The flush of embarrassment stained Muir's face which he promptly focused on his drink. "Of course not." He bit through the words trying to take the sting out of his rebuke and changed the subject. "I have to be gone a couple of days."

Thomas cocked a brow in surprise.

"No choice," Muir continued, "a personal matter has come up. Will there be work and time enough for me to finish earning a good share?"

"Oh, aye," his grizzled companion affirmed, slouching back in his chair. "Aye, you're not to worry. I'm sure Gordon will have need of your services."

His lips pressed tight, Muir felt unexpectedly discomfited by that promise. He'd not met Gordon, but the man's reputation was enough to put anyone's teeth on edge. Still, Thomas seemed fit enough. He was surviving unscathed the unenviable position of having to teach Struan the business as well as keep him out of trouble. All that being true, Muir did not look forward to coming face to face with Gordon.

"Fine," was all Muir finally uttered and, to his dismay, it squeaked out, making him sound like a frightened mouse.

A deep-throated chuckle reverberated from Gray. "There now, lad, don't fret. You be straight with Gordon, he'll treat you right. If you cross him," the man lifted his brows and shoulders in a sympathetic shrug and finished, "I wouldn't want to be you."

Anxiously, Fia waited in Kate's drawing room for Martin's return from the quay. She was grateful through all this that Muir seemed to have found another place to spend his time and she was spared dealing with him. Every night since it was decided he would take Alayne to Edinburgh, Martin had wandered the quay taverns to no avail, at least not where news of either Forbes brother was concerned. On the second night, however, he'd returned with the news that the King had died. If they'd lived closer to London, they'd possibly have felt the death of George II more acutely. As it was, it was the late King's brother, the Duke of Cumberland, who'd left his horrible stamp forever on the Scots when he'd led the Crown's troops at Culloden. Now, the King's grandson would be George III and time would tell what kind of ruler he would be.

This was Martin's last night of watching; tomorrow, he'd be gone. Alayne had finished the dress for Mistress Ingram, seen both Ingrams happily off after the gown had been modeled and declared a stunning success by the couple. So tomorrow, Fia would part with Martin, breaking the oath she'd hoped would never be challenged. Whenever he came into the room, her heart caught in her throat; she was ever surprised and scarcely able to believe he was really there. The closeness they'd developed at his croft continued to blossom and deepen, and they shared an intimacy so complete the thought of it left her incredulous and breathless. The loneliness she'd endured since the death of her parents, the lack of warmth and caring–of love–Martin remedied a thousand fold. And her own capacity to love and to give to Martin not only thrived but increased daily. What Fia couldn't fathom was how she would get through the coming days without him. It hadn't been long since he'd come back into her life, but somehow Fia was sure she'd forgotten how to be alone. Already she missed him.

Upon hearing the door open, Fia leaped from the chair and greeted her husband's return with a crushing embrace that easily betrayed her dread of their coming separation. Yet she presented a smile to accompany her adoring gaze.

Martin's heart squeezed painfully at her pretense. He hung up his greatcoat while Fia bent to ruffle Arthur's fur and have her hand nuzzled insistently in return greeting.

"Did you hear or see anything tonight?" she asked.

Martin ran cold fingers through his burnished curls. "The taverns were quiet, just like last night and the two before."

Fia straightened and inquired further, "Are you hungry?"

"Not for food," he declared, brushing his lips against hers. "I want to take you upstairs, undress you, brush your hair, and hold you in my arms all night."

"I like your plan very much," Fia murmured appreciatively, her body beginning to hum with desire and anticipation of his bare skin, warm and stirring against her own. They mounted the stairs and Martin called over his shoulder, "Come, Arthur."

At the invitation, the large hound bounded the stairs past them and waited impatiently by the bedroom door until they arrived.

"You don't know, lad, how fortunate you are that your Aunt Kate allows you to stay in the house," Martin commented, opening the door and watching Arthur prance into the room, tail swinging a broad arc, to settle near the hearth.

Fia rejoined, "And you don't know, my love, how fortunate you are that Aunt Kate doesn't know you refer to Arthur as her nephew."

"It's an honorary title," Martin huffed good-naturedly.

"Arthur is an exquisite fellow," Fia stated before adding skeptically, "I'm just not convinced Aunt Kate would think it much of an honor."

At that moment Arthur flopped to his side, stretched his full length and sighed mightily his contentment, causing Martin and Fia to laugh.

Turning to her husband, Fia whispered, "Speaking of exquisite fellows..." Her eyes smoldered darkly and she eagerly pulled his shirt from his breeches, enough to slide her fingers beneath and onto the sculptured planes of his chest, its hardness softened only slightly by the light covering of hair. Her hands explored and caressed before pulling his shirt up and over his head. When Martin's sleek torso was free of its sheath, Fia kissed the hollow of his throat, traced her way across each breast, paused at the silver scar below his ribs. Then she was unbuttoning his breeches.

"I thought I was going to un...undress you," he sputtered with difficulty.

"You can," she replied, easing his breeches from his hips, "when it's your turn." Fia's fingers stroked his thighs and his lower back where his waist curved into his buttocks. "I love this curve; it's very sensual, very enticing." She pressed her willing body against his.

"I say it's my turn now, Fia," he murmured. Gently he pulled from her, kicked off his boots, hose and then the breeches from where they lay round his ankles. Martin gathered her into his arms, kissing her thoroughly. He deftly unlaced her waistcoat, unhooked her petticoats, untied her panniers and lifted her shift over her head.

He laid her on the bed where she sank deeply into the feather tick. As his kisses coursed their way down her body, he heard her catch her breath. Her body began to move in response. She bent her knees and opened her thighs wider as his searching mouth found and settled in the moistness between. He roused her passion until her pleas became nearly frantic. She needed to feel his weight on her body and him inside her.

Blissfully, Martin obliged, plunging deep and with such force they both gasped; Fia shivered in ecstasy. She clutched his narrow hips trying to force him even deeper, driven by the need to pull his whole being inside her so they could never be parted.

Martin shared her sense of urgency with a depth of desperation he could never have guessed possible. It was not just her silken skin and lithe body that made him mad with desire, but also her sweetness and the courage she possessed in every fiber of her being. He was touched by Fia's generous nature, her innocence and passion. Everything he could have wanted thrived in this one beautiful, alluring woman–his wife. "I never imagined a woman such as you," he whispered and succumbed with her to the convulsing waves of release that gripped and held him inside her.

They strained together, capturing the last of that euphoric haze and lay locked in each other's arms waiting for nature to part them.

After long minutes during which Fia's heartbeat slowed to normal, she stroked his smooth back from shoulder to hip and offered, "I'm grateful you want me and love me."

Martin stared at her, incredulous. "I wanted and loved you before we were parted. And I was heartsick and bitter those months when I thought you'd chosen another. I never stopped longing for, loving you or wanting you."

"There was never another." She assured and pressed his hand to her breast. "I didn't choose to love you, Martin, I was born to it, whether or not you returned the feeling–plain and simple. I'm eternally thankful that you do."

"What I feel for you my love, is nothing that I've ever experienced before. And because you love me, I now have a healed soul and heart that live for you, Fia."

They shared a lingering kiss and contented sigh. Fia rested her head on his chest, hearing and reassured by the strong beat of his heart.

"I still want to brush your hair." Martin stroked her tangled curls lovingly, and raised a lock of it to his lips. "It gives me such pleasure."

"And me," she responded. "But the brush is on the vanity. Are you sure you want to get up to fetch it?"

"Aye. Just keep my place warm." Martin pushed himself from the bed.

"And which of your 'places' exactly, do you wish me to keep warm?" she teased.

His grin lit the shadows. "All of them!"

Too soon, the sun's appearance heralded the morning and Martin's departure. He and Fia said goodbye with a tender kiss, standing in the entryway while Kate kept a discreet distance. As she watched the couple murmur together, foreheads touching and faces held in hands, she nearly cried for them. It wouldn't be long though–no more than two weeks depending on when the Court met. Kate wanted to cry for her son and daughter-in-law as well. If only things had been different–but they weren't.

"Goodbye, Mistress," Martin was saying. "Please watch over Fia. I've asked Simon to help, I hope that doesn't bother you."

Kate shook her head. "No. Your cousin is welcome here. And Fia will be in good hands. Safe journey, and you take good care of my daughter-in-law."

"That I will." Martin gazed at his wife again, turned her palm up and pressed his lips to it. "I love you. I'll be with you again as soon as it's humanly possible."

Fia barely nodded, trusting herself only to say, "I'll be waiting, my love."

With a fleeting smile, Martin swung onto Odhar's back, Barley's reins gripped in one hand. Fia was lending her horse to Alayne for the trip to Edinburgh; he was in better shape than the horse Alayne usually borrowed from Kate, and Fia wanted to do what she could to speed the journey's outcome.

Martin bade Arthur stay with Fia then headed toward the millinery to fetch Alayne. Only once did Martin glanced back as they turned the corner and went out of sight of the Douglas Row house.

It had done nothing but alternate rain and sleet since he'd left Edinburgh yesterday morning. Now, as dusk set in, Muir noticed the steel gray sky becoming more leaden by the minute. His mount stumbled over a deep rut in the road and, jarred, Muir cursed under his breath as the horse regained its footing. He hated horses. But, the sudden pricking of the steed's ears and tossing of its head captured Muir's attention. He reined in and sat listening to the sound of the drizzle. He heard nothing, though he noticed the horse still attentive to something up ahead. There...he thought he heard voices.

Muir quickly urged his beast off the road and down the side of a hillock far enough to provide cover, but near enough for him to observe whoever was passing by. Dismounting, Muir swiftly wrapped his neck handkerchief through the metal fittings of his horse's bridle to keep them from jingling and drawing attention. Then he waited, but not for long.

The party was soon near enough not only to be seen, but also to be recognized. Muir almost laughed at the sight of his dear, drenched wife and her companions: that devil Ross, bedraggled and soggy now, and a black-haired gent Muir could only guess was the solicitor. On their way to Edinburgh no doubt, Muir thought, to obtain a divorce. Grinning a demented grin, Muir allowed himself an almost audible chuckle. "Won't they be surprised?" he murmured in the palest of whispers.

The approach to Inverness up the great glen was tedious, the landscape stark in its autumn undress. Day had broken an odd umber glow and the sky still held a tinge of brown that Elizabeth found unsettling. First, the Loch, and now the River Ness resembled tarnished silver, dingy and uninviting.

Elizabeth pulled her hood closer against her face, the fox edging warming her cold-reddened cheeks. This day should be the last of their journey north. Each night, she had insisted on her own room and Andrew had grudgingly obliged.

A sidelong glance brought her former lover's profile into view. Where once she'd found his square jaw and strong, almost blunt features and roguish ways appealing, Elizabeth found herself increasingly repelled. His features she now noted were cold and cruel, his nature cloying and demonic. How could she not have noticed before?

Wryly, Elizabeth also discerned Andrew seemed quite at ease this morning. She was certain that he'd spilt his seed in some trollop the previous night. Too well Elizabeth recognized his complacent, satiated look–she'd seen it often. "Well," she thought, "fine with me." Elizabeth never again intended to lie with the monster.

Suddenly, the hair prickled the back of Andrew's neck and he turned, catching Elizabeth's venomous glower. An unexpected chill surged through him as he wondered what made her cast him such a look. He had no answer. He'd been very clever about his dalliance the night before and felt certain of Elizabeth's ignorance of that encounter.

Warily, Andrew moved his horse closer to hers. "Are you well Elizabeth? Cold? Is the pace too much?"

"Warm enough and well enough, thank you," she responded. "Will we be in Inverness soon? I'm tired of riding in this saddle."

"That's not all you're tired of these days," he ventured. "You haven't been as...attentive... lately."

"I'm not tired of riding *you*, Andrew. Since I lost my son, I honestly haven't wanted or felt the need."

"Our son," he dutifully corrected.

She ignored him. "I'm sure it's difficult on a man of your passionate nature. I just ask that you be patient, Andrew."

For a long moment, he studied her, muscle twitching the length of his cheek. The silvery scar resembled a dancing worm, Elizabeth thought, and bit her lip to keep from laughing at the comparison she'd drawn.

Andrew covered her gloved hand where it held the reins of her mount. "Of course I'll be patient, my dear. I wish you had told me sooner what troubled you. I've been quite perplexed."

"Perhaps I should have," she acknowledged, "Only it's a difficult thing for me to talk about. I ask your understanding."

His voice took on a sudden huskiness. "Just know that, when you're ready, I can help you forget the tragedy befallen you and remind you what it's like to really live."

"Us," she said, staring at him. To his obvious bewilderment, Elizabeth elaborated, "The tragedy befallen *us*."

"O...of course," he muttered, coloring violently.

"And as for your offer," she strained through taut lips, "I'll remember."

"So this is your lady," Thomas Gray dipped a bow toward Elizabeth, who stood in the small parlor, surprised that it existed in this excuse for an inn. It didn't look the kind of place any gentlewoman would visit. But this visit was, apparently, necessary. They had to know what Struan was doing that had caused Gray to summon–she glanced at Andrew. So he went by the name "Gordon."

"Aye, Thomas," Andrew replied. "Miss Elizabeth Graham. My betrothed," he added.

The ruddy fellow cast a rather speculative eye on the dark-haired young woman. He knew that Andrew had a partner named Graham, related to the chit who was supposed to have married Struan and gifted them all with her beach. After having met Struan, Gray thought the Graham in question to be an astute judge of character for having run off. Besides, the lack of a wedding hadn't hampered operations.

Elizabeth scowled. "You're being rude, staring at me like that."

Thomas snapped to attention. "Begging your pardon, Miss, I was only wondering if you were related to the Gra–"

"Distant cousin," Andrew broke in and turned to Elizabeth. "Please sit, my dear. Let me order you some Atholl Brose and you can rest from the journey. This shouldn't take long."

Elizabeth did as he requested and when the warm liquor eased her parched throat, she began to revive and take an interest in the discussion going on over her head as the men continued to stand.

"Your brother's dangerous," Gray was saying. "He says what he wants, when he wants, no matter who's in earshot. The profit is all that interests him."

"We're all interested in profit, Thomas," Andrew prompted. "What else?"

"In the tap room, he said he was only here because his brother, Gordon, had to stay out of sight after his folly up north." Gray saw Andrew stiffen. "People know Gordon. They don't know Andrew Forbes. Linking Gordon to himself–stating they're brothers–that's risking us all and you know it."

Andrew scratched the blue-black stubble on his chin, knowing Gray was right. "It was very careless of him," Andrew conceded. "What's he been doing since you sent the message to me?"

"Drinking, grousing, whori–" Gray stopped short with a glance at Elizabeth. "Pardon, Miss."

"Whoring," Elizabeth repeated. "I've heard the word Mr. Gray, no need to apologize."

Gray shrugged. "I've a man who's been in my employ these last five years, four spent in the Indies. He's desperate to earn a share of the next run. He took Struan hunting–wasn't happy about it, but willing to do about anything, I'd wager, to make some good money fast. Anything," he emphasized.

Andrew's brows drew down. "And where is this man?"

"He's in town. We can fetch him anytime."

"Where's Struan?"

"At the moment, I don't know. But I've discovered that, if I don't bring up the subject of business, he's content to dawdle about and never mention it himself."

Elizabeth sighed. "I'm tired, Andrew. Can't we deal with Struan tomorrow?"

"The problem, my love, is that I'm not sure when or how I want to deal with my brother. Still, it is late and it's been a very long day." He turned to Gray. "Where is Struan staying?"

"Here."

"Then we'll stay elsewhere; I don't want him to know we're here until I'm ready. Would you recommend someplace suitable for Miss Graham should our business require me to leave her alone for a bit?"

"The White Rose," Gray answered. "It's about the best there is. I think it'll meet with your approval."

Elizabeth studied Thomas for a moment. His physical appearance was like many others' who spent their lives at sea: his complexion reddened by long exposure to sun and wind, his slate gray curls askew and seldom introduced to a comb. He was stocky, solid–not fat–and his age, indeterminate. Nothing special, yet Elizabeth found herself impressed by his keen awareness of the sensitivity of dealing with Andrew–about his brother and his woman. She thought she would like Thomas Gray. Finally, she nodded her approval and, standing, extended her hand.

Thomas glanced at Andrew, whose thoughts were already racing elsewhere.

Gray's deference to Andrew–no doubt a healthy respect for a man capable of murder–did not escape Elizabeth's notice.

Gray took Elizabeth's hand and bowed over it as he heard her say, "Thank you for your consideration."

"My pleasure," he responded, avoiding her jet-black eyes. "I'll escort the two of you to the inn and, tomorrow, Andrew, you and I must make a plan."

Once again, Gray had Andrew's attention. "Indeed we must."

Chapter Thirty-Three

"*Miss Graham*," *Thomas* Gray spoke, bowing slightly, "may I present Muir Matheson, a colleague of mine."

"And so of my fiancé as well," Elizabeth surmised, eyeing the tall, blond man. His face was arresting in its boyish good looks and that boyishness betrayed by a wide, sensual mouth. Liking what she saw, Elizabeth extended her hand and dipped a curtsey as he accepted it. "Mr. Matheson."

Muir bowed slightly over her hand, staring into her dark eyes. "It is my great pleasure, Miss Graham," he intoned smoothly and boldly placed his lips to her fingers where they lingered a moment longer than good manners allowed.

A faint pink stain crept above her neckline and grew deeper at his bold perusal. Elizabeth was at once flattered and annoyed. Her voice hardened to ask, "Have you met my fiancé?"

Muir shot a look at Thomas who shook his head. As he straightened, Muir replied, "It seems not, Miss. May I ask who is the fortunate gentleman?"

Elizabeth watched guardedly Muir's reaction as she offered the name by which his comrades referred to him. "I believe you would know him as 'Gordon'." Muir's gaze flicked nervously to Thomas who nodded this time, then back to Elizabeth's satisfied smirk.

"Indeed," Muir responded, "I've not had that pleasure."

"Soon you will," Thomas reinserted himself into the conversation. "He's due here momentarily. I invited you, Muir, because Gordon has a special request to make of you."

Muir looked somewhat mystified which caused Elizabeth to chuckle. "Please sit, Mr. Matheson. We should become better acquainted for my fiancé's entreaty involves me."

Unable to think what Gordon's plea might be, Muir simply sat opposite Elizabeth. He found he could not speak. Her heart-shaped face, hair the color of jet, and flawless skin held him spellbound.

Elizabeth recognized the look of the conquered, but pretended not to notice the effect on him when she deliberately adjusted the gauze neck handkerchief that barely concealed the generous curve of her breasts. And to leave no room for doubt of her triumph, she leaned forward slightly on pretext of straightening her petticoat exposing more of what the handkerchief struggled to cover. When she raised herself again, she was gratified to see her companion shift slightly in his chair, lick his lips, and jerk his gaze toward Thomas, who stood by the door awaiting Gordon's arrival.

Elizabeth cleared her throat, drawing Muir's attention once more as footfalls were heard on the stairs. "We'll talk later, Mr. Matheson. There's a great deal we have to learn about one another."

With scarcely enough breath to answer, Muir replied, "I look forward to it."

"Ah, there you are, Gordon," Thomas welcomed, stepping aside for Andrew to enter.

Muir nearly leapt from his chair at the entrance of the formidable man. Immediately, he sensed the possible danger that his attention to Elizabeth represented and resolved to keep his wits about him—no matter the request Gordon was about to make.

Andrew's eyes swept the small parlor at the "White Rose" where he and Elizabeth had taken rooms. Elizabeth's back was to him and a lean, yellow-haired man stood near her chair.

"You are Muir Matheson?" Andrew asked in his friendliest hiss.

"Aye, Sir, ready to be of service to you in any way I can." Muir was pleased that his voice hadn't failed him.

"Please Mr. Matheson," Andrew said smoothly, indicating the chair Muir had just vacated, "sit. I would speak with you."

"Certainly," Muir replied, and tried with minimal success to ignore Elizabeth's eyes on him as he reseated himself and attempted to look comfortable on the wooden chair. He tried to focus on the infamous Gordon: not overly tall, but burly, with a voice that grated and a dark look that menaced–even when it was meant to be friendly as Muir assumed was the case now. Fleetingly, he wondered how Gordon had earned the scar on his face.

Thomas stood to one side as Andrew placed himself on the settee beside Elizabeth.

"Thomas tells me you are a man to be trusted," Andrew said, losing no time.

"I am that," Muir confirmed.

"You took my brother grousing I hear."

"I did, Sir."

"And?" Andrew prompted.

Muir felt honesty would serve him best and offered, "We got off to a bad start. Your brother was not willing to place his confidence in me so I threatened to leave him out on the moor. But we overcame that; your brother wanted birds and I needed the money."

"And have you been keeping an eye on Struan since then?"

"No, Sir. I had business in Edinburgh and only just returned."

"What kind of business?" Andrew asked.

"It was personal business,"Muir replied.

Andrew pursued, "What kind of personal business?"

Elizabeth watched Muir's eyes steel as he replied, "*My* personal business." His bravado intrigued her.

After a long moment where Andrew and Muir stared at each other and Thomas rolled his eyes at Muir's less-than-cooperative response, Andrew snickered, "Well said."

Slowly, Muir let out the breath he'd been holding. He had no idea how much, or when he should push his luck with Gordon. It made him extremely nervous. However, his personal life was none of the man's concern as long as Muir successfully carried out the tasks Gordon and Thomas gave him.

Andrew stretched his legs and crossed them at the ankles. "Do you still need money?" he bluntly asked.

"Aye."

Through narrowed eyes Andrew pressed, "For what? A man in need of money can change his loyalties quickly enough."

"I want to buy into the next shipment. I've worked for Thomas for nearly five years; I like this work, but I want to return to the Indies. Better climate."

"And no wife and mother nagging," Thomas chuckled, eliciting a stony glower from Muir.

"I no longer have to concern myself with the wife," he sneered.

Gray's brows rose as did Elizabeth's, each wondering the significance of Muir's statement.

Apparently satisfied, Andrew reined the conversation back to meet his own need. "There are two things I would like you to do and one thing I don't want you to do." Andrew draped his arm along the back of the settee and began to casually finger Elizabeth's neck handkerchief. Muir thought he detected a slight stiffening in Elizabeth's posture.

Andrew, oblivious, continued, "First, I'd like you to keep my brother occupied during the next few days, hunting, most likely, but I leave that to you."

"Easily," Muir confirmed his ability to carry out the first request, though the thought of so much time spent with Struan Forbes was distasteful. His eyes widened as he watched Andrew run his forefinger across his fiancé's milky skin, along the neckline of her gown. Except that Andrew's eyes betrayed his interest, Muir would have thought his gesture absent-minded, born of long practice.

"Second, each day, from tea until she wishes to retire for the evening, I ask you to put yourself at the disposal of my betrothed. Since business dictates that I can't spend my evenings with her, I would like Miss Graham to have a companion I can trust."

On hearing Andrew's second request, Muir abruptly raised his eyes to Elizabeth's. Unsure what reaction he expected to see, Muir was surprised to find a fixed smile on her pale lips–and malice in her eyes. Muir could not respond except to nod.

"Excellent," Andrew purred. "Now the thing you will *not* do. Under no circumstance is Struan to know Miss Graham and I are in Inverness–not until I say so. Do you understand?"

"Perfectly," Muir replied, beginning to feel a gnawing of sudden dread mixed with annoyance at the man's continued pawing of his fiancé; putting his stamp on her so there would be no mistaking to whom she belonged. Inexplicably, he felt the room closing in and abruptly he stood saying, "I'll do as you bid until I receive new orders."

Turning to Elizabeth, Muir bowed. "Miss Graham, I'll call for you just at four o'clock." He then left the room with all the dignity he could muster. Gordon was powerful and rich and had an enticing, beautiful, sophisticated woman at his side–all things Muir craved for himself. When *he* became wealthy and all-powerful–and he promised himself he would–he'd like it just fine if his own woman was as intriguing and provocative as Elizabeth Graham.

"So, Miss Graham," Muir asked as tea, including a plate of scones and almond cake, was set before them, "how would you like to spend your evening? It is already too dark to show you the sights of Inverness, such as they are."

"Perhaps not too late though," Elizabeth demurred. "We may chance upon something that will give me ideas for the nights to come."

"Then by all means I will be happy to show you the town," Muir conceded. He waited to follow the woman's example with the tea since he could scarcely remember the last time he'd partaken in the ritual. Moreover, Elizabeth's presence made him anxious. He congratulated himself that, so far, he seemed to have concealed the fact. Still, it was important to him not to appear coarse before her.

During his musings, Elizabeth poured the tea and passed the plate to him from which he lifted a slice of the cake. When it lay safely on his plate, Muir rested one arm on that of his chair in a casual pose masking his nervousness rather well, he thought.

Elizabeth was not totally unaware of his discomfort. They shared a table in a small room with the flimsy door closed as a precaution against the possibility of Struan accidentally stumbling into the "White Rose". No one believed he would purposely patronize an establishment so far above his normal haunts, but it was important that they not be discovered. In the interim, Elizabeth found herself in a cozy, secluded space with a fine looking young man who she fancied was enamored of her–and she wasn't even trying very hard! Oh, this did have delicious potential.

"Why are you staring at me Miss Graham?" Muir asked, clearing his throat.

With a blink, Elizabeth smiled. "Was I? I didn't intend to be rude Mr. Matheson. I was just thinking...." Her lashes swept downward as she prolonged the moment.

"Thinking what?" Muir prompted, as she expected him to.

She raised confident, challenging eyes to his. "That I like sharing this snug little spot with you. That you're perhaps a wee bit uncomfortable because we don't know each other well–"

"And you're Gordon's betrothed," he blurted.

Elizabeth shrugged. "That wouldn't bother you if you didn't feel some measure of attraction to me would it?"

Muir's face hardened, but his voice was like sweet cream, "You're testing me."

"Why would I do that?"

"So you can report to Gordon whether I'm worthy of trust...of being alone with you."

She studied every feature of him that she could see from her chair: broad cheekbones; azure eyes and sun-colored hair; smooth, almost beardless skin; the wide, sculpted mouth; squared shoulders. He withstood her perusal, flushing only slightly. Elizabeth's gaze returned to his mouth and she shifted slightly feeling a moistness between her thighs that had long been absent. For an instant, she imagined the magic those lips might work in that damp. "You are mistaken," she assured, somewhat short of breath. "My fiancé trusts Thomas Gray's opinion...and Mr. Gray has vouched for you."

Muir challenged, "Then why do you tease me?"

"Because I like you and believe we shall enjoy each other's company," Elizabeth decreed, reaching for the sugar. "I wish you wouldn't be uncomfortable. I'll tell you something about myself. I'm a woman who knows her mind. I know what I want and am not afraid to go after it. Don't let that bother you though; it's one quality of mine that you just might grow to appreciate."

Muir was silent, feeling the heat of her gaze on him and not knowing himself where it was safe to look. Already he appreciated the potential only slightly hidden in her words and her bold perusal of his own attributes. He felt the stirring of longing and chanced a look at her heart-shaped face, catching his breath upon seeing her intent stare and slightly parted lips.

"Are you afraid of me?" she asked with a touch of gloating in her tone.

"Only of the possibility of getting lost in you," he said, quite forgetting about Gordon.

Elizabeth chuckled quietly. "Entertain me well while I'm here, Mr. Matheson, and who knows, you may get that opportunity."

Muir forced his fluster to calm. Was she serious or playing him for a fool? Well, no matter. An innocent flirtation couldn't really hurt. He leaned forward, lifted her hand and placed his lips against her fingers. "Tell me when you're ready for a better look at Inverness," he breathed. "I can't wait to see you enjoying yourself."

So tell me, my dear," Andrew remarked, "what kind of companion is Matheson?"

"Solicitous," she replied. "He'll do in your absence."

"He's not ugly," Andrew remarked too casually, standing near the mussed bed in her room.

Elizabeth turned a steady gaze on him. "No, he's not. But remember, Andrew, you chose him, not I. So I thank you for your thoughtfulness in not saddling me with a troll."

Andrew snorted. "Choosing a troll to keep you company would have only drawn attention to you by the contrast, my beauty."

Elizabeth smiled her thanks for the compliment and, on this meager encouragement, Andrew caught the back of her neck in his grip and forced his mouth against hers in a rough kiss, the kind she used to eagerly seek. It took her breath away, which Andrew excitedly interpreted as a spark of passion. Without hesitating, he lifted the hem of her dressing gown, grasped her buttocks in his massive hands, and thrust his hips against her belly. Repulsed, Elizabeth put her hands to his chest, intent on shoving him away, when she was saved the trouble–and no doubt an unpleasant scene–by a knock on her door.

"What is it?" Andrew growled impatiently.

"My apologies," Thomas Gray replied in tones muffled by the door's thickness. "You told me to tell you when I had word on the whereabouts of the Portuguese."

"All right. Wait for me a moment." Andrew's smoldering eyes encountered Elizabeth's black, unreadable ones. He gave one last hard squeeze to her exquisite flesh–almost lifting her from the floor–and released her. "Forgive me, my dear. I've waited for news of this ship."

"Business calls, I understand," she acknowledged graciously. "Will I see you later?"

Andrew stood and straightened himself. "I can't promise, so I would suggest you plan your day without me."

"As you say, Andrew."

He briefly considered her reply, wondering if she weren't just a bit too agreeable. But he shook off the feeling and, kissing her again, took his leave.

Martin's worried gaze lingered on Alayne's defeated posture. He moved Odhar closer and reached to cover her hands in which Barley's reins lay slack.

At length, Alayne roused from her grievous thoughts to glance over at her companion. She swallowed hard the bitterness clogging her throat, preventing her from speaking. Finally she croaked, "I would never have thought Muir cared enough to trouble himself."

They'd been too late–too late to present Alayne's case before the Commissary Court because Muir had gotten there first. Muir had obtained the divorce Alayne so eagerly sought after years of abandonment. And he'd been granted the decree based on adultery.

"Simon," Alayne whimpered. "How will I tell Simon that I ca...," her voice caught, "can't marry him because the Court has declared that he...he..." She dissolved into hard-fought tears–the first she'd shed.

Martin grimly recognized her sobs as a sign that the initial shock on learning of Muir's treachery was beginning to wear off. He was numb himself and considered Muir's behavior villainous: abandoning his wife, returning after years without a word, then lying, accusing Alayne of adultery with Simon to win a divorce. Martin clamped his jaw. All this was to Muir, he thought, was a game; Muir was playing a game with the future of two innocent people. The Court had forbidden marriage–ever–between Alayne and Simon as the partner in her adultery. "Damn him," Martin uttered through clenched teeth.

Alayne weakly pressed his hand. "Aye," she concurred, "damn him." None of her solicitor's pleading could undo what had been done. Muir claimed to have seen Simon and her together within the last two weeks at the shop after closing. She rolled her eyes as they teared up again knowing exactly the night to which Muir must have referred–the night Simon had come to the shop upon learning she was going to Edinburgh. While nothing had happened between them, she couldn't prove it.

It would be two more days before she and Martin reached Inverness. As they neared the point where the road split, one fork turning toward Fort William, Alayne faced the solicitor who had had little to say while she and Martin spent much of the homeward journey up to that point going over the same exclamations of disbelief.

"Before you leave us and continue on to Fort William," Alayne said, "I want you to know that I appreciate what you tried to do for me."

Mr. Francis offered, "I wish it could have been more. Your hus...former husband, is a rogue and I truly hope he lives to rue the day he treated you so contemptibly. Now," he continued, "you must try to find a way to accept this hand the Court has dealt. Truth is that couples forbidden to marry have sometimes wed despite the Court's decision. I can't advocate it, but the future may not be quite as bleak as it seems in this dark hour." He addressed Martin, "Dr. Ross, I know this is painful for you as well with your cousin waiting, so full of hope, at the end of your journey."

"Aye," Martin agreed, "painful indeed."

"I'm so sorry." The man peered down the road. "My path to Fort William lies just ahead. May God be with you both and give you strength."

Martin held back on Odhar's reins to clasp the gentleman's hand. "You have our thanks, Mr. Francis. God speed."

Alayne offered the solicitor a nod of her head and an echoed "God speed," as she watched the man she once hoped would provide her salvation leave them alone to continue on to Inverness. Her hand crept to the back of her neck and rubbed it hard; her eyes darted in vain over the landscape.

Martin watched her, his personal and professional curiosity surfacing. "Are you unwell?" he asked, concerned.

"Not yet," she muttered before adding, "but I may be soon."

"What do you mean?"

She cast him a rueful look and replied, "I occasionally suffer from headaches. If...if I don't catch them in time, I'm fairly incapacitated, vomit a lot. It's very...unpleasant," she finished lamely.

"I would think so," he agreed and narrowed his eyes. "Does anything help?"

Now she flushed, slightly embarrassed. "Icy water on the back of my neck."

He arched a brow and returned, "I'm surprised that helps. Heat is normally better–it helps the blood flow to the head."

"Cold numbs me and that's how I get through it," Alayne offered with a shrug.

"Well, it's not likely we'll find such a remedy here," Martin stated. "Let me see if I can help."

Alayne waited as Martin dismounted, untied and unrolled his cache of medicines. As she looked on, he lay a linen square on Odhar's saddle. From a leather pouch, he extracted several pinches of some dried herb, tied the linen around it, and handed it to Alayne.

"Breathe this in for a bit," he said as he repacked his medicines.

"What is it?" she asked, sniffing the linen bag tentatively.

"Meadowsweet. Excellent for headaches and, I daresay, more pleasant than freezing water on your neck. It can't hurt and just may help. When we stop tonight, if your head still hurts, I'll brew you some tea."

"Of this?"

With a shake of his head Martin replied, "Betony."

Alayne didn't respond, only placed the bag of meadowsweet under her nose and breathed deeply the pungent fragrance. As Martin remounted, he stared skyward. Her own gaze followed and immediately she blinked as a snowflake touched her eye.

To her unspoken question Martin remarked, "I think it'll be light. Even so, we need to hasten; we don't want to spend a full week returning from Edinburgh."

"No delay will make my task any easier," she replied gloomily, her thoughts returning to the cause of her aching head.

"No, it won't," he sympathized, "but Fia and I will be there for you both."

"I know." Alayne smiled crookedly and confessed, "I was looking forward to being your cousin, you know." Martin returned her smile but it faded when she added acidly, "Thanks to Muir, I'm not even kin to your wife anymore."

After two evenings of flirting with, and testing Andrew's hand-picked attendant, Elizabeth decided Muir would do nicely as a companion. He was strong but malleable, and he reminded her not a whit of Andrew–a fact certainly in his favor. Now, in the "White Rose", she goaded him a bit. "Since you aren't much of a dancer and you aren't good at parlor games, I think perhaps the theater might make for a more successful evening."

Muir pursed his lips in a playful pout. "I'm greatly out of practice with the games and the dance."

Elizabeth simpered, "Don't take my comments to heart. I'm sure you are quite adept at other methods of keeping a woman happily occupied."

Muir stood closer to her chair and leaned to whisper, "Ah, but you haven't asked yet for the diversion I'm best at."

Her brows arched in challenge. "Assuming from your posture that you brag of your talents in seduction, how do you think Andrew would react if he found out you had attempted to bed me... with or without my permission?"

Muir paled but didn't hesitate his answer, "If I were him, I'd kill me." Belatedly he noted the use of her fiancée's real name.

Elizabeth stood amidst a whispering rustle of silk skirts and stopped an inch before him. "Aye, he would kill you. That's why I'm protecting you from your lustful urges."

His hand closed gently but firmly around her upper arm, fingers brushing the side of her sumptuous breast. "And I venture to say, from your own passions as well while you tease me mercilessly."

"Tease you?" she prompted, bestowing her most innocent look.

The pressure of his fingers against her breast increased. "Aye," he purred, "a woman without passion could not tantalize a man as you do. You know the effect of your every move before you make it."

"You flatter me."

"I tell the truth," Muir returned.

Elizabeth studied him boldly. "Perhaps," she allowed and returned the discussion to its original purpose. "I honestly do want to attend the theater tonight. I don't go often but find it immensely diverting."

Muir bent over her hand, turned the palm up and pressed his lips to her flesh. "Then diverted you shall be. I can't begin to tell you what a delight it is to spend my evenings with you after ushering Struan around during the day."

"I'm not sure I'm complimented that you mention me in the same sentence with that boor," she huffed.

"I'd be grateful for time with you under any circumstance. Still, after Struan, being with you is a reward. Now," Muir changed the subject, "I'll change my clothes and return in time to have dinner with you first."

"Why don't you let me accompany you to your home?" Elizabeth asked and was curious to see Muir start.

"That isn't a good idea, Miss. It's not my own home I'm staying at, it's my mother's. She's none too pleased with me these days. Bringing you there would not further endear me to her."

Elizabeth looked at him shrewdly. "Why are you out of favor?"

Muir assured, "It's a tiring story which, forgive me, I have no time for now if I'm to return and share supper with you."

"All right," Elizabeth conceded, "if you'll answer one question for me."

His eyes narrowed suspiciously. "And what might that be?"

She lightly laid a hand against his chest and gazed up at him with innocence she'd lost years before. "What did you mean the day we met when you said that you no longer had to concern yourself with your wife?"

For a long moment he studied her before confessing, "I divorced my wife early last week in Edinburgh–a fact Mither is unaware of as yet. That's the private business I was on."

"Oh," she declared, genuinely astonished. "Can we talk of it more later on?"

"I don't know why you'd want to, it's of no consequence." He bowed and departed, leaving Elizabeth to ponder what he'd revealed. Divorce. Her curiosity piqued.

The late-November cold forced him to quicken his pace. Muir admitted to himself that he scarcely knew what to think of Elizabeth Graham and, in her presence, his senses so often reeled he could barely think at all. Certainly he didn't want to talk about Alayne–not to anyone–but most especially not to Elizabeth. My God Elizabeth was a tease...and he wanted her. He groaned inwardly and almost immediately tried to douse the flame that burned for her body with the icy visage of, "Gordon," he grumbled, then corrected, "Andrew." Muir had seen no evidence that supported the man's reputation for being a rogue, and a nasty one at that, despite his great talent for the free trade. Part of Muir wanted Forbes' reputation to be all show though he didn't feel he could afford to risk being wrong. It could be costly indeed. What puzzled Muir mightily was the relationship Forbes had with Elizabeth. Obviously the man craved her–and Muir understood that. Elizabeth, he was convinced, had blood hotter than a Jamaican summer. Yet there was a distance between the two that was damnably curious for a betrothed couple.

"Well, no matter," he thought, shedding his musings. "I'll enjoy the scintillating Elizabeth's company as long as I can. If there's a line not to be crossed with her she'll let me know where the line is." A moment's tingling fear grazed him as he wondered if he could trust her enough to keep himself from running afoul of Forbes. Muir reached the steps of his mother's house just as she, his cousin and Ross' mutt rounded the corner. He ducked inside cursing his poor timing and nearly ran headlong into Flora.

"Why are you sneaking around so?" he snapped at her.

"I wasn't," she replied stiffly, pulling herself to her full height and looking him in the eye. "You burst in and nearly knocked me over." Before he could argue, she announced, "Your mother isn't home."

"Too bad," he said harshly. "I'm only here to change anyway." With that, he leapt the stairs three at a time and disappeared down the hall.

Flora heard his door slam and sneered after him. "What an ungrateful whelp," she muttered. "Mistress Kate does not deserve a son of his ilk. And what's he doing that he's been coming and going at such odd hours?" She shook her head; it was all very strange. The door opened again and with the cold draft came Kate, Fia and Arthur. Both women greeted Flora warmly and she fluttered to help them out of their mantles while Arthur made his way to the hearth. "Both of you go in; I've just built up the fire and will bring you tea."

"Oh, Flora, you're such a dear to have everything ready just as we arrive," Kate praised.

When Kate was seated and Fia stood with her fingers outstretched to the peat flames, Flora delivered the teapot, shortbread, scones and gooseberry preserves. Fia breathed deeply of the scones. "Mmm, no one makes better scones than you do, Flora."

Pleased, Flora chuckled, "Why you sound just like your husband when you say that."

Fia felt a jab of loneliness as she was caught a bit off guard by the remark, but smiled broadly when she realized she had indeed heard Martin pay a similar compliment on more than one occasion. She took a seat across from Kate.

Kate looked up from the plate she held and noticed that Flora hovered looking suddenly doleful and restless. She inquired, "Flora what is it? Is something on your mind?"

"It's just that your son's here," Flora burst. "He's upstairs changing to go out again. His behavior gets stranger by the day, Mistress."

Kate's lips pressed together making a thin, grim line. She sighed then stood. "Excuse me."

Fia said nothing as her aunt left the drawing room and mounted the stairs almost noiselessly. The young woman turned her disheartened gaze on Flora. "I doubt talking to him will do any good."

As Flora withdrew, Fia's thoughts turned troubled. She stared into the fire, wishing with all her heart just to see Martin's face, touch him. If they traveled quickly, her husband and her friend would have maybe eight days on the road. Who knew how long they'd have to wait for an audience at the Commissary Court. Fia stretched her legs toward the heat. A brick of peat slipped from the andirons making a muted hissing sound and putting a temporary end to Fia's musings. She prayed her husband and friend would return quickly. Suddenly, Fia heard raised voices coming from above stairs, then from the entryway landing where Kate and her son now stood engrossed in a heated argument.

"Mither, where I go, when or with whom is not your affair."

"I don't understand what you fear in telling me," Kate responded. "You're my son and it concerns me that you come and go at all hours, dressed in tattered clothing one minute, your best woolen breeches and frockcoat the next. I'm very confused."

"My business doesn't concern you, Mither, I told you that," Muir harped. "These are business dealings, nothing more, nothing less."

Kate's eyes narrowed considerably. "And does your 'business' always wear the same scent that clings to your shirts?"

Muir thrust his face into Kate's. "Are you going around *sniffing* my clothes? I can't believe it!"

She straightened her shoulders and vented, "I still pick up your clothes when you throw them on the floor though God knows why I do after all these years. Now answer my question." Kate demanded. "You are a married man–"

"You forget that Alayne is on her way to divorce me as we speak."

"Do you care? If you did, why would you reek of some strumpet's perfume? You were brought up to be a gentleman like your father. Why can't you behave like one just once in your life?"

Muir's expression turned murderous and he jeered, "And this is the mother who loves me and missed me and was glad I wasn't dead after all. The mother who takes my mousy wife's part in every spat and disagreement. Behave like a gentleman, you say? I was taken from Inverness by force and have done nothing wrong. But to you, *everything* I do is wrong. A fine mother you are," he spat.

Kate's palm resounded on his cheek. Muir lurched in shock and stinging pain. He raised his hand as if to retaliate when Fia's cold anger halted him. "Touch her and I'll have the Sheriff after you."

He spun to face his cousin, who stood in the doorway armed with the fire poker, the mutt at her side, snarling. Always, Fia was in his way. If it was the only worthwhile thing he did in the rest of his life he would make her pay for her nosiness. "You shouldn't interfere, Cousin. You may come to regret it." Slowly he turned his glower back to his mother. "I'm leaving now. I don't want to see or talk to either of you when I return. And get that damned mongrel out of here!" he screamed, slamming the door behind him.

"*Why did he* come back?" Kate squalled. "If he has so little regard for me and scorns all my attempts to reach out to him, why did he ever bother to return?"

As best she could, Fia comforted her distraught aunt, plying her with tea, patting her on the back and offering soothing little utterances. Already, she had answered this question, but she was prepared to answer it as many times as it was asked. "I think he wants something, Aunt Kate. We just haven't discovered what it is."

"And he spoke so wickedly to you," Kate added, despairingly. "Muir *threatened* you, Fia."

"He was angry," Fia replied with outward calm. Inside, she had been shaken by the malice in his eyes. Her own ire had sustained her through the confrontation, but unease had begun to gnaw.

Kate blew her nose on her handkerchief and replied, "That's no excuse." She mopped her reddened eyes and threw up her hands and begged, "What am I to do?"

Fia poured brandy for her aunt and wished she could offer an answer. The truth of it was she was reluctant to offer advice for fear of being blamed later for coming between Kate and her son. "Only you can answer that question," she finally replied.

It was another hour before Kate had quieted enough to retire. Arthur raced ahead of Fia who trudged into the room she and Martin shared. When the dog was inside, Fia sagged against the closed door, again reminded of how acutely she missed her husband and how his absence hurt. She hugged herself remembering how she'd believed her days without him beside her were over when they wed.

Trying to shake off her mood, Fia shed her clothes but for her shift. However, when she eyed the bed, looming large and cold, Fia resorted to her old habit and curled into the window seat, tucking a blanket round her, pillows propping her up. What good was the bed without Martin to share it? For that matter, what good was anything without him?

A chill coursed through her and Fia pulled the blanket closer, noting that the chill seemed to emanate from within. Muir was the cause of it, she felt sure. He worried her. She'd seen his temper—now had it turned on her, and she believed his threat to be real. With her husband away Fia only saw one option. "Tomorrow, I'll speak to Simon. He may have some advice."

Fia snuggled down into the blanket, but felt no real comfort even with her decision to talk to Simon. She hated to bring yet more worry to Simon and Martin knowing that neither would leave Inverness until they dealt with Andrew. She both dreaded and sought the confrontation. With Struan in town for days now, Fia was beginning to feel a prisoner, always alert for a glimpse of him. If they could deal with Andrew, she and Martin could leave. She wasn't eager to leave her aunt, Alayne or Simon. She simply wanted to be free to begin a real life with Martin in his home. That's where she wanted their children to be born. Her eyes misted again because she could think of nothing she wanted more than to bear Martin's children—except to ensure his safety in the inevitable encounter with Andrew. "Lord, watch over him," she prayed into the dark, her warm breath misting the pane against which she leaned her head.

Without warning, Arthur jumped onto the window seat and lay with his head across her belly. She hugged him, grateful for his presence and warmth. "I know you miss Martin too. We'll wait together."

"*I'm pleased you* obtained box seats," Elizabeth noted as Muir removed her mantle, exposing the milky paleness of her breasts barely constrained by the neckline of her gown. His sharp intake of breath at the sight coaxed a smirk from Elizabeth. She had taken care to greet him already cloaked and delighted in his reactions to her sensual little surprises. How quickly his body betrayed his needs! By his often obvious discomfort, Elizabeth reasoned he'd either not lain with a woman in months or he had an appetite for lovemaking that might rival her own. Someday, she determined, she would reward this man handsomely for reawakening the ardor she thought Andrew had killed—just as he had killed their son. She trembled with sudden, rekindled anger.

Muir's hand went to the small of her back as he leaned in and asked, "What's wrong?"

"I...it was an unpleasant memory. It...caught me off guard."

"Can I help you at all? Perhaps you should sit," he urged.

Elizabeth sank into her chair saying, "I think I'll sit."

Muir pulled his own chair close to hers. In the brief time he'd known this woman, he'd never glimpsed a weak moment—he almost believed her incapable of it. He was intrigued by her obvious upset.

Once composed, Elizabeth turned her gaze on him. She was surprised by the concern in his expression. A warm glow momentarily replaced some of the hatred she bore Andrew. Might Muir actually care about her? She had the strong urge to kiss him in gratitude; but settled instead for a slim smile and, "Thank you. I trust my momentary lapse won't ruin the evening for you."

Muir boldly grasped her hand where it rested in her lap. "Only if you're still distressed."

"Then we'll have a fine evening for I'm fully recovered; I swear it."

Their banter was light, slightly forced. Elizabeth was content to leave her hand in Muir's. She even enjoyed the soft caresses of his fingers stroking hers until the first player appeared on stage, then her attention was fixed to the drama about to unfold before her. When the second character took the stage, Elizabeth found herself transfixed. There was something very familiar about the fellow, but she was hard-pressed to say just what it was: his voice, face, the way he held himself? "I must have seen him on stage in Edinburgh or Glasgow," she murmured after some contemplation.

"Did you say something, Elizabeth?" Muir whispered.

She flicked her hand, dismissing his question as she might an insect hovering too near her face.

As the play progressed, Elizabeth tried to concentrate on the story itself, yet found her attention returning to the dark-haired actor, his movements lithe, his voice clear—almost recognizable.

During an interlude in which jugglers took the stage to entertain, Elizabeth turned restlessly to her escort who'd been watching her covertly throughout the entertainment. The frown that had settled between her delicate brows perplexed him, but she didn't keep him waiting. "Do you know who the man playing the Captain is?"

"I don't believe so. Though he does remind me of someone, I can't think who." He studied her intently. "Is that what's bothering you?"

"I confess, it does nag me."

"Well, if it will help," he offered, "I'll ask someone."

In his absence, Elizabeth amused herself by debating the ways in which she might express her appreciation to Muir for his attentiveness. She hadn't quite decided, when the jugglers were replaced by a man whose baritone boomed out a tune she'd never heard. He was so loud that Elizabeth clamped her hands over her ears so she felt, rather than heard, the curtain behind her rustle as Muir returned, his face unreadable though his mouth registered a sneer.

"Well," she asked over the singer's melody, "what did you find out?"

"It's ironic," he announced. "You wouldn't know the man but, as it turns out, I do."

"Really?"

"Aye. He's the man for whom my former wife lusts–the one I named in the divorce proceedings as her lover."

"Truly?" she gushed over this delicious bit of insight into a personal life Muir had been reluctant to share. "Still, it doesn't explain why I thought him so familiar."

"No, I can't explain that unless you've seen him elsewhere in the theater. If you remove his wig, he's got pale hair but, other than that, MacLaren has no distinguishing features."

"MacLaren?" Elizabeth prompted.

Muir nodded. "Simon MacLaren. I should have known the little cuckold was an *actor*."

Elizabeth felt her hands grow icy, her mouth, parched. Simon MacLaren. Pale haired? Could it be... it could only be the same Simon MacLaren who attended her miscarriage with his cousin... "Martin Ross," she breathed into the very moment the baritone finished his song.

Muir's head snapped around and he stared at her. "What did you say?"

Elizabeth didn't respond; her mind raced. If MacLaren was here, Martin Ross might be as well. And since the deluded doctor had insisted on searching for her own tramp of a cousin, perhaps he'd found her–here–in Inverness. As the possible implications crowded in on her, Elizabeth sucked a harsh breath through clenched teeth. Her attention was jarred back to the stage as she heard MacLaren's voice, clearly recognizable now that she could match it with his name.

"Elizabeth," Muir shook her, irritated that she continued to ignore him.

She hissed, "I have to get out of here." Snatching up her mantle, Elizabeth fought her way through the uncooperative curtain, an astounded Muir close behind her.

Once outside in the bracing air, Elizabeth gulped deep breaths, trying to calm herself. Muir relieved her of her mantle, wrapping it roughly around her shoulders. "You'll catch your death and I'll be blamed," he complained, then demanded, "Now...you tell me what's going on."

She flashed him a clearly annoyed look. "I really don't see that it's your business."

Now Muir's own anger flared. Quickly, he forced her back to the theater wall, pinning her there with his body. "I'm really tired of your games. Either you trust me or you don't," he delared.

"You're being paid to keep me company, not to threaten me," she retorted. "That hardly earns my trust."

"I'm not threatening you, and you're very much aware, I think, of my interest in you."

"As opposed to the money, you mean?" she simmered.

"The two need not be exclusive," he responded. "Either you trust me or you don't," he repeated. "Where do you know MacLaren from?"

"That's not important," she finally gritted. "What is important is whether he's alone in town or with his cousin."

"His cousin?" Muir barked a laugh. "Are you telling me that you know that pest Ross?" He could tell by the look on her face that, indeed, she knew him. "My," he smirked, "how interesting."

"So you've met Dr. Ross?" Elizabeth inquired, her excitement barely controlled.

Muir backed a step away from her. "Don't tell me you're enamored of that saint?"

"Saint?" Elizabeth queried.

"Aye," Muir emphasized. "He and that busy-body wife of his are always mixing in the business of others, trying to make sure each person they meet is as blissfully happy as they claim to be."

"Dr. Ross has taken a w...wife?" Elizabeth squeaked, feeling lightheaded.

Muir's eyes lit with devilment. "Ah, so you are infatuated with the venerable Doctor. I certainly hate to be the one to spoil your dreams, my dear, but your man is well married to my very own cousin Fia Gra...Graham."

Muir stepped from her, his hand thoughtfully rubbing his smooth chin. "Fia Graham...Elizabeth Graham. Related to you as well, then?" he asked.

"Also a cousin," she grudgingly admitted, straightening her gown where he had crushed it moments before.

"So, you know dear Fia also."

Something in his tone made Elizabeth take note. "Fia isn't really that dear to you is she?"

"I admit she's caused me some trouble."

"She excels at that," Elizabeth assured him.

"Not so adored by you either it would seem." Slowly, Muir moved close to her again, this time resting his hands on her waist. "I don't know just what these people mean to you, Elizabeth, but I believe we have much to talk about."

She leaned tantalizingly against him and lifted her chin. "And what would you say to showing a proper greeting to your new-found, albeit quite distant, cousin?"

"I'd say it's long overdue," he breathed against her mouth as he covered it insistently with his own.

Elizabeth responded ardently, as much from long-dormant passion as from anticipation of what their talks about her hated cousin might reveal. The one pang of regret she felt–and it was a meager one–was that Fia had succeeded in bewitching Martin Ross into marriage. The man had been there when Elizabeth needed him and he didn't deserve life with a harpy like Fia. But Elizabeth *had* warned him, after all.

The pressure of Muir's hips against her own and his hand at her breast made her fervently wish they had somewhere to go. Alas, there really wasn't anywhere. She broke the kiss and said as much.

"Then let's return to the 'White Rose'," he suggested. "At least we can talk in the privacy of the little room."

Her eyes glittered mischievously as she remembered the coziness the little nook provided. "By all means," she agreed.

Chapter Thirty-Four

There was a knock on Kate's door and a feeble response, "Aye?"

"Mistress Kate, it's Flora. Are you all right?" she asked in a worried voice. "You're so late abed this morning."

"I'm fine Flora, dear, thank you. Just a small headache which I believe has begun to go away."

Headache named Muir most likely, Flora thought, but said, "Is there nothing I can do for you then?"

"Thank you, no. I'll be down within the hour," Kate promised. "Don't bother with breakfast."

Flora frowned but replied, "As you wish."

Kate heard the housekeeper's retreating footsteps and sighed her despair. "Douglas, what am I to do?" she asked. Since his departure, Kate often found herself having solitary conversations with Douglas Sutherland. She missed his good sense, his sound advice, his honesty. And, if *she* were honest, she also missed his attentiveness, his comfortable face and easy smile. She missed his touch.

Thrusting herself from her chair, Kate paced. "How could that be? He's barely touched me at all," she railed to herself. The truth was though, that it had been enough. If she closed her eyes, Kate could conjure the feel and smell and look of him each time their hands or lips had met.

"Stop this," Kate demanded. "You aren't a starry-eyed maiden anymore. You're a grown woman with a grown son who becomes more wicked by the day. Douglas isn't here to help. You have to stand on your own," she scolded.

But Kate had no answers to her problems with Muir, just pain. And the pain of Douglas' absence seemed to hurt her every bit as much–but in a very different way.

"An answer will come to me," Kate determined in her most convincing tone. "It has to. Things can't go on this way much longer."

Andrew Forbes scowled perpetually. Thomas wondered what he could say or do that would make a difference but everything seemed to irritate his partner. The cause, Gray assumed, was the brother...and maybe the woman.

Gray had never met their silent partner, George Graham, whom he'd always assumed had the money but not the belly for smuggling. He found himself wondering if Graham's daughter mirrored her father in any way. He doubted it. If Graham had half the presence of his daughter, Andrew would not have maintained their partnership for long–he loved the power and control far too much. In fact, Gray was surprised that Andrew planned to marry Elizabeth who seemed to equal Forbes in tenacity and command, though she was more discreet about how and when she showed it. The fact that Elizabeth was shapely and had a handsome, if somewhat disdainful face was no hardship. And it was clear that Andrew believed his intended doted upon him. Thomas sensed, though, that not all was as it should be between the pair. Andrew's brusquely delivered instructions broke through his reverie.

"Have Matheson bring my brother to you at the end of their hunt tomorrow. You'll give Struan his instructions and not let him out of your sight until the two of you arrive for the landing." He rubbed a hand across his freshly shaven face in anticipation. "I'll be waiting."

The idea of mixing business with retribution made Thomas nervous. "Begging your pardon, Andrew, but do you think it's the best course to deal with your brother while handling an off-loading?"

Andrew shot the man a cross look. "Can't handle it, Thomas?"

Gray shrugged. "I only have to get him there then he's yours to do with as you please. I just don't want the crew distracted."

"Maybe it would do the crew some good to see how I deal with someone who crosses me."

Thomas had known this man a long time; knew fully how dangerous he was. He recognized the predatory look in Andrew's eyes and nearly shivered. Instead, he forced a laugh which brought a glower from his boss. "Poor simple crofters are your off-loading crew, Andrew. They are grateful for the work and fiercely loyal. In some ways you're more important to them than God. Because of you, they eat fairly regularly and can afford some means of shelter over their heads. There's no need to scare them; they already work their hardest."

"A God, you say? More likely the Devil." Andrew grunted his approval then grinned. "I'll concede to dealing with my brother in an unobtrusive manner, that's all I can promise."

"That's all I ask." Thomas replied.

Andrew poured himself a glass of claret. "Is Matheson's performance acceptable to you?" he bluntly changed the subject.

Gray cocked an eyebrow. "I'd say it's more important that *you* find it acceptable."

"Of course it is," he snapped. "But you know the man...what he's capable of?"

"He's doing what you asked of him. During the day, he keeps your brother occupied and he hasn't killed him, though grasping his throat with both hands must be a tempting prospect."

"By that you mean...?" Andrew rumbled, but Gray didn't flinch.

"I mean, Struan's a bombastic, reckless turd who invites trouble, and not just for himself. That's why I summoned you. It's only right that you know of his disloyalty and determine his fate." Thomas reverted to the original subject. "Matheson also squires your woman around at night–as you ordered." A thought suddenly occurred to him. "Do you want me to find someone else to do that?"

"No," Andrew replied slowly, "he seems to amuse Elizabeth."

Treading carefully, Thomas suggested, "Perhaps you'd rather someone amuse her less?"

Andrew snorted a laugh. "Elizabeth is devoted to me...and she knows what would happen if she betrayed me," he added menacingly. "You just give my brother his orders and watch over him as I asked." He lifted his glass and gulped its contents. Andrew felt less than reassured about Matheson, but he was busily revising his plan for dealing with Struan. He'd see just what Matheson would do for money–indeed he would.

As he watched Andrew, Thomas Gray imagined he could see the man's mind at work. He was profoundly glad that he and Andrew had always seen eye to eye and he hoped to keep it that way for he never wanted to be the target of Andrew's wrath. He fervently preferred that he have nothing to do with the brother or the fiancé but that was not to be. At least the business side of life was going well–no sign of nosy excise men, every sign of a profitable delivery on the morrow. He was thankful that it was almost over. Andrew would go home then, perhaps take Struan and Elizabeth, and his own life could get back to normal. He was eager at the prospect.

As she lay on her bed, the watery light of early morning faintly illuminating her skin, Elizabeth ran her hands over her nakedness enjoying the sensation, though somewhat sorry that it was not Muir's hand that stroked and caressed her. She regretted having had no place to go to seal their plan. They had groped and fondled in the little dining room, but there was no way to ensure privacy there. She moaned, fingers slipping between her thighs to press the flesh where she most wanted to feel his. The extremely limited experience she had with his touch proved it different than Andrew's–not as rough, but every bit as exciting. Muir had showed no hint of Andrew's temperament, but had a mind just as keen and a slightly more subtle drive for success. She'd discovered that when they talked about Fia.

"So your father was brother to Fia's," Muir repeated.

"And your mother and her's were sisters," Elizabeth had answered, receiving his nod in response. "Why we didn't think of her relatives in Inverness when she ran off, I'll never understand."

Muir cocked an eyebrow. "Ran off? What do you mean?"

"We'd betrothed her to–" Elizabeth broke off, looking startled and amused at the same time. "Oh...you'll enjoy this," she promised. "Fia was to wed Struan."

"Forbes?" Muir blurted and promptly choked on his surprise.

Elizabeth pounded his back until he'd recovered enough to gasp, "You really don't like Fia, do you?"

With a shrug, Elizabeth responded, "That had much less to do with it than the fact that it was a good business move."

"How so?"

"The land Andrew is using east of here–"

"The landing site?" Muir interrupted with lowered voice.

"Precisely. It happens to belong to Fia; her father left it to her." Elizabeth turned the stem of her wine glass between slender fingers and contemplated the gentle swirl of red liquid in its bowl. "We thought a legitimate claim to the land–through her marriage to Struan–would be useful."

"And if anything went wrong," Muir guessed astutely, "there was no provable connection to you or your lover."

Elizabeth's palm shot forward and connected resoundingly with his face. Beyond the buzzing in his ears, tearing eyes and stinging cheek, Muir heard her growl, "Never, *never* call Andrew my lover."

When he'd managed to shake off his stun, Muir rose quickly, jerked her from her chair, and caught her in a vise-like grip. "What was that for?" he snarled as she struggled in vain against his grasp.

"Let me go," she hissed.

"No," Muir decreed. "Not until you tell me why you struck me–and not until you apologize."

"It's none of your business," she strained through clenched teeth.

"Oh, but it is," he disagreed. "We're about to become partners."

Abruptly, Elizabeth ceased her struggle. "Partners?" she queried cautiously. "In what?"

Muir said innocently, "Why in getting even of course."

"Getting even...with whom?"

"You tell me. It could be Fia, Struan...or Andrew. It depends on who we want to get even with and how we plan to do it."

Elizabeth studied him for a long moment before offering, "I'm listening; let me go."

"Apologize," he demanded.

Her lips touched his teasingly and she murmured, "I'm very sorry."

A slow, sly grin captured his mouth. "That'll do for now." Muir released her and they sat. "Fia has insinuated herself into my life working at Mither's millinery with my ex-wife; living at Mither's house. Fia has crossed me several times–made life not just uncomfortable for me, but even dangerous. Her husband, your friend," he added contemptuously, "has even threatened to kill me."

Elizabeth kept her face carefully blank while she wondered what Muir had done to engender a threat on his life. She reined in her thoughts in time to hear Muir finish his sentence, "... Struan, whom I find pompous, cloying and simply the most obnoxious man I've ever crossed paths with."

"And what have you got against Andrew?" she questioned brusquely.

Muir leaned toward her, his intense blue gaze locked on her black one. "Wealth, power...and you hate him."

Elizabeth slowly smiled her satisfaction. "Struan is merely an annoyance," she allowed. "I don't care about him. As for Fia and Andrew, we must plan very carefully. Whatever we do, we don't want to hurt the business."

"Decidedly not. And who knows," Muir offered, "depending on how cannily we scheme, you may influence the choice for Andrew's successor, should he no longer...show interest, shall we say?"

Elizabeth cut him a shrewd look. "Perhaps."

Muir nodded, pleased with himself, then asked, "When will you tell me why you hate Andrew?"

"I won't," she answered starkly.

He considered her response and decided that it didn't matter. He had what he really wanted, her implied acceptance of himself as the new 'Gordon', so, with a shrug of his broad, lean shoulders, Muir replied, "Suit yourself."

They plotted and revised their plot of how best to exact revenge on their enemies, how best to cause irreparable damage. Their ideas fed off each other's and their excitement grew. They aroused each other so thoroughly with their wicked brilliance that Muir suddenly swept her from her chair onto his lap and, in a moment, had one hand behind her neck guiding her mouth to his, his other hand diving under her skirts easily urging her thighs apart to accept his stroking, probing fingers.

Muir's boldness and touch inflamed and unleashed a flood of long-checked desire in Elizabeth. She would have gladly straddled his hardness then and there but for the fear of being caught and having all their plans ruined.

Elizabeth pressed against him then broke their kiss. "Not here," she panted.

"I want you," he demanded, which elicited a husky chuckle from his partner.

"I noticed...but not here...not now. It's too easy to be discovered, too public. We'll celebrate," she promised, stroking his hardness, "when our plan has succeeded."

Intently, Muir studied her and reluctantly extracted his hand from between her legs, placed his damp fingers to his mouth and slowly drew them across his lips before kissing her again. "To success."

That display had nearly peaked her passion; remembering it now fueled her own fingers, bringing her to a shuddering, convulsing, welcome release.

"Miss Graham? Miss Fia Graham?"

Fia started, at once confused and frightened at being addressed by her maiden name. She turned swiftly in the direction of the voice, pulling the edge of the kertch closer to her face, even as Simon placed himself between her and the ginger-haired man who'd spoken.

Next to the knife grinder's cart, Fia beheld, "Charles Drummond?" As he smiled and nodded his response, relief rushed through her and she extended her greeting, "What an unexpected pleasure to see you again." She dipped a curtsey and received his bow in return.

"The pleasure is mine, dear lady. I never thought to see you in Inverness."

"I'm living here temporarily with my husband."

Now Drummond looked confused, glance darting between Simon and Fia. Seeing this, Fia quickly offered, "This is Simon MacLaren, my husband's cousin. Simon," she added, "This is Lieutenant Charles Drummond whom I met in Glasgow last Hogmany."

Each man bowed a formal greeting then Drummond attempted a discreet inquiry. "So, you married as your uncle had arranged."

"Oh, no," Fia hurried to explain. "I didn't marry Struan, Lieutenant. My husband's name is Martin Ross. I met him after you and I became acquainted. But, as it happens, Struan is here in Inverness right now," she stated and bestowed a curious look on him. Dropping her voice, she asked, "Does that have anything to do with why *you're* here and out of uniform?"

"Ah," Drummond acknowledged, "you remember our conversation."

"I do, indeed," Fia confirmed and, to Simon, quietly added, "Lieutenant Drummond works with the excise men."

Simon fixed his attention on the soldier. "Are you here specifically for Forbes?" he asked bluntly, his budding excitement making him careless.

Drummond glanced casually around before replying, "The Market has too many ears."

"But the shop doesn't," Fia suggested. "Let me make one more purchase for Aunt Kate and we'll go to the millinery."

The two men escorted her to a tinker who gladly took her coins in exchange for several packets of hooks and eyes. Twenty minutes later, Kate looked up as the three entered the shop. She blinked wide-eyed at the stranger.

"Is anything wrong?" Kate inquired warily.

Fia assured, "No, Aunt Kate. This is an acquaintance of mine, Lieutenant Charles Drummond, whom Simon and I came across at Market. Lieutenant, this is my aunt, Katherine Matheson." As the two exchanged greetings, Fia continued, "The Lieutenant and I were together when Uncle George informed me that I was to marry Struan."

Kate was about to declare her surprise when Simon, who could wait no longer, burst, "Tell us about Forbes!"

"What have you to do with Struan Forbes, Lieutenant Drummond?" Kate asked, mystified.

"Andrew, actually," came the response, "not Struan."

Fia bleached a shade paler and in a small voice begged, "Is Andrew here?"

Drummond offered, "I've received that report. And it is Andrew who is behind one of the most prolific groups of free traders in Scotland."

"Aye, and one of the most ruthless, no doubt," Simon gritted. "He's murdered four people that we know of, and goes by the name 'Gordon'."

With a shrewd eye, Drummond remarked, "It appears I'm not the only person who's looking for Andrew Forbes."

"No, you aren't," Simon affirmed grimly. "My cousin and I have been awaiting his arrival."

"May I ask why?"

"He killed my brother-in-law's father and brother. And he has threatened Fia on more than one occasion. We want to find him before he finds her."

Drummond turned to Fia. "This is true? Because you didn't marry his brother?"

"It's a long story," Fia rejoined. "Have you time to hear it?"

At the dining table, Kate and Simon were finishing an animated discussion about the earlier exchange at the shop with Drummond–so animated, they didn't notice Fia's unnatural silence while picking at the haddock on her plate.

"What a stroke of luck to have run into Drummond," Simon expounded. "The information we gave him about Fia's land should be invaluable. And, thankfully, he provided fair warning that Andrew is nearby."

"Most fortunate," Kate agreed, then addressed her niece. "Don't you think so, Fia? This way we can better protect you."

Fia's somber look matched her tone, "And who will protect Martin and Simon when they go after Andrew?"

Simon put his hands up in a gesture that bade her stop. "You heard me tell Drummond that Martin and I would let him and his troops take care of Andrew."

Fia dismissed his statement and accused, "You'll want to be there to settle your own score; you won't be patient enough to wait for the army to do its job."

"How can you say that?" he asked bewildered.

"Because you and Martin are both unbelievably stubborn where the subject of Andrew is concerned, that's how. If you only *would* leave the matter to Lieutenant Drummond."

Simon lay a hand on her arm. "You're understandably upset with Andrew possibly here."

"Aye," she flared, "I'm upset for you and Martin. You're intentions are noble, I've no doubt. But I've pleaded with Martin before to stay away from Andrew–he won't listen to me. Andrew is a killer. Martin heals people. And you," she pointed at Simon, "make people forget their troubles for a few hours. You're good, decent men. Andrew is ruthless and he thinks he's invincible. That's a powerful combination."

"He doesn't know Martin or me, doesn't know we're looking for him and won't feel threatened by us. That's our advantage," Simon argued.

Fia narrowed her eyes and spat, "You just proved my point. Did you hear yourself? That you and Martin have an *advantage*! Tell me again how you intend to let the Lieutenant do his job."

Simon began a retort, but quickly realized she was right. He hung his head slightly. "I'm sorry, Fia."

"As am I. What good will it do Alayne or I if you or Martin get hurt...or worse, God forbid." Fia dropped her fork and pushed herself from the table.

Speechless at the intensity of their exchange, Kate finished her claret in one gulp.

Arthur, who had been lying just inside the dining room door raised his head and ears suddenly and uttered a soft, "woof," drawing Fia's attention. Just as abruptly, he leaped up and disappeared into the entryway. Now Simon and Kate were also watching, but Fia had left her chair. They heard the door open and Arthur began excited yipping and gave them glimpses of his prancing body and furiously swinging tail.

"Martin!" Fia cried. Before she reached the dining room door, Martin appeared in it–lines of weariness etched in his grimy face–never a more welcome sight to his wife. No sooner were his arms open than Fia filled them, clenching him hard, her cheek pressed to the sound of his heart beating strong and sure.

Martin clung tightly, grateful for her warmth and softness, her scent, her love.

Simon leapt from his chair, hurried past Martin in search of Alayne, and returned, his face ripe with confusion. "Where's Alayne?" he asked eagerly.

"At the millinery," Martin replied. "It didn't occur to us that you'd be here."

"I have to see her," Simon exclaimed, starting for the door.

Martin gripped Simon's arm and his grave expression made the hair on the back of Simon's neck stand up. "It's not good news, I'm afraid," Martin stated.

"What...what do you mean? It could only be good news."

"There's no easy way to tell you this," Martin responded grimly. "Muir got there first. He got the divorce...by charging you and Alayne with adultery. According to the Court, you and Alayne are forbidden to wed, ever."

From afar, Martin heard Kate's gasp and Fia's strangled cry, "God in heaven, no!"

Simon stuttered uncomprehendingly, "For...forbidden? But we've done nothing...nothing wrong," he protested.

"The Court decreed otherwise," Martin noted bitterly.

"I have to see Alayne," Simon declared again.

Martin nodded and loosed his grip. "Aye, you must."

Still trying to absorb Martin's news, Simon ran toward the millinery. It wasn't important that he understood, only that he be with Alayne. If she needed him just half as much as he did her, she was desperate.

The brief distance to the shop took a lifetime to travel. As he reached the stoop, his gaze swept the shop and he noted only the barest hint of light from within. He began to pound on the door.

"Go away," she responded in muffled tones.

"I won't," he swore, "*ever*! So you might as well let me in now. Martin told me what happened," he added.

After a moment of silence, Alayne said, "Then you know there's nothing for you here."

"Everything I want is on the other side of this door. Now open it, Alayne. I tell you again, I will not go away–and you *know* how persistent I can be."

An eternity later, he heard her turn the key and the door swung open with a lengthy creak. "For all the good your persistence has done you," she uttered dejectedly and turned her wan face from him. The slump in her shoulders spoke clearly her fatigue and defeat.

Simon's heart ached when he saw her in the meager light. He closed and locked the door behind him and faced her.

Alayne reluctantly raised her gaze to his, felt rather than saw him step toward her then she was caught in his embrace, her face buried against his neck, his cheek resting on her silken hair. Alayne shuddered as she sobbed quietly her anguish. It was his request that stilled her abruptly.

"Marry me, Alayne."

"M...marry you?" she gulped the last of her tears and looked up at him with red-rimmed eyes.

"Aye."

Her confusion was obvious. "I thought...you said Martin told you what happened."

"He did."

"Muir saw us here; the Court says we're adulterers." She pushed back to see him better, to make sure her thoughts were clear–his nearness seemed to be muddling them. The Court forbade us to wed. You didn't hear the judgment of the Court," she stated.

"I've heard it now." He assured, "I just don't intend to abide by it."

"But–"

"Do you love me?" he intervened.

"I do, of course, but–"

"And do you want me as your husband?"

Reluctant to have her hopes raised only to be disappointed bitterly again, Alayne tempered, "Aye, but what do my desires matter against the Court's ruling?"

"Everything," he resolved. "If you believe in our love, then we will find a way."

Alayne studied him; his eyes, blue, clear and vibrant, swam before her and infused her with the first glimmer of hope she'd experienced in days, even if that hope was unfounded. His belief in what they shared was infectious–but she was also afraid of what he was suggesting. "If we wed in defiance of the Court we'd be criminals," she cautioned.

"God would not agree," he declared solemnly. "We'd be together, husband and wife, as He meant us to be."

A sudden shiver racked her frame.

"Are you cold?" he asked, rubbing her arms.

Alayne shook her head.

"I can build the fire." Simon inclined his head toward the hearth.

"The one upstairs," she suggested, glancing uneasily at the window. "I feel so...exposed here." With the rush lamp in her hand, Alayne led the way.

Simon followed her gently-swaying skirts upward, hesitating as he topped the steps. This, he realized, was where Muir had accused them of committing adultery. Glancing around, Simon found a cozy and inviting room with an open door at the opposite side. He assumed it was the bedroom. His eyes lit easily on Alayne, still pale and hurting. Anger at Muir flared in him, fueling his determination to find some way to make Alayne his wife–and quickly. Simon turned his attention and frustration on the hearth.

No sooner had he got the fire lit and the blaze steady than Alayne turned to him and fretted, "How? How can we possibly make this happen?"

"Give me a little time and I'll think of something, I promise. In the meantime, stay out of Matheson's way. Don't give him the satisfaction of seeing the results of his conniving." Simon's mind was churning already, searching for ideas. He scowled, wondering how someone as decent as Kate could have begot such a selfish devil. His attention was drawn back to Alayne and he stopped his pondering to ask, "What did you say?"

"I said Mr. Francis told me that people sometimes married though the Court forbade it."

"If that's true and common knowledge, then what's to stop us from doing the same?" Simon asked, hardly daring to hope the answer could be that simple.

Alayne shook her head vehemently. "Muir would alert the Sheriff to our breaking the law, I'm sure of it. He will always be our real problem, Simon. Until he goes away, he will never leave us in peace; he will always deny us happiness." She sank onto one of the wooden chairs.

Simon knew she spoke the truth. They remained thoughtful and silent for some moments until Simon hesitantly suggested, "We could go away."

Now Alayne gazed blankly at him. "Go away?"

"Who's to say it must be Muir who leaves? We could go anywhere that he's not, be married, and live the rest of our lives together without his ghost to interfere."

"Leave?" she repeated as the idea made its way through the maze of reasons why they couldn't just leave...reasons Alayne desperately wanted to discard one after another. "Where would we go?" she inquired in a tentative whisper.

Simon knelt and grasped her hands, excitement over a possible solution growing. "Anywhere you'd like. I've been to France, Spain and Italy. We would get along fine in any of those countries. And then there's America. I spent a great deal of time in the colonies–and you have family there," he finished expectantly.

Though her eyes took on a wistful gleam at the thought of her family, Alayne questioned, What about your family?"

Promptly, Simon responded, "You must meet them before we leave, of course," and added, "well, you already know Mairi."

"No, I mean would you want to leave them again? Be so far away? And what about Martin and Fia? I admit I long to see my kin again, but you'd be giving up yours, that's not fair," she reminded, her voice rising with the dream while the realities struggled still to hold her in check.

"To be with you," he spoke solemnly, "is my choice. I want nothing more in this life." His eyes washed over her. "That doesn't mean I don't love them and won't miss them, but I'll have what's most important if we're together."

"Simon, we aren't just fooling ourselves with this fantasy are we?" He stroked her cheek tenderly. "No," he answered with conviction. "We aren't fooling ourselves."

"Then will you do something for me?"

"Anything, my love."

Her eyes searched his face with a returning hint of desperation, this time, for their fantasy to become true. "Make me believe it as strongly as you do."

Simon cupped her face between his hands and began convincing her with a deep, searching kiss that caused them to rise together and left each short of breath. His lips released hers to ask, "Do you believe me?"

Alayne's scarce whisper, "I need a great deal more assurance," made his breathing quicken. She crossed to the door he'd noticed earlier. "It's very late," she suggested. "Will you stay?"

The air seemed to thicken around him and he moved through it slowly as though it tried to hold him back. When he stood before Alayne and set his hands on her slight waist, her eyes, barely discernable in the paltry light, told him all he needed to know. "I'll stay...always."

Their lips met impatiently now, long-suppressed hunger engulfing them.

Simon spun with her through the darkened door, stumbled across and fell onto the bed with her. He stopped thinking about everything but this woman for whom he'd waited his whole life.

Between kisses, they fumbled over clothing, at times working on the same buttons, laces or hooks. They shared nervous, breathy laughter as they got in each other's way repeatedly.

Finally ridding themselves of all but Alayne's hose and shift, she commanded, "Wait!" and to Simon's surprise, bounded from the bed and dashed into the other room.

The shock of her ripping herself from his grasp forced Simon to his feet. "Alayne? What is it? Did I–"

She quickly returned with the sputtering rush lamp, her shining, ravenous gawk appraising his tautly muscled limbs and chest. Setting the lamp on the small table at bedside, her warm hands eagerly trailed her gaze.

Simon allowed himself a sublime, selfish moment to revel in her admiring exploration before he could stand it no longer. He grasped the ends of her shift, whisked it upward and tossed it aside. He crushed her pliant body against his, pressing his lips to the hollow of her throat.

Alayne's fingers wandered and tangled in his hair urging him lower till he nuzzled her breast. His hardness taunted her, roused her until she rocked him backward onto the bed, straddling his thighs. Her fingers kneaded and stroked, her mouth coaxed.

"N...not yet," he stuttered. Already he felt ready to burst, but he would not rush this joining—they'd waited far too long. He rolled, bringing her body beneath his and slid his hands up her stockinged legs. Nearly crying out when his fingers touched her smooth, bare thighs above the softly-woven wool, he pressed a kiss to her lips so profoundly stirring that Alayne plucked at his back and hips, urging his entry. His kiss left her feeling at once set free and thoroughly possessed.

Simon trailed kisses, licks and nibbles across her breasts, down her belly, and into the moist warmth between her thighs. She jerked convulsively and arched herself to his unspoken demands.

"Please, Simon...please, my love," she finally gasped. "Don't torture..."

He ecstatically complied, surging into her with a force that brought a shuddering cry from him and a whimper of sweet relief from her own lips.

Alayne paused to savor the feel of him filling her before the frenzy of the long-awaited and oft-imagined union overtook them both. Their hips moved as one; raw passion roused them to a fevered pitch.

His fingers tangled in her honey-red hair. Simon was dazzled by the intensity of his lover. Alayne's reddened, parted lips and smoldering eyes thrilled him. There was much he wanted to say to her; he settled for an impassioned declaration, "God's life, I love you, Alayne."

Shivering, Alayne leaned over him, her hair creating a veil that shut out all but his face. "And I love you, Simon, more than I thought I was even capable of." She kissed him fervently and repeatedly bore down and rose up over him until Simon crushed her body once more against his chest and smothered her mouth with his.

His body and senses throbbed with the feel of her; her scent made him light-headed.

Alayne's body tensed and, with a guttural groan, she was overtaken by waves of sweet release rippling through her. Simon, urged by the pulsing flood within Alayne, cried out as his own passion peaked and they collapsed, panting, still clinging together tightly, tears mingling on their cheeks.

As his breathing and heartbeat neared normal, Simon stoked Alayne's hair and back, exploring the curve of her shoulder, the gentle swell that separated hip from waist. He sighed, shifted to better see her. "Thank you, my love, for bringing in the lamp."

She pushed closer to him. "You've seen me before; I confess I brought the lamp in so that I could see you. Tonight, I didn't want to rely on my imagination."

"So," he smiled blissfully, "you dreamed of me as I did of you."

"Often," she assured, feathering his sweat-glistened chest lightly with her fingers.

"I vividly remember how you looked at the waterfall," he said. "As beautiful as you were then, as much as I wanted you...watching you as we made love...you are an exquisite woman, Alayne." he swallowed hard.

"And yours, forever," she assured solemnly. "I thank God for the day you nearly knocked me into the mud."

"The happiest day of my life–until this one." His face clouded and Alayne voiced his thoughts.

"If only we were husband and wife in *every* way," she lamented.

His arms tightened round her as his resolve strengthened. "We will be."

In a wretchedly somber mood, Martin and Fia retreated to the kitchen, Arthur the only one showing unrestrained joy as he repeatedly vaulted ahead and returned to dance around Martin's legs and receive a ruffling or scratch for his efforts.

Kate had retired to her room, weighed down with the guilt of knowing her son was responsible for so much misery.

On a chair before the fire, Martin sat heavily, the weariness and strain of the last days clearly visible. The steaming water Flora had provided for his bath went unnoticed.

Fia pondered how best to help her husband. She knew that touching him would make *her* feel better, so she came up behind him and wrapped her arms around his shoulders, placed her cheek against his and stared, as he did, into the flames.

Rather absently, Martin patted her arms where they crossed over his breast bone. When his hand dropped, Fia knelt before him to remove his mud-spattered boots. But Martin stopped her, putting his hands out to gently squeeze hers.

"No," he whispered. "I don't want you to wait on me, Fia." He pulled her onto his lap and encircled her hips. "I don't want to take you for granted *ever*."

Fia soothed, "My love, you aren't. I just wanted to do something to help you, make you more comfortable at least. I'm sorry."

He studied her face, pushing her hair back for a better look at the features he'd long ago committed to memory–features that never ceased to stir him anew each time he looked at her. "There's no reason for you to be sorry." He hesitated then asked, "Do you remember when you were at my croft?"

"Of course I do," she replied, puzzled slightly.

"You would do or say things that seemed normal and sensible to you and, in response, I either chided or growled at you."

"Why are you bringing that up?"

"Because it was wrong of me to always make you feel as though you'd made a mistake and needed to apologize."

"I didn't always apologize," she grinned and his grip tightened.

"And I'm glad you didn't!" he said vehemently.

"That was long ago," she forgave.

"Not so long that I can forget it. I've learned much since that foolish time, Fia, and my life has changed in many ways. I no longer fear the law; I no longer harbor resentment and anger at my brother and first wife. I pity what became of them for they never knew the pure rapture I know with you–their deceit couldn't allow it. The most important change is that you are my love and my life. Never again should you fret over what's the right or wrong thing to say or do. There is no right or wrong between us. Be with me, Fia. Love me...that's all you ever need do for me... nothing else is of any consequence."

Tears filled her eyes and Fia framed his face with her palms kissed his forehead then his mouth. "I will always be with you, and will always, *always* love you. God only knows how deeply because, when I try to tell you, no matter how earnestly, my words are always shallow compared to what I feel."

Martin turned his head to place a kiss into her palm. "I understand your dilemma, Sweetheart,

I suffer the same. But when you're in my arms, we express ourselves eloquently. Come," he urged, setting her on her feet and rising. "I need to wash this grime off."

"I'd like to help you wash," she offered, eliciting a grin from him.

"By all means."

She hesitated. "Do you want to talk about the trip with Alayne?"

Martin caressed the back of her neck and trailed his fingers lightly round the front to the curve of her breast. "Aye...but not now. I think this tub is big enough for two." He suggested, pulled his shirt over his head and flung it aside.

Fia eyed the tub with skepticism; it was hardly larger than a half-hogshead. She returned her attention to Martin, now naked and staring longingly at her. Her eyes grew dark with appreciation. As she drank in his perfect form, her doubt about the tub evaporated. "I believe you're right."

Hours later, Fia woke suddenly, unsure where she was, her heart pounding. The feel of Martin's still-damp hair against her breast and his warm skin under her hand quickly soothed her. She searched her thoughts to find the cause for her start. Fia had been dreaming about the moors of Culloden—the icy rain and stinging sleet. The din of battle, a distant commotion now in her waking memory, left her with an uneasiness she could not fathom. Was it a memory of the night she'd found herself face-to-face with Martin's grandfather? Martin's face was turned from her now, but Fia didn't need to see it to recall the striking resemblance, and how it had shaken her into the only faint of her life. As she thought about it, it dawned on Fia that she hadn't been dreaming about that experience at all, but definitely about the Moor and a feeling of acute panic.

Martin stirred but did not wake. Closer he snuggled, his hand coming to rest low on her belly, his fingers caressing her even in sleep. It immediately roused her blood and a desire to repeat their passion of a few hours earlier. It had been particularly poignant and achingly sweet, and left each dazed and utterly convinced that the other filled every emptiness, and healed every pain they'd ever felt.

Once, Fia stroked the length of Martin's back as far as she could reach and decided simply to bask in her happiness while it was so complete, so perfect. Life was unlikely to grant her many such moments, even with this remarkable man at her side. Tomorrow, she would know the terrible story of Muir's wicked lies and the reality of its outcome. And she would have to tell Martin that Andrew Forbes had arrived in Inverness.

Chapter Thirty-Five

Elizabeth looked up from her breakfast plate into the heavily-hooded eyes of her betrothed and wondered if she and Muir weren't foolishly tempting fate. In the full, cold light of day, their scheme didn't seem quite so perfect. She started from her musing when Andrew spoke tersely.

"Why are you looking at me so oddly?"

Deftly, she commented, "It's just such a rare treat these days that you would join me at a meal."

He grunted, "Today and tomorrow will be rather hectic, my dear, and I wanted to assure you that I'd not forgotten about you. Quite the contrary."

Her eyes narrowed slightly as she contemplated his words. "I understand," Elizabeth assured him and, to vex him a bit, added, "I've been entertained reasonably well in your absence."

"Aye, well, I'll need Matheson back so I'm afraid you'll have to fend for yourself tonight."

While Elizabeth was disappointed in his blunt response, more importantly, his revelation surprised her. Silently, she scolded herself for being caught off guard and for not having paid more attention to how Andrew's plans were proceeding. Tonight. "As you say," she murmured.

"You'll...not miss his company?" Andrew baited.

Elizabeth shrugged. "A little I suppose, though not for long. And, after all, he works for you. If you need him..." She let the thought trail as she picked up a piece of toast and changed the subject. "So, tonight you'll be working?"

"Aye."

"And have you decided what role, if any, your beloved brother will play?"

"I have. I'll be seeing him this evening. It's time he take responsibility for both his actions and his mouth."

"I'd give a great deal to see Struan squirm," Elizabeth said, her eyes dancing with the thought.

"That I can't risk. Still, Matheson might tell you about it later," he said casually, but watched her reaction keenly.

Her eyes swiftly rose to his. She was clearly startled though she tried quickly to cover it. "You need him elsewhere; I don't expect to see him again. Surely we will leave this God-forsaken burgh and return to Glasgow after you complete the business transactions tonight."

Andrew's cool gaze made her shiver. "There may be a few loose ends to tie up tomorrow." He wiped his mouth and stood. "Regrettably, I must leave you now." He stood behind her and slid his hands over her shoulders and inside her dressing gown to clutch her breasts. "When we return to Glasgow," he promised in her ear, "I will have you again. You are too ripe and exquisite to go to waste. We'll both return to the land of the living and put our grief behind us once and for all." He squeezed her flesh until she bit her lip to keep from crying out–then he was gone.

Elizabeth was dazed. She stared down at her bruising flesh and, as she recovered herself, felt a surge of hostility. It renewed her faith in the intrigue she and Muir had concocted. How was she to get word to him though that Andrew's own plans might interfere? She didn't have a clue where to look for him. Suddenly, she stood and strode to the window, bracing the frame with her palms as she surveyed the lane below. Gray would know how to reach Muir, but Elizabeth couldn't trust him–he was Andrew's man. She couldn't walk the streets looking for him either; the chance of running into Fia, Struan, Martin or Simon was too great. Besides, Muir would be with Struan shortly if he wasn't already. "Damn, why didn't I think of this possibility?" she cursed. "I can't reach him."

Searching for an answer, Elizabeth glanced at the sky. The leaden clouds lay heavy and threatening on the horizon. Perhaps it would delay the landing and she could get to Muir. If not, she would have to trust that Muir was nimble enough to make whatever adjustments were necessary so as not to ruin everything. Elizabeth believed he was smart enough–and motivated enough.

While she thought the temptation of a tryst with her appealing to Muir, she knew that Andrew's place in the business was what he desired above all else. She had to count on his greed. "Aye, he'll play smart," she decided, "he has to."

It was early. Muir hoped early enough that all in his mother's house still slept. He pulled on his hose in a rough, haphazard manner–it was only Struan he had to impress this morning. He frowned as his immediate concern surfaced–Martin Ross. Muir'd seen Ross' horse in the stable last night. The good Doctor's return meant potential trouble on two fronts: everyone now knew of the divorce, and last minute changes may be needed to ensure the plan Muir had crafted with Elizabeth would work.

After stepping into his shoes and stuffing the tail of his shirt into his breeches, Muir picked up his coat and headed downstairs, determined to leave before being seen. As he reached the top landing, however, his hopes were dashed. Below, looking up at him, was his mother. Muir sucked a deep, preparing breath, and descended to hear her disappointment in him–again.

Kate, in turn, steeled herself for another tirade, more lies and bitter realities. "Why did you do this to Alayne?" she accused.

"Do what? Expose her for the whore she is?" he sneered.

Kate clenched her hands before her, forcing herself to refrain from striking him again. "Alayne is not a whore and you know it."

"Is that so, Mither? Then why is it that the night I went to the shop to plead once more with my wife not to divorce me, I saw her in the arms of Simon MacLaren?"

Kate was taken aback slightly but rallied, "You had no intention of asking her to rebuild your marriage. You don't want Alayne. You only want her to be alone, just as she has been since you went away."

He growled in a tightly controlled voice, "I was *stolen* from my home and you are conveniently ignoring the most important part of what I just said. She was in *his* arms. What choice did I have? I'm the one who's been made a cuckold. I'm the one who's been wronged you simply refuse to accept it. Why is that, Mither?"

"Because you've lied to me over and over, ever since you returned home. Never once have you behaved or spoken as though you were truly happy to be here, that you regretted the years you'd been away, or that you missed me or Alayne." Her eyes hardened as she finished, "You have misjudged me if you believe that I'm so easily fooled because you're my son and I love you."

"Lo...*love* me?" his voice rose in astonishment.

"Aye," she declared, "despite every wicked thing you do, I love you. Why do you think it pains me so when you treat me like a stranger and you threaten your cousin and lie about your wife?"

Muir snidely reminded, "Ex-wife."

"All *right*," Kate stamped her foot in exasperation, "ex-wife. You're playing at words with me proving once more that you don't care who you hurt as long as you gain from it." She walked from him and opened the door onto the heavy, gray morning. "You are not the son I knew. I don't care to know the man you are now. Send word where you want your belongings delivered and I'll make sure they get there." She stood waiting as Muir stared at her, mouth open, unmoving.

For the briefest moment, he felt a twinge of pain–at least, he thought it was pain. His mother could no longer abide him, did not want to see him again. Then the ire roiled inside him, as much for feeling the pain as for how much more difficult this would make it to lay hold of her money.

"This is them talking not you," he proclaimed. "It's Alayne, Ross and...Fia. You would not turn me out if it weren't for them."

"It's your actions toward them that helped bring me to this, nothing they've done." Kate stiffened her spine as she tried to remain firm in her resolve. "Send me word, Muir, and look inside yourself–you'll see where the fault lies. Then ask God for forgiveness."

His azure eyes flashed fury at her as he pushed past nearly toppling her to the floor in his rage. They would all come to regret this disownment. He'd already punished Alayne and that milksop lover of hers. Now he was more determined than ever to reap vengeance on his cousin, and bring the meddling bastard she called 'husband' down with her.

Martin opened his eyes and found himself staring into his wife's gray-blue ones. Before he could speak, Fia covered his mouth in a lingering, rousing kiss which he willingly returned, moving his hands over her warm flesh.

Fia's response was immediate. She pushed the blankets aside, knowing that Martin's body generated such heat that she would scarcely feel the frigid air in the bedroom. His lean, sculpted form, ready to love her, almost teared her eyes, "I love looking at you," she finally spoke. "You are so beautiful, so perfect."

Martin glanced at her under furrowed brows. These things she'd said before–and he was proud that she felt them. There was something in her voice though, a catch of some kind that concerned him. He caressed her cheek and studied her until she looked away from him. His heart balked in fear and he clutched her against him. "What is it, Fia?" he whispered his dread. "What makes you turn from me?"

"No...not yet." she insisted, fighting a rising panic.

Now he sat up and held her at arms' length, her reluctance feeding his anxiety. "What is it? Please, lass, I know something is very wrong."

A flood of emotions washed her face, her breathing shallowed, and she fought all her instincts to swallow the words, finally blaring, "Andrew is here," and bit her lip to still the tears that threatened to pour.

Martin gathered her in again and gently rocked her, his own insides in turmoil. "How do you know?" he asked at last. "Have you seen him?"

Fia gulped, "Simon and I ran into an acquaintance of mine at Market, Lieutenant Drummond. He works with excise men and followed Andrew here. He thinks there'll be a landing within the next several days."

He stroked her cheek. "I'm sorry I wasn't here when you found out, my love."

"It would...wouldn't have changed anything," she replied.

"No," he agreed, "but I'm sorry just the same."

"I don't suppose you could leave all this to Lieutenant Drummond?" His silence was her answer. "I didn't think so," she murmured miserably, "since nothing I've ever said about Andrew has made a difference."

"Look at me, Fia," he requested. "I will talk to Drummond, try to work with him, I promise. I just want the threat of Andrew gone. Only then can we truly start our life together, on our own. You see, I'm being very selfish."

"And I want that more than anything–our life together. I want you with me. You don't know Andrew like I do. You've seen the results of his evil and treachery, but have never been his adversary. He is a man of no conscience, Martin–he is lethal."

Martin nodded. "Let me talk to Drummond then you and I will talk again. Maybe there is some way I can put your mind and heart at ease."

She merely nodded, knowing there was no more to say on the subject. The ardor that teased them short minutes earlier was gone–buried under the weight of uncertainty.

Outside the door of the quay tavern where Muir met Struan every morning, Thomas Gray waited, cape of his greatcoat pulled close around his neck, uncocked hat surrounding his gray head like a soiled, floppy halo. He pondered silently why he always felt colder on landing days than on other days. Perhaps it was the care he had to give every detail that helped slow his blood and keep him from ever being warm. And this day...this was like no other. Andrew was here to oversee the operation–nothing so unusual in that. Yet, there was the business with the brother. Thomas didn't like the feel of things, didn't care for Andrew's attention being on anything but the landing itself. Still, there was no sign of excise men, and he'd heard of no fresh troops. That was good.

Over the rise in the lane, Gray caught sight of Matheson's knit cap, low over his ears, his arms flapping across his chest for warmth. Gray briefly thought that maybe today, it really was colder. He raised one hand in greeting, catching the younger man's attention.

"You're out at an ungodly hour, aren't you Thomas?" Muir goaded, knowing the man's penchant for late evenings and equally late mornings.

"Aye, so you know there's got to be a good reason for it."

"Oh? And what might that be?" Muir stopped close to his mentor and caught the stench of stale mead and spilled ale seeping from the tavern behind them.

"Orders," Thomas replied.

"From Gordon?" Muir replied casually.

"Aye. You're to deliver Struan back here to me after today's foray for grouse." Thomas shook his head. "On my life, I can't figure what the man wants with so many birds."

Muir chuckled sourly. "He doesn't kill many. While he'd have you think otherwise, the younger Mr. Forbes is not much of a hunter. He's noisy, clumsy and, to be honest, a bad shot."

"Well," commented Thomas, "luck for the birds. Anyway, don't let him go looking for a whore; he must be returned here."

It occurred to Muir that there was a major change of plans afoot. For his sake, and Elizabeth's, he needed to know what change. "So is this night a good night?" he asked Gray.

"Aye," replied Gray, then he shifted thoughts. "Gordon wishes to talk to you also. You should go to the 'White Rose' after leaving Struan with me. I believe your days of squiring Miss Graham are at an end." Thomas saw a bit of surprise flicker across Muir's face. "I hope you enjoyed your time with the lady," Thomas stated, "but not too much."

The comment drew a narrow look of impatience from the younger man.

Thomas shrugged and reminded, "Not a word to Struan about tonight, eh?"

"Not a word," Muir breathed harshly, and entered the tavern to wait for Struan to stumble downstairs. He sat at a table and impatiently waved away the maid who approached to serve him. Now what did all this mean, Thomas' talk? A landing tonight, certainly. No more minding Struan–God be praised–no more time with Elizabeth. Well, let them think that anyway. Likely, what this did mean was no chance to speak with her privately. They'd be all right he determined confidently. He and Elizabeth had desires in common that went beyond the carnal ones.

Though thinking back to last evening when he'd so easily aroused her–and she him–the anticipation of coupling with her stirred his blood more than he'd ever remembered being affected by a woman–certainly not by his mouse of an ex-wife.

Muir's attention was drawn to a noise on the stairs–a loud grumbling belch. Struan. Muir was so happy at the thought of these being his last moments with the lout that he broke a huge smile. "Good morning, Mr. Forbes. It's going to be a lovely day."

"*She wanted no* breakfast this morning Mistress Fia. She and her son had words again just a short while ago, then she went out," Flora finished.

"To the shop?" Fia asked, worry puckering her brow.

"I don't think so because Mistress Kate told me she'd visit the shop later."

Martin placed Fia's mantle over her shoulders and donned his greatcoat. "We'll go on to the shop, Flora. If Mistress Kate returns, please tell her we hope to see her there."

"I will, Sir," she replied, handing him his blue woolen bonnet.

Fia smiled her thanks and followed her husband out the door, which he closed once Arthur was out.

Martin surveyed the sky and breathed deeply. How he wished it were night and he and Fia safely tucked up once more in their bed. That would mean that they'd gotten through the day–no matter what it held in store–and could find solace in each other again.

They began the trek to the millinery. Martin held Fia's hand and grasped Odhar's reins in his other hand intending to exercise the horse after meeting with Lieutenant Drummond. Fia had suggested leaving him behind the shop. "Sensible," Martin smiled at her. "Simon and I are going together to see Drummond. He fell silent then and kept his face forward, but his eyes darted everywhere he caught movement. Never would he say it to Fia, but he feared that Andrew Forbes would catch him slacking, leaving her vulnerable.

Acutely aware of Martin's vigilance, Fia frowned. He would never rest until the matter of Andrew was resolved. Fia bore the weight of knowing that it was she who'd brought Andrew into Martin's life. Now she realized it was she who must help him settle the matter any way she could. When she spoke, though, it was on another subject altogether. "Do you think Simon's with Alayne at the shop?"

He nodded and, when they at last arrived, they left Odhar in the stable and entered through the workroom, the prediction proved true.

The four friends fell into each others' arms, each with their own tumultuous thoughts, too overcome with emotion for words. When they reluctantly began to loosen their grips, there were shy smiles on Alayne's and Simon's faces.

Martin glanced quickly between them, realizing they'd already moved past Muir's treachery. "Well?" he asked expectantly and with relief.

"We have a plan," Simon announced quietly.

Fia asked, "You have? Already?"

Vigorously, Alayne nodded and wove her fingers with Simon's. "It's not without pain, but we believe it's the only way to be together as husband and wife."

"That's what matters most," Fia replied earnestly.

Martin nodded his agreement. "What have you decided?"

Simon cautioned, "We'll tell no one but you. At all costs, it must be kept from falling into Muir's hearing."

Alayne touched Fia's arm lightly. "That means Kate can't know, though I'll talk to her when the time is right."

"I understand," Fia responded. "She loves you, Alayne." She faced Simon, adding, "and she has come to care about you."

Simon smiled and allowed, "I believe that's true. But this is how it must be."

"Then it'll be as you say," Martin stated.

"Mr. Francis said that some people forbidden to wed do so despite the Court's decree," Alayne began. "Simon and I realize that, as long as Muir is here, we won't be able to do that–he'll never leave us in peace."

Simon continued, "Since we can't count on Muir to leave, we will. I'll take Alayne to Strathcarron to meet my family. Then we will sail to America by way of France where we'll be married."

"America?" Fia repeated and addressed Alayne, "Because of your family there?"

"That's one reason we chose the colonies. The other is, well, Simon tells me it's a place ripe for new beginnings." She studied first Fia then Martin. "You see, this is where the pain comes in; we'll have to leave the two of you, Simon's family, and even Kate behind. It'll be very lonely."

Fia's voice quavered slightly but she tried to infuse it with enthusiasm. "But your family will be waiting, and you've missed them for too long."

"It's a good plan," Martin said and added, "likely the best option you've got."

Simon said, "Perhaps the only one that can possibly succeed. Truthfully though, we'll miss you both more than we can say."

"Aye, and if you try to say," Fia reckoned, "I, for one, will bawl like a bairn so we won't do that!"

They all broke into self-conscious laughter, knowing Fia wouldn't be alone in her tears. Finally, Martin offered, "You'll doubtless want to leave as soon as you can. Simon, I can tie up the loose ends here. You and Alayne do what you must."

Simon started and glanced at Fia. "What did Fia tell you?"

"That Andrew is in Inverness," Martin replied.

"*What*?" Alayne gasped.

"He is," Simon confirmed and, to Martin, "Is that what you mean by tying up loose ends?"

"Aye, I can work with this Drummond fellow and–"

"No!" Simon interjected. "We'll work with him together, look out for each other. I promised as much to Fia."

The thought of Andrew Forbes in Inverness caused Alayne to lapse into a brief, horrified trance where she saw the night of beauty and love shared with Simon as their first...and possibly last. So focused had she been on the danger for Fia, the fact that Simon could also be in peril hadn't sunk in. She tried to speak his name, but her throat was so parched, no sound emerged. She tried to catch Fia's eye, but Fia stared at her hand clutched in Martin's. Alayne heard Simon telling Martin of the argument he and Fia had at supper just last night and... "Who is Drummond?" she finally squeaked, needing to know if she could trust this man with Simon's life.

Simon's attention locked on Alayne as he realized for the first time that he stood to lose someone and something very precious if this didn't go just right. He drew her close and responded, "A friend. He commands the troops assigned here to rid the area of smugglers. He told us Forbes was here."

Fia added, "I mentioned him once. I met him the night I learned of my betrothal, do you remember?"

A light of recognition flickered in Alayne's eyes but it did not overcome her concern. "Simon, I'm worried," she began, and vaguely was aware that Martin and Fia withdrew toward the hearth to afford them some privacy. Alayne continued, "I can't make any arguments that Fia hasn't already made a dozen times to Martin and maybe several times to you. But don't forget, I just got you all to myself. I will not stand to lose you–not now–not in a hundred years. The thought of you putting yourself in Forbes' way frightens me terribly."

Simon's conviction in his own abilities was impenetrable; he sought to ease her mind. "I will take every precaution and come back to you, my love, a whole man as I am now. I'll come back to love you, marry you, have bairns with you and grow old with you. I've waited all my life for you. I don't intend to let go now that I have you." He wrapped his arms round her and embraced, then kissed her. "I love you, Alayne."

"As I do you, Simon MacLaren."

Fia, deep in thought, sat on a stool at the work table. Next to her, Martin leaned, resting his elbows on the wooden surface and his thigh against her knee.

Simon and Alayne returned to stand opposite them and Simon spoke to Martin, "So you and I need to speak to Drummond–the sooner, the better."

"Aye. The more time we have to learn what Drummond plans, the better prepared we'll be."

"Of course," Alayne agreed.

"Fia?" Simon queried.

Fia nodded a bit too vigorously and echoed, "Of course."

"Good," declared Simon.

Martin cautioned, "We can't leave the two of you by yourselves though, not with Andrew in town."

Simon readily agreed and offered, "Let me run to the theater. I've made friends there with the fellow who tosses out the rowdy patrons. His name is Halbert. He's a bit simple, but sweet-natured and doggedly loyal. I bet he would stay here while Martin and I talk to Drummond."

"I'll go with you," Alayne announced, but Simon kissed her and replied, "I can move faster on my own, lass. I'll be back here before you know I've gone."

True to his word, Simon returned quickly with a sleepy but agreeable man in tow, hair stuck straight up like the comb of a rooster.

"Martin, Alayne, Fia, I'd like you to meet Halbert. He assures me he'd be happy to keep you ladies company while Martin and I see Drummond."

Fia curtseyed and Halbert responded with a low, dramatic bow–no doubt learned from watching too many actors on stage. "I'm pleased to meet you, Halbert. Simon has told you about Andrew?"

"Aye, he has," the man replied. "I will protect you and your friend," he promised nodding at Alayne and bowing to her as well.

"It's very kind of you, Halbert," Martin allowed, shaking the man's hand. "You're doing us a great service."

"Anything for my friend Simon," he responded with a huge grin.

Simon patted his shoulder. "We won't forget this favor, Halbert." He turned to Martin. "It's only a few minutes until the shop opens. Shall we go then, Martin?"

Martin nodded, then drew up a stool and sat with Fia, catching her fingers in his.

Halbert discovered Arthur and proceeded to get acquainted.

Simon and Alayne drifted out of earshot again as they alternately murmured, touched and kissed.

"I'm so happy for them," Fia offered to her expectant husband.

"Aye," he replied, "Fia–"

"I wish I were as brave as Alayne," she interrupted, "or at least that I could more successfully hide my concerns."

"You are one of the bravest people I know, my love. Admitting fear for Simon and me doesn't make you weak; you're trying to protect those you love. I think that's very brave."

She brought his fingers to her lips and kissed them. "I'm amazed that you can see so fine a sentiment in my actions."

Martin puzzled, "What actions?"

Her gaze held his; she wouldn't allow herself to look away this time. "I've failed to support your need to find and deal with Andrew, not just for me, but for the promise you made Simon's family. I don't want our life together to be burdened with you looking over your shoulder every minute of every day. I'm also ashamed of myself."

"Fia, you've no reason to feel shame. You want me to be safe, as I do you," Martin declared vehemently.

Fia slid from her perch to stand between his knees and place her hands on his thighs. "Nevertheless, I am…but not after this moment. You concentrate only on Andrew. I'll give you no more cause to fret on my account, you have my word. As I fear and loath Andrew–and you know that I do–I have far more confidence in your ability to do whatever you set your mind to."

Until she had said it, Martin hadn't realized that he really was preoccupied with Fia's fears and doubts. Why wouldn't he be? He loved her. Finally, he asked, "Why the change of heart? This morning you didn't give Simon and me much hope for success."

"As I saw you watch every leaf that blew across our path on the way here, I realized that you couldn't succeed unless your mind was clear, your thoughts focused. Andrew is evil. But you, my darling, are good. Simon is good. And you're both very honest, intelligent men. Andrew is devious and cruel. Martin, you have the tools to beat him. My distracting you is the only thing holding you back. I know that now."

"Thank you, Fia," he whispered, holding her tight against him. "Your confidence means everything to me." Their lips met, their gaze never breaking, and the truth of all that they spoke and felt was there to see. Only as Simon cleared his throat did they reluctantly part.

"It's time to go, Cousin," Simon reminded.

Fia reached to grasp Simon's hand. "Good luck; please be careful."

Simon pondered the distinct difference in Fia's perspective as he replied, "That we will." He glanced at Martin and saw a difference in him as well. Not sure what it was, Simon was encouraged that the change was a good one. He squeezed Fia's hand in return and jerked his head toward the door. "Shall we?"

Martin nodded and ordered, "Arthur, stay here." To Fia, he said, "There's no sense in letting Struan see him if he's about."

Arthur whined but accepted his fate, standing where his haunch touched Fia's petticoat and she could easily console him with a few strokes of his shiny, black fur.

Lieutenant Drummond had taken a room in a boarding house, quite close to the quay. He distanced himself from the excise man, still dressed in frock coat and breeches, so as to move about the town and not attract attention. His troops were quartered outside Inverness, again to minimize the possibility of tipping Andrew's hand to their presence. He was surprised by the knock on his door; he was expecting no one, and he was instinctively cautious. "I've ordered nothing," he called through the closed door.

"It isn't your landlord," came the response. "It's Simon MacLaren. I've brought my cousin. We'd like to talk to you."

Martin chimed in, "If we're too early we–" He halted as the door swung open, and he beheld a trim fellow with a pleasant, freckled face and pale ginger-colored hair.

Drummond smiled and held out his hand to Simon. "This is unexpected, but welcome. Come in."

Simon took the offered hand then, stepping inside, turned to introduce, "My cousin, Martin Ross, who returned to Inverness last night."

Drummond executed a formal bow then extended his hand. "I'm very pleased to meet you, Mr. Ross. And may I offer congratulations on your recent marriage. I admire your wife and am very pleased for the happiness she's found."

"Thank you," Martin replied. "I'm an exceedingly fortunate man. Please call me Martin."

Drummond nodded and inquired, "Have the two of you breakfasted? Shall I ask for something to be sent up?"

Simon assured, "That's kind of you but we're fine. Is this a good time for you to talk?"

"Indeed, please sit and tell me why you're here. I apologize; the room isn't set up for visitors." Drummond sat on the edge of the bed after Simon took the chair and Martin perched atop a trunk.

"You won't be surprised to hear that we want to talk about Andrew Forbes," Simon began. "We want to offer any assistance we can that will help you catch and punish him."

Coolly, Drummond responded, "Well, I'm a bit surprised. Fia–oh," he turned to Martin. "Please forgive my familiarity."

"Fia wouldn't mind," Martin assured, "so I don't either."

"Thank you. Fia seemed quite anxious at the possibility that you might attempt to take an active part in bringing Andrew to justice."

Martin stated, "She knows the man's ways too well." A hardness edged Martin's voice, but faded as he continued, "Fia is apprehensive. Still, she wanted us to speak to you and offer what help we can. She just doesn't want us to be foolish about it and get ourselves hurt in the process."

Drummond nodded his understanding, then said, "First, let me tell you what I know and we'll see how best you might assist."

"Of course," Simon agreed.

"I believe a landing will be made tonight. Last evening, I visited a tavern you suggested, Simon. There I heard two men whispering that they had to be rested for tonight. They were rather loud; too much ale I think. They also lamented the cold dank along the shore. One dropped the name 'Thomas'. I'm guessing it's the Thomas Gray you told me about, Simon."

"They had surprisingly loose tongues," Martin commented dryly. "Your interpretation seems well-founded."

Simon added, "Congratulations, Drummond. You heard more than anyone could have reasonably hoped for last night."

"Aye, with a sizable bit of luck," he admitted. "Do either of you know exactly where this landing site is?"

"I've not been there," Simon replied, "but I can find it. If you'd like, I can take you there," he offered buoyantly, his excitement growing at the prospect.

"We," Martin swiftly corrected.

Simon glanced sheepishly at him. "Of course, we."

With some hesitation, Drummond said, "I'd have to have your solemn word that neither of you would try to help in the capture. That task is my sworn duty, and I've no business bringing you along except that you can guide me to the landing point."

"We'll stay out of your way," Martin promised. "I can identify one brother and Simon, both if that will help you."

"I assume you know I've met Struan," Drummond stated and Martin nodded. "Is there any information you can provide that Simon can't?"

"No, but I'm a doctor. I've tended three people that died at the hand of Andrew Forbes. And I promised Simon's family I will see this through with him. I can treat anyone who may get wounded."

Drummond was hesitant but could not deny that it would be prudent to have a doctor with them, since the opportunity was at hand. Finally, he asked, "Can you meet me here at half past three o'clock?"

"We can." Simon affirmed.

A smile broke Drummond's freckled face. "Then it's settled. If all goes well, you'll be home before dawn. Now, let me tell you what will likely happen so you'll have some idea what to expect."

The two women stood staring at the closed door for a long minute–only Arthur's whine punctured the silence, but he was soon distracted by Halbert's attentions. Then Fia and Alayne turned and hugged one another, not speaking of concerns they still harbored for what their men might soon face before the day was done.

Finally, they moved apart and entered the shop. Fia unlocked the door and placed the small 'Open' sign in the window; when she turned, Alayne was already busy with her first task. "So, you're going away," Fia said in a small, clear voice.

"We must," Alayne confirmed.

"The thought of you and Simon leaving gives me an empty feeling."

"I have much the same feeling." Alayne empathized as she took shears to a length of linen destined to become several shifts.

Fia picked up her needle and sat matching fabric edges in order to begin a waistcoat seam. "Will you settle where you have some family?" she questioned.

"In truth, Simon and I haven't discussed that," she responded. "I believe much depends on where there is a theater. After all, I can work anywhere."

"Aye, that you can," Fia replied then fell silent. Her immediate thought that, once they left Scotland, she and Martin would likely never see their friends again made her terribly sad; but she would not show it. She realized that leaving was Alayne and Simon's only hope of sharing a life in peace. Finally, she offered, "I'm so happy that you and Simon have found a solution to this nightmare that Muir inflicted on you. I'm even happier that you and Simon are together–in every sense, I believe." She flashed a smile to Alayne who beamed and blushed.

"So am I, I assure you," Alayne emphatically agreed.

They chattered on about less personal matters, keeping their minds and fingers occupied. A few customers came and went and, when Alayne looked up later, she exclaimed her surprise that it was after ten o'clock. "I thought you said that Kate had planned to join us," she quipped.

Fia snipped a thread and responded, "She told Flora she would but didn't say when."

"Do you think she misses Douglas?" Alayne asked wistfully.

"I think she misses him and thinks of him often. In fact, I believe she–"

The door crashed open causing the women to jump and the shop to shudder. A thin, tallish lad stood framed in the opening, gulping air. "Which...which of you," he struggled.

Both women hastened toward him, but were beaten by Halbert, who blocked the boy's path. Arthur barked furiously at the sudden upheaval.

"Arthur, hush," Fia commanded, stroking the dog.

Alayne assured, "This is not Andrew, Halbert," and turned to the lad urging, "Go slow. What is it?"

"Mis...Mistress Ross? Which?" His gaze hopped from one to the other of the startled faces before him, anticipating an answer to his question.

"I'm Mistress Ross," Fia responded, mouth suddenly dry. "What is it you want?" she asked.

He almost had his breath now. "Been an...accident. Your husband has–*ouch*!" he yelped as Fia's fingers dug painfully into his flesh.

"What accident, *where*?" she pressed.

Struggling with her own rising panic, Alayne pried her friend's white-knuckled fingers loose. "Fia, let the lad speak." She turned and prodded, "Now, lad, what accident?"

"Bad accident near the Firth east of town; I was sent to fetch Mistress Ross. Your husband is hurt something fierce."

"Why would he be there?" Alayne asked.

Fia's knees turned watery; her belly leaden. Then she heard the boy add, "He's calling for you!"

Her strength surging back, Fia thrust her face close to his. "Who sent you?" she demanded.

The lad edged from her, nervously, and bumped into the solid form of Halbert, who clamped a hand on his shoulder. "I...I don't know his name. He...he had yellow hair, blue eyes."

Alayne and Fia's shocked stares met, and they declared in unison, "Simon!"

"I have to get Barley." Fia scurried to the workroom for her mantle.

"I'm going with you," Alayne stated, close on her heels.

"No," Fia replied emphatically. "Someone has to stay and tell Aunt Kate what's happened."

"But, Fia, you can't–"

"*Please*, Alayne, I haven't time to argue." She threw on her wrap.

"Don't worry, Alayne," Halbert said, "I'm going with her. The only thing is, that leaves you alone."

Alayne bit her lip. "That's all right, Halbert, Andrew doesn't know me. It's Fia he's after." She squeezed his arm. "Thank you. I would worry so much more if you weren't with her."

Fia added, "Aye, Halbert, thank you. You heard him say Martin's badly injured. I'd be grateful if you were with me."

"Wait a moment," Alayne said and dashed back to the shop. She ripped a long length of linen and returned, folding it around her shears. "Put these in your pocket. You may need bandages–I pray not."

Fia reached through the slit in her petticoat and secured the bundle in her pocket. Quickly she hugged Alayne. "Thank you."

"Now, lad, exactly where is my husband?"

"Head east from town," the boy instructed. "Where the road bends south, ride a short ways north off the road towards the Firth. You'll find them there."

Startled, Alayne demanded, "Aren't you going to take them there?"

Vigorously, the lad shook his head. "I wasn't supposed to be there in the first place. My mam will take a large switch to me if she finds out." He glanced at Fia, then away. "You can't miss them."

Fia noticed Arthur madly pacing, infected by the excitement. "Alayne, would you keep Arthur here? He won't be able to keep up for as far as Halbert and I might need to go."

"I'd feel better if you took him," Alayne grumbled, "but you're right. Arthur would kill himself trying to keep up." She grabbed the passing dog and held on, a deep shiver coursing through her. "Be very careful, Fia," she counseled solemnly.

"I will." Fia and Halbert raced to Kate's stable, saddled Barley and Kate's horse faster than Fia though possible and set their horses thundering down the lane.

When Alayne turned her attention from the struggling hound back to the lad, he was gone. She hoped he was headed to his mother's but the uneasiness in her belly swelled at his quick departure. "Please, dear God, let Martin be all right; and Simon; and Fia; and Halbert too." She had to believe Simon was well–he'd sent the lad after all.

Arthur squirmed and whimpered in her grasp and Alayne grappled with him, finally getting him inside.

Once she let Arthur loose, he picked up his pacing once more, whining and barking his unhappiness, scratching at the door.

"Arthur, *please*," the woman begged. "I can't have you doing this. Now hush, please."

His distress she found particularly unsettling and determined, "As soon as Kate gets here, I'll follow Fia. I know I can help." Yet she quickly found herself pacing with the dog, unable to concentrate on her work. It was only the arrival of an occasional customer that kept her sane.

It was going on noon; still, Kate had not arrived, and Alayne was now frantic. "I can't wait any longer," she declared and, as she strode to the window to remove the 'Open' sign, the door swung toward her. She came face to face with Martin.

Alayne's jaw dropped, eyes swept him up and down looking for blood, breaks, holes or gashes. Finding none, she seized him in a violent hug. "Thank God you weren't badly hurt after all," she exclaimed, then begged, "Is Simon all right?"

"I'm here; I'm fine," Simon stepped around Martin and received his hug with no surprise–except at its fierceness.

"I'm not hurt at all," Martin responded belatedly and bent to rub the ecstatic and noisy hound. "What's this about? Where's Fia?"

Shock ran coldly through Alayne. "What...what do you mean, 'Where's Fia'? She's with you: she's supposed to be with you." As panic gripped her anew, Alayne pushed the two men aside and burst into the street, praying they had stupidly left Fia standing in the lane. They had not.

Distantly, Alayne heard Martin again asking, "What do you mean, she's supposed to be with me? *Alayne?*"

Alayne whipped around, sudden tears of dread streaming her cheeks. "A lad stormed in here saying there had been an accident. You," she pointed an accusing finger at Martin, "were badly hurt. And you," she turned to Simon, "sent the boy racing here to fetch Fia."

"*Me?*" Simon gaped. "He said I sent him?"

"He...he said a yellow-haired, blue-eyed man. Fia and I assumed it was...you." Alayne jammed her knuckles against her mouth to keep the building scream from erupting. Neither Martin nor Simon had any idea what was going on. That meant only one thing–Andrew Forbes did.

Martin shook her shoulders just enough to refocus her attention. "Where did she go, Alayne?" Martin demanded. He knew all too well what she was thinking, and he willed the thought away.

"E...east. Where the road turns south, she was to head north off the road toward the Firth for a short way. The lad said she could not miss finding you."

"When did she leave?" Martin croaked, his voice choked with fear.

"Just after ten," she sobbed and turned to grasp Simon's arm for support.

"Almost two hours ago?" Martin roared, "By *herself?*"

Alayne's pitch rose to match his. "*No!* Halbert is with her. She wouldn't let me go. We expected Kate at any moment and I was supposed to tell her what had happened, that they'd taken the horses, then I was going to follow." Her tortured gaze went from one to the other. "Kate never got here."

Without another word, Martin raced through the shop and out toward the stable and Odhar. Arthur beat him there, Simon and Alayne were right behind him.

"Let me fetch Devenick and go with you," Simon pleaded.

Martin shook his head as he brought Odhar from his stall. "You have to go with Drummond. He may be our best bet in the long run, don't you see? At least Halbert is with Fia. I pray he can protect her." Martin added, "I'm taking Arthur. Maybe he can pick up Fia's scent...if she dismounts for any reason."

Alayne grabbed his arm. "Listen, what's that?"

They all froze, all heard a voice calling "Alayne."

"It's Kate!" Alayne hiked up her skirts and sprinted back into the shop and was caught off guard to see not just Kate, but a young woman with dark hair and heart-shaped face. Ignoring the customer she cried, "Kate, where have you been?"

Kate said distractedly, "Alayne, would you help this woman? She is asking about you."

Alayne ignored her and demanded again, "Where have you been? Something horrible has happened."

"Trouble in paradise?" the stranger asked with an ill-concealed grin that brought Alayne up short; every hair on her body prickling in fear.

Something about the woman was familiar though Alayne knew she'd never seen her. Alayne's eyes narrowed. Andrew was in Inverness, and she guessed, "Elizabeth Graham."

"E...Elizabeth?" Kate stuttered, finally rousing from her own thoughts to look more closely at the woman.

Elizabeth's attention shifted to Alayne and she raised her chin a notch. "Have we met?"

"No, but we're about to become much better acquainted," she promised acidly.

Immediately relieved that Fia was nowhere in sight, Kate finally asked in alarm, "Alayne, what's going on here?"

Everything was becoming frighteningly clear now. Alayne bellowed, "Simon, Martin, get in here *now!*"

Elizabeth lurched forward. She hadn't expected to see Martin Ross. She *couldn't* see him. Damn, if only she'd stayed away from the shop. But she just *had* to seek out Muir's former wife; her curiosity clouding her judgment. Now the harpy had sounded the alarm. Elizabeth turned and reached for the door, ready to flee, but Kate jumped in front of her, blocking her way.

"No you don't. I don't know what's going on here, but you aren't leaving until Martin sees you."

Trapped, Elizabeth glowered at Kate–Muir's mother. No wonder he wanted to get away from Inverness, she thought irately. Her head snapped up as Martin appeared in the doorway, Simon at his shoulder.

His eyes blazed when he saw her. Elizabeth's presence confirmed his dread that Andrew Forbes was behind Fia's disappearance. His belly danced wildly with fear, and he was before her in an instant. "Where's my wife?" he demanded.

"Your wife?" Elizabeth stalled, struggling to hide her anxiety.

"Don't trifle with me, Elizabeth. Where is Fia?"

"Fia? You mean you married her despite my advice?"

Martin's hand shot out and gripped her upper arm tightly making her wince. "Where...is... she?"

Simon added, "For the love of God, Elizabeth, tell him."

"How nice to see your handsome face again, Simon," she spoke with remarkable calm, which boosted her confidence.

A startled Alayne turned to him. "You've *met* her?"

"In Glasgow. Now," Simon turned back to Elizabeth, "tell Martin where she is."

Martin shook her, "Is she unharmed?"

Elizabeth regarded him carefully; his hold on sanity was tenuous. "I haven't seen her since she left Glasgow so who knows? When I saw her last, she was in one piece."

Before anyone could move, Kate's hand shot out and slapped Elizabeth hard across the face. "You viper," she raged. "You knew Forbes was hatching some horrible plot against my niece. Tell Martin where she is now or I'll have the Sheriff here."

Elizabeth, angered from the sting of Kate's hand and the throbbing of her arm under Martin's grip, growled, "If you want your precious Fia back, you'll be nicer to me."

"We're wasting time, Elizabeth," Martin said. "I well know how you feel about Fia, and you know that I love her. I'll not let you or your lover take her from me. Andrew loves you; but he hates Fia. He'll hurt her, perhaps worse."

Elizabeth grimaced at the thought of Andrew loving her but said only, "Worse?"

Simon, who was indignant that Martin had to cajole her into giving information, spat, "Aye, worse! Andrew's killed four people that we know of."

"Is that all?" she asked.

"*All?*" Martin screeched. "Isn't that enough? Tell me where Fia is!"

She remained silent and Martin finally snapped. He catapulted her ahead of him through the workroom and out the door. "You *will* help me find her."

"You're hurting me," Elizabeth cried.

"And you're hurting *me*," he retorted. "The difference is that you delight in doing so."

Nearly throwing her onto Odhar's back, Martin swung up behind Elizabeth before she could bolt.

The others had tumbled out the door behind them and Kate pushed her way to the horse's head and grasped the bridle. "If harm comes to Fia, I'll see that you're punished."

Shockingly, Elizabeth laughed. "You have more to worry about than Fia, old woman."

"What...what do you mean?"

"Sorry, Kate," Elizabeth sneered haughtily, "Martin's in a hurry, I can't talk now."

Kate released the reins, thoroughly befuddled, but knowing that Elizabeth spoke the truth. "Go, Martin. Bring Fia back safe."

Brusquely, Martin ordered, "Simon, Alayne, keep Arthur here. I have a new guide."

Chapter Thirty-Six

Muir tried hard not to show his upset. He'd left Struan Forbes with Thomas as he'd been ordered, then proceeded to the "White Rose" to meet with Gordon. It was 11:30 when he'd arrived and mounted the stairs to Andrew Forbes' room. Now, sitting opposite the imposing man, considering the request he'd just made, Muir felt almost sick–not at Andrew's request, but that he'd so underestimated his opponent's ruthlessness.

"You want me to...kill...your brother," Muir repeated slowly.

With a frigid smile, Andrew asked, "Didn't you understand me?"

"I wasn't sure I'd heard you correctly."

"You did, I assure you." Andrew studied the man closely. "What's your answer?"

Caught completely off guard, Muir stalled. "I...I just didn't dream this would be how you believed I could best serve you." As a meager thought popped into his head, Muir peered at Andrew through narrowed eyes. "You're testing me," he guessed, "testing my loyalty, whether you can trust me. I thought I passed that test when you entrusted your betrothed to me."

Andrew smirked, "You aren't as dull-witted as you look. Still, I'm quite serious in my desire to be rid of Struan. You'll do it?"

For a long few moments, Muir weighed what he stood to gain and lose by his next utterance. This seemed to be the opportunity he and Elizabeth had counted on. Instead of manipulating it himself, it had fallen into his lap. Finally he responded, "No, I won't do it."

The look of surprise on Andrew's face was so comical Muir almost laughed. But he had to move quickly while surprise was still his small advantage and the words began to spill from his lips. "If you want a demonstration of loyalty and trustworthiness, I can do better than killing that worthless lump you call a brother–anyone can do that. It so happens that, in my possession, is something you want more than almost anything in this world, at least that's what I've been led to believe. I may be willing to give it to you, but I would expect something beyond your gratitude for this gift."

With a menacing look, Andrew growled, "You're playing games with me."

Muir sensed the tide shifting and knew he was about to gain the upper hand. That in itself would probably make Andrew angry, yet a surge of confidence was building and Muir was determined to play it out. "I assure you, *Andrew*," he experimented, "I'm not playing games. I'm telling you plainly, I have something you want, and I want something in return."

"And what is it you want, pray tell?"

"I want the Indies–that part of the business."

Andrew asked coolly, "The Indies?"

"What I offer is well worth the Indies and, once I deliver on my end of the bargain, I will still be loyal and trustworthy. And doesn't that get us right back where we started? Except, that is that you have to find someone else to tend to your brother."

Andrew felt a splinter of grudging respect for Muir. In his request for the Indies, Muir had asked for a lucrative piece of the business. The question was whether that part of the business was worth what Muir had to trade. How could it be? Yet, if the trade was good enough, then Andrew would just tell Thomas Gray to take care of Struan, and he might come out farther ahead than he'd reckoned even a few minutes ago. He just couldn't imagine what this man could possibly have that he'd want. But Andrew, a gambling man by nature, conceded, "All right, I'm willing to listen. If what you have to offer me is worthwhile, I'll give you the Indies and find someone else to rid me of my pesky, careless brother."

Muir wondered briefly what Elizabeth would think. The circumstances weren't exactly what they'd envisioned but, even so, Muir thought they could both get what they truly wanted...to be rid of Andrew and Fia. "I'll have to take you there," Muir began, but Andrew balked.

"No," he insisted, "you will tell me now."

A fox-like grin split Muir's face as he announced, "I have Fia Graham."

Shock drained the blood from Andrew's face–anticipation brought it surging back. Barely could he string the words together, "You...*you* have Fia Graham?"

Muir congratulated himself on his obvious coup. "So," he said quietly, "it's true."

"What's true," Andrew licked his lips, "that I want that harlot in my grasp?"

"More that anything..." Muir prompted.

"Oh, aye," Andrew conceded, eyes blazing, voice hissing, "it is true."

Muir was more than surprised by Andrew's passion as well as by his unguarded comments. It was clear that Fia was an enormous weakness for Andrew–the only weakness Muir had glimpsed. He now understood clearly why Elizabeth hated Fia and made him wish he'd bartered for more with his prize. His musing ceased abruptly when he realized that he was the object of Andrew's pointed glower. "What is it?" he asked.

"How did you know about Fia Graham?"

"Your lady-love and I discovered that we are each cousin to Fia and that neither of us bear her any great affection. The rest fell into place."

"By that you mean?" Andrew prodded.

"Fia and her husband–" The jerk of Andrew's head prompted a hasty explanation from Muir. "She's married to a meddlesome bastard. Anyway, they live with my mother, Fia's aunt. I arranged to lure Fia away and she is now in my safekeeping." Muir could see Andrew's mind racing and watched a series of emotions flick across the man's countenance. At length, Muir chuckled. "Don't fret, Andrew. She may not be a virgin anymore, but experience should make her that much better able to satisfy your needs."

"You forget yourself!" Andrew growled and drummed his fist on the table before him. "Where are you keeping her?"

"Have I earned the Indies?" Muir asked.

"If you waste no more of my time you have. Perhaps more."

"I'll take you there."

Andrew, who chaffed at being led anywhere, had no choice but to go along. "All right. First though, we must pay a visit to Struan and Thomas. Come with me." Andrew snatched up his cloak and tricorne, plotting quickly his next move.

Muir exhaled his relief. When he dealt with Andrew and Fia, Elizabeth would be far away. He did not have to worry about her. His hand touched his belt just where his dirk rested. Concealed by his coat was his pistol. He hoped it would be enough.

Odhar disappeared down the lane and Kate whirled to Alayne and Simon. "I...how did this happen?" Before one of them could respond, she wailed, "This is my fault...my punishment for disowning my son this very morning."

"You what?" they gaped.

Kate paced the stable yard wringing her hands. "Oh, why didn't I just come here this morning? Dear God, what will happen now?" Kate retreated into silence then, and Alayne urged her inside where she collapsed onto a chair by the workroom hearth. Immediately, Arthur came to rest his furry black muzzle across the older woman's thigh, seeking solace for having been left behind. Kate's hand methodically stroked the hound's head.

Simon and Alayne retreated to the stairway landing. There was nothing they could do for Kate at this moment.

"Thank God Halbert went with Fia," Alayne said. "Though knowing of Elizabeth and Andrew's involvement, I fear Halbert is in danger as well."

Tightening his grip on her fingers, Simon urged, "You won't be good at this, but please try not to fret. It won't help and you need to be thinking clearly to deal with Kate after I leave." To her startled look, he gently stated, "I have to meet Drummond. The landing is tonight and I'm to lead him there. I know it's going to be hard on you, my love, waiting."

"Waiting for you, waiting for Martin and Fia, waiting for Kate to come around. Aye," she agreed, "it'll be difficult. But no one's task is easy this day. Why did I let her go, Simon," she lamented, "even with Halbert to accompany her?"

He raised her palm to his lips and kissed it. "You couldn't have stopped Fia and you know it."

Abjectly, she shrugged.

Simon stared across the room at Kate. "I feel sorry for her. Imagine feeling you have no choice but to disown your only child."

Nodding, Alayne added, "And then to have one you love like a child snatched almost from under your roof. She'll need looking after. That's my responsibility today."

"That, and to wait." Simon grimly repeated.

"Now what am I going to do?" Elizabeth pondered. Perched on the back of the largest horse she'd ever sat, she was galloping down the road at break-neck speed, an enraged and desperate Martin Ross holding her fast in place. Elizabeth had never expected to see Martin again; she didn't *want* to see him, or his pain. Elizabeth actually liked the man despite his blind and unfathomable attachment to her cousin. If her life depended on it, Elizabeth would never understand how such a dull woman inspired such devotion and emotion. But she'd seen her cousin inspire emotion–at least lust–in Andrew, as well. Explain it? Elizabeth couldn't. This wasn't about Martin though, oddly enough not even about Fia. This was about getting even with Andrew–nothing more, nothing less.

Still, her present predicament was a problem she'd not reckoned on. How Muir had managed to dupe Fia into leaving the shop with Martin in town she couldn't guess. She had no actual role in this whole affair but to wait for Muir to tell her it was all over. Perhaps if she had, she wouldn't have had time to let her curiosity get the better of her. Why, oh why had she decided to go to the millinery just to get a look at the woman Muir rejected? Stupidity, she thought, colossal, careless, unforgivable blundering.

But now she had to save herself. If she refused to cooperate, she didn't truly believe Martin would hurt her more than he already had when he grabbed her arm and tossed her onto the saddle. She had to admit though that people changed when cornered; she knew that first-hand. The doctor may have dedicated himself to healing people, but she sensed something feral in his depths and found herself pondering the lengths to which he'd go to retrieve his wife. For a long moment, Elizabeth closed her eyes and concentrated. His body was so taut she could feel it hum like a plucked bow string. She chanced a look at his bearded face and involuntarily shuddered at its fierce glower. His focus was completely on his task; he'd not spoken, and she didn't exist until he needed her.

An unexpected stab of jealousy rocked her causing Martin to tighten his grip. "You'll not jump and break your neck before I find Fia," he declared.

"I wasn't going to jump," she retorted, stung.

"Then what?" he grilled.

"Why doesn't Andrew love me like you do that simpering cousin of mine?" she shot back without thinking.

Martin was stunned by her revelation, but now that Elizabeth had broken the silence, her long-held resentment tumbled forth. "Andrew always put his needs first."

"What do you mean?" Martin interjected.

"You call yourself a doctor," she snarled. "Andrew killed my bairn. It was the wine; he put something in my wine."

Astounded, Martin simply demanded, "What's this got to do with Fia?"

"Since Andrew first laid eyes on her, he's wanted her. He denied me what I wanted most, my son. I will deny him what he wants most–your wife!"

Martin pulled fiercely on the reins, bringing Odhar to a stop. "What are you talking about?" he panicked, grasping her chin and jerking her face to his. "You just told me that he killed your son. You speak as though this kidnapping was your idea."

Elizabeth's mouth clamped shut, as she realized belatedly, she'd said too much. "No...no one is going to kill Fia," she offered, shakily, ignoring the comment about her role in Fia's disappearance.

Martin growled, "I don't believe you," to which Elizabeth had no response. He thrust her face from his and kicked Odhar forward again, his mind frantically racing in front of his speeding mount.

Grudgingly, Elizabeth found herself feeling sorry for Martin. While she didn't understand his love for Fia, it was obviously genuine and he would suffer greatly if harm were to come to her.

While harming Fia gave Elizabeth no pause, hurting Martin, she surprised herself to realize, was less palatable. He had helped her through her worst loss with more compassion than she'd ever known. Still, he was not her problem she reminded herself.

As the two men entered the tavern, Thomas Gray noted a fevered gleam in Andrew's eyes that he'd never seen. He tensed, unsure what was happening. The smug look on Muir's face told him to expect trouble.

With a jerk of his head, Andrew asked, "Is he upstairs?"

"He is," Thomas nodded. "What's afoot here?" he added.

"A change of plan," came Andrew's reply. "Let's pay a visit to my brother." And he took the steps two at a time, the others hurrying to keep up.

Thomas' qualms deepened; it was not like Andrew to keep things from him.

Outside the room containing the unwary Struan, Andrew stopped and motioned to Muir. "I want a word with Thomas. You go in and keep my brother busy a moment; don't mention me."

Muir chaffed at his dismissal, but did as he was told. As the door was closing behind him, the men in the hall heard Struan snivel, "You again? I'm tired of you. What is it you want now?"

When the door latched shut, Gray turned to his employer and demanded in a low voice, "What in Hell is going on here?"

Taking the grizzled man by the arm, Andrew moved them several steps away. "Something's come up that I can't ignore, Thomas."

"Talk sense, man," Thomas urged.

"Matheson has found Fia Graham."

Gray's eyes bulged wide. "Fia Graham?"

"Aye. After I talk to Struan, I'm going after her."

"Andrew, I know she's important to you but, really, this is not the time."

"Since when do you dictate to me?" Andrew demanded, glowering.

Swallowing hard, Gray responded, "I'm not dictating to you. I'm trying to remind you that there is a great deal at stake tonight. Vengeance on Fia Graham can wait."

"You are perfectly capable of handling tonight, are you not?" Andrew challenged.

Thomas knew he was trapped. "Aye."

"Fine. There will be a change though."

Once again, Thomas was on guard. "What kind of change?"

"You'll have to do without Matheson, he's coming with me."

"Do...do without my *watch*?" sputtered Gray, astonished. "We only have one to begin with."

"Oh, you'll have a watch; Struan will do it."

Now Gray could hide neither his frustration nor his anger. He raised his hands in denial of what he was hearing and spoke sharply, "Do you want to get us all killed? He's never been the watch; he's only been to one landing here. If one thing goes wrong because you've taken Matheson, we could lose everything. Are you going to ruin all we've built over your obsession with this woman?"

Past the ability to recognize the truth in Gray's words, Andrew seized the man by his throat and thrust him against the wall. "I run this operation; I make the decisions," he threatened, hand tightening little by little. "Don't try to second-guess me."

"That's...what you...pay me...for," Thomas choked, pulling at Andrew's fingers with his own frantic ones. "To...point out things...you may...have missed."

Andrew peered at him narrowly. "You're right, I do," he said, and abruptly released the man. "But not this time."

Thomas sagged against the wall, silent, seething, glad to be drawing breath.

"Struan will stand the watch," Andrew was saying, "and then, no matter how fine a job he does, I want him killed. Do you understand me?"

"Perfectly," Thomas croaked.

"Then come," Andrew commented and led the way back to Struan's room.

"You and Gray treat me like a captive," Struan pouted. He looked up when the opening door squeaked, saw his brother, and turned ashen. "Andrew," he declared and, upon recovery, said, "no one told me you were arriving today."

"No?" Andrew replied. "That was remiss of someone." Pulling a chair up in front of his brother, Andrew sat and asked, "How do you like Inverness?"

His tone seemed so casual, Struan was tempted to relax. However, the presence of the two men hovering a few feet away persuaded him not to be lulled so easily. "I'm ready to go home, if that's what you mean."

Andrew asked, "And what of your education? Your first-hand experience with the business?"

"I was at the last landing," Struan replied sullenly.

"And?"

With a slight hesitation, Struan pronounced, "It was cold and wet and I didn't care for it."

Leaning back and crossing his arms before him, Andrew said, "So I've heard. Perhaps you'd like it better if you had a real job to perform." Abruptly, he stood. "That's why I'm giving you one. Tonight you'll accompany Thomas and *you* will be the watch. It's not quite as cold and damp up on the machair as it is in the cave so it should suit you better."

"But that's Matheson's job," Struan declared.

"Not tonight." Andrew held up his hand to stop further protest. "I'll make you a bargain, Brother. If you don't enjoy yourself tonight, you won't ever have to participate again. Can I be more fair than that?"

"It...sounds fair," Struan replied warily.

"Excellent!" Andrew smiled. "Now, I have someplace to go. Thomas," he said, turning to the grizzled man, "once more, I leave Struan in your capable hands."

He opened the door, turned back to eye his brother's rangy frame. "Goodbye, Struan," he said with an icy smile, and was gone, Muir trailing after him.

At the makeshift barracks where the troops waited, Drummond changed into his uniform and contemplated what MacLaren had recounted–the probable disaster befallen Fia Ross. It both saddened and angered him, and served as a forceful reminder how easily good intentions could be thwarted. When up against a man as crafty and greedy as Andrew Forbes, nothing could be left to chance–nothing taken for granted. He wanted this business with Forbes done.

Drummond took a long moment to pray for Fia's safe deliverance before returning to the anteroom where Simon impatiently paced, and where the soldiers stood ready. He could feel the tension of anticipation crackling the air. He'd shared Simon's tale of Fia's kidnapping with his troops to incite them to greater care, vigilance and enthusiasm for the task ahead. It was almost dusk. "Time to go," he announced.

Fia thought her eyes were open, yet there was only darkness. Musty, dank air was all she could breathe and it added to her befuddlement. She was cold. Her mantle was clasped still at her throat but the folds of it seemed to be behind her. "I'm alive," she deduced and knew it to be true because her head throbbed mercilessly and her jaw ached almost beyond bearing. With a jolt she remembered Martin was hurt, calling for her. Swiftly, she tried to rise only to find herself incapable of doing more than lurching to one side. Fia moaned her wretchedness and was surprised to hear how muffled a sound it was. Only then did she realize she'd been gagged.

Fia felt herself drifting back into oblivion but fought to keep her eyes open and to think. Slowly, as she tested her limbs, Fia discovered her hands were bound behind her; her legs tied at the ankles and knees. A flash of memory rocked her: she'd been yanked from Barley's back, Halbert knocked to the ground and hit with the butt of a musket. Fia cringed recalling she'd heard a shot; she remembered nothing else.

The longer Fia kept her eyes open, the more shapes became clear before them. "So there's some light somewhere," she thought, though there was no hint as to its source.

On her side, she lay heaving frustration and pain. Fia could not survey much of her surroundings, but she felt packed dirt beneath her; beyond her knees appeared to be an earthen crock, tilted on its side. There was the frigid, hard outline of rock against her back. "A cave?" she guessed. If so, she was far back inside it and in a cramped space. While she could not see them, Fia sensed the walls and roof of the cave only inches beyond her. Briefly she thought of the cave on her property, but there was no sound of the sea in the stillness, so she surmised she was somewhere else.

No one she loved knew where she was and the pain in her head along with her trussed body forced Fia to despair of ever being able to escape and look for her husband. "Martin," her mind called out as she tried to swallow a sob of anxiety, "What have I done?"

The cold was bone-numbing, adding to Martin's worries about Fia. The coming storm rendered the sky soft and heavy, looking scarcely able to bear its own weight. He prayed the tempest would hold off until he found his wife.

A blur of movement far to his left caught his eye and fluttered his heart. Martin slowed Odhar. A lump of desperation weighed Martin's soul as he spied Barley, saddle empty, reins flapping, speeding head-long toward his stable mate. Odhar snorted and pawed the ground as Fia's horse came alongside.

"There, Barley, there," Martin soothed, "you're with friends now." He leaned to catch a dangling rein, brought the horse's head close, and rubbed the strong jaw and muzzle. Looking the horse over for injury, Martin saw none. "Where's your mistress, Barley?" he whispered plaintively, his frantic gaze darting across the landscape. In the direction from which Barley had come, Martin glimpsed Kate's horse, grazing on the stunted grass. A tangled mass lay near the horse's muzzle and Martin's belly flopped wildly. Turning Odhar and Barley in that direction, Martin soon drew up along side. With a gruff, "Stay where you are," aimed at Elizabeth, Martin leapt from the saddle and crouched beside the still figure of Simon's friend, Halbert.

"Is...is he all right?" Elizabeth reluctantly asked.

Martin turned a murderous glare on her. "*Does he look all right to you?*" he thundered, rolling Halbert to his back and revealing the right side of his head, a bloody pulp.

Elizabeth gasped her shock, but could not look away from the grizzly scene. She felt vaguely ill and watched in silence as Martin removed the man's coat and wrapped it around the shattered head. He lifted Halbert's limp form and, struggling under the dead weight, managed to lay it across the waiting horse's back.

Elizabeth unwisely demanded, "I'll ride that horse now," pointing at Barley.

"Like Hell you bloody will," Martin growled between clenched teeth. "You ride with me!" He lashed Halbert's body down before tying the reins up to Barley's saddle. With Barley's reins now in hand, Martin remounted.

"Do you m...mean," Elizabeth stuttered in disbelief, "we're taking *him* with us?"

"I've no choice. If I leave him, some animal will find him. He was a friend of Simon's... probably had a family. I can't let the horse wander the countryside with him dead on his back."

"I think—"

"I don't *care* what you think," he broke in roughly, "unless you want to tell me where Fia is and stop wasting time."

Stomach still churning from their gruesome discovery, Elizabeth finally admitted that the plan had gone disastrously awry. She needed to save herself at all costs, for no one would doubt she was part of the scheme to steal Fia away. Whether Fia was at the cairns or not, Muir would kill Andrew after leading him there. And Elizabeth knew, if it came to it, she could easily mollify Muir regarding Fia's "escape" by naming him to take Andrew's place in the business. Muir would have all the money he could want and, if Elizabeth chose, he would have her as well. It was more than a fair trade for handing Fia to her husband.

She looked at Martin's white-knuckled hands on the reins before her and felt a light tremor of fear. If she helped Martin rescue his wife, would he be grateful enough to let her go? In that moment it was clear to her that she had no real choice. In a small voice, Elizabeth said, "Will you take her away so I never have to see her again?"

"What?" Martin asked cautiously.

"Just answer my question," she snapped impatiently.

"You'll never see her or me again."

"And I can go free? I didn't really *do* anything."

"Aye, free. Just give me my wife," he pleaded.

Elizabeth knew she could trust his word. She made her decision, took a deep breath and inquired, "Do you know Culloden?"

The jolt that ran through Martin's body clearly answered her question.

"Head towards Culloden. Fia is not far beyond, on the east side of the River Nairn."

As he wheeled Odhar east, Martin dredged up distant memories of the landscape near Culloden and came to only one conclusion as to where they could hide Fia along the east bank of the Nairn. "She's at Clava? Is that what you're telling me?"

"Aye, that's where–" Elizabeth grabbed a handful of mane as the horse lunged forward, Fia's horse and Halbert's bounding with him.

Muir felt safe only on his own feet. He was never at home on a horse, used one only if he had no choice, and never went faster than a trot. Yet so eager was Andrew to reach Fia that Muir found himself urging his mount to a far faster gait and clinging to its neck like a child. To Muir's chagrin, Andrew kept pace without a sign of discomfort. When he dismounted at the cairns, Muir hoped his legs would support his weight. They'd been riding for some time and he could feel his thighs wobbling from the strain of trying to keep his seat.

"How much farther?" Andrew demanded. "Where are we going?"

"Out past Culloden," Muir responded.

"What, have you got her in that ramshackle croft at the edge of the moor?"

"No. I said *past* Culloden."

"What is there past Culloden?" Andrew pressed.

"You'll see," Muir snapped. He wanted Andrew to shut up; he needed all his wits to remain in the saddle. "Try to be patient, will you?" Stay alert, Muir reminded, focusing his thoughts again on himself. There was no room for error. He and Andrew were fast approaching the river and the weight of what he was about to do almost equaled the weight of the pistol he'd use to do it. While he was not interested in killing Struan for being annoying, killing Andrew would in all likelihood make him wealthy. For that, he could kill the man. And his bonus would be Eliza–

Muir sailed through the air, landing hard on his back, his leg beneath him. Agonizing pain tore through his body. There was a roar in his ears and blackness before his eyes, both of which faded rapidly. Still, the pain was intense. His body jerked to the sound of a shot, and the torment worsened. Belatedly, he saw Andrew over him. "What happened?" Muir gasped.

"I killed your horse," Andrew responded. "It broke its leg when it stepped in a rabbit burrow... broke yours too," he observed, casually as he reloaded.

"W...what?" Muir struggled to sit up and peer at his leg, but fell back and nearly fainted when he saw the distorted limb.

"Be brave, lad," Andrew sneered. "Now, tell me where Fia is."

Muir's eyes bulged in disbelief. "Fia will keep. I need help!"

"The sooner you tell me where she is, the sooner you'll get your help," Andrew said and squatted next to the injured man. "You have no choice, so don't keep me waiting."

His belly wrenching with fear, Muir realized Andrew was right. He had to tell where to find Fia. "Just north of Culloden, cross the river. Keep straight till you see a meager grouping of trees. A number of standing stones are in the grove there along with three burial cairns. My cousin is in the middle one."

"Thank you, Matheson." Andrew stood and began to walk away.

Muir raised on one elbow. "*Wait*," he called in panic. "You promised to help me."

"Did I?" Andrew paused a moment, returned, knelt, grasped the ankle of Muir's broken leg and gave a mighty tug.

Muir screamed in agony.

"Now," came Andrew's gruff voice through the wave of pain," I've helped. If you live, you won't be a cripple." He rose and again walked away.

Muir gathered his strength to ask, "When...when will you be back?"

Andrew stopped and turned to the injured man. "Back? I've no intention of coming back. You're a clever, enterprising fellow. If you make it to Inverness...or anywhere...this experience will be an invaluable lesson. You should thank me." He plucked up the reins of his horse and mounted.

Muir gathered his wits, remembering his pistol, and fumbled to free it as waves of nausea rolled over him. By the time he'd pulled the weapon from his waistband, Andrew was too far away.

Muir was in shock. Truly Andrew Forbes was more evil than anyone knew. With his leg not set and his witless horse dead, Muir's hopes of surviving were few. Damn Andrew Forbes; damn that reckless horse; and damn Fia Graham

He looked around him, desperately searching for anything he could use to splint his leg. He saw nothing but his horse and, in the distance, a lone spindly tree. With no choice, he began the torturous process of dragging himself toward that tree, all the while continuing his cursing diatribe.

Crossing the Nairn had at least not been bad, the river was shallow. A few more minutes, Martin thought, before the cairns came into view. Just a few...there! Blood pounded in his ears and he heard his heart thundering. "Please, God," he prayed, suddenly bringing the horses to a halt. As he slid from the saddle, he was vaguely aware of, and sorry for, their labored breathing. He'd make it up to them later. Loosely, he tied Odhar's and Barley's reins to the trunk of a small tree in the sparse grove near the cairns. He stood surveying the area. It was deathly quiet, only the patter of the beginning rain could be heard above the panting horses. Turning, he pulled Elizabeth off Odhar.

"What are you doing?" she demanded and was rewarded with a hand clamped over her mouth.

"Be quiet," he whispered his command. "I don't know if there's anyone about. I don't want you riding off and stranding us here; you can't reach the stirrup without help. Now, do you know which cairn Fia is in?" He slowly removed his hand.

"I have no...idea," she finished somberly as she look at the grove from ground level for the first time. A sharp chill traversed her spine and every hair on her neck and arms stood up. She'd seen this before. It was the copse of trees, the standing stones and the round cairns of her dream— the dream in which Martin Ross always appeared. Elizabeth shrank back against the steaming flank of the horse.

"What is it?" he asked, instantly alert.

Elizabeth shook her head.

"Elizabeth!" he whispered urgently.

Quietly, she offered, "I've dreamed of this place, nothing more."

Exasperated, Martin said, "I'm going to find Fia." From the slim cover the trees provided, his gaze darted across the glade trying to spot a possible ambush. He couldn't trust Elizabeth. Clearly, the roof of the cairn closest to him had collapsed long ago. Suddenly, fear that Fia wasn't here at all propelled him forward to crouch behind the nearest standing stone. More stones stood at odd angles to the right and left of him, silently guarding the tombs.

"Go on," Elizabeth urged in a hiss, "she's waiting."

Martin glanced at her, fleetingly wondering at her impatience. She flicked her hands signaling him to move, and Martin thrust himself up, sprinted past the cairn to the entrance of the next. For a long moment, he listened at the black opening before softly calling, "Fia? Are you there?"

Nothing stirred.

Again he called, more loudly this time, and was rewarded with a muffled noise, the sound of which barely escaped the impenetrable black of the entrance tunnel. On his hands and knees, Martin scampered into the narrow opening.

Chapter Thirty-Seven

"Cruel," *Fia thought*; cruel that her mind played wicked tricks. So clearly, she'd heard Martin's voice calling her name, but that wasn't possible. He was hurt, and only God, Simon, and that lad knew where he was. A sudden scraping, shuffling noise caused her to tense then a hand was plucking at her skirted thigh. Panicked, Fia recoiled and felt the jabs of the cold rock wall in her back. But there was no escape; the invading hand was joined by another which grasped her arm, touched her shoulder, and her face. She tried to lurch away but fingers yanked at the hair behind her neck until her gag fell loose. Then she was pulled into arms that clutched her in a bone-crushing embrace and near a mouth that sobbed, "Thank God I found you."

Darkness and terror confused her. She couldn't identify the touch or the voice, but Martin's tantalizing scent seeped through Fia's fright and jolted her. Intense relief and joy surged through her and Fia rocked toward him, making a strangled sort of sound. Impossibly, he held her more tightly then retrieved his dirk, reached behind her and carefully cut the rope binding her wrists.

Fia wanted to fling her arms around him and never let go, but they were cold and numb and refused to work.

Martin seemed to understand and began chafing her arms vigorously, forcing her blood to move faster, to help warm her. He talked all the while and she reveled in the sound of his voice. Next, he found and attacked the rope at her knees, cursing the blackness that blinded him. As he severed that rope, he moved down to her ankles and freed her from the final binding.

Fia's mind cleared and she finally croaked, "Where are you hurt?"

He replied in a voice thick with emotion,"They lied to you, Sweetheart. There was no accident." Martin began rubbing her legs, trying to awaken them. "Did they hurt you?"

"I'm not hurt. Oh, Martin, thank God you're safe."

He held her close once more. "But you aren't, my love. I must get you away from here."

Guardedly testing her arms and legs, Fia said, "I'll follow you."

"Aye, but wait at the entrance until I tell you to come out, just in case someone is there." Martin started to move, but Fia stopped him. "Kiss me."

He obliged with a hard, desperate kiss then whispered, "We have to go."

With Fia close behind, Martin made his way back to the cairn's opening and observed the vista spread out before him: stark, silent, wet.

Elizabeth heard the approaching horse and struggled with her next move. It wouldn't do for Muir to come face to face with Martin. Elizabeth hurriedly emerged from the sparse cover of the trees intending to warn him away. The horse she'd heard appeared over a nearby rise and, a moment later, Elizabeth realized that it was Andrew who was astride the horse. By the sudden change in his posture, she guessed he recognized her as well.

Panicked, she hoisted her skirts and swiftly ran back through the copse of trees, keeping her eyes on the cairn ahead. She heard the heavy footfalls of Andrew who'd leapt from his mount and was closing behind her.

The standing stones loomed somber in the gloaming, indifferent to the dread of the black-haired woman who burst into the open glade intent now on giving her warning to Martin Ross. Elizabeth spied him, crouched beside the cairn, just as he'd been in her dream. *"Martin,"* she wailed.

At the terrified sound of Elizabeth's voice, Martin reeled abruptly, saw her, and a man bearing down on her.

Suddenly, her pursuer stopped, extended his arm in her direction, and fired the pistol he held.

"Mar–" Searing pain cut short Elizabeth's warning. She pitched forward to the ground and lay unmoving.

The Borrowed Days

For a moment, the choking smoke from the discharged pistol enshrouded the man's face–a face Martin had never seen, but knew just the same. It could only be Andrew Forbes. And now he leaped over Elizabeth and was coming at a run–for Fia.

"Martin, what was that?" Fia called anxiously as she crawled from the cairn struggling to make her legs hold her.

"Fia, get back," he bellowed, whirling to shield her as Andrew raised his second pistol in their direction and fired it. As it hit, the force threw Martin against the cairn's outer wall. He landed in a crumpled heap at its base.

Fia screamed and dove toward her husband, but was brought up short by Andrew who grabbed her arm and jerked her away. She struggled, clawing, kicking and pounding Andrew. "Let go, let me *go!*" she demanded frantically. And each time she thought she would touch Martin, Fia was pulled farther from him.

"No, no, *Mistress Ross,*" Andrew hissed. "Your husband doesn't need your help anymore."

His words were like a fist in her face; blotches of light and spots of black danced before her eyes, obscuring Martin from her vision. "No...it isn't *true,*" she denied vehemently. Fia's knees began to buckle, yet rage and despair churned the pit of her stomach and surged new strength into her. Wheeling, Fia dug her nails into Andrew's face with such force, he momentarily staggered, yelping from the sharp sting.

With a grip of steel, Andrew's hands closed around her wrists, immobilizing her attack. "Enough of this," he ordered and began dragging her away, an arduous task as she fought and pulled against him. Tiring of it quickly, Andrew tugged with such force Fia stumbled, landing on her face.

Andrew cursed and, yanking her upright, heard her horrified gasp, "Elizabeth?" for it was Elizabeth whom she'd fallen over. Fia gaped in disbelief at the scarlet stain spreading over her cousin's back; Elizabeth was the only person she'd thought safe from Andrew. "*You killed her.*"

"It seems so. Come," he commanded.

"*Martin!*" she screamed and battled anew, sheer terror added now to her despair and hatred. Tiring of her hysterics, Andrew slapped Fia so hard she fell again, incoherent. He hoisted her over his shoulder where, for the time being, he didn't have to look at her tear, blood and dirt-stained face. Easily, Andrew lifted her onto the saddle and swung up behind her. Pulling the reins sharply to the right, Andrew kicked his horse back toward Culloden.

On Martin's forehead, Fia's hand was cool. A steady throbbing pained his head and, as she washed his face, he could taste blood in his mouth. "F...Fia," Martin uttered with difficulty. "My love?" He was perplexed that she wouldn't answer him; he could still feel her tender touch. Martin's eyelids flicked open in the light of the dying day only to close again as everything came flooding back to him. He had warned Fia, then there had been screams–he knew they were hers. Somehow, he had to find his wife. Because there was still meager light, he guessed Andrew could not be far away. The gentle rain that Martin realized he'd mistaken for Fia's comforting palm, might already have erased any trace of the direction they'd taken. He prayed not.

His shoulder burned fiercely. Slowly, painfully, Martin pulled himself up by bracing his back against the cairn. That cursed cairn. Gingerly, he felt his left shoulder beneath his greatcoat and drew his hand away, warm and sticky with blood. He been shot from behind and, with any luck, it came through clean. Hitting his head on the cairn had dazed him–and probably saved his life. If Andrew hadn't thought him dead, he surely would have finished the job.

Martin gingerly pulled his arm from his greatcoat, untied the stock from around his neck, tossed one end over his shoulder, pulled it under his arm to meet the other end and knotted it tightly. He hoped the bleeding would stop and slipped his arm back through the sleeve of the coat.

Pushing himself from the cairn, Martin moved unsteadily toward Odhar, who was still tied to a tree next to Barley and the horse bearing Halbert's body. And why not? Andrew had no fear of the dead following him. As he reached Elizabeth, Martin knelt and checked, with no hope, for a pulse. "Thank you for trying to warn me," he murmured. With no backward glance, Martin searched the ground near the horses for any signs of the direction Andrew had taken. He spotted the barest impression of hooves heading back toward the river. Though Andrew was likely congratulating himself on getting away with murder–literally–Martin knew he'd still try to cover

372

his tracks. He guessed Andrew would head for the river and travel in its shallows before seeking shelter with Fia for the night. The thought made him gag with fear for her. "God," he implored, "keep her safe."

Untying Odhar's reins, Martin leaned a moment against the horse, trying to draw strength from the beast. He loosed Barley's reins as well and, once mounted on Odhar, muttered to Fia's horse, "Sorry, Barley. You'll have to fend for yourself for a bit," and urged Odhar in the direction of the river.

As he looked around the treeless landscape, Simon wondered how the soldiers could ever catch the smugglers. The steadily falling rain at least muffled the noise of the advancing troops and the deepening dark afforded them as much cover as it did to the smugglers. Drummond had a company of men with him; Simon hoped it would be enough.

He pulled his coat close at the neck and was exceedingly happy to have worn an uncocked hat which was the only thing keeping the rain from his eyes. In low tones, he asked Drummond, "They wouldn't postpone a landing for this weather would they?"

Drummond shook his head. "There's almost no wind tonight. If there were, or if the sea were heavy, they might consider it. But, otherwise, it's highly unlikely. A landing takes a great deal of planning and coordination as well as audacity."

Simon nodded. "How can I help once we arrive?"

"What I anticipate is taking care of the watch first. My informer tells me there's only one which is unusual. If the watch lives, I want you to guard him." Drummond gave Simon a look so stern he could feel it penetrate the gloom. "Under no circumstance do I want you on the beach where you could be mistaken for a trader."

Though disappointment plucked at him, Simon knew Drummond was right. He was not a soldier and could easily hamper the operation or get hurt in the process. Nor would Alayne forgive him if he ended up injured–or dead. Her enticing face appeared before him forcefully reminding him that he didn't want to take risks he didn't have to. "You have my word, Sir," he pledged, then asked, "What will happen to the ship?"

"A cruiser is in the firth, on its way to this area as we speak. What becomes of the ship depends on how well the cruiser and its crew perform."

They trudged on for what seemed endless miles until Drummond raised his hand and halted the march. On their walk, eyes had become accustomed to the dark. Now, any anomaly in the landscape stood out. But what Drummond was looking at was off shore. Two tiny lights betrayed the presence of the ship, and signaled a change in approach and direction for the soldiers.

The excise man, who was to have taken up watch himself for illicit activity, had not appeared. Drummond grumbled a curse then issued a second signal. The company separated; half veered northeast toward the sea, the rest, including Simon, moved forward with the Lieutenant, parallel to the shoreline. When he stopped them again, they were just below the crest of a hill. Simon's heart quickened as he saw on the top of a rise, a lone figure.

Silently, the soldiers waited while Drummond and his second-in-command, Lamont, methodically searched the dimness for signs of any other watch–the informer could have been mistaken. When satisfied there was no other, at least not in sight, Lamont took two men and moved ahead of the rest, low to the ground and stealthy.

It took an astonishingly short time for them to reach their target, subdue him and signal the rest to advance.

When they arrived, they found the watch seated in the wet heath, bound and gagged. The others crouched around him, only Simon stood, in case any smuggler were to look that way, his silhouette being the only one without a military guise.

"This is a surprise," chuckled Drummond quietly. "Struan Forbes."

Simon's attention jerked downward for a look at the now upturned face.

"Mr. Forbes," Drummond was whispering, "you are under arrest in the name of His Majesty, King George III. You will wait here with two men to guard you until we have finished our business on the strand below." He rose, gestured to his rawest recruit to remain behind with Simon.

As the troops moved away, Simon eyed Struan. What a pitiful excuse for a man: slouched, soaked and scared. Aye, he could see the fright in the man's limpid eyes. Then he could see recognition. Forbes knew Simon from their encounter at the tavern, but Simon didn't know what Struan was thinking, nor did he care.

An eternity passed before the crack of musket fire erupted from below the cliff. Simon's attention was riveted in the direction of the sound. He could see nothing and exchanged worried glances with the young recruit over Struan's head as sporadic gunfire and the yells and screams of the desperate and wounded reached their ears.

From the darkness, they saw perhaps ten figures, including one pack horse with its rope sling flapping wildly against its sides, scurrying away into the obscuring rain. The waiting, Simon found hard to bear. He began to pace a bit and nearly fell over Struan in the process. From behind Struan's gag, Simon heard whimpering.

"Contemptible," was all Simon said. And then four men were approaching, three soldiers with their weapons trained on one stocky fellow of medium height, gray hair reflecting what little light there was.

"Andrew Forbes was not there," Drummond conceded. "Damn bad luck."

"What of your men?" Simon began. "What hap–" and stopped, realizing that if Andrew wasn't where he was expected to be, it likely meant he was with Fia. Unable to speak, Simon gulped air, trying to calm his spiraling dread. He and Drummond exchanged sour looks of disappointment then Simon shook his head. "Your men?"

"Lost two, five wounded," Drummond admitted bitterly.

Simon eyed the prisoner thoughtfully. "I've seen him down at the quay," he remarked, nodding at the stocky man.

"This is Thomas Gray. I believe he's Andrew's right hand man. "He won't tell us where Forbes is," Drummond stated.

Gray spat his contempt, landing the gob in the officer's face.

Drummond returned the gesture then calmly wiped his own face clean. "Gag and bind him. He may not talk, but he'll hang for killing two of my men."

As a soldier stepped forward to follow Drummond's orders, Thomas Gray lurched to one side, not only throwing one of his escorts off balance, but grabbing the man's dirk from its sheath.

"Watch out...*Seize him!*"

But in a flash, Gray lunged for Struan, jerked up his chin and drew the dirk across the man's throat with such ferocity, he cut nearly mid-way through his neck.

Blood spurted onto the young soldier standing guard with Simon, and it rapidly spread its stain down Struan's chest. Simon had a moment to see Struan's look of surprise before the vacancy of death filled his eyes. Only then did he realize that Drummond was struggling to disarm and subdue Gray.

It was over quickly. Gray was face down on the ground, one of Drummond's knees on his back, the other foot across the wrist of the hand that still clutched the bloody dirk.

When Gray was safely bound, Simon leaned toward him and asked, "Why did you kill Struan?"

To the surprise of all, Gray spoke. "He deserved it; and it's as easy to hang for killing three as it is for two. I've nothing to lose."

"Then tell us where Andrew Forbes is," Drummond pressed.

The hatred in Gray's eyes burned through the soggy murk. "I would if I knew where he was. He left that lump," he jerked his head in Struan's direction, "to watch for *you*. He never should have done it: he betrayed us all."

Gray would say no more. He had nothing to lose, nor had he anything to gain by talking, and he determined to say nothing else.

Struan's lifeless body lay on the heath and Simon turned away fretting over how they would ever find Forbes now. He noticed activity in the darkness, troops moving around securing prisoners and the smuggled goods, but was uninterested in the process. So he wandered toward the shore and stood looking down at the strip of sand, eerily pale, smudged with casks, crates, people and horses. The black water made hungry inroads on the strand. It made him restless and fed his disappointment that the raid, successful though it had been, had failed to capture Andrew. Surely he would lay low for some time to come when word of this night reached him. They might never have another opportunity as good as tonight's to put an end to Andrew Forbes.

Suddenly, Simon felt the sting of sleet on his cheeks and smelled the salt from the spray carried on the rising wind. It woke him from his glum musings and made him shiver. He was seized by the need to feel Alayne filling his arms: warm, sweet, molding her body to his. Turning on his heel, Simon strode back to Drummond, intent on doing what he could to hurry the process that would hasten his return to his love.

Along the riverbank, Martin fought rising despair and a persistent throbbing in his shoulder, concentrating instead on finding some way to track his wife and her kidnapper. He suddenly reined in Odhar and cocked his head, listening to the night. The wind was all he heard but, to Martin, it had an oddly human timbre to its sighing. A shiver coursed his spine and the urge to cross the river right where he stood seized him–almost as if he'd done it before. "Why?" his logic questioned. The gust spoke to him again, this time calling his name. Tears of gratitude shimmered in his eyes; Martin knew who his guide was, who would accompany him to Culloden just as he had fourteen years earlier.

Turning Odhar, Martin urged him across the river and, when they reached the other side, into a run. The animal sensed the return of confidence in his master and flew over the soggy, uneven ground.

When Fia roused, it was nearly dark; she was on a horse cantering rhythmically. Her husband was dead. "Martin," Fia sobbed.

Behind her, Andrew heard her lament and immediately his lips were at her ear, vilely promising, "You'll soon forget any man but me ever touched you."

Repulsion snapped Fia's stupor and unleashed a howl of rage that chilled even Andrew's blood. Thrusting her head back, Fia hit her captor full in the face, breaking his nose.

A screech erupted from Andrew, who instinctively jerked back hard on the reins. The sudden force of it brought the horse up so fast it lost its footing on the wet turf.

Without thinking, Fia flung herself from the toppling steed. She landed hard, but rolled to safety, scratched and bruised and tangled in her mantle. The horse landed with a crash; Andrew with a loud thud and another cry of pain.

Swiftly, Fia picked herself up. Unsure whether Andrew had been thrown clear or been injured, she had no intention of waiting to find out. Lunging to catch the horse's reins, the beast, standing again and thoroughly spooked, shied at the sudden movement and bolted. "*No!*" Fia begged, but the horse was quickly swallowed up by the murky light.

Fia had to get back to Martin...but where was he? Which direction? Once more, as at the beginning of the borrowed days, Fia was stranded with Andrew Forbes; the thought nearly paralyzed her. The last time, she'd discovered Martin–but what awaited her now? Without him, it mattered little what became of her. But Andrew mattered. She vowed he would not escape punishment for murdering her husband.

Nearby, Andrew growled a curse. The sound willed Fia to move her feet. The deepening dark threatened every step she took, yet Fia embraced the unknown and fled. Brush snagged her mantle and skirts, scratched her hands and arms, but didn't slow her. Fia could only run; she could not think...*refused* to think lest it weaken her body or her resolve. A low-growing gorse loomed suddenly in her path and thorns grabbed Fia's petticoats, tangling her legs. Trying to wrench free, she sprawled to the ground.

Fia heard the crunch of grasses and heather under Andrew's feet and realized that he could hear when she moved as well. Her heart leaped to her throat–there was nothing now but silence as Andrew had stopped. When he spoke, Fia jumped–he was too close.

"You won't escape me...no one does. You know that, Fia."

Grabbing her skirts, she stood and plunged ahead. The earth rose suddenly and Fia tumbled again, landing on her belly, losing her breath.

Dazed and gulping air, Fia rolled to her side and winced as she felt a rock under her hip. It took a long moment before she realized it wasn't a rock at all, but the cloth-wrapped scissors Alayne insisted she take. Trembling, Fia fished out the shears, unwrapped and gripped them tightly. Slithering down the small hillock that had tripped her, she waited...but not for long.

The wind seemed to breathe life into the night, and Fia jerked sharply around, sensing movement on all sides, but seeing nothing. Then, from a distance, came the clang of metal, the shouts and moans of many men.

Heart pounding, Fia squeezed shut her eyes, and nearly cried out as the skirl of bagpipes floated to her. She knew exactly where she was–Culloden! And the Jacobite army was once more on the field of battle. Did Andrew hear it, she fleetingly wondered...know what it was? Did it strike fear in him or cause confusion? Fia prayed it did. She welcomed the sounds, oddly comforted by the knowledge that Martin's grandfather must be near. "Help me, Hugh," she murmured, careless in her relief.

In an instant, Andrew was on her, landing heavily, stunning her and pinning her arms.

"At last," he snarled, "under me where you belong." His mouth crushed hers; his injured nose dripping blood.

Fia twisted her head violently to the side, breaking his loathsome hold on her lips. Kicking and thrashing about–desperate to loosen his grip, Fia couldn't budge him. In panicked frenzy, she screamed, "*Hugh!*"

Andrew shifted his weight, grinding her body into the heath beneath his own. "So fickle," he hissed. "Wanting another and your husband not cold yet? I'm happy to oblige." Abruptly, he seized her face, intent on stilling her voice, but not her struggles, which excited him.

Her hands suddenly free, Fia swung her right arm up as far as she could and plunged the shears into his back.

Andrew howled, rising to his knees, frantically swiping at his back to locate the weapon.

Fia shoved him hard, toppling him and freeing her legs in the process. She scurried to her feet.

Now, there was movement all around her and Fia hoped to lose herself in it. Yet when she ran forward the specters retreated, staying beyond reach. Befuddled, Fia hesitated. In the next second, a monstrous yank on her skirt buckled her knees. With a bone-jolting thud, Fia sat. She jerked round to face Andrew.

He clawed at her legs, dragging himself up her body.

Fia saw that the scissors were gone, replaced by a wet, black stain. Frenziedly feeling around for the shears, her fingers skittered over, then gripped a rock she could just get her fingers around. With all her might, Fia brought the rock down hard on the seeping wound.

In the bedlam of the battle raging around them, Andrew's wail was lost–almost.

Martin heard it pierce the din and blindly turned Odhar toward the sound. The noise of struggle reached Martin and, disoriented by the clamor, he reined in his mount and shuddered at the familiarity of the racket.

Martin slid from Odhar's saddle and clutched his dirk, gritting his teeth against a stabbing pain radiating from his wound. "Where is she, Hugh?" he beseeched.

A sudden stirring of mist ahead to his left revealed the answer and Martin gathered his strength, bounding forward, every ounce of him strung tight, alert. The phantoms slid aside creating a path that he followed without hesitation. Martin heard a woman's voice in the cacophony around him. He drew a breath to call to her, but it stuck in his throat. No. Andrew Forbes would get no warning from him. If the man panicked, Fia might die. There they were! Martin saw in the dim, his wife's struggle to separate herself from Forbes.

A lucky twist of her body landed Fia's knee in Andrew's rib cage and, at last, she wrested herself from his grasp, leapt to her feet and stopped dead in her tracks. It wasn't the ghost of Hugh approaching through the icy shroud, but that of her husband. It was Martin who would protect her this time, not his grandfather after all. Fia's eyes blurred with tears of pain and joy at the spectral sight. The tears spilled, streaking the grime on her face and mingling with the rain.

A quick movement and labored grunt brought Andrew's hands around Fia's throat. Her fingers frantically clawed at his.

"You...killed me," Andrew rasped over an odd gurgling in his throat. Blood-flecked spittle showered Fia; his fingers tightened.

Martin sprinted toward them. "*Forbes! Let her go!*" he howled. Thrusting his good arm around his enemy's neck, Martin drove his dirk up into Andrew's back, just below the ribs, with such force that only the hilt was visible. The jolt to Martin's wound momentarily blacked his vision.

Andrew convulsed, losing his strangle-hold on Fia.

Grasping Andrew's shoulder, Martin spun him so they were face to face. "My wife won't be the last thing you see in this life."

A final time, Andrew tried to speak...but the breath was his last.

Martin let Forbes' body fall away from his grasp, then faced his wife, his guise reflecting the pain and emotion sweeping through him. It was a feral and intensely stirring visage and Fia's blood pounded.

"Please don't be a ghost," she implored, and stretched her fingers toward him.

Martin clutched them in his right hand and stifled her cry of elation against his mouth. They seized each other, unable to get close enough, unable to kiss hard enough, and sobbed joyously their relief in between attempts.

Suddenly, Fia pulled away, her gaze sweeping him in alarm. "Martin, where are you shot? How–" She abruptly stopped upon seeing the edge of the bandage, soaked dark with blood, through his open greatcoat,. Urgently, Fia demanded, "Tell me how to help." Already, she was fishing under her petticoats to rip a large chunk of linen from her shift.

Martin whistled sharply and Odhar was soon beside them. "Will you get my medicines," he pointed to the saddlebags, "and the whiskey?"

Fia quickly found both and held open the pouch containing small jars and smaller pouches of herbs.

Martin easily found an ointment and handed it to her. "This is yarrow and will help stop the bleeding. The whiskey will clean the wound. But first," he directed, "drink some yourself. It'll help warm you."

Without question, Fia gulped a small amount and handed him the skin. "You, too."

Martin obeyed then dropped his coat to the ground and sat on it. "Take these bandages off and pour the whiskey...both sides. After that, apply the ointment."

Fia cringed at his reaction to the whiskey on his open wounds; he rocked violently forward with a groan that, if he'd unclenched his teeth, might have been a scream. But she quickly blotted the wound and spread the yarrow ointment as he'd directed.

While she was doing that, Martin recovered his composure and pointed to the strips from her shift. "Can you split that to make a pad for each side then tie it?"

Fia wadded the cloth, packed the front and back of his wound, and tied them in place with another strip of linen. "You need to rest," she observed, wiping bloody hands on her skirt.

"Aye, but not here," Martin shook his head and she helped him rise. "I'm sorry I won't be much help to get you on to Odhar's back, lass."

"I'll manage," she replied, and helped him back into his greatcoat; he would need it to keep him warm. While she repacked the saddlebags, Martin bent over Andrew's body and retrieved his dirk, wiping the blade clean on the wet heath before sheathing it.

Fia looked around and saw a fair size rock peeking above the heath about fifteen paces away. She led Odhar over to it but it was still a struggle for Martin to mount, even with Fia's help. She got the toe of her shoe into Odhar's stirrup and pulled herself into the saddle in front of Martin before swinging her right leg over the horse's neck. She heard Martin's labored breathing and worriedly asked, "Will you be all right?"

"I think so if we got the bleeding stopped," he replied bluntly.

"Hold to me," she insisted and Martin responded by crossing his good arm around her, holding her fast. Fia counseled, "There's a croft nearby, I'm certain of it. I can take better care of you there."

"I remember the croft, but where is it?" Martin pondered and, in response to his question, a new path began to take shape before him as the icy rain abruptly blew past them and the warrior ghosts faded with its passing.

Fia didn't question, but guided Odhar in the direction of the parting mist. She cast a long, grateful look skyward and silently thanked God for Martin's life and for her own. And for Hugh Stewart and the others who'd given their lives at Culloden and helped them this night, Fia asked God to grant them peace.

Chapter Thirty-Eight

Fia stood shivering on the quay, her hand clutched tightly in Martin's, Arthur sitting at her feet. The March wind was erratic buffeting them from all directions, making it hard to stand still and harder still to keep warm. She raised her eyes to the furled sails of the ship that would carry their dearest friends to America.

Martin lifted her hand to his cheek and nuzzled it as he had many times since the night Andrew Forbes died. It was a small gesture, yet important to them both–an unspoken reassurance that they were alive and together and she, no longer the target of ruthless people. So many times the odds had been against them, even after they'd left Andrew behind at Culloden.

By the time they'd reached the croft, Martin leaned heavily on Fia and that frightened her. She had no way of knowing what was happening of how much blood he'd lost. After Fia tied up Odhar, Martin slid from the saddle and, with her help, entered the deserted building.

He sat, propped against the wall near the hearth. Thin light from a half moon and a sprinkling of stars now visible, turned Fia into a ragged shadow searching for something with which to build a fire.

At length she declared, "There are a few peat bricks still and a bit of kindling...but nothing to light it."

"There's a tinder box in Odhar's saddlebags."

With relief, Fia hurried outside and returned with the saddlebags as well as the blanket she'd pulled from Odhar's back after unsaddling him. She was so grateful for the stone wall outside the croft without which she could never have reached high enough to remove the saddle. She fished out the flask and gave it to Martin before draping the blanket over his legs.

Gratefully, he drank before handing the flask back. "Here. You have to still be cold."

"Maybe after I get the fire going," she replied. "I'm really not cold; moving around is keeping me warm." There wasn't much left in the skin and Fia wanted to save what there was in case Martin needed it.

In short order, a meager flame was licking round the peat bricks. The fire wouldn't last long enough, she feared, but every bit of light and warmth helped. "I'll step out and see if there's more kindling in the byre."

"We should check the bleeding, first," Martin said.

Fia eased the greatcoat from his shoulder and removed the existing bandage. She tore part of his shirt to further expose his shoulder.

"You'll need more bandages," said Martin, offering the obvious.

What was left of her shift came off in Fia's hand and she untied the embroidered pocket beneath her gown.

Martin's eyes followed her every move and he teased softly, "You'll be naked in a moment and me in no shape to press the advantage."

His little joke brought a lump to her throat which Fia cleared to declare, "When this is behind us, I expect you to make it up to me many times over." She kissed him, lips lingering a long moment against his.

"I don't see any fresh blood." she told him. "That's a good sign, aye?"

"It is, lass," he responded.

Her need to help him pushed her past thoughts of Andrew's death when she pulled Martin's dirk from its sheath and cut her pocket in half to replace the padding she had used at Culloden. Fia used the last strip from her shift to tie them in place and helped him lie down with the blanket beneath him. The dirt floor was cold.

"I'll just lie quietly," he said, as much for his own benefit as for hers. Then he slowly turned

378

his head in the dim, black-gold light of the peat fire and stared at her, aghast. "God's blood, Fia. I've not even asked if you're all right; not since Clava."

"I'm fine," she hastened to assure. "Scratches and bruises, nothing more."

Fia saw tears in his eyes. "Thank God...thank God," he muttered then begged, "Forgive me."

"For what?" she asked, confused. "There's nothing to forgive."

"There is," he disagreed, grasping her hand. "I broke my promise. I wasn't with you when you needed me most."

She stroked his hair with a blood-caked hand. "Oh, but you are, Martin. I need you most now, and tomorrow, and the day after that. Andrew knew the right bait to lure me from Inverness. For me to face life without you beside me everyday...*that* would be unforgivable. Nothing else."

Martin's tears spilled over and he kissed the palm of her hand. He searched her stained, scratched face. "You're a remarkable woman," he proclaimed.

"I was a terrified woman," she corrected, gripping his fingers, "angry and desperate. I thought he'd taken you from me forever." Fia hesitated then whispered shakily, "I killed him, Martin."

Martin shook his head. "*I* did, Fia," he insisted, not willing to let any thought that she was to blame haunt her.

"But I stabbed him. He *told* me I killed him."

"You know he was evil and you can't believe him. And you know he was alive when I reached him. I stabbed him...and *I* killed him," he repeated.

Silently, Fia studied him. Maybe it was Martin's dirk that was the final blow, but stabbing Andrew with her scissors had played a major part in his death. She was sure it had and could live with that; he had tried to take her husband from her. Yet she guessed Martin was taking the blame to protect her. And she found herself unwilling to rob him of his comfort in doing so. She nodded, and let it go at that. "You sleep now. I'll check the byre and be right back."

He began, "Tomorrow–"

"Will come soon enough," she gently interrupted. "We'll deal with everything when you're rested and stronger." She pulled the edges of his greatcoat together and buttoned it to help keep him warm. "You need to rest now, my love, no argument." He gave her none, falling asleep almost instantly.

Fia stepped outside and took several deep breaths, turned toward the byre and vomited; the fear and anxiety overwhelming her. Her hand on the cold stone of the croft for support, she thought she should now feel relief. But Martin might still be in trouble so there was no reprieve yet.

She moved toward the byre and, kneeling, Fia wiped her hands on the wet grass to rid them of some of the blood before rubbing them against her face where Andrew had spewed drops of his blood.

She could only see a few feet into the dark doorway of the byre. There were a few small pieces of wood she could just make out but, before she picked them up, Fia untied Odhar and led him into the shelter. The horse chuffed at her and dipped his head for her to stroke. The gesture brought forth a stream of tears from Fia that she let flow for a few long moments. "Thank you, Odhar," she placed her forehead against his while she stroked his neck. "I promise you the best rubdown and grooming you've ever had when we get back to Aunt Kate's."

Inside again, she added the sticks to the fire before wrapping her ragged cloak around her and laying down pressed next to Martin's uninjured right side.

Around mid-morning, Martin felt strong enough to rise. He'd slept soundly, unlike Fia who'd watched him half the night, then dozed fitfully until daybreak.

Fia again took advantage of the wall at the croft to help in her saddle Odhar. It made mounting the horse easier for each of them. Deliberately, they set a moderate pace toward the cairns, under a startlingly blue sky, air edged with the cold damp of the previous night. With relative ease, they found Barley and his companion horse with its sad burden, at the river's edge. Fia gathered up the reins, stopping long enough to stroke each horse and utter a few comforting words.

Martin assured, "I'll be alright on Odhar; I won't fall off." So Fia clambered onto Barley's back and they began the trek back to Inverness.

At last the town came into view and Fia said, "I'll take you to Kate's, then locate the Sheriff."

"No, lass," Martin gently disagreed, "the Sheriff first."

Vigorously, Fia protested, "Martin, you're exhausted. You need rest, clean bandages and more medicine."

"All true. Nevertheless, we see the authorities first. I want to leave no doubt as to the truth of what happened on the moor. Also, the Sheriff may still have light enough left to retrieve Elizabeth and Andrew."

Reluctantly, Fia relented and led the way. As they traversed the lanes, she became aware of the stares, pointing and whispering their appearance engendered: torn, bloody, ragged with poor Halbert's body draped across his horse. It was no wonder people were agog.

The stir they caused resulted in word of their arrival reaching the Sheriff before they did. Not only were they met by the Sheriff, but also by Lieutenant Drummond, who was there to request help in searching for Martin and Fia.

"By God," Drummond exuded, rushing forward to grip the bridles, "it's a relief to see you both alive."

"Help Martin," Fia begged. "He's been shot."

Her own dismount was dismal, her legs so numb, they nearly felled her. Fia staggered to clutch the arm of the Sheriff and follow Martin, who was half carried inside by Drummond who immediately set about working on Martin's shoulder. After ordering his deputy to care for Halbert's body, the Sheriff generously provided whiskey, which burned Fia's throat but immediately began to warm her. She spilled out the story as she knew it, holding Martin's good hand all the while. Then Martin filled in the tale's missing pieces.

When they finished, the Sheriff scratched his head and, astonished, remarked, "You are both beyond fortunate to be alive, but you know that. From what I've heard and seen, my guess is that no further inquiry will be needed. And from what the Lieutenant was telling me before you arrived, I feel certain this all happened just as you described it." He drew a deep resigned breath. "And it looks like I have two bodies to retrieve. I'd best get at it; and you'd best get home."

"Sheriff, do you need my help?" Drummond inquired.

"Thank you, no. I think Dr. and Mistress Ross need your assistance far more; and you owe them a debt. After all, they've put an end to your smuggler once and for all."

"They have indeed," Drummond agreed, "and I have some news to share with them about Struan Forbes." He turned to the puzzled looks of Martin and Fia. "When you're ready to go, I'll see you to Mistress Matheson's. Simon and Alayne are with her. It's a gross understatement to say they'll be relieved and thrilled to see you."

Alayne flew out Kate's doorway crying, "*Fia! Martin!*," before the riders could dismount.

Simon and Kate were close behind her and their tearful reunion in the lane caused yet more passersby to gape and wonder what had befallen the bedraggled, bloodied riders.

"I'll take care of the horses," Lieutenant Drummond offered.

Fia protested, "You've done so much already, Charles, it isn't necessary. Come inside instead."

But Drummond politely declined. "I know what happened to you and Martin. I'll leave it to Simon to tell you details of the landing and Struan's death. These steeds have been through their own ordeals and need tending. You need your family."

Martin stood beside Fia and extended a hand to the soldier. "We can't thank you enough for your kindnesses."

Drummond grasped Martin's hand. "Don't forget, you've done me and countless others a great service as well. I'm just so pleased at the outcome for all of us."

Fia reached up and kissed his cheek. "You are a true friend."

The others offered their thanks as well before Drummond walked the horses toward the stable. Kate then hustled the group inside to share their stories, have a bite to eat, rest, and savor their good fortune.

After the bodies of Elizabeth and Andrew had been retrieved, Lieutenant Drummond turned over those of the Forbes brothers to the excise man. Accompanied by a blistering scolding for not having been on duty the night of the landing, Drummond told the man, "You deal with this lot; at least you can do that!" He volunteered himself to accompany Elizabeth's body to her father's home in Glasgow, a generous offer Fia and Martin gratefully accepted. Fia had no intention of seeing her uncle. If he were to turn to her for comfort, she didn't think she could give it. Yet Fia vowed to do nothing to cause him more grief than he would have to bear at losing his only child. For Martin's part, despite the fact that Elizabeth had sounded the warning of Andrew's arrival, she had plotted to rob Martin of his wife. He felt pity for the woman, but could never forgive her.

The loss of Halbert grieved everyone. None of them could have guessed the price he would pay for his willingness to help someone in need. And though only Simon had really known him, Halbert's sacrifice had forever given him a place in their hearts and prayers. Halbert had no family of his own, but Simon, Alayne, Martin, Fia and Kate buried him with great honor, and all mourned him as if he had been their kin.

Kate had her own loss to bear for, once more, Muir had disappeared. No one had seen him since the morning Fia was kidnapped. Kate had stoically resigned herself to the probability that he'd run off when she'd disowned him.

Alayne was dubious and not willing to risk his reappearance and the trouble that would almost certainly follow. She and Simon could not risk staying in Scotland. And that's what had led Martin and Fia to this moment on the quay.

Fia leaned her head against Martin's shoulder, good as new, his wound completely healed in the nearly three months since Andrew shot him. The scar would fade with time–all their scars would.

"My love," Martin murmured, "why don't you step inside for a bit and warm yourself. Simon is heading this way and that means Alayne is alone in the tavern."

Reaching up, Fia caressed his comely face. "Do you know how very much I love you?"

He grinned and kissed her. "Aye, but I never tire of hearing it."

"And I'll never tire of telling or showing you," she replied, returning his kiss. Leaning over, Fia patted Arthur's side, then left for Alayne's corner of the public room. When she found her friend, Alayne looked glum, but the woman's expression cleared at the sight of Fia approaching.

"I should have taken your advice and stayed at Kate's while all this was going on," Alayne admitted, waving her hand in the direction of the door overlooking the quay. "It makes me nervous."

Fia sat opposite her and asked devilishly, "More nervous than when you met Simon's family?"

"Oh," Alayne threw back her head and laughed, "not nearly *that* nervous. I've never been so frazzled."

Fia smiled broadly. "I was a bit skittish myself with the four of us descending on Strathcarron and surprising his family. And not just by our arrival but with all the news we bore. As much as we had to tell them, I think they took it all with uncommon grace."

"Including Simon's and my wish to wed," Alayne inserted. "Our handfasting in Strathcarron...I wish it hadn't been necessary though to explain why Simon and I will marry again in France before heading to the colonies," Alayne added wistfully.

"Your handfasting was their favorite part of the visit and rightly so. Muir's treachery was beyond anyone's control. The MacLarens were very supportive and understanding, and so eager to share your joy. And on another happy note," she added with a grin, "you gave Mairi the opportunity to wear her new gown."

Alayne laughed softly, remembering her sister-in-law's exuberance at seeing what was to have been her own wedding dress. "I wish you and Martin had stayed longer than a week."

"It would have been lovely. But you know, with the two of you settling in the American colonies, it's a very real possibility that your visit with Simon's kin might be the last. You needed to make the most of your time with them."

Alayne vowed, "What wonderful people, the MacLarens, to welcome both you and me so warmly into the family."

The two women grew silent, awkwardly searching for words to express their sorrow at parting. If only that last problem had been resolved...

"If we hear anything about Muir," Fia offered, "we'll send word."

"Thank you," Alayne said stiffly then grumbled, "Poor Kate. It's just like him to disappear again and cause her more misery. But then he caused her misery when he was here. I guess you never really can disown a child, no matter how well deserved. You always love them." Then she flashed a shaky smile. "Kate was extremely generous to me and Simon, you know. Her wedding gift will go a long way toward helping us start our life together."

"She loves you," Fia reminded. "And I'm convinced she's got a rather large soft spot in her heart for Simon as well."

Alayne nodded. "Your aunt is an amazing woman–I'm glad we resolved our differences. Still, I can't help but wonder what she intends to do with the shop now that you and I are moving on."

Fia shrugged, "As far as I know, she hasn't decided yet."

Again, a strained silence fell. Alayne swallowed a lump in her throat. "I wish I were going to be here when your bairn comes."

Rapidly, Fia blinked back tears and spread her fingers across her belly. "Me too. But you know I'll be in good hands."

"The best!" Alayne agreed.

Hastily, the two rose and met around the table in a staunch hug. "I'll miss you so," Alayne said, "you and your Martin."

The cousins watched as the last load of freight was moved to storage below decks to be secured for the upcoming voyage. "Is Fia still suffering nightmares?" Simon asked, punctuated by a sidelong look of concern.

"Not as often," Martin replied, digging his frigid hands into the pockets of his new greatcoat. "It's been nearly three weeks since the last one. I think that's a good sign."

With a nod, Simon added, "It's a wonder to me that she is recovering this quickly from what Forbes put her through. Your support and love have been the key."

"And yours, Alayne's and Kate's." Martin added. "We're so grateful to you all. But Fia's is strong inside, Simon," Martin declared proudly. "The fact that she bested Forbes is testament to that."

"And how are you?" Simon inquired.

"How should I be? My beloved wife is free from danger; she's carrying my child." Then Martin smiled ruefully. "Indeed, the only thing amiss in my life is that you and Alayne are leaving."

Simon's look was a sorrowful one. "We've no choice, Martin."

Laying a hand on Simon's shoulder, Martin reassured, "I know...but knowing makes it no easier. Simon, I owe you so much."

"Martin–"

"It's true," Martin interrupted. "Without you, I'd still be hiding from people who would punish me for crimes I didn't commit. You banished my demons and shared your family with me, something I'd sorely missed. And worse, I may never have brought myself to look for Fia; and your family led me to her."

"And now you're starting one of your own." Simon's voice caught slightly, "I...I wish I could see the bairn when it arrives, be here for you."

"In spirit, you will be," Martin assured.

"Finding you," Simon vowed soberly, "was one of the best things I ever did."

Martin hugged his cousin. "Ah, but the very best, without doubt, was when you married Alayne."

Fia stretched in the soft bed, savoring the feel of the clean sheets against her skin.

Martin's arm slid across her belly and pulled her closer. His lips brushed her shoulder. "Today, we go home, lass," he whispered.

"I can hardly wait," she sighed, shivering a little at the prospect.

"Are you cold?" Martin asked, rising to his elbow and brushing a lock of hair from her cheek.

Fia assured, "While we share a bed, my love, that will never be a problem. You generate the heat of a forge," She rolled toward him, slipping her leg over his thigh, and her arm round his neck. "No," she admitted. "My shiver was one of anticipation. I never believed I would return here to Annie's and, when I left, it was with no hope of ever being with you, even seeing you again. I've never known such misery." She gulped tears of happiness. "How things have changed. That night I spent in this very room, I had horrid nightmares." Martin's grip tensed, but Fia continued, "I woke in despair and cried. I stood with my face pressed to that door, craving your presence, yet convinced you wanted someone else."

Martin's voice was hard. "Jean's damnable lies."

Fia searched his face in the half light of morning. "She didn't want to lose you."

"I wasn't hers to lose," he declared vehemently.

Fia touched her forehead to his. "I certainly understand the fear though...of losing you."

"You need never fear that again, lass." Holding her tightly, Martin confessed, "That same night...I stopped at your door. I needed to be with you so desperately–to sleep on the floor in the same room would have been enough. But I thought...well, I just couldn't stay, separated from you by so much more than that door. All night I walked the village, wallowing so in my own pain that I couldn't see yours. Annie could see though, when I was blind, that we hurt...that we loved each other." Unexpectedly, Martin chuckled. "It was good of her not to gloat too much when we arrived yesterday."

"I think Annie was too pleased for us to carry on for long. Besides," Fia added, "she believes in true love."

Martin cupped her chin in his hand and drank in her eyes with his own, love-filled gaze. "So do I, lass."

Outside the "Rowan and Thistle" Annie promised, "Donald will cart your things out as soon as they arrive, dear."

"I hate to put you to so much trouble," Fia protested from her perch on Barley's back. "It's only one small trunk."

Annie waved her concern away. "It's not a bit of trouble. Donald would welcome anything that doesn't involve having me tell him what to do all day." Turning to Martin, who stood beside her, she said, "And you," patting his cheek fondly, "will make such a wonderful father. I know– I've watched you with my Donald."

Martin smiled broadly to her compliment and Annie teased, "You aren't happy about the prospect, are you, lad?"

"Euphoric," he assured and reached up to squeeze Fia's hand and receive an adoring smile in return.

With no warning, Annie burst into tears. Martin hastily gripped her shoulders. "Annie, what-ever's wrong?"

"Oh, Martin," she sniffed, "these tears are p...pure joy...for you. You have n...no idea what happiness it gives me to see you and Fia together, so in love, as I always said you were," she hastened to remind.

Martin hugged her, deeply touched. Over her head, he caught Fia's eye and saw her own shimmering tears. Finally, he stepped away and kissed Annie's cheek. "Thank you, Annie, for seeing what we couldn't. Without your belief in our love for each other, we might never have come together and come here again. And thank you for letting us stay last night and generously sharing some of your supplies so we won't starve while we get the croft going again."

"Well," she observed, dabbing her eyes, "you're entirely welcome. I'd like you to stay longer, but know and understand you're anxious to be in your own home. Just don't be strangers." She smoothed her hair and apron. "You'd best mount up now. Even that hound of yours is eager to be off," she observed, nodding in the direction of Arthur's darting, prancing form.

Martin swung onto Odhar's back and whistled for the dog.

"We can never thank you enough, Annie. We'll visit soon," Fia said, urging Barley to meet Odhar's gentle gait.

It would be nearly dark by the time they arrived at the croft; it couldn't be soon enough to suit Fia. The long months since she'd left in such dispair were about to end. Now, she was Martin's wife; she carried his child inside her. Fia had never known such happiness–scarcely guessed it existed–much less that it would be hers to savor. As they rode along, Fia openly admired her husband's striking profile, the lazy reddish curls that feathered at his shoulders. Once more, she marveled at his trim, perfectly formed body knowing the fierce, compassionate man he was. Love and pride swelled her heart.

Martin glanced over, then stared, riveted by the ethereal glow of Fia's expression.

The intensity of his perusal started Fia's pulse racing.

"I can scarcely wait to get you home," he breathed softly.

Fia grinned, "I was thinking much the same thing about you, Husband."

He reined-in Odhar, reaching to pull back on Barley's bridle at the same time. "It's not much further," Martin offered, "but there's something I'm missing."

Dismounting, Martin tied Odhar up to Barley's saddle and joined Fia on her horse. He wrapped his arms around his wife and kissed the back of her neck, causing a shiver of delight to pass through her. They resumed their journey, snuggled for warmth and to enjoy each other's nearness. At one point, Martin spread his palm across her belly, gently caressing it.

"You grow more beautiful every day," he vowed.

Fia laughed softly. "Thank you, my love."

Martin's arms brought her closer, and he brushed his cheek against hers.

They rode on and, at dusk, Arthur shot ahead, the croft faintly visible in the distance.

"I'm afraid it'll take some time after I start the fire to take the chill from inside, lass," Martin apologized.

"It doesn't matter, I won't go anywhere," she assured and received a pleased smile and a kiss in return.

When, at last, Fia stood inside, memories swept over her with such power, she gripped the edge of the table to steady herself: the loom where he'd told her about Hugh; the trunk from which he'd pulled many a treasure, including the whistle he'd played while she danced; the medical book still lying on the rough-hewn mantle. Suddenly she was uncertain as to her place in this world which was so intimately Martin's.

Arthur's wagging body burst past her, shattering her musings. He was followed by Martin, arms full of wood and peat bricks.

Silently, Fia watched as he set and nursed the fire to a blaze. Martin was about to suggest she rest in the chair by the hearth while the croft warmed when, seeing the unsettled look on her face, he came to her side instead.

"Fia, what is it? Are you tired?"

She turned wide, questioning eyes on him. "This is your home, Martin," she replied, voice tremulous. "How will it become mine as well?"

"It's been your home, Fia, since the day you entered it." He hesitated a moment before asking solemnly, "Do you know how it came to be that Simon found me?"

Puzzled, Fia replied, "You know he told me he'd been searching for you."

"Yet he never would have found me if I hadn't left here. I left because without you, it wasn't my home anymore. Your presence was everywhere and in everything. Fia, I was just existing when we met, not living. And when you left, I only wanted to lose myself."

"But you can't escape from yourself," she said.

"As I discovered night after night," he agreed. "Now I breathe again, because you're with me and you love me."

"And I do love you, from the depths of my heart and my soul." Her declaration was also her promise. Fia slid her hands down his back to rest on his narrow hips. "Isn't it time we stirred the embers of the other fire that will take the chill off?"

Martin grinned broadly and returned her embrace. "I know the very one you mean," he declared, and covered her eager lips with his own.

Douglas Sutherland rose from his desk and padded down the hall on slippered feet. It was late. Murdoch had fetched his sister, Agnes, several hours ago, leaving Douglas alone with his thoughts. It was just as well, for he had to admit he hadn't been very good company lately, not since he'd received word of all that had happened in Inverness this past December.

Notes from Fia and Alayne had arrived early in January bearing news that alternately made him tremble with anger or rejoice with happiness. Kate, on the other hand–dear Kate–had been silent. Douglas feared her son's disappearance had devastated her once again, and she was too embarrassed or simply had no desire to turn to Douglas for comfort. The man sighed, trying to resign himself anew to having no place in the lady's life.

As he passed through the hall, Douglas felt chilled and pulled his quilted, brocade dressing gown closer around his lean frame. A tentative knock sounded on his door and, inwardly, Douglas groaned. Late arrivals invariably turned out to be clients with problems of a more sordid sort. Resigned, he pulled the door open and gaped at who he beheld.

"You invited me to come to Glasgow, do you remember?" she asked quietly.

"Kate! I do...I...do," he repeated, stupefied.

She nodded past him. "May I?"

"Oh!" Douglas jumped back. "Of course, Kate, I beg your pardon. Please...please come in," Douglas sputtered his surprise. He relieved her of her valise and closed the door once she was inside.

Douglas removed her mantle, hung it on a peg near the door and faced her. Eagerness and concern flooded his face; he could not speak, so many things did he want to say to her.

Kate saw his struggle and was deeply moved. "I hoped you'd be glad to see me, not angry at my foolishness."

He vehemently stated, "You've never been foolish in my eyes, Kate, and... I'm overjoyed to see you here."

Kate's lower lip quivered, her doe-eyes moistened. "Thank you for that."

Cautiously, Douglas said, "You know, don't you, that I've heard from Fia and Alayne." To her nod, he resumed, "Will you tell me about your son?"

With a shrug, Kate allowed, "There's nothing to tell. Muir's gone with no word; he won't come back this time."

"How can you know that?"

"Because he never wanted to be home," she said, resigned. "First, he hid the fact that he'd returned, and he was always so unhappy, unsettled and...angry. You no doubt know about his horrid role in the divorce. And I...I disowned him just before that terrifying kidnapping of Fia. I haven't seen or heard from him since. No, I can't believe he'd ever come back again of his own free will. Somehow, he found the opportunity he needed, and he left."

"I'm very sorry." Douglas nodded his understanding then asked, "Have you found new seamstresses? Who is minding your shop?"

"The new owners. I sold it. I only kept Martin's cloths." She hesitated for a long moment. "I'm also selling my home." Kate looked into Douglas' astonished eyes and recognized anticipation and deep affection in them. She hoped it was a *very* deep affection and rushed on before her courage flagged, "I've missed you dreadfully, Douglas. Not just because you were always truthful with me and supportive of me when it came to my son, and not just for opening my eyes where Alayne was concerned. I'm grateful for all that–will be so eternally." She blushed. "I used to talk to you when I was alone. But, Douglas...I miss *you*: your tenderness and compassion, your intellect and wit...your company." Kate boldly pressed her palm to his smooth, angular cheek. "I missed this beautiful, expressive face...I missed your kiss, your touch. That's why I'm here, Douglas."

"For...me?" he questioned cautiously, not trusting that he was hearing what he longed for most.

"For you," Kate assured, fiercely.

His fingers fumbled to clutch hers. "Then...will you stay with me?" he asked, his voice strained by spiraling emotion.

"I would be so very honored," she answered. "I love you, Douglas."

Douglas gazed down at her from his great height and saw the truth of her words in her serene, adoring gaze. His face creased in a bliss-filled smile and his arms encircled her trim body, pulling her close. "Then we'll send for the rest of your things tomorrow, my dearest Kate, for I intend never to let you go."

About the Author

Susan M. Walls was born in Washington, DC. She received a Bachelor's degree in history from James Madison University. An author and editor, she enjoyed a 30+ year career with the U.S. Agency for International Development and received its highest award, Distinguished Career Service, upon retirement. She volunteers with historical and lineage-based societies to which she belongs and currently resides in the Shenandoah Valley of Virginia with her husband and their cats in a farmhouse dating to 1787.